Cupid's Arrows

story and art by
Thom Zahler

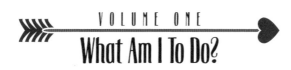

VOLUME ONE
What Am I To Do?

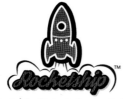

Rocketship Entertainment, LLC

Tom Akel, CEO & Publisher
Rob Feldman, CTO
Jeanmarie McNeely, CFO
Brandon Freeberg, Dir. of Campaign Mgmt.
Jed Keith, Social Media

rocketshipent.com

CUPID'S ARROWS originally published online at WEBTOON

CUPID'S ARROWS VOLUME 1
ISBN PAPERBACK: 978-1-952126-15-4
ISBN HARDBACK: 978-1-952126-16-1
First printing. March 2021.
Printed in China.

"Aim True"

I think I got asked to present this story because my personal work has one theme in common: love. Whether it's the last romantic antihero or a super-thief forced to become a superhero against his will, my comix (and plays) center around matters of the heart. Misfits wrestling with their feelings. Frankly, it's embarrassing. Nobody wants to witness a hero cry, much less a bruiser clutch at his chest hairs pining for his better half. That's uncivilized. It's soft.

Even though I've dedicated my career to telling such sentimental tales, I like to imagine myself a tough guy who wouldn't dare get caught up in the soap opera of other people's conquests and heartbreaks. Besides, I'm in my 50s. I've already experienced unrequited love and failed relationships. I don't necessarily believe in soul mates. I trust in transparent communication, honest loyalty, and a belly full of laughs. But this isn't about me. This is about Thom Zahler. A talented gentleman with a charming smile who's as generous as he is genuine.

When I cracked *Cupid's Arrows*, my faux-machismo was exposed within five pages. See, Eros has gone missing and the magic of love has diminished. Two wingless agents of romance, better known as Cupids, are in charge of matchmaking couples whose relationships will change the world as curated by an ancient Book of Love. Wait – what? I needed to know more!

Joshua Wolf Shenk, writer and current editor-in-chief of The Believer magazine, wrote a book called *Powers Of Two*. It's about "how relationships drive creativity." In *Cupid's Arrows*, Thom introduces the concept of people who are designated to spark greatness if only they could just meet and fall in love. This is the eternal mission statement of our two hitmen of love to help make a better tomorrow with the elevation of erotica. Sounds like one of my comix!

Romantic relationships driving creativity or greatness is a fascinating concept worth investigating. It makes me think about Christo and Jeanne-Claude, John Lennon and Yoko Ono, Marina Abramović and Ulay, Robert Mapplethorpe and Patti Smith, Gertrude Stein and Alice B. Toklas, Sonny & Cher, Ike and Tina Turner, Johnny Cash and June Carter Cash. The list goes on and on.

Whether these clashes of titans only lasted a short while or ended up being toxic and abusive, we get to be the recipient of their magical collaborations. But what about the life-inspiring relationships we don't know about? The ones we never hear or see but, through the cosmic algorithms of life, we benefit from? The spiritual passion that endow our love stories?

Great mythology, literature, poetry, songs, and theater aside, my favorite way to indulge romance is through the silver screen. From William Wyler's *Wuthering Heights*, Elia Kazan's *On The Waterfront*, Robert Wise and Jerome Robbins' *West Side Story*, Mike Nichols' *Who's Afraid Of Virginia Woolf?*, Hal Ashby's Harold And Maude, Alex Cox's *Sid And Nancy*, Tony Scott's *True Romance*, Ang Lee's *Brokeback Mountain*, Damien Chazelle's *La La Land*, to Guillermo del Toro's *The Shape Of Water*, there are so many ways to contextualize the complications of love. And, with the recent cinematic paradigm shift, we've come to indulge blockbuster romances influenced by America's greatest invention, the comic book.

Superman and Lois Lane. Captain America and Agent Carter. Wonder Woman and Steve Trevor. Archie, Betty and Veronica. Reed and Sue Richards. Spider-Man and Mary Jane. Batman and Catwoman. Harley Quinn and The Joker. Apollo and Midnighter. Marv and Goldie. Scott Pilgrim and Ramona Flowers. Jesse Custer and Tulip O'Hare. Agent 355 & Yorick Brown. Alana and Marko. Billy Dogma and Jane Legit. And now Rick and Lora from *Cupid's Arrows* join the ranks of classic comix romances.

Cupid's Arrows makes me think about my own relationships. How did they impact my creativity? What did we make together that couldn't have existed otherwise? What did my relationships afford you? What have your relationships gifted me? Was it free will or fate that put us together? How many relationships went unrequited because Cupid missed its target? These are some of the questions this tome asks.

A heartfelt cross between *Men In Black* by way of *Moonlighting* with a love tap from *Wings Of Desire*, *Cupid's Arrows* is Thom Zahler's funny Valentine to comics.

If you're feeling a little lonely and you notice a curious quiver flying towards you, don't dodge it. Rip open your shirt, puff out your chest, and fall in love.

--*Dean Haspiel,*
*creator of **Billy Dogma** and **The Red Hook***
February, 2021

For Jesse and Linda
Raising the bar in so many ways

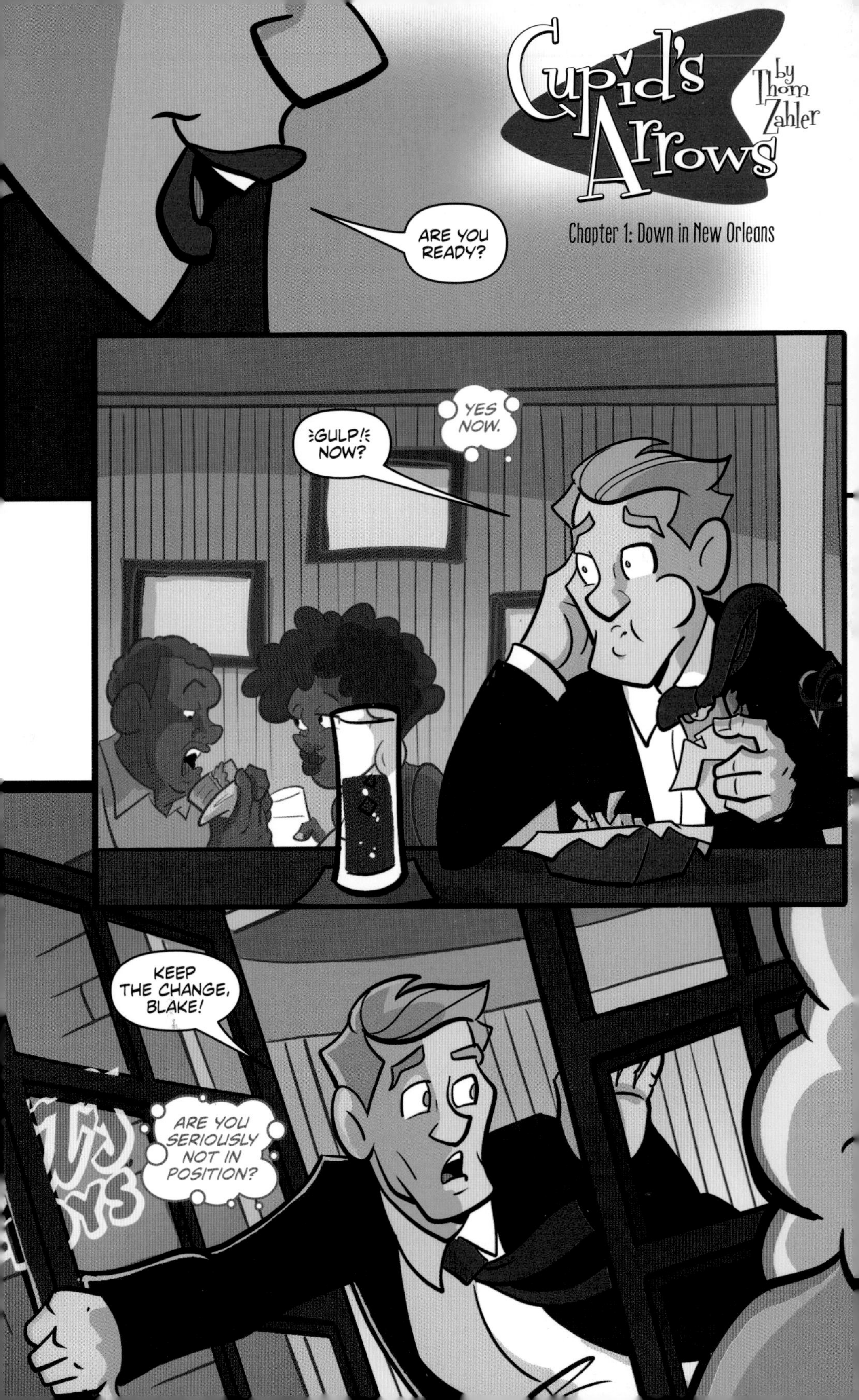
Cupid's Arrows
by Thom Zahler
Chapter 1: Down in New Orleans
ARE YOU READY?
GULP! NOW?
YES NOW.
KEEP THE CHANGE, BLAKE!
ARE YOU SERIOUSLY NOT IN POSITION?

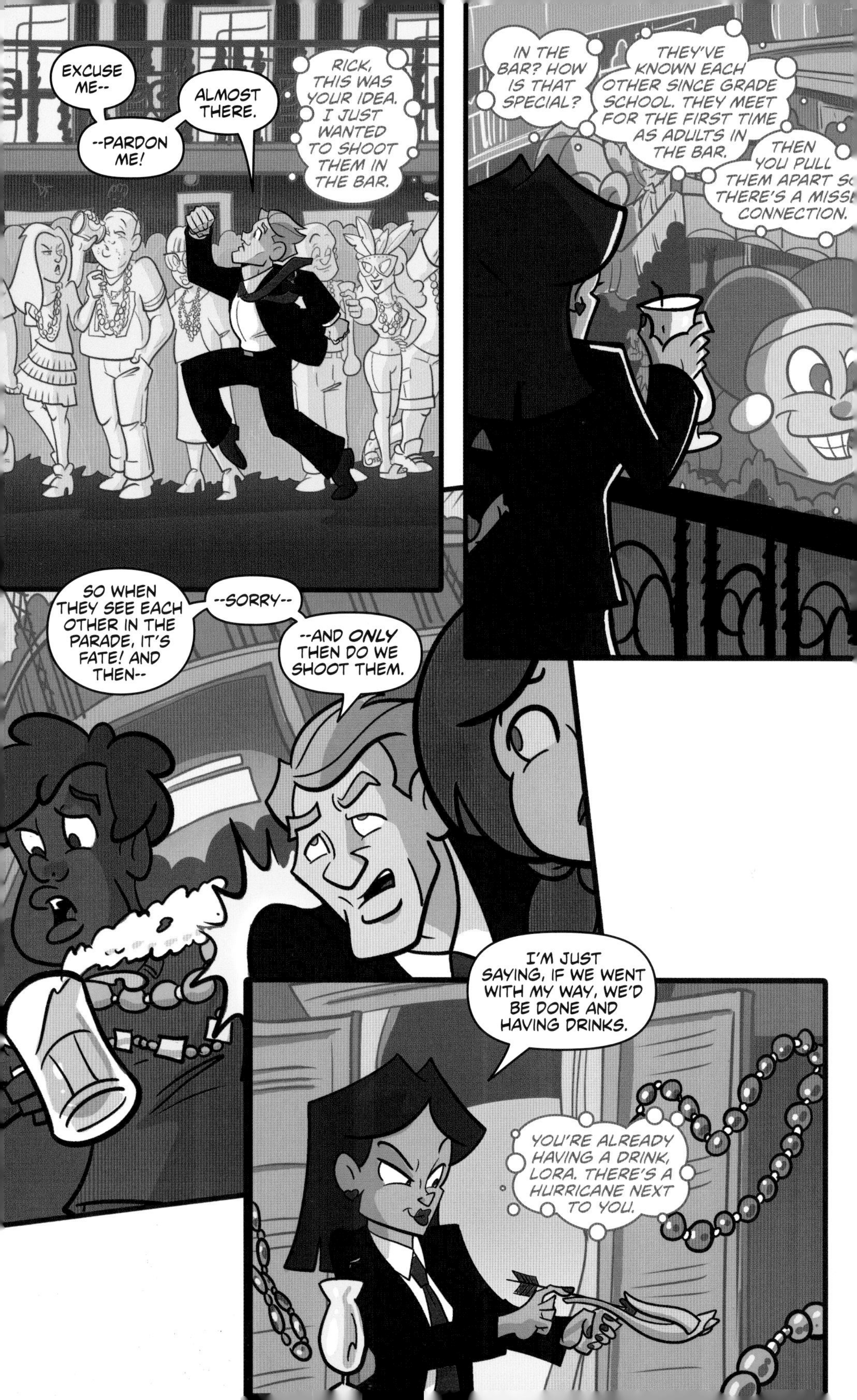
EXCUSE ME--
--PARDON ME!
ALMOST THERE.
RICK, THIS WAS YOUR IDEA. I JUST WANTED TO SHOOT THEM IN THE BAR.
IN THE BAR? HOW IS THAT SPECIAL?
THEY'VE KNOWN EACH OTHER SINCE GRADE SCHOOL. THEY MEET FOR THE FIRST TIME AS ADULTS IN THE BAR.
THEN YOU PULL THEM APART SO THERE'S A MISSED CONNECTION.
SO WHEN THEY SEE EACH OTHER IN THE PARADE, IT'S FATE! AND THEN--
--SORRY--
--AND ONLY THEN DO WE SHOOT THEM.
I'M JUST SAYING, IF WE WENT WITH MY WAY, WE'D BE DONE AND HAVING DRINKS.
YOU'RE ALREADY HAVING A DRINK, LORA. THERE'S A HURRICANE NEXT TO YOU.

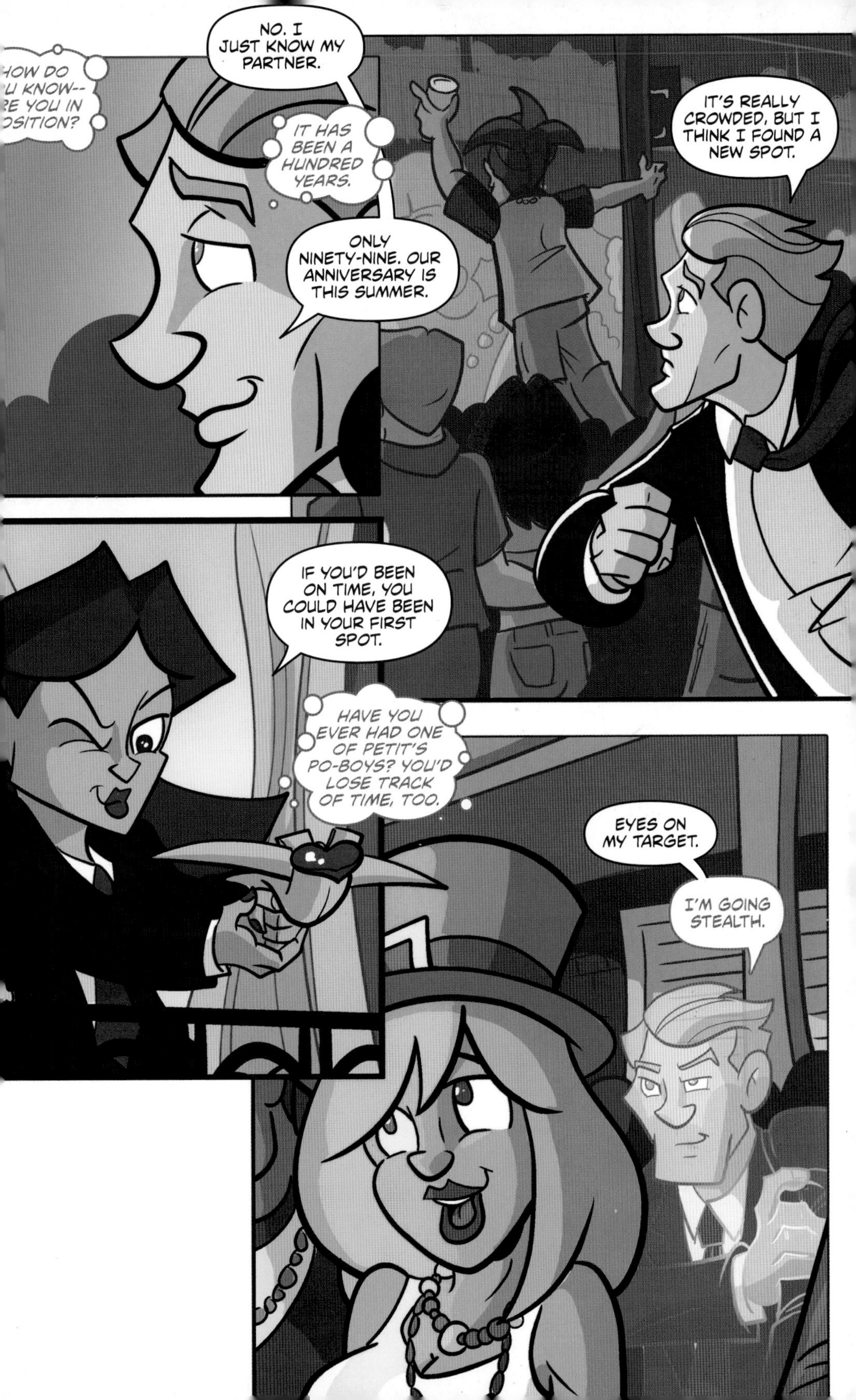

HOW DO
U KNOW--
RE YOU IN
OSITION?
NO. I
JUST KNOW MY
PARTNER.
IT HAS
BEEN A
HUNDRED
YEARS.
ONLY
NINETY-NINE. OUR
ANNIVERSARY IS
THIS SUMMER.
IT'S REALLY
CROWDED, BUT I
THINK I FOUND A
NEW SPOT.
IF YOU'D BEEN
ON TIME, YOU
COULD HAVE BEEN
IN YOUR FIRST
SPOT.
HAVE YOU
EVER HAD ONE
OF PETIT'S
PO-BOYS? YOU'D
LOSE TRACK
OF TIME, TOO.
EYES ON
MY TARGET.
I'M GOING
STEALTH.

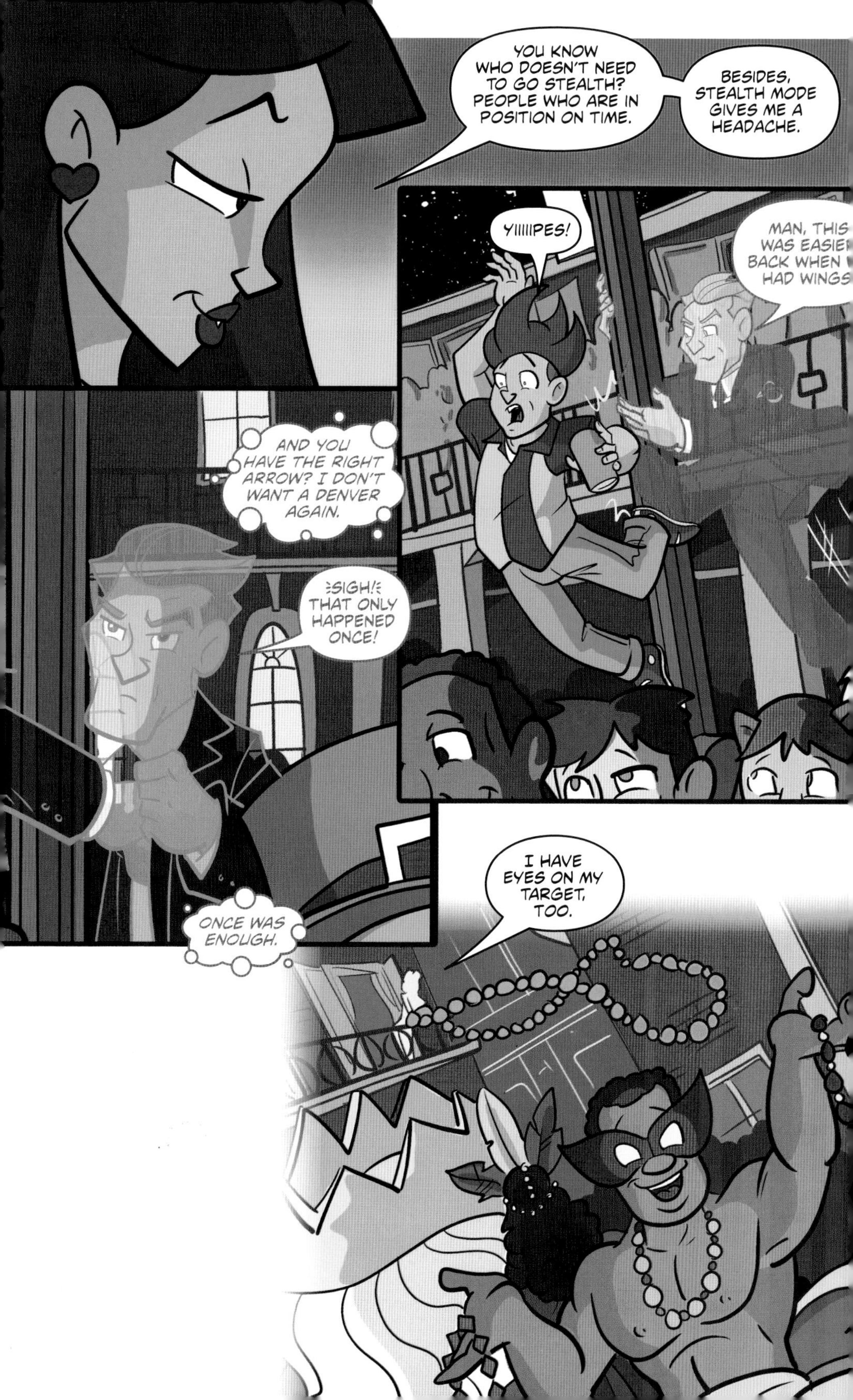
YOU KNOW WHO DOESN'T NEED TO GO STEALTH? PEOPLE WHO ARE IN POSITION ON TIME.
BESIDES, STEALTH MODE GIVES ME A HEADACHE.
YIIIIIPES!
MAN, THIS WAS EASIER BACK WHEN I HAD WINGS.
AND YOU HAVE THE RIGHT ARROW? I DON'T WANT A DENVER AGAIN.
SIGH! THAT ONLY HAPPENED ONCE!
ONCE WAS ENOUGH.
I HAVE EYES ON MY TARGET, TOO.

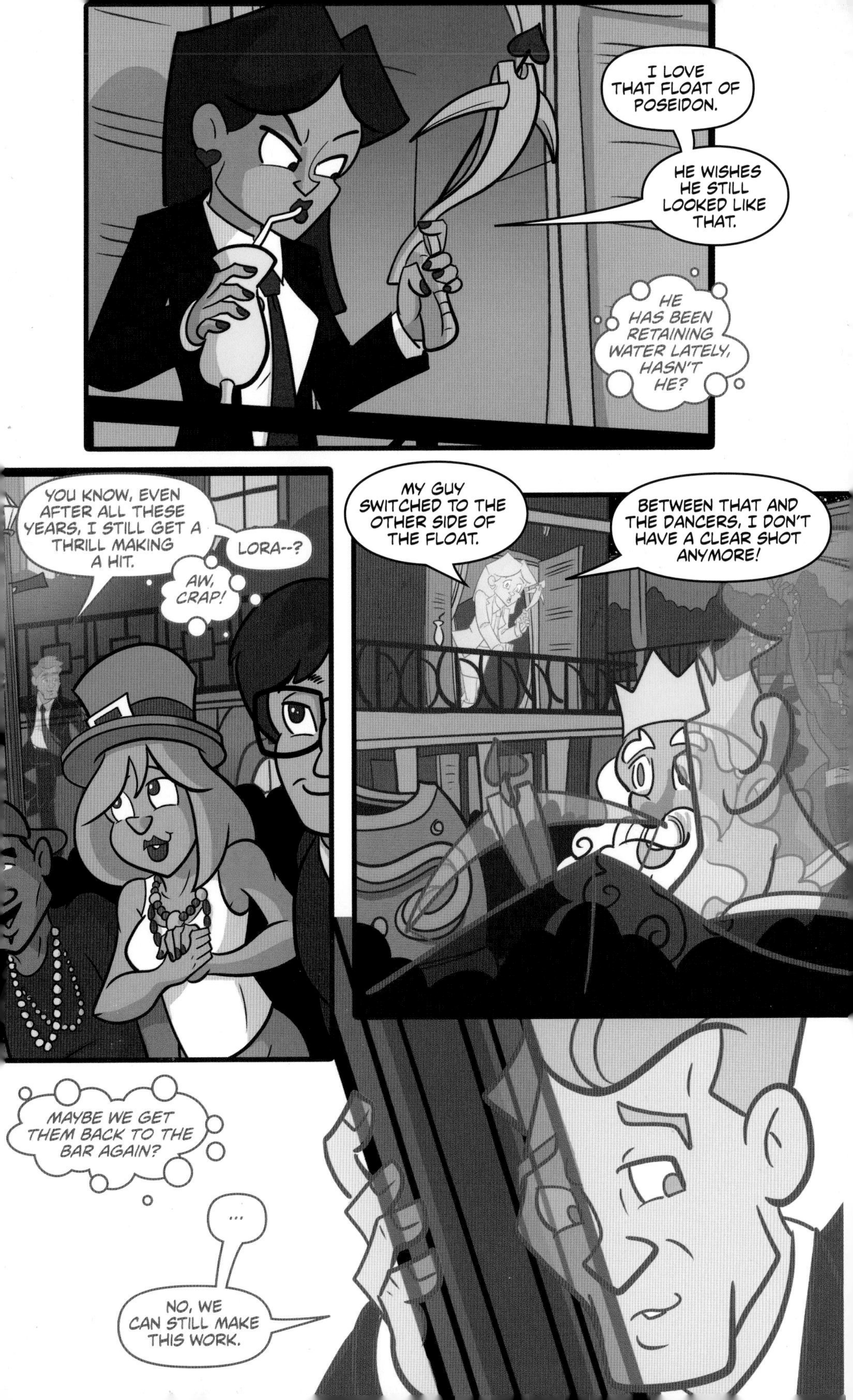
I LOVE THAT FLOAT OF POSEIDON.
HE WISHES HE STILL LOOKED LIKE THAT.
HE HAS BEEN RETAINING WATER LATELY, HASN'T HE?
YOU KNOW, EVEN AFTER ALL THESE YEARS, I STILL GET A THRILL MAKING A HIT.
LORA--?
AW, CRAP!
MY GUY SWITCHED TO THE OTHER SIDE OF THE FLOAT.
BETWEEN THAT AND THE DANCERS, I DON'T HAVE A CLEAR SHOT ANYMORE!
MAYBE WE GET THEM BACK TO THE BAR AGAIN?
...
NO, WE CAN STILL MAKE THIS WORK.

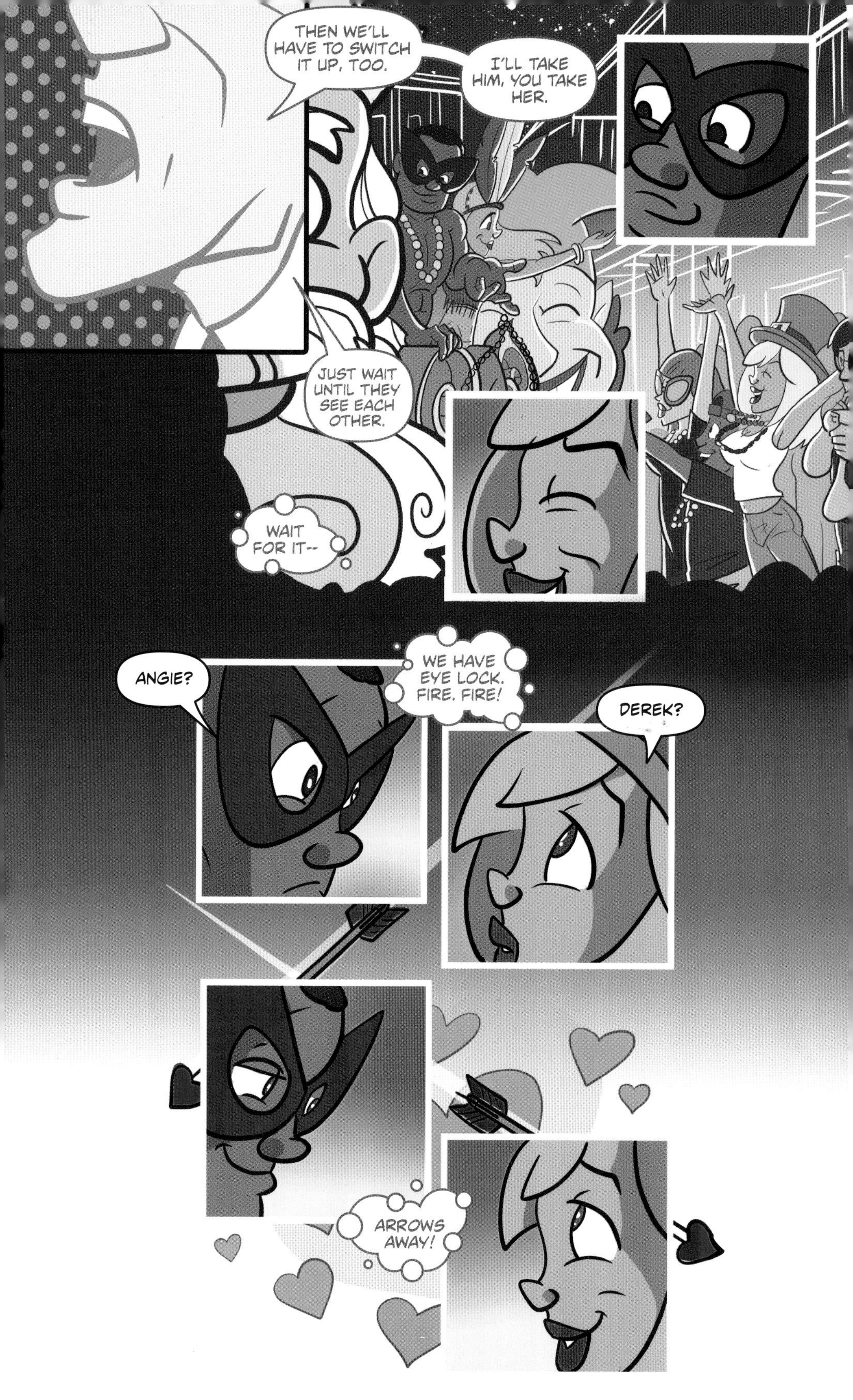
THEN WE'LL HAVE TO SWITCH IT UP, TOO.
I'LL TAKE HIM, YOU TAKE HER.
JUST WAIT UNTIL THEY SEE EACH OTHER.
WAIT FOR IT--
ANGIE?
WE HAVE EYE LOCK. FIRE. FIRE!
DEREK?
ARROWS AWAY!

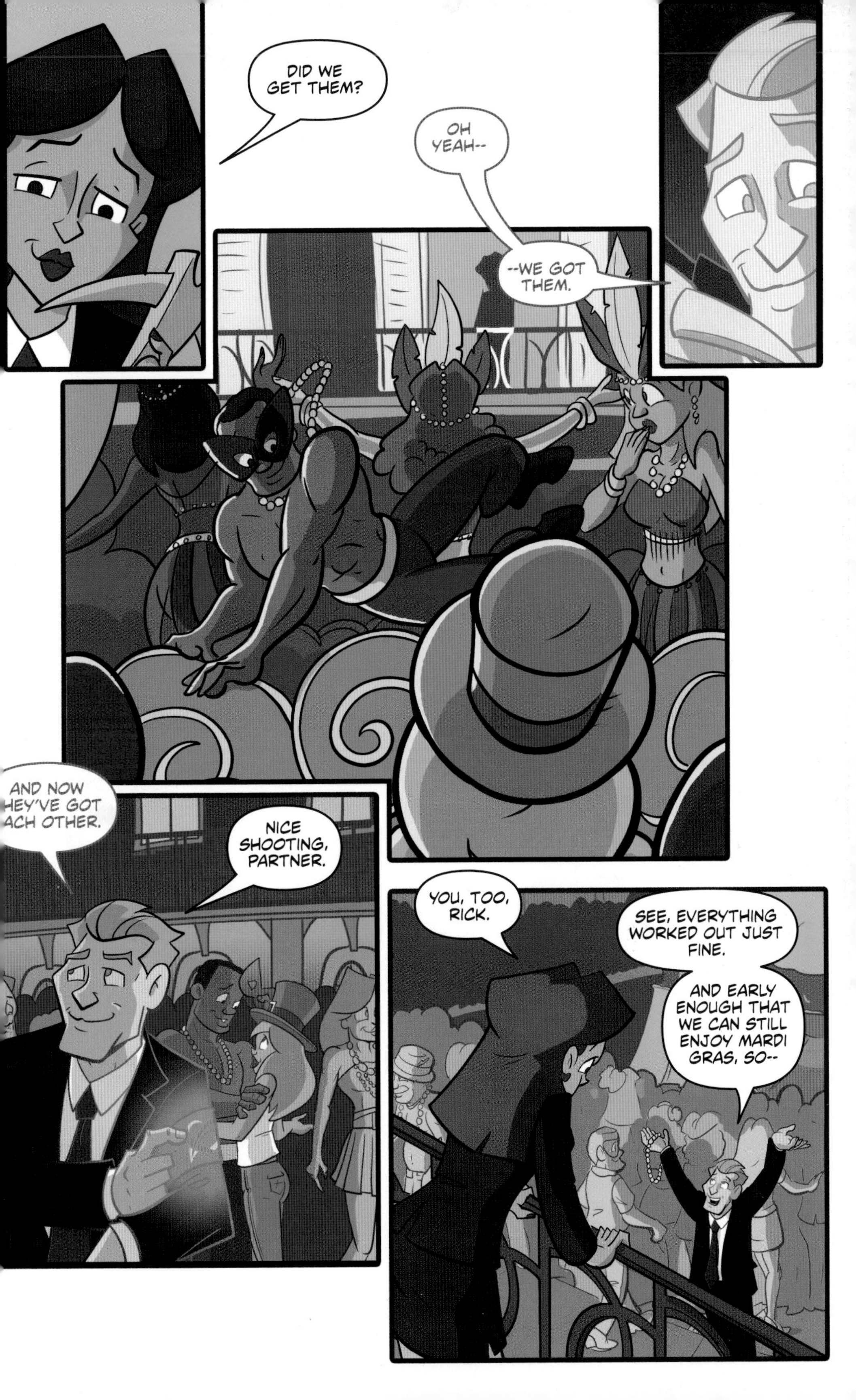
DID WE GET THEM?
OH YEAH--
--WE GOT THEM.
AND NOW HEY'VE GOT ACH OTHER.
NICE SHOOTING, PARTNER.
YOU, TOO, RICK.
SEE, EVERYTHING WORKED OUT JUST FINE.
AND EARLY ENOUGH THAT WE CAN STILL ENJOY MARDI GRAS, SO--

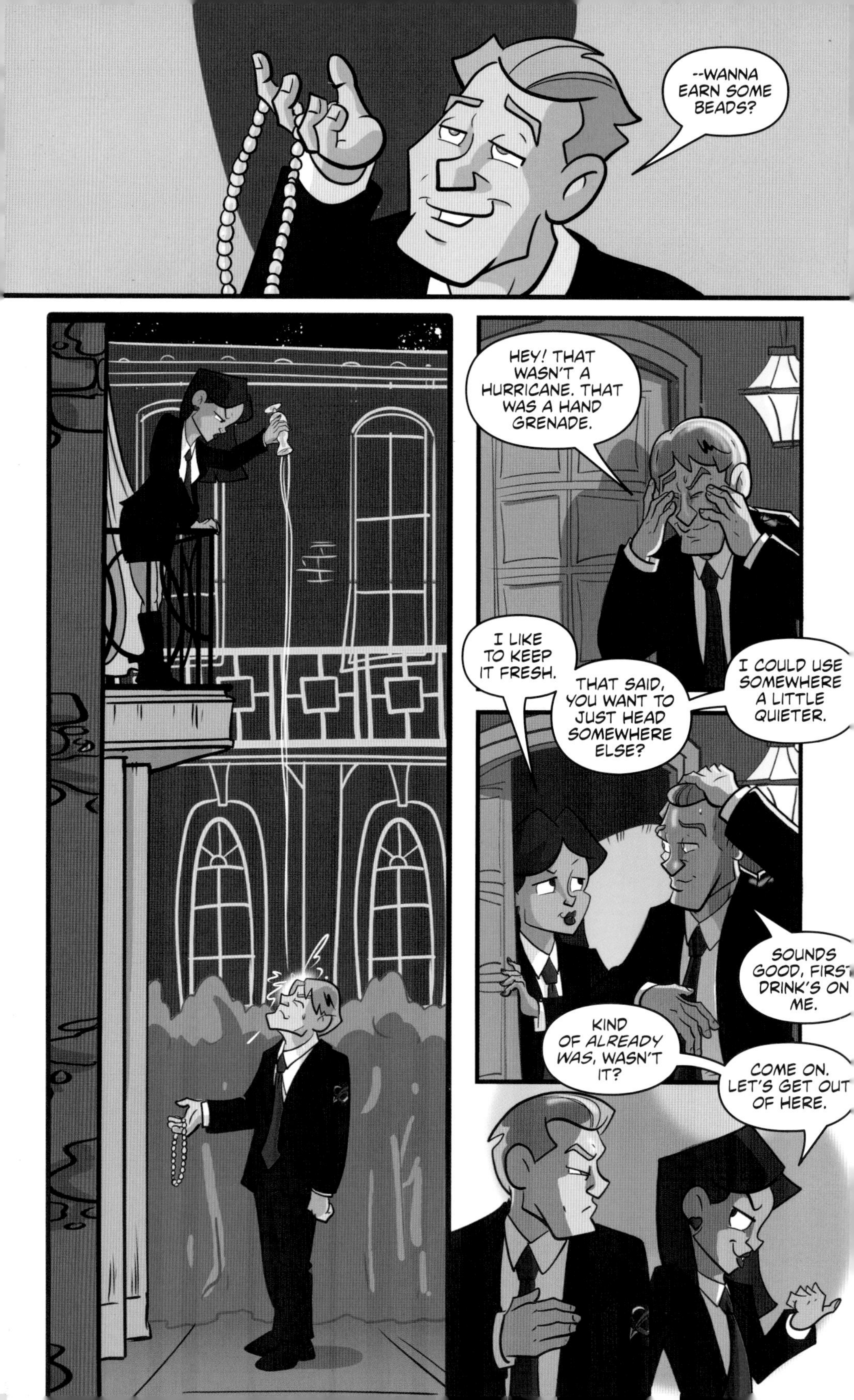
--WANNA EARN SOME BEADS?
HEY! THAT WASN'T A HURRICANE. THAT WAS A HAND GRENADE.
I LIKE TO KEEP IT FRESH.
THAT SAID, YOU WANT TO JUST HEAD SOMEWHERE ELSE?
I COULD USE SOMEWHERE A LITTLE QUIETER.
SOUNDS GOOD, FIRST DRINK'S ON ME.
KIND OF ALREADY WAS, WASN'T IT?
COME ON. LET'S GET OUT OF HERE.

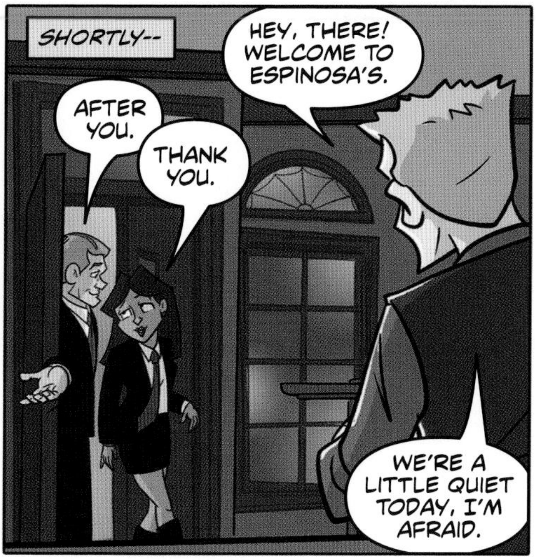
SHORTLY--
HEY, THERE! WELCOME TO ESPINOSA'S.
AFTER YOU.
THANK YOU.
WE'RE A LITTLE QUIET TODAY, I'M AFRAID.

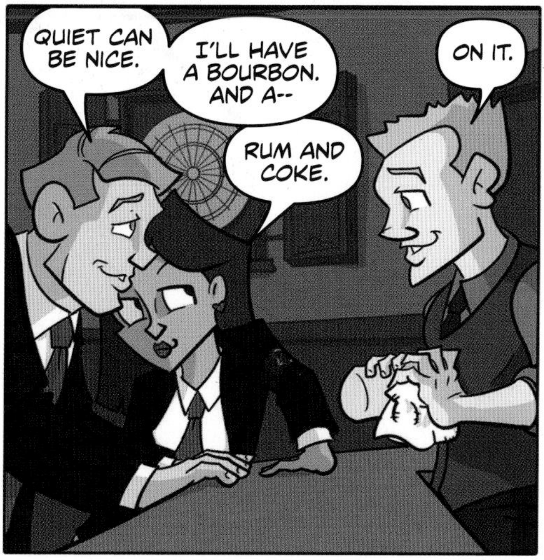
QUIET CAN BE NICE.
I'LL HAVE A BOURBON. AND A--
RUM AND COKE.
ON IT.

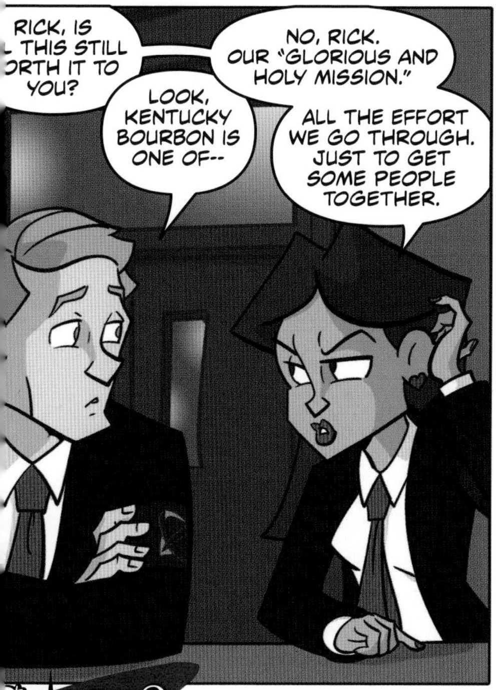
RICK, IS
L THIS STILL
ORTH IT TO
YOU?
NO, RICK. OUR "GLORIOUS AND HOLY MISSION."
LOOK, KENTUCKY BOURBON IS ONE OF--
ALL THE EFFORT WE GO THROUGH. JUST TO GET SOME PEOPLE TOGETHER.

hapter 2

Where Everybody Knows Your Name

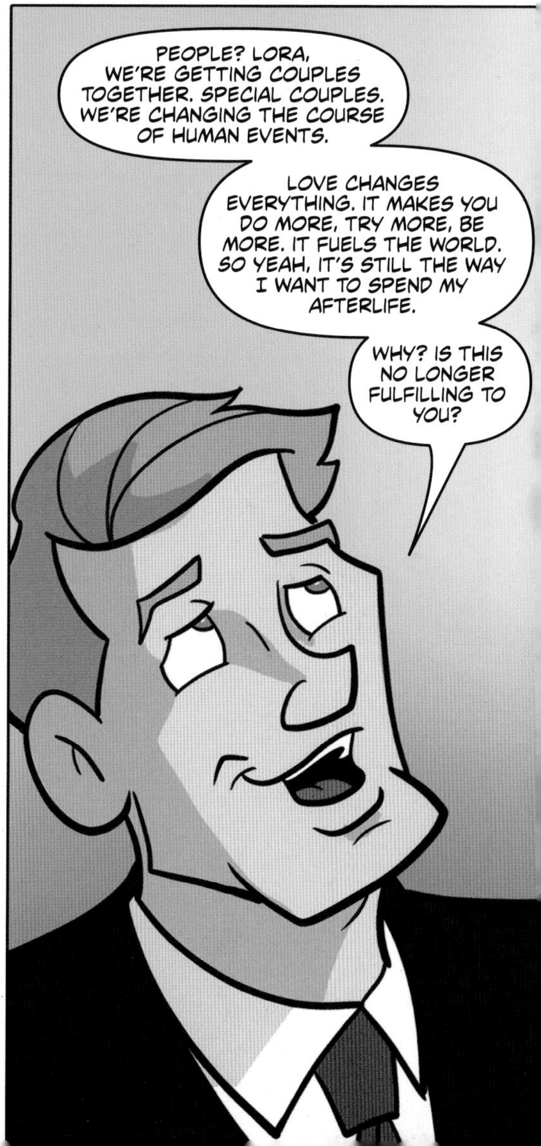
PEOPLE? LORA, WE'RE GETTING COUPLES TOGETHER. SPECIAL COUPLES. WE'RE CHANGING THE COURSE OF HUMAN EVENTS.
LOVE CHANGES EVERYTHING. IT MAKES YOU DO MORE, TRY MORE, BE MORE. IT FUELS THE WORLD. SO YEAH, IT'S STILL THE WAY I WANT TO SPEND MY AFTERLIFE.
WHY? IS THIS NO LONGER FULFILLING TO YOU?

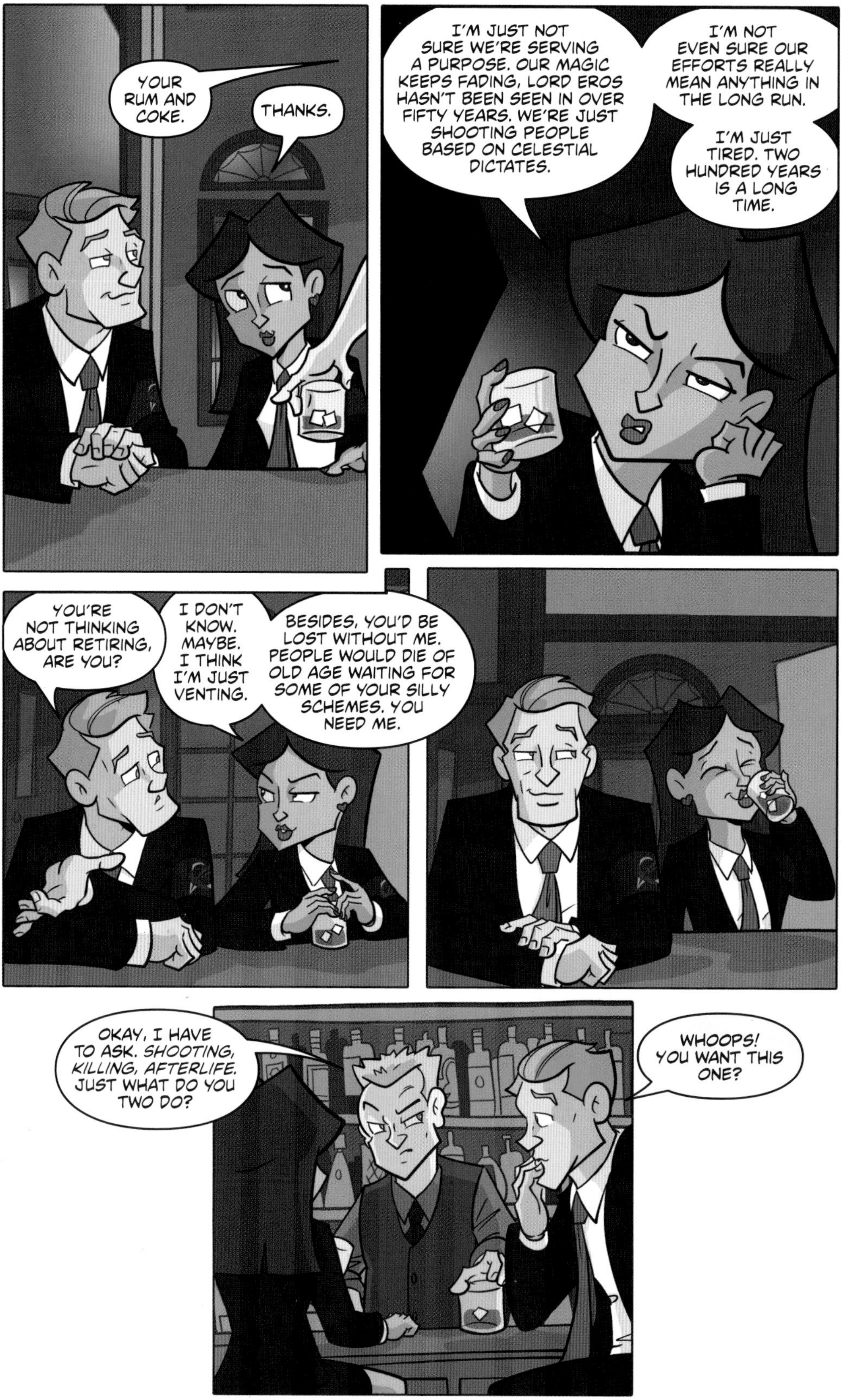
YOUR RUM AND COKE.
THANKS.
I'M JUST NOT SURE WE'RE SERVING A PURPOSE. OUR MAGIC KEEPS FADING, LORD EROS HASN'T BEEN SEEN IN OVER FIFTY YEARS. WE'RE JUST SHOOTING PEOPLE BASED ON CELESTIAL DICTATES.
I'M NOT EVEN SURE OUR EFFORTS REALLY MEAN ANYTHING IN THE LONG RUN.
I'M JUST TIRED. TWO HUNDRED YEARS IS A LONG TIME.
YOU'RE NOT THINKING ABOUT RETIRING, ARE YOU?
I DON'T KNOW. MAYBE. I THINK I'M JUST VENTING.
BESIDES, YOU'D BE LOST WITHOUT ME. PEOPLE WOULD DIE OF OLD AGE WAITING FOR SOME OF YOUR SILLY SCHEMES. YOU NEED ME.
OKAY, I HAVE TO ASK. *SHOOTING, KILLING, AFTERLIFE.* JUST WHAT DO YOU TWO DO?
WHOOPS! YOU WANT THIS ONE?

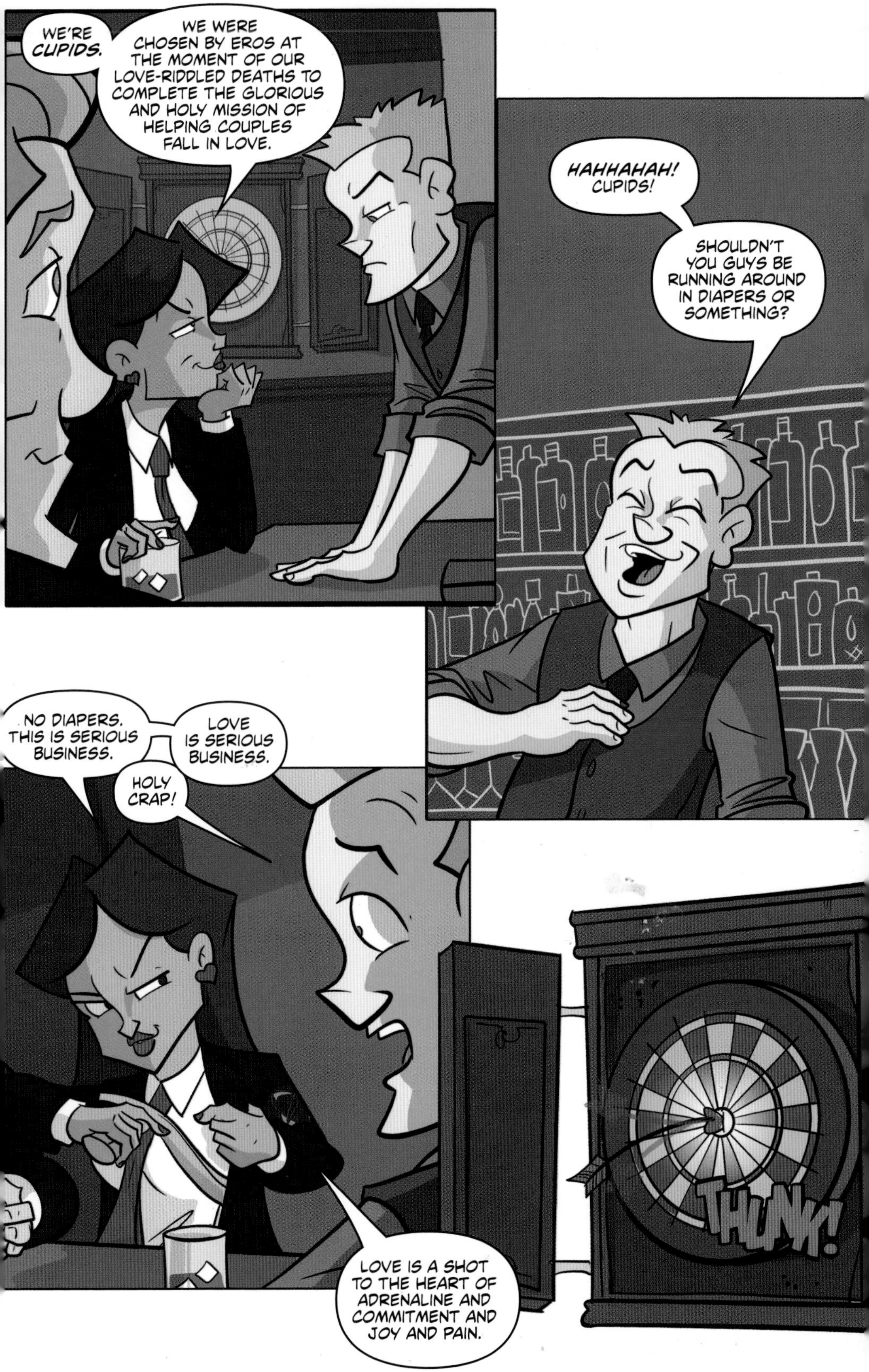
WE'RE *CUPIDS.*
WE WERE CHOSEN BY EROS AT THE MOMENT OF OUR LOVE-RIDDLED DEATHS TO COMPLETE THE GLORIOUS AND HOLY MISSION OF HELPING COUPLES FALL IN LOVE.
HAHHAHAH! CUPIDS!
SHOULDN'T YOU GUYS BE RUNNING AROUND IN DIAPERS OR SOMETHING?
NO DIAPERS. THIS IS SERIOUS BUSINESS.
LOVE IS SERIOUS BUSINESS.
HOLY CRAP!
LOVE IS A SHOT TO THE HEART OF ADRENALINE AND COMMITMENT AND JOY AND PAIN.
THUNK!

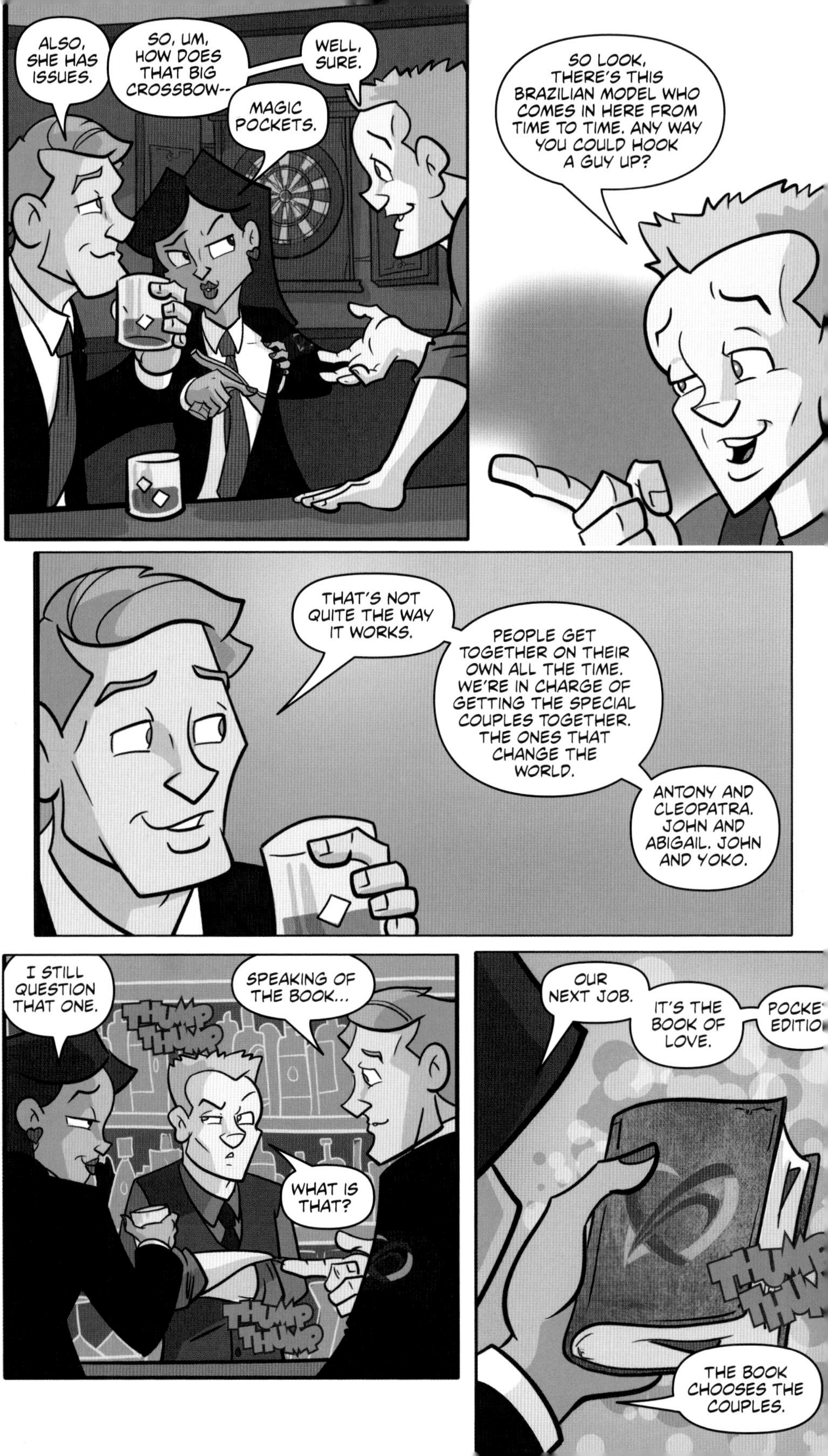
ALSO, SHE HAS ISSUES.
SO, UM, HOW DOES THAT BIG CROSSBOW--
WELL, SURE.
MAGIC POCKETS.
SO LOOK, THERE'S THIS BRAZILIAN MODEL WHO COMES IN HERE FROM TIME TO TIME. ANY WAY YOU COULD HOOK A GUY UP?
THAT'S NOT QUITE THE WAY IT WORKS.
PEOPLE GET TOGETHER ON THEIR OWN ALL THE TIME. WE'RE IN CHARGE OF GETTING THE SPECIAL COUPLES TOGETHER. THE ONES THAT CHANGE THE WORLD.
ANTONY AND CLEOPATRA. JOHN AND ABIGAIL. JOHN AND YOKO.
I STILL QUESTION THAT ONE.
SPEAKING OF THE BOOK...
THUMP THUMP
WHAT IS THAT?
THUMP THUMP
OUR NEXT JOB.
IT'S THE BOOK OF LOVE.
POCKE EDITIO
THE BOOK CHOOSES THE COUPLES.

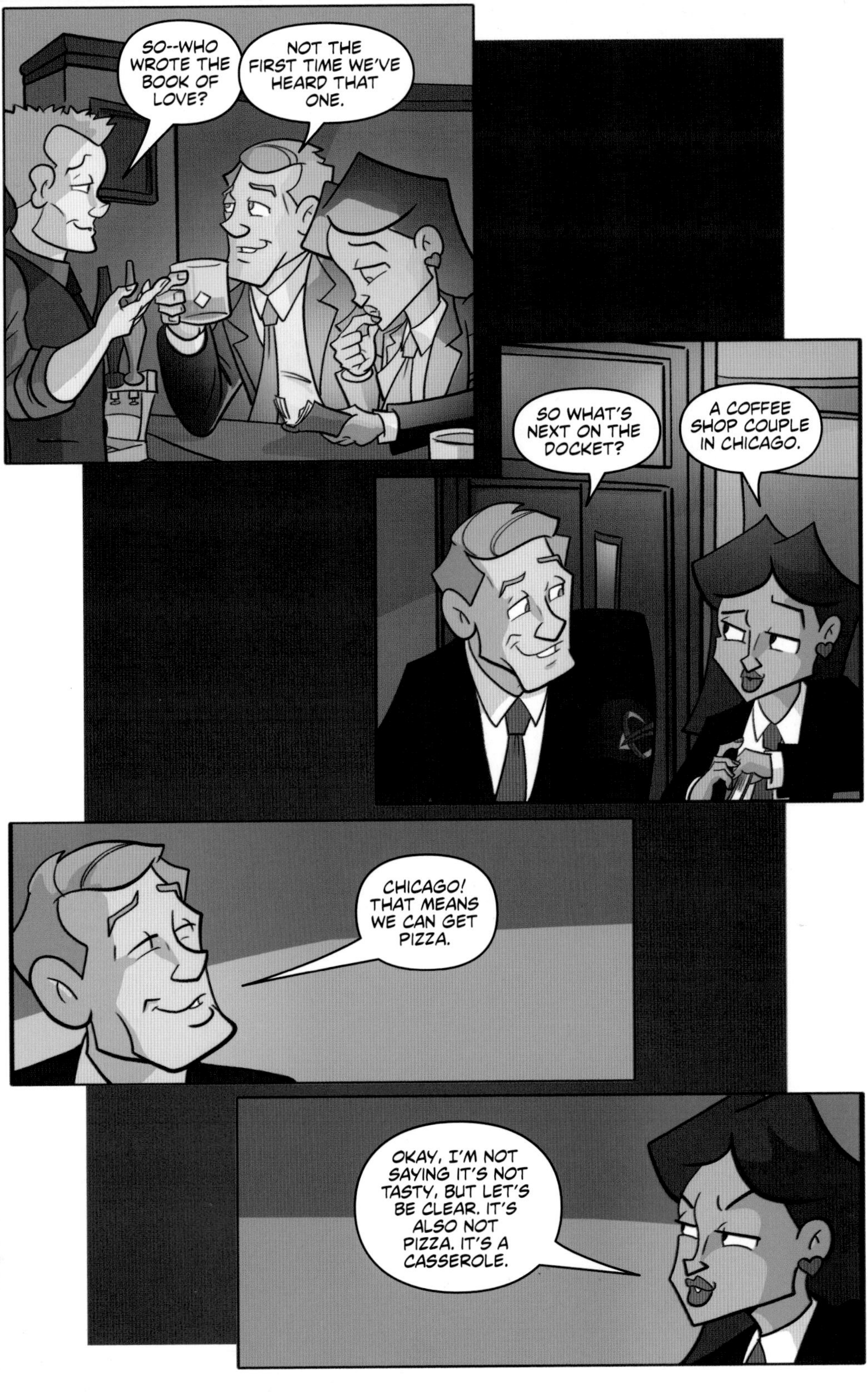
SO--WHO WROTE THE BOOK OF LOVE?
NOT THE FIRST TIME WE'VE HEARD THAT ONE.
SO WHAT'S NEXT ON THE DOCKET?
A COFFEE SHOP COUPLE IN CHICAGO.
CHICAGO! THAT MEANS WE CAN GET PIZZA.
OKAY, I'M NOT SAYING IT'S NOT TASTY, BUT LET'S BE CLEAR. IT'S ALSO NOT PIZZA. IT'S A CASSEROLE.

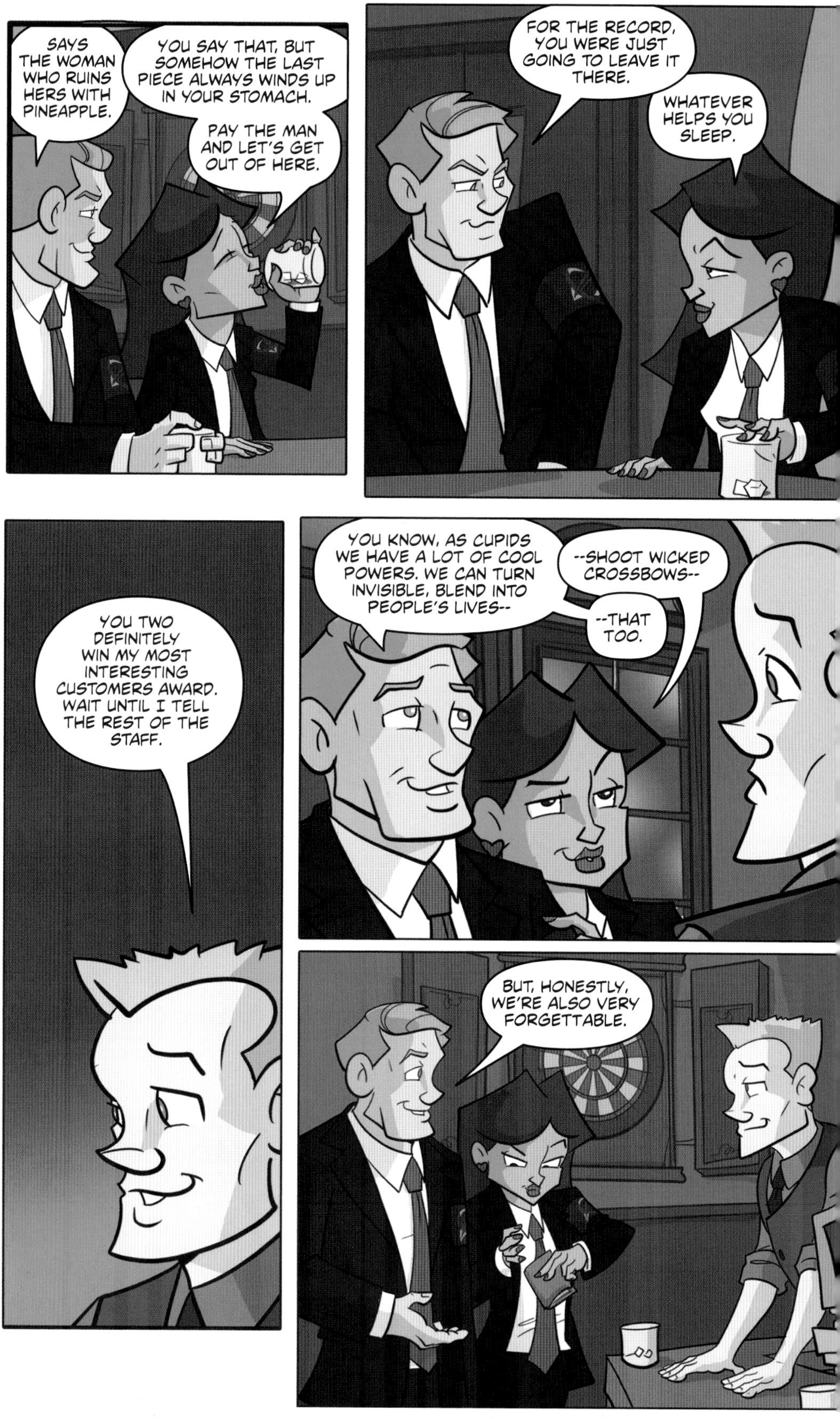
SAYS THE WOMAN WHO RUINS HERS WITH PINEAPPLE.
YOU SAY THAT, BUT SOMEHOW THE LAST PIECE ALWAYS WINDS UP IN YOUR STOMACH.
PAY THE MAN AND LET'S GET OUT OF HERE.
FOR THE RECORD, YOU WERE JUST GOING TO LEAVE IT THERE.
WHATEVER HELPS YOU SLEEP.
YOU TWO DEFINITELY WIN MY MOST INTERESTING CUSTOMERS AWARD. WAIT UNTIL I TELL THE REST OF THE STAFF.
YOU KNOW, AS CUPIDS WE HAVE A LOT OF COOL POWERS. WE CAN TURN INVISIBLE, BLEND INTO PEOPLE'S LIVES--
--SHOOT WICKED CROSSBOWS--
--THAT TOO.
BUT, HONESTLY, WE'RE ALSO VERY FORGETTABLE.

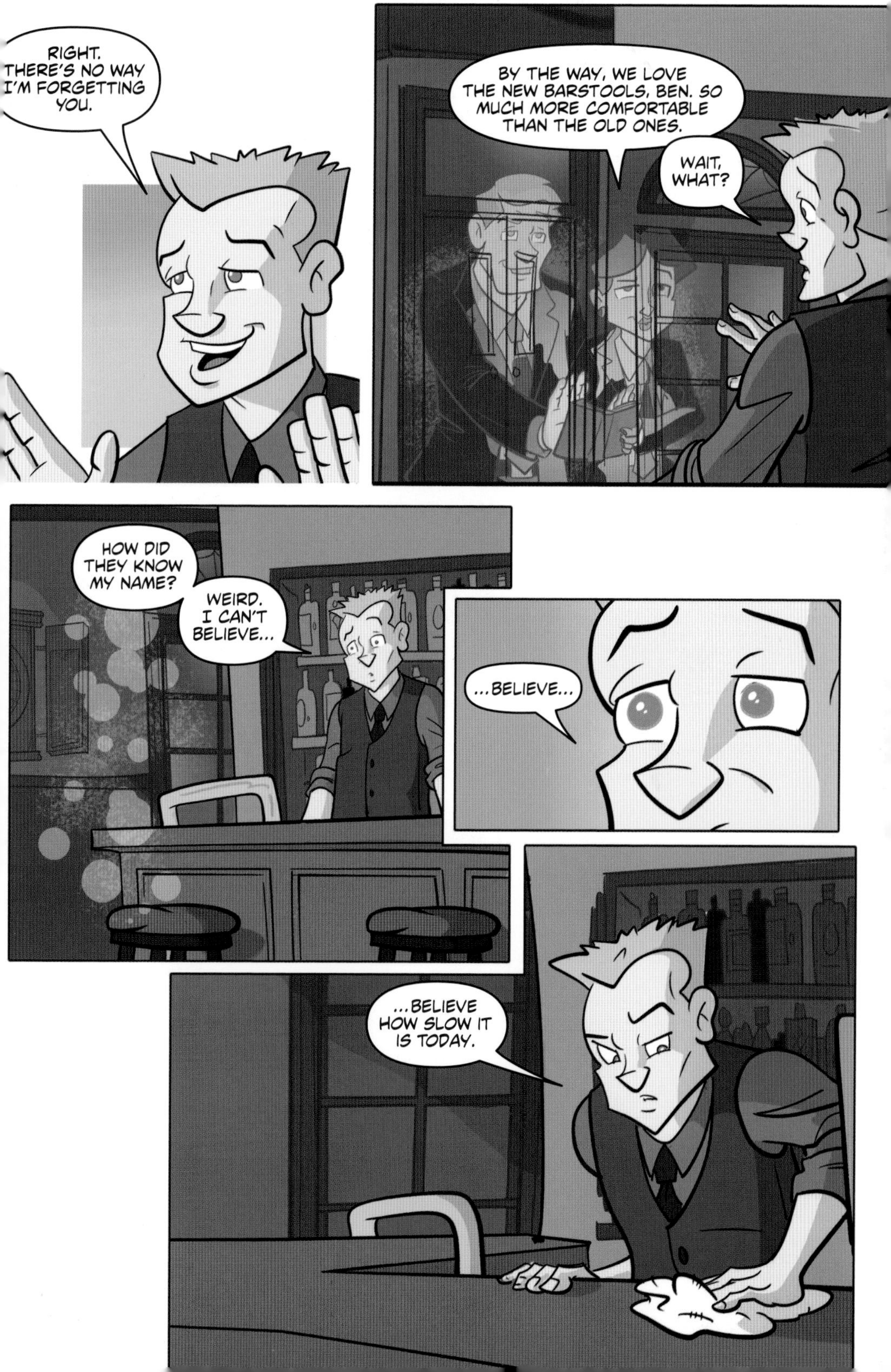
RIGHT. THERE'S NO WAY I'M FORGETTING YOU.
BY THE WAY, WE LOVE THE NEW BARSTOOLS, BEN. SO MUCH MORE COMFORTABLE THAN THE OLD ONES.
WAIT, WHAT?
HOW DID THEY KNOW MY NAME?
WEIRD. I CAN'T BELIEVE...
...BELIEVE...
...BELIEVE HOW SLOW IT IS TODAY.

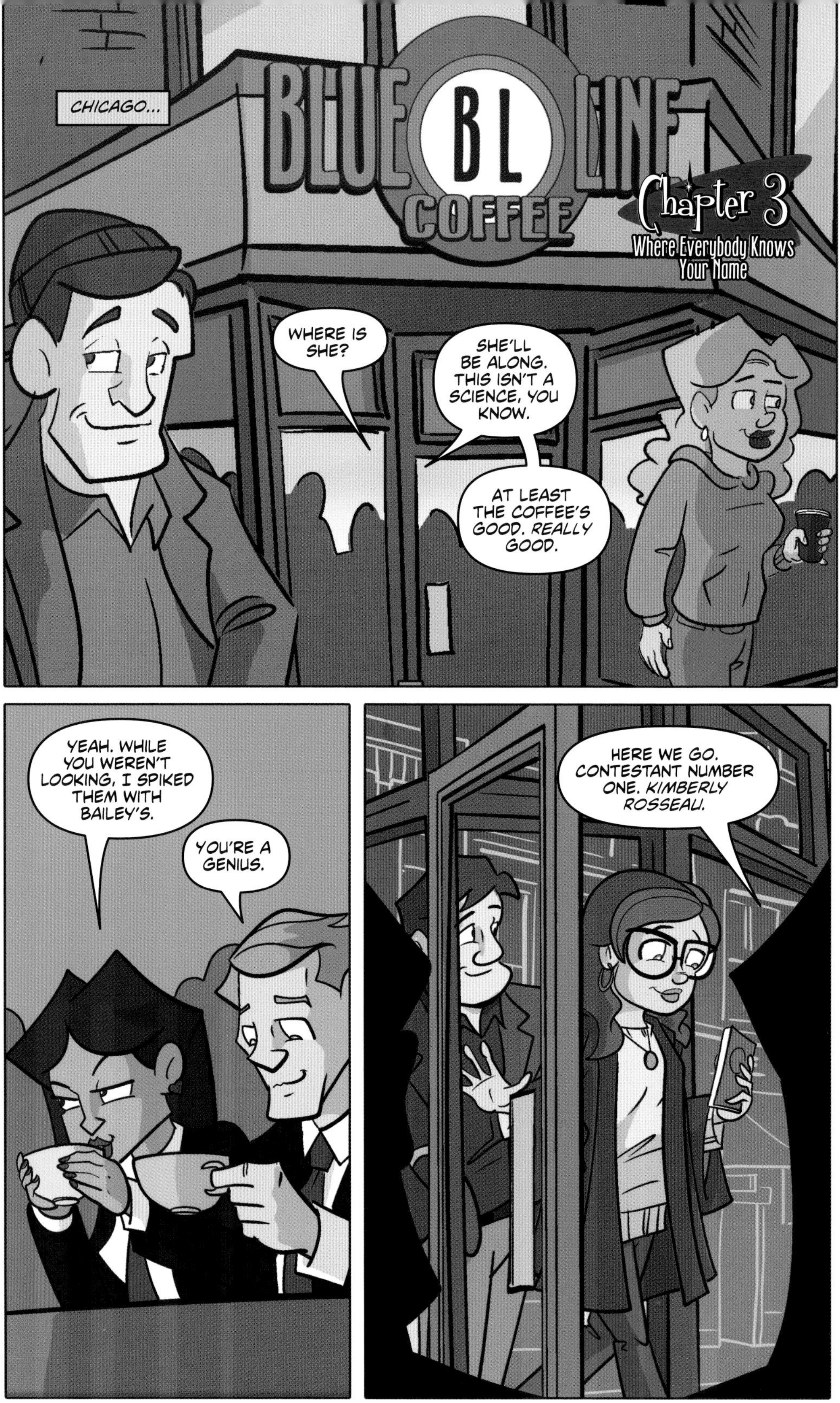
CHICAGO...
BLUE BL LINE COFFEE
Chapter 3
Where Everybody Knows Your Name
WHERE IS SHE?
SHE'LL BE ALONG. THIS ISN'T A SCIENCE, YOU KNOW.
AT LEAST THE COFFEE'S GOOD. REALLY GOOD.
YEAH. WHILE YOU WEREN'T LOOKING, I SPIKED THEM WITH BAILEY'S.
YOU'RE A GENIUS.
HERE WE GO. CONTESTANT NUMBER ONE. KIMBERLY ROSSEAU.

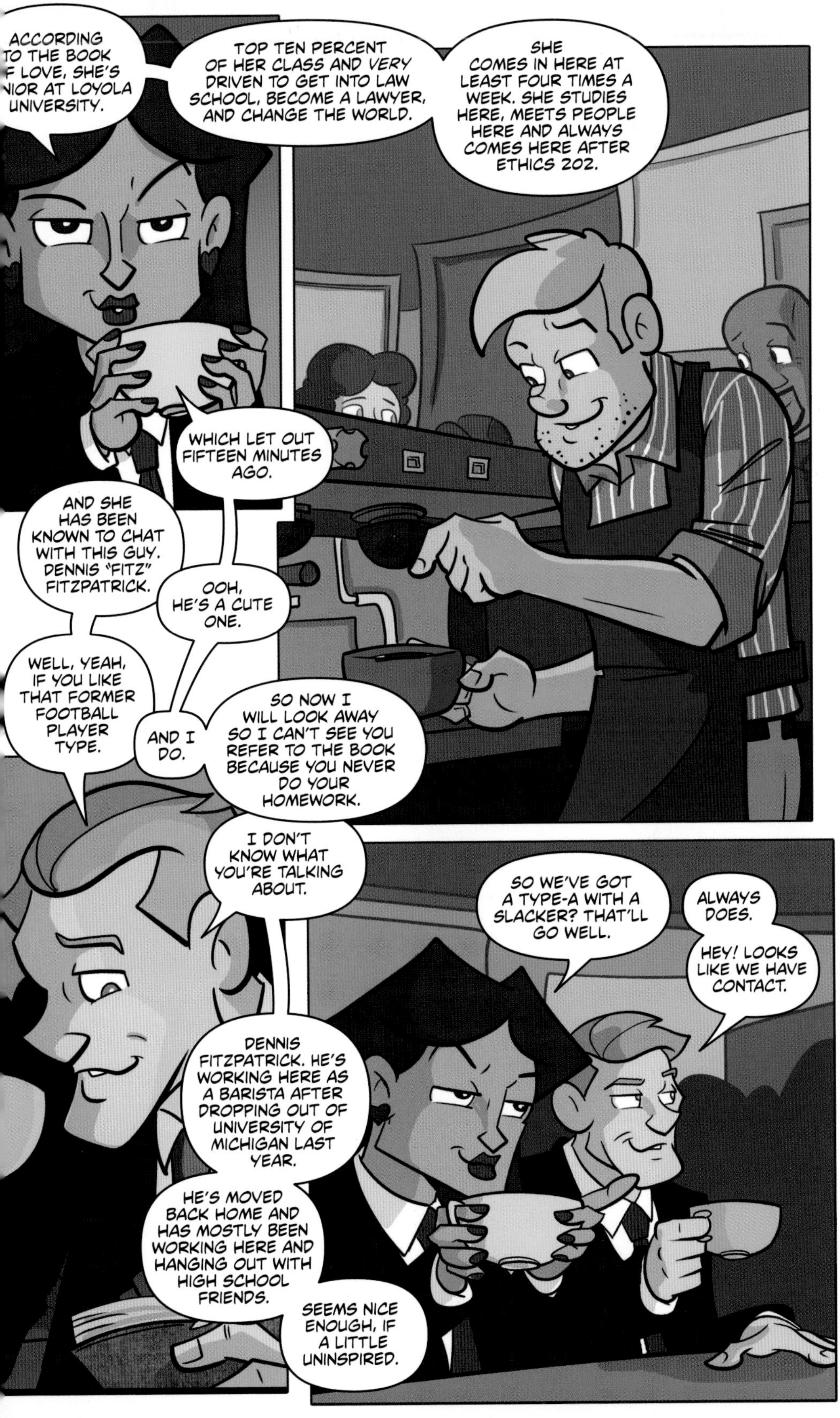
ACCORDING TO THE BOOK F LOVE, SHE'S NIOR AT LOYOLA UNIVERSITY.
TOP TEN PERCENT OF HER CLASS AND *VERY* DRIVEN TO GET INTO LAW SCHOOL, BECOME A LAWYER, AND CHANGE THE WORLD.
SHE COMES IN HERE AT LEAST FOUR TIMES A WEEK. SHE STUDIES HERE, MEETS PEOPLE HERE AND ALWAYS COMES HERE AFTER ETHICS 202.
WHICH LET OUT FIFTEEN MINUTES AGO.
AND SHE HAS BEEN KNOWN TO CHAT WITH THIS GUY. DENNIS "FITZ" FITZPATRICK.
OOH, HE'S A CUTE ONE.
WELL, YEAH, IF YOU LIKE THAT FORMER FOOTBALL PLAYER TYPE.
AND I DO.
SO NOW I WILL LOOK AWAY SO I CAN'T SEE YOU REFER TO THE BOOK BECAUSE YOU NEVER DO YOUR HOMEWORK.
I DON'T KNOW WHAT YOU'RE TALKING ABOUT.
DENNIS FITZPATRICK. HE'S WORKING HERE AS A BARISTA AFTER DROPPING OUT OF UNIVERSITY OF MICHIGAN LAST YEAR.
HE'S MOVED BACK HOME AND HAS MOSTLY BEEN WORKING HERE AND HANGING OUT WITH HIGH SCHOOL FRIENDS.
SEEMS NICE ENOUGH, IF A LITTLE UNINSPIRED.
SO WE'VE GOT A TYPE-A WITH A SLACKER? THAT'LL GO WELL.
ALWAYS DOES.
HEY! LOOKS LIKE WE HAVE CONTACT.

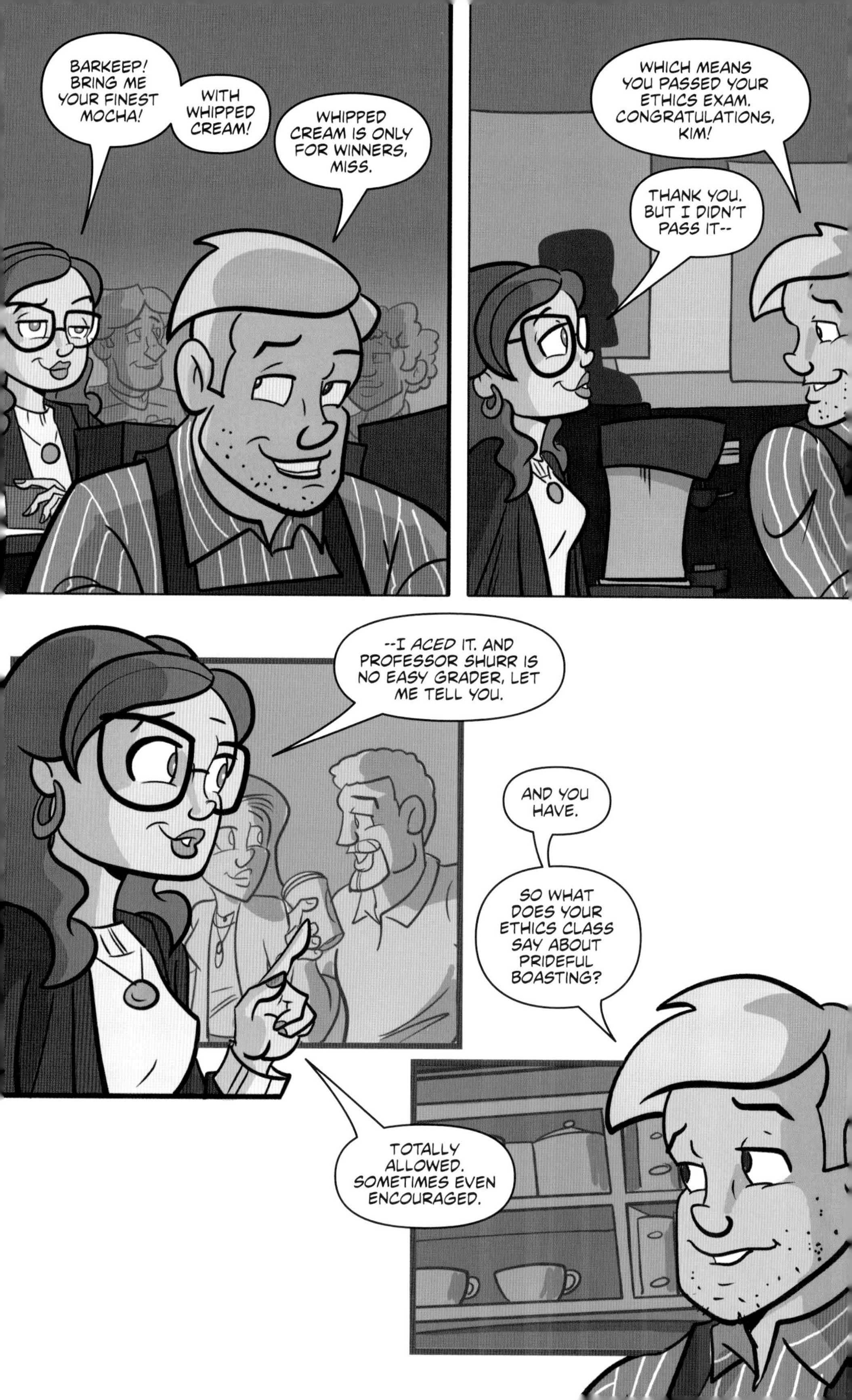
BARKEEP! BRING ME YOUR FINEST MOCHA!
WITH WHIPPED CREAM!
WHIPPED CREAM IS ONLY FOR WINNERS, MISS.
WHICH MEANS YOU PASSED YOUR ETHICS EXAM. CONGRATULATIONS, KIM!
THANK YOU. BUT I DIDN'T PASS IT--
--I *ACED* IT. AND PROFESSOR SHURR IS NO EASY GRADER, LET ME TELL YOU.
AND YOU HAVE.
SO WHAT DOES YOUR ETHICS CLASS SAY ABOUT PRIDEFUL BOASTING?
TOTALLY ALLOWED. SOMETIMES EVEN ENCOURAGED.

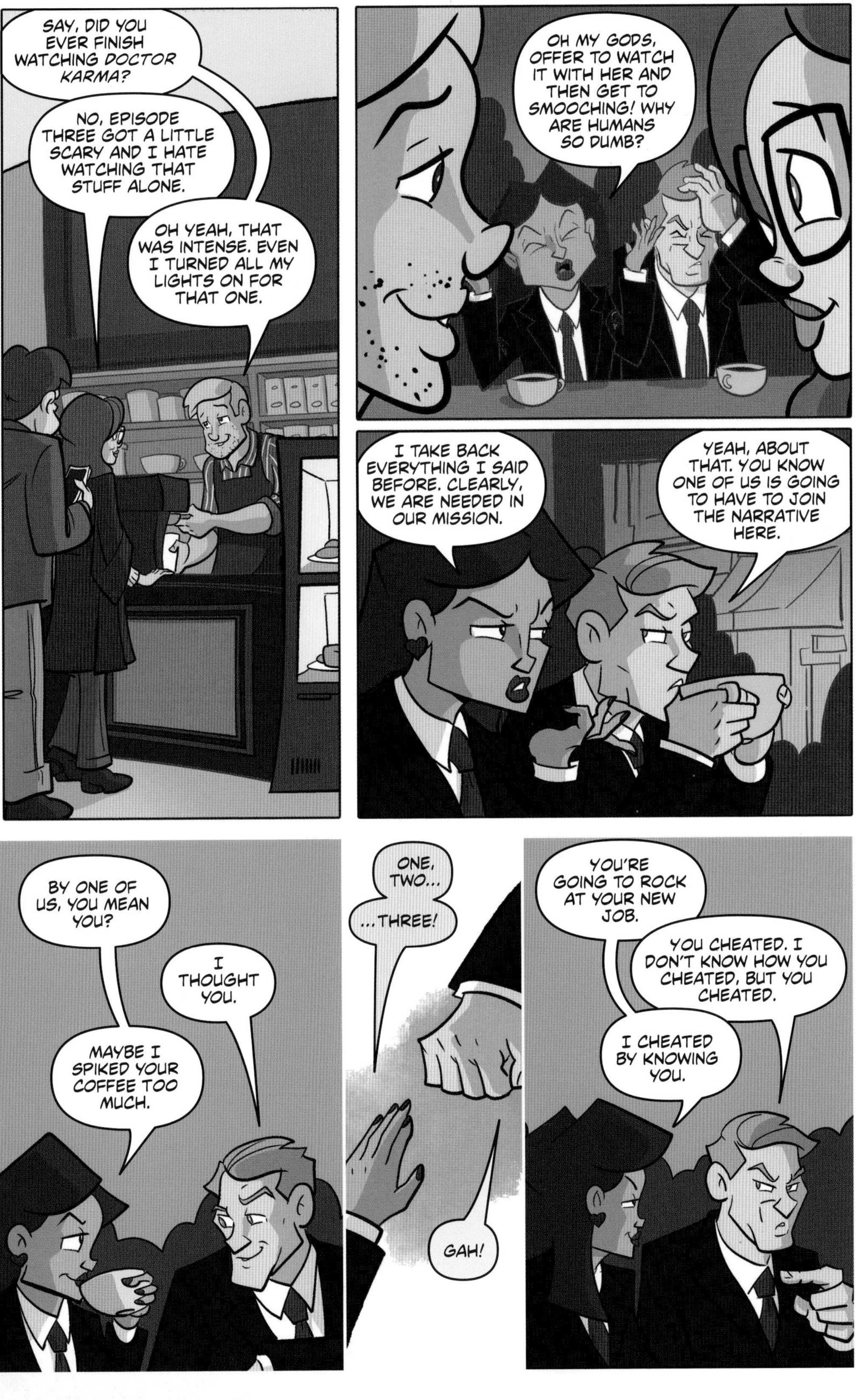
SAY, DID YOU EVER FINISH WATCHING *DOCTOR KARMA*?
NO, EPISODE THREE GOT A LITTLE SCARY AND I HATE WATCHING THAT STUFF ALONE.
OH YEAH, THAT WAS INTENSE. EVEN I TURNED ALL MY LIGHTS ON FOR THAT ONE.
OH MY GODS, OFFER TO WATCH IT WITH HER AND THEN GET TO SMOOCHING! WHY ARE HUMANS SO DUMB?
I TAKE BACK EVERYTHING I SAID BEFORE. CLEARLY, WE ARE NEEDED IN OUR MISSION.
YEAH, ABOUT THAT. YOU KNOW ONE OF US IS GOING TO HAVE TO JOIN THE NARRATIVE HERE.
BY ONE OF US, YOU MEAN YOU?
I THOUGHT YOU.
MAYBE I SPIKED YOUR COFFEE TOO MUCH.
ONE, TWO...
...THREE!
GAH!
YOU'RE GOING TO ROCK AT YOUR NEW JOB.
YOU CHEATED. I DON'T KNOW HOW YOU CHEATED, BUT YOU CHEATED.
I CHEATED BY KNOWING YOU.

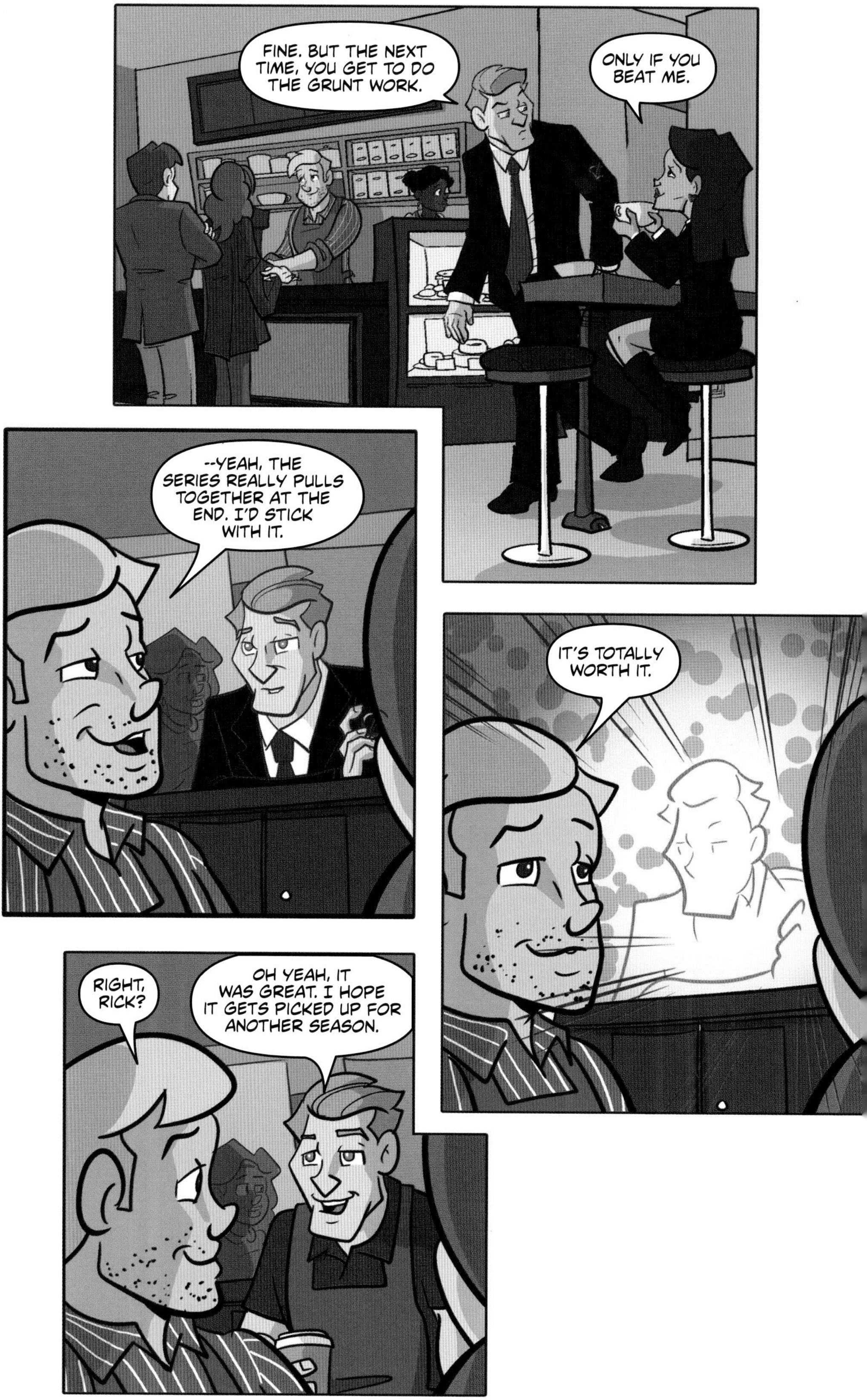
FINE. BUT THE NEXT TIME, YOU GET TO DO THE GRUNT WORK.
ONLY IF YOU BEAT ME.
--YEAH, THE SERIES REALLY PULLS TOGETHER AT THE END. I'D STICK WITH IT.
IT'S TOTALLY WORTH IT.
RIGHT, RICK?
OH YEAH, IT WAS GREAT. I HOPE IT GETS PICKED UP FOR ANOTHER SEASON.

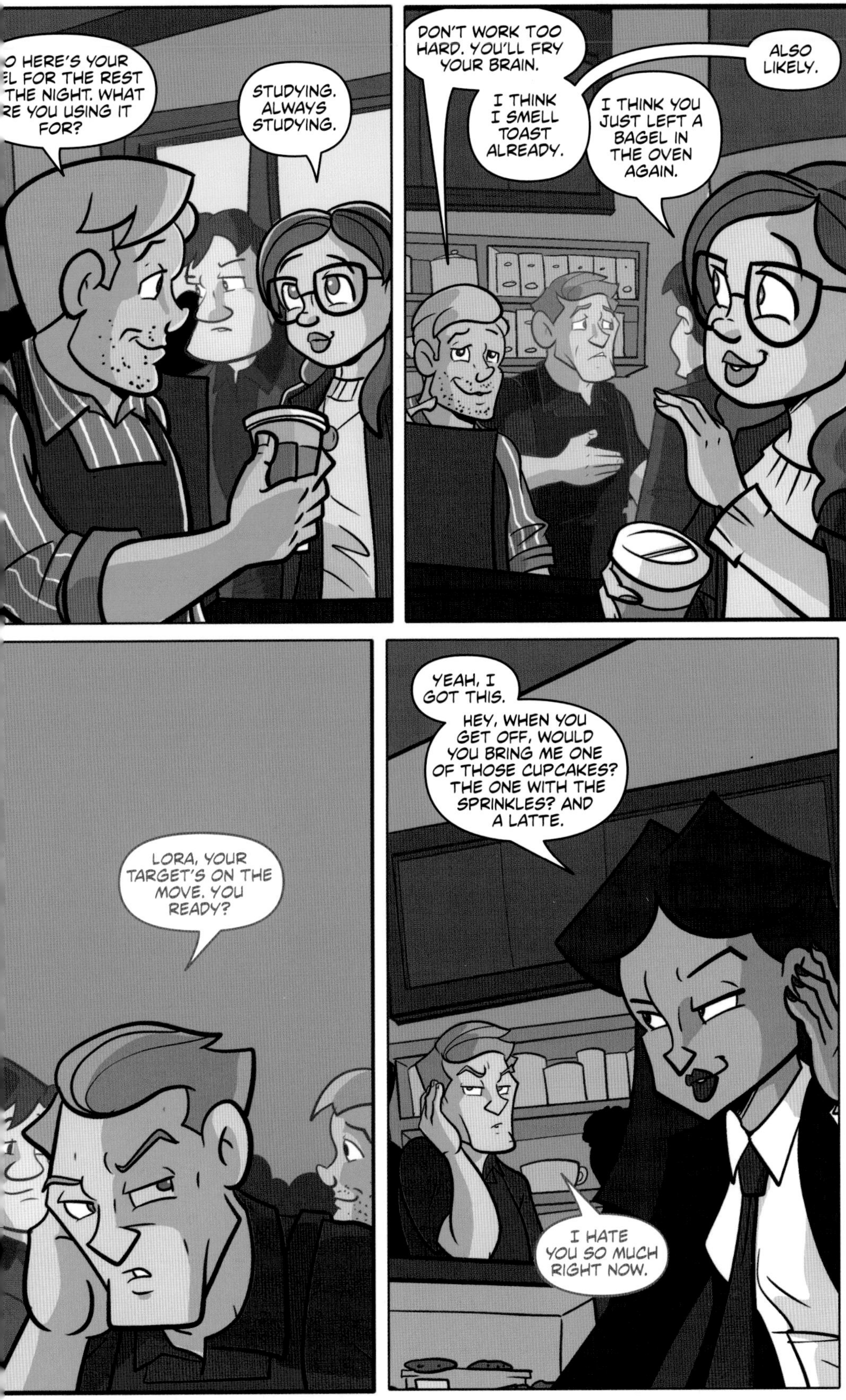
O HERE'S YOUR
EL FOR THE REST
THE NIGHT. WHAT
RE YOU USING IT
FOR?
STUDYING. ALWAYS STUDYING.
DON'T WORK TOO HARD. YOU'LL FRY YOUR BRAIN.
I THINK I SMELL TOAST ALREADY.
I THINK YOU JUST LEFT A BAGEL IN THE OVEN AGAIN.
ALSO LIKELY.
LORA, YOUR TARGET'S ON THE MOVE. YOU READY?
YEAH, I GOT THIS.
HEY, WHEN YOU GET OFF, WOULD YOU BRING ME ONE OF THOSE CUPCAKES? THE ONE WITH THE SPRINKLES? AND A LATTE.
I HATE YOU SO MUCH RIGHT NOW.

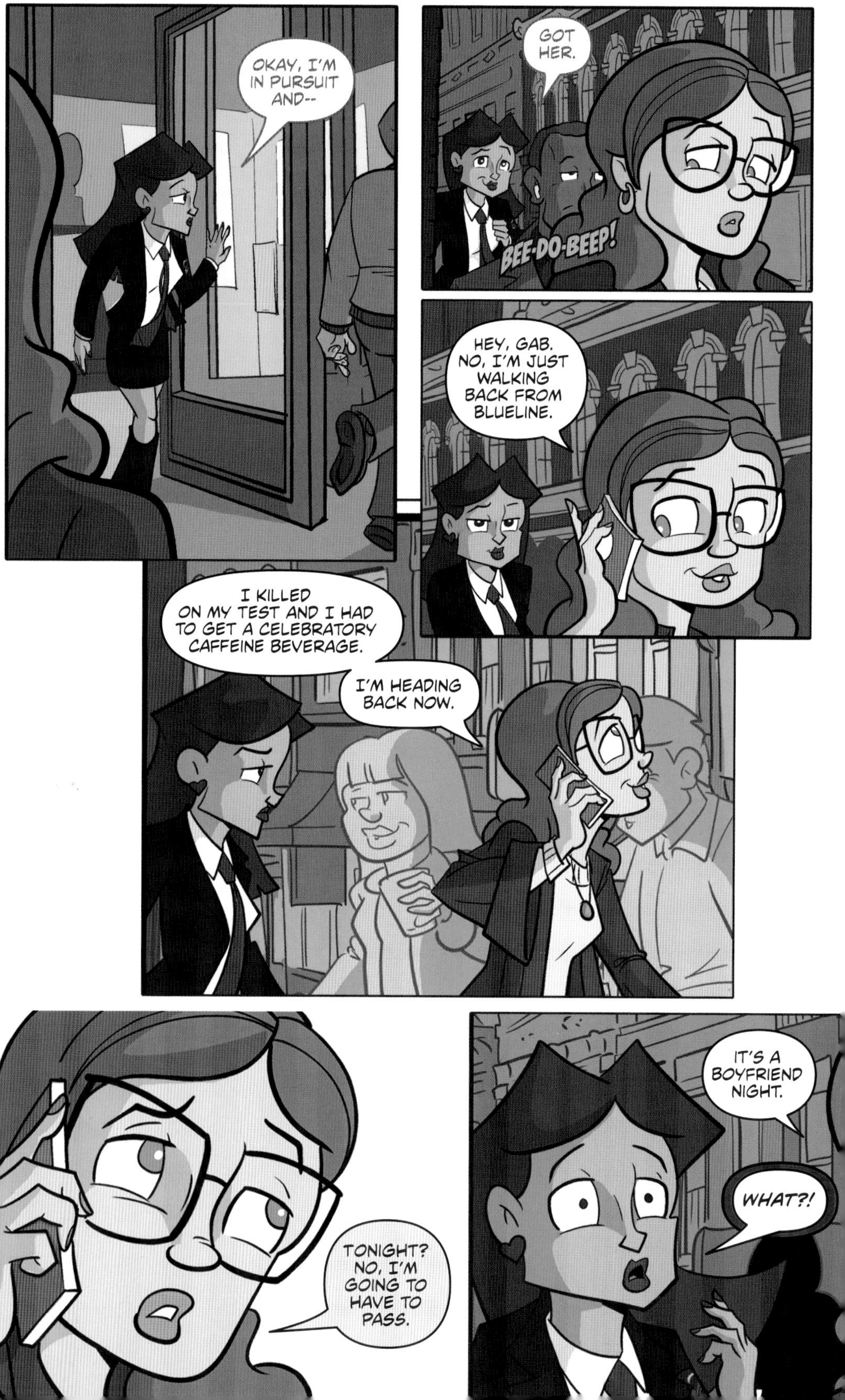
OKAY, I'M IN PURSUIT AND--
GOT HER.
BEE-DO-BEEP!
HEY, GAB. NO, I'M JUST WALKING BACK FROM BLUELINE.
I KILLED ON MY TEST AND I HAD TO GET A CELEBRATORY CAFFEINE BEVERAGE.
I'M HEADING BACK NOW.
TONIGHT? NO, I'M GOING TO HAVE TO PASS.
IT'S A BOYFRIEND NIGHT.
WHAT?!

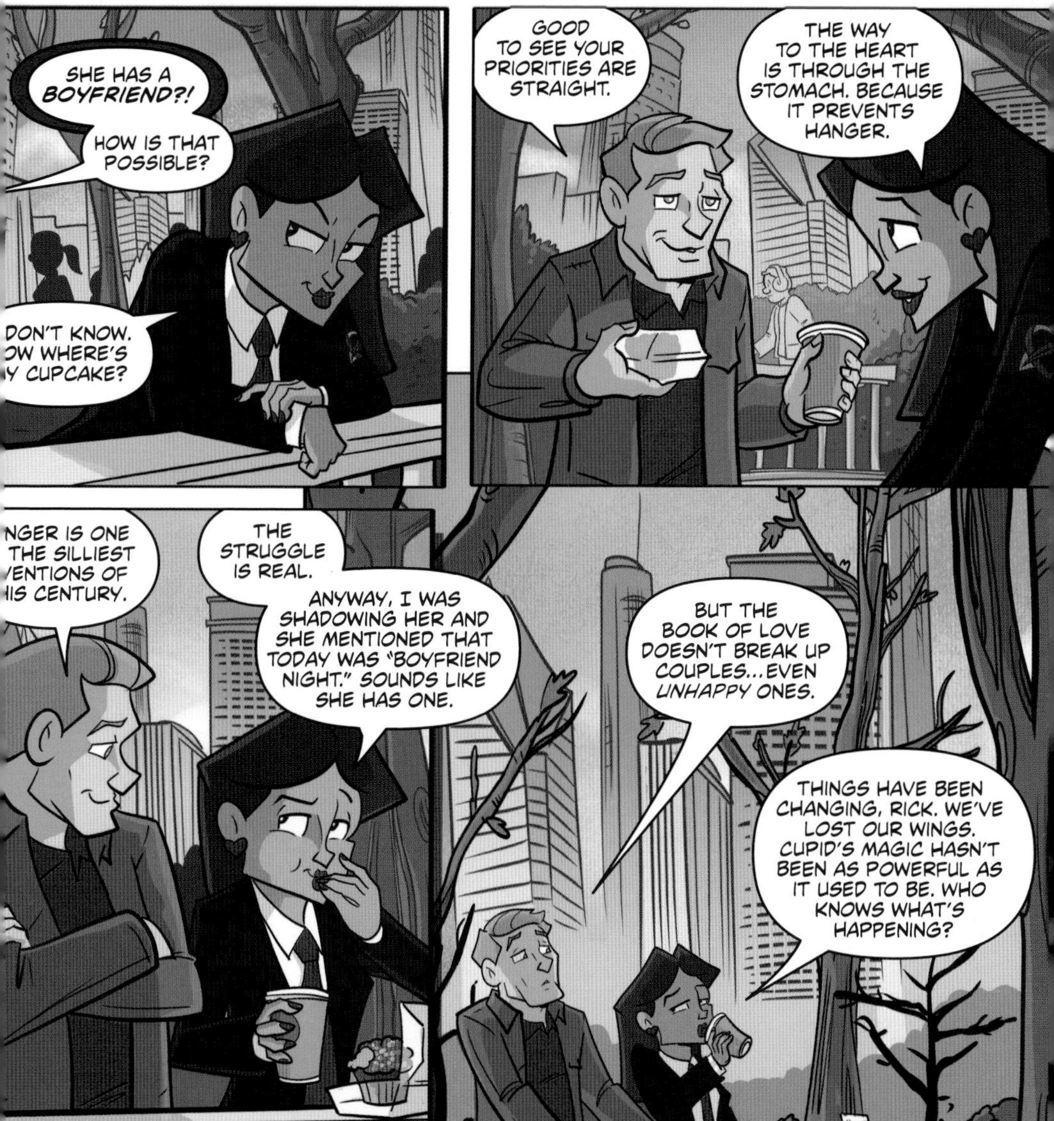
SHE HAS A *BOYFRIEND?!*
HOW IS THAT POSSIBLE?
DON'T KNOW. OW WHERE'S Y CUPCAKE?
GOOD TO SEE YOUR PRIORITIES ARE STRAIGHT.
THE WAY TO THE HEART IS THROUGH THE STOMACH. BECAUSE IT PREVENTS HANGER.
NGER IS ONE THE SILLIEST VENTIONS OF IIS CENTURY.
THE STRUGGLE IS REAL.
ANYWAY, I WAS SHADOWING HER AND SHE MENTIONED THAT TODAY WAS "BOYFRIEND NIGHT." SOUNDS LIKE SHE HAS ONE.
BUT THE BOOK OF LOVE DOESN'T BREAK UP COUPLES...EVEN *UNHAPPY* ONES.
THINGS HAVE BEEN CHANGING, RICK. WE'VE LOST OUR WINGS. CUPID'S MAGIC HASN'T BEEN AS POWERFUL AS IT USED TO BE. WHO KNOWS WHAT'S HAPPENING?

Chapter 4

Foolproof Face

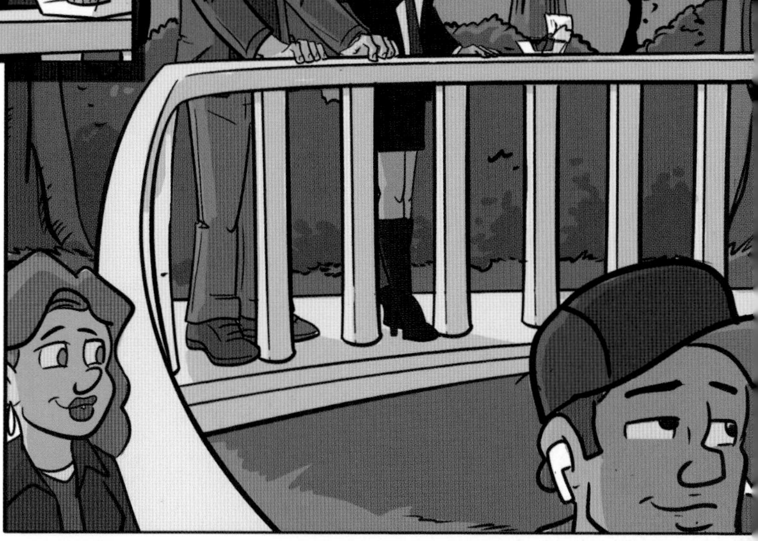

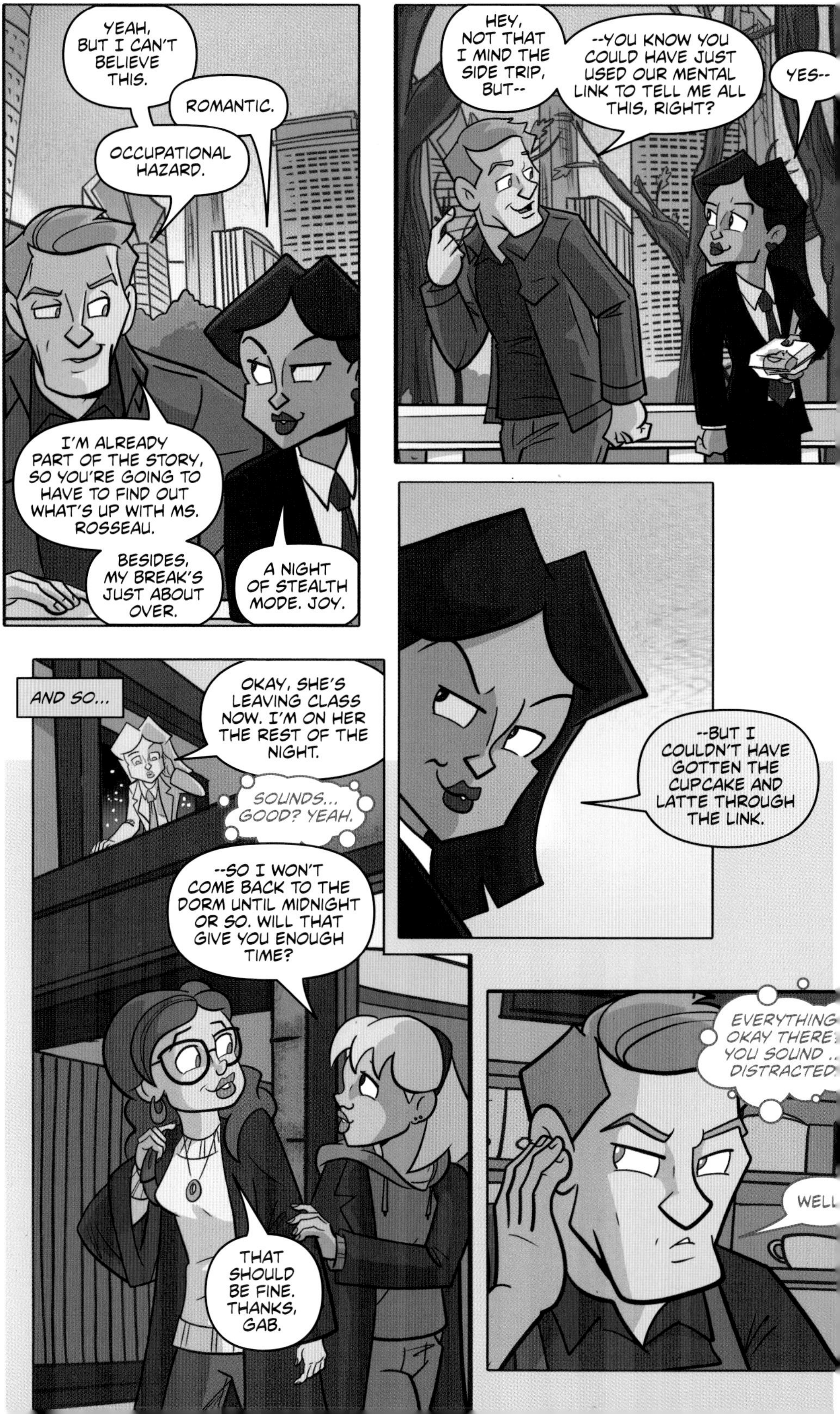

YEAH, BUT I CAN'T BELIEVE THIS.
ROMANTIC.
OCCUPATIONAL HAZARD.
I'M ALREADY PART OF THE STORY, SO YOU'RE GOING TO HAVE TO FIND OUT WHAT'S UP WITH MS. ROSSEAU.
BESIDES, MY BREAK'S JUST ABOUT OVER.
A NIGHT OF STEALTH MODE. JOY.
HEY, NOT THAT I MIND THE SIDE TRIP, BUT--
--YOU KNOW YOU COULD HAVE JUST USED OUR MENTAL LINK TO TELL ME ALL THIS, RIGHT?
YES--
--BUT I COULDN'T HAVE GOTTEN THE CUPCAKE AND LATTE THROUGH THE LINK.
AND SO...
OKAY, SHE'S LEAVING CLASS NOW. I'M ON HER THE REST OF THE NIGHT.
SOUNDS... GOOD? YEAH.
--SO I WON'T COME BACK TO THE DORM UNTIL MIDNIGHT OR SO. WILL THAT GIVE YOU ENOUGH TIME?
THAT SHOULD BE FINE. THANKS, GAB.
EVERYTHING OKAY THERE? YOU SOUND ... DISTRACTED.
WELL

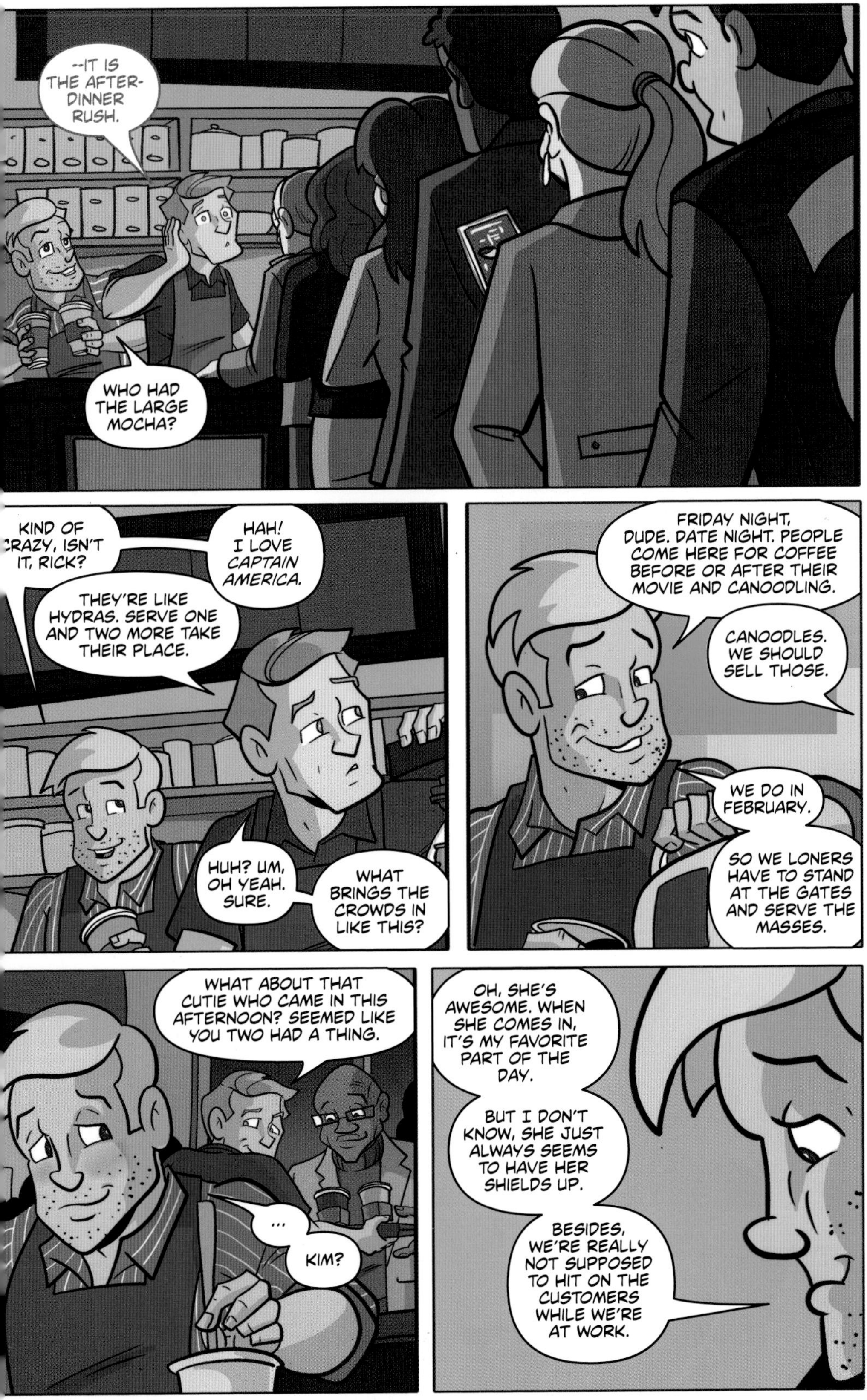
--IT IS THE AFTER-DINNER RUSH.
WHO HAD THE LARGE MOCHA?
KIND OF CRAZY, ISN'T IT, RICK?
HAH! I LOVE CAPTAIN AMERICA.
THEY'RE LIKE HYDRAS. SERVE ONE AND TWO MORE TAKE THEIR PLACE.
HUH? UM, OH YEAH. SURE.
WHAT BRINGS THE CROWDS IN LIKE THIS?
FRIDAY NIGHT, DUDE. DATE NIGHT. PEOPLE COME HERE FOR COFFEE BEFORE OR AFTER THEIR MOVIE AND CANOODLING.
CANOODLES. WE SHOULD SELL THOSE.
WE DO IN FEBRUARY.
SO WE LONERS HAVE TO STAND AT THE GATES AND SERVE THE MASSES.
WHAT ABOUT THAT CUTIE WHO CAME IN THIS AFTERNOON? SEEMED LIKE YOU TWO HAD A THING.
...
KIM?
OH, SHE'S AWESOME. WHEN SHE COMES IN, IT'S MY FAVORITE PART OF THE DAY.
BUT I DON'T KNOW, SHE JUST ALWAYS SEEMS TO HAVE HER SHIELDS UP.
BESIDES, WE'RE REALLY NOT SUPPOSED TO HIT ON THE CUSTOMERS WHILE WE'RE AT WORK.

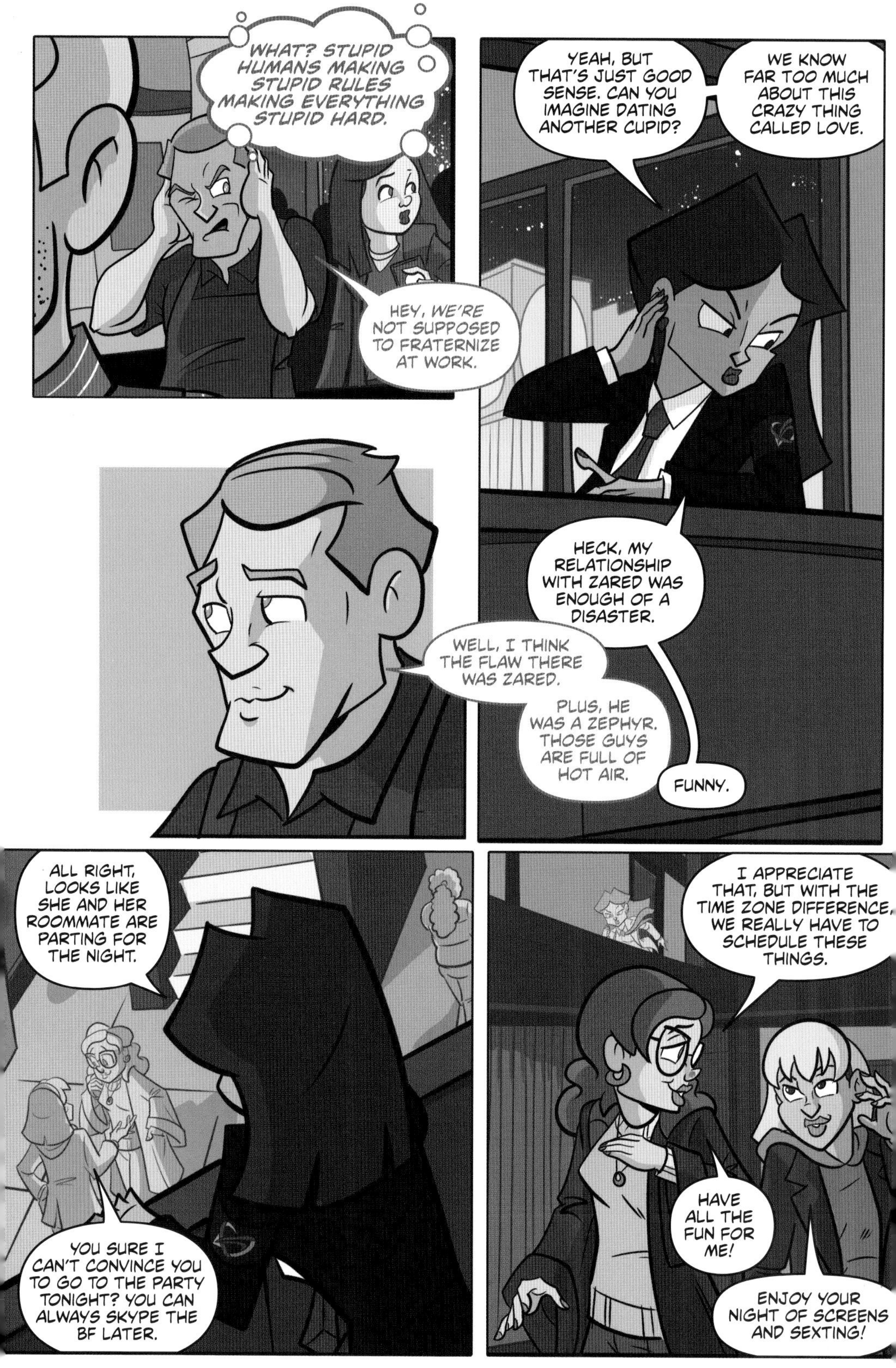
WHAT? STUPID HUMANS MAKING STUPID RULES MAKING EVERYTHING STUPID HARD.
HEY, WE'RE NOT SUPPOSED TO FRATERNIZE AT WORK.
YEAH, BUT THAT'S JUST GOOD SENSE. CAN YOU IMAGINE DATING ANOTHER CUPID?
WE KNOW FAR TOO MUCH ABOUT THIS CRAZY THING CALLED LOVE.
HECK, MY RELATIONSHIP WITH ZARED WAS ENOUGH OF A DISASTER.
WELL, I THINK THE FLAW THERE WAS ZARED.
PLUS, HE WAS A ZEPHYR. THOSE GUYS ARE FULL OF HOT AIR.
FUNNY.
ALL RIGHT, LOOKS LIKE SHE AND HER ROOMMATE ARE PARTING FOR THE NIGHT.
YOU SURE I CAN'T CONVINCE YOU TO GO TO THE PARTY TONIGHT? YOU CAN ALWAYS SKYPE THE BF LATER.
I APPRECIATE THAT, BUT WITH THE TIME ZONE DIFFERENCE, WE REALLY HAVE TO SCHEDULE THESE THINGS.
HAVE ALL THE FUN FOR ME!
ENJOY YOUR NIGHT OF SCREENS AND SEXTING!

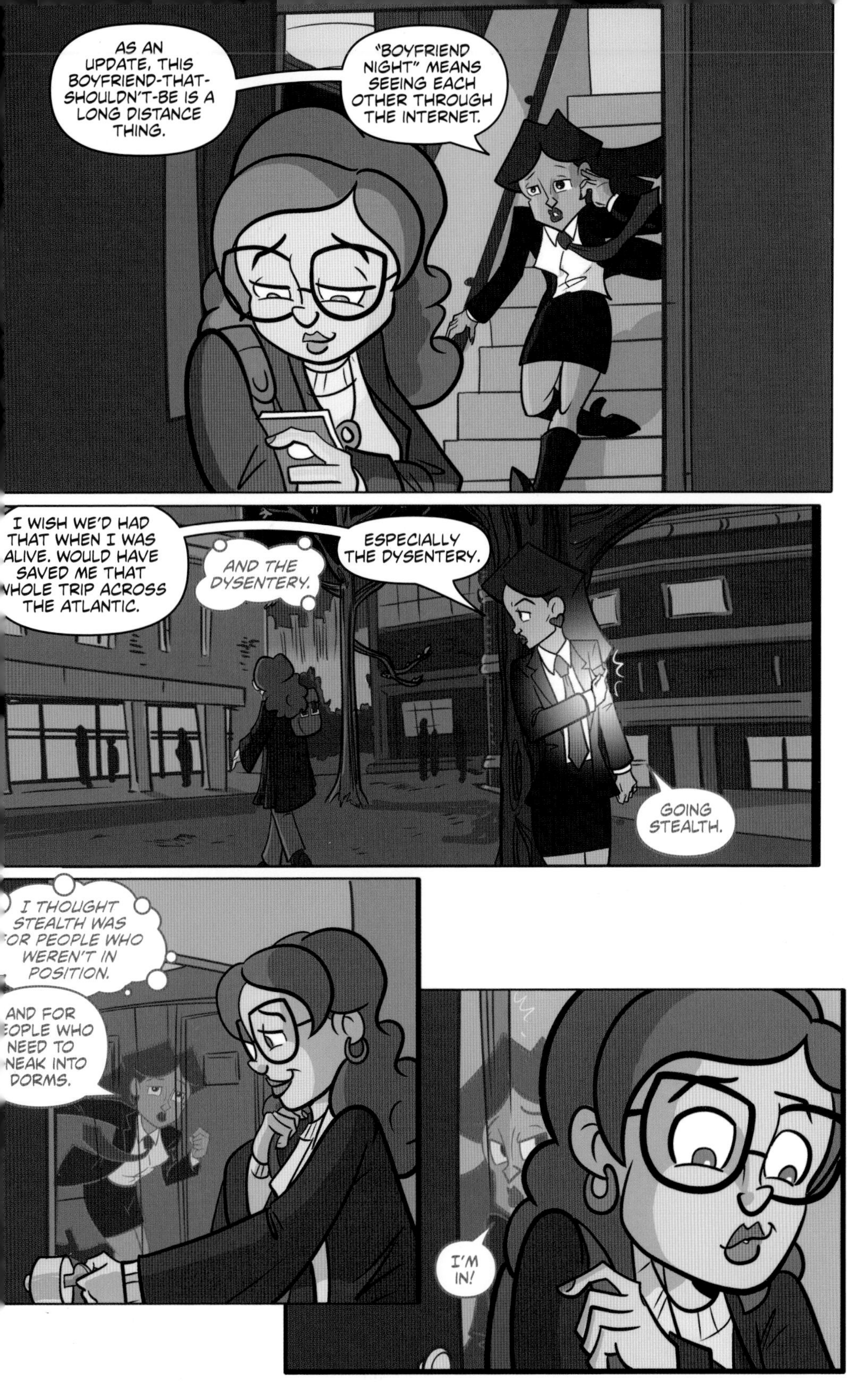
AS AN UPDATE, THIS BOYFRIEND-THAT-SHOULDN'T-BE IS A LONG DISTANCE THING.
"BOYFRIEND NIGHT" MEANS SEEING EACH OTHER THROUGH THE INTERNET.
I WISH WE'D HAD THAT WHEN I WAS ALIVE. WOULD HAVE SAVED ME THAT WHOLE TRIP ACROSS THE ATLANTIC.
AND THE DYSENTERY.
ESPECIALLY THE DYSENTERY.
GOING STEALTH.
I THOUGHT STEALTH WAS FOR PEOPLE WHO WEREN'T IN POSITION.
AND FOR PEOPLE WHO NEED TO SNEAK INTO DORMS.
I'M IN!

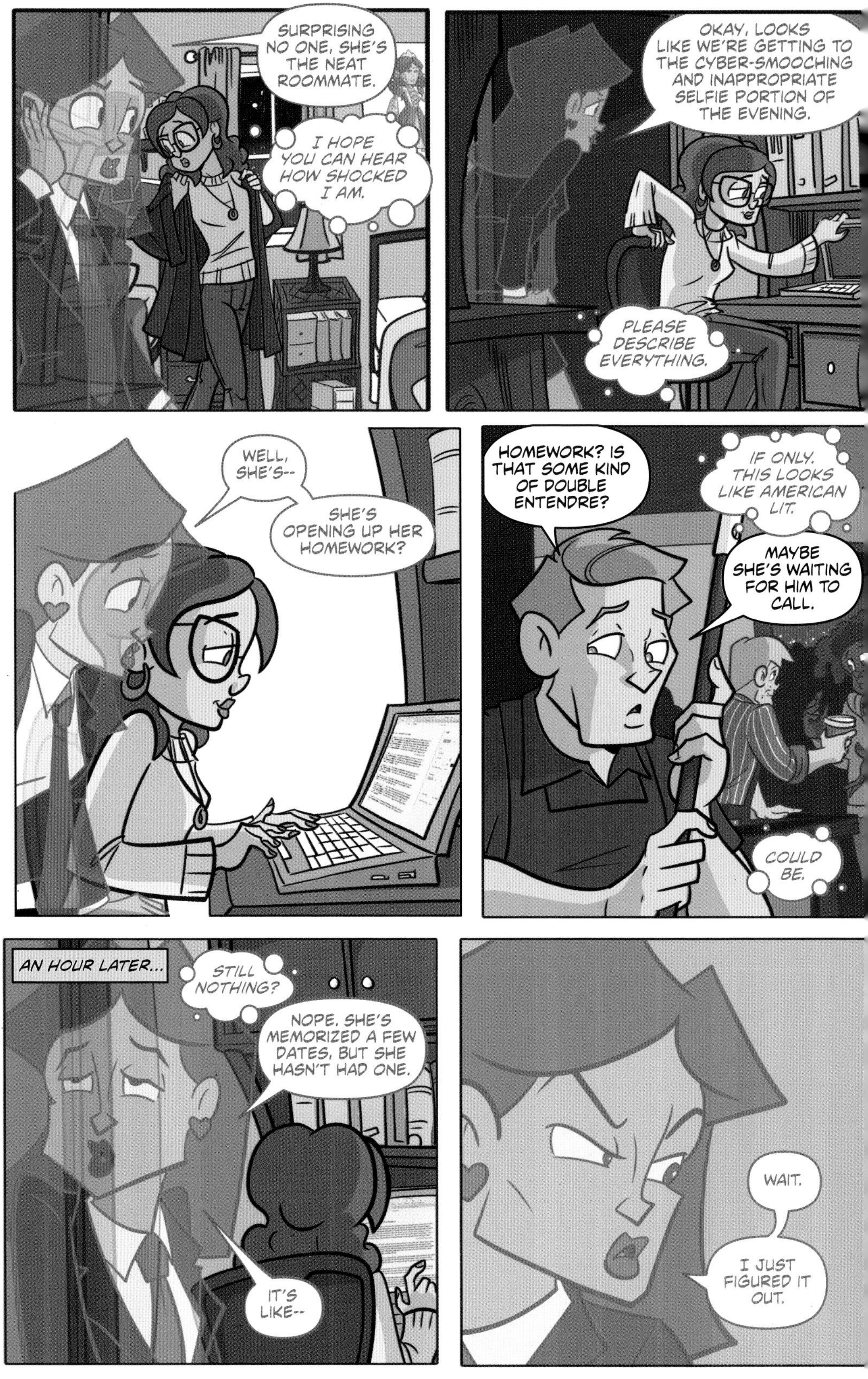
SURPRISING NO ONE, SHE'S THE NEAT ROOMMATE.
I HOPE YOU CAN HEAR HOW SHOCKED I AM.
OKAY, LOOKS LIKE WE'RE GETTING TO THE CYBER-SMOOCHING AND INAPPROPRIATE SELFIE PORTION OF THE EVENING.
PLEASE DESCRIBE EVERYTHING.
WELL, SHE'S--
SHE'S OPENING UP HER HOMEWORK?
HOMEWORK? IS THAT SOME KIND OF DOUBLE ENTENDRE?
IF ONLY. THIS LOOKS LIKE AMERICAN LIT.
MAYBE SHE'S WAITING FOR HIM TO CALL.
COULD BE.
AN HOUR LATER...
STILL NOTHING?
NOPE. SHE'S MEMORIZED A FEW DATES, BUT SHE HASN'T HAD ONE.
IT'S LIKE--
WAIT.
I JUST FIGURED IT OUT.

Chapter 5 My Dirty Little Secret

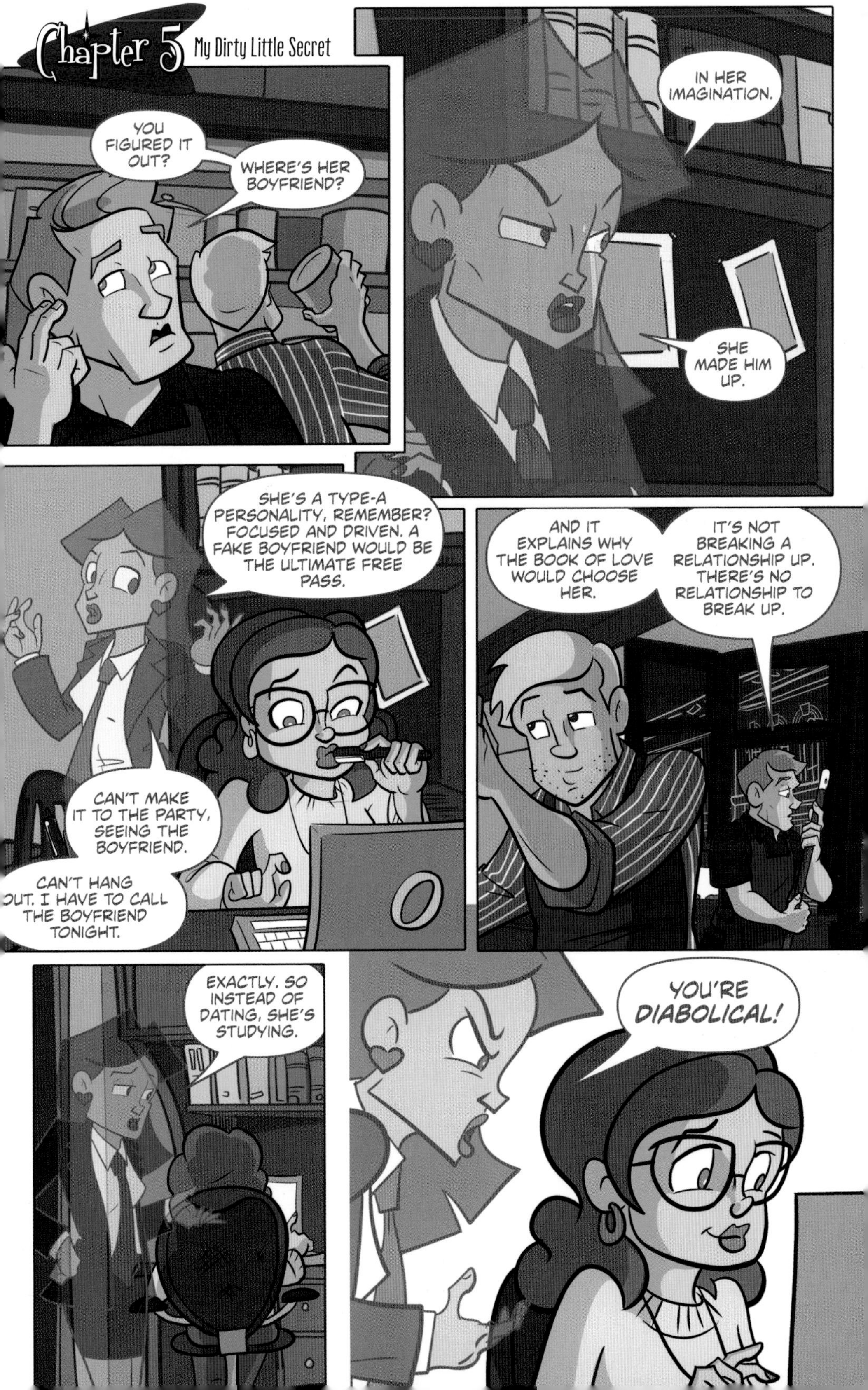
YOU FIGURED IT OUT?
WHERE'S HER BOYFRIEND?
IN HER IMAGINATION.
SHE MADE HIM UP.
SHE'S A TYPE-A PERSONALITY, REMEMBER? FOCUSED AND DRIVEN. A FAKE BOYFRIEND WOULD BE THE ULTIMATE FREE PASS.
CAN'T MAKE IT TO THE PARTY, SEEING THE BOYFRIEND.
CAN'T HANG OUT. I HAVE TO CALL THE BOYFRIEND TONIGHT.
AND IT EXPLAINS WHY THE BOOK OF LOVE WOULD CHOOSE HER.
IT'S NOT BREAKING A RELATIONSHIP UP. THERE'S NO RELATIONSHIP TO BREAK UP.
EXACTLY. SO INSTEAD OF DATING, SHE'S STUDYING.
YOU'RE *DIABOLICAL!*

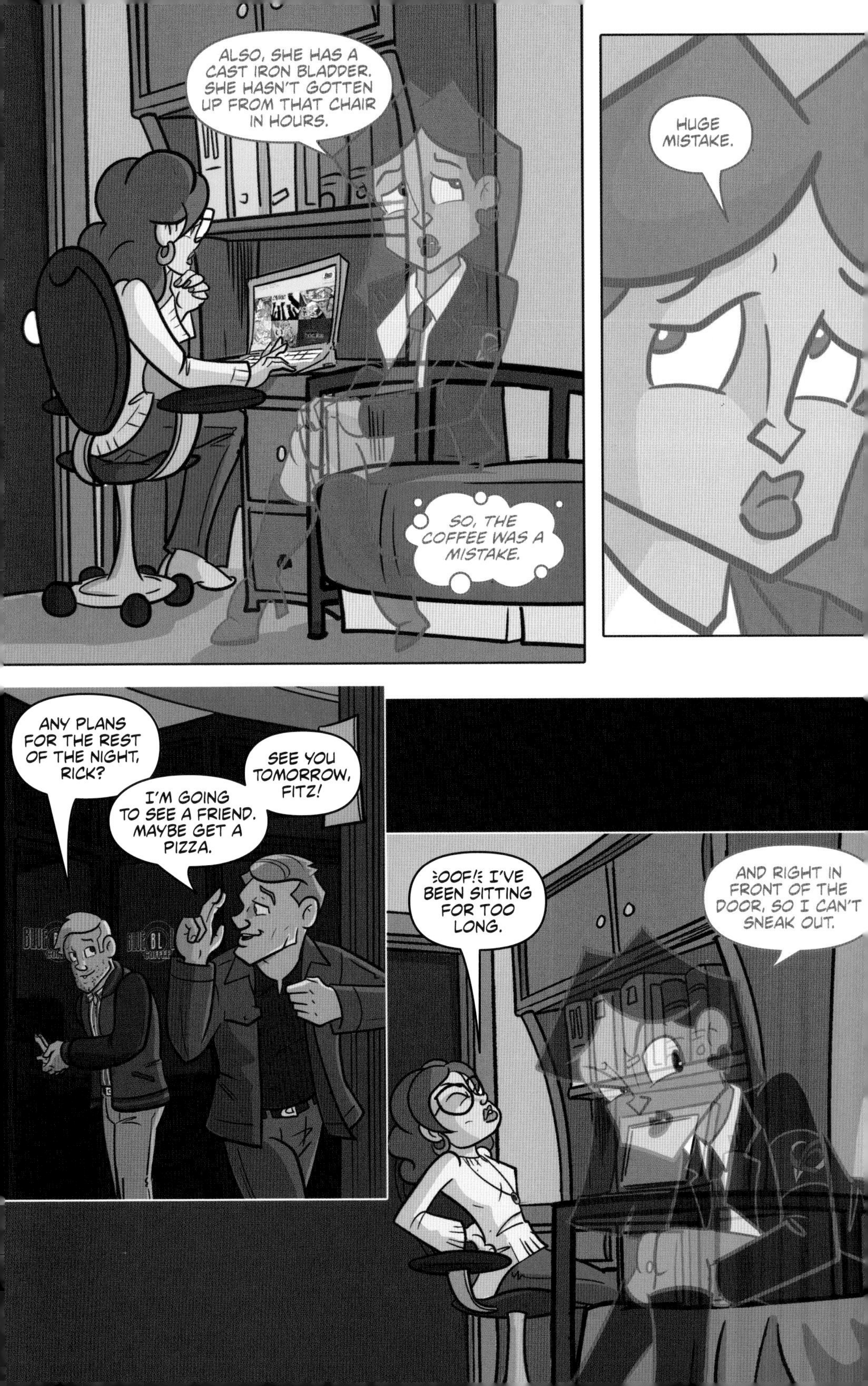
ALSO, SHE HAS A CAST IRON BLADDER. SHE HASN'T GOTTEN UP FROM THAT CHAIR IN HOURS.
SO, THE COFFEE WAS A MISTAKE.
HUGE MISTAKE.
ANY PLANS FOR THE REST OF THE NIGHT, RICK?
I'M GOING TO SEE A FRIEND. MAYBE GET A PIZZA.
SEE YOU TOMORROW, FITZ!
OOF! I'VE BEEN SITTING FOR TOO LONG.
AND RIGHT IN FRONT OF THE DOOR, SO I CAN'T SNEAK OUT.

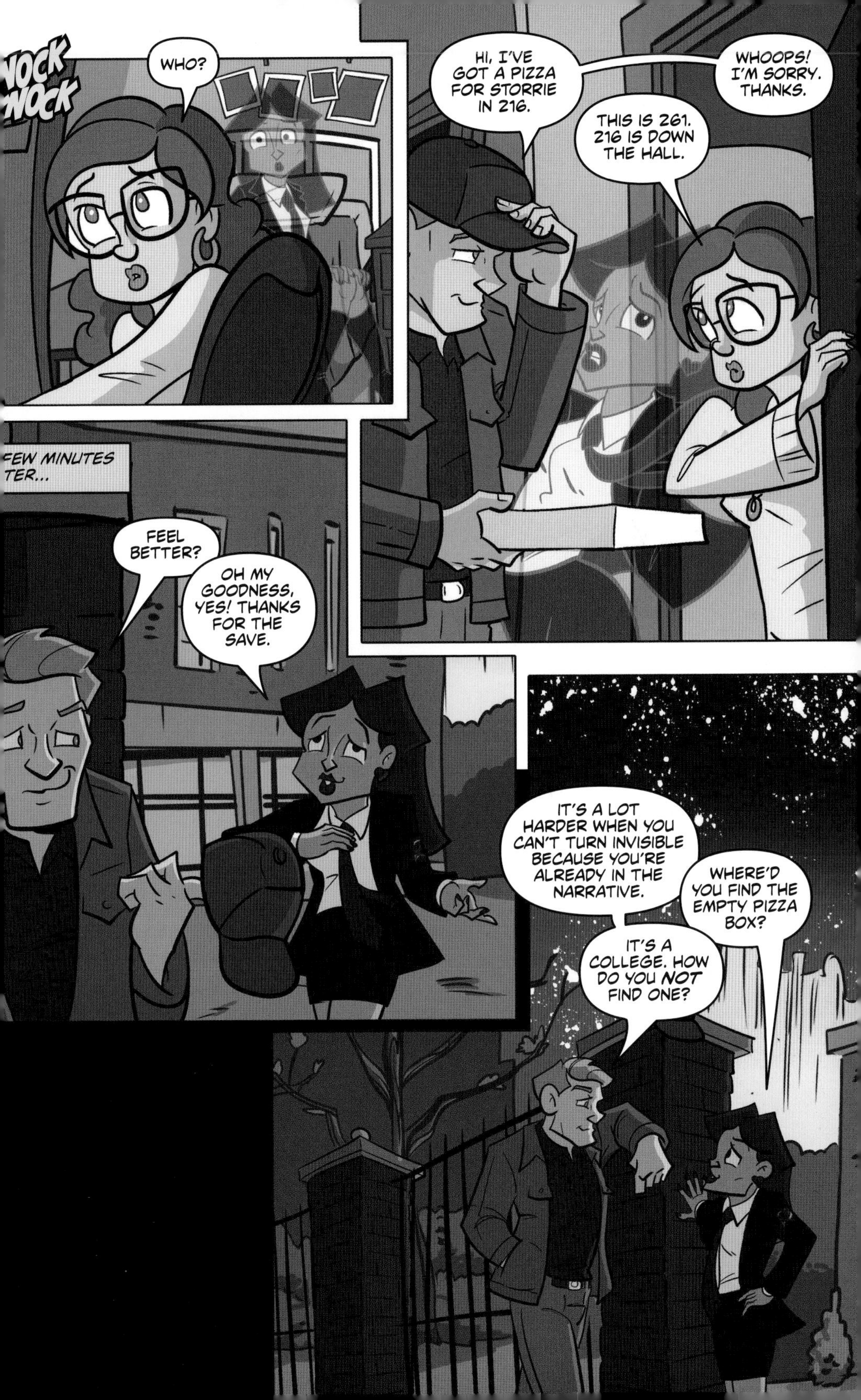
NOCK
NOCK
WHO?
HI, I'VE GOT A PIZZA FOR STORRIE IN 216.
THIS IS 261. 216 IS DOWN THE HALL.
WHOOPS! I'M SORRY. THANKS.
FEW MINUTES
TER...
FEEL BETTER?
OH MY GOODNESS, YES! THANKS FOR THE SAVE.
IT'S A LOT HARDER WHEN YOU CAN'T TURN INVISIBLE BECAUSE YOU'RE ALREADY IN THE NARRATIVE.
WHERE'D YOU FIND THE EMPTY PIZZA BOX?
IT'S A COLLEGE. HOW DO YOU NOT FIND ONE?

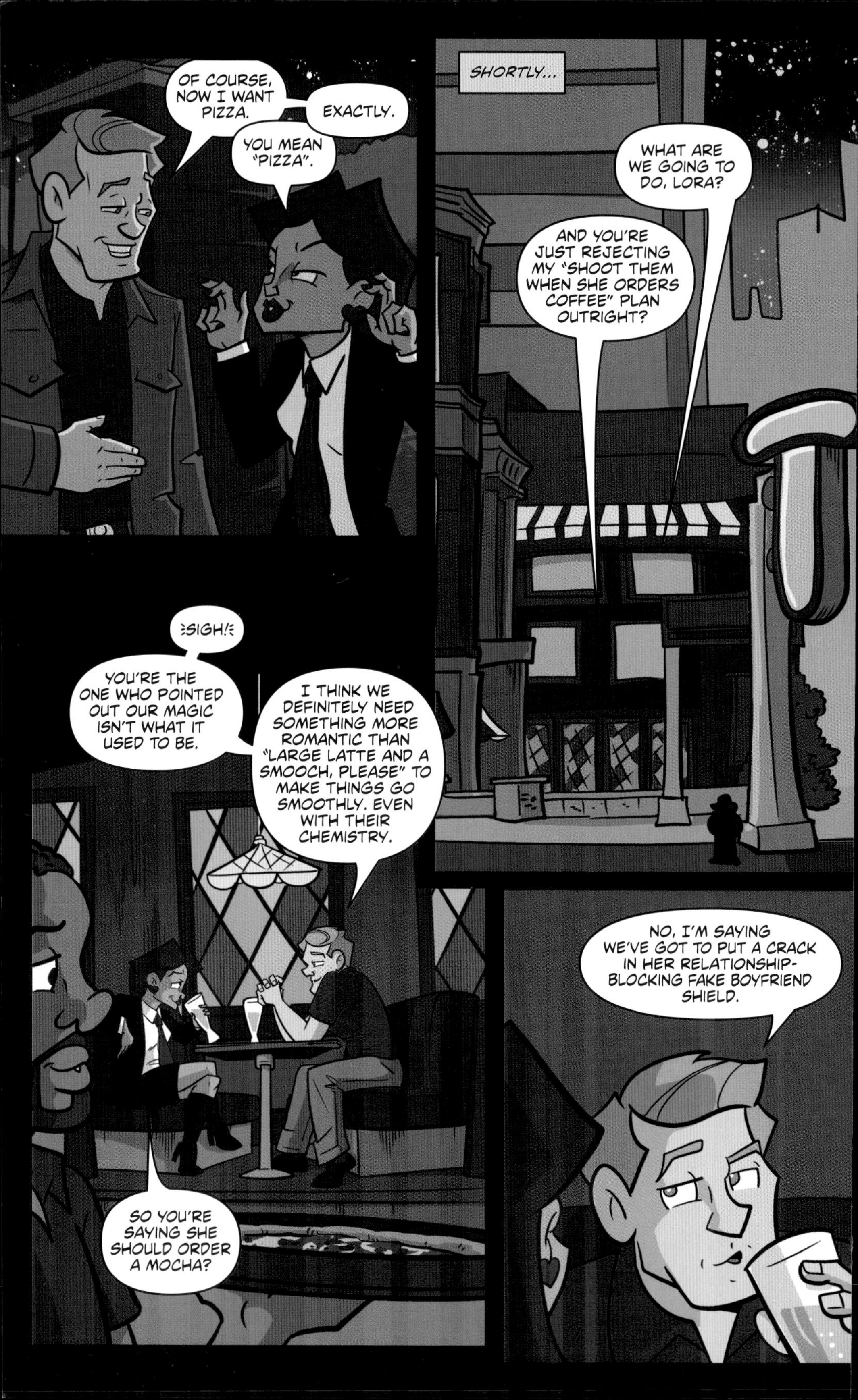
OF COURSE, NOW I WANT PIZZA.
YOU MEAN "PIZZA".
EXACTLY.
SHORTLY...
WHAT ARE WE GOING TO DO, LORA?
AND YOU'RE JUST REJECTING MY "SHOOT THEM WHEN SHE ORDERS COFFEE" PLAN OUTRIGHT?
SIGH!
YOU'RE THE ONE WHO POINTED OUT OUR MAGIC ISN'T WHAT IT USED TO BE.
I THINK WE DEFINITELY NEED SOMETHING MORE ROMANTIC THAN "LARGE LATTE AND A SMOOCH, PLEASE" TO MAKE THINGS GO SMOOTHLY. EVEN WITH THEIR CHEMISTRY.
SO YOU'RE SAYING SHE SHOULD ORDER A MOCHA?
NO, I'M SAYING WE'VE GOT TO PUT A CRACK IN HER RELATIONSHIP-BLOCKING FAKE BOYFRIEND SHIELD.

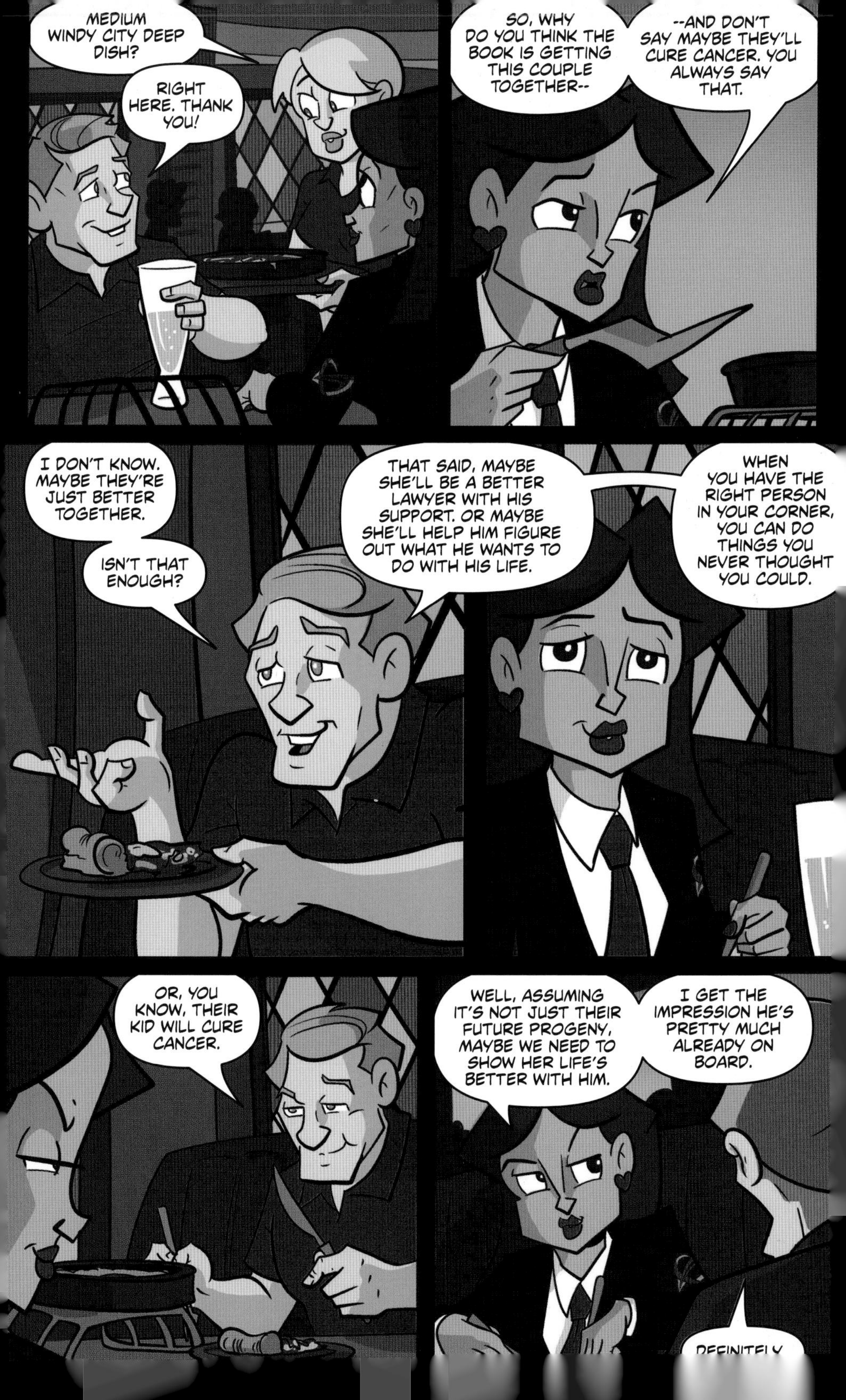
MEDIUM WINDY CITY DEEP DISH?
RIGHT HERE. THANK YOU!
SO, WHY DO YOU THINK THE BOOK IS GETTING THIS COUPLE TOGETHER--
--AND DON'T SAY MAYBE THEY'LL CURE CANCER. YOU ALWAYS SAY THAT.
I DON'T KNOW. MAYBE THEY'RE JUST BETTER TOGETHER.
ISN'T THAT ENOUGH?
THAT SAID, MAYBE SHE'LL BE A BETTER LAWYER WITH HIS SUPPORT. OR MAYBE SHE'LL HELP HIM FIGURE OUT WHAT HE WANTS TO DO WITH HIS LIFE.
WHEN YOU HAVE THE RIGHT PERSON IN YOUR CORNER, YOU CAN DO THINGS YOU NEVER THOUGHT YOU COULD.
OR, YOU KNOW, THEIR KID WILL CURE CANCER.
WELL, ASSUMING IT'S NOT JUST THEIR FUTURE PROGENY, MAYBE WE NEED TO SHOW HER LIFE'S BETTER WITH HIM.
I GET THE IMPRESSION HE'S PRETTY MUCH ALREADY ON BOARD.

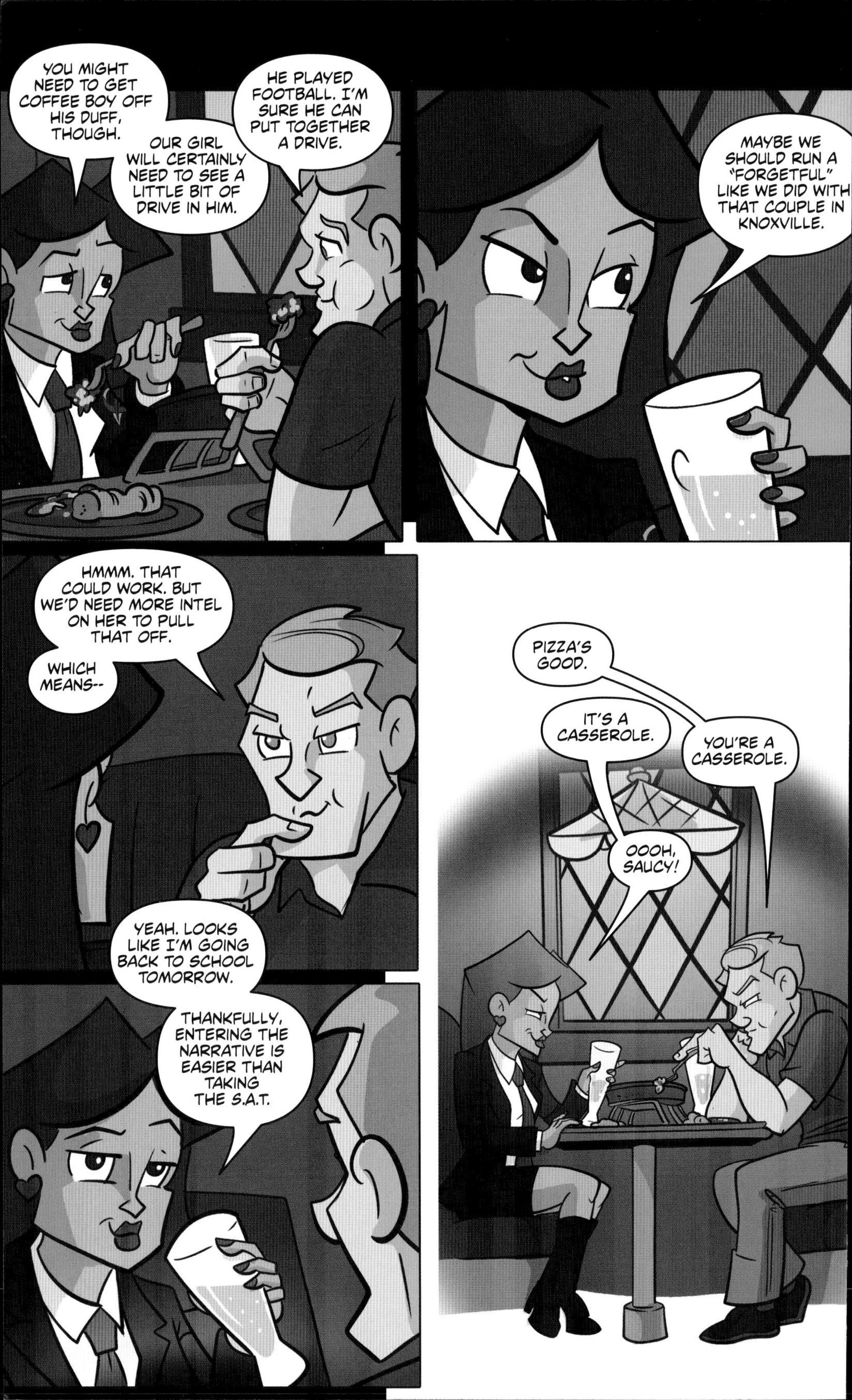
YOU MIGHT NEED TO GET COFFEE BOY OFF HIS DUFF, THOUGH.
OUR GIRL WILL CERTAINLY NEED TO SEE A LITTLE BIT OF DRIVE IN HIM.
HE PLAYED FOOTBALL. I'M SURE HE CAN PUT TOGETHER A DRIVE.
MAYBE WE SHOULD RUN A "FORGETFUL" LIKE WE DID WITH THAT COUPLE IN KNOXVILLE.
HMMM. THAT COULD WORK. BUT WE'D NEED MORE INTEL ON HER TO PULL THAT OFF.
WHICH MEANS--
YEAH. LOOKS LIKE I'M GOING BACK TO SCHOOL TOMORROW.
THANKFULLY, ENTERING THE NARRATIVE IS EASIER THAN TAKING THE S.A.T.
PIZZA'S GOOD.
IT'S A CASSEROLE.
YOU'RE A CASSEROLE.
OOOH, SAUCY!

Chapter 6

Study Buddies

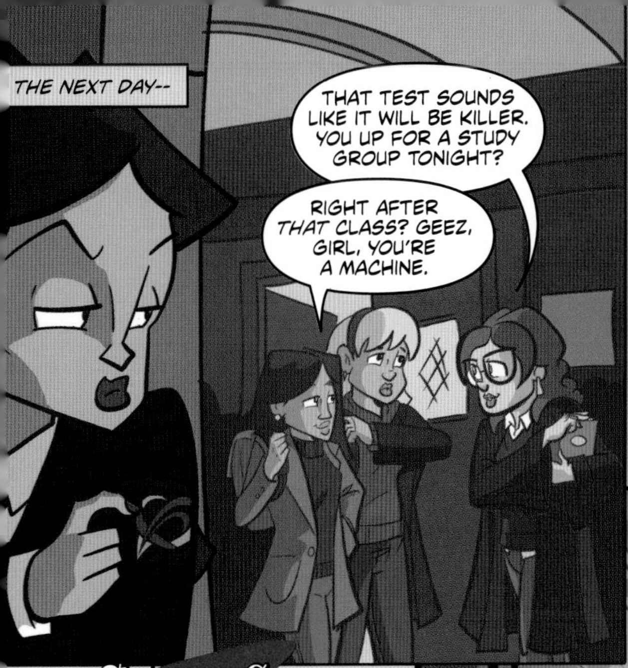
THE NEXT DAY--
THAT TEST SOUNDS LIKE IT WILL BE KILLER. YOU UP FOR A STUDY GROUP TONIGHT?
RIGHT AFTER *THAT CLASS?* GEEZ, GIRL, YOU'RE A MACHINE.

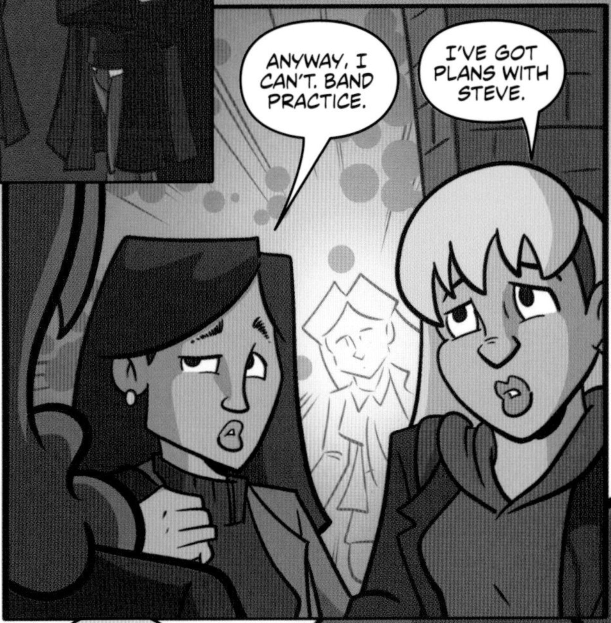
ANYWAY, I CAN'T. BAND PRACTICE.
I'VE GOT PLANS WITH STEVE.

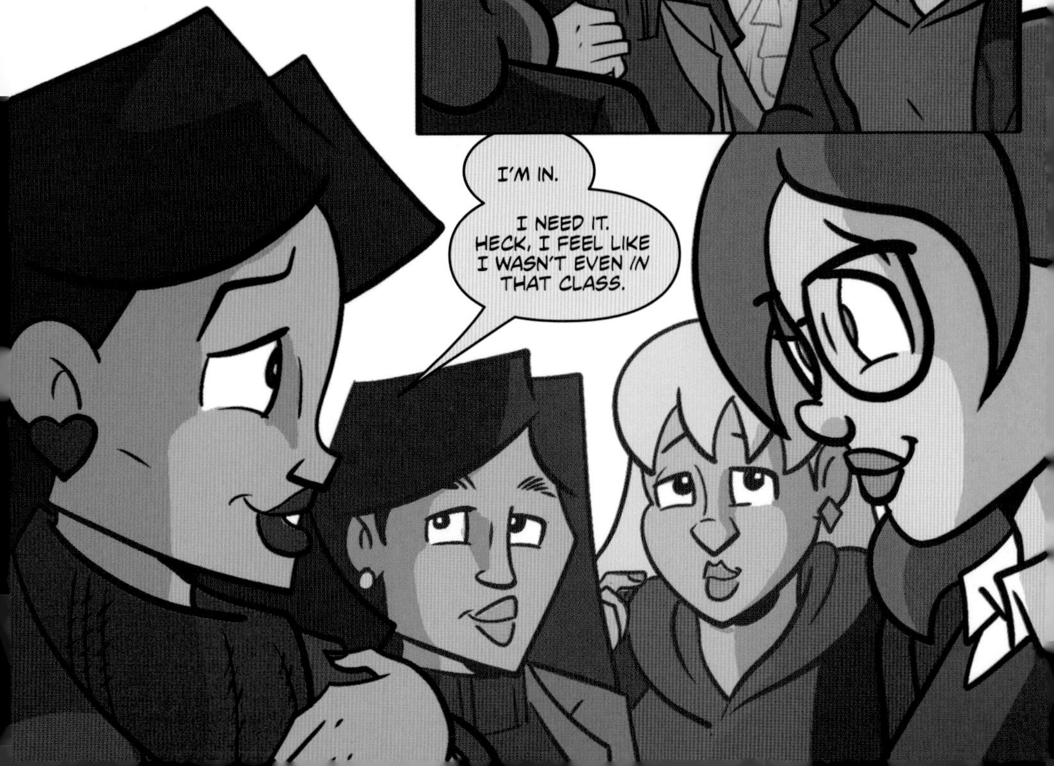
I'M IN.
I NEED IT. HECK, I FEEL LIKE I WASN'T EVEN *IN* THAT CLASS.

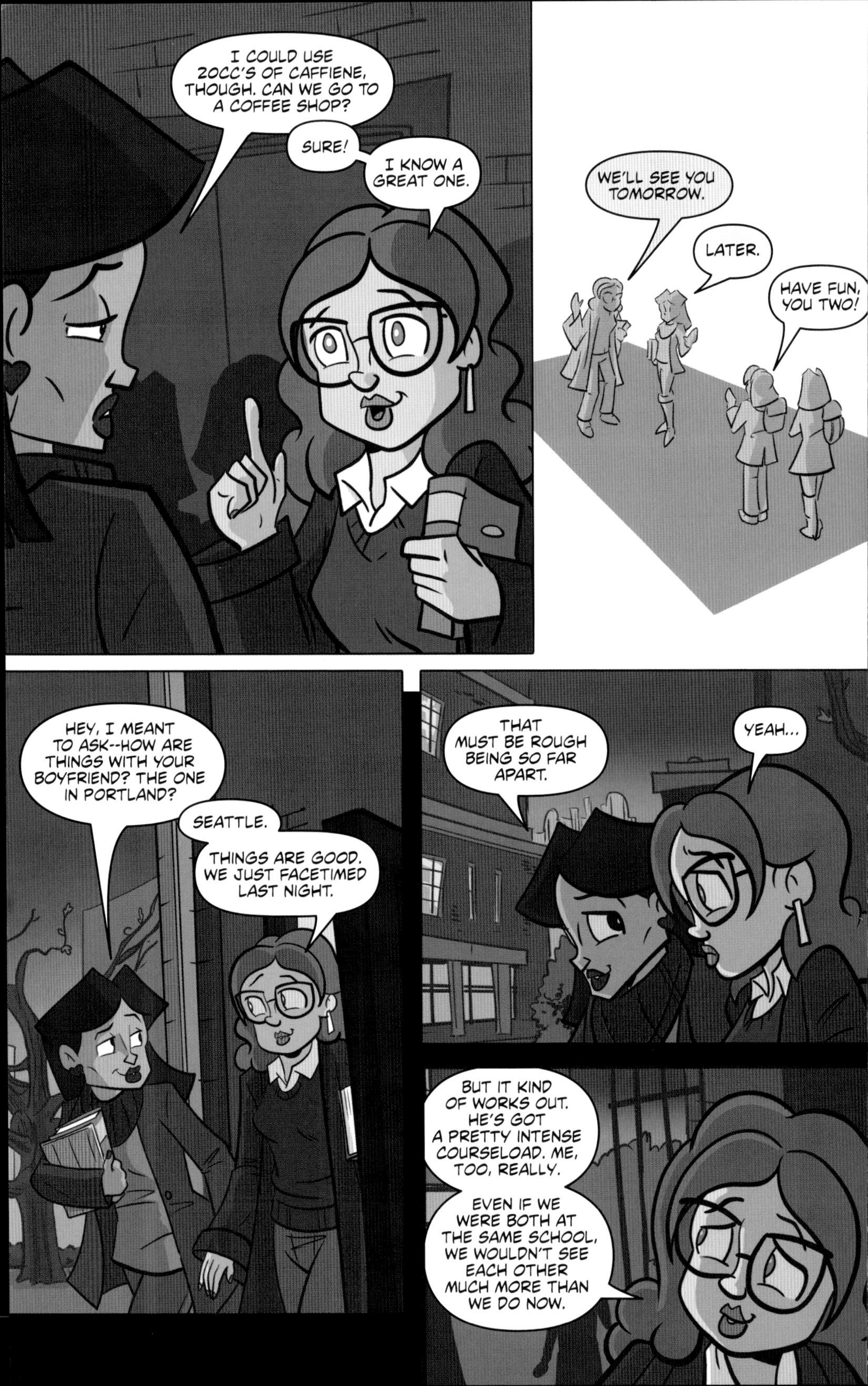
I COULD USE 20CC'S OF CAFFIENE, THOUGH. CAN WE GO TO A COFFEE SHOP?
SURE!
I KNOW A GREAT ONE.
WE'LL SEE YOU TOMORROW.
LATER.
HAVE FUN, YOU TWO!
HEY, I MEANT TO ASK--HOW ARE THINGS WITH YOUR BOYFRIEND? THE ONE IN PORTLAND?
SEATTLE.
THINGS ARE GOOD. WE JUST FACETIMED LAST NIGHT.
THAT MUST BE ROUGH BEING SO FAR APART.
YEAH...
BUT IT KIND OF WORKS OUT. HE'S GOT A PRETTY INTENSE COURSELOAD. ME, TOO, REALLY.
EVEN IF WE WERE BOTH AT THE SAME SCHOOL, WE WOULDN'T SEE EACH OTHER MUCH MORE THAN WE DO NOW.

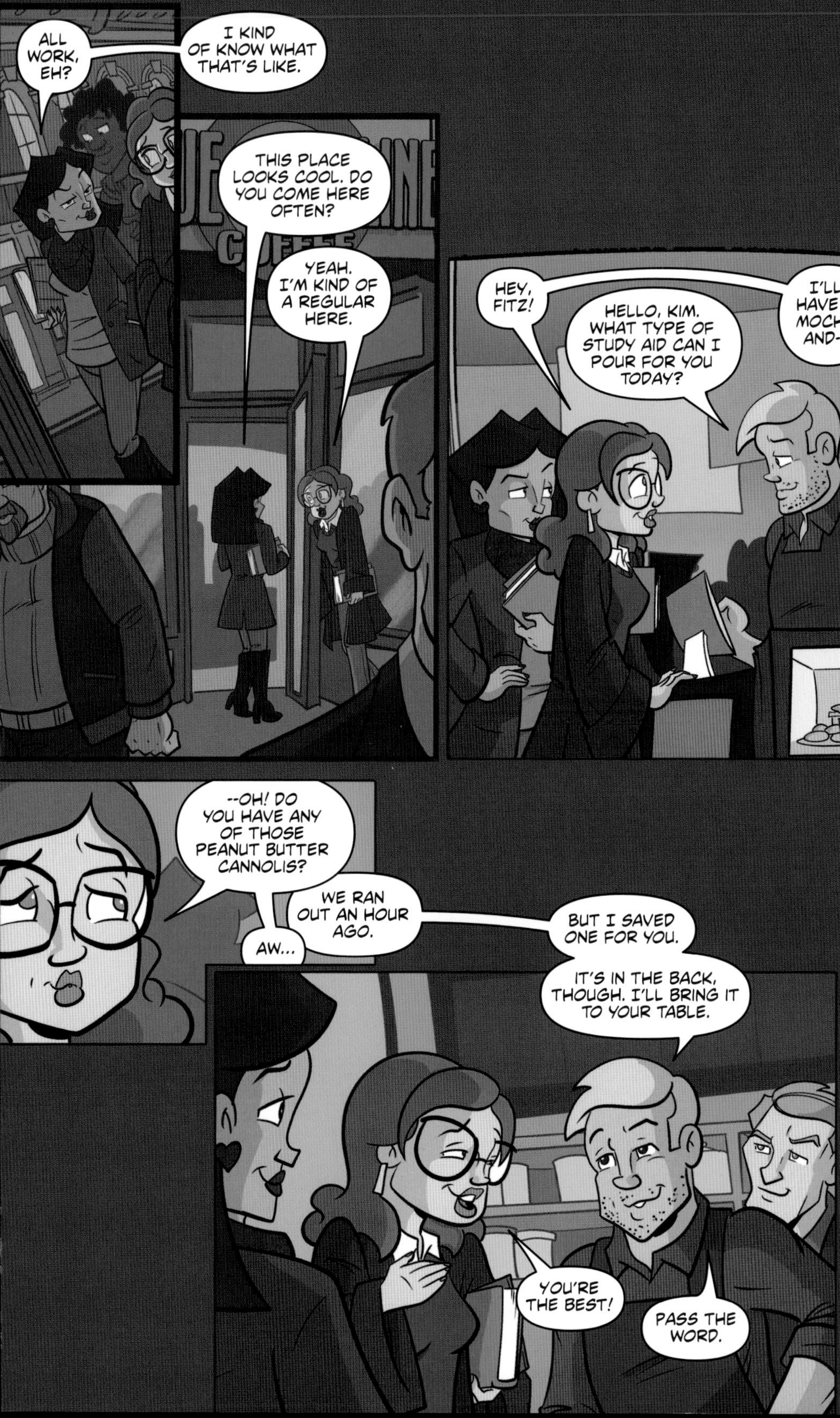
ALL WORK, EH?
I KIND OF KNOW WHAT THAT'S LIKE.
THIS PLACE LOOKS COOL. DO YOU COME HERE OFTEN?
YEAH. I'M KIND OF A REGULAR HERE.
HEY, FITZ!
HELLO, KIM. WHAT TYPE OF STUDY AID CAN I POUR FOR YOU TODAY?
I'LL HAVE A MOCHA AND--
--OH! DO YOU HAVE ANY OF THOSE PEANUT BUTTER CANNOLIS?
WE RAN OUT AN HOUR AGO.
AW...
BUT I SAVED ONE FOR YOU.
IT'S IN THE BACK, THOUGH. I'LL BRING IT TO YOUR TABLE.
YOU'RE THE BEST!
PASS THE WORD.

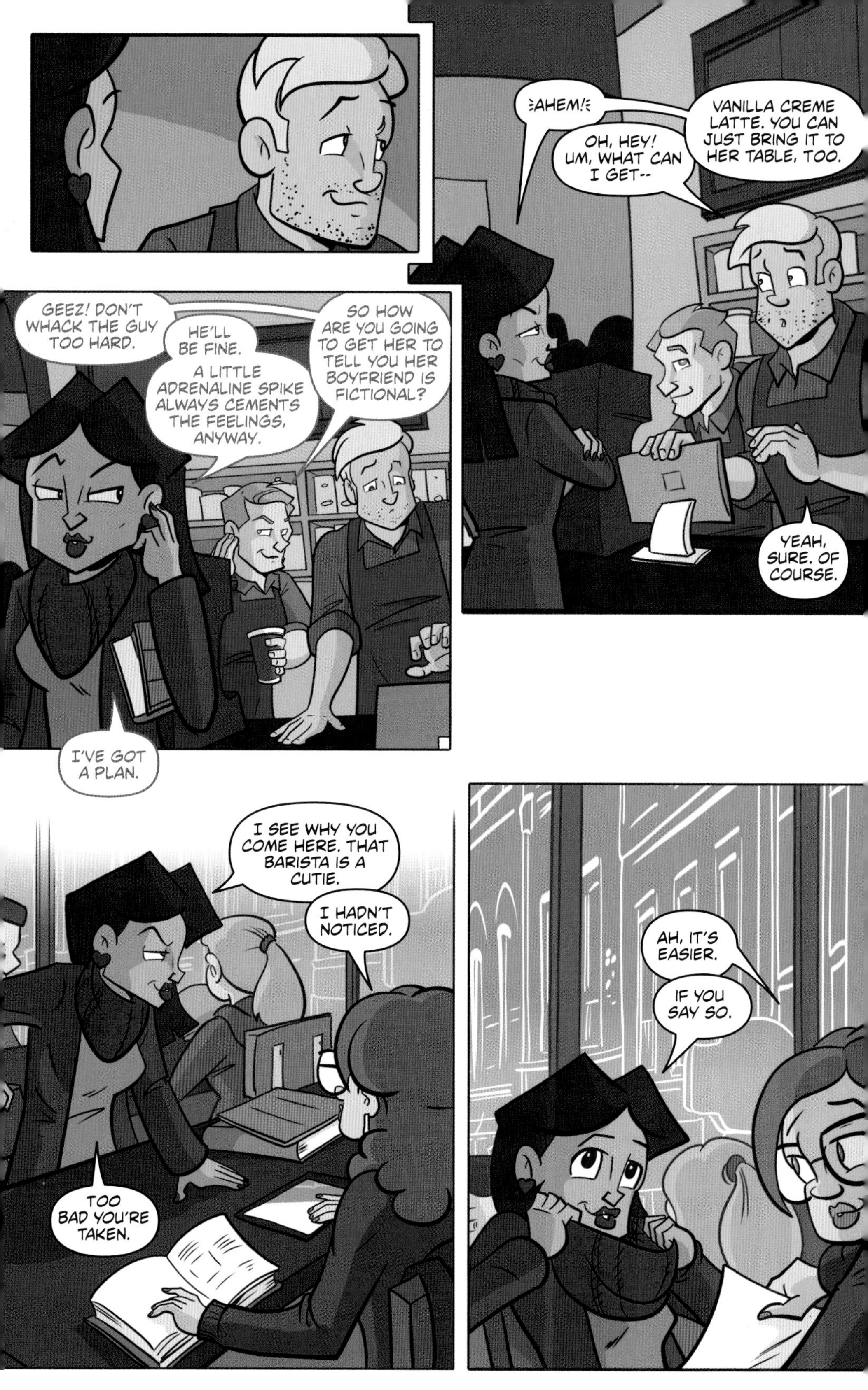

AHEM!
OH, HEY! UM, WHAT CAN I GET--
VANILLA CREME LATTE. YOU CAN JUST BRING IT TO HER TABLE, TOO.
YEAH, SURE. OF COURSE.
GEEZ! DON'T WHACK THE GUY TOO HARD.
HE'LL BE FINE.
A LITTLE ADRENALINE SPIKE ALWAYS CEMENTS THE FEELINGS, ANYWAY.
SO HOW ARE YOU GOING TO GET HER TO TELL YOU HER BOYFRIEND IS FICTIONAL?
I'VE GOT A PLAN.
I SEE WHY YOU COME HERE. THAT BARISTA IS A CUTIE.
I HADN'T NOTICED.
TOO BAD YOU'RE TAKEN.
AH, IT'S EASIER.
IF YOU SAY SO.

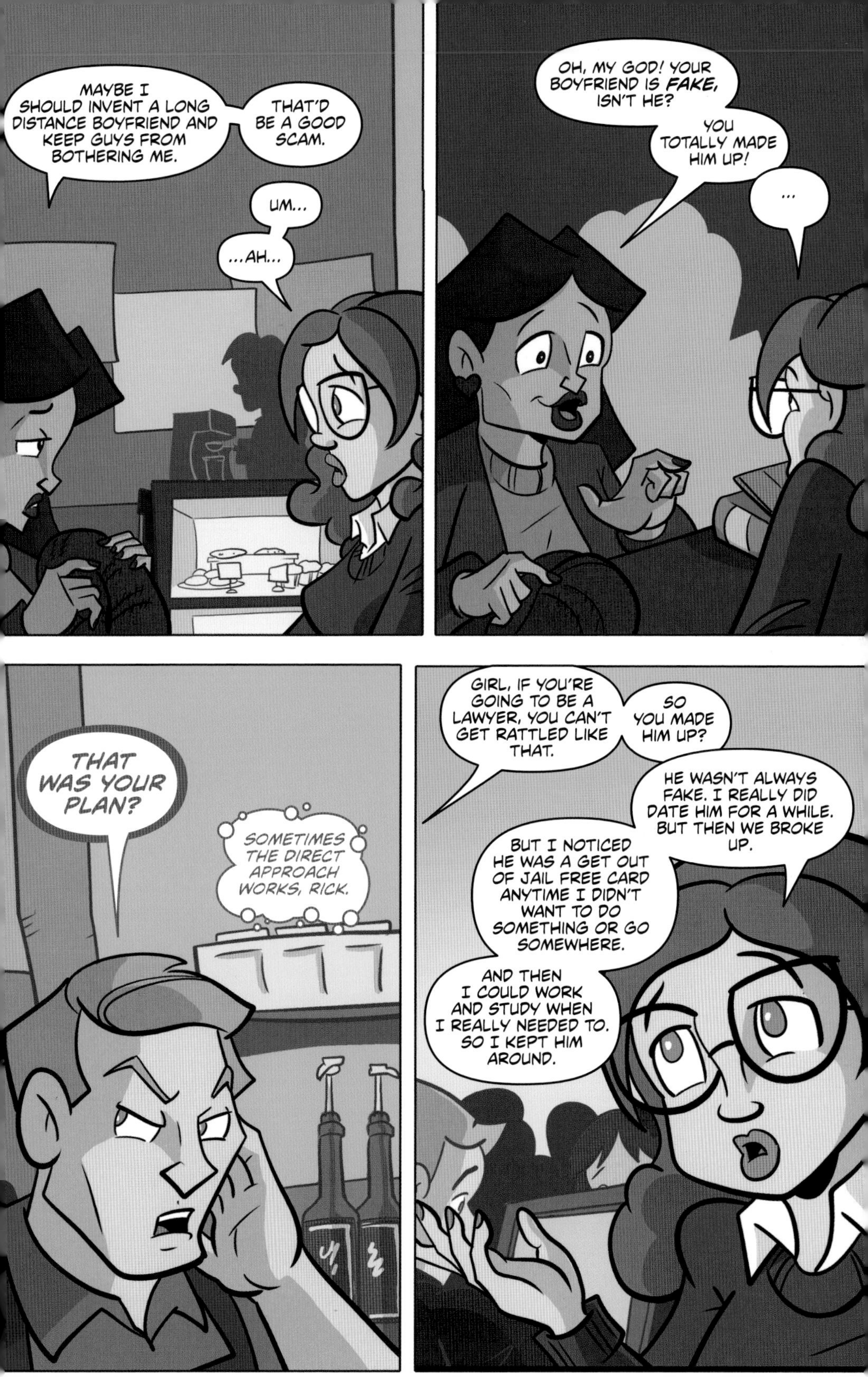
MAYBE I SHOULD INVENT A LONG DISTANCE BOYFRIEND AND KEEP GUYS FROM BOTHERING ME.
THAT'D BE A GOOD SCAM.
UM...
...AH...
OH, MY GOD! YOUR BOYFRIEND IS *FAKE,* ISN'T HE?
YOU TOTALLY MADE HIM UP!
...
THAT WAS YOUR PLAN?
SOMETIMES THE DIRECT APPROACH WORKS, RICK.
GIRL, IF YOU'RE GOING TO BE A LAWYER, YOU CAN'T GET RATTLED LIKE THAT.
SO YOU MADE HIM UP?
HE WASN'T ALWAYS FAKE. I REALLY DID DATE HIM FOR A WHILE. BUT THEN WE BROKE UP.
BUT I NOTICED HE WAS A GET OUT OF JAIL FREE CARD ANYTIME I DIDN'T WANT TO DO SOMETHING OR GO SOMEWHERE.
AND THEN I COULD WORK AND STUDY WHEN I REALLY NEEDED TO. SO I KEPT HIM AROUND.

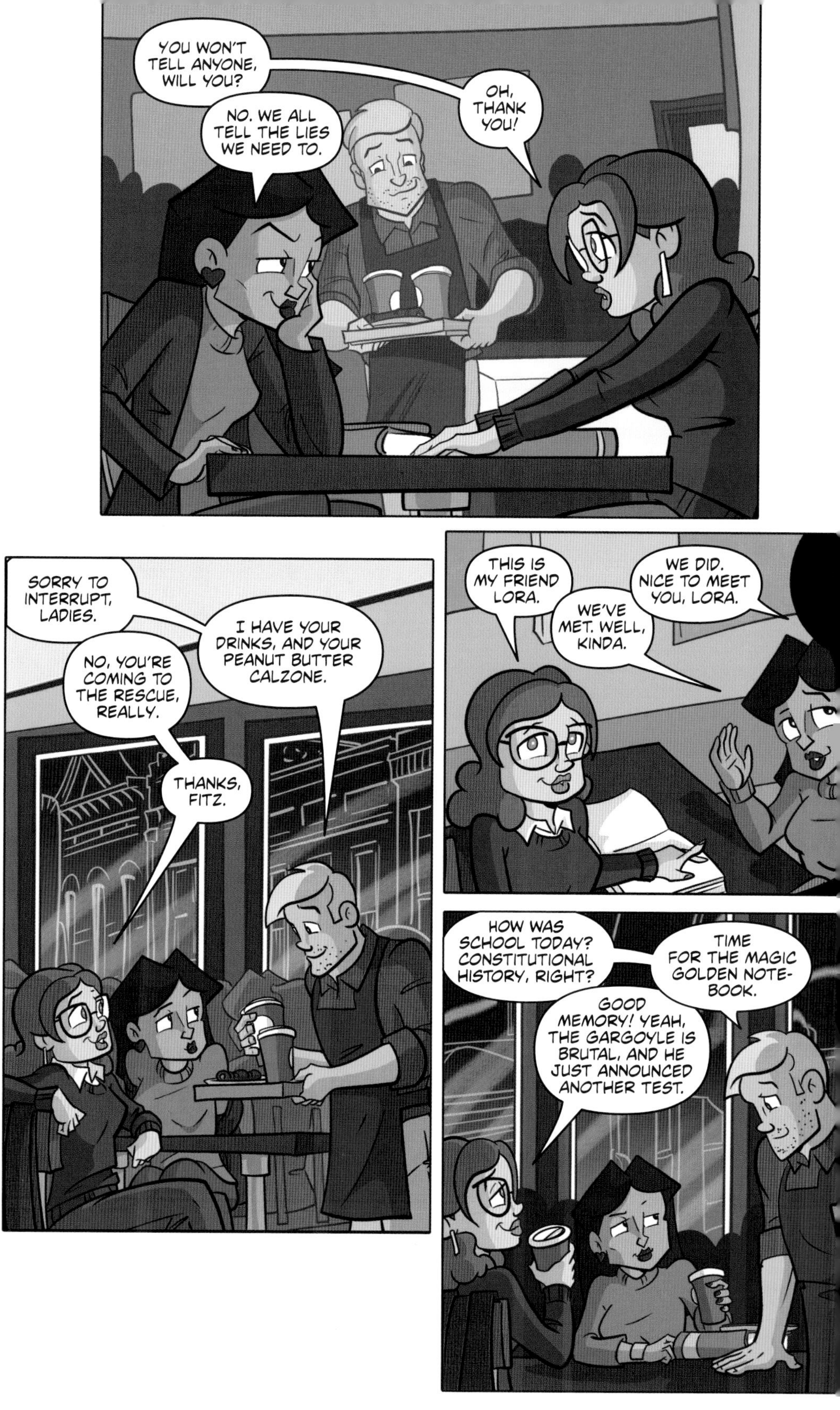
YOU WON'T TELL ANYONE, WILL YOU?
NO. WE ALL TELL THE LIES WE NEED TO.
OH, THANK YOU!
SORRY TO INTERRUPT, LADIES.
I HAVE YOUR DRINKS, AND YOUR PEANUT BUTTER CALZONE.
NO, YOU'RE COMING TO THE RESCUE, REALLY.
THANKS, FITZ.
THIS IS MY FRIEND LORA.
WE'VE MET. WELL, KINDA.
WE DID. NICE TO MEET YOU, LORA.
HOW WAS SCHOOL TODAY? CONSTITUTIONAL HISTORY, RIGHT?
TIME FOR THE MAGIC GOLDEN NOTE-BOOK.
GOOD MEMORY! YEAH, THE GARGOYLE IS BRUTAL, AND HE JUST ANNOUNCED ANOTHER TEST.

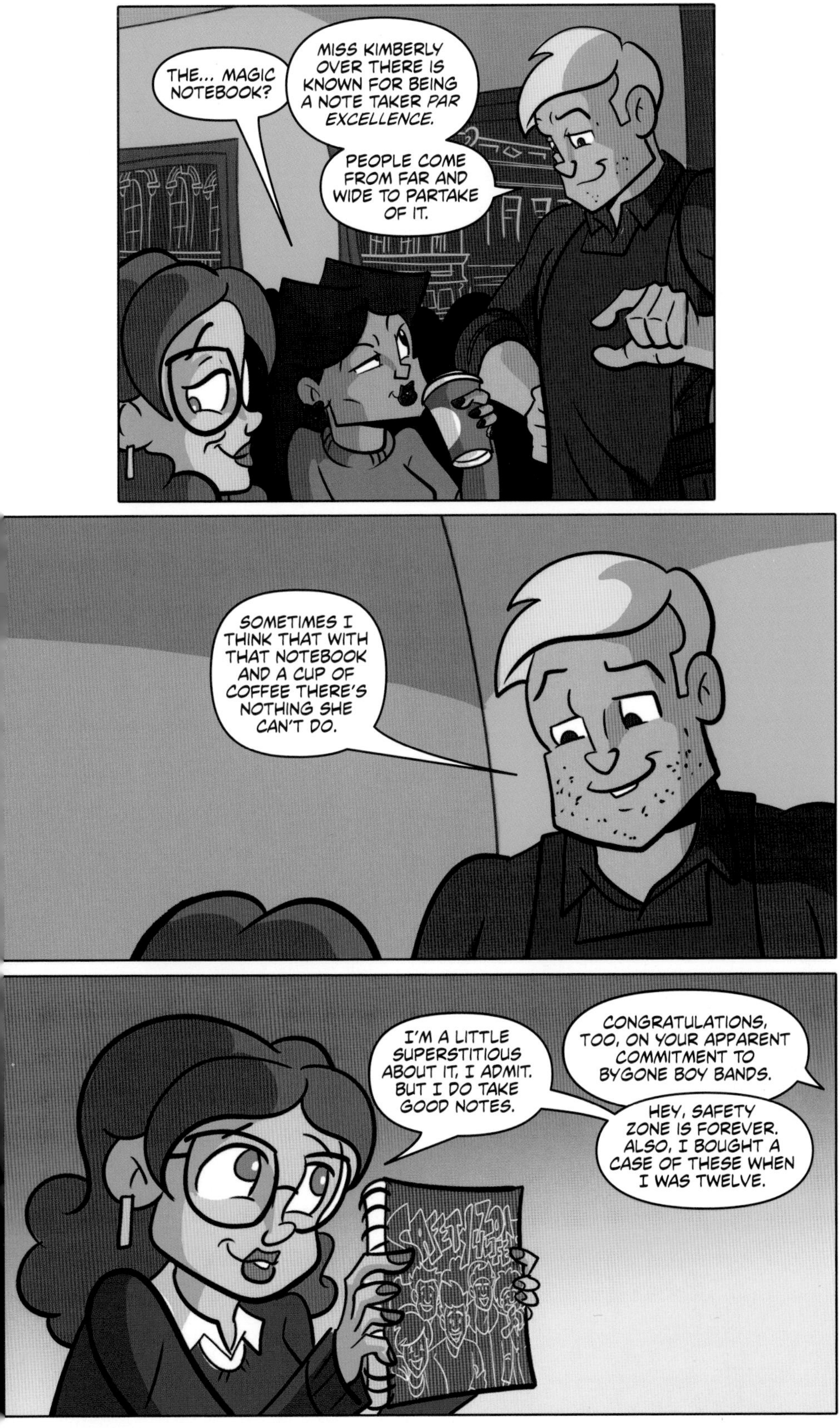
THE... MAGIC NOTEBOOK?
MISS KIMBERLY OVER THERE IS KNOWN FOR BEING A NOTE TAKER *PAR EXCELLENCE*.
PEOPLE COME FROM FAR AND WIDE TO PARTAKE OF IT.
SOMETIMES I THINK THAT WITH THAT NOTEBOOK AND A CUP OF COFFEE THERE'S NOTHING SHE CAN'T DO.
I'M A LITTLE SUPERSTITIOUS ABOUT IT, I ADMIT. BUT I DO TAKE GOOD NOTES.
CONGRATULATIONS, TOO, ON YOUR APPARENT COMMITMENT TO BYGONE BOY BANDS.
HEY, SAFETY ZONE IS FOREVER. ALSO, I BOUGHT A CASE OF THESE WHEN I WAS TWELVE.

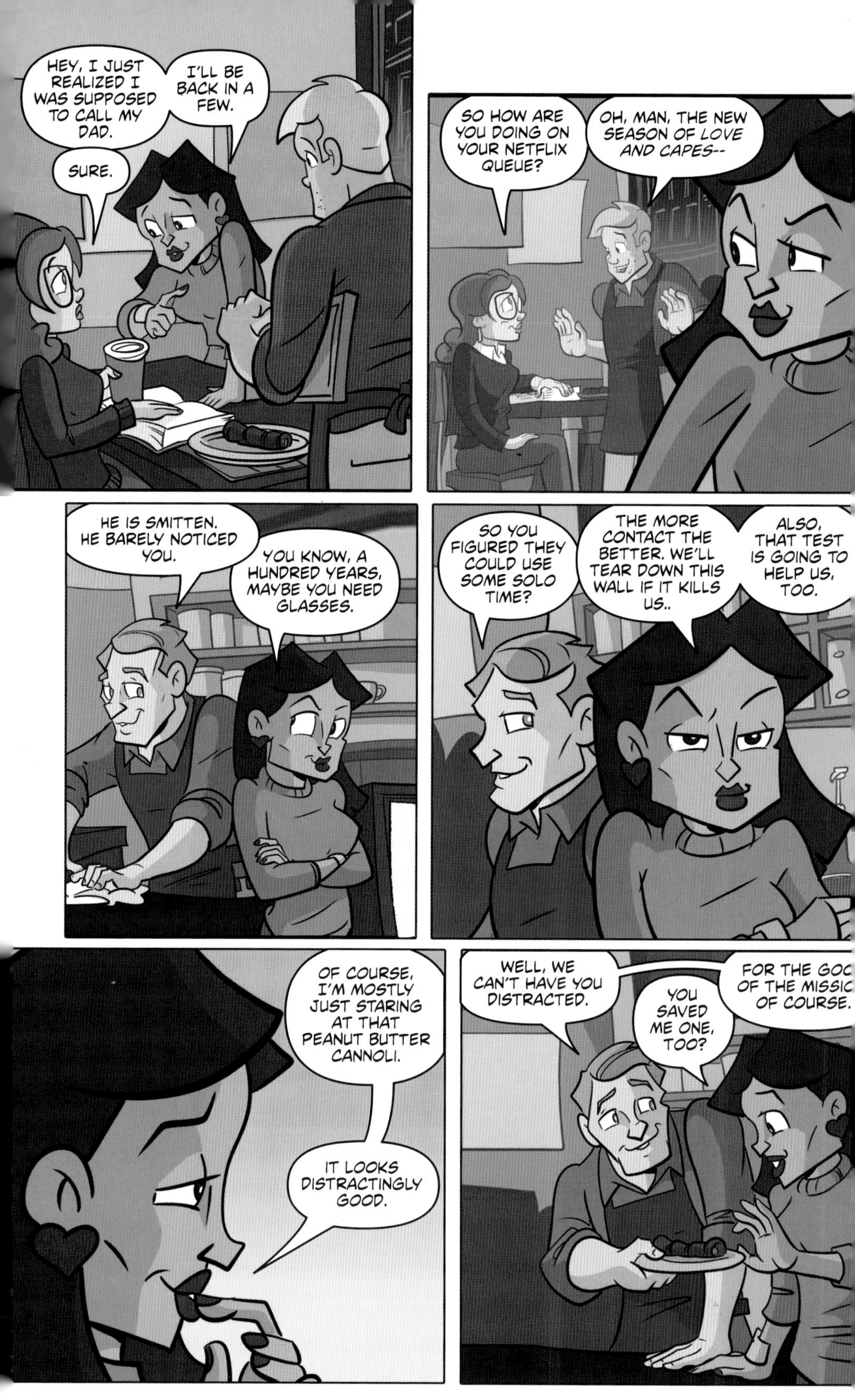

HEY, I JUST REALIZED I WAS SUPPOSED TO CALL MY DAD.
I'LL BE BACK IN A FEW.
SURE.
SO HOW ARE YOU DOING ON YOUR NETFLIX QUEUE?
OH, MAN, THE NEW SEASON OF *LOVE AND CAPES*--
HE IS SMITTEN. HE BARELY NOTICED YOU.
YOU KNOW, A HUNDRED YEARS, MAYBE YOU NEED GLASSES.
SO YOU FIGURED THEY COULD USE SOME SOLO TIME?
THE MORE CONTACT THE BETTER. WE'LL TEAR DOWN THIS WALL IF IT KILLS US..
ALSO, THAT TEST IS GOING TO HELP US, TOO.
OF COURSE, I'M MOSTLY JUST STARING AT THAT PEANUT BUTTER CANNOLI.
IT LOOKS DISTRACTINGLY GOOD.
WELL, WE CAN'T HAVE YOU DISTRACTED.
FOR THE GOO OF THE MISSIC OF COURSE.
YOU SAVED ME ONE, TOO?

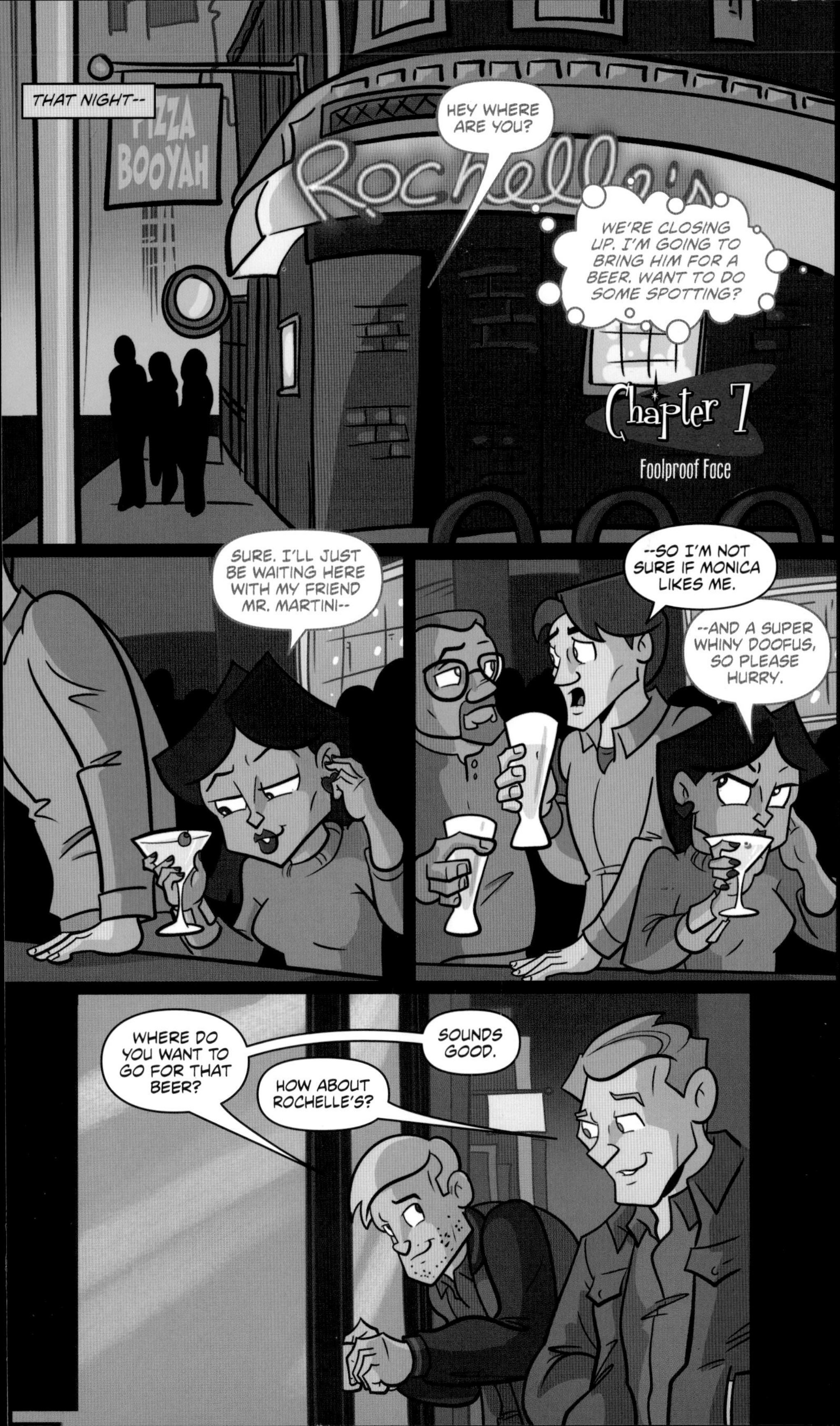
THAT NIGHT--
PIZZA BOOYAH
Rochelle's
HEY WHERE ARE YOU?
WE'RE CLOSING UP. I'M GOING TO BRING HIM FOR A BEER. WANT TO DO SOME SPOTTING?
Chapter 7
Foolproof Face
SURE. I'LL JUST BE WAITING HERE WITH MY FRIEND MR. MARTINI--
--SO I'M NOT SURE IF MONICA LIKES ME.
--AND A SUPER WHINY DOOFUS, SO PLEASE HURRY.
WHERE DO YOU WANT TO GO FOR THAT BEER?
HOW ABOUT ROCHELLE'S?
SOUNDS GOOD.

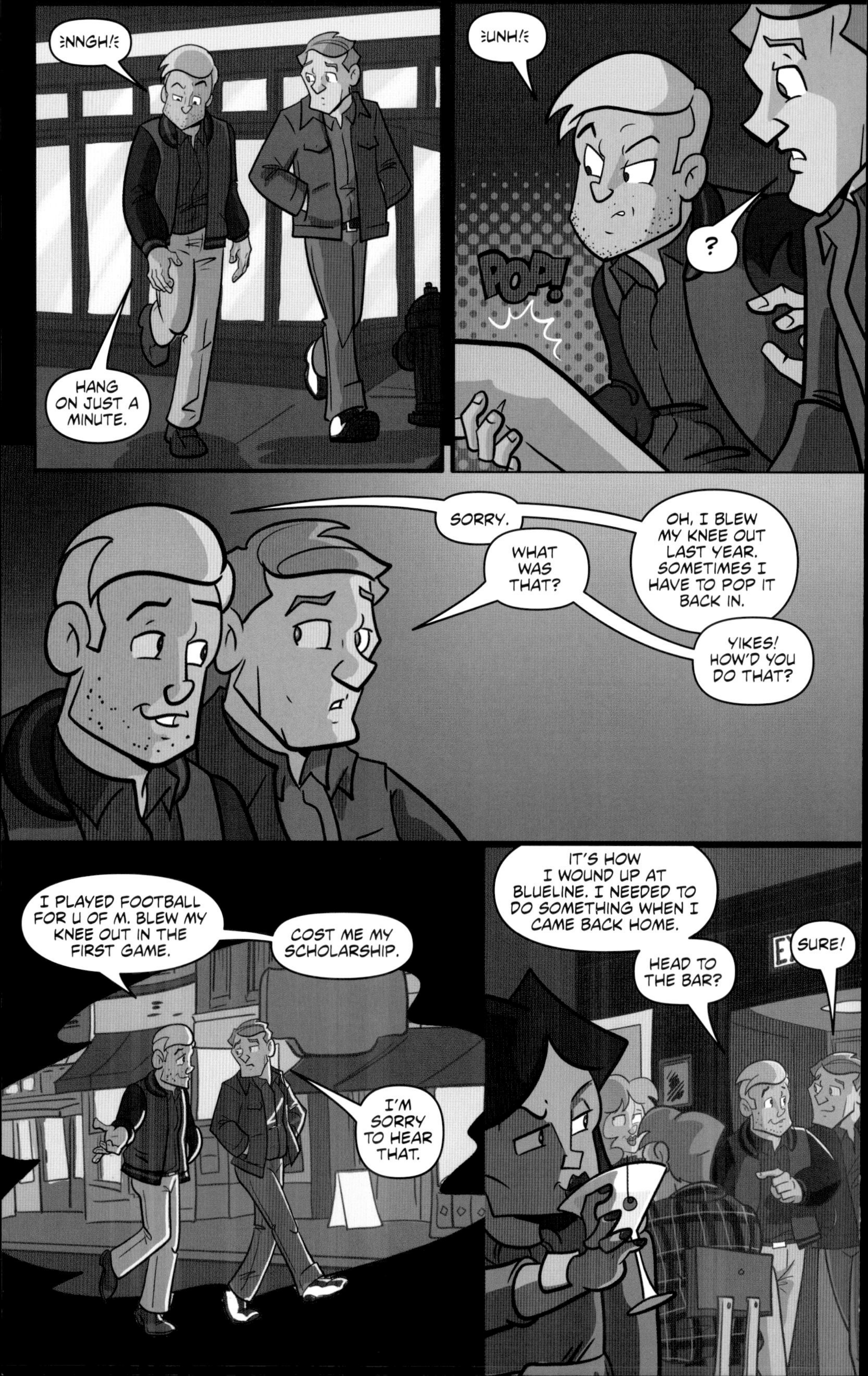
NNGH!
HANG ON JUST A MINUTE.
UNH!
POP!
?
SORRY.
WHAT WAS THAT?
OH, I BLEW MY KNEE OUT LAST YEAR. SOMETIMES I HAVE TO POP IT BACK IN.
YIKES! HOW'D YOU DO THAT?
I PLAYED FOOTBALL FOR U OF M. BLEW MY KNEE OUT IN THE FIRST GAME.
COST ME MY SCHOLARSHIP.
I'M SORRY TO HEAR THAT.
IT'S HOW I WOUND UP AT BLUELINE. I NEEDED TO DO SOMETHING WHEN I CAME BACK HOME.
HEAD TO THE BAR?
SURE!

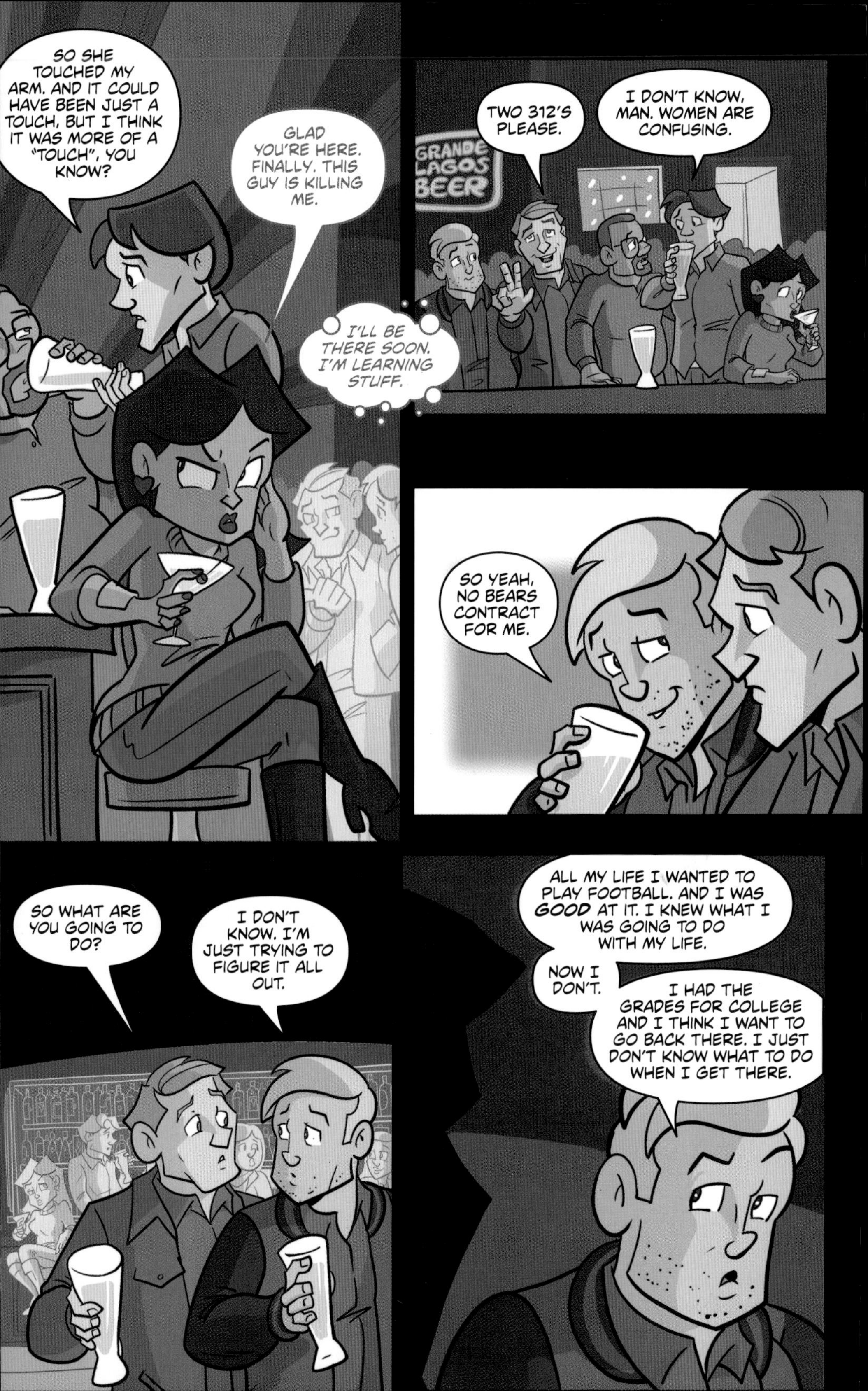
SO SHE TOUCHED MY ARM. AND IT COULD HAVE BEEN JUST A TOUCH, BUT I THINK IT WAS MORE OF A "TOUCH", YOU KNOW?
GLAD YOU'RE HERE. FINALLY. THIS GUY IS KILLING ME.
I'LL BE THERE SOON. I'M LEARNING STUFF.
TWO 312'S PLEASE.
I DON'T KNOW, MAN. WOMEN ARE CONFUSING.
GRANDE LAGOS BEER
SO YEAH, NO BEARS CONTRACT FOR ME.
SO WHAT ARE YOU GOING TO DO?
I DON'T KNOW. I'M JUST TRYING TO FIGURE IT ALL OUT.
ALL MY LIFE I WANTED TO PLAY FOOTBALL. AND I WAS GOOD AT IT. I KNEW WHAT I WAS GOING TO DO WITH MY LIFE.
NOW I DON'T.
I HAD THE GRADES FOR COLLEGE AND I THINK I WANT TO GO BACK THERE. I JUST DON'T KNOW WHAT TO DO WHEN I GET THERE.

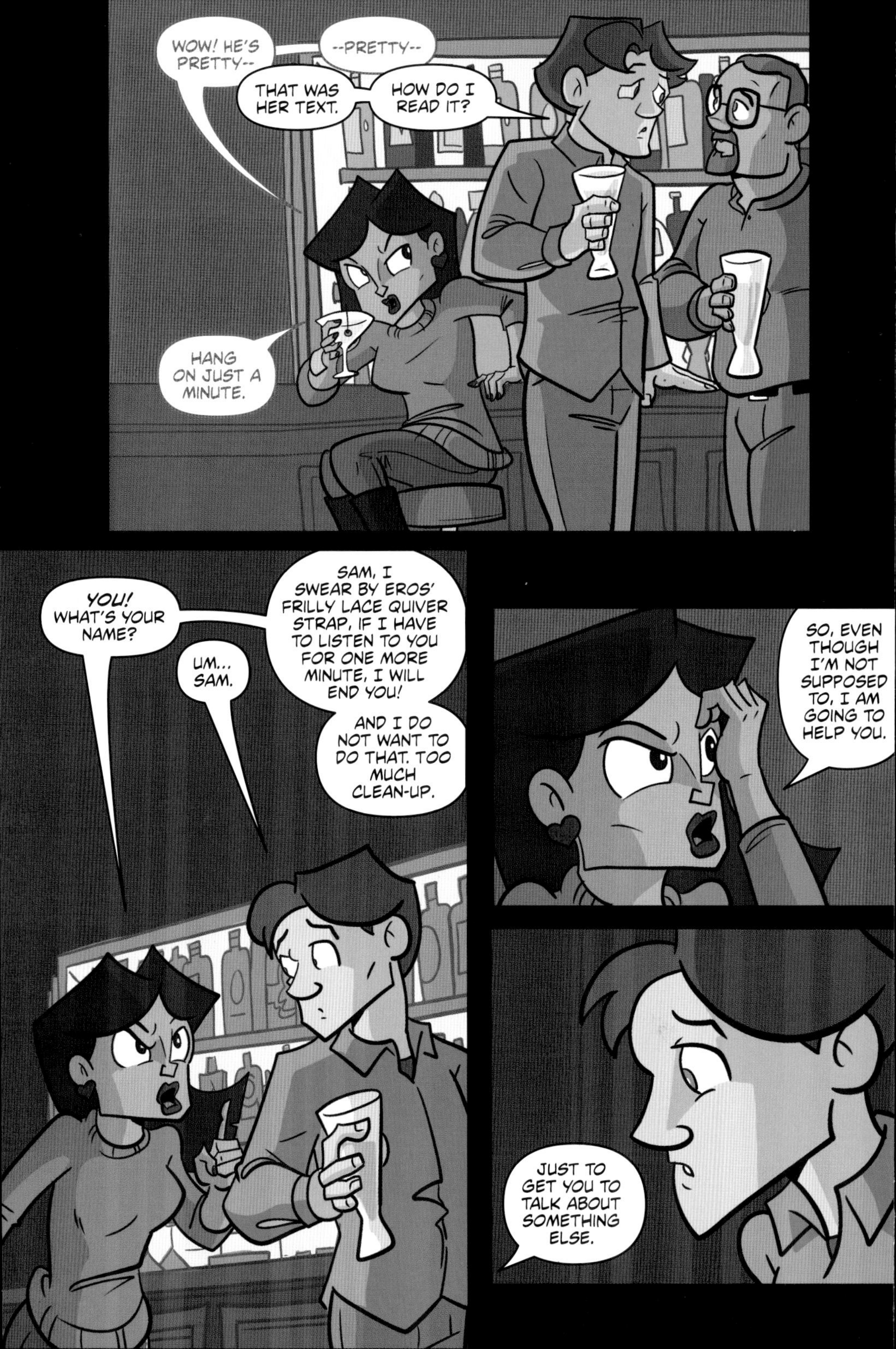

WOW! HE'S PRETTY--
--PRETTY--
THAT WAS HER TEXT.
HOW DO I READ IT?
HANG ON JUST A MINUTE.
YOU! WHAT'S YOUR NAME?
UM... SAM.
SAM, I SWEAR BY EROS' FRILLY LACE QUIVER STRAP, IF I HAVE TO LISTEN TO YOU FOR ONE MORE MINUTE, I WILL END YOU!
AND I DO NOT WANT TO DO THAT. TOO MUCH CLEAN-UP.
SO, EVEN THOUGH I'M NOT SUPPOSED TO, I AM GOING TO HELP YOU.
JUST TO GET YOU TO TALK ABOUT SOMETHING ELSE.

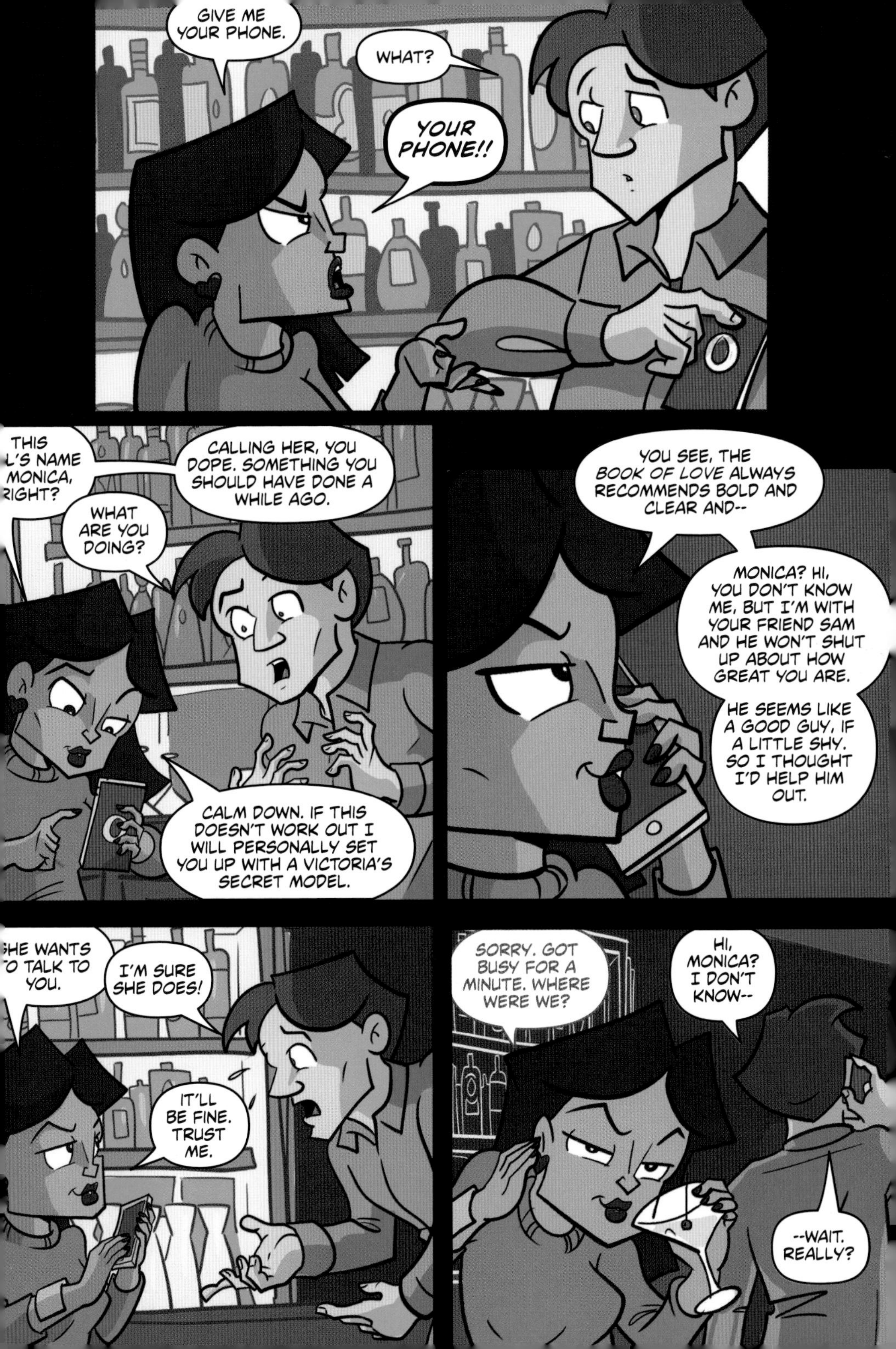
GIVE ME YOUR PHONE.
WHAT?
YOUR PHONE!!
THIS
'L'S NAME
MONICA,
RIGHT?
CALLING HER, YOU DOPE. SOMETHING YOU SHOULD HAVE DONE A WHILE AGO.
WHAT ARE YOU DOING?
CALM DOWN. IF THIS DOESN'T WORK OUT I WILL PERSONALLY SET YOU UP WITH A VICTORIA'S SECRET MODEL.
YOU SEE, THE BOOK OF LOVE ALWAYS RECOMMENDS BOLD AND CLEAR AND--
MONICA? HI, YOU DON'T KNOW ME, BUT I'M WITH YOUR FRIEND SAM AND HE WON'T SHUT UP ABOUT HOW GREAT YOU ARE.
HE SEEMS LIKE A GOOD GUY, IF A LITTLE SHY. SO I THOUGHT I'D HELP HIM OUT.
HE WANTS
O TALK TO
YOU.
I'M SURE SHE DOES!
IT'LL BE FINE. TRUST ME.
SORRY. GOT BUSY FOR A MINUTE. WHERE WERE WE?
HI, MONICA? I DON'T KNOW--
--WAIT. REALLY?

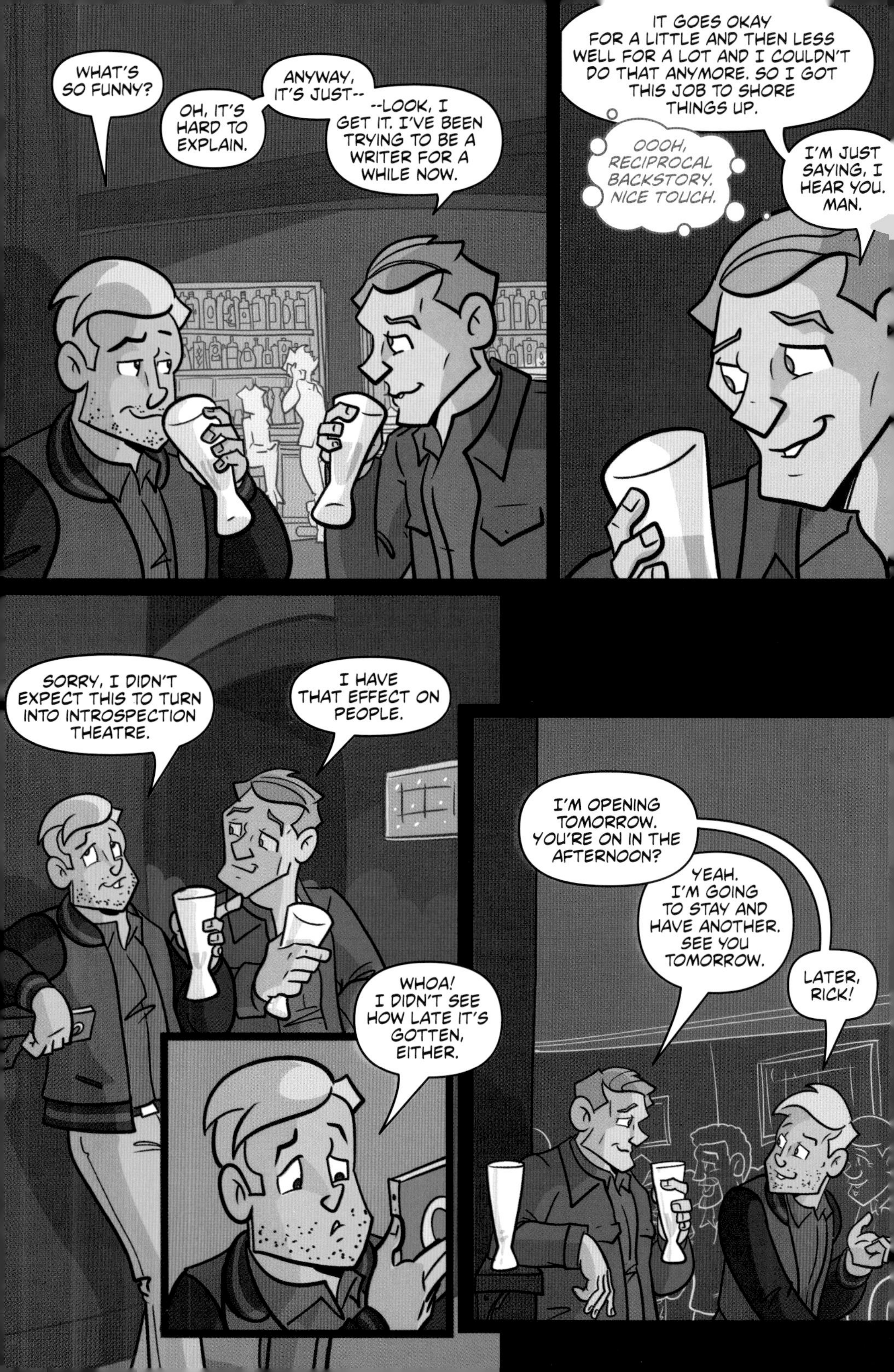
WHAT'S SO FUNNY?
OH, IT'S HARD TO EXPLAIN.
ANYWAY, IT'S JUST--
--LOOK, I GET IT. I'VE BEEN TRYING TO BE A WRITER FOR A WHILE NOW.
IT GOES OKAY FOR A LITTLE AND THEN LESS WELL FOR A LOT AND I COULDN'T DO THAT ANYMORE. SO I GOT THIS JOB TO SHORE THINGS UP.
OOOH, RECIPROCAL BACKSTORY. NICE TOUCH.
I'M JUST SAYING, I HEAR YOU. MAN.
SORRY, I DIDN'T EXPECT THIS TO TURN INTO INTROSPECTION THEATRE.
I HAVE THAT EFFECT ON PEOPLE.
WHOA! I DIDN'T SEE HOW LATE IT'S GOTTEN, EITHER.
I'M OPENING TOMORROW. YOU'RE ON IN THE AFTERNOON?
YEAH. I'M GOING TO STAY AND HAVE ANOTHER. SEE YOU TOMORROW.
LATER, RICK!

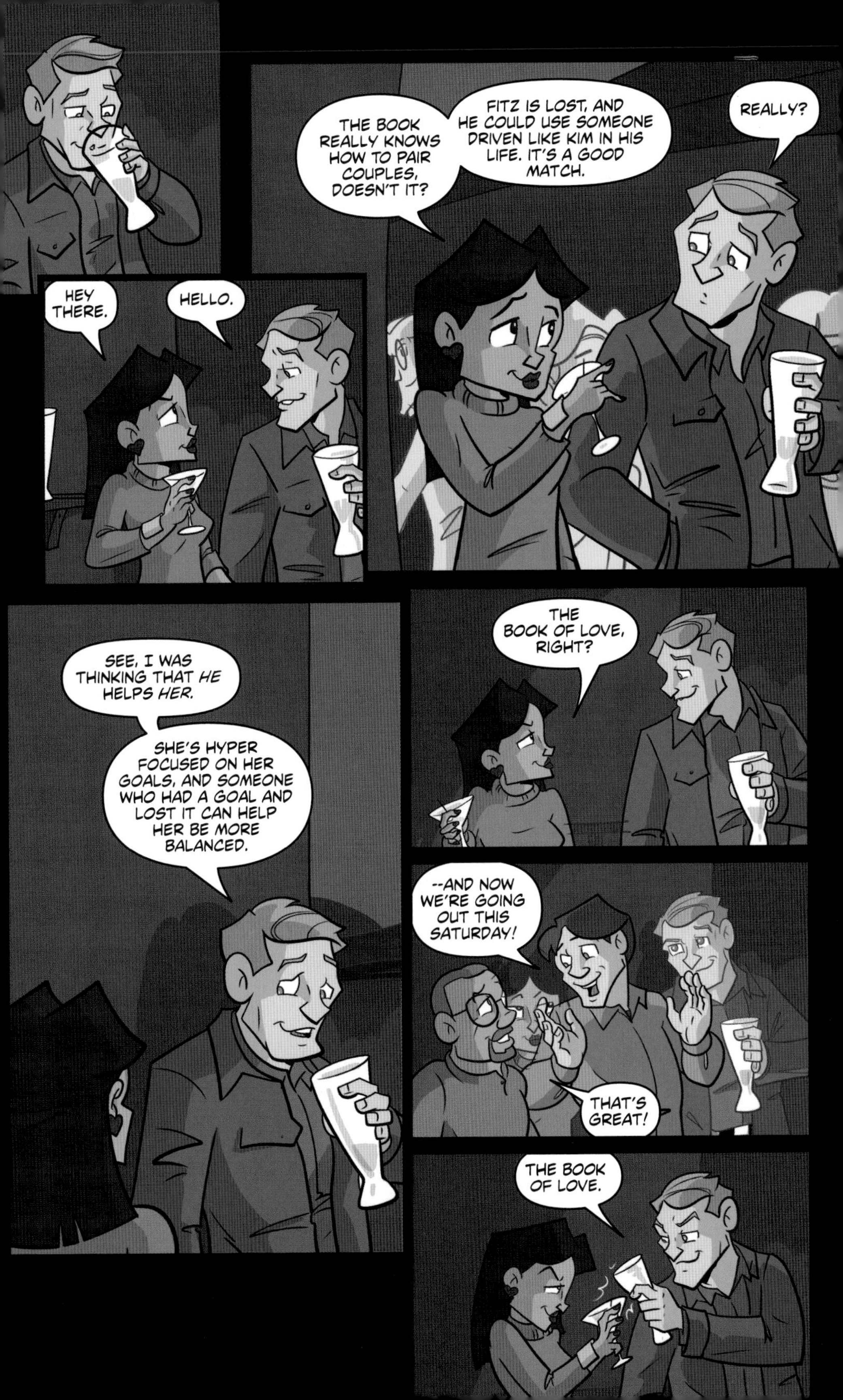
HEY THERE.
HELLO.
THE BOOK REALLY KNOWS HOW TO PAIR COUPLES, DOESN'T IT?
FITZ IS LOST, AND HE COULD USE SOMEONE DRIVEN LIKE KIM IN HIS LIFE. IT'S A GOOD MATCH.
REALLY?
SEE, I WAS THINKING THAT *HE* HELPS *HER*.
SHE'S HYPER FOCUSED ON HER GOALS, AND SOMEONE WHO HAD A GOAL AND LOST IT CAN HELP HER BE MORE BALANCED.
THE BOOK OF LOVE, RIGHT?
--AND NOW WE'RE GOING OUT THIS SATURDAY!
THAT'S GREAT!
THE BOOK OF LOVE.

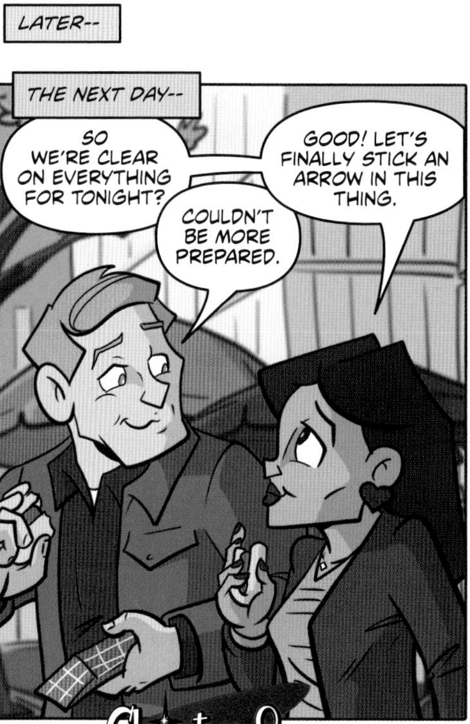
LATER--
THE NEXT DAY--
SO WE'RE CLEAR ON EVERYTHING FOR TONIGHT?
COULDN'T BE MORE PREPARED.
GOOD! LET'S FINALLY STICK AN ARROW IN THIS THING.

Chapter 8

On Your Marks

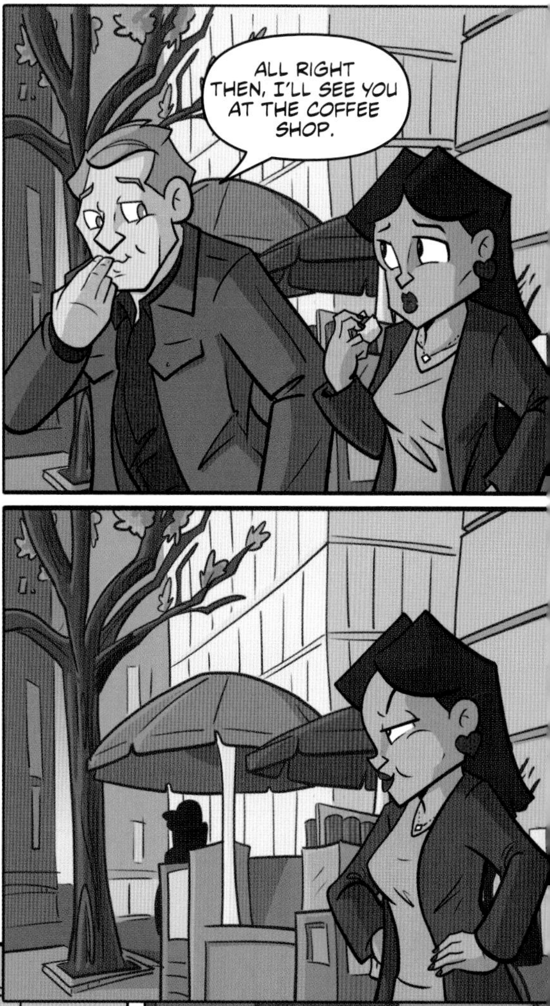
ALL RIGHT THEN, I'LL SEE YOU AT THE COFFEE SHOP.

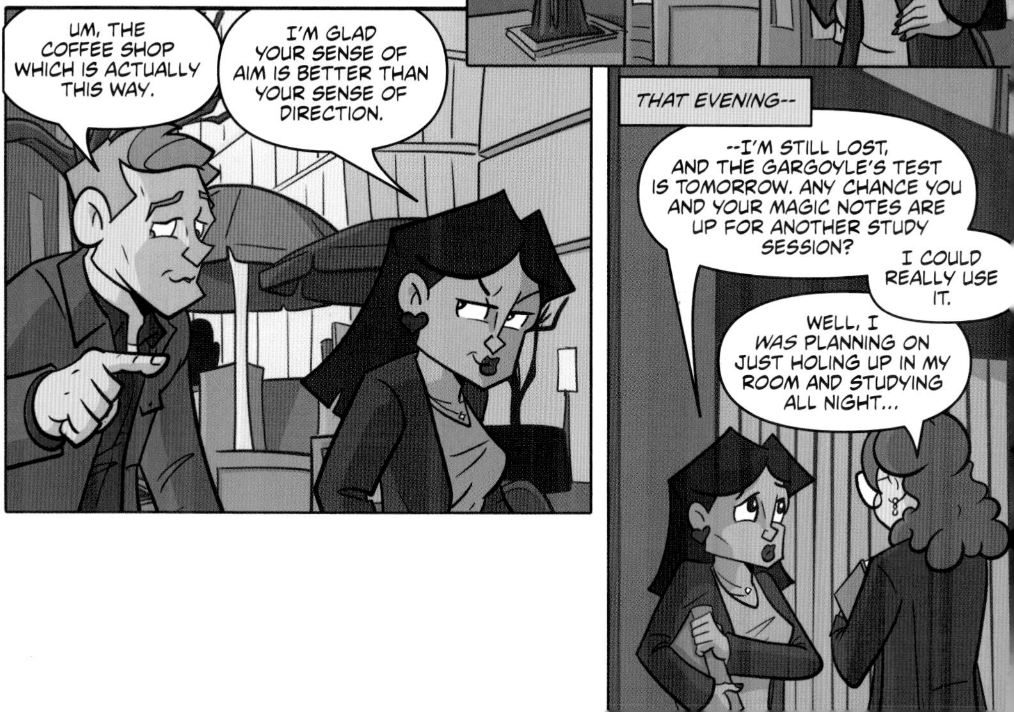
UM, THE COFFEE SHOP WHICH IS ACTUALLY THIS WAY.
I'M GLAD YOUR SENSE OF AIM IS BETTER THAN YOUR SENSE OF DIRECTION.
THAT EVENING--
--I'M STILL LOST, AND THE GARGOYLE'S TEST IS TOMORROW. ANY CHANCE YOU AND YOUR MAGIC NOTES ARE UP FOR ANOTHER STUDY SESSION?
I COULD REALLY USE IT.
WELL, I WAS PLANNING ON JUST HOLING UP IN MY ROOM AND STUDYING ALL NIGHT...

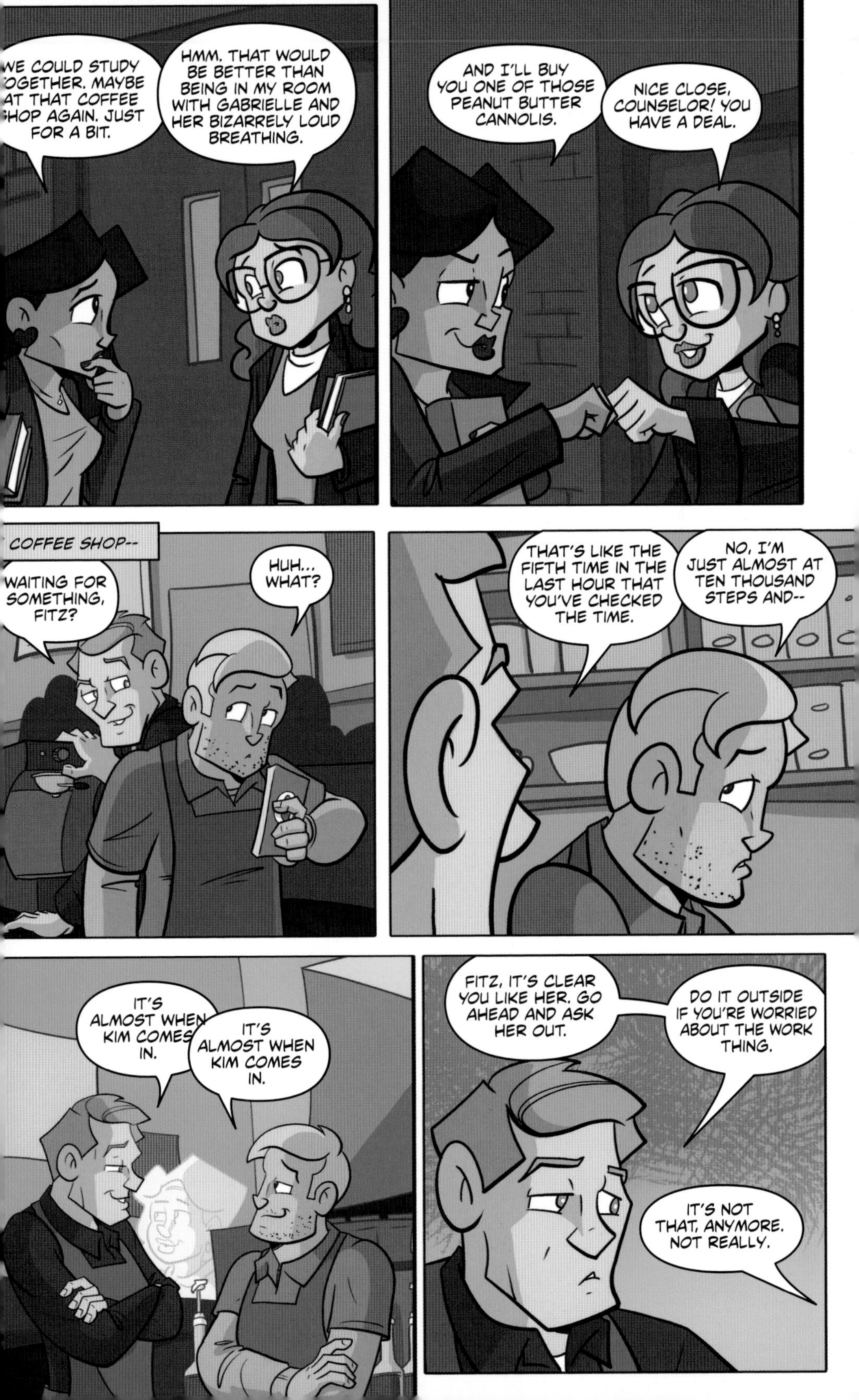
WE COULD STUDY OGETHER. MAYBE AT THAT COFFEE HOP AGAIN. JUST FOR A BIT.
HMM. THAT WOULD BE BETTER THAN BEING IN MY ROOM WITH GABRIELLE AND HER BIZARRELY LOUD BREATHING.
AND I'LL BUY YOU ONE OF THOSE PEANUT BUTTER CANNOLIS.
NICE CLOSE, COUNSELOR! YOU HAVE A DEAL.
COFFEE SHOP--
WAITING FOR SOMETHING, FITZ?
HUH... WHAT?
THAT'S LIKE THE FIFTH TIME IN THE LAST HOUR THAT YOU'VE CHECKED THE TIME.
NO, I'M JUST ALMOST AT TEN THOUSAND STEPS AND--
IT'S ALMOST WHEN KIM COMES IN.
IT'S ALMOST WHEN KIM COMES IN.
FITZ, IT'S CLEAR YOU LIKE HER. GO AHEAD AND ASK HER OUT.
DO IT OUTSIDE IF YOU'RE WORRIED ABOUT THE WORK THING.
IT'S NOT THAT, ANYMORE. NOT REALLY.

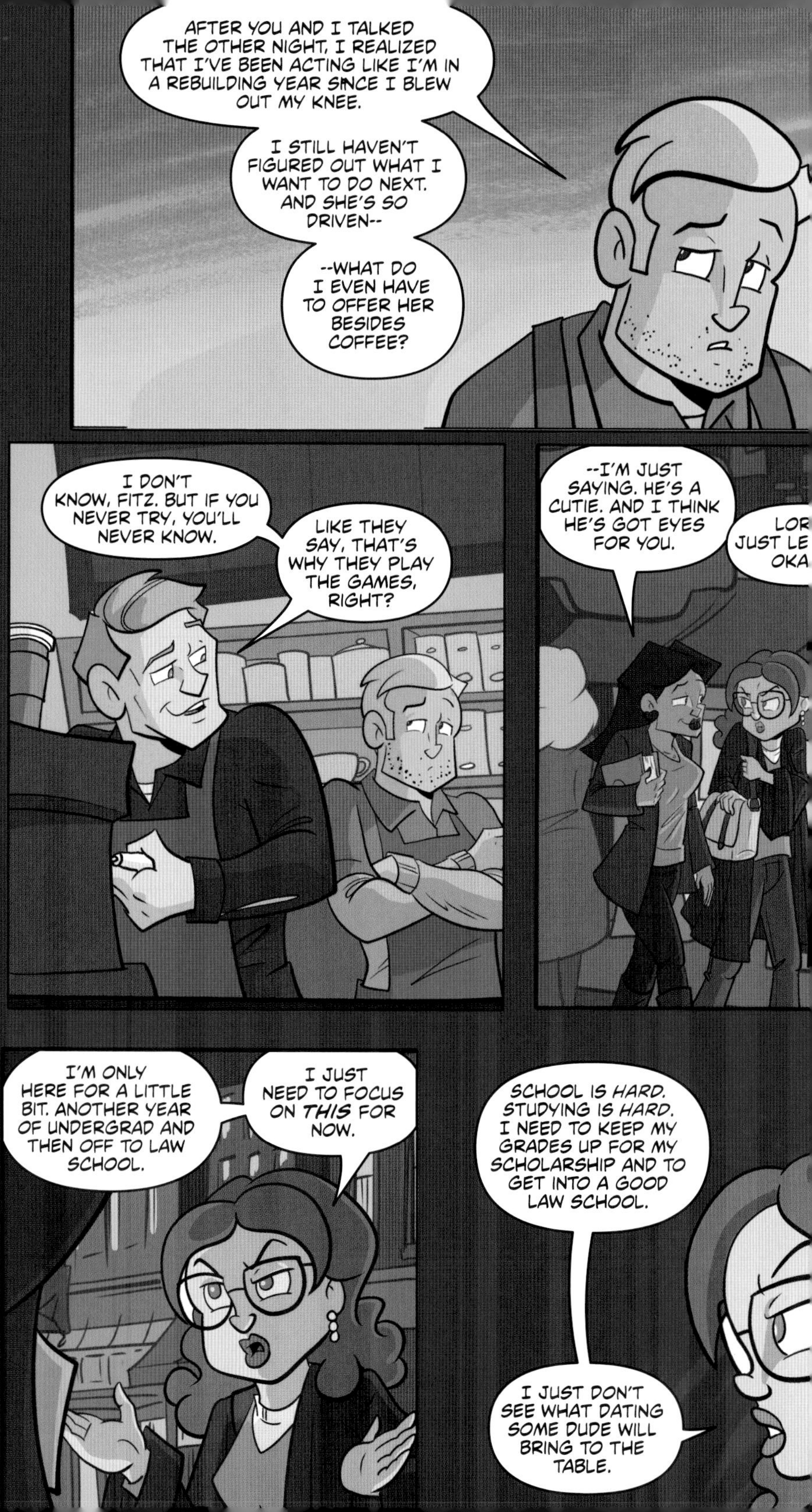
AFTER YOU AND I TALKED THE OTHER NIGHT, I REALIZED THAT I'VE BEEN ACTING LIKE I'M IN A REBUILDING YEAR SINCE I BLEW OUT MY KNEE.
I STILL HAVEN'T FIGURED OUT WHAT I WANT TO DO NEXT. AND SHE'S SO DRIVEN--
--WHAT DO I EVEN HAVE TO OFFER HER BESIDES COFFEE?
I DON'T KNOW, FITZ. BUT IF YOU NEVER TRY, YOU'LL NEVER KNOW.
LIKE THEY SAY, THAT'S WHY THEY PLAY THE GAMES, RIGHT?
--I'M JUST SAYING. HE'S A CUTIE. AND I THINK HE'S GOT EYES FOR YOU.
I'M ONLY HERE FOR A LITTLE BIT. ANOTHER YEAR OF UNDERGRAD AND THEN OFF TO LAW SCHOOL.
I JUST NEED TO FOCUS ON *THIS* FOR NOW.
SCHOOL IS *HARD*. STUDYING IS *HARD*. I NEED TO KEEP MY GRADES UP FOR MY SCHOLARSHIP AND TO GET INTO A GOOD LAW SCHOOL.
I JUST DON'T SEE WHAT DATING SOME DUDE WILL BRING TO THE TABLE.

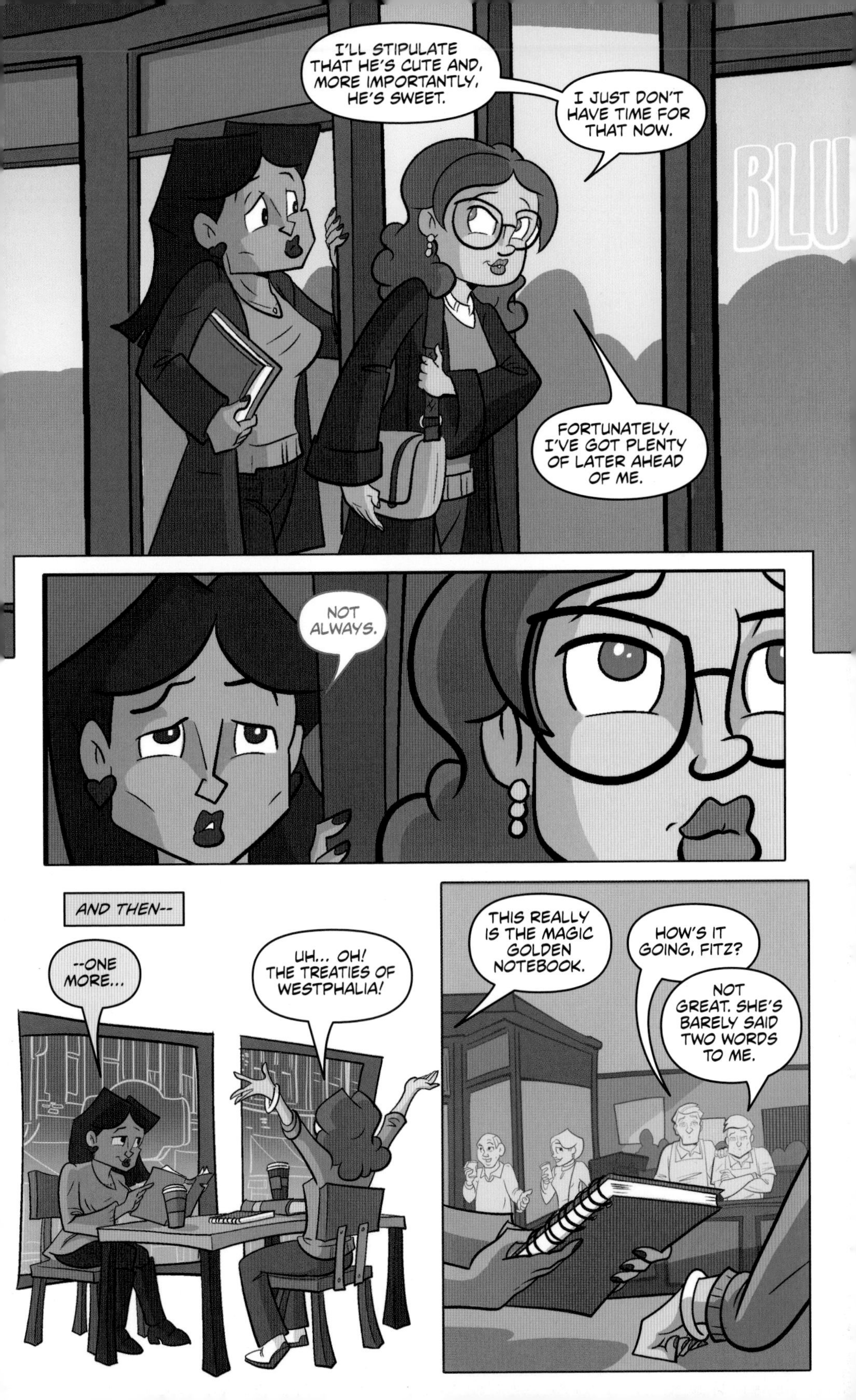
I'LL STIPULATE THAT HE'S CUTE AND, MORE IMPORTANTLY, HE'S SWEET.
I JUST DON'T HAVE TIME FOR THAT NOW.
BLU
FORTUNATELY, I'VE GOT PLENTY OF LATER AHEAD OF ME.
NOT ALWAYS.
AND THEN--
--ONE MORE...
UH... OH! THE TREATIES OF WESTPHALIA!
THIS REALLY IS THE MAGIC GOLDEN NOTEBOOK.
HOW'S IT GOING, FITZ?
NOT GREAT. SHE'S BARELY SAID TWO WORDS TO ME.

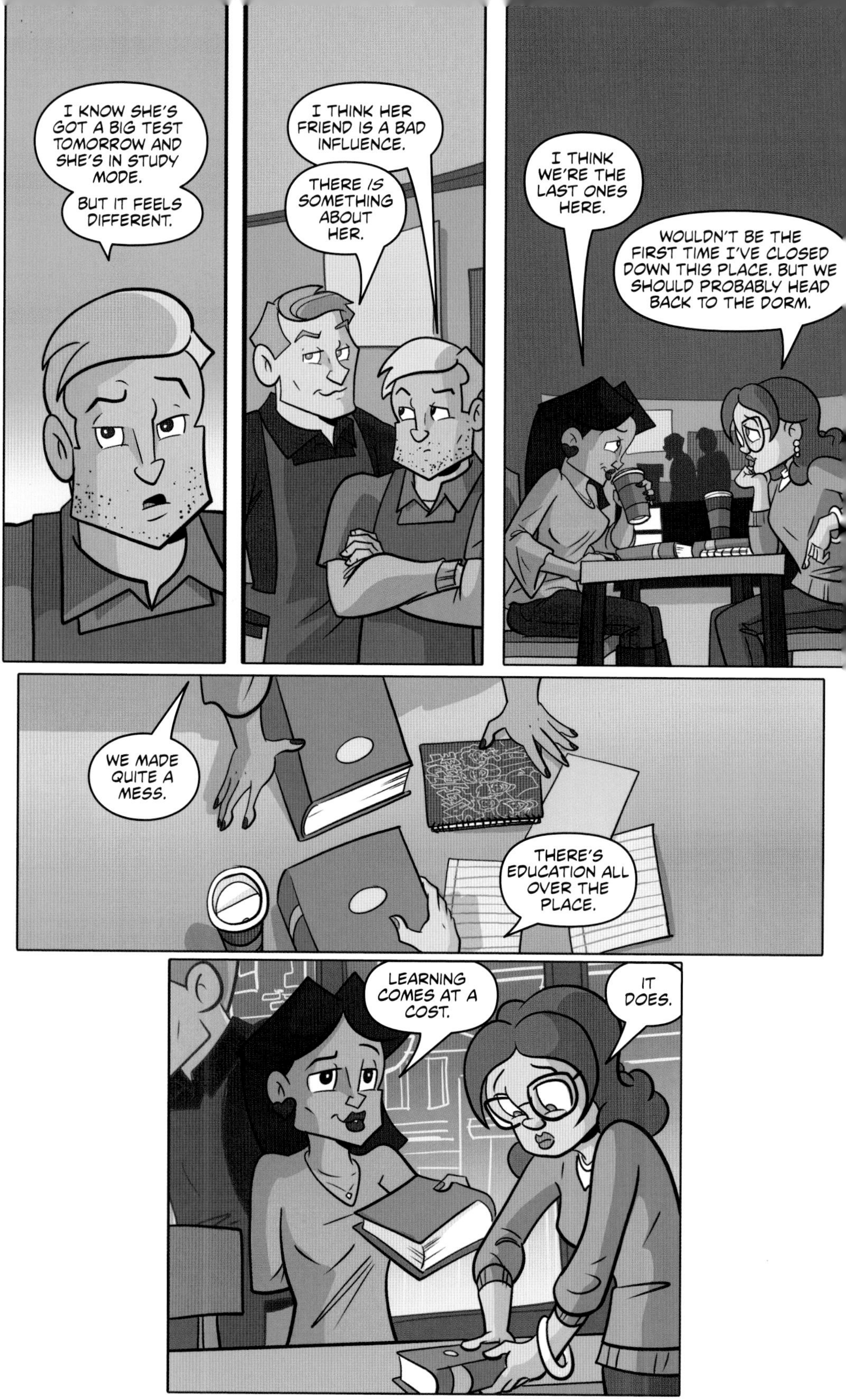
I KNOW SHE'S GOT A BIG TEST TOMORROW AND SHE'S IN STUDY MODE.
BUT IT FEELS DIFFERENT.
I THINK HER FRIEND IS A BAD INFLUENCE.
THERE IS SOMETHING ABOUT HER.
I THINK WE'RE THE LAST ONES HERE.
WOULDN'T BE THE FIRST TIME I'VE CLOSED DOWN THIS PLACE. BUT WE SHOULD PROBABLY HEAD BACK TO THE DORM.
WE MADE QUITE A MESS.
THERE'S EDUCATION ALL OVER THE PLACE.
LEARNING COMES AT A COST.
IT DOES.

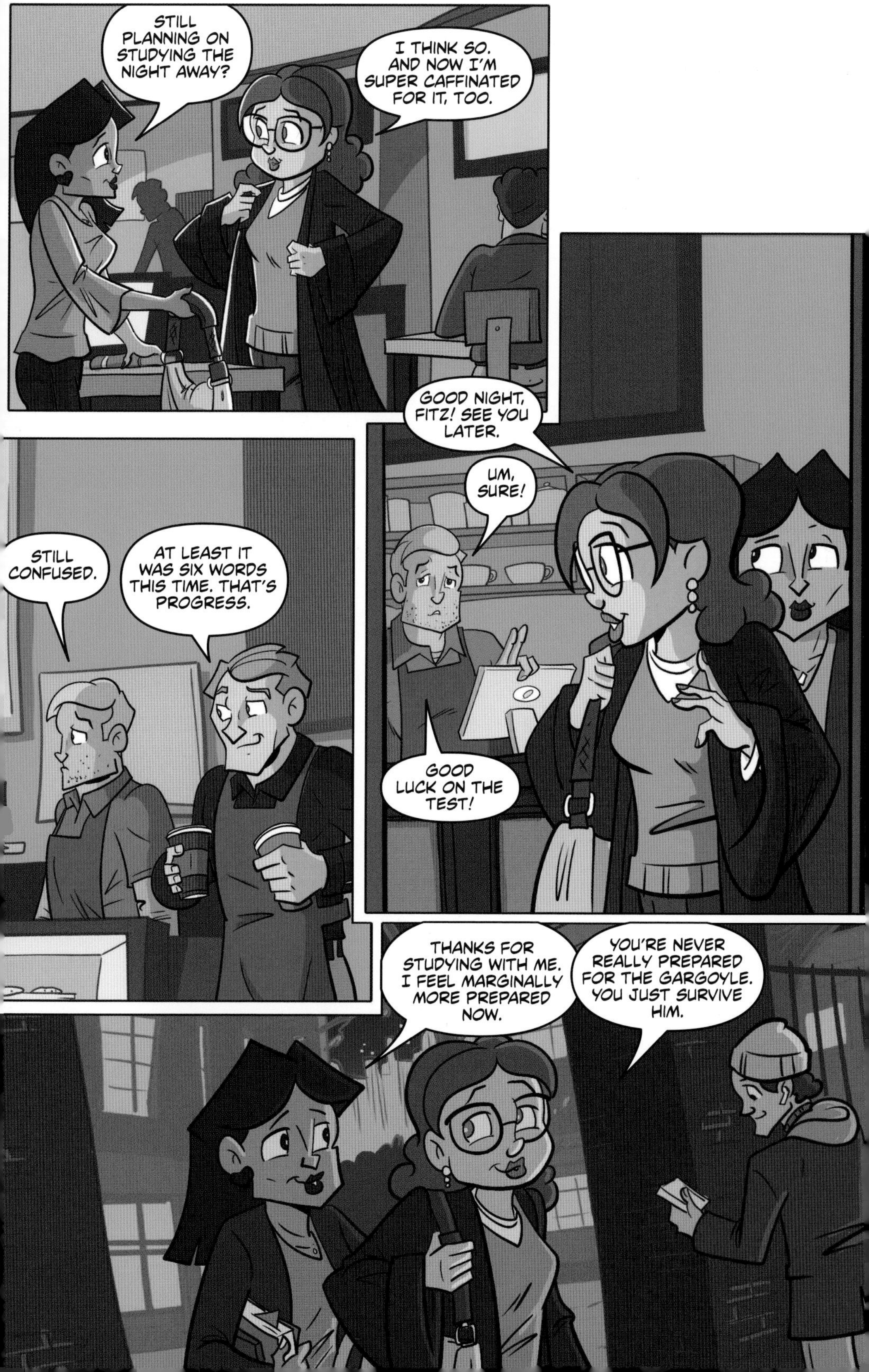
STILL PLANNING ON STUDYING THE NIGHT AWAY?
I THINK SO. AND NOW I'M SUPER CAFFINATED FOR IT, TOO.
STILL CONFUSED.
AT LEAST IT WAS SIX WORDS THIS TIME. THAT'S PROGRESS.
GOOD NIGHT, FITZ! SEE YOU LATER.
UM, SURE!
GOOD LUCK ON THE TEST!
THANKS FOR STUDYING WITH ME. I FEEL MARGINALLY MORE PREPARED NOW.
YOU'RE NEVER REALLY PREPARED FOR THE GARGOYLE. YOU JUST SURVIVE HIM.

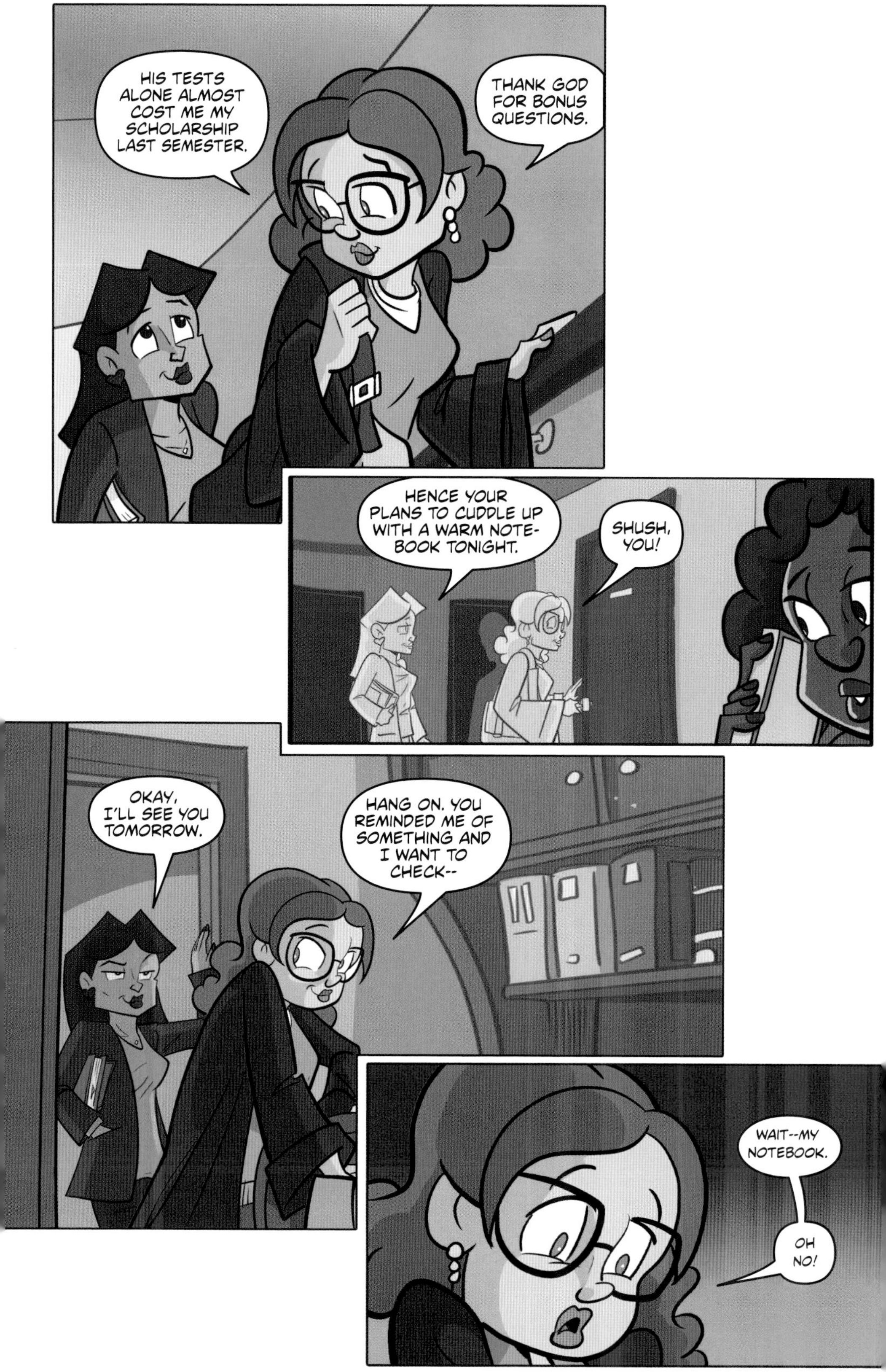
HIS TESTS ALONE ALMOST COST ME MY SCHOLARSHIP LAST SEMESTER.
THANK GOD FOR BONUS QUESTIONS.
HENCE YOUR PLANS TO CUDDLE UP WITH A WARM NOTE-BOOK TONIGHT.
SHUSH, YOU!
OKAY, I'LL SEE YOU TOMORROW.
HANG ON. YOU REMINDED ME OF SOMETHING AND I WANT TO CHECK--
WAIT--MY NOTEBOOK.
OH NO!

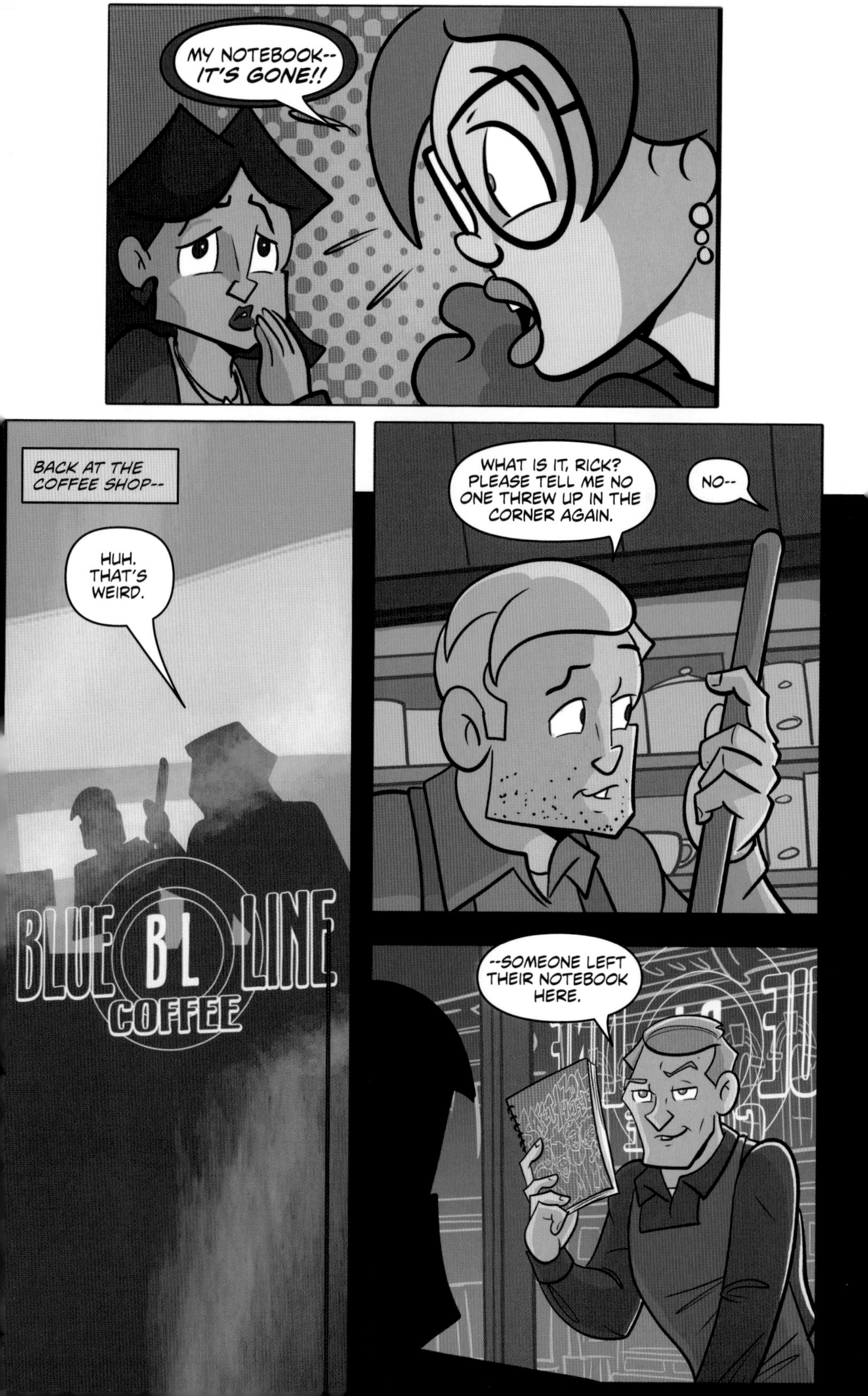
MY NOTEBOOK-- IT'S GONE!!
BACK AT THE COFFEE SHOP--
HUH. THAT'S WEIRD.
BLUE BL LINE COFFEE
WHAT IS IT, RICK? PLEASE TELL ME NO ONE THREW UP IN THE CORNER AGAIN.
NO--
--SOMEONE LEFT THEIR NOTEBOOK HERE.

Chapter 9

Running Out of Time

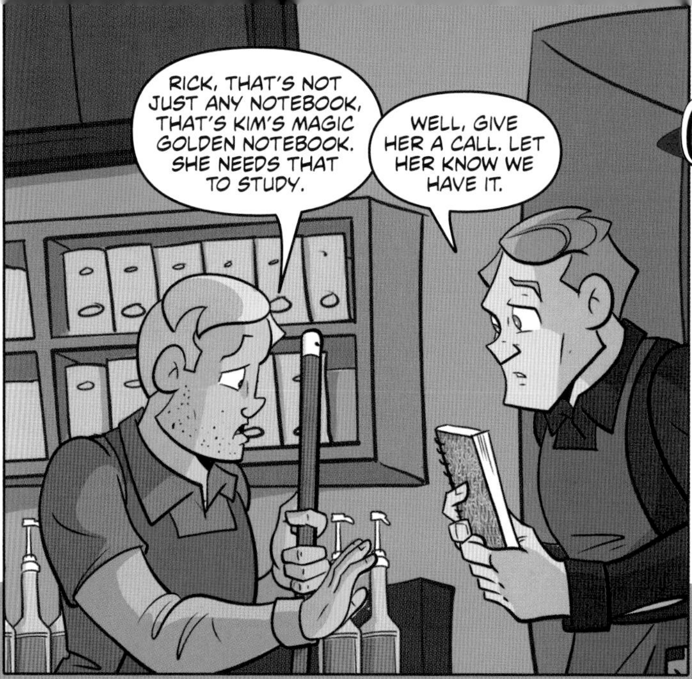
RICK, THAT'S NOT JUST ANY NOTEBOOK, THAT'S KIM'S MAGIC GOLDEN NOTEBOOK. SHE NEEDS THAT TO STUDY.
WELL, GIVE HER A CALL. LET HER KNOW WE HAVE IT.

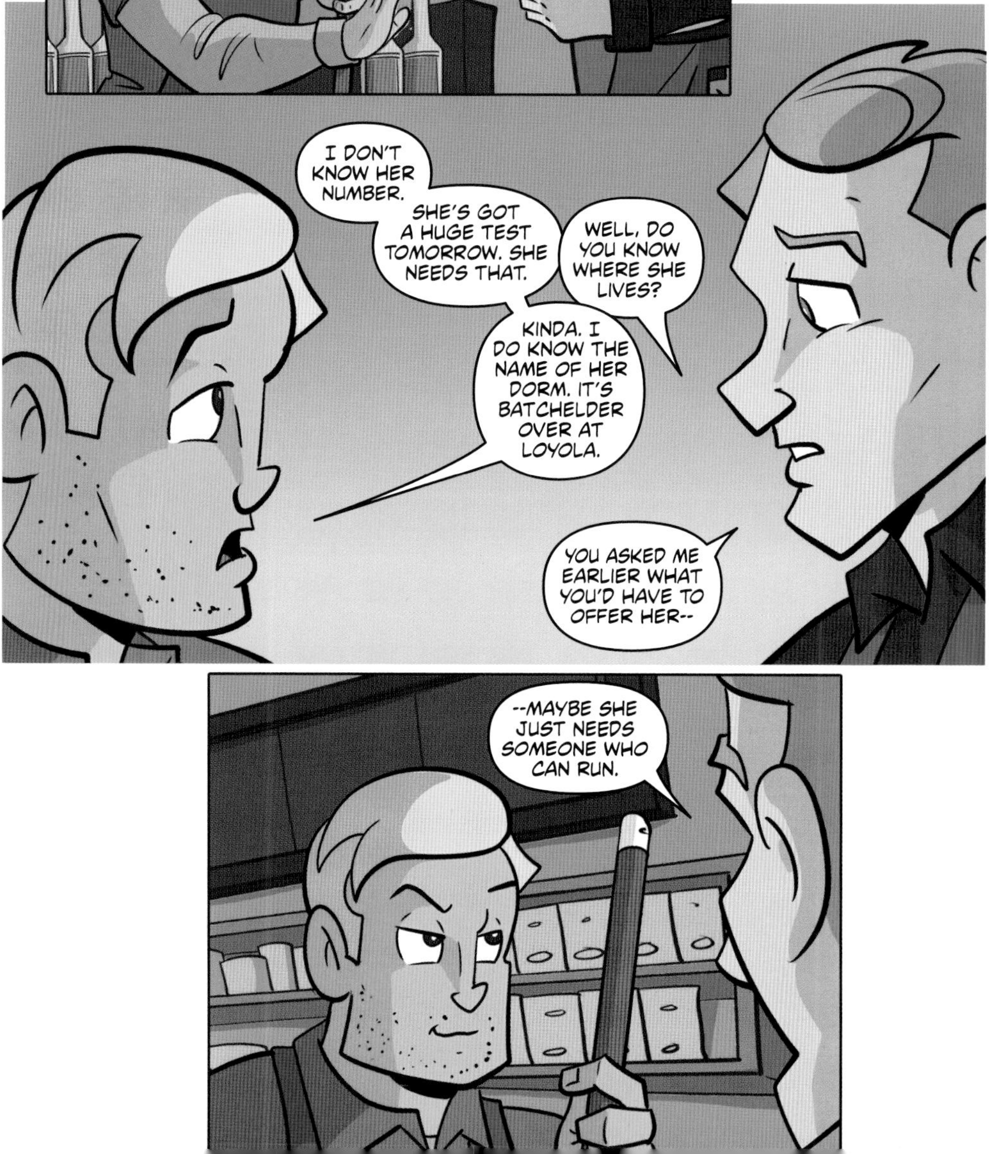
I DON'T KNOW HER NUMBER.
SHE'S GOT A HUGE TEST TOMORROW. SHE NEEDS THAT.
WELL, DO YOU KNOW WHERE SHE LIVES?
KINDA. I DO KNOW THE NAME OF HER DORM. IT'S BATCHELDER OVER AT LOYOLA.
YOU ASKED ME EARLIER WHAT YOU'D HAVE TO OFFER HER--
--MAYBE SHE JUST NEEDS SOMEONE WHO CAN RUN.

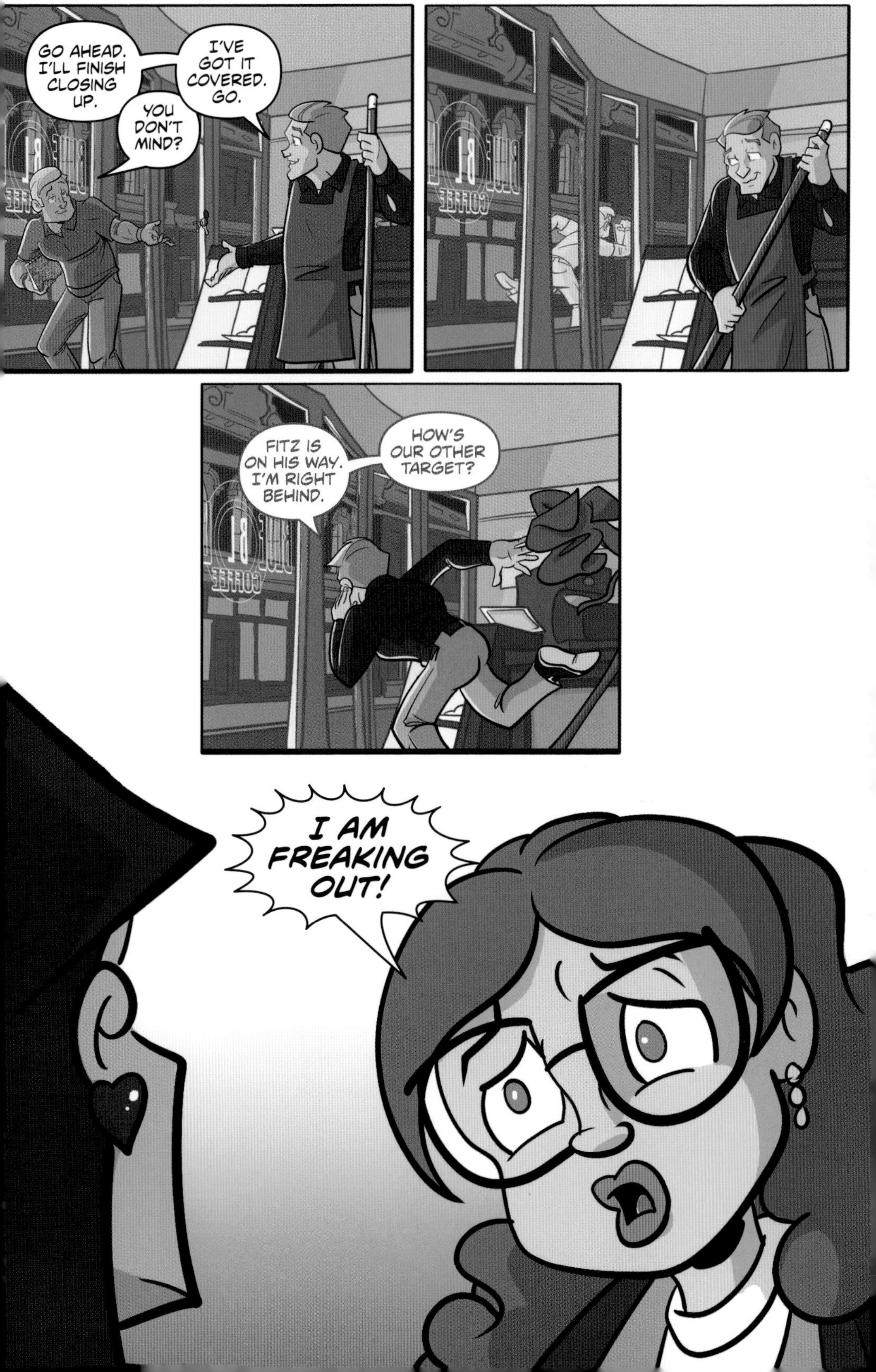
GO AHEAD. I'LL FINISH CLOSING UP.
YOU DON'T MIND?
I'VE GOT IT COVERED. GO.
FITZ IS ON HIS WAY. I'M RIGHT BEHIND.
HOW'S OUR OTHER TARGET?
I AM FREAKING OUT!

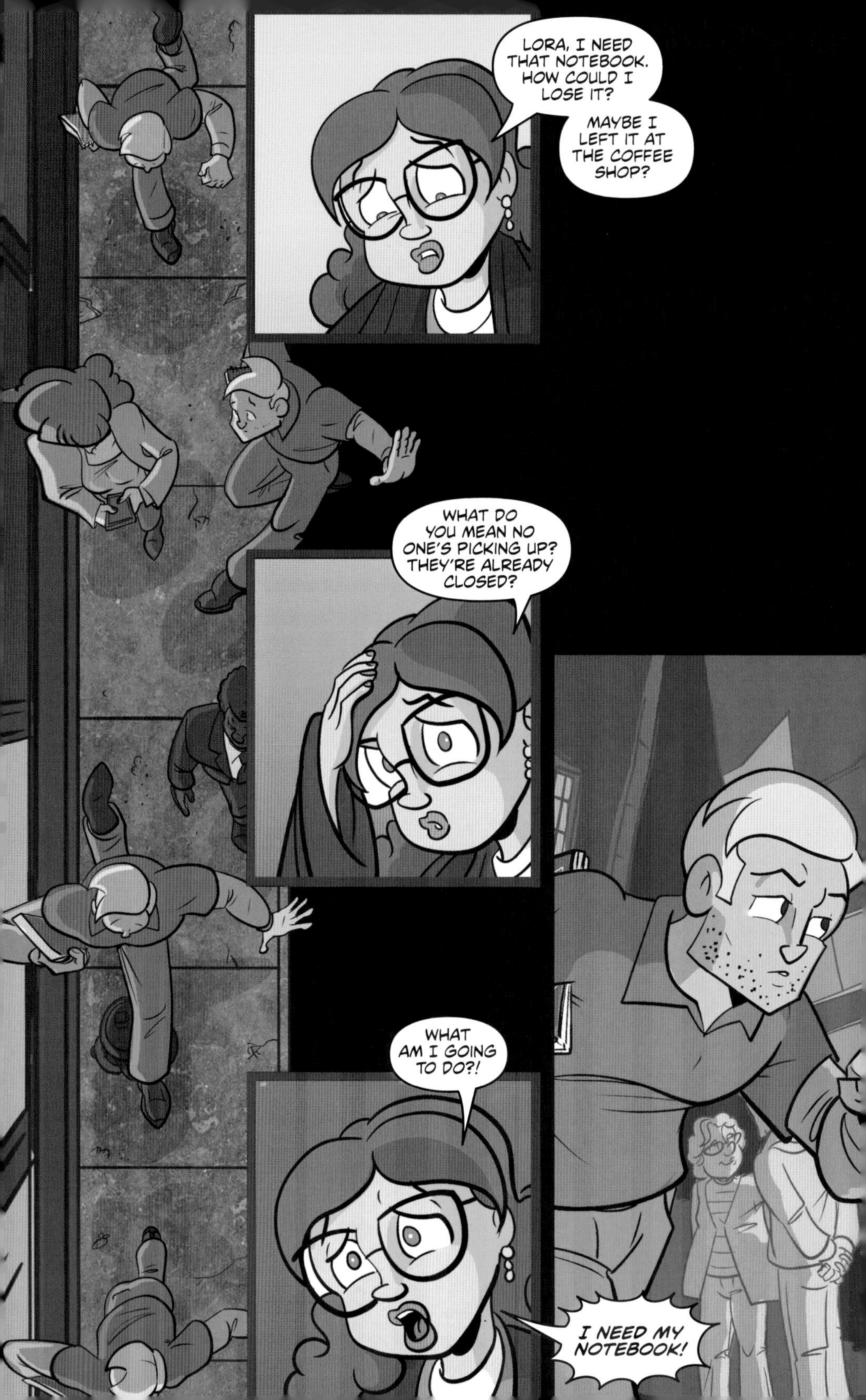
LORA, I NEED THAT NOTEBOOK. HOW COULD I LOSE IT?
MAYBE I LEFT IT AT THE COFFEE SHOP?
WHAT DO YOU MEAN NO ONE'S PICKING UP? THEY'RE ALREADY CLOSED?
WHAT AM I GOING TO DO?!
I NEED MY NOTEBOOK!

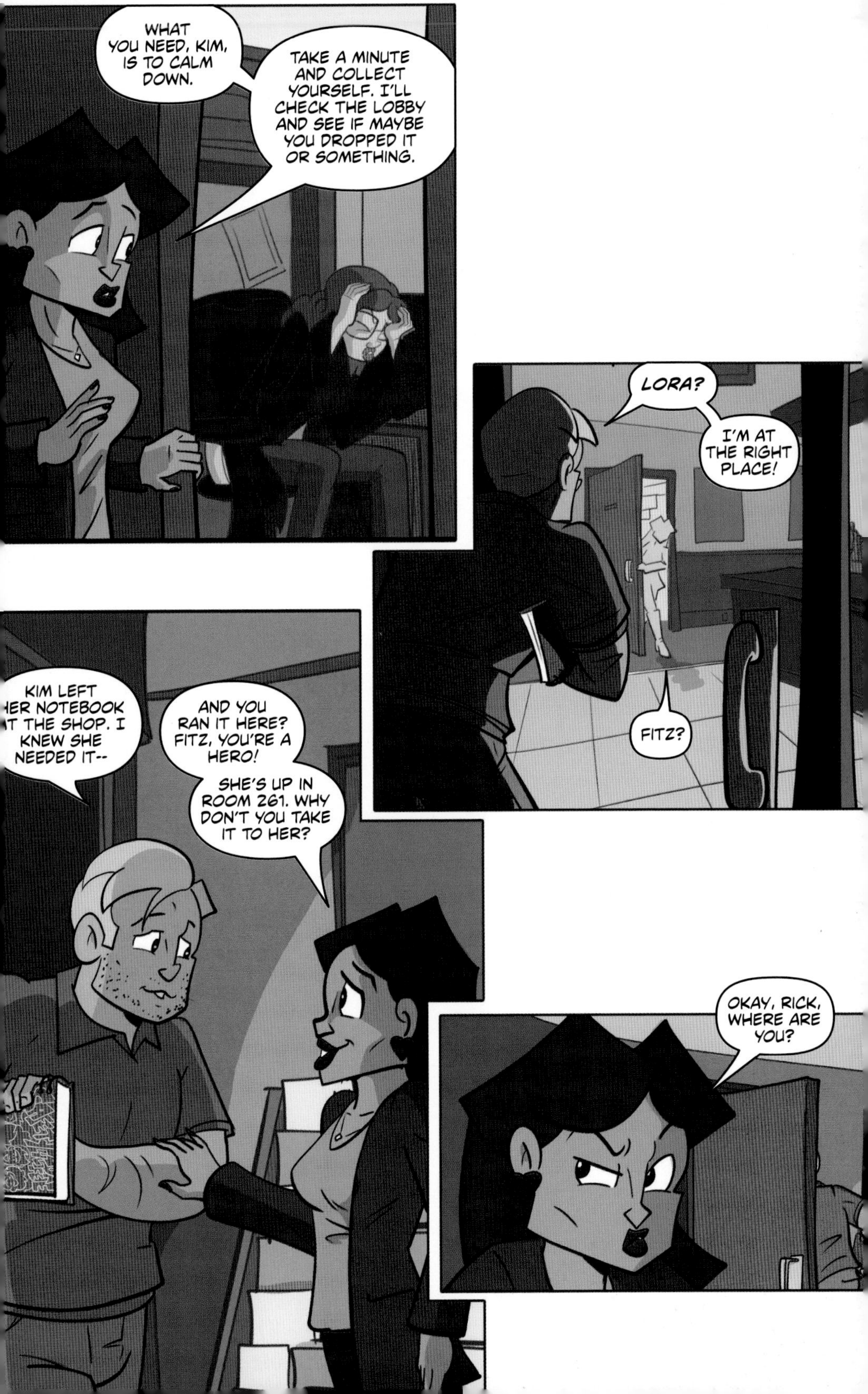
WHAT YOU NEED, KIM, IS TO CALM DOWN.
TAKE A MINUTE AND COLLECT YOURSELF. I'LL CHECK THE LOBBY AND SEE IF MAYBE YOU DROPPED IT OR SOMETHING.
LORA?
I'M AT THE RIGHT PLACE!
FITZ?
KIM LEFT HER NOTEBOOK AT THE SHOP. I KNEW SHE NEEDED IT--
AND YOU RAN IT HERE? FITZ, YOU'RE A HERO!
SHE'S UP IN ROOM 261. WHY DON'T YOU TAKE IT TO HER?
OKAY, RICK, WHERE ARE YOU?

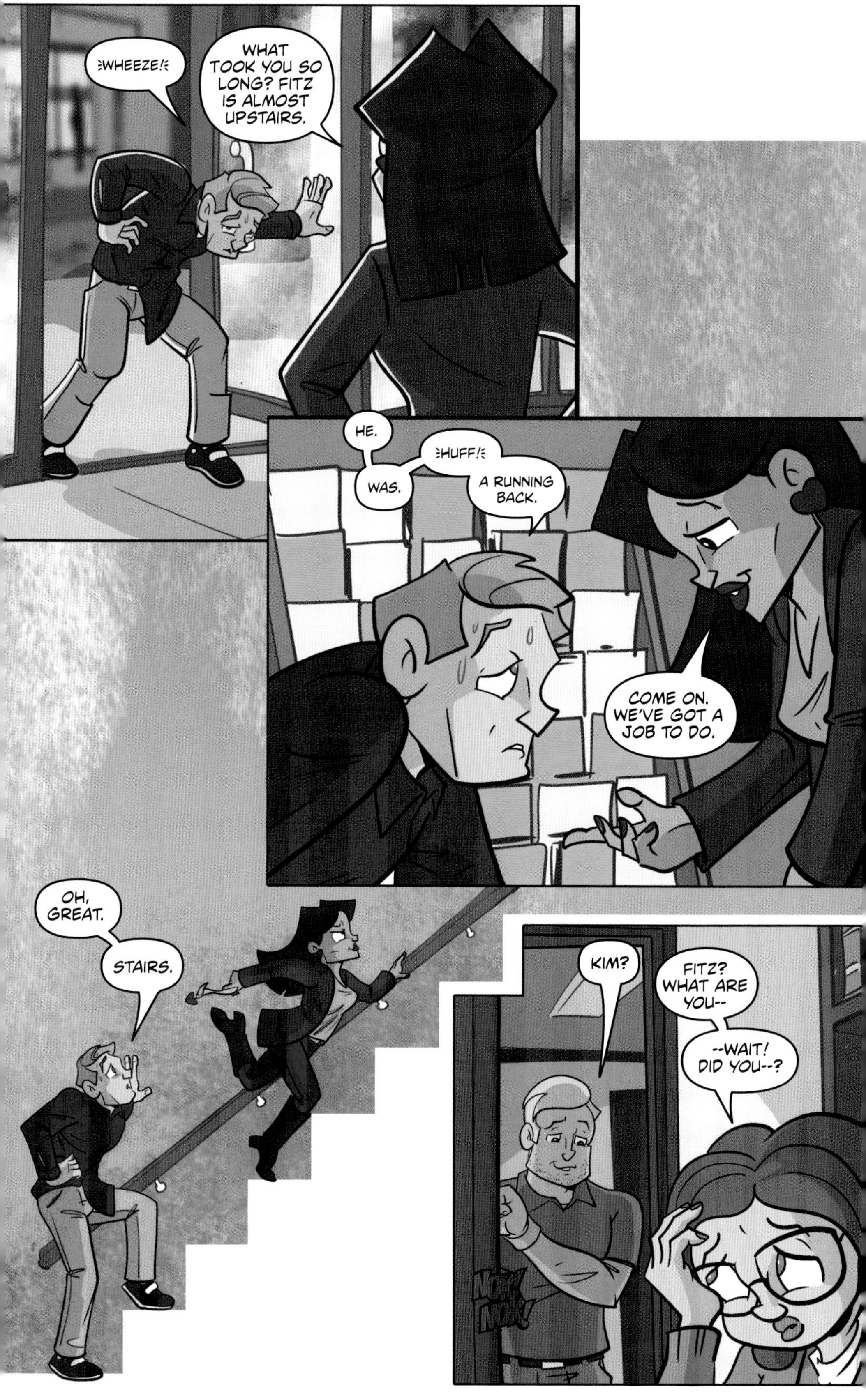

⁝WHEEZE!⁝
WHAT TOOK YOU SO LONG? FITZ IS ALMOST UPSTAIRS.
HE.
WAS.
⁝HUFF!⁝
A RUNNING BACK.
COME ON. WE'VE GOT A JOB TO DO.
OH, GREAT.
STAIRS.
KIM?
FITZ? WHAT ARE YOU--
--WAIT! DID YOU--?

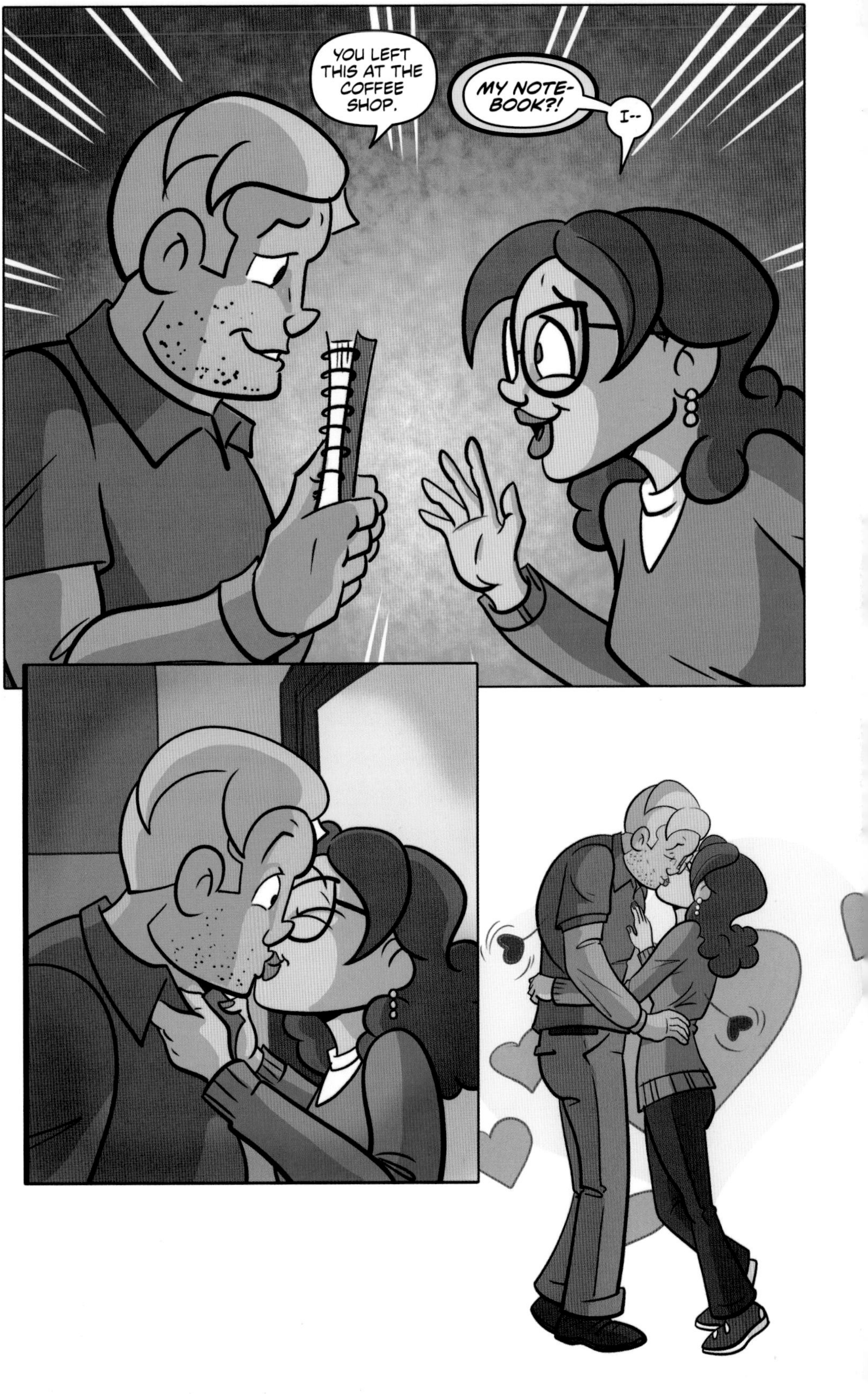
YOU LEFT THIS AT THE COFFEE SHOP.
MY NOTE-BOOK?!
I--

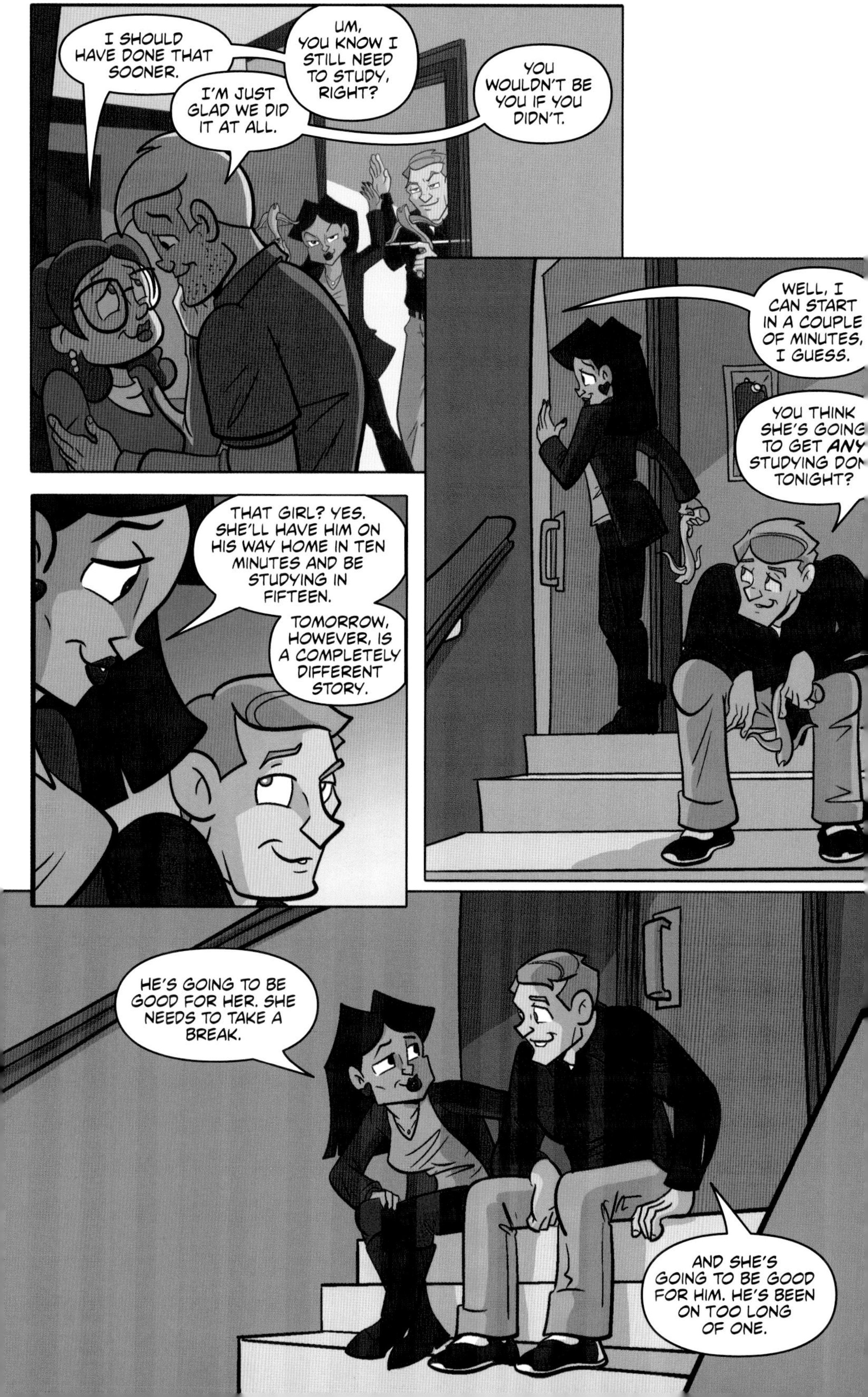
I SHOULD HAVE DONE THAT SOONER.
UM, YOU KNOW I STILL NEED TO STUDY, RIGHT?
I'M JUST GLAD WE DID IT AT ALL.
YOU WOULDN'T BE YOU IF YOU DIDN'T.
WELL, I CAN START IN A COUPLE OF MINUTES, I GUESS.
YOU THINK SHE'S GOING TO GET *ANY* STUDYING DON TONIGHT?
THAT GIRL? YES. SHE'LL HAVE HIM ON HIS WAY HOME IN TEN MINUTES AND BE STUDYING IN FIFTEEN.
TOMORROW, HOWEVER, IS A COMPLETELY DIFFERENT STORY.
HE'S GOING TO BE GOOD FOR HER. SHE NEEDS TO TAKE A BREAK.
AND SHE'S GOING TO BE GOOD FOR HIM. HE'S BEEN ON TOO LONG OF ONE.

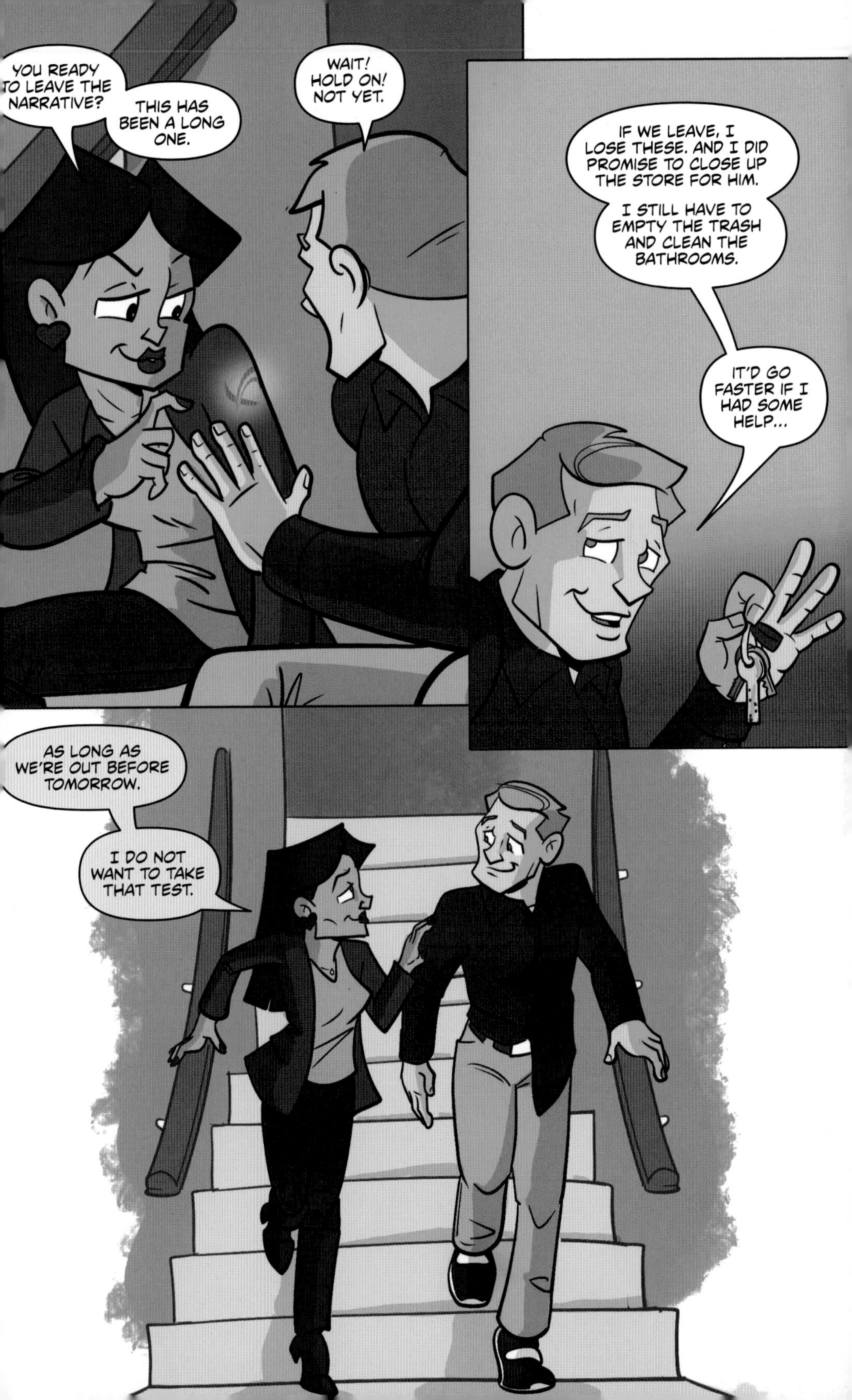
YOU READY TO LEAVE THE NARRATIVE?
THIS HAS BEEN A LONG ONE.
WAIT! HOLD ON! NOT YET.
IF WE LEAVE, I LOSE THESE. AND I DID PROMISE TO CLOSE UP THE STORE FOR HIM.
I STILL HAVE TO EMPTY THE TRASH AND CLEAN THE BATHROOMS.
IT'D GO FASTER IF I HAD SOME HELP...
AS LONG AS WE'RE OUT BEFORE TOMORROW.
I DO NOT WANT TO TAKE THAT TEST.

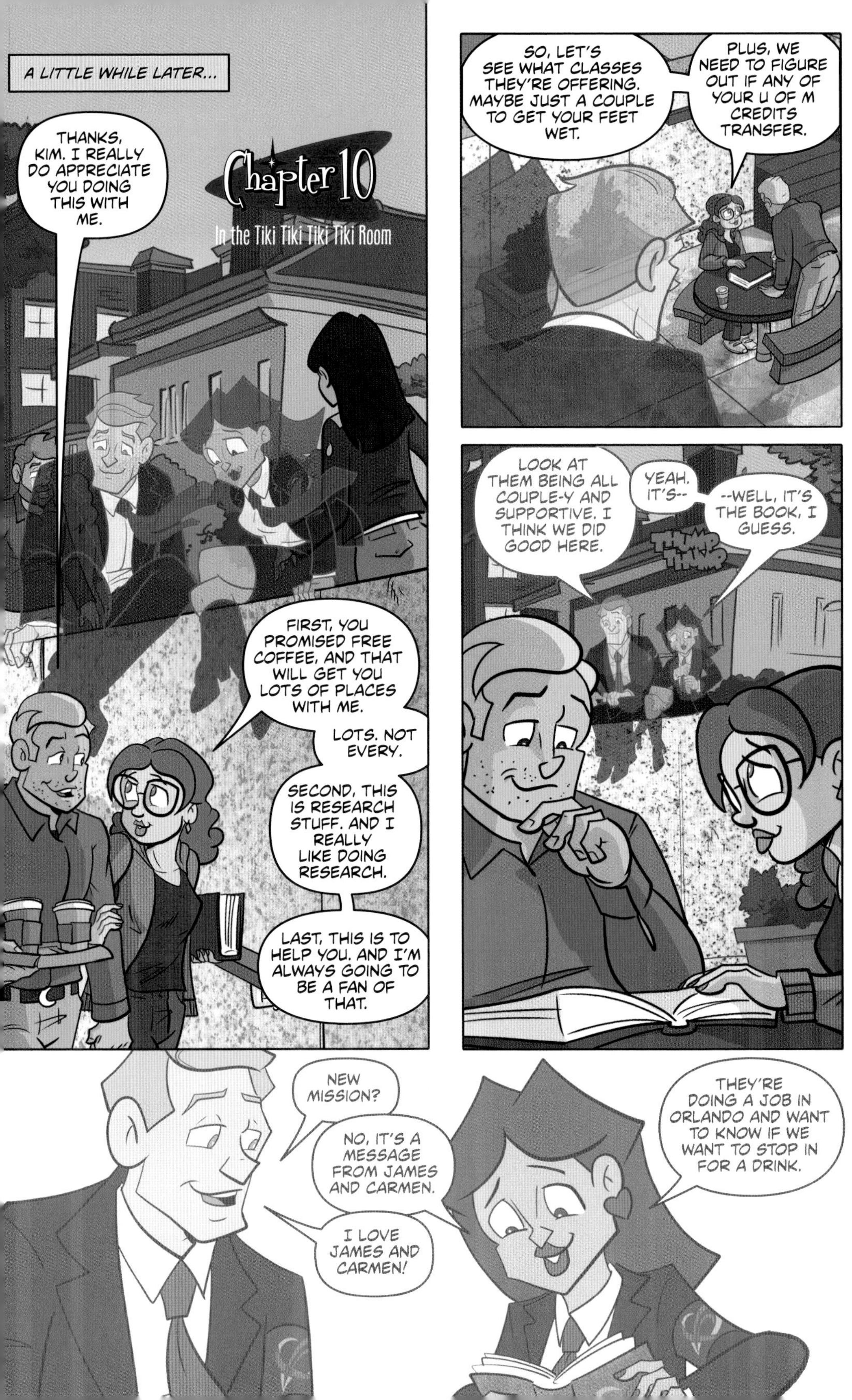
A LITTLE WHILE LATER...
THANKS, KIM. I REALLY DO APPRECIATE YOU DOING THIS WITH ME.
Chapter 10
In the Tiki Tiki Tiki Tiki Room
FIRST, YOU PROMISED FREE COFFEE, AND THAT WILL GET YOU LOTS OF PLACES WITH ME.
LOTS. NOT EVERY.
SECOND, THIS IS RESEARCH STUFF. AND I REALLY LIKE DOING RESEARCH.
LAST, THIS IS TO HELP YOU. AND I'M ALWAYS GOING TO BE A FAN OF THAT.
SO, LET'S SEE WHAT CLASSES THEY'RE OFFERING. MAYBE JUST A COUPLE TO GET YOUR FEET WET.
PLUS, WE NEED TO FIGURE OUT IF ANY OF YOUR U OF M CREDITS TRANSFER.
LOOK AT THEM BEING ALL COUPLE-Y AND SUPPORTIVE. I THINK WE DID GOOD HERE.
YEAH. IT'S--
--WELL, IT'S THE BOOK, I GUESS.
THUMP THUMP
NEW MISSION?
NO, IT'S A MESSAGE FROM JAMES AND CARMEN.
THEY'RE DOING A JOB IN ORLANDO AND WANT TO KNOW IF WE WANT TO STOP IN FOR A DRINK.
I LOVE JAMES AND CARMEN!

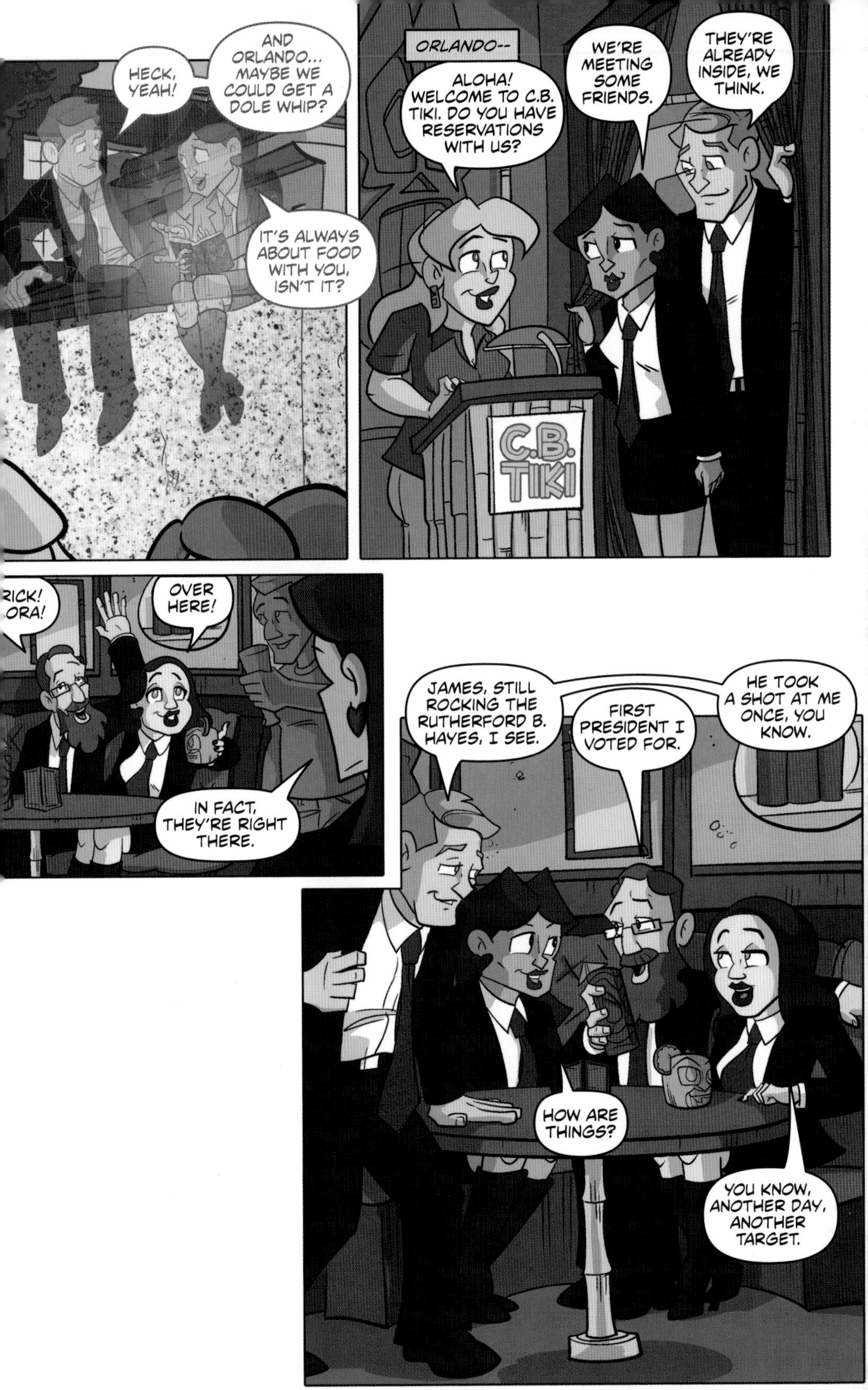
HECK, YEAH!
AND ORLANDO... MAYBE WE COULD GET A DOLE WHIP?
IT'S ALWAYS ABOUT FOOD WITH YOU, ISN'T IT?
ORLANDO--
ALOHA! WELCOME TO C.B. TIKI. DO YOU HAVE RESERVATIONS WITH US?
WE'RE MEETING SOME FRIENDS.
THEY'RE ALREADY INSIDE, WE THINK.
C.B. TIKI
RICK! ORA!
OVER HERE!
IN FACT, THEY'RE RIGHT THERE.
JAMES, STILL ROCKING THE RUTHERFORD B. HAYES, I SEE.
FIRST PRESIDENT I VOTED FOR.
HE TOOK A SHOT AT ME ONCE, YOU KNOW.
HOW ARE THINGS?
YOU KNOW, ANOTHER DAY, ANOTHER TARGET.

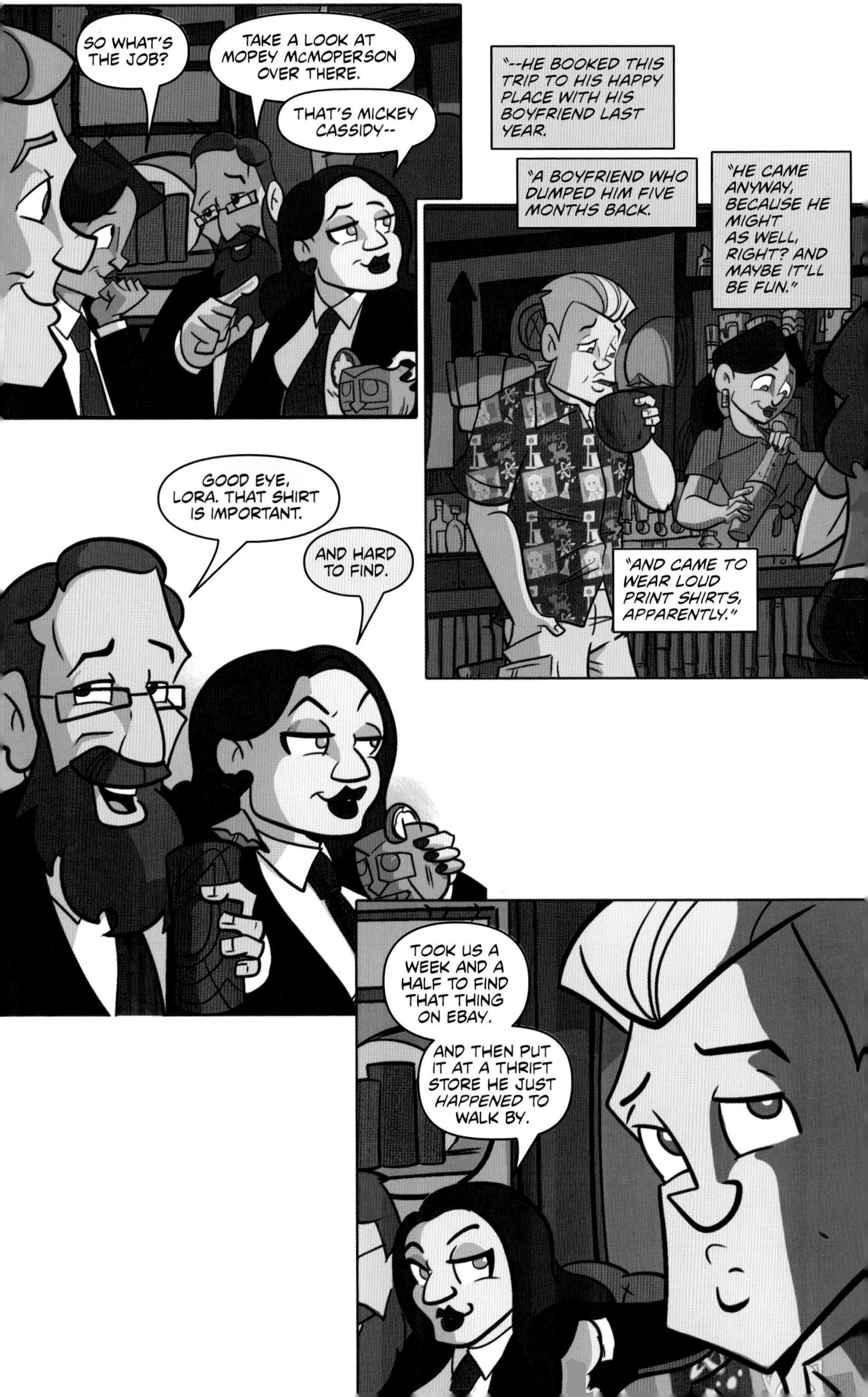

SO WHAT'S THE JOB?
TAKE A LOOK AT MOPEY McMOPERSON OVER THERE.
THAT'S MICKEY CASSIDY--
"--HE BOOKED THIS TRIP TO HIS HAPPY PLACE WITH HIS BOYFRIEND LAST YEAR.
"A BOYFRIEND WHO DUMPED HIM FIVE MONTHS BACK.
"HE CAME ANYWAY, BECAUSE HE MIGHT AS WELL, RIGHT? AND MAYBE IT'LL BE FUN."
"AND CAME TO WEAR LOUD PRINT SHIRTS, APPARENTLY."
GOOD EYE, LORA. THAT SHIRT IS IMPORTANT.
AND HARD TO FIND.
TOOK US A WEEK AND A HALF TO FIND THAT THING ON EBAY.
AND THEN PUT IT AT A THRIFT STORE HE JUST *HAPPENED* TO WALK BY.

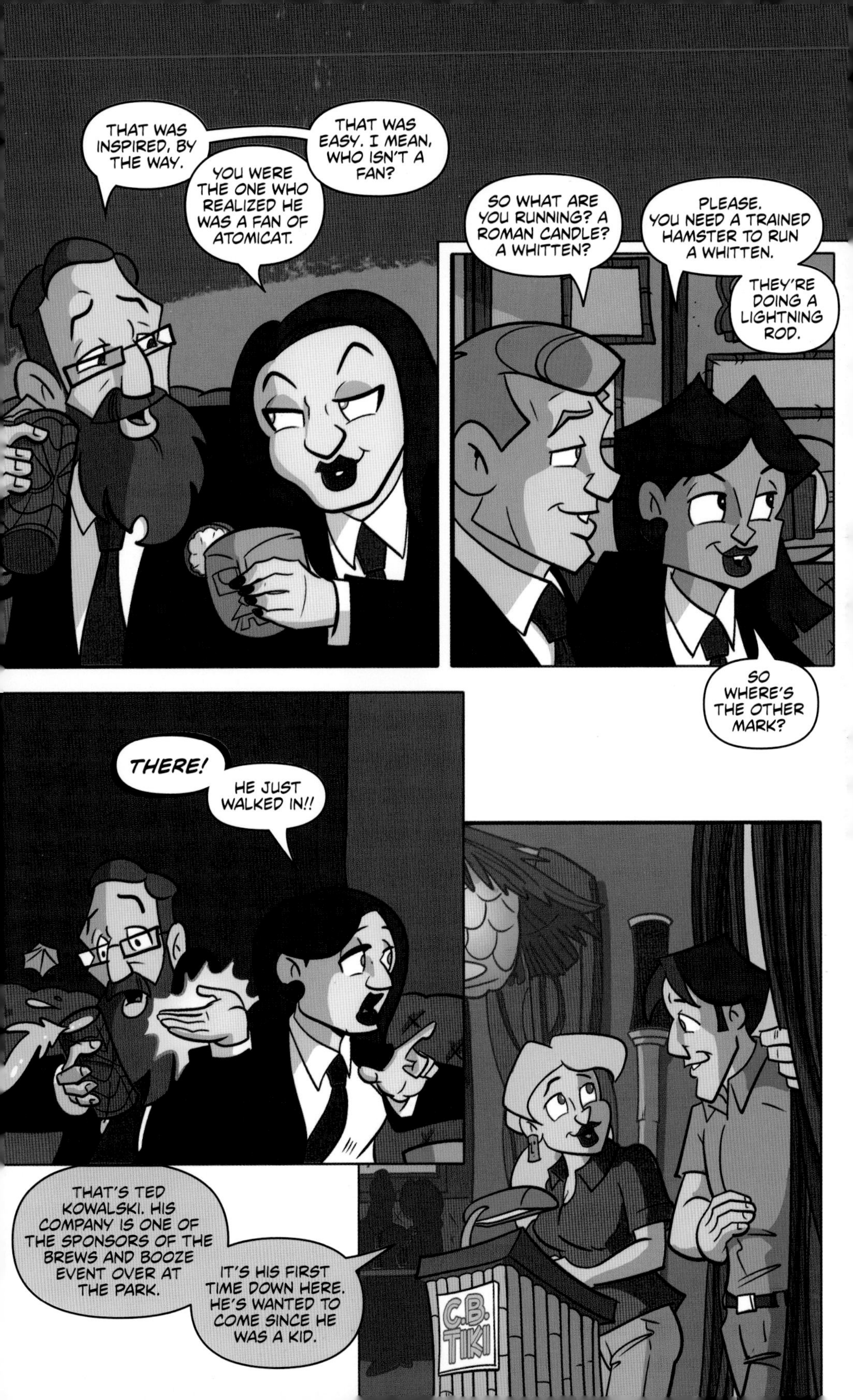
THAT WAS INSPIRED, BY THE WAY.
THAT WAS EASY. I MEAN, WHO ISN'T A FAN?
YOU WERE THE ONE WHO REALIZED HE WAS A FAN OF ATOMICAT.
SO WHAT ARE YOU RUNNING? A ROMAN CANDLE? A WHITTEN?
PLEASE. YOU NEED A TRAINED HAMSTER TO RUN A WHITTEN.
THEY'RE DOING A LIGHTNING ROD.
SO WHERE'S THE OTHER MARK?
THERE!
HE JUST WALKED IN!!
THAT'S TED KOWALSKI. HIS COMPANY IS ONE OF THE SPONSORS OF THE BREWS AND BOOZE EVENT OVER AT THE PARK.
IT'S HIS FIRST TIME DOWN HERE. HE'S WANTED TO COME SINCE HE WAS A KID.
C.B. TIKI

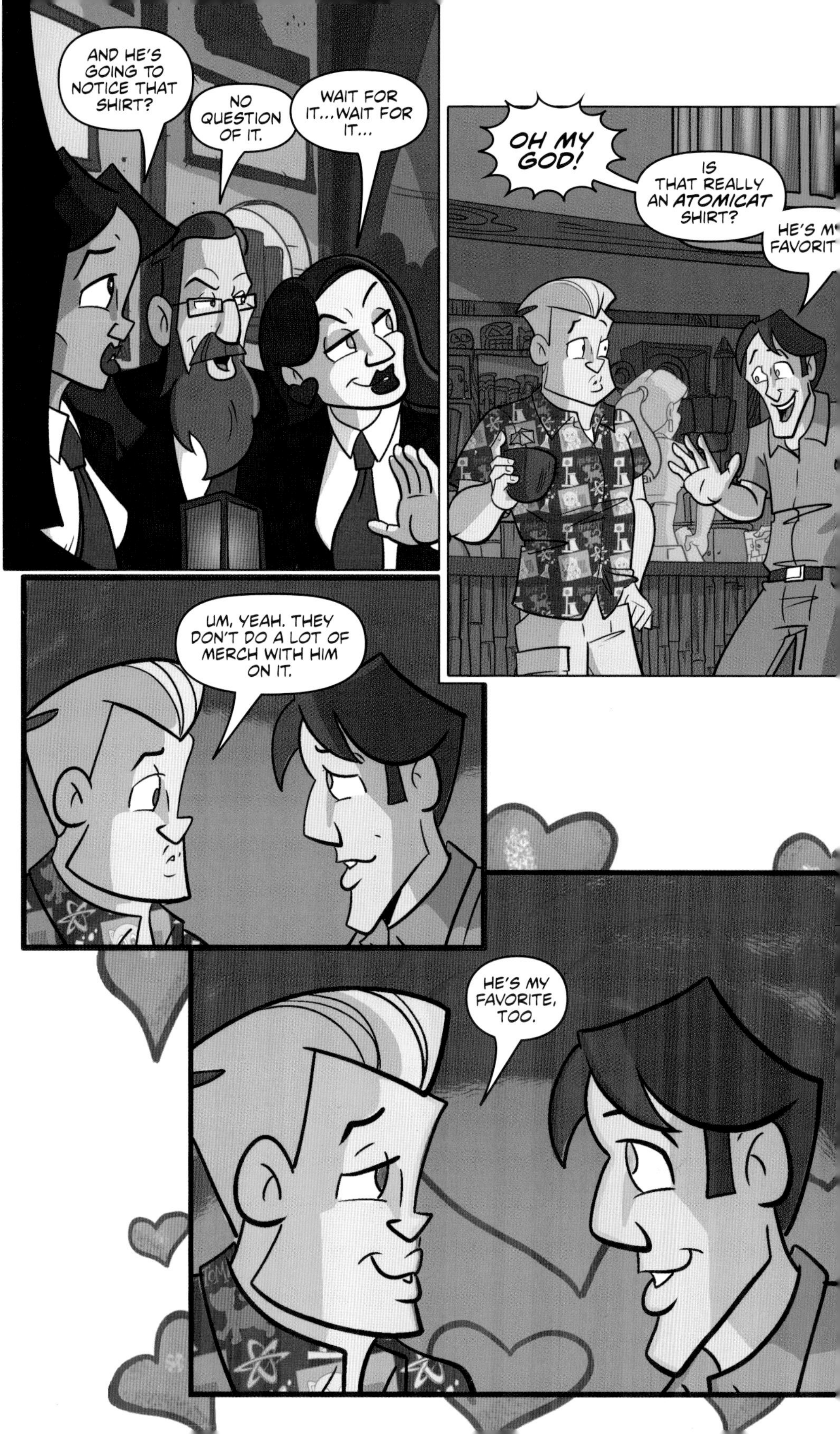
AND HE'S GOING TO NOTICE THAT SHIRT?
NO QUESTION OF IT.
WAIT FOR IT...WAIT FOR IT...
OH MY GOD!
IS THAT REALLY AN *ATOMICAT* SHIRT?
HE'S M' FAVORIT
UM, YEAH. THEY DON'T DO A LOT OF MERCH WITH HIM ON IT.
HE'S MY FAVORITE, TOO.

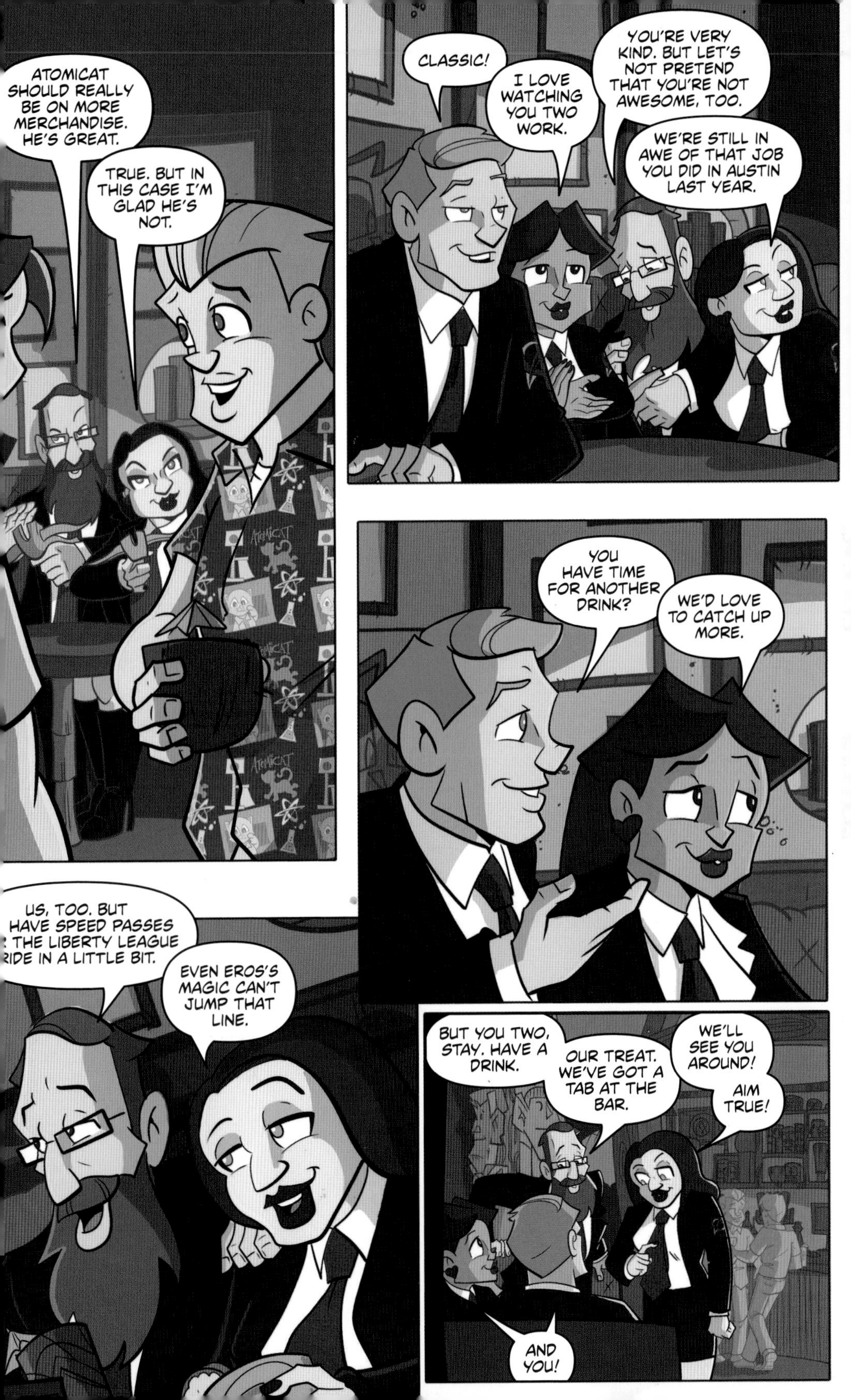
ATOMICAT SHOULD REALLY BE ON MORE MERCHANDISE. HE'S GREAT.
TRUE. BUT IN THIS CASE I'M GLAD HE'S NOT.
ATOMICAT
CLASSIC!
I LOVE WATCHING YOU TWO WORK.
YOU'RE VERY KIND. BUT LET'S NOT PRETEND THAT YOU'RE NOT AWESOME, TOO.
WE'RE STILL IN AWE OF THAT JOB YOU DID IN AUSTIN LAST YEAR.
YOU HAVE TIME FOR ANOTHER DRINK?
WE'D LOVE TO CATCH UP MORE.
US, TOO. BUT HAVE SPEED PASSES THE LIBERTY LEAGUE RIDE IN A LITTLE BIT.
EVEN EROS'S MAGIC CAN'T JUMP THAT LINE.
BUT YOU TWO, STAY. HAVE A DRINK.
OUR TREAT. WE'VE GOT A TAB AT THE BAR.
WE'LL SEE YOU AROUND!
AIM TRUE!
AND YOU!

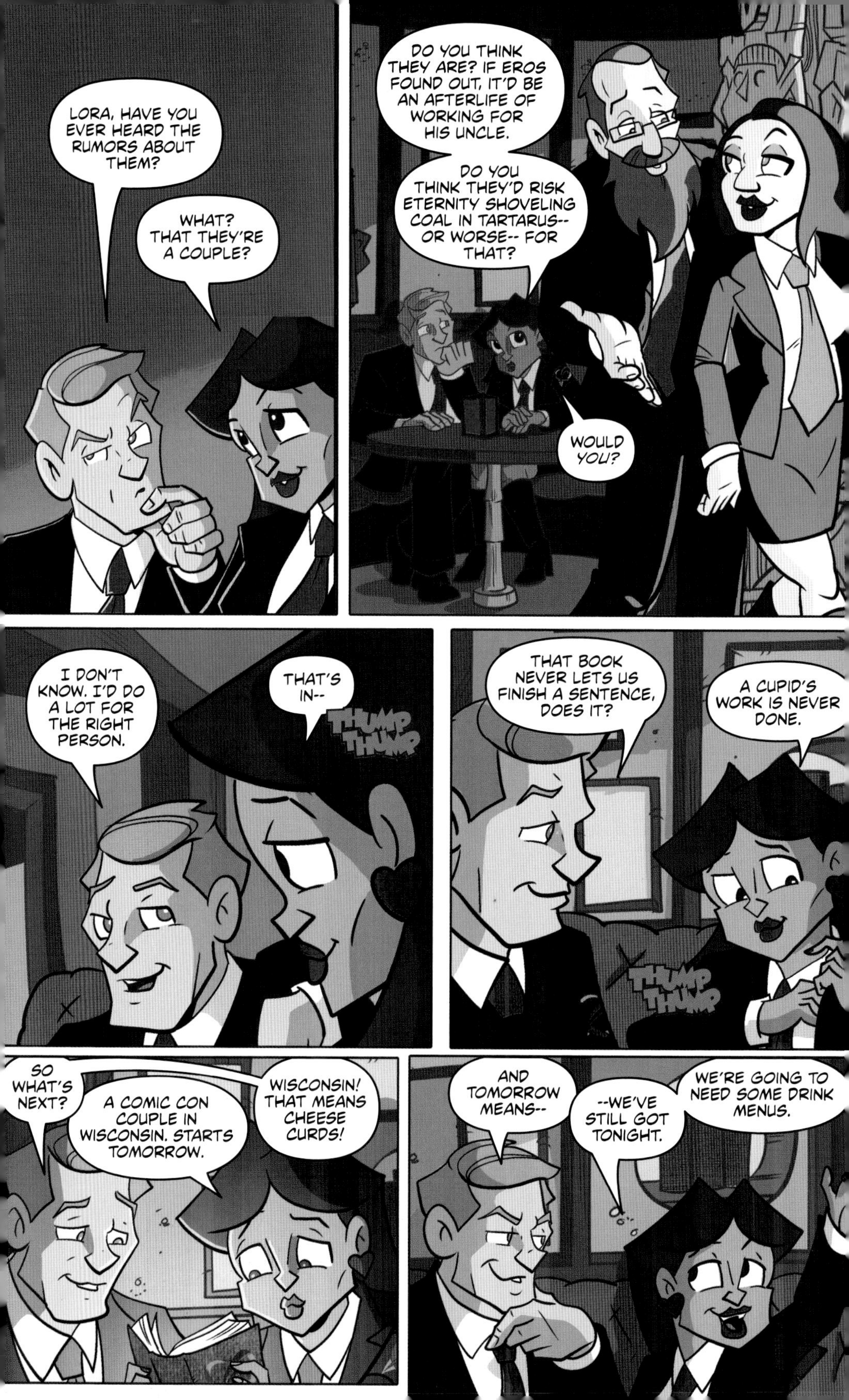
LORA, HAVE YOU EVER HEARD THE RUMORS ABOUT THEM?
WHAT? THAT THEY'RE A COUPLE?
DO YOU THINK THEY ARE? IF EROS FOUND OUT, IT'D BE AN AFTERLIFE OF WORKING FOR HIS UNCLE.
DO YOU THINK THEY'D RISK ETERNITY SHOVELING COAL IN TARTARUS-- OR WORSE-- FOR THAT?
WOULD YOU?
I DON'T KNOW. I'D DO A LOT FOR THE RIGHT PERSON.
THAT'S IN--
THUMP THUMP
THAT BOOK NEVER LETS US FINISH A SENTENCE, DOES IT?
A CUPID'S WORK IS NEVER DONE.
THUMP THUMP
SO WHAT'S NEXT?
A COMIC CON COUPLE IN WISCONSIN. STARTS TOMORROW.
WISCONSIN! THAT MEANS CHEESE CURDS!
AND TOMORROW MEANS--
--WE'VE STILL GOT TONIGHT.
WE'RE GOING TO NEED SOME DRINK MENUS.

Chapter 11

The Cheese Stands Alone

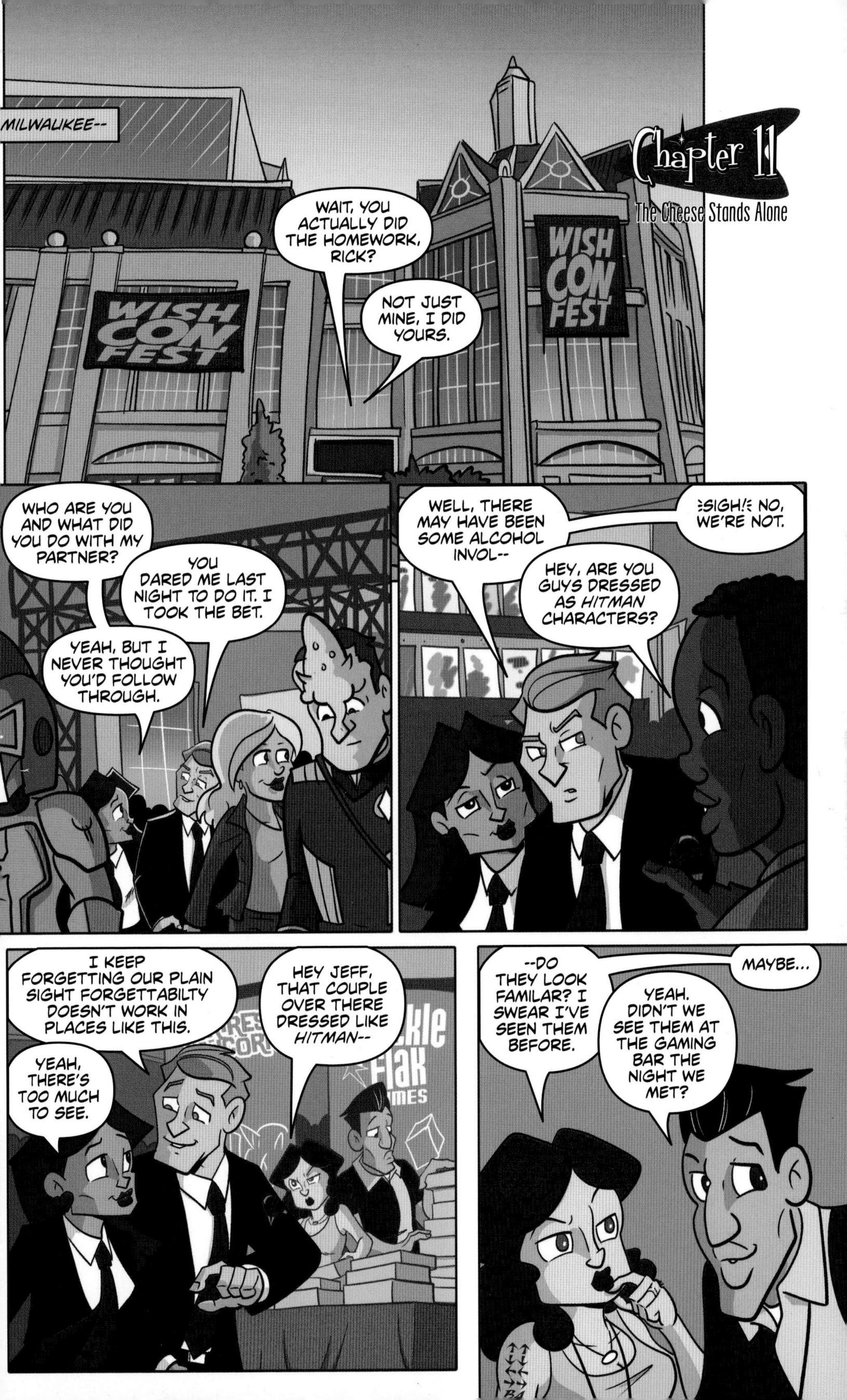

MILWAUKEE--
WISH CON FEST
WAIT, YOU ACTUALLY DID THE HOMEWORK, RICK?
NOT JUST MINE, I DID YOURS.
WHO ARE YOU AND WHAT DID YOU DO WITH MY PARTNER?
YOU DARED ME LAST NIGHT TO DO IT. I TOOK THE BET.
YEAH, BUT I NEVER THOUGHT YOU'D FOLLOW THROUGH.
WELL, THERE MAY HAVE BEEN SOME ALCOHOL INVOL--
HEY, ARE YOU GUYS DRESSED AS *HITMAN* CHARACTERS?
SIGH! NO, WE'RE NOT.
I KEEP FORGETTING OUR PLAIN SIGHT FORGETTABILTY DOESN'T WORK IN PLACES LIKE THIS.
YEAH, THERE'S TOO MUCH TO SEE.
HEY JEFF, THAT COUPLE OVER THERE DRESSED LIKE *HITMAN*--
--DO THEY LOOK FAMILAR? I SWEAR I'VE SEEN THEM BEFORE.
YEAH. DIDN'T WE SEE THEM AT THE GAMING BAR THE NIGHT WE MET?
MAYBE...

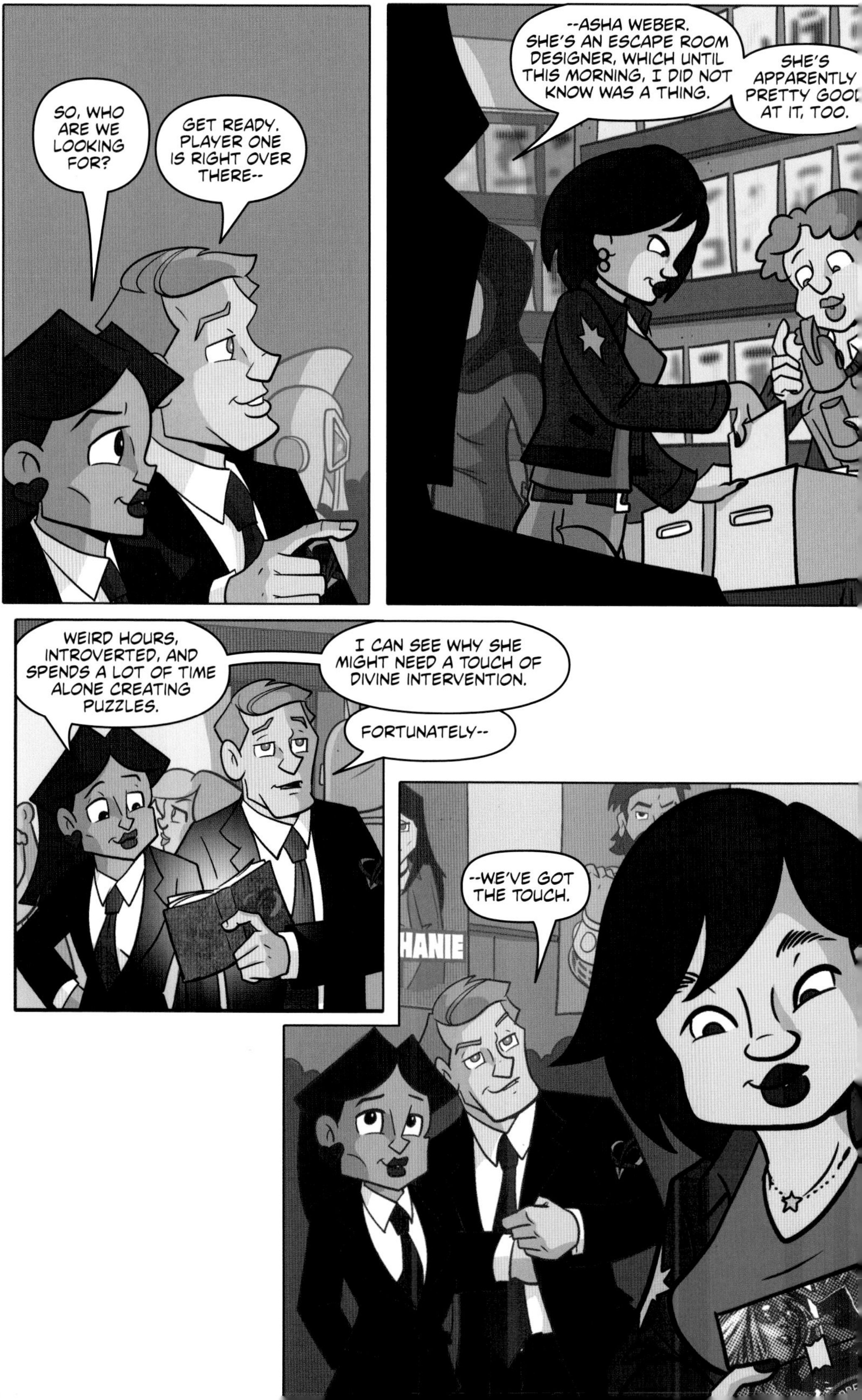

SO, WHO ARE WE LOOKING FOR?
GET READY. PLAYER ONE IS RIGHT OVER THERE--
--ASHA WEBER. SHE'S AN ESCAPE ROOM DESIGNER, WHICH UNTIL THIS MORNING, I DID NOT KNOW WAS A THING.
SHE'S APPARENTLY PRETTY GOO AT IT, TOO.
WEIRD HOURS, INTROVERTED, AND SPENDS A LOT OF TIME ALONE CREATING PUZZLES.
I CAN SEE WHY SHE MIGHT NEED A TOUCH OF DIVINE INTERVENTION.
FORTUNATELY--
HANIE
--WE'VE GOT THE TOUCH.

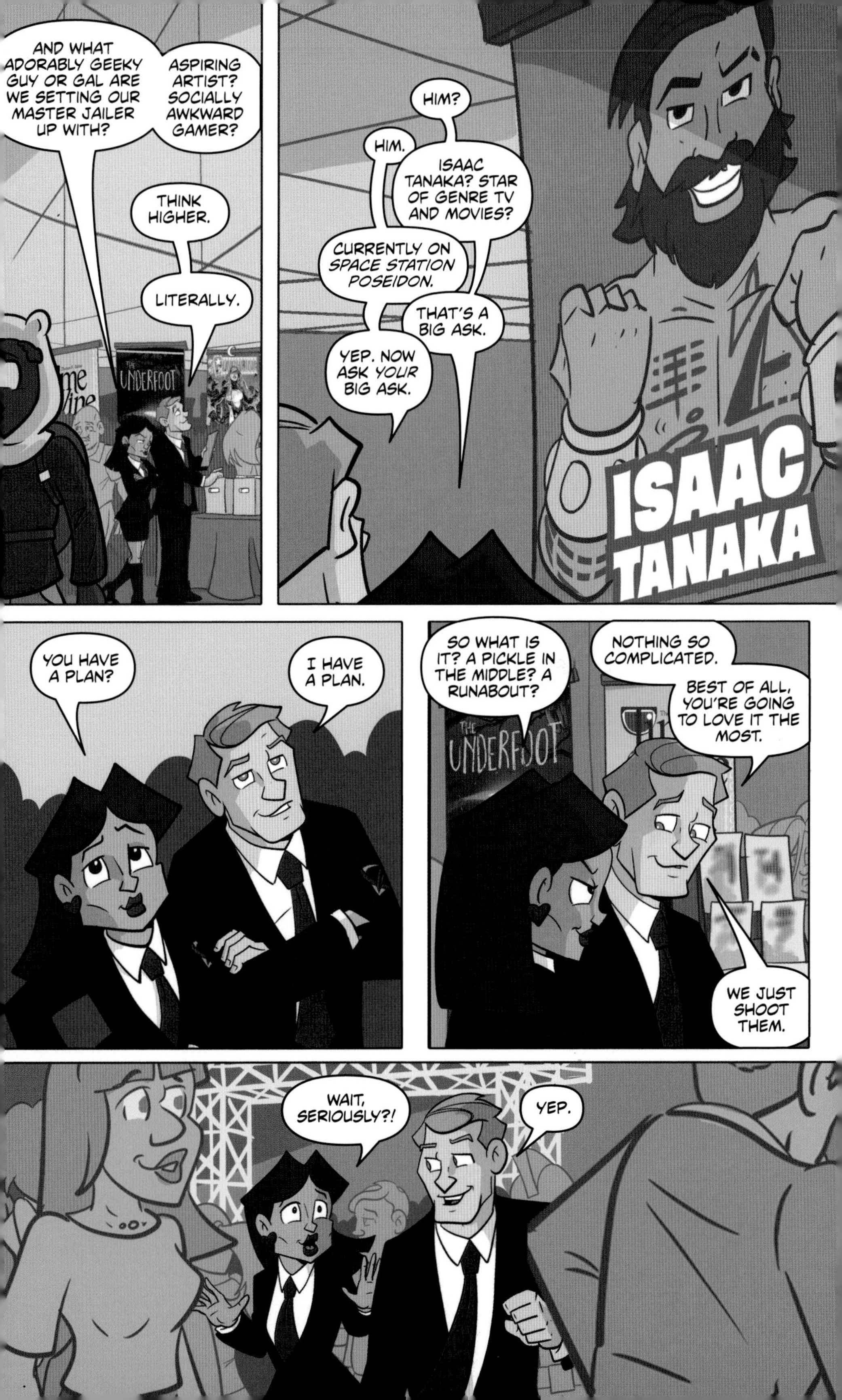
AND WHAT ADORABLY GEEKY GUY OR GAL ARE WE SETTING OUR MASTER JAILER UP WITH?
ASPIRING ARTIST? SOCIALLY AWKWARD GAMER?
THINK HIGHER.
LITERALLY.
THE UNDERFOOT
HIM?
HIM.
ISAAC TANAKA? STAR OF GENRE TV AND MOVIES?
CURRENTLY ON SPACE STATION POSEIDON.
THAT'S A BIG ASK.
YEP. NOW ASK YOUR BIG ASK.
ISAAC TANAKA
YOU HAVE A PLAN?
I HAVE A PLAN.
SO WHAT IS IT? A PICKLE IN THE MIDDLE? A RUNABOUT?
NOTHING SO COMPLICATED.
BEST OF ALL, YOU'RE GOING TO LOVE IT THE MOST.
THE UNDERFOOT
WE JUST SHOOT THEM.
WAIT, SERIOUSLY?!
YEP.

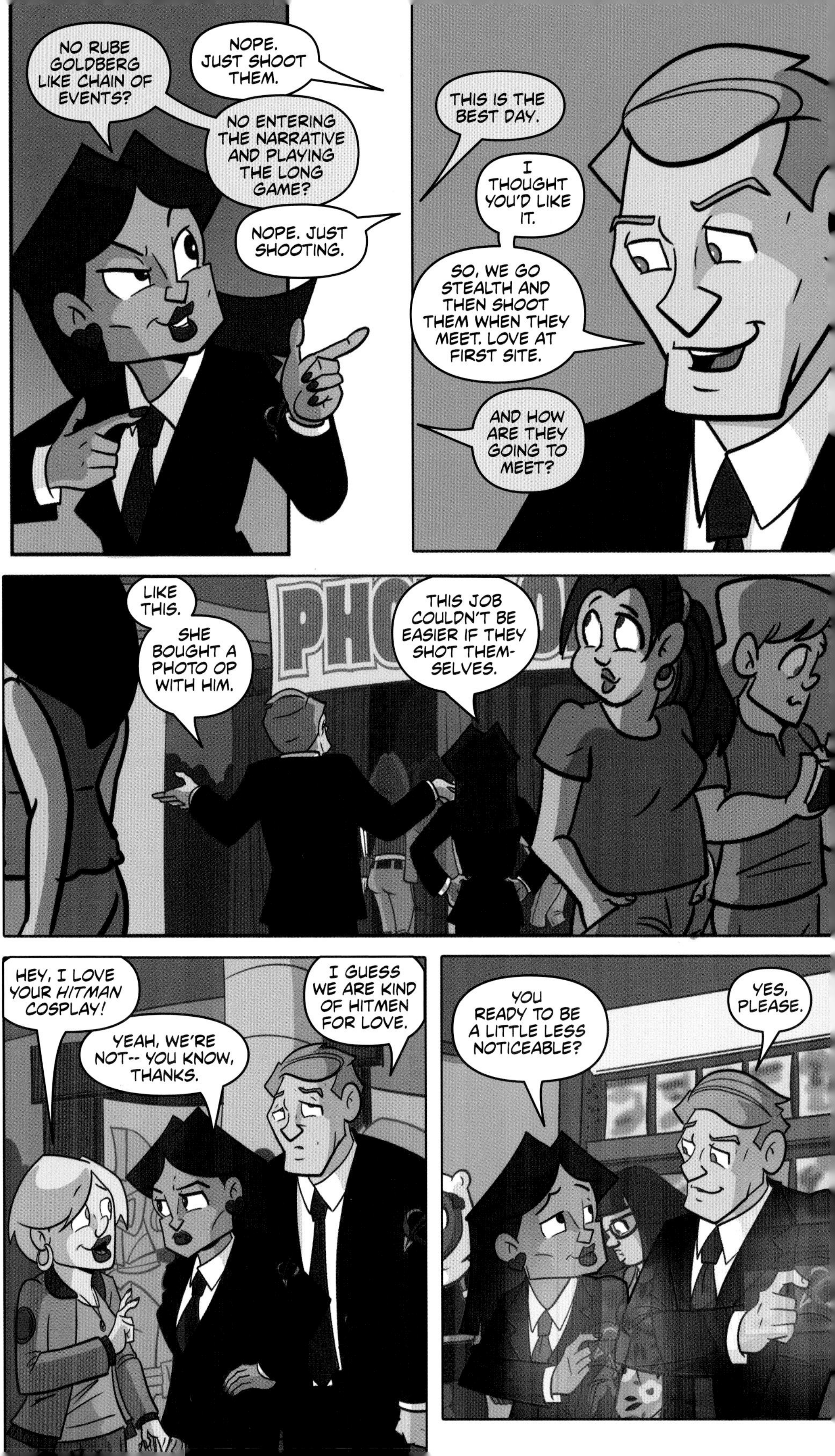
NO RUBE GOLDBERG LIKE CHAIN OF EVENTS?
NOPE. JUST SHOOT THEM.
NO ENTERING THE NARRATIVE AND PLAYING THE LONG GAME?
NOPE. JUST SHOOTING.
THIS IS THE BEST DAY.
I THOUGHT YOU'D LIKE IT.
SO, WE GO STEALTH AND THEN SHOOT THEM WHEN THEY MEET. LOVE AT FIRST SITE.
AND HOW ARE THEY GOING TO MEET?
LIKE THIS.
SHE BOUGHT A PHOTO OP WITH HIM.
THIS JOB COULDN'T BE EASIER IF THEY SHOT THEM-SELVES.
HEY, I LOVE YOUR *HITMAN* COSPLAY!
YEAH, WE'RE NOT-- YOU KNOW, THANKS.
I GUESS WE ARE KIND OF HITMEN FOR LOVE.
YOU READY TO BE A LITTLE LESS NOTICEABLE?
YES, PLEASE.

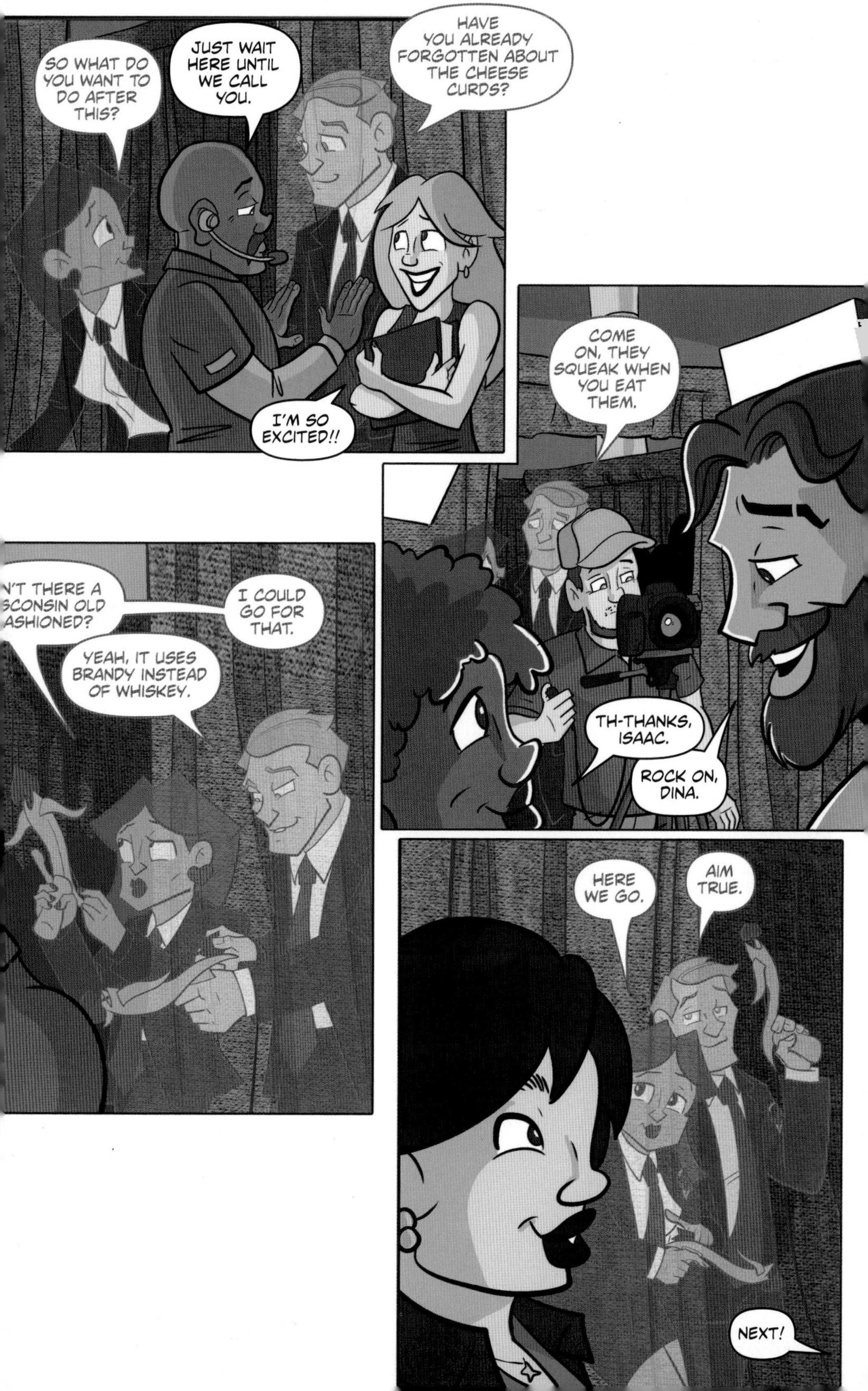
SO WHAT DO YOU WANT TO DO AFTER THIS?
JUST WAIT HERE UNTIL WE CALL YOU.
HAVE YOU ALREADY FORGOTTEN ABOUT THE CHEESE CURDS?
I'M SO EXCITED!!
COME ON, THEY SQUEAK WHEN YOU EAT THEM.
TH-THANKS, ISAAC.
ROCK ON, DINA.
N'T THERE A SCONSIN OLD ASHIONED?
I COULD GO FOR THAT.
YEAH, IT USES BRANDY INSTEAD OF WHISKEY.
HERE WE GO.
AIM TRUE.
NEXT!

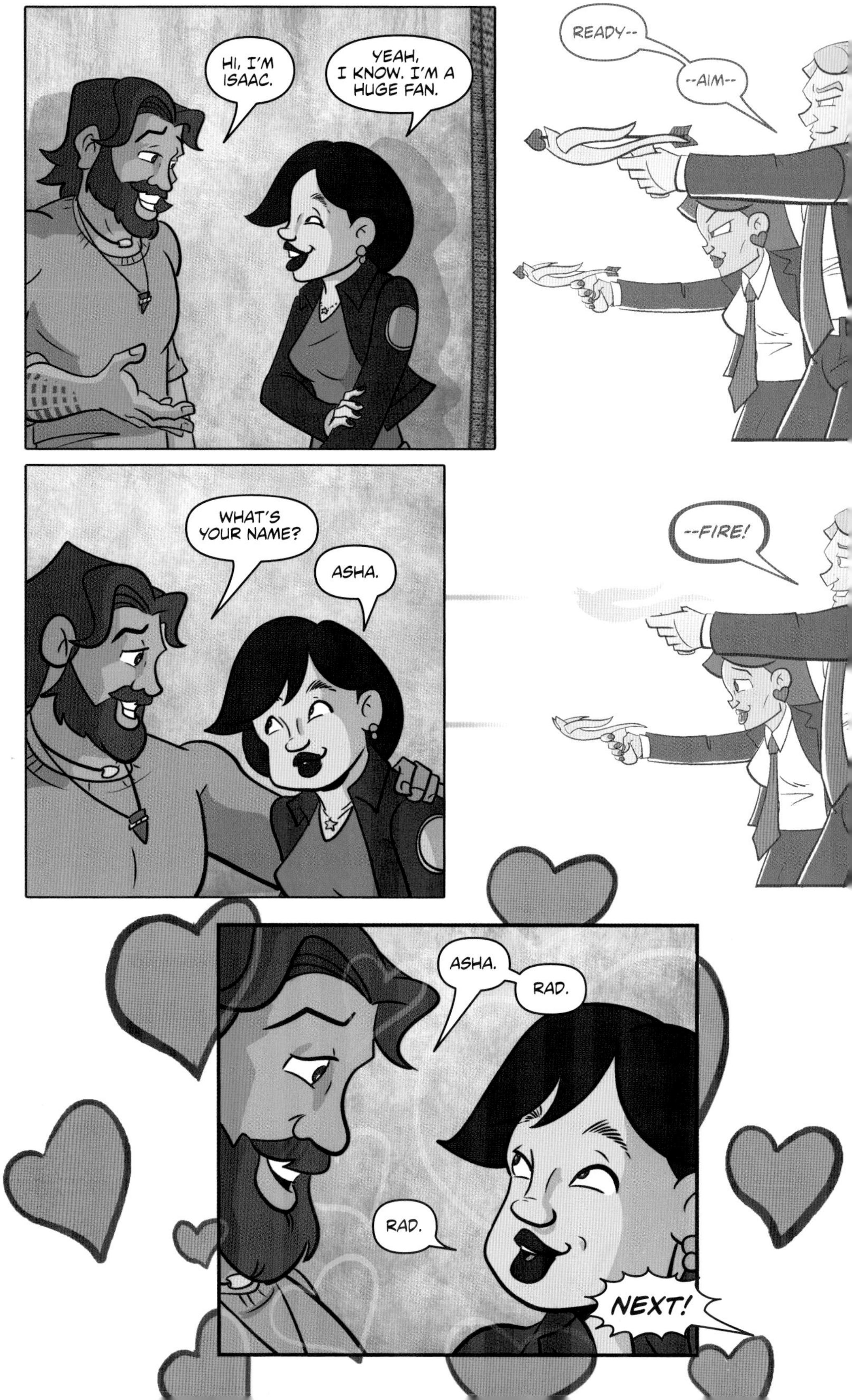
HI, I'M ISAAC.
YEAH, I KNOW. I'M A HUGE FAN.
READY--
--AIM--
WHAT'S YOUR NAME?
ASHA.
--FIRE!
ASHA.
RAD.
RAD.
NEXT!

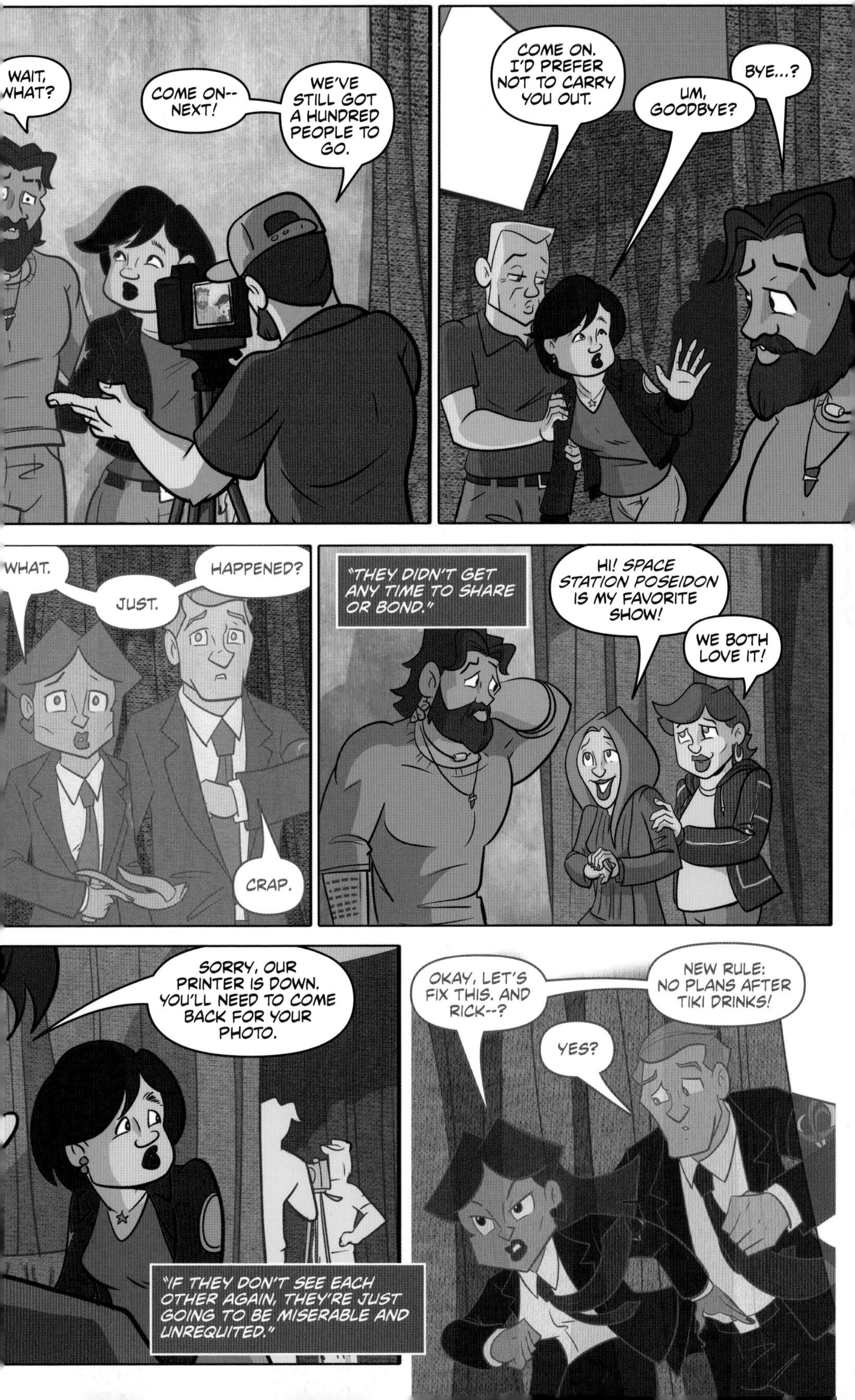
WAIT, WHAT?
COME ON-- NEXT!
WE'VE STILL GOT A HUNDRED PEOPLE TO GO.
COME ON. I'D PREFER NOT TO CARRY YOU OUT.
UM, GOODBYE?
BYE...?
WHAT.
JUST.
HAPPENED?
CRAP.
"THEY DIDN'T GET ANY TIME TO SHARE OR BOND."
HI! SPACE STATION POSEIDON IS MY FAVORITE SHOW!
WE BOTH LOVE IT!
SORRY, OUR PRINTER IS DOWN. YOU'LL NEED TO COME BACK FOR YOUR PHOTO.
"IF THEY DON'T SEE EACH OTHER AGAIN, THEY'RE JUST GOING TO BE MISERABLE AND UNREQUITED."
OKAY, LET'S FIX THIS. AND RICK--?
NEW RULE: NO PLANS AFTER TIKI DRINKS!
YES?

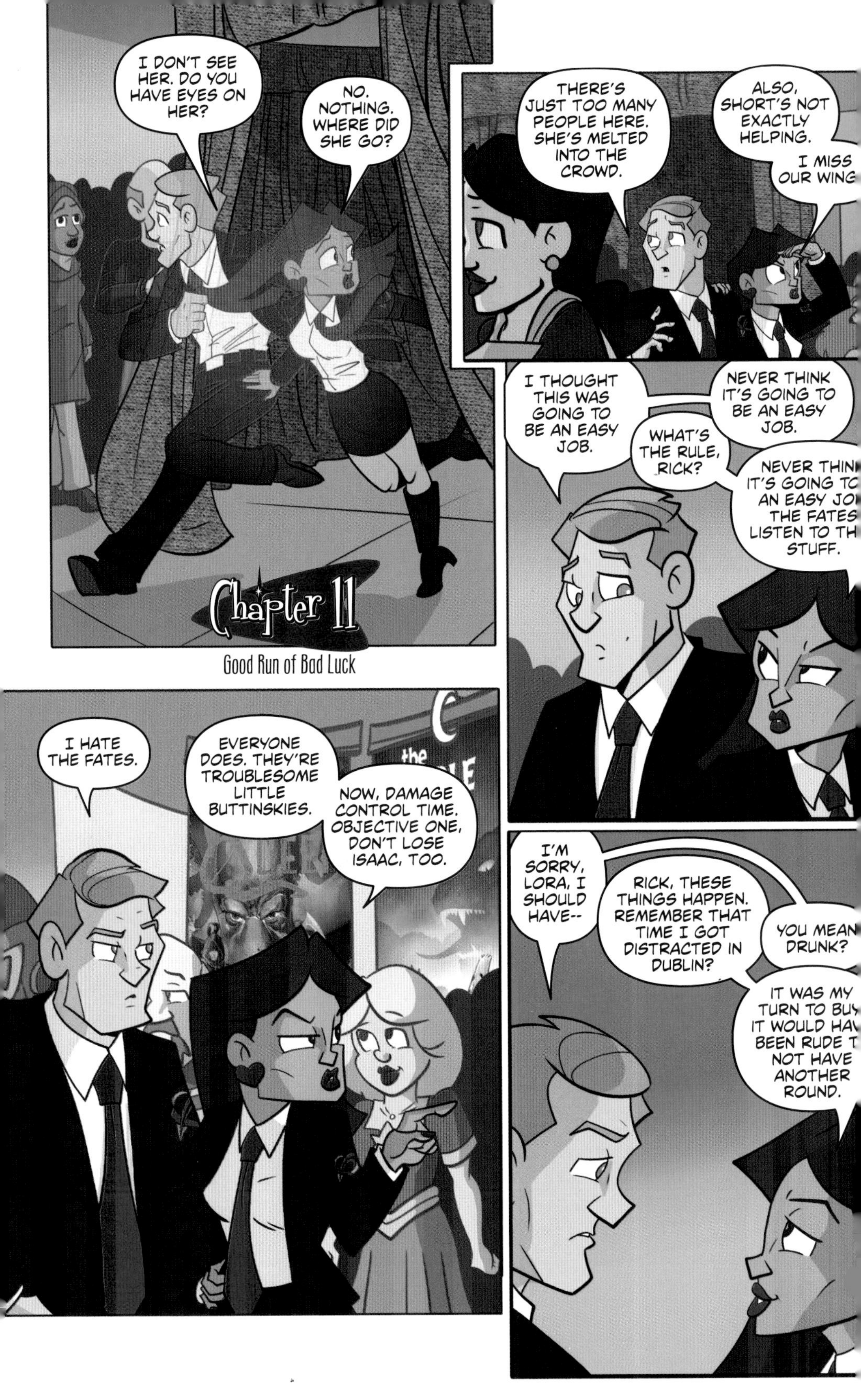
I DON'T SEE HER. DO YOU HAVE EYES ON HER?
NO. NOTHING. WHERE DID SHE GO?
Chapter 11
Good Run of Bad Luck
THERE'S JUST TOO MANY PEOPLE HERE. SHE'S MELTED INTO THE CROWD.
ALSO, SHORT'S NOT EXACTLY HELPING.
I MISS OUR WING
I THOUGHT THIS WAS GOING TO BE AN EASY JOB.
WHAT'S THE RULE, RICK?
NEVER THINK IT'S GOING TO BE AN EASY JOB.
NEVER THIN IT'S GOING TO AN EASY JO THE FATES LISTEN TO TH STUFF.
I HATE THE FATES.
EVERYONE DOES. THEY'RE TROUBLESOME LITTLE BUTTINSKIES.
NOW, DAMAGE CONTROL TIME. OBJECTIVE ONE, DON'T LOSE ISAAC, TOO.
I'M SORRY, LORA, I SHOULD HAVE--
RICK, THESE THINGS HAPPEN. REMEMBER THAT TIME I GOT DISTRACTED IN DUBLIN?
YOU MEAN DRUNK?
IT WAS MY TURN TO BU IT WOULD HA BEEN RUDE T NOT HAVE ANOTHER ROUND.

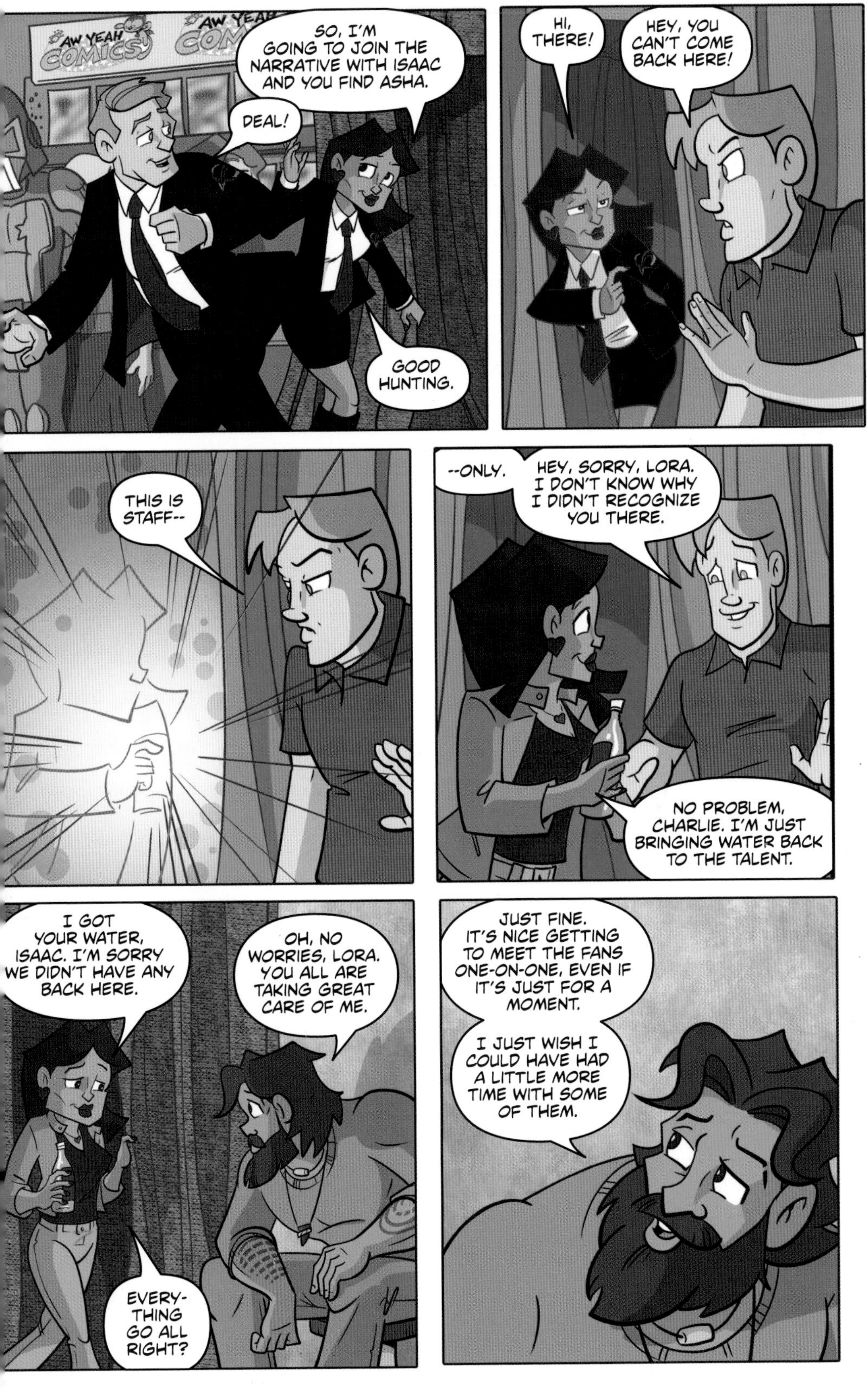
AW YEAH COMICS
AW YEAH COMICS
SO, I'M GOING TO JOIN THE NARRATIVE WITH ISAAC AND YOU FIND ASHA.
DEAL!
GOOD HUNTING.
HI, THERE!
HEY, YOU CAN'T COME BACK HERE!
THIS IS STAFF--
--ONLY.
HEY, SORRY, LORA. I DON'T KNOW WHY I DIDN'T RECOGNIZE YOU THERE.
NO PROBLEM, CHARLIE. I'M JUST BRINGING WATER BACK TO THE TALENT.
I GOT YOUR WATER, ISAAC. I'M SORRY WE DIDN'T HAVE ANY BACK HERE.
OH, NO WORRIES, LORA. YOU ALL ARE TAKING GREAT CARE OF ME.
EVERY-THING GO ALL RIGHT?
JUST FINE. IT'S NICE GETTING TO MEET THE FANS ONE-ON-ONE, EVEN IF IT'S JUST FOR A MOMENT.
I JUST WISH I COULD HAVE HAD A LITTLE MORE TIME WITH SOME OF THEM.

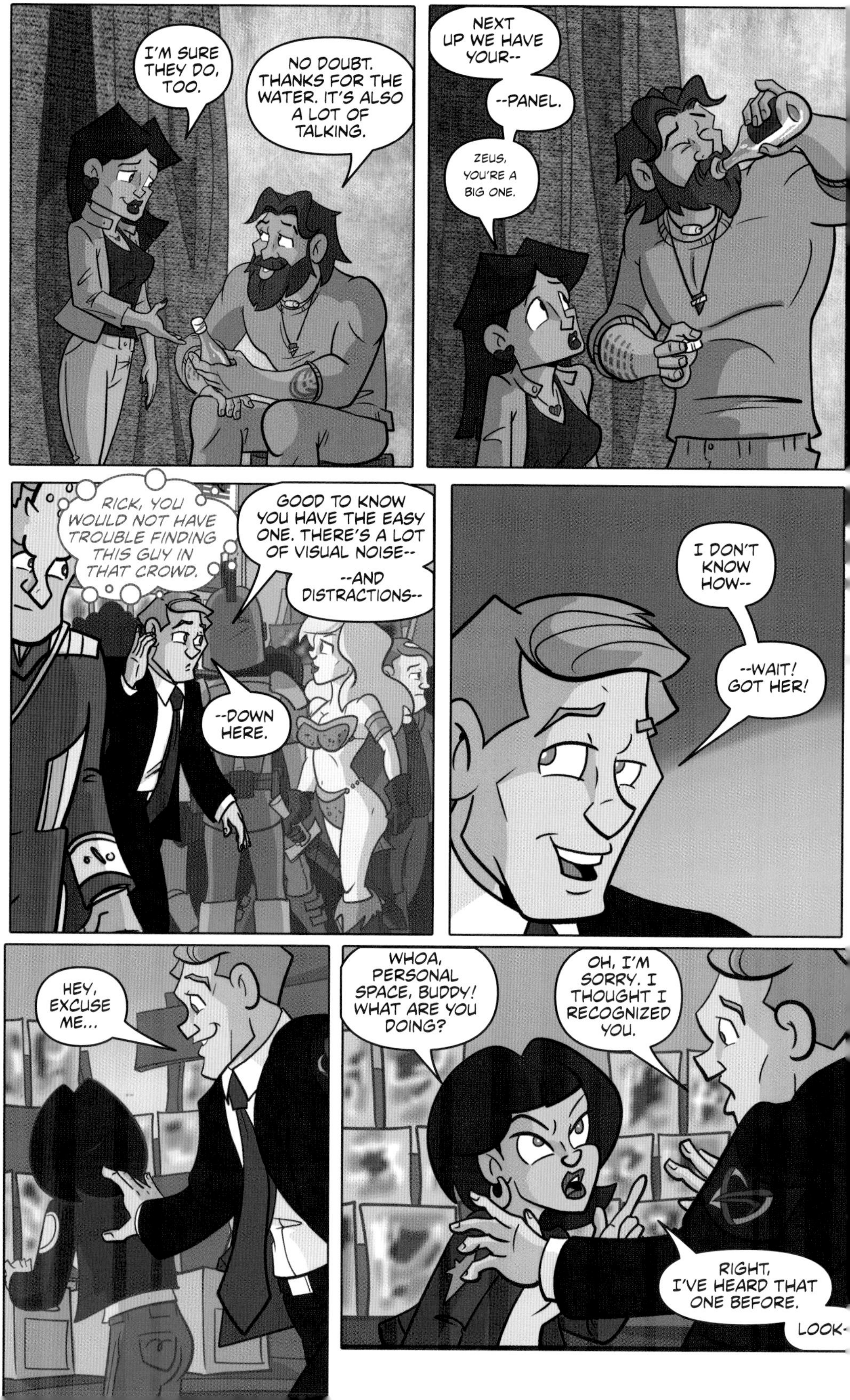
I'M SURE THEY DO, TOO.
NO DOUBT. THANKS FOR THE WATER. IT'S ALSO A LOT OF TALKING.
NEXT UP WE HAVE YOUR--
--PANEL.
ZEUS, YOU'RE A BIG ONE.
RICK, YOU WOULD NOT HAVE TROUBLE FINDING THIS GUY IN THAT CROWD.
GOOD TO KNOW YOU HAVE THE EASY ONE. THERE'S A LOT OF VISUAL NOISE--
--AND DISTRACTIONS--
--DOWN HERE.
I DON'T KNOW HOW--
--WAIT! GOT HER!
HEY, EXCUSE ME...
WHOA, PERSONAL SPACE, BUDDY! WHAT ARE YOU DOING?
OH, I'M SORRY. I THOUGHT I RECOGNIZED YOU.
RIGHT, I'VE HEARD THAT ONE BEFORE.
LOOK-

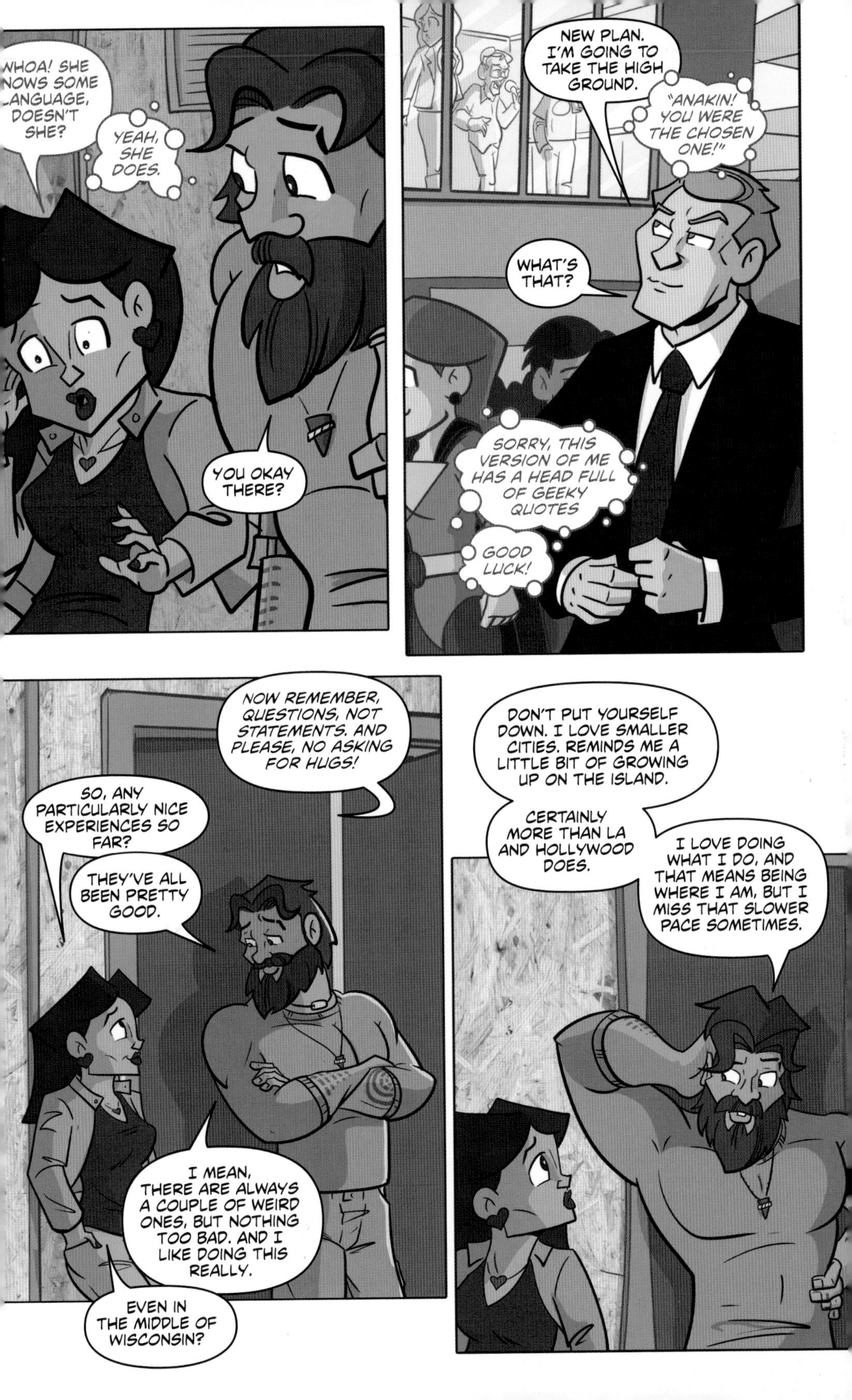
WHOA! SHE KNOWS SOME LANGUAGE, DOESN'T SHE?
YEAH, SHE DOES.
YOU OKAY THERE?
NEW PLAN. I'M GOING TO TAKE THE HIGH GROUND.
"ANAKIN! YOU WERE THE CHOSEN ONE!"
WHAT'S THAT?
SORRY, THIS VERSION OF ME HAS A HEAD FULL OF GEEKY QUOTES
GOOD LUCK!
NOW REMEMBER, QUESTIONS, NOT STATEMENTS. AND PLEASE, NO ASKING FOR HUGS!
SO, ANY PARTICULARLY NICE EXPERIENCES SO FAR?
THEY'VE ALL BEEN PRETTY GOOD.
I MEAN, THERE ARE ALWAYS A COUPLE OF WEIRD ONES, BUT NOTHING TOO BAD. AND I LIKE DOING THIS REALLY.
EVEN IN THE MIDDLE OF WISCONSIN?
DON'T PUT YOURSELF DOWN. I LOVE SMALLER CITIES. REMINDS ME A LITTLE BIT OF GROWING UP ON THE ISLAND.
CERTAINLY MORE THAN LA AND HOLLYWOOD DOES.
I LOVE DOING WHAT I DO, AND THAT MEANS BEING WHERE I AM, BUT I MISS THAT SLOWER PACE SOMETIMES.

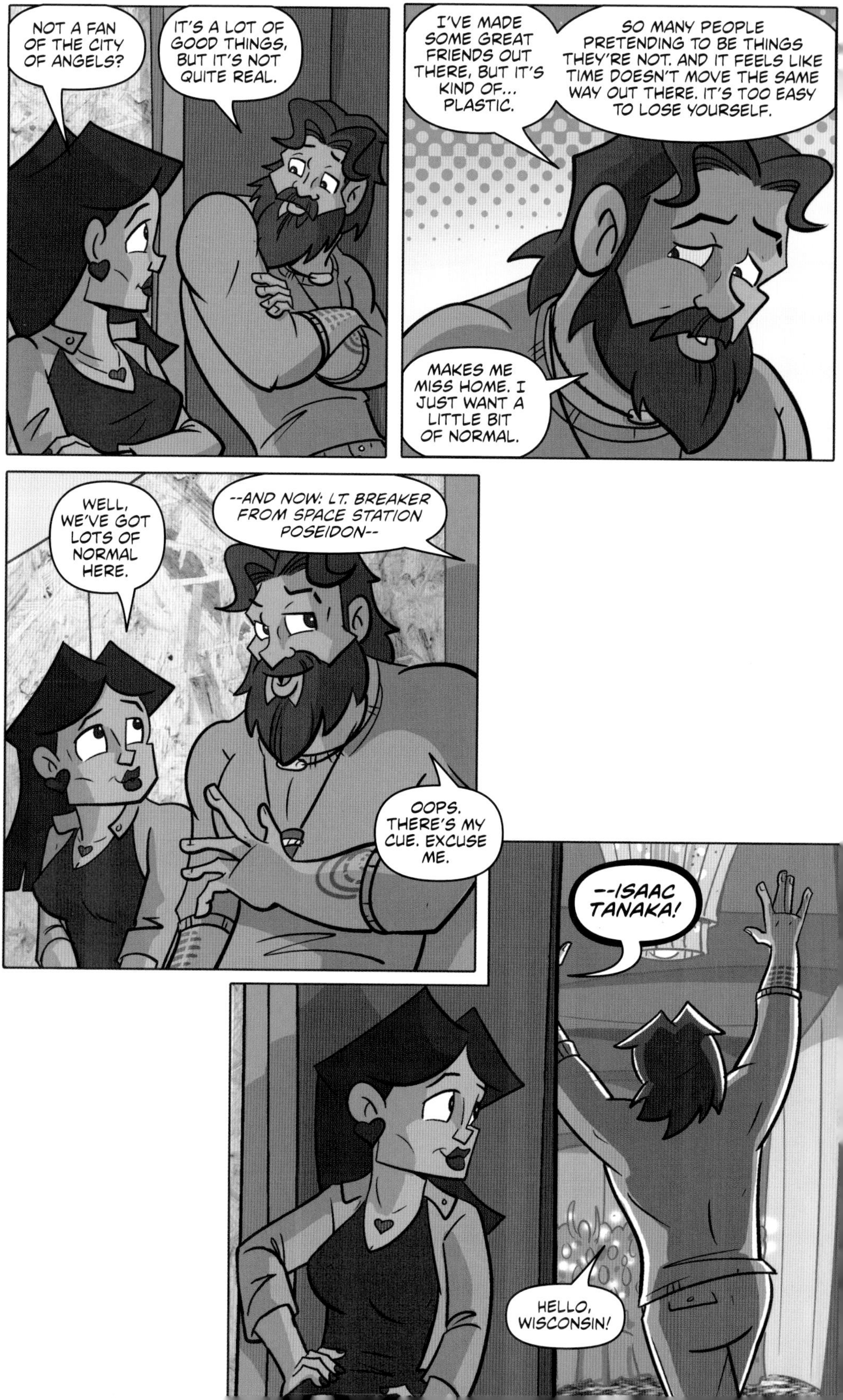
NOT A FAN OF THE CITY OF ANGELS?
IT'S A LOT OF GOOD THINGS, BUT IT'S NOT QUITE REAL.
I'VE MADE SOME GREAT FRIENDS OUT THERE, BUT IT'S KIND OF... PLASTIC.
SO MANY PEOPLE PRETENDING TO BE THINGS THEY'RE NOT. AND IT FEELS LIKE TIME DOESN'T MOVE THE SAME WAY OUT THERE. IT'S TOO EASY TO LOSE YOURSELF.
MAKES ME MISS HOME. I JUST WANT A LITTLE BIT OF NORMAL.
WELL, WE'VE GOT LOTS OF NORMAL HERE.
--AND NOW: LT. BREAKER FROM SPACE STATION POSEIDON--
OOPS. THERE'S MY CUE. EXCUSE ME.
--ISAAC TANAKA!
HELLO, WISCONSIN!

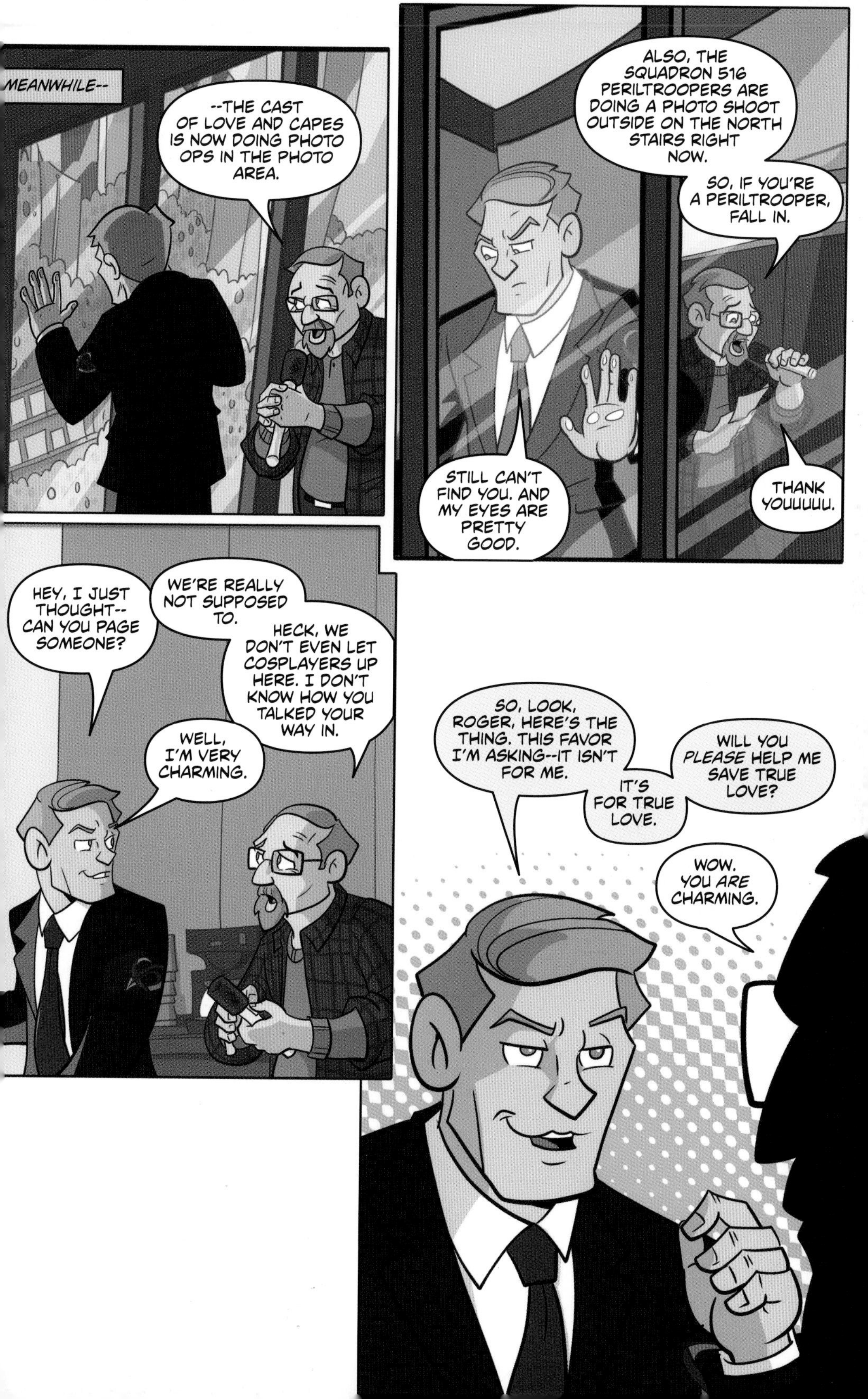
MEANWHILE--
--THE CAST OF LOVE AND CAPES IS NOW DOING PHOTO OPS IN THE PHOTO AREA.
ALSO, THE SQUADRON 516 PERILTROOPERS ARE DOING A PHOTO SHOOT OUTSIDE ON THE NORTH STAIRS RIGHT NOW.
SO, IF YOU'RE A PERILTROOPER, FALL IN.
STILL CAN'T FIND YOU. AND MY EYES ARE PRETTY GOOD.
THANK YOUUUUU.
HEY, I JUST THOUGHT-- CAN YOU PAGE SOMEONE?
WE'RE REALLY NOT SUPPOSED TO.
HECK, WE DON'T EVEN LET COSPLAYERS UP HERE. I DON'T KNOW HOW YOU TALKED YOUR WAY IN.
WELL, I'M VERY CHARMING.
SO, LOOK, ROGER, HERE'S THE THING. THIS FAVOR I'M ASKING--IT ISN'T FOR ME.
IT'S FOR TRUE LOVE.
WILL YOU *PLEASE* HELP ME SAVE TRUE LOVE?
WOW. YOU ARE CHARMING.

Chapter 13

Heaven is One Step Away

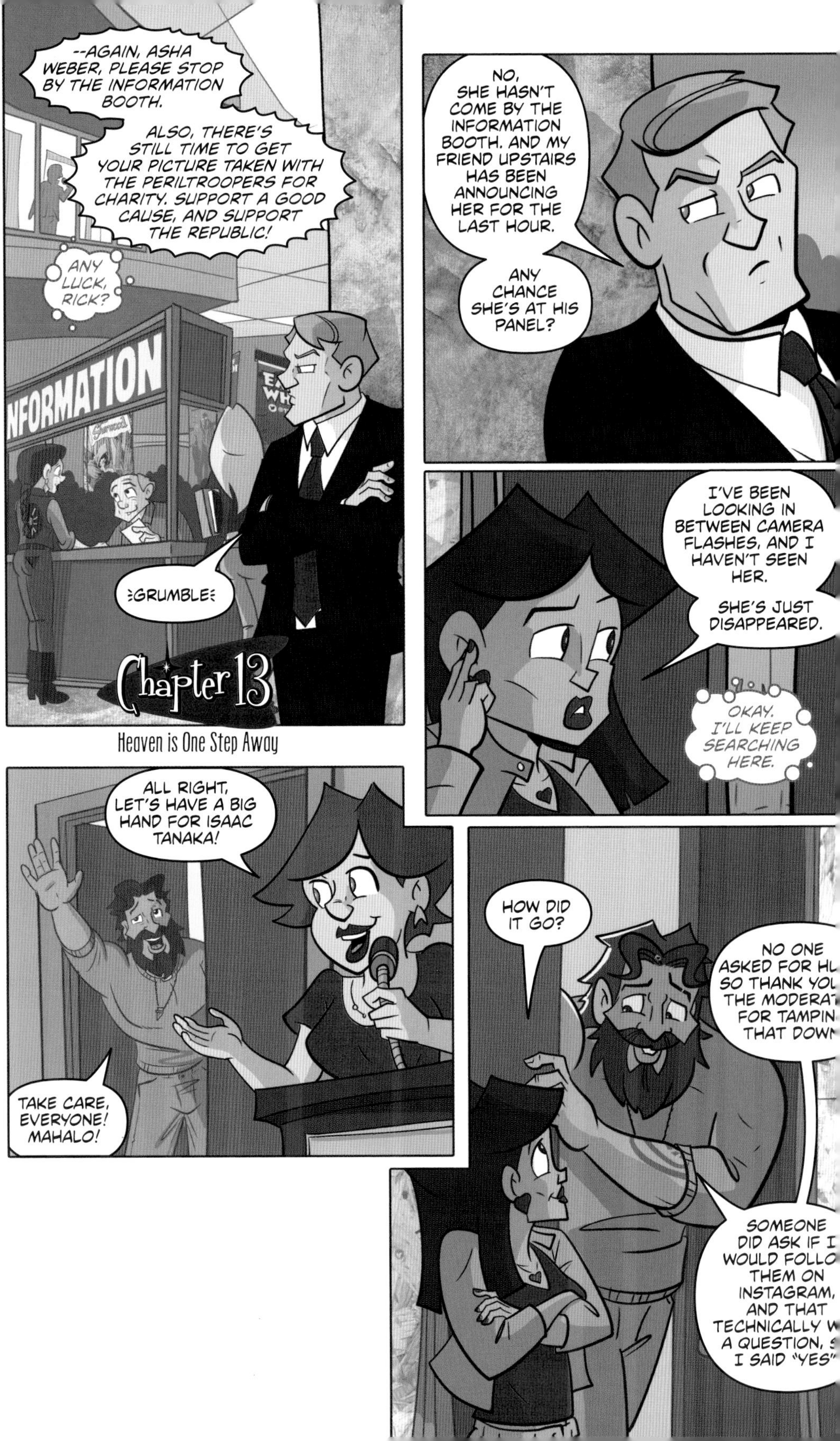
--AGAIN, ASHA WEBER, PLEASE STOP BY THE INFORMATION BOOTH.
ALSO, THERE'S STILL TIME TO GET YOUR PICTURE TAKEN WITH THE PERILTROOPERS FOR CHARITY. SUPPORT A GOOD CAUSE, AND SUPPORT THE REPUBLIC!
ANY LUCK, RICK?
INFORMATION
GRUMBLE
Chapter 13
NO, SHE HASN'T COME BY THE INFORMATION BOOTH. AND MY FRIEND UPSTAIRS HAS BEEN ANNOUNCING HER FOR THE LAST HOUR.
ANY CHANCE SHE'S AT HIS PANEL?
I'VE BEEN LOOKING IN BETWEEN CAMERA FLASHES, AND I HAVEN'T SEEN HER.
SHE'S JUST DISAPPEARED.
OKAY. I'LL KEEP SEARCHING HERE.
ALL RIGHT, LET'S HAVE A BIG HAND FOR ISAAC TANAKA!
TAKE CARE, EVERYONE! MAHALO!
HOW DID IT GO?
NO ONE ASKED FOR H SO THANK YOU THE MODERAT FOR TAMPIN THAT DOWN
SOMEONE DID ASK IF I WOULD FOLLO THEM ON INSTAGRAM, AND THAT TECHNICALLY W A QUESTION, S I SAID "YES"

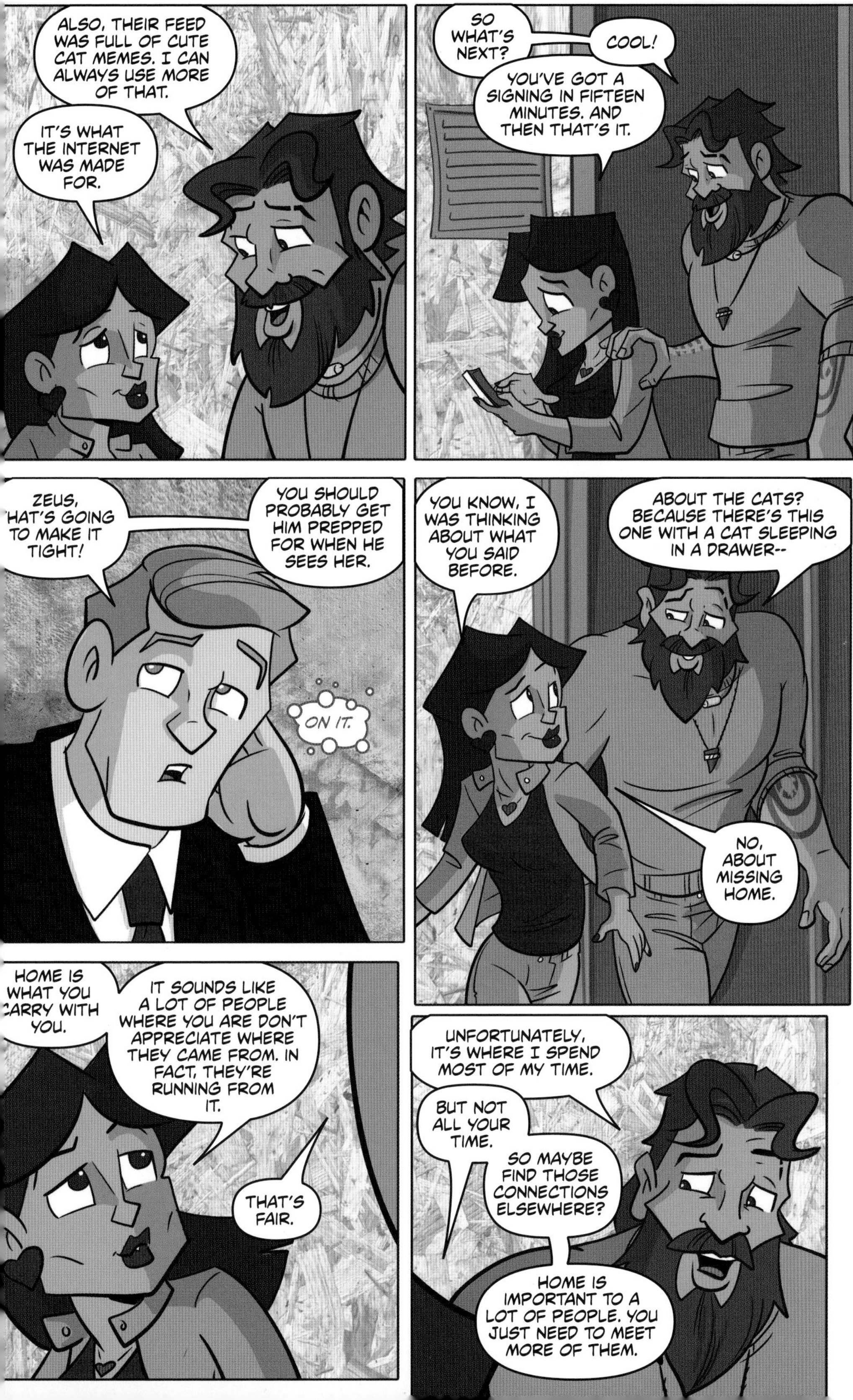
ALSO, THEIR FEED WAS FULL OF CUTE CAT MEMES. I CAN ALWAYS USE MORE OF THAT.
IT'S WHAT THE INTERNET WAS MADE FOR.
SO WHAT'S NEXT?
COOL!
YOU'VE GOT A SIGNING IN FIFTEEN MINUTES. AND THEN THAT'S IT.
ZEUS, HAT'S GOING TO MAKE IT TIGHT!
YOU SHOULD PROBABLY GET HIM PREPPED FOR WHEN HE SEES HER.
ON IT.
YOU KNOW, I WAS THINKING ABOUT WHAT YOU SAID BEFORE.
ABOUT THE CATS? BECAUSE THERE'S THIS ONE WITH A CAT SLEEPING IN A DRAWER--
NO, ABOUT MISSING HOME.
HOME IS WHAT YOU ARRY WITH YOU.
IT SOUNDS LIKE A LOT OF PEOPLE WHERE YOU ARE DON'T APPRECIATE WHERE THEY CAME FROM. IN FACT, THEY'RE RUNNING FROM IT.
THAT'S FAIR.
UNFORTUNATELY, IT'S WHERE I SPEND MOST OF MY TIME.
BUT NOT ALL YOUR TIME.
SO MAYBE FIND THOSE CONNECTIONS ELSEWHERE?
HOME IS IMPORTANT TO A LOT OF PEOPLE. YOU JUST NEED TO MEET MORE OF THEM.

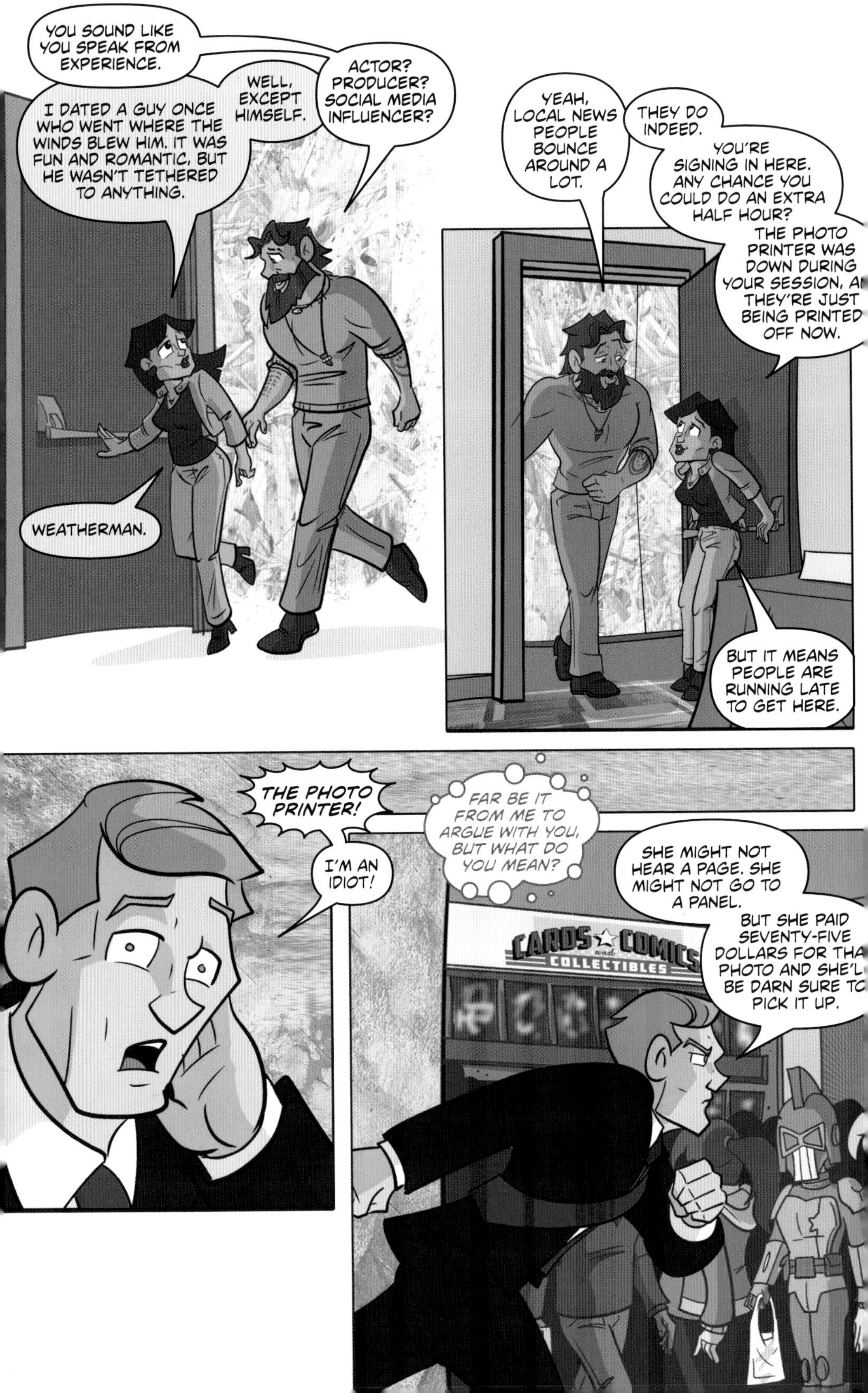
YOU SOUND LIKE YOU SPEAK FROM EXPERIENCE.
I DATED A GUY ONCE WHO WENT WHERE THE WINDS BLEW HIM. IT WAS FUN AND ROMANTIC, BUT HE WASN'T TETHERED TO ANYTHING.
WELL, EXCEPT HIMSELF.
ACTOR? PRODUCER? SOCIAL MEDIA INFLUENCER?
WEATHERMAN.
YEAH, LOCAL NEWS PEOPLE BOUNCE AROUND A LOT.
THEY DO INDEED.
YOU'RE SIGNING IN HERE. ANY CHANCE YOU COULD DO AN EXTRA HALF HOUR?
THE PHOTO PRINTER WAS DOWN DURING YOUR SESSION, A THEY'RE JUST BEING PRINTED OFF NOW.
BUT IT MEANS PEOPLE ARE RUNNING LATE TO GET HERE.
THE PHOTO PRINTER!
I'M AN IDIOT!
FAR BE IT FROM ME TO ARGUE WITH YOU, BUT WHAT DO YOU MEAN?
SHE MIGHT NOT HEAR A PAGE. SHE MIGHT NOT GO TO A PANEL.
BUT SHE PAID SEVENTY-FIVE DOLLARS FOR THA PHOTO AND SHE'L BE DARN SURE TO PICK IT UP.
CARDS COMICS and COLLECTIBLES

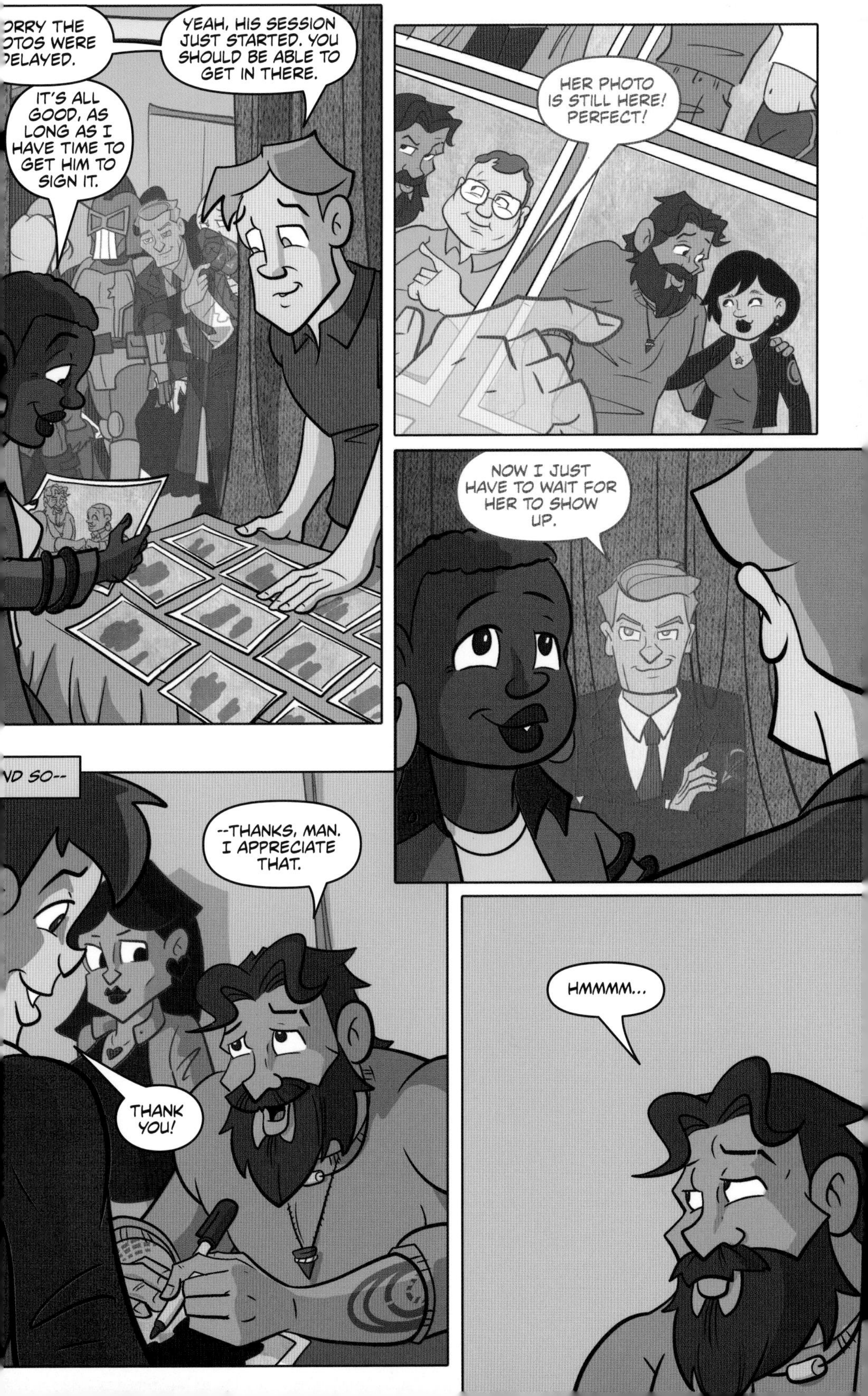
ORRY THE
OTOS WERE
DELAYED.
YEAH, HIS SESSION JUST STARTED. YOU SHOULD BE ABLE TO GET IN THERE.
IT'S ALL GOOD, AS LONG AS I HAVE TIME TO GET HIM TO SIGN IT.
HER PHOTO IS STILL HERE! PERFECT!
NOW I JUST HAVE TO WAIT FOR HER TO SHOW UP.
ND SO--
--THANKS, MAN. I APPRECIATE THAT.
THANK YOU!
HMMMM...

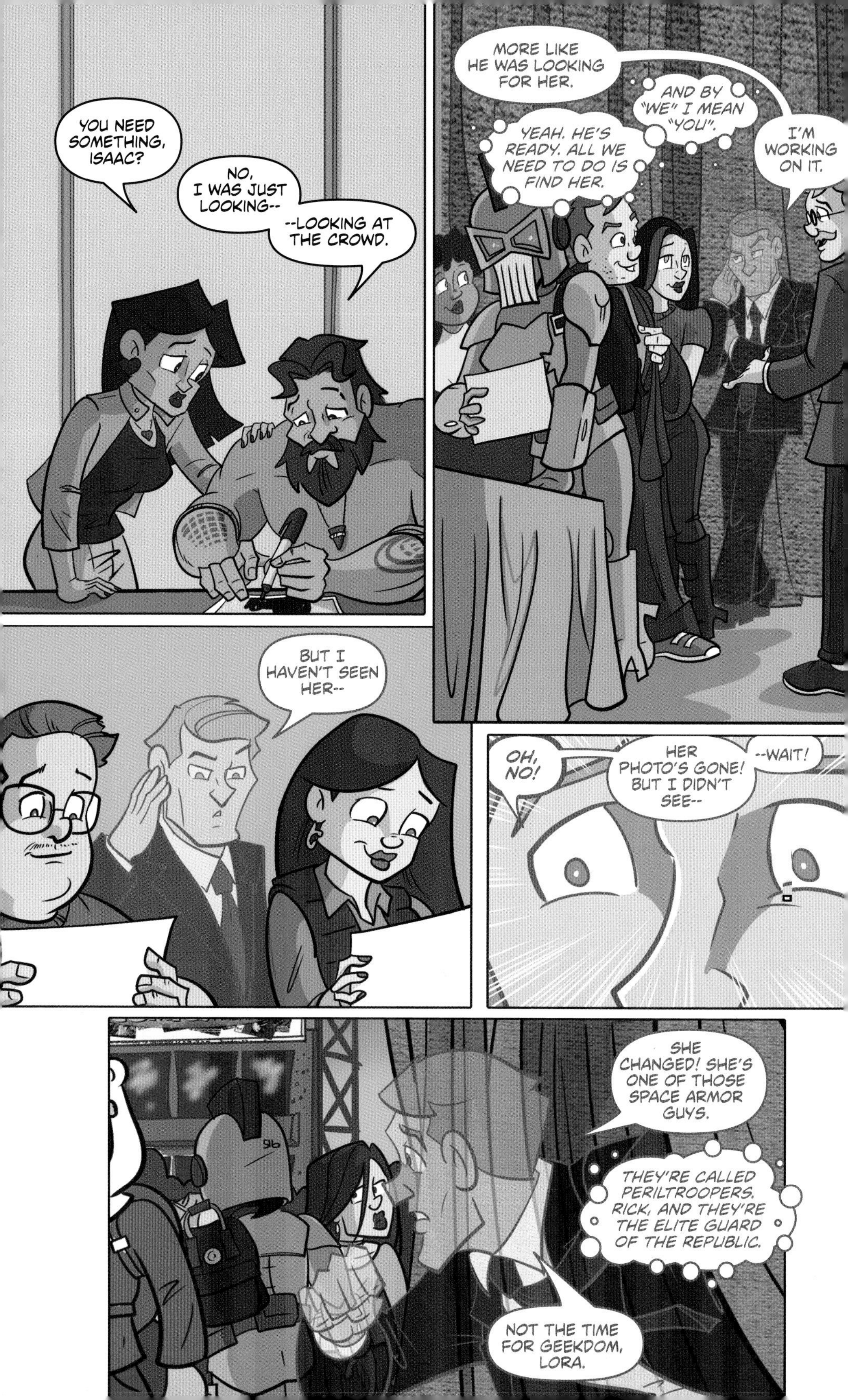
YOU NEED SOMETHING, ISAAC?
NO, I WAS JUST LOOKING--
--LOOKING AT THE CROWD.
MORE LIKE HE WAS LOOKING FOR HER.
YEAH. HE'S READY. ALL WE NEED TO DO IS FIND HER.
AND BY "WE" I MEAN "YOU".
I'M WORKING ON IT.
BUT I HAVEN'T SEEN HER--
OH, NO!
HER PHOTO'S GONE! BUT I DIDN'T SEE--
--WAIT!
SHE CHANGED! SHE'S ONE OF THOSE SPACE ARMOR GUYS.
THEY'RE CALLED PERILTROOPERS. RICK, AND THEY'RE THE ELITE GUARD OF THE REPUBLIC.
NOT THE TIME FOR GEEKDOM, LORA.

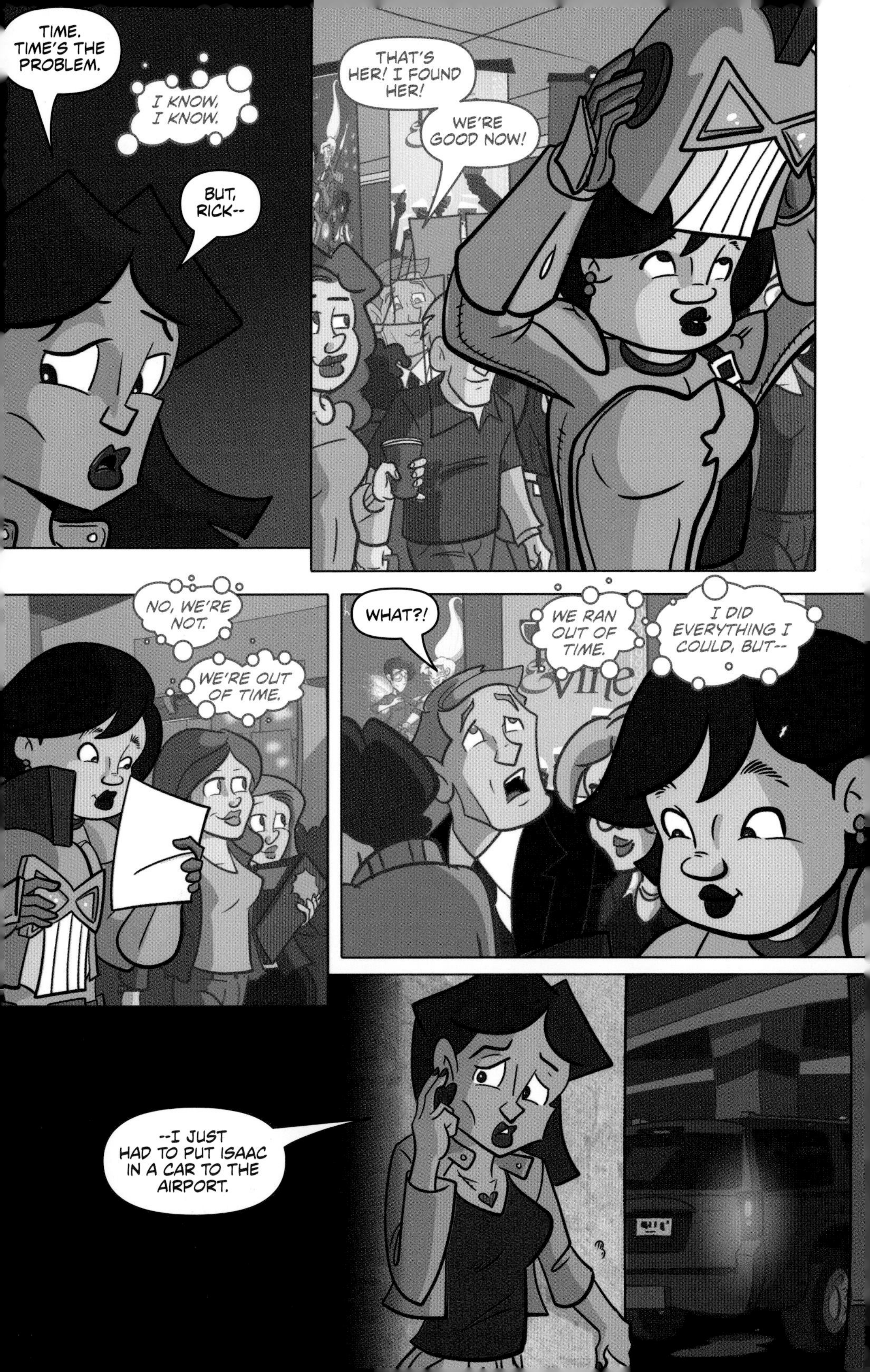
TIME. TIME'S THE PROBLEM.
I KNOW, I KNOW.
BUT, RICK--
THAT'S HER! I FOUND HER!
WE'RE GOOD NOW!
NO, WE'RE NOT.
WE'RE OUT OF TIME.
WHAT?!
WE RAN OUT OF TIME.
I DID EVERYTHING I COULD, BUT--
--I JUST HAD TO PUT ISAAC IN A CAR TO THE AIRPORT.

Chapter 14
Telling Me Just What a Fool I've Been

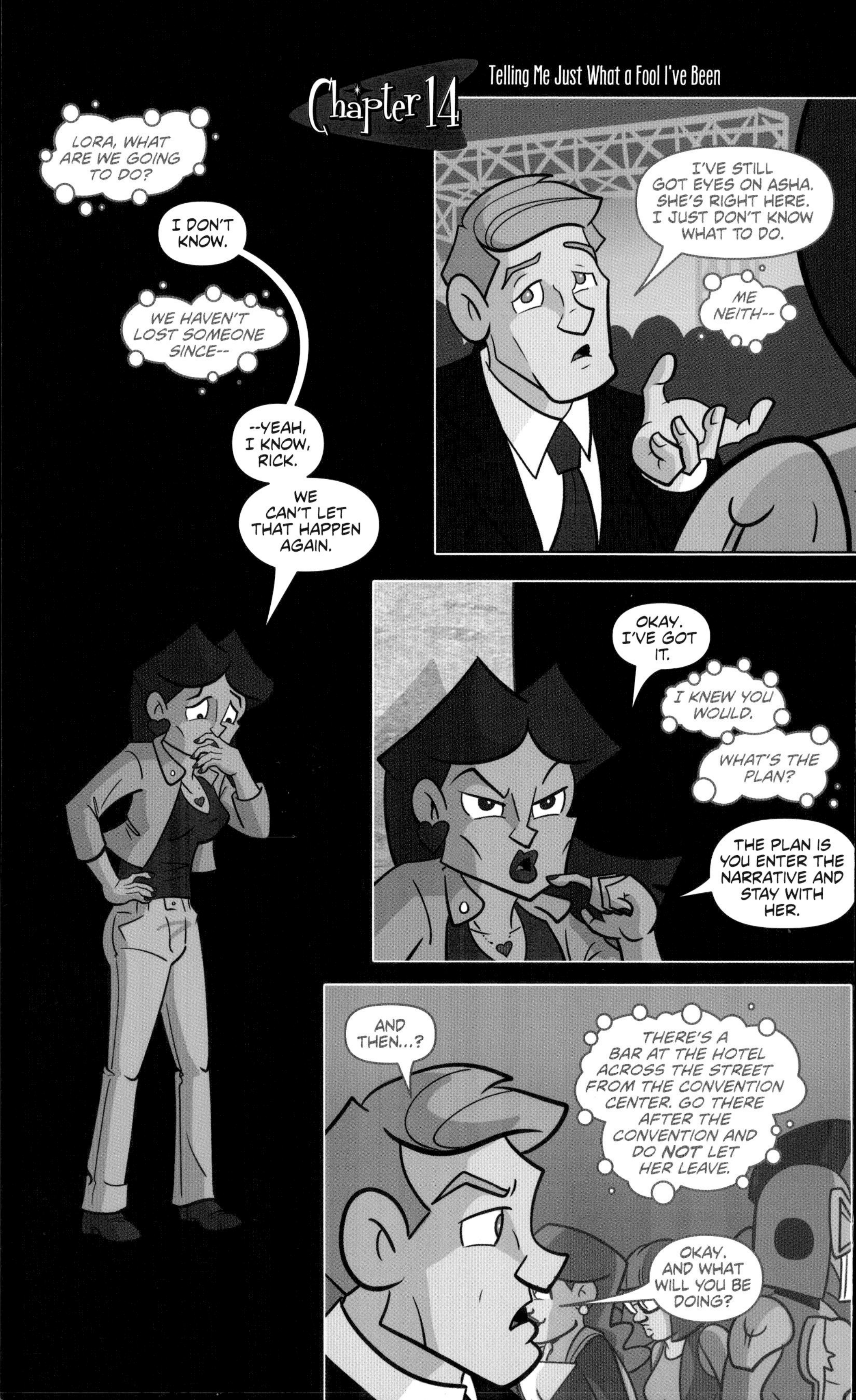
LORA, WHAT ARE WE GOING TO DO?
I DON'T KNOW.
WE HAVEN'T LOST SOMEONE SINCE--
--YEAH, I KNOW, RICK.
WE CAN'T LET THAT HAPPEN AGAIN.
I'VE STILL GOT EYES ON ASHA. SHE'S RIGHT HERE. I JUST DON'T KNOW WHAT TO DO.
ME NEITH--
OKAY. I'VE GOT IT.
I KNEW YOU WOULD.
WHAT'S THE PLAN?
THE PLAN IS YOU ENTER THE NARRATIVE AND STAY WITH HER.
AND THEN...?
THERE'S A BAR AT THE HOTEL ACROSS THE STREET FROM THE CONVENTION CENTER. GO THERE AFTER THE CONVENTION AND DO NOT LET HER LEAVE.
OKAY. AND WHAT WILL YOU BE DOING?

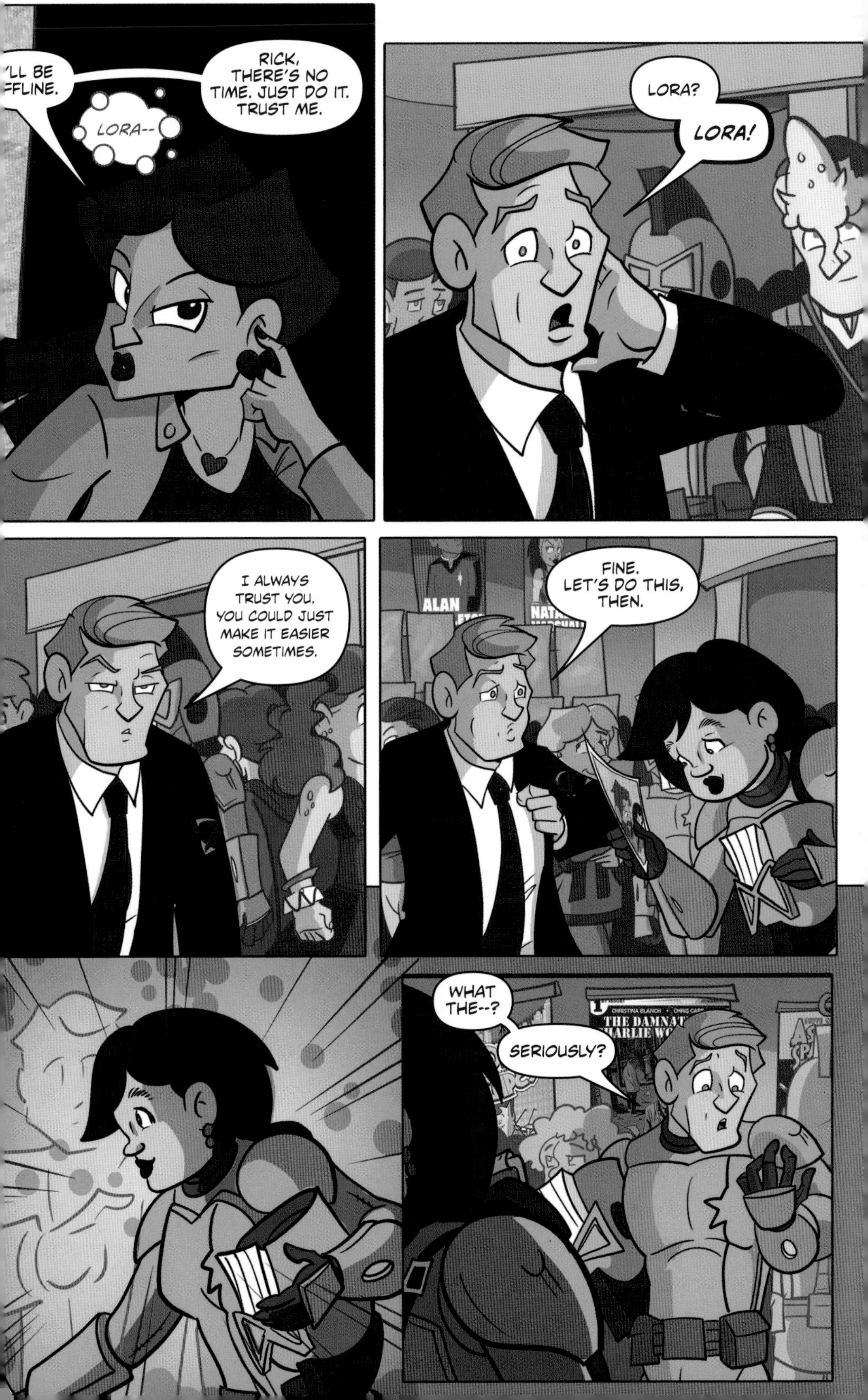
'LL BE
FFLINE.
LORA--
RICK, THERE'S NO TIME. JUST DO IT. TRUST ME.
LORA?
LORA!
I ALWAYS TRUST YOU. YOU COULD JUST MAKE IT EASIER SOMETIMES.
ALAN
FINE. LET'S DO THIS, THEN.
WHAT THE--?
SERIOUSLY?
CHRISTINA BLANCH
THE DAMNAT
CHARLIE WO

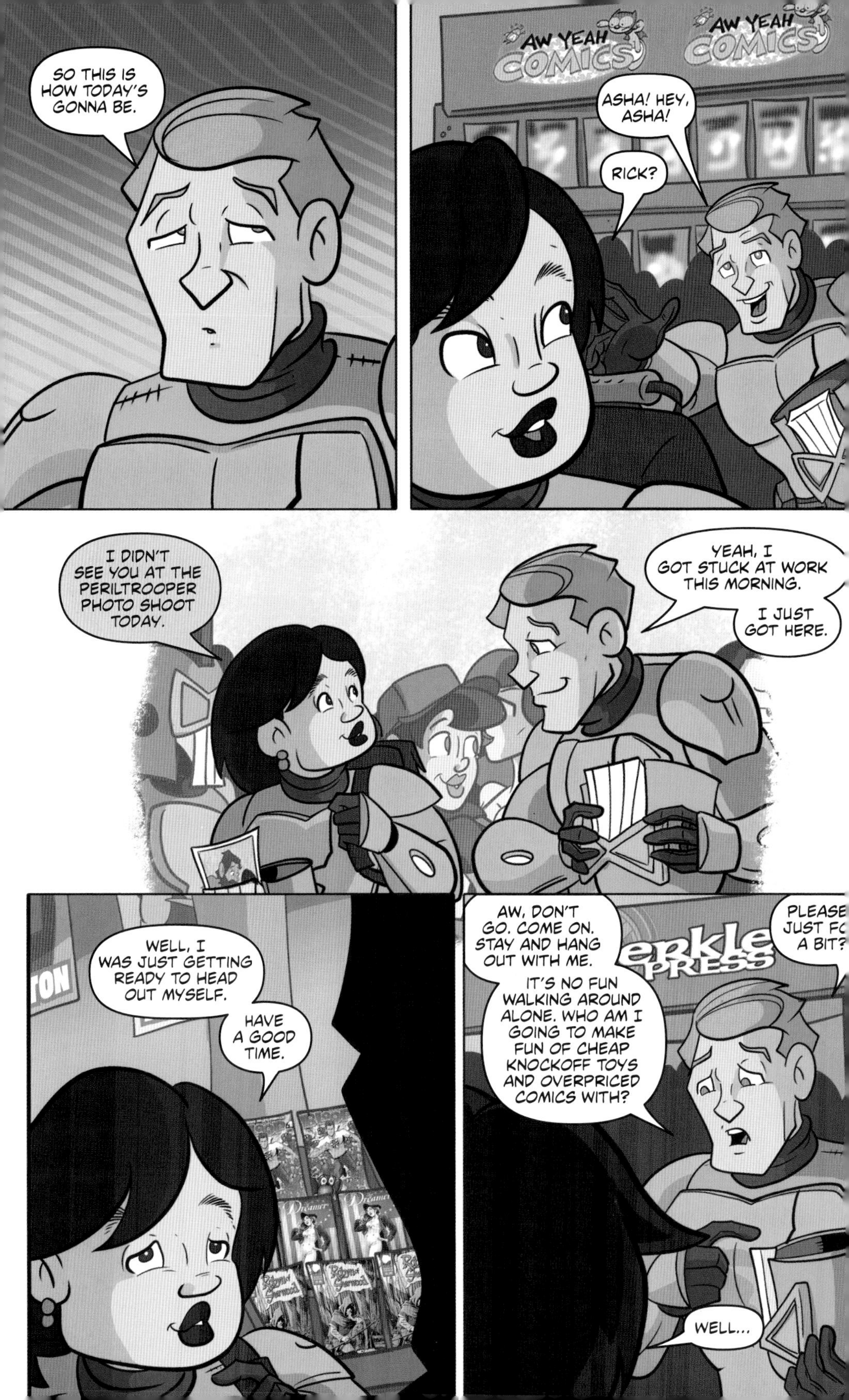
SO THIS IS HOW TODAY'S GONNA BE.
AW YEAH COMICS
AW YEAH COMICS
ASHA! HEY, ASHA!
RICK?
I DIDN'T SEE YOU AT THE PERILTROOPER PHOTO SHOOT TODAY.
YEAH, I GOT STUCK AT WORK THIS MORNING.
I JUST GOT HERE.
WELL, I WAS JUST GETTING READY TO HEAD OUT MYSELF.
HAVE A GOOD TIME.
AW, DON'T GO. COME ON. STAY AND HANG OUT WITH ME.
IT'S NO FUN WALKING AROUND ALONE. WHO AM I GOING TO MAKE FUN OF CHEAP KNOCKOFF TOYS AND OVERPRICED COMICS WITH?
PLEASE JUST FO A BIT?
WELL...

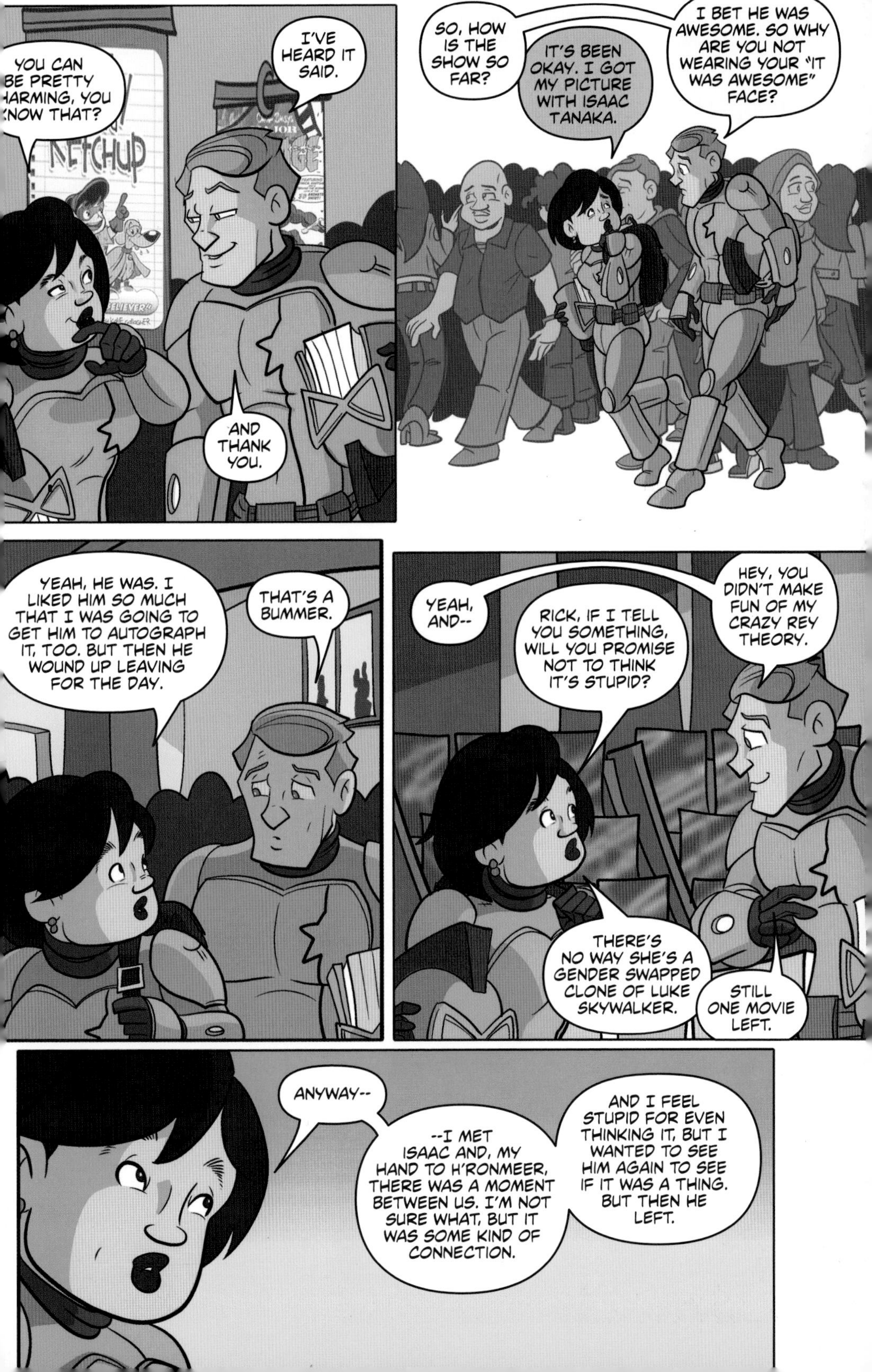
YOU CAN BE PRETTY HARMING, YOU KNOW THAT?
I'VE HEARD IT SAID.
AND THANK YOU.
SO, HOW IS THE SHOW SO FAR?
IT'S BEEN OKAY. I GOT MY PICTURE WITH ISAAC TANAKA.
I BET HE WAS AWESOME. SO WHY ARE YOU NOT WEARING YOUR "IT WAS AWESOME" FACE?
YEAH, HE WAS. I LIKED HIM SO MUCH THAT I WAS GOING TO GET HIM TO AUTOGRAPH IT, TOO. BUT THEN HE WOUND UP LEAVING FOR THE DAY.
THAT'S A BUMMER.
YEAH, AND--
HEY, YOU DIDN'T MAKE FUN OF MY CRAZY REY THEORY.
RICK, IF I TELL YOU SOMETHING, WILL YOU PROMISE NOT TO THINK IT'S STUPID?
THERE'S NO WAY SHE'S A GENDER SWAPPED CLONE OF LUKE SKYWALKER.
STILL ONE MOVIE LEFT.
ANYWAY--
--I MET ISAAC AND, MY HAND TO H'RONMEER, THERE WAS A MOMENT BETWEEN US. I'M NOT SURE WHAT, BUT IT WAS SOME KIND OF CONNECTION.
AND I FEEL STUPID FOR EVEN THINKING IT, BUT I WANTED TO SEE HIM AGAIN TO SEE IF IT WAS A THING. BUT THEN HE LEFT.

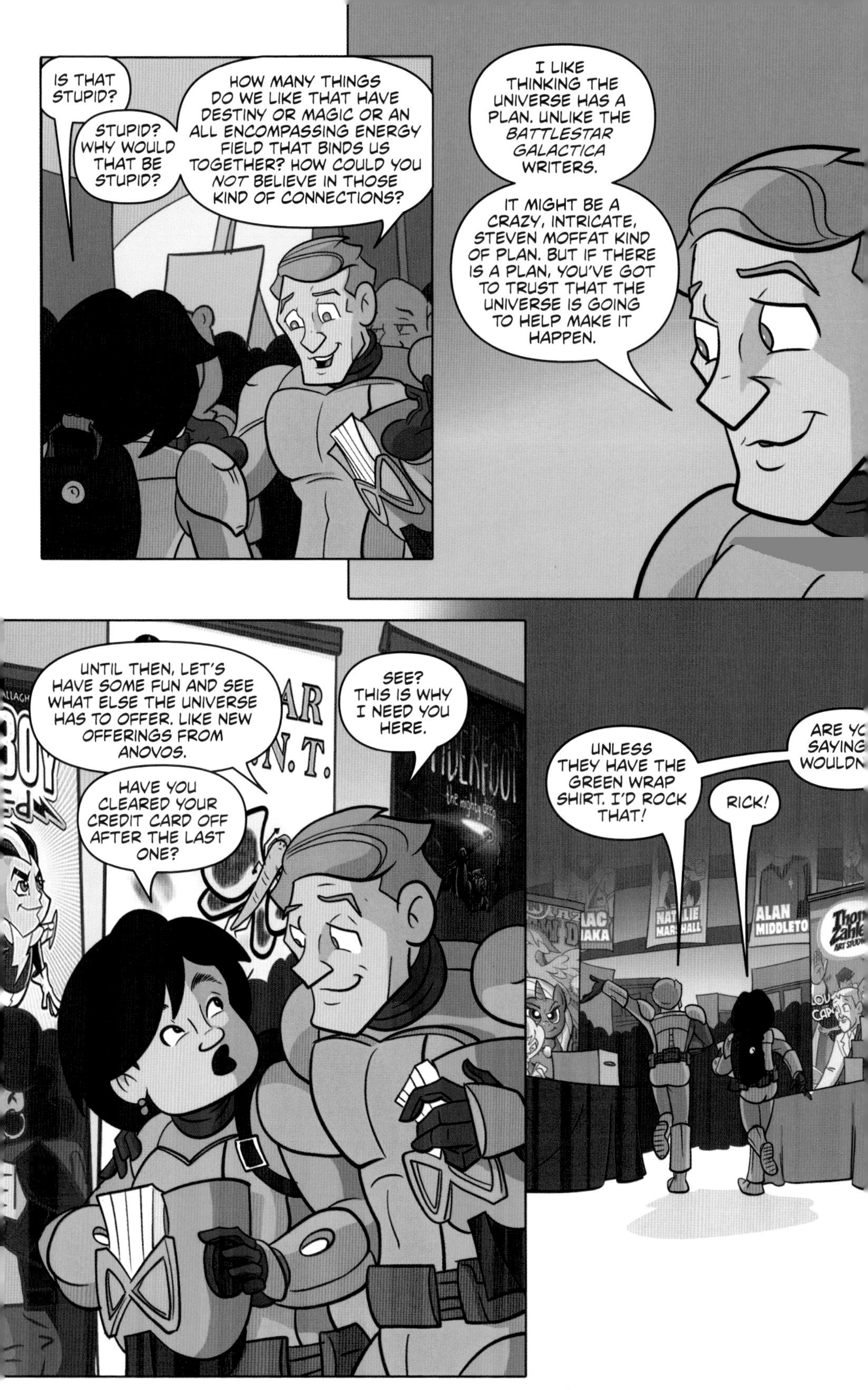
IS THAT STUPID?
STUPID? WHY WOULD THAT BE STUPID?
HOW MANY THINGS DO WE LIKE THAT HAVE DESTINY OR MAGIC OR AN ALL ENCOMPASSING ENERGY FIELD THAT BINDS US TOGETHER? HOW COULD YOU *NOT* BELIEVE IN THOSE KIND OF CONNECTIONS?
I LIKE THINKING THE UNIVERSE HAS A PLAN. UNLIKE THE *BATTLESTAR GALACTICA* WRITERS.
IT MIGHT BE A CRAZY, INTRICATE, STEVEN MOFFAT KIND OF PLAN. BUT IF THERE IS A PLAN, YOU'VE GOT TO TRUST THAT THE UNIVERSE IS GOING TO HELP MAKE IT HAPPEN.
UNTIL THEN, LET'S HAVE SOME FUN AND SEE WHAT ELSE THE UNIVERSE HAS TO OFFER. LIKE NEW OFFERINGS FROM ANOVOS.
SEE? THIS IS WHY I NEED YOU HERE.
HAVE YOU CLEARED YOUR CREDIT CARD OFF AFTER THE LAST ONE?
UNLESS THEY HAVE THE GREEN WRAP SHIRT. I'D ROCK THAT!
ARE YO
SAYING
WOULDN
RICK!
NATALIE MARSHALL
ALAN MIDDLETO

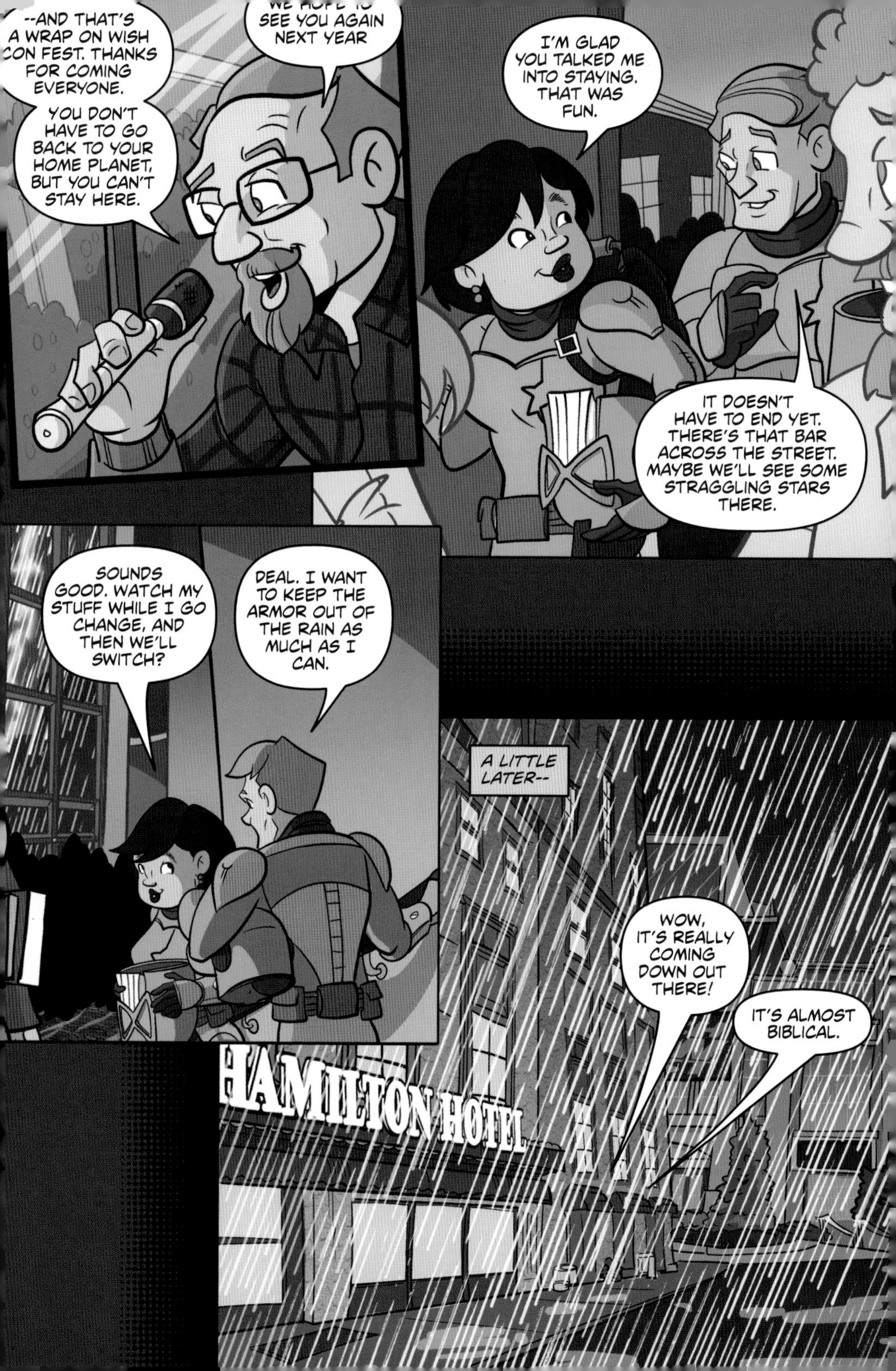
--AND THAT'S A WRAP ON WISH CON FEST. THANKS FOR COMING EVERYONE.
YOU DON'T HAVE TO GO BACK TO YOUR HOME PLANET, BUT YOU CAN'T STAY HERE.
SEE YOU AGAIN NEXT YEAR
I'M GLAD YOU TALKED ME INTO STAYING. THAT WAS FUN.
IT DOESN'T HAVE TO END YET. THERE'S THAT BAR ACROSS THE STREET. MAYBE WE'LL SEE SOME STRAGGLING STARS THERE.
SOUNDS GOOD. WATCH MY STUFF WHILE I GO CHANGE, AND THEN WE'LL SWITCH?
DEAL. I WANT TO KEEP THE ARMOR OUT OF THE RAIN AS MUCH AS I CAN.
A LITTLE LATER--
HAMILTON HOTEL
WOW, IT'S REALLY COMING DOWN OUT THERE!
IT'S ALMOST BIBLICAL.

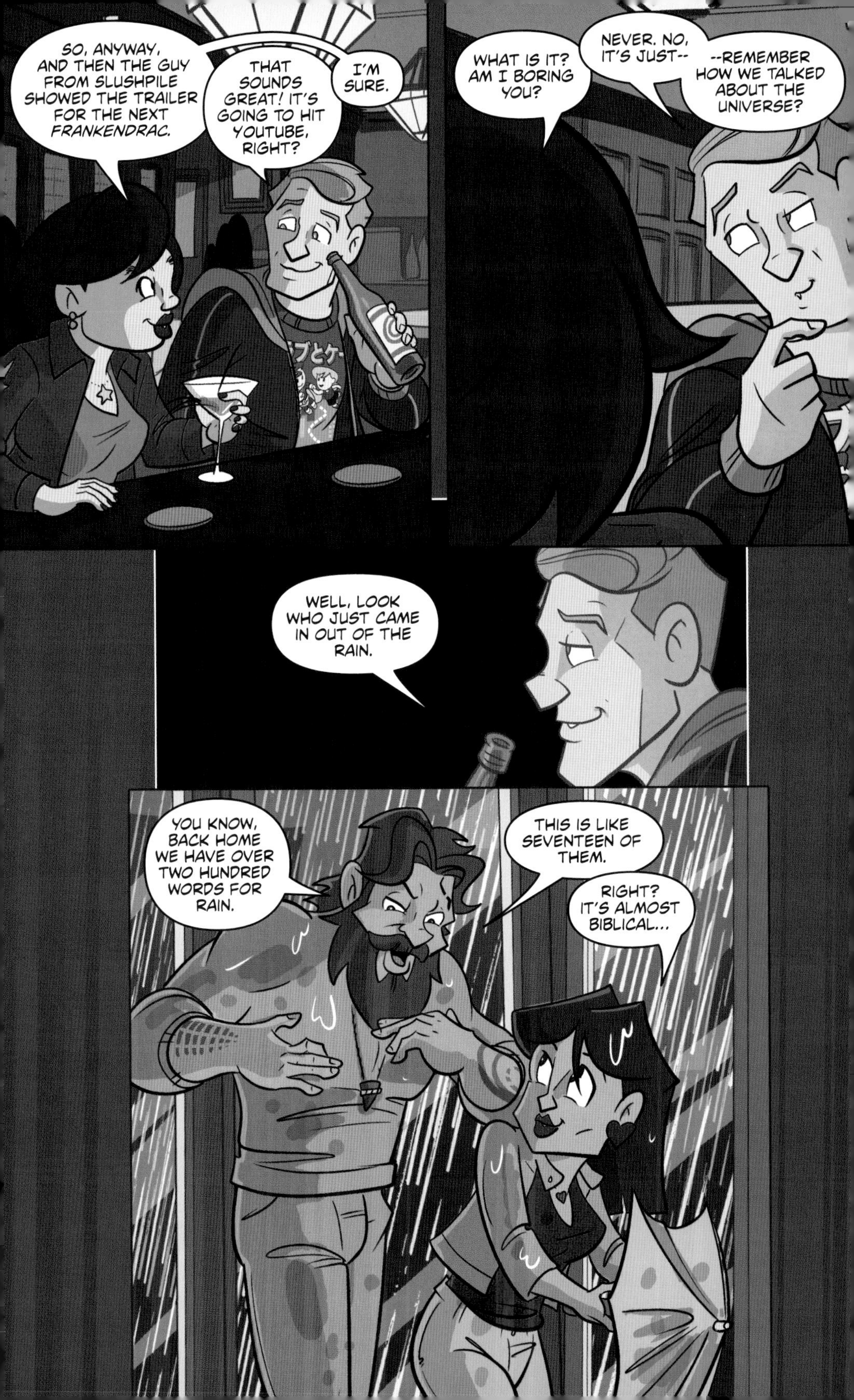
SO, ANYWAY, AND THEN THE GUY FROM SLUSHPILE SHOWED THE TRAILER FOR THE NEXT *FRANKENDRAC.*
THAT SOUNDS GREAT! IT'S GOING TO HIT YOUTUBE, RIGHT?
I'M SURE.
WHAT IS IT? AM I BORING YOU?
NEVER. NO, IT'S JUST--
--REMEMBER HOW WE TALKED ABOUT THE UNIVERSE?
WELL, LOOK WHO JUST CAME IN OUT OF THE RAIN.
YOU KNOW, BACK HOME WE HAVE OVER TWO HUNDRED WORDS FOR RAIN.
THIS IS LIKE SEVENTEEN OF THEM.
RIGHT? IT'S ALMOST BIBLICAL...

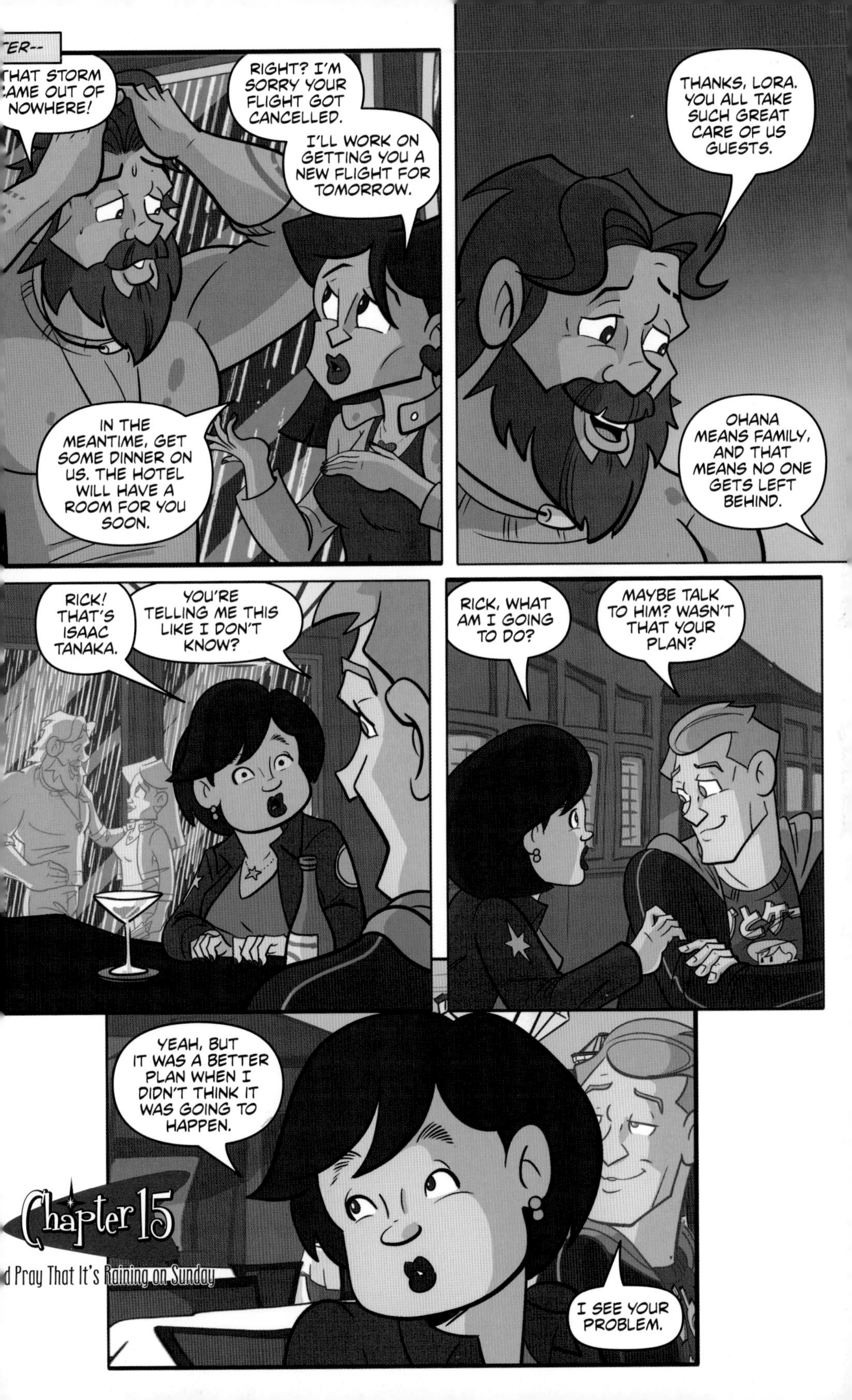
TER--
THAT STORM CAME OUT OF NOWHERE!
RIGHT? I'M SORRY YOUR FLIGHT GOT CANCELLED.
I'LL WORK ON GETTING YOU A NEW FLIGHT FOR TOMORROW.
IN THE MEANTIME, GET SOME DINNER ON US. THE HOTEL WILL HAVE A ROOM FOR YOU SOON.
THANKS, LORA. YOU ALL TAKE SUCH GREAT CARE OF US GUESTS.
OHANA MEANS FAMILY, AND THAT MEANS NO ONE GETS LEFT BEHIND.
RICK! THAT'S ISAAC TANAKA.
YOU'RE TELLING ME THIS LIKE I DON'T KNOW?
RICK, WHAT AM I GOING TO DO?
MAYBE TALK TO HIM? WASN'T THAT YOUR PLAN?
YEAH, BUT IT WAS A BETTER PLAN WHEN I DIDN'T THINK IT WAS GOING TO HAPPEN.
I SEE YOUR PROBLEM.
Chapter 15
d Pray That It's Raining on Sunday

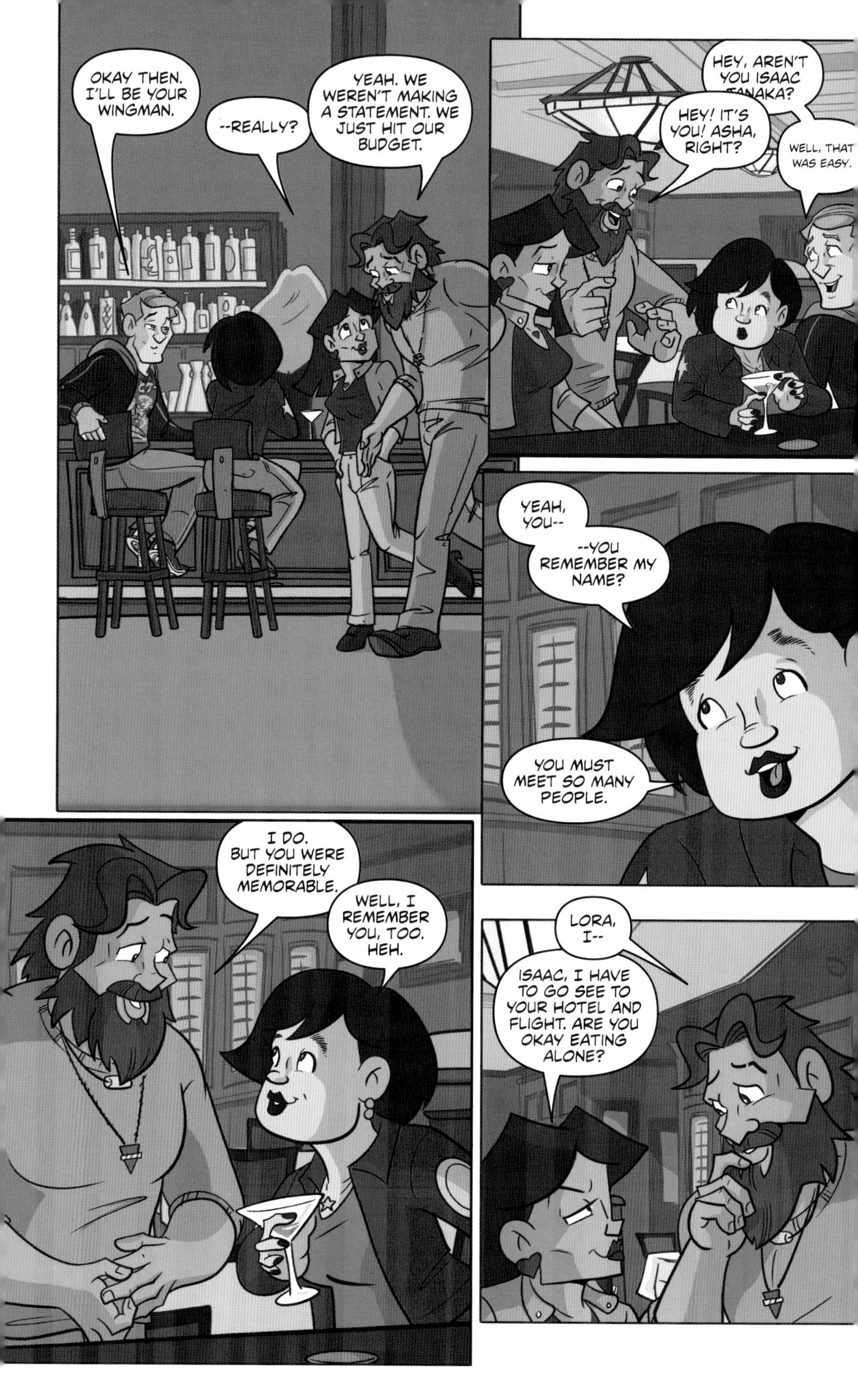
OKAY THEN. I'LL BE YOUR WINGMAN.
--REALLY?
YEAH. WE WEREN'T MAKING A STATEMENT. WE JUST HIT OUR BUDGET.
HEY, AREN'T YOU ISAAC TANAKA?
HEY! IT'S YOU! ASHA, RIGHT?
WELL, THAT WAS EASY.
YEAH, YOU--
--YOU REMEMBER MY NAME?
YOU MUST MEET SO MANY PEOPLE.
I DO. BUT YOU WERE DEFINITELY MEMORABLE.
WELL, I REMEMBER YOU, TOO. HEH.
LORA, I--
ISAAC, I HAVE TO GO SEE TO YOUR HOTEL AND FLIGHT. ARE YOU OKAY EATING ALONE?

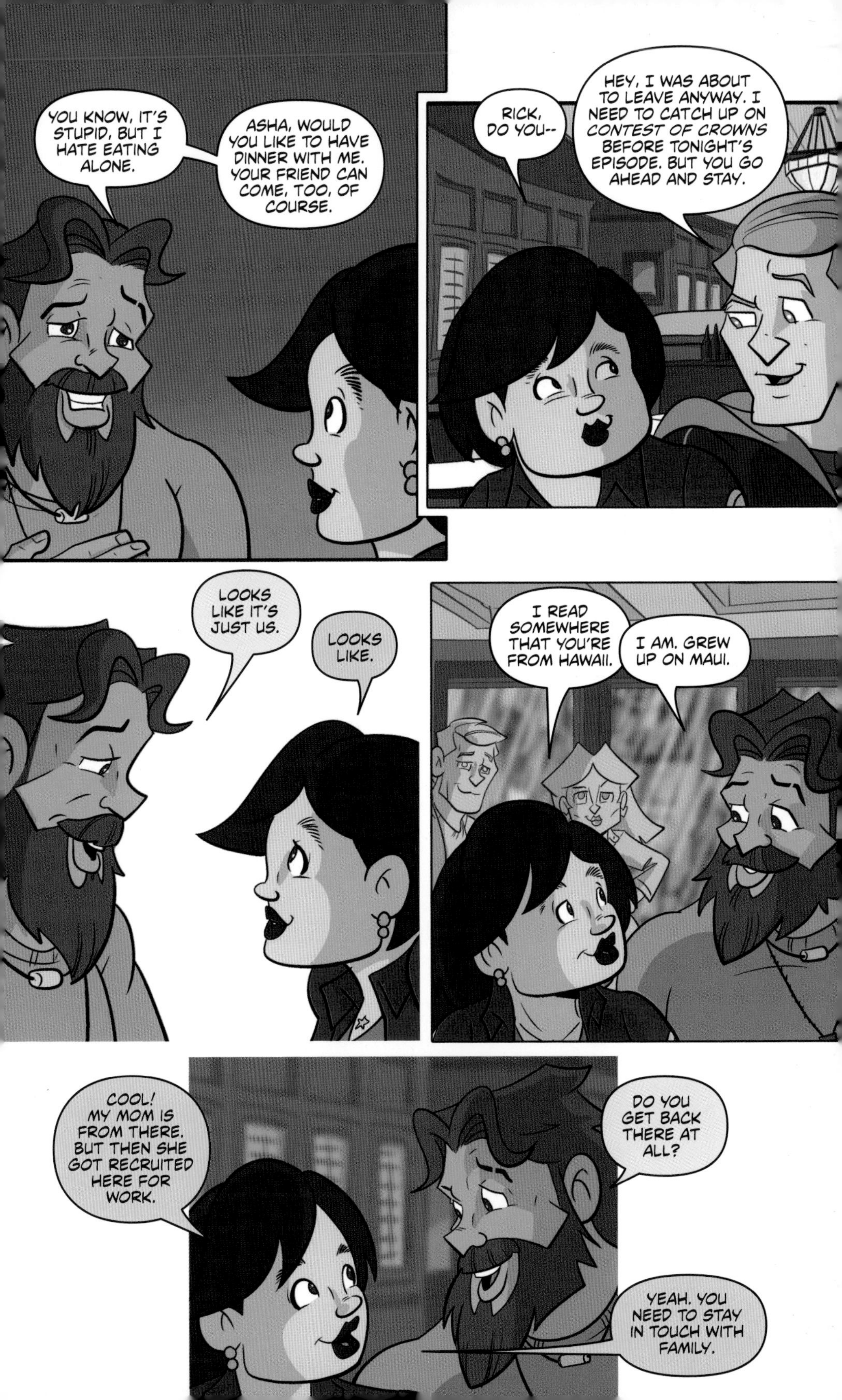
YOU KNOW, IT'S STUPID, BUT I HATE EATING ALONE.
ASHA, WOULD YOU LIKE TO HAVE DINNER WITH ME. YOUR FRIEND CAN COME, TOO, OF COURSE.
RICK, DO YOU--
HEY, I WAS ABOUT TO LEAVE ANYWAY. I NEED TO CATCH UP ON *CONTEST OF CROWNS* BEFORE TONIGHT'S EPISODE. BUT YOU GO AHEAD AND STAY.
LOOKS LIKE IT'S JUST US.
LOOKS LIKE.
I READ SOMEWHERE THAT YOU'RE FROM HAWAII.
I AM. GREW UP ON MAUI.
COOL! MY MOM IS FROM THERE. BUT THEN SHE GOT RECRUITED HERE FOR WORK.
DO YOU GET BACK THERE AT ALL?
YEAH. YOU NEED TO STAY IN TOUCH WITH FAMILY.

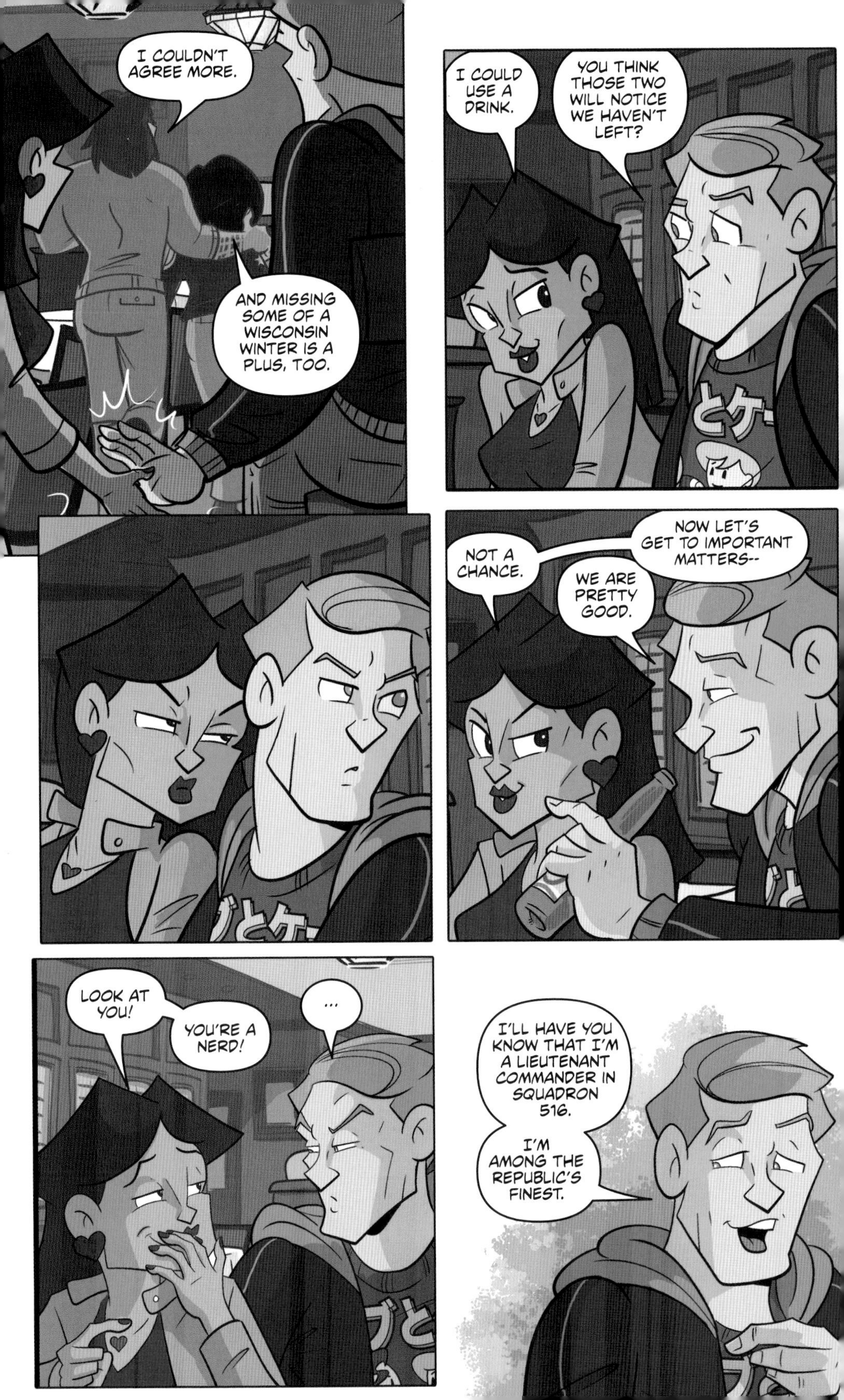
I COULDN'T AGREE MORE.
AND MISSING SOME OF A WISCONSIN WINTER IS A PLUS, TOO.
I COULD USE A DRINK.
YOU THINK THOSE TWO WILL NOTICE WE HAVEN'T LEFT?
NOT A CHANCE.
NOW LET'S GET TO IMPORTANT MATTERS--
WE ARE PRETTY GOOD.
LOOK AT YOU!
YOU'RE A NERD!
...
I'LL HAVE YOU KNOW THAT I'M A LIEUTENANT COMMANDER IN SQUADRON 516.
I'M AMONG THE REPUBLIC'S FINEST.

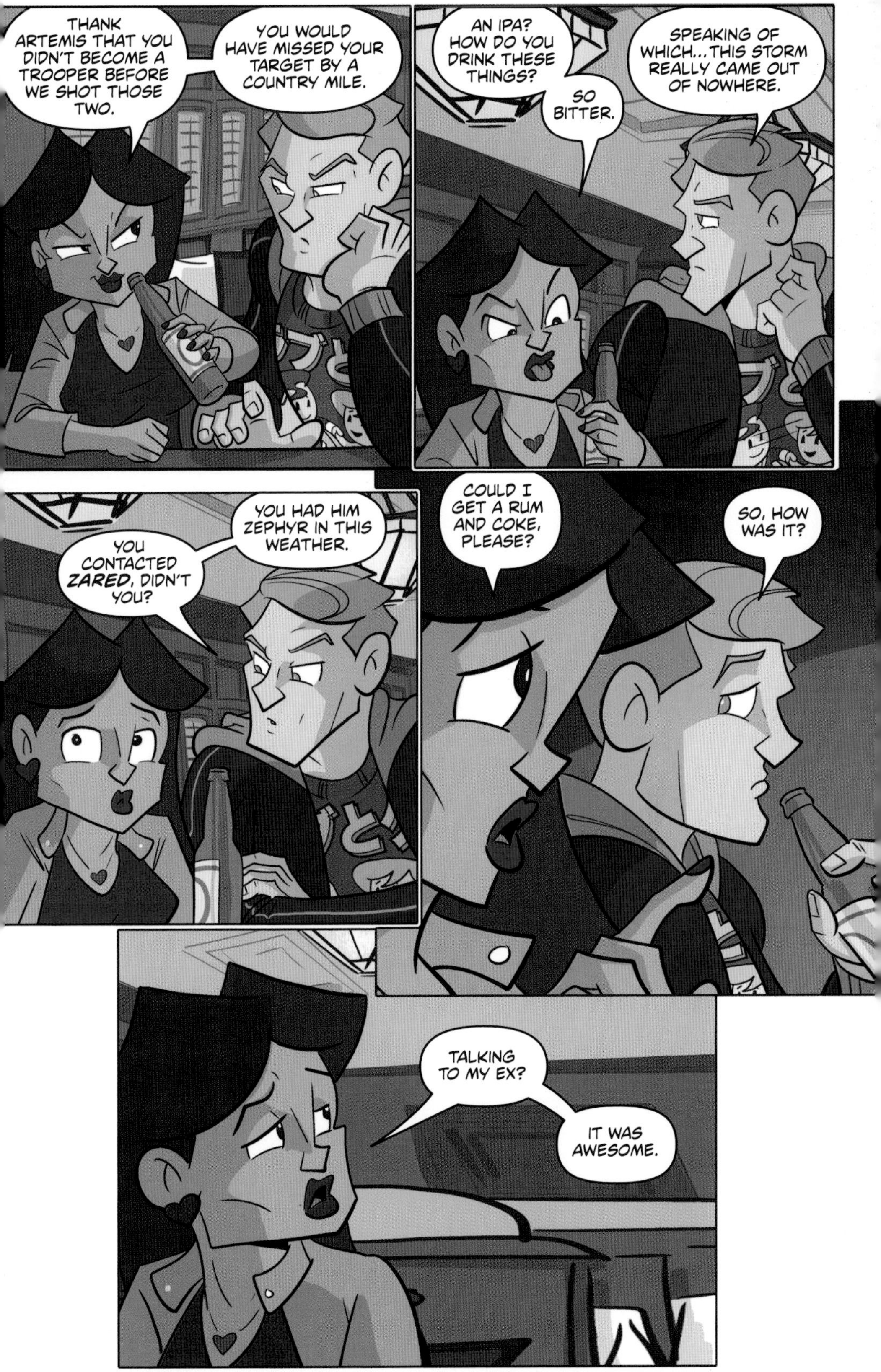
THANK ARTEMIS THAT YOU DIDN'T BECOME A TROOPER BEFORE WE SHOT THOSE TWO.
YOU WOULD HAVE MISSED YOUR TARGET BY A COUNTRY MILE.
AN IPA? HOW DO YOU DRINK THESE THINGS?
SO BITTER.
SPEAKING OF WHICH...THIS STORM REALLY CAME OUT OF NOWHERE.
YOU CONTACTED ZARED, DIDN'T YOU?
YOU HAD HIM ZEPHYR IN THIS WEATHER.
COULD I GET A RUM AND COKE, PLEASE?
SO, HOW WAS IT?
TALKING TO MY EX?
IT WAS AWESOME.

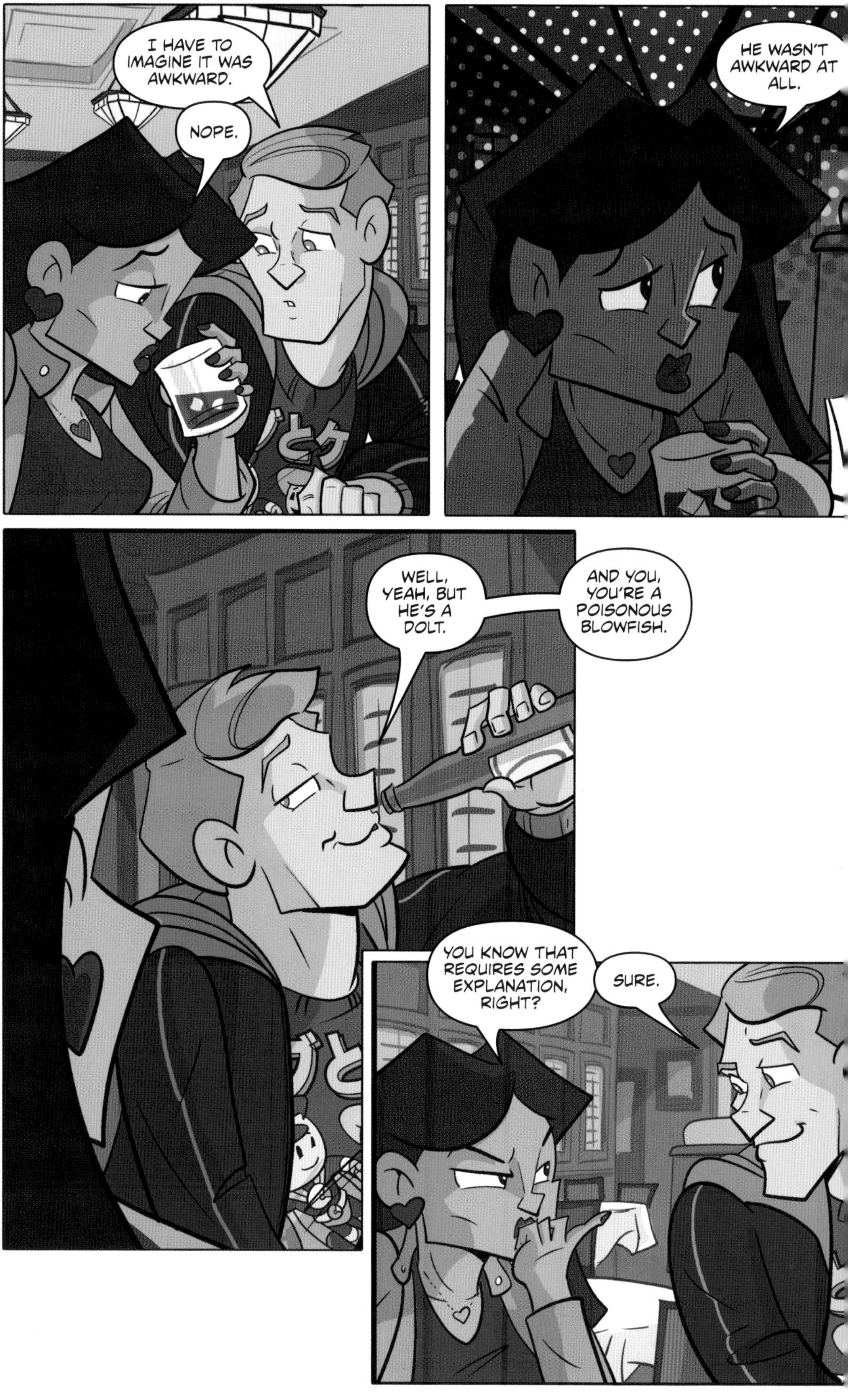

I HAVE TO IMAGINE IT WAS AWKWARD.
NOPE.
HE WASN'T AWKWARD AT ALL.
WELL, YEAH, BUT HE'S A DOLT.
AND YOU, YOU'RE A POISONOUS BLOWFISH.
YOU KNOW THAT REQUIRES SOME EXPLANATION, RIGHT?
SURE.

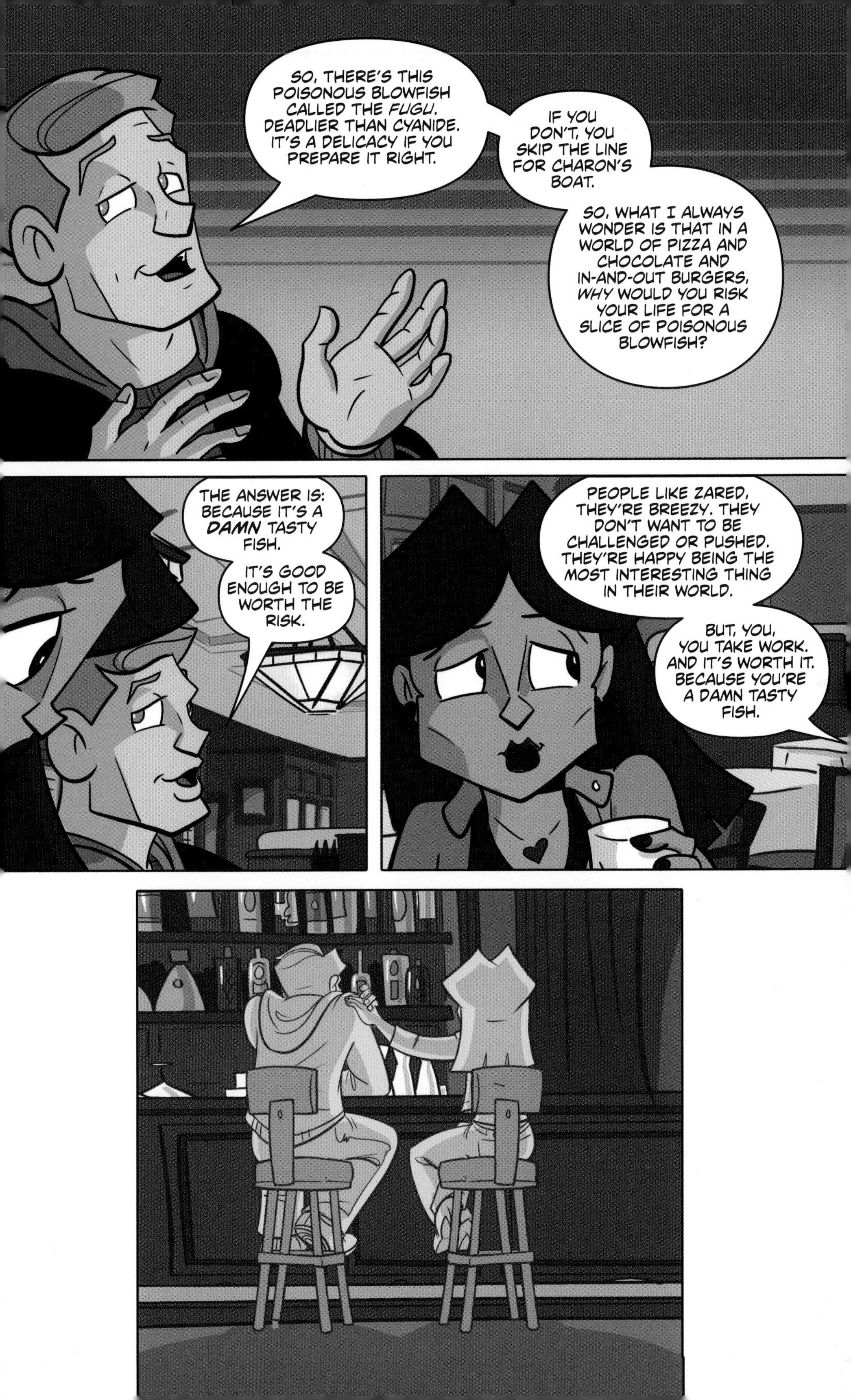
SO, THERE'S THIS POISONOUS BLOWFISH CALLED THE *FUGU*. DEADLIER THAN CYANIDE. IT'S A DELICACY IF YOU PREPARE IT RIGHT.
IF YOU DON'T, YOU SKIP THE LINE FOR CHARON'S BOAT.
SO, WHAT I ALWAYS WONDER IS THAT IN A WORLD OF PIZZA AND CHOCOLATE AND IN-AND-OUT BURGERS, *WHY* WOULD YOU RISK YOUR LIFE FOR A SLICE OF POISONOUS BLOWFISH?
THE ANSWER IS: BECAUSE IT'S A **DAMN** TASTY FISH.
IT'S GOOD ENOUGH TO BE WORTH THE RISK.
PEOPLE LIKE ZARED, THEY'RE BREEZY. THEY DON'T WANT TO BE CHALLENGED OR PUSHED. THEY'RE HAPPY BEING THE MOST INTERESTING THING IN THEIR WORLD.
BUT, YOU, YOU TAKE WORK. AND IT'S WORTH IT. BECAUSE YOU'RE A DAMN TASTY FISH.

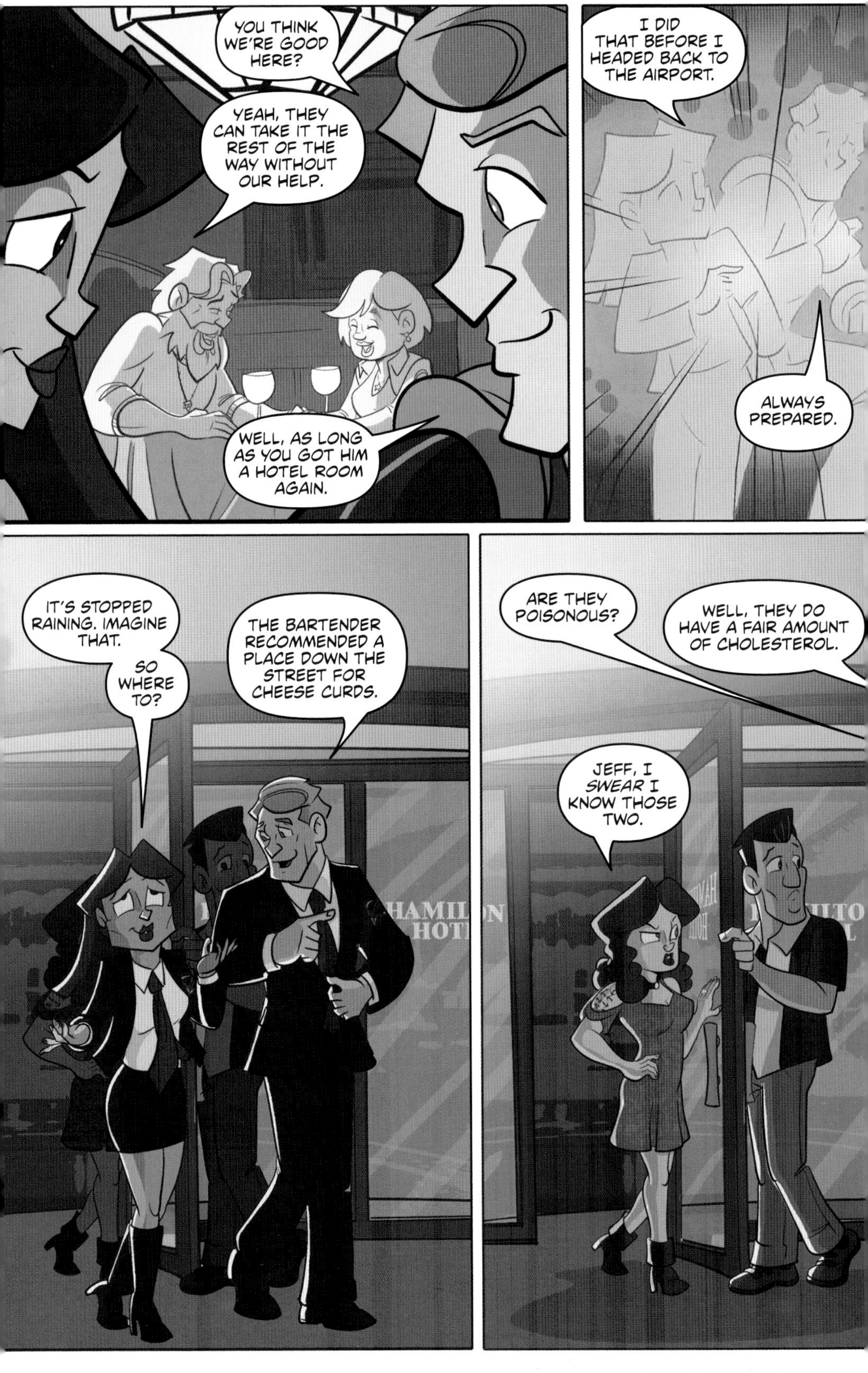
YOU THINK WE'RE GOOD HERE?
YEAH, THEY CAN TAKE IT THE REST OF THE WAY WITHOUT OUR HELP.
WELL, AS LONG AS YOU GOT HIM A HOTEL ROOM AGAIN.
I DID THAT BEFORE I HEADED BACK TO THE AIRPORT.
ALWAYS PREPARED.
IT'S STOPPED RAINING. IMAGINE THAT.
SO WHERE TO?
THE BARTENDER RECOMMENDED A PLACE DOWN THE STREET FOR CHEESE CURDS.
ARE THEY POISONOUS?
WELL, THEY DO HAVE A FAIR AMOUNT OF CHOLESTEROL.
JEFF, I SWEAR I KNOW THOSE TWO.

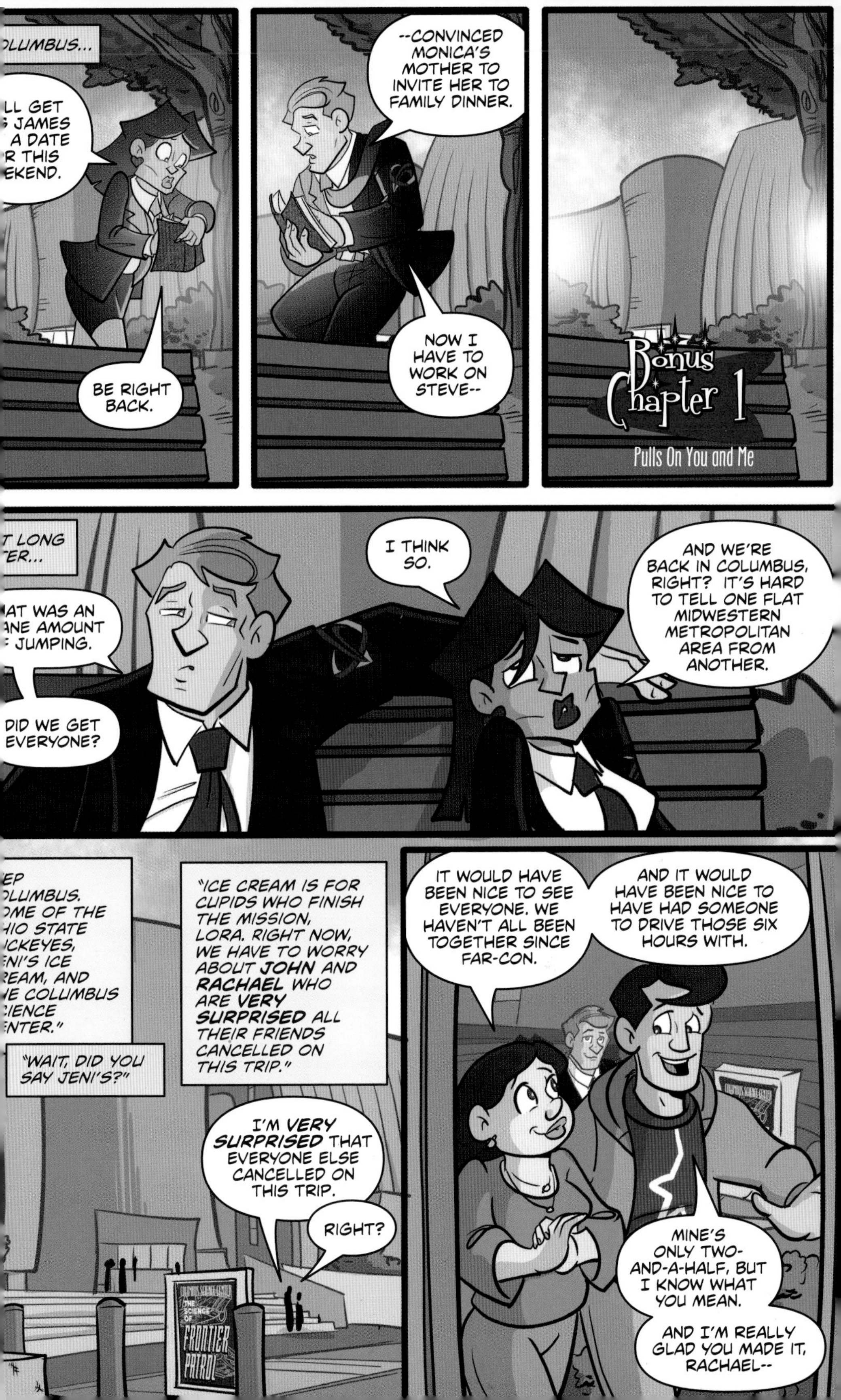

OLUMBUS...
LL GET
JAMES
A DATE
R THIS
EKEND.
BE RIGHT BACK.
--CONVINCED MONICA'S MOTHER TO INVITE HER TO FAMILY DINNER.
NOW I HAVE TO WORK ON STEVE--
Bonus Chapter 1
Pulls On You and Me
T LONG
TER...
IAT WAS AN
ANE AMOUNT
F JUMPING.
DID WE GET EVERYONE?
I THINK SO.
AND WE'RE BACK IN COLUMBUS, RIGHT? IT'S HARD TO TELL ONE FLAT MIDWESTERN METROPOLITAN AREA FROM ANOTHER.
EP
OLUMBUS.
OME OF THE
HIO STATE
ICKEYES,
ENI'S ICE
REAM, AND
IE COLUMBUS
CIENCE
ENTER."
"WAIT, DID YOU SAY JENI'S?"
"ICE CREAM IS FOR CUPIDS WHO FINISH THE MISSION, LORA. RIGHT NOW, WE HAVE TO WORRY ABOUT JOHN AND RACHAEL WHO ARE VERY SURPRISED ALL THEIR FRIENDS CANCELLED ON THIS TRIP."
I'M VERY SURPRISED THAT EVERYONE ELSE CANCELLED ON THIS TRIP.
RIGHT?
COLUMBUS SCIENCE CENTER
THE SCIENCE OF FRONTIER PATROL
IT WOULD HAVE BEEN NICE TO SEE EVERYONE. WE HAVEN'T ALL BEEN TOGETHER SINCE FAR-CON.
AND IT WOULD HAVE BEEN NICE TO HAVE HAD SOMEONE TO DRIVE THOSE SIX HOURS WITH.
MINE'S ONLY TWO-AND-A-HALF, BUT I KNOW WHAT YOU MEAN.
AND I'M REALLY GLAD YOU MADE IT, RACHAEL--

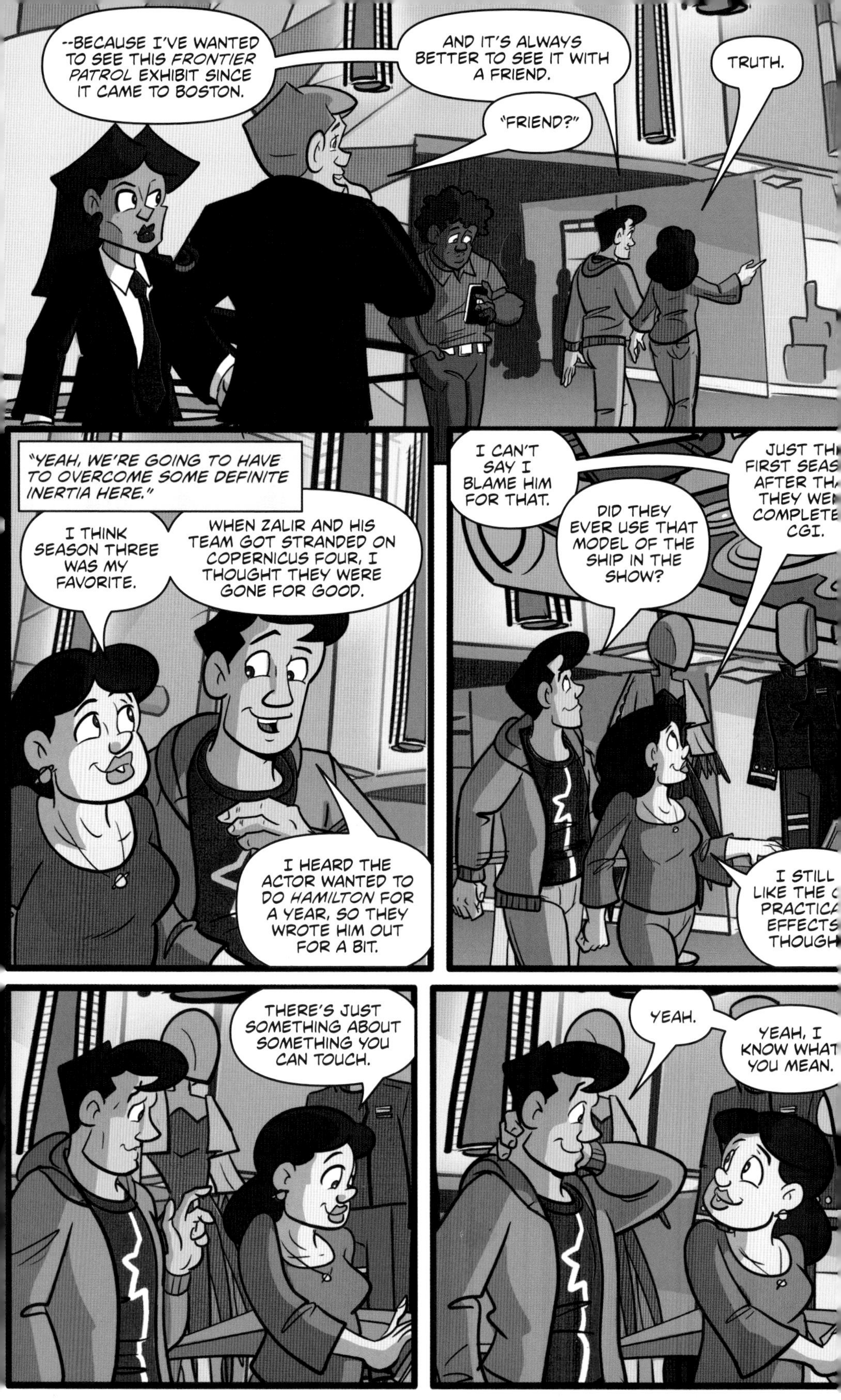
--BECAUSE I'VE WANTED TO SEE THIS *FRONTIER PATROL* EXHIBIT SINCE IT CAME TO BOSTON.
AND IT'S ALWAYS BETTER TO SEE IT WITH A FRIEND.
"FRIEND?"
TRUTH.
"YEAH, WE'RE GOING TO HAVE TO OVERCOME SOME DEFINITE INERTIA HERE."
I THINK SEASON THREE WAS MY FAVORITE.
WHEN ZALIR AND HIS TEAM GOT STRANDED ON COPERNICUS FOUR, I THOUGHT THEY WERE GONE FOR GOOD.
I HEARD THE ACTOR WANTED TO DO *HAMILTON* FOR A YEAR, SO THEY WROTE HIM OUT FOR A BIT.
I CAN'T SAY I BLAME HIM FOR THAT.
DID THEY EVER USE THAT MODEL OF THE SHIP IN THE SHOW?
JUST TH FIRST SEAS AFTER TH THEY WE COMPLETE CGI.
I STILL LIKE THE PRACTICA EFFECTS THOUGH
THERE'S JUST SOMETHING ABOUT SOMETHING YOU CAN TOUCH.
YEAH.
YEAH, I KNOW WHAT YOU MEAN.

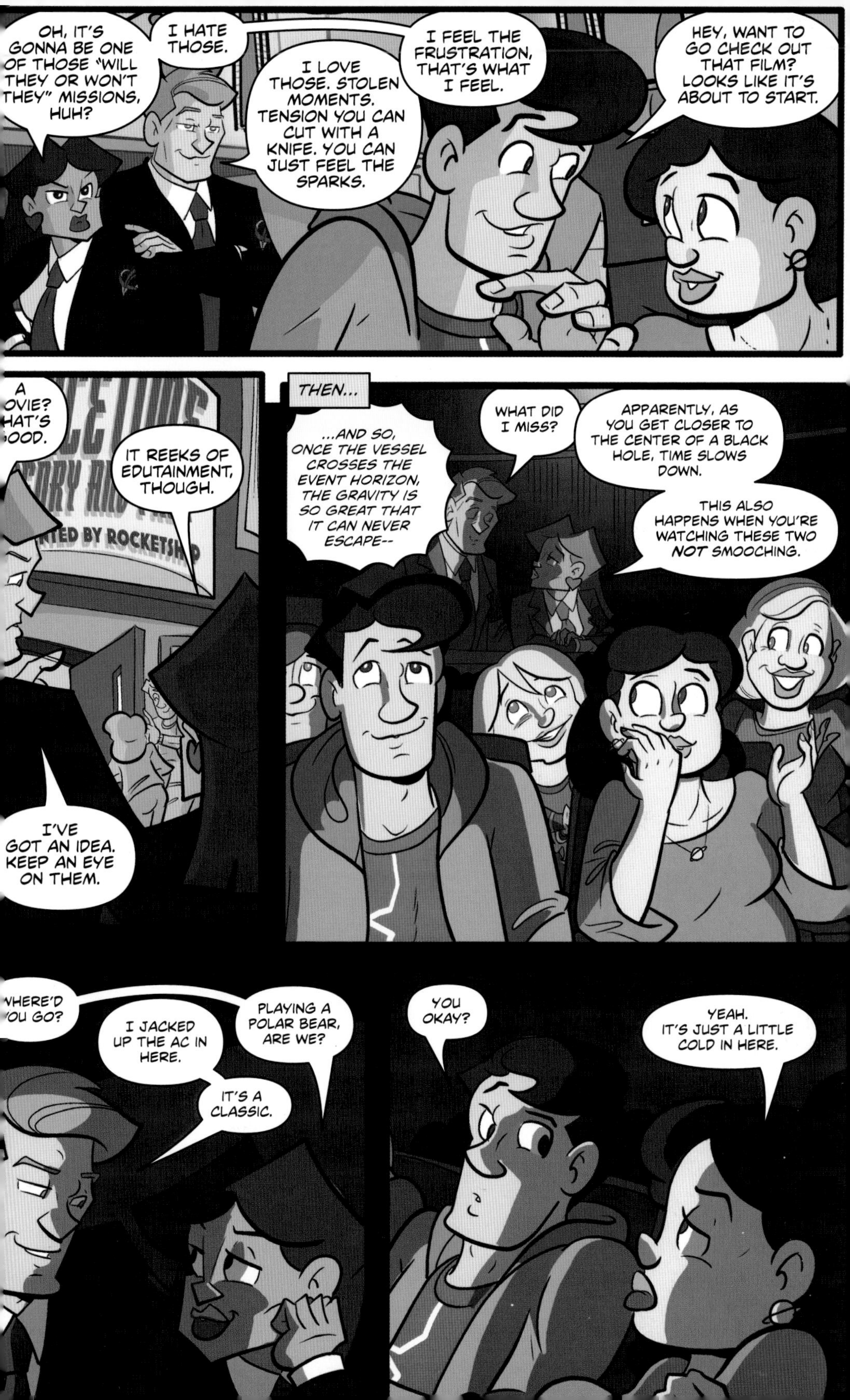
OH, IT'S GONNA BE ONE OF THOSE "WILL THEY OR WON'T THEY" MISSIONS, HUH?
I HATE THOSE.
I LOVE THOSE. STOLEN MOMENTS. TENSION YOU CAN CUT WITH A KNIFE. YOU CAN JUST FEEL THE SPARKS.
I FEEL THE FRUSTRATION, THAT'S WHAT I FEEL.
HEY, WANT TO GO CHECK OUT THAT FILM? LOOKS LIKE IT'S ABOUT TO START.
A OVIE? HAT'S OOD.
IT REEKS OF EDUTAINMENT, THOUGH.
NTED BY ROCKETSH
I'VE GOT AN IDEA. KEEP AN EYE ON THEM.
THEN...
...AND SO, ONCE THE VESSEL CROSSES THE EVENT HORIZON, THE GRAVITY IS SO GREAT THAT IT CAN NEVER ESCAPE--
WHAT DID I MISS?
APPARENTLY, AS YOU GET CLOSER TO THE CENTER OF A BLACK HOLE, TIME SLOWS DOWN.
THIS ALSO HAPPENS WHEN YOU'RE WATCHING THESE TWO NOT SMOOCHING.
HERE'D OU GO?
I JACKED UP THE AC IN HERE.
PLAYING A POLAR BEAR, ARE WE?
IT'S A CLASSIC.
YOU OKAY?
YEAH. IT'S JUST A LITTLE COLD IN HERE.

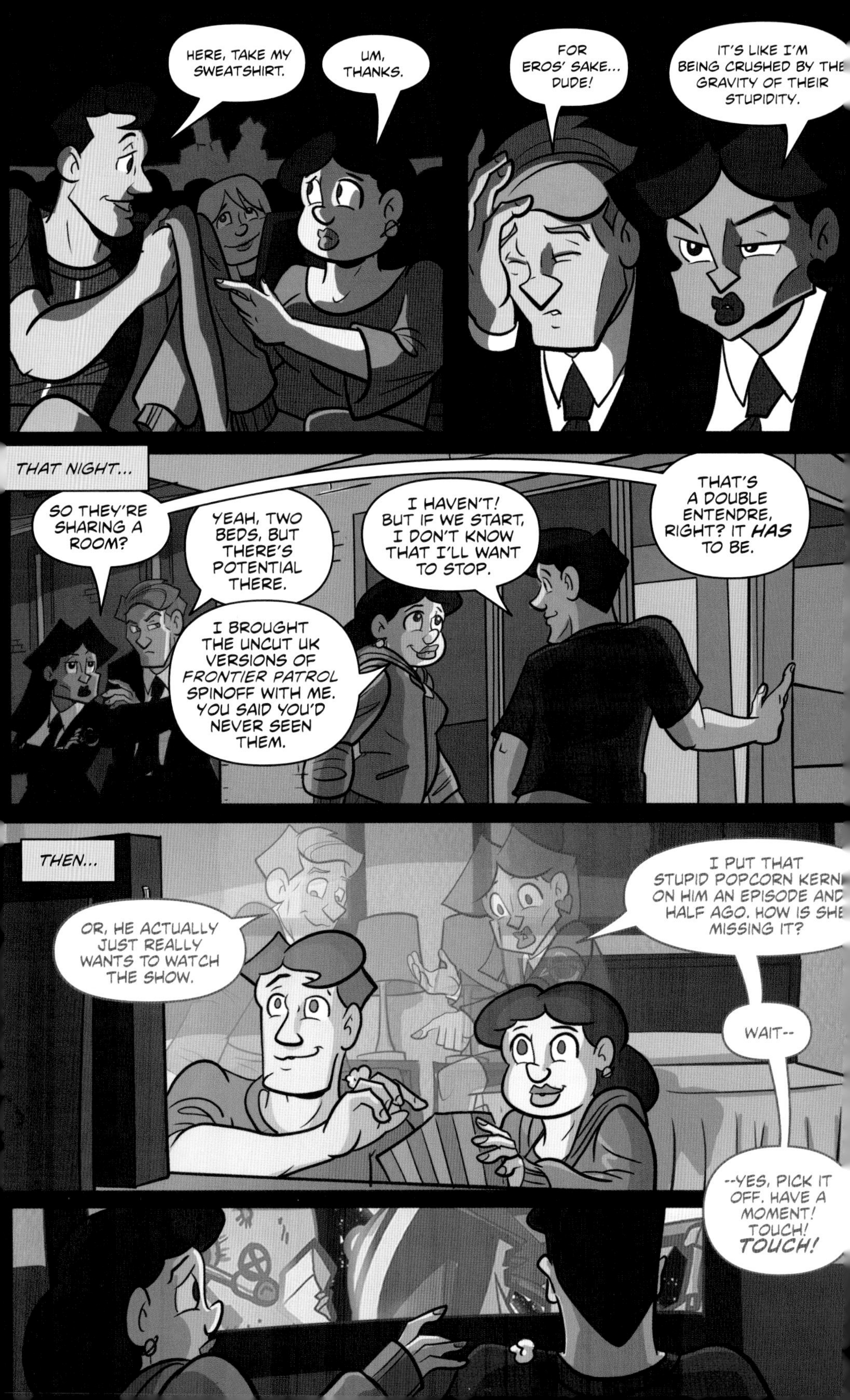
HERE, TAKE MY SWEATSHIRT.
UM, THANKS.
FOR EROS' SAKE... DUDE!
IT'S LIKE I'M BEING CRUSHED BY THE GRAVITY OF THEIR STUPIDITY.
THAT NIGHT...
SO THEY'RE SHARING A ROOM?
YEAH, TWO BEDS, BUT THERE'S POTENTIAL THERE.
I BROUGHT THE UNCUT UK VERSIONS OF FRONTIER PATROL SPINOFF WITH ME. YOU SAID YOU'D NEVER SEEN THEM.
I HAVEN'T! BUT IF WE START, I DON'T KNOW THAT I'LL WANT TO STOP.
THAT'S A DOUBLE ENTENDRE, RIGHT? IT HAS TO BE.
THEN...
OR, HE ACTUALLY JUST REALLY WANTS TO WATCH THE SHOW.
I PUT THAT STUPID POPCORN KERN ON HIM AN EPISODE AND HALF AGO. HOW IS SHE MISSING IT?
WAIT--
--YES, PICK IT OFF. HAVE A MOMENT! TOUCH! TOUCH!

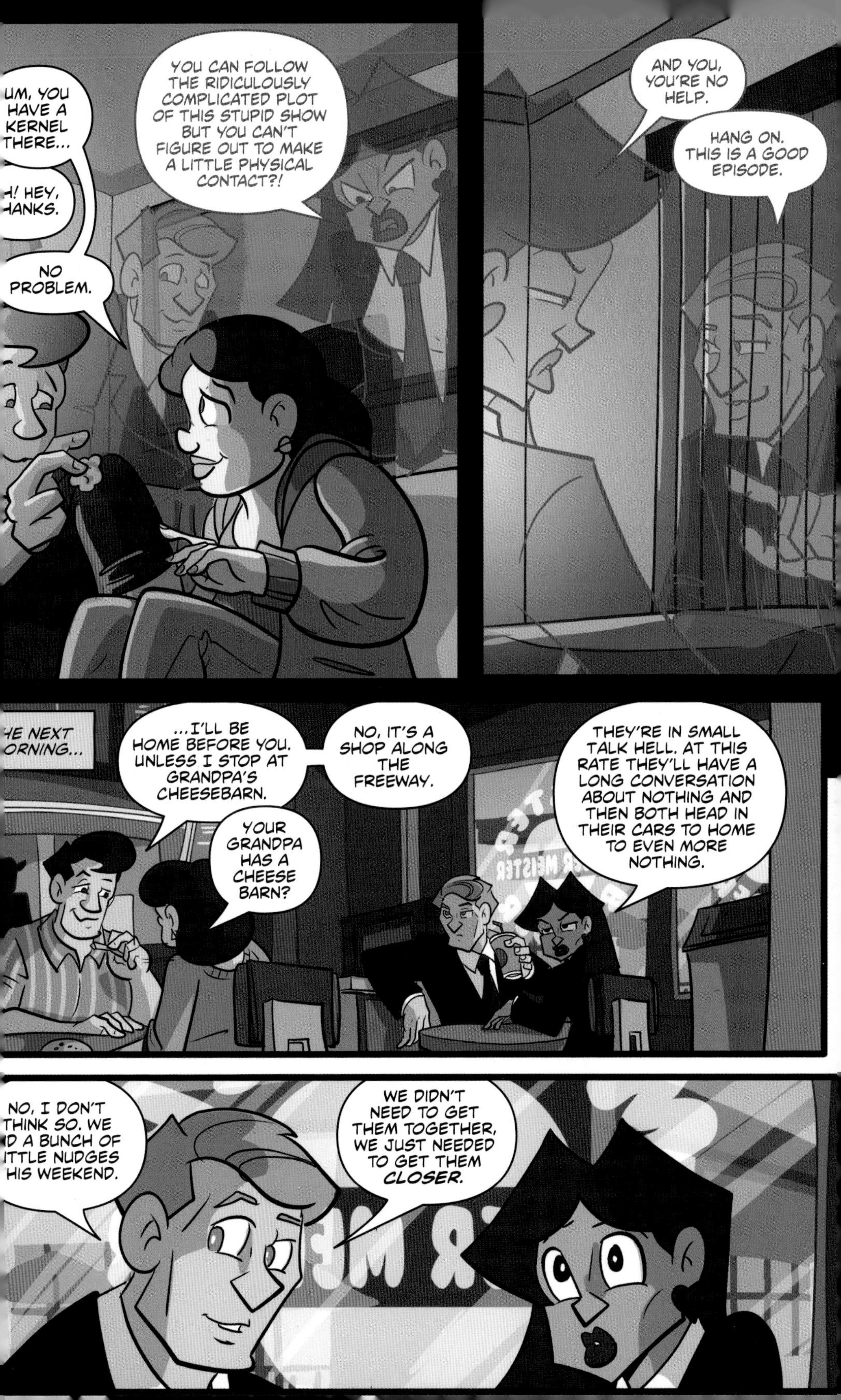
UM, YOU HAVE A KERNEL THERE...
H! HEY, HANKS.
NO PROBLEM.
YOU CAN FOLLOW THE RIDICULOUSLY COMPLICATED PLOT OF THIS STUPID SHOW BUT YOU CAN'T FIGURE OUT TO MAKE A LITTLE PHYSICAL CONTACT?!
AND YOU, YOU'RE NO HELP.
HANG ON. THIS IS A GOOD EPISODE.
HE NEXT ORNING...
...I'LL BE HOME BEFORE YOU. UNLESS I STOP AT GRANDPA'S CHEESEBARN.
YOUR GRANDPA HAS A CHEESE BARN?
NO, IT'S A SHOP ALONG THE FREEWAY.
THEY'RE IN SMALL TALK HELL. AT THIS RATE THEY'LL HAVE A LONG CONVERSATION ABOUT NOTHING AND THEN BOTH HEAD IN THEIR CARS TO HOME TO EVEN MORE NOTHING.
NO, I DON'T THINK SO. WE D A BUNCH OF ITTLE NUDGES HIS WEEKEND.
WE DIDN'T NEED TO GET THEM TOGETHER, WE JUST NEEDED TO GET THEM *CLOSER.*

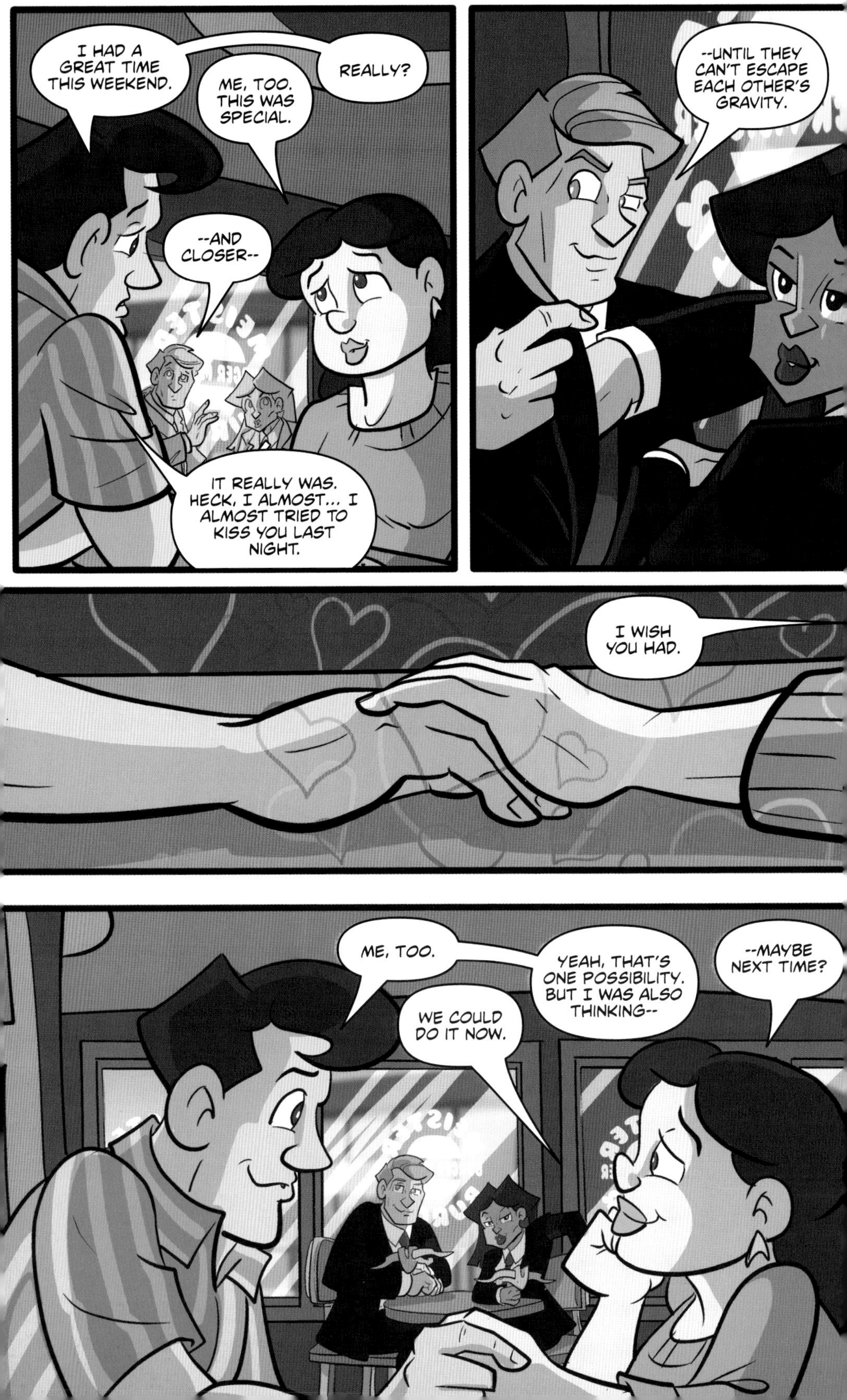
I HAD A GREAT TIME THIS WEEKEND.
REALLY?
ME, TOO. THIS WAS SPECIAL.
--AND CLOSER--
IT REALLY WAS. HECK, I ALMOST... I ALMOST TRIED TO KISS YOU LAST NIGHT.
--UNTIL THEY CAN'T ESCAPE EACH OTHER'S GRAVITY.
I WISH YOU HAD.
ME, TOO.
YEAH, THAT'S ONE POSSIBILITY. BUT I WAS ALSO THINKING--
--MAYBE NEXT TIME?
WE COULD DO IT NOW.

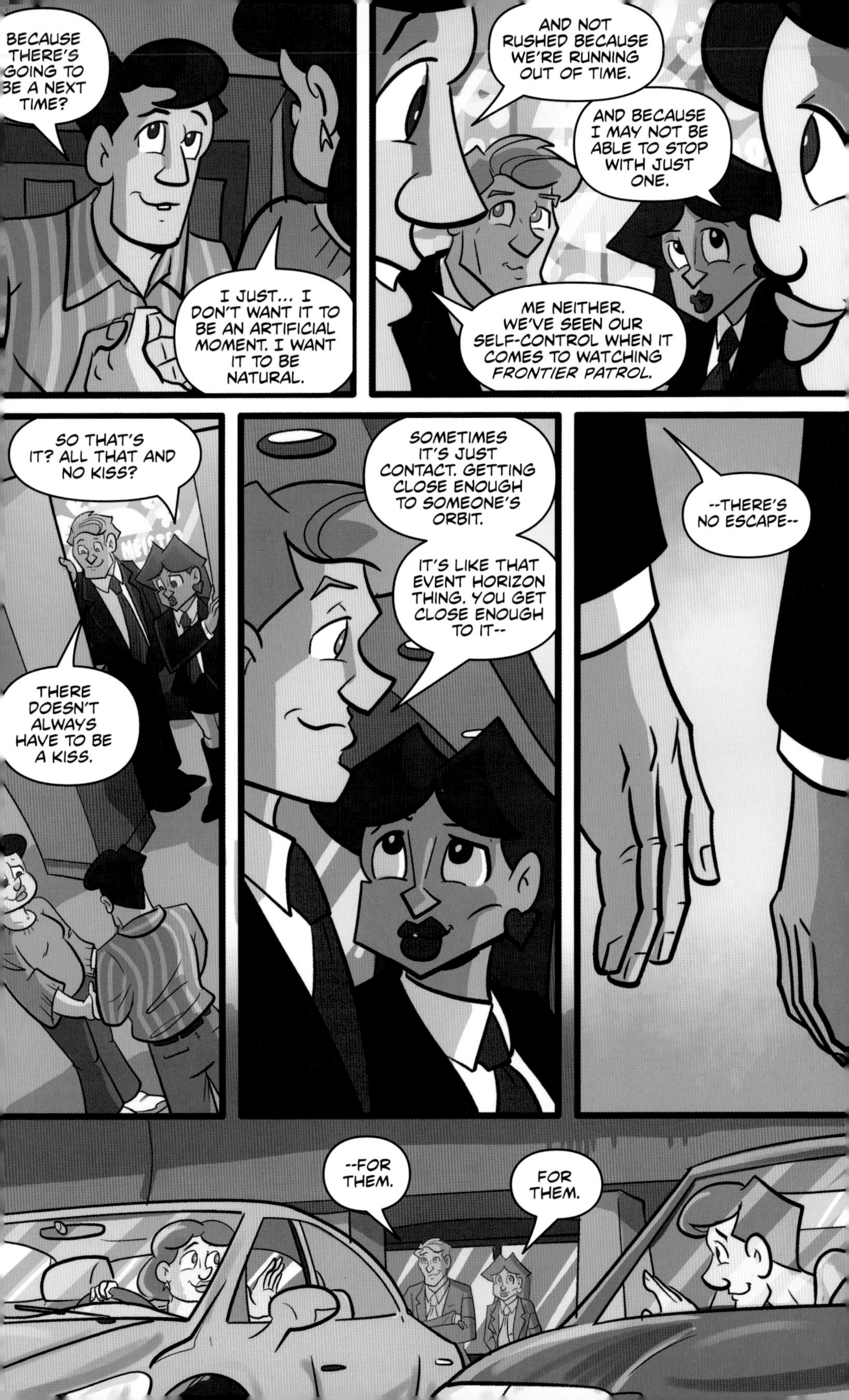
BECAUSE THERE'S GOING TO BE A NEXT TIME?
I JUST... I DON'T WANT IT TO BE AN ARTIFICIAL MOMENT. I WANT IT TO BE NATURAL.
AND NOT RUSHED BECAUSE WE'RE RUNNING OUT OF TIME.
AND BECAUSE I MAY NOT BE ABLE TO STOP WITH JUST ONE.
ME NEITHER. WE'VE SEEN OUR SELF-CONTROL WHEN IT COMES TO WATCHING *FRONTIER PATROL.*
SO THAT'S IT? ALL THAT AND NO KISS?
THERE DOESN'T ALWAYS HAVE TO BE A KISS.
SOMETIMES IT'S JUST CONTACT. GETTING CLOSE ENOUGH TO SOMEONE'S ORBIT.
IT'S LIKE THAT EVENT HORIZON THING. YOU GET CLOSE ENOUGH TO IT--
--THERE'S NO ESCAPE--
--FOR THEM.
FOR THEM.

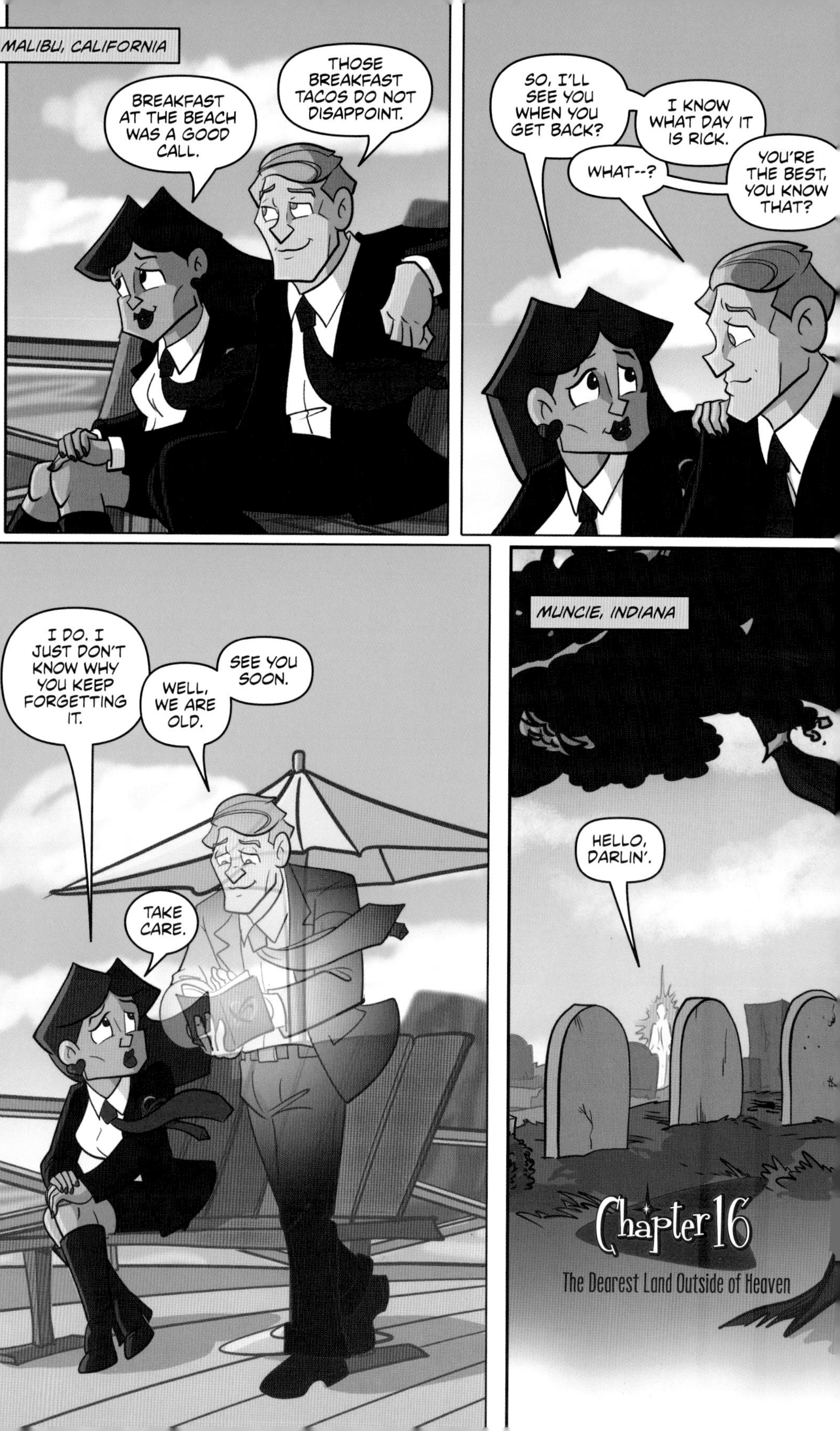
MALIBU, CALIFORNIA
BREAKFAST AT THE BEACH WAS A GOOD CALL.
THOSE BREAKFAST TACOS DO NOT DISAPPOINT.
SO, I'LL SEE YOU WHEN YOU GET BACK?
I KNOW WHAT DAY IT IS RICK.
WHAT--?
YOU'RE THE BEST, YOU KNOW THAT?
I DO. I JUST DON'T KNOW WHY YOU KEEP FORGETTING IT.
WELL, WE ARE OLD.
SEE YOU SOON.
TAKE CARE.
MUNCIE, INDIANA
HELLO, DARLIN'.
Chapter 16
The Dearest Land Outside of Heaven

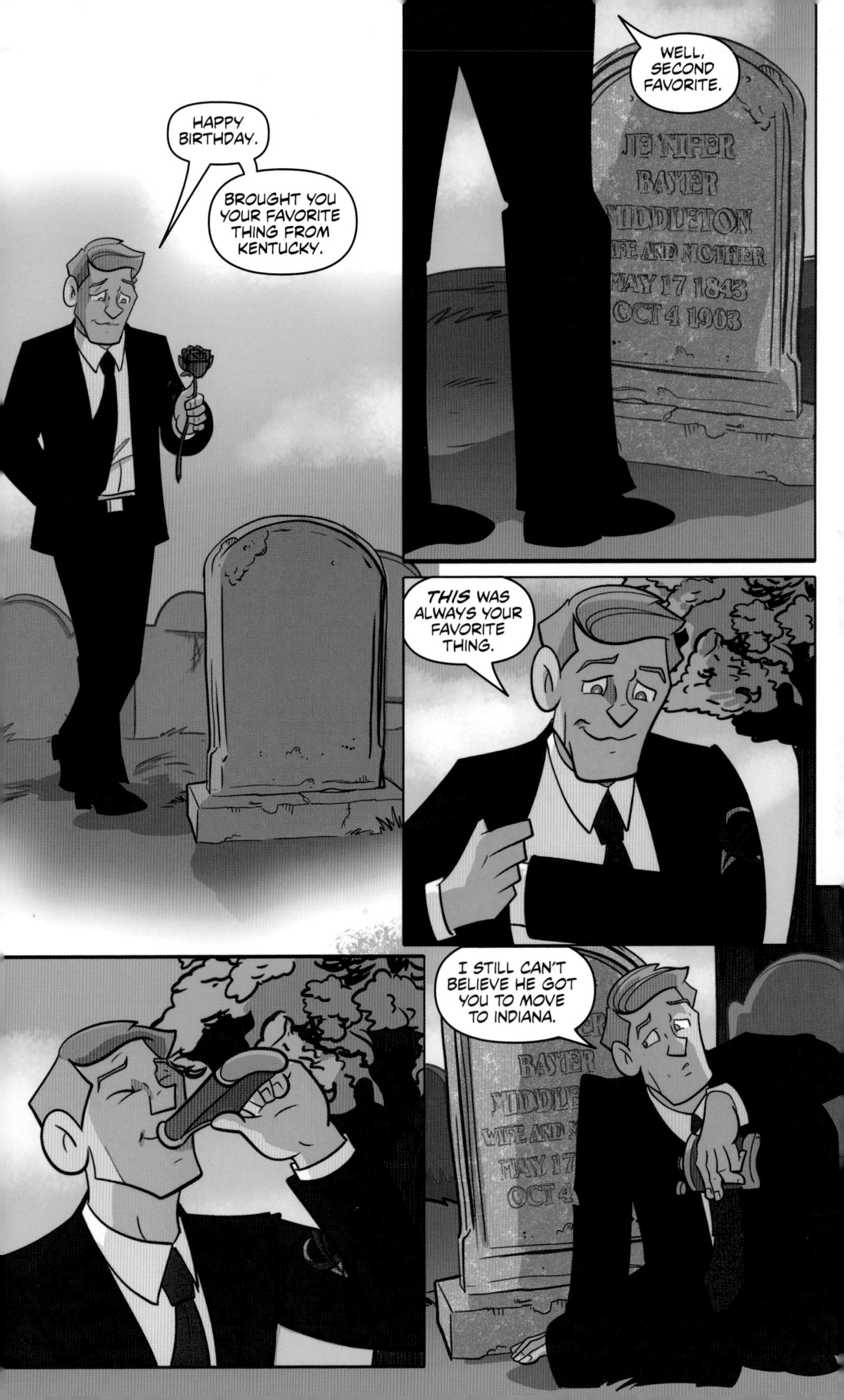
HAPPY BIRTHDAY.
BROUGHT YOU YOUR FAVORITE THING FROM KENTUCKY.
WELL, SECOND FAVORITE.
JENNIFER BAYER MIDDLETON WIFE AND MOTHER MAY 17 1843 OCT 4 1903
THIS WAS ALWAYS YOUR FAVORITE THING.
I STILL CAN'T BELIEVE HE GOT YOU TO MOVE TO INDIANA.

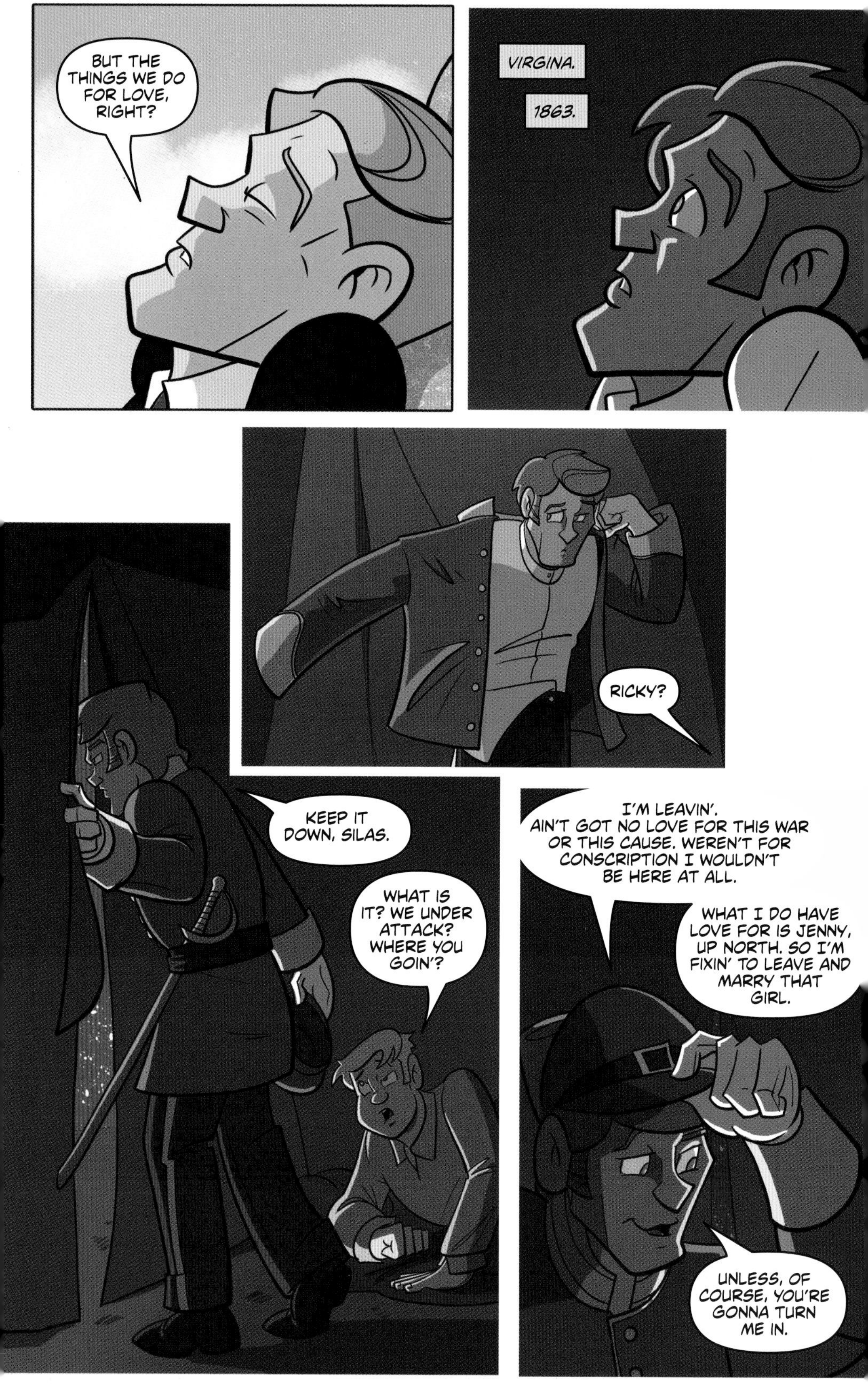
BUT THE THINGS WE DO FOR LOVE, RIGHT?
VIRGINA.
1863.
RICKY?
KEEP IT DOWN, SILAS.
WHAT IS IT? WE UNDER ATTACK? WHERE YOU GOIN'?
I'M LEAVIN'. AIN'T GOT NO LOVE FOR THIS WAR OR THIS CAUSE. WEREN'T FOR CONSCRIPTION I WOULDN'T BE HERE AT ALL.
WHAT I DO HAVE LOVE FOR IS JENNY, UP NORTH. SO I'M FIXIN' TO LEAVE AND MARRY THAT GIRL.
UNLESS, OF COURSE, YOU'RE GONNA TURN ME IN.

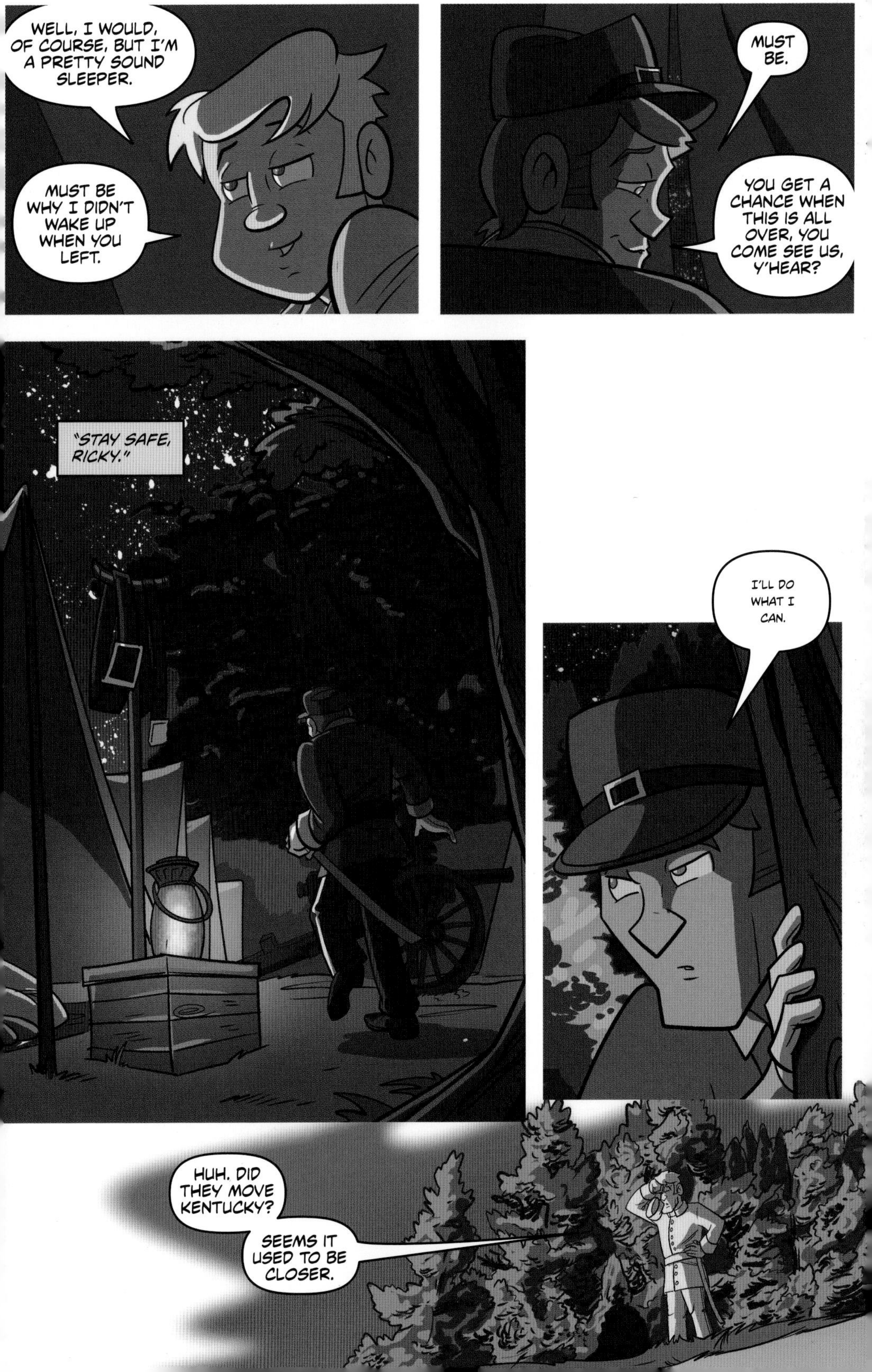
WELL, I WOULD, OF COURSE, BUT I'M A PRETTY SOUND SLEEPER.
MUST BE WHY I DIDN'T WAKE UP WHEN YOU LEFT.
MUST BE.
YOU GET A CHANCE WHEN THIS IS ALL OVER, YOU COME SEE US, Y'HEAR?
"STAY SAFE, RICKY."
I'LL DO WHAT I CAN.
HUH. DID THEY MOVE KENTUCKY?
SEEMS IT USED TO BE CLOSER.

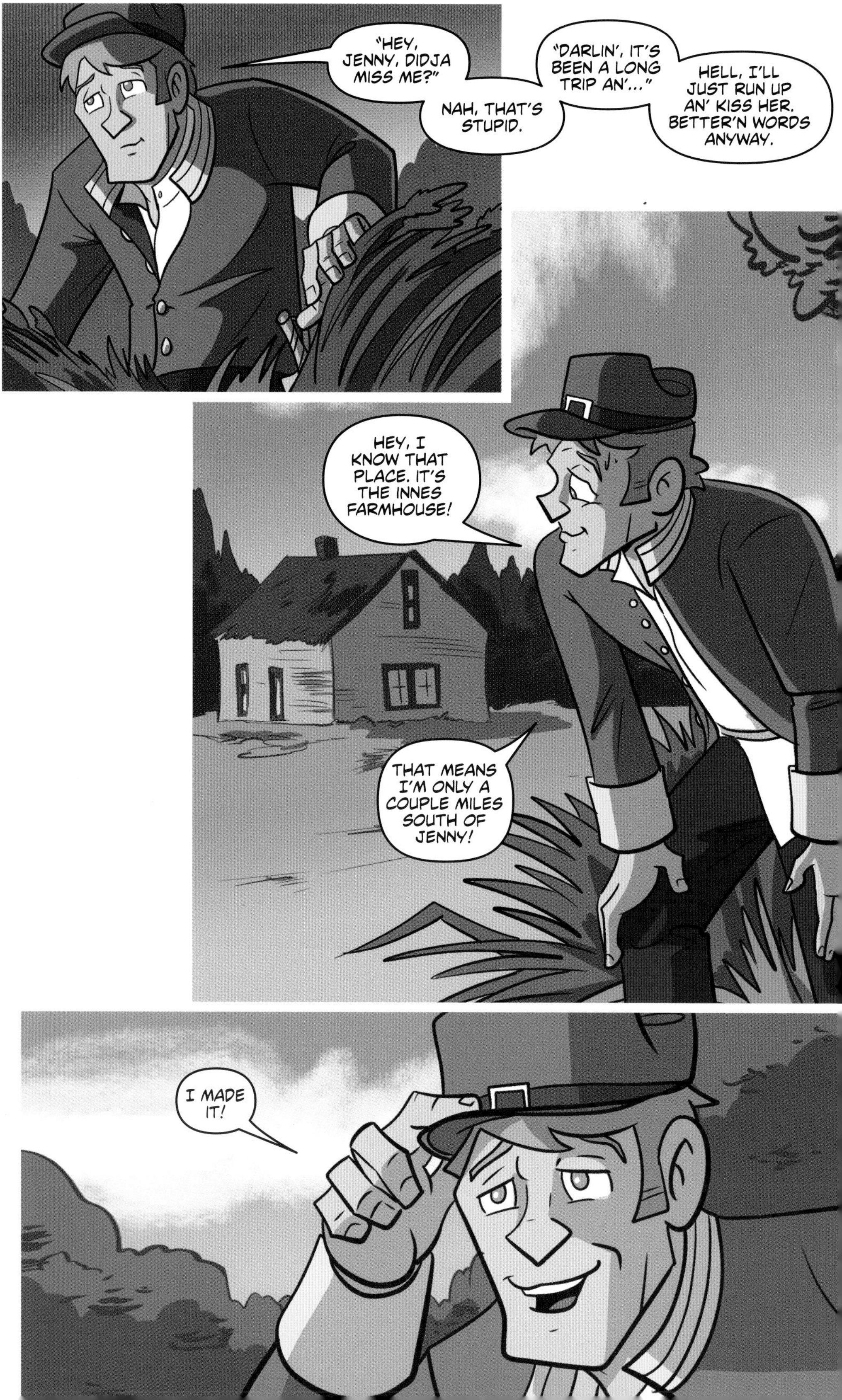
"HEY, JENNY, DIDJA MISS ME?"
NAH, THAT'S STUPID.
"DARLIN', IT'S BEEN A LONG TRIP AN'..."
HELL, I'LL JUST RUN UP AN' KISS HER. BETTER'N WORDS ANYWAY.
HEY, I KNOW THAT PLACE. IT'S THE INNES FARMHOUSE!
THAT MEANS I'M ONLY A COUPLE MILES SOUTH OF JENNY!
I MADE IT!

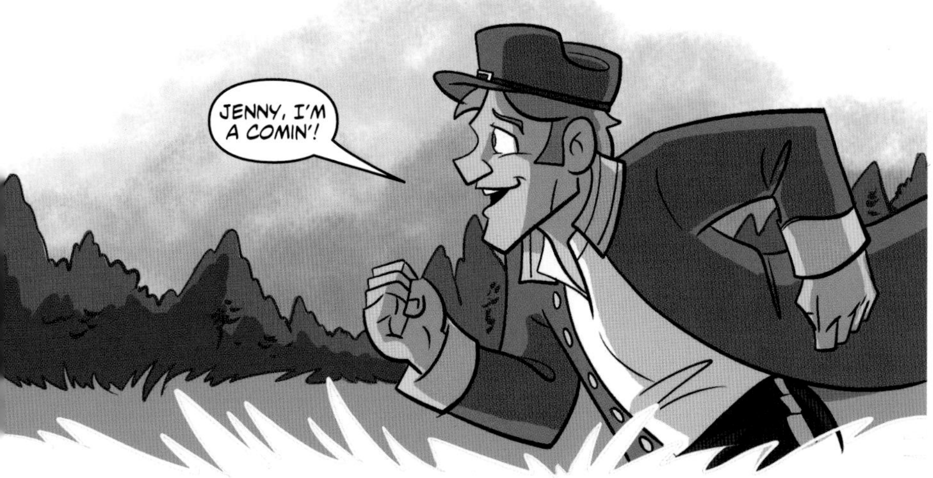
JENNY, I'M A COMIN'!

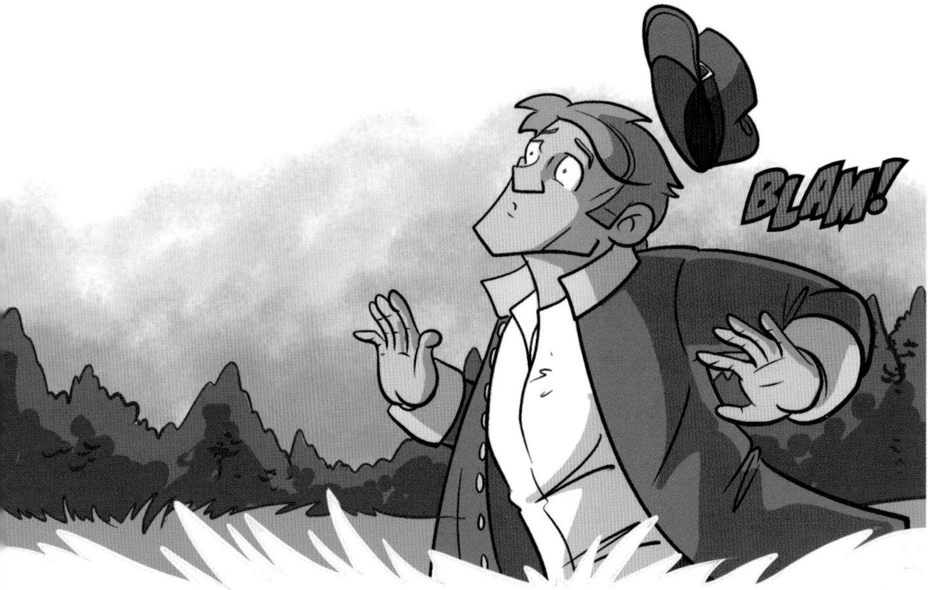
BLAM!

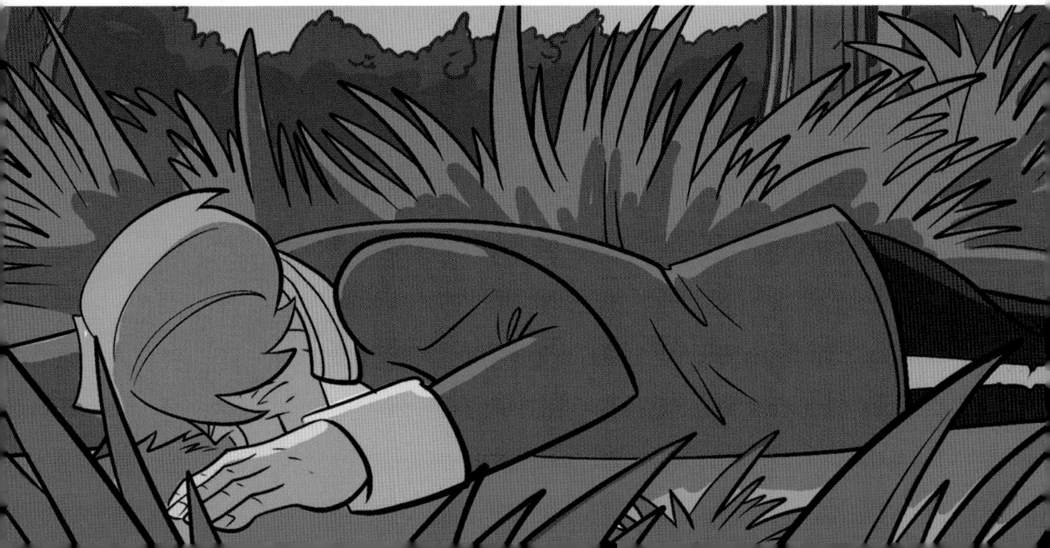

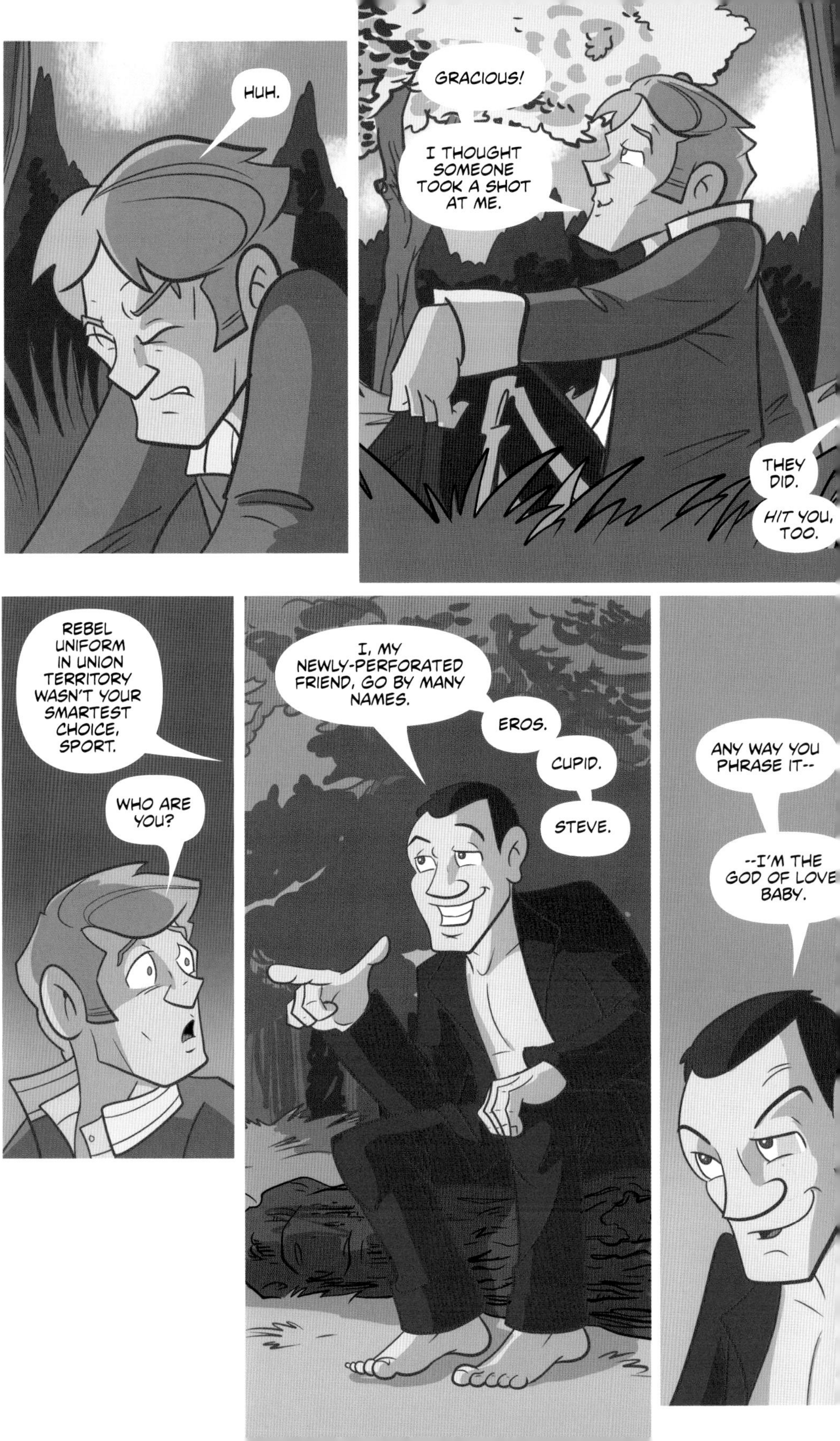
HUH.
GRACIOUS!
I THOUGHT SOMEONE TOOK A SHOT AT ME.
THEY DID.
HIT YOU, TOO.
REBEL UNIFORM IN UNION TERRITORY WASN'T YOUR SMARTEST CHOICE, SPORT.
WHO ARE YOU?
I, MY NEWLY-PERFORATED FRIEND, GO BY MANY NAMES.
EROS.
CUPID.
STEVE.
ANY WAY YOU PHRASE IT--
--I'M THE GOD OF LOVE BABY.

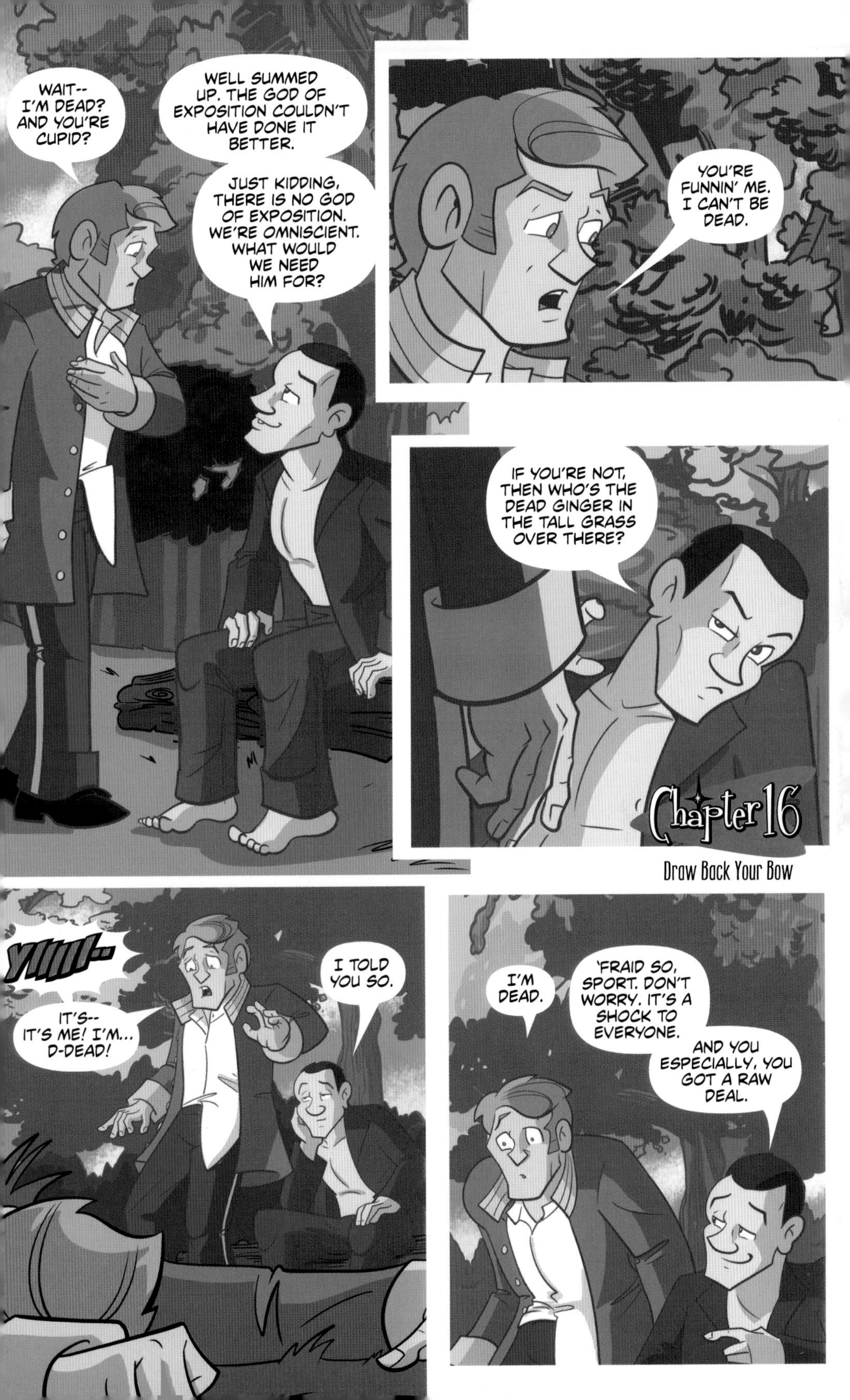
WAIT-- I'M DEAD? AND YOU'RE CUPID?
WELL SUMMED UP. THE GOD OF EXPOSITION COULDN'T HAVE DONE IT BETTER.
JUST KIDDING, THERE IS NO GOD OF EXPOSITION. WE'RE OMNISCIENT. WHAT WOULD WE NEED HIM FOR?
YOU'RE FUNNIN' ME. I CAN'T BE DEAD.
IF YOU'RE NOT, THEN WHO'S THE DEAD GINGER IN THE TALL GRASS OVER THERE?
Chapter 16
Draw Back Your Bow
YIIIII-
IT'S-- IT'S ME! I'M... D-DEAD!
I TOLD YOU SO.
I'M DEAD.
'FRAID SO, SPORT. DON'T WORRY. IT'S A SHOCK TO EVERYONE.
AND YOU ESPECIALLY, YOU GOT A RAW DEAL.

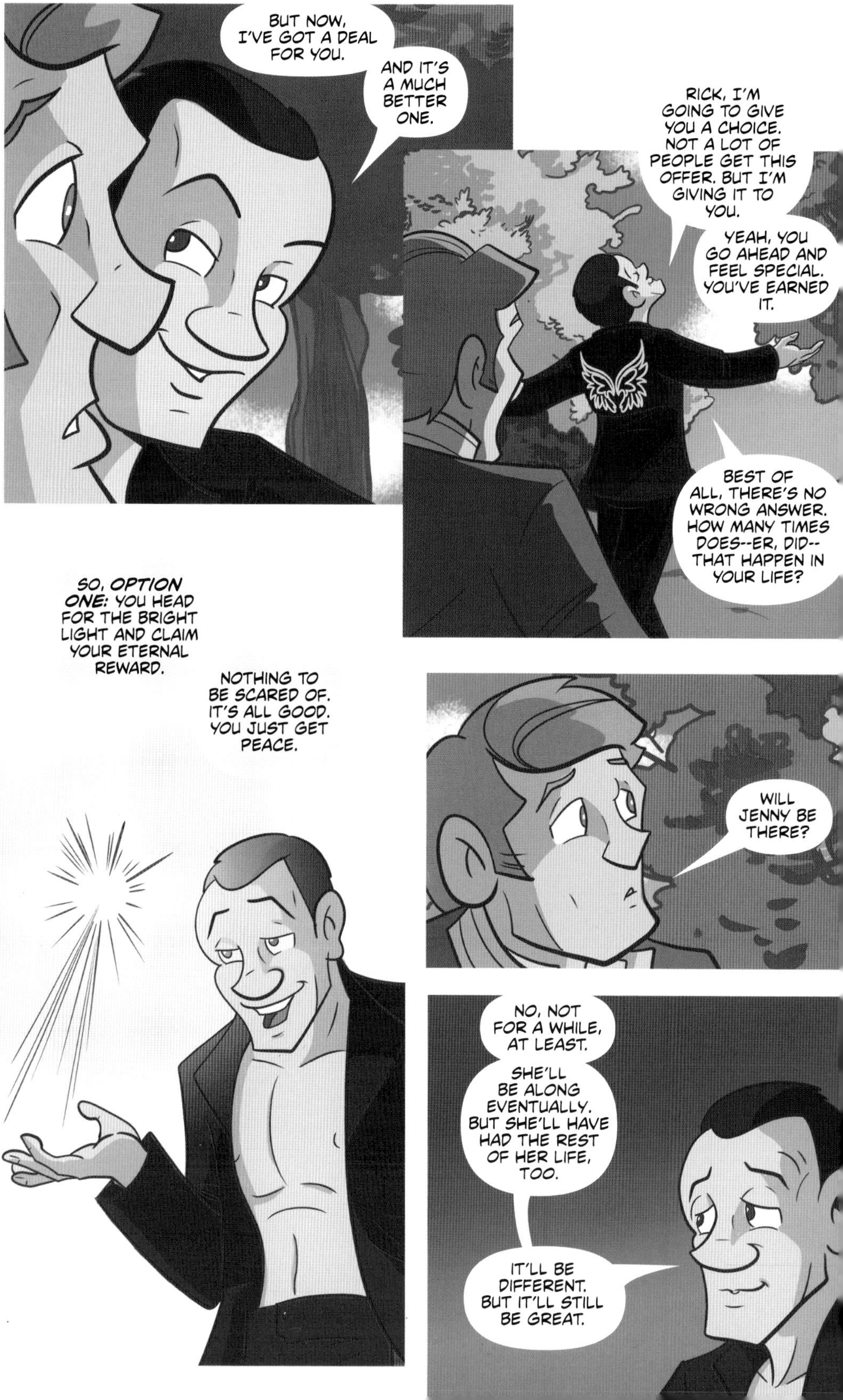
BUT NOW, I'VE GOT A DEAL FOR YOU.
AND IT'S A MUCH BETTER ONE.
RICK, I'M GOING TO GIVE YOU A CHOICE. NOT A LOT OF PEOPLE GET THIS OFFER. BUT I'M GIVING IT TO YOU.
YEAH, YOU GO AHEAD AND FEEL SPECIAL. YOU'VE EARNED IT.
BEST OF ALL, THERE'S NO WRONG ANSWER. HOW MANY TIMES DOES--ER, DID--THAT HAPPEN IN YOUR LIFE?
SO, OPTION ONE: YOU HEAD FOR THE BRIGHT LIGHT AND CLAIM YOUR ETERNAL REWARD.
NOTHING TO BE SCARED OF. IT'S ALL GOOD. YOU JUST GET PEACE.
WILL JENNY BE THERE?
NO, NOT FOR A WHILE, AT LEAST.
SHE'LL BE ALONG EVENTUALLY. BUT SHE'LL HAVE HAD THE REST OF HER LIFE, TOO.
IT'LL BE DIFFERENT. BUT IT'LL STILL BE GREAT.

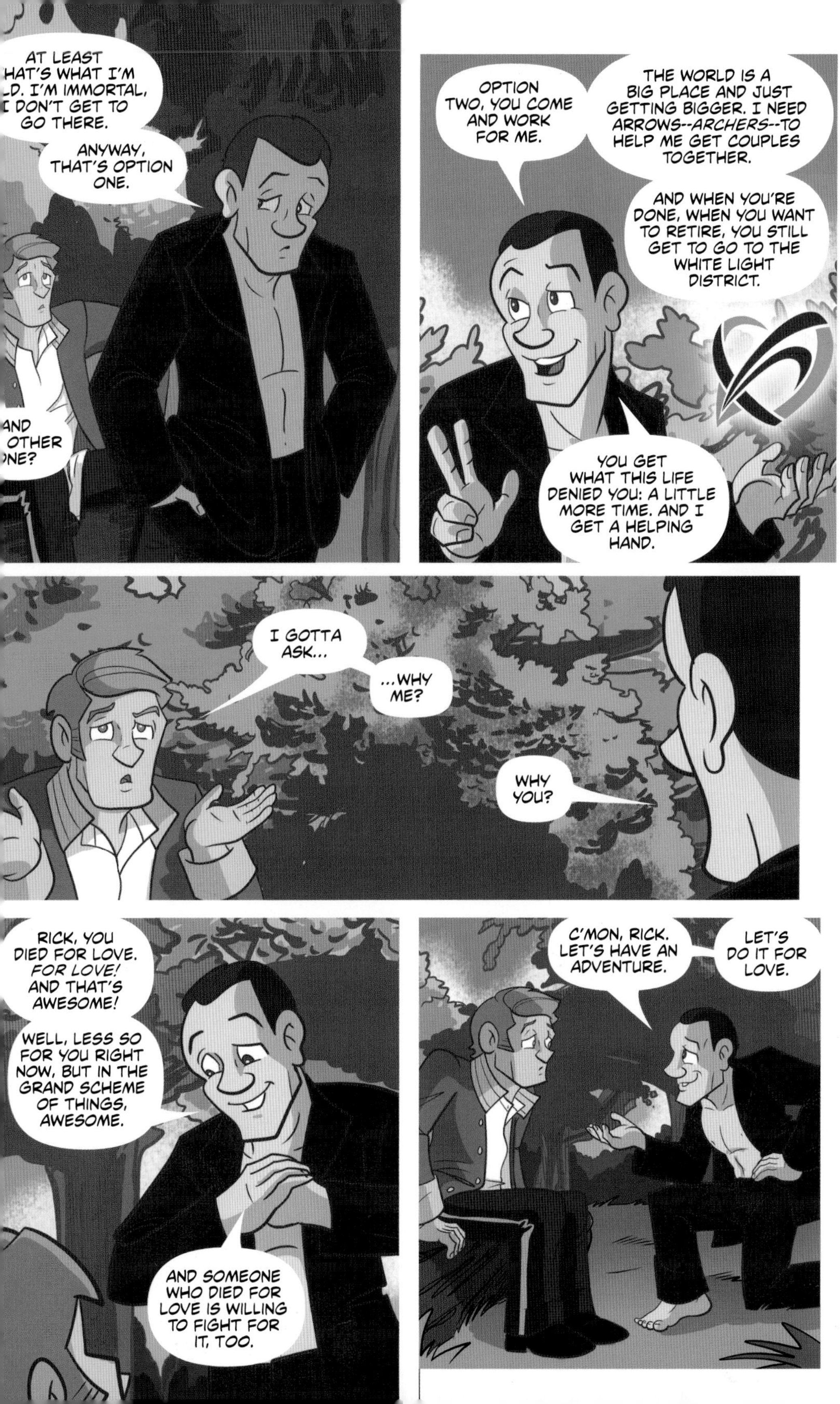
AT LEAST
HAT'S WHAT I'M
LD. I'M IMMORTAL,
I DON'T GET TO
GO THERE.
ANYWAY, THAT'S OPTION ONE.
AND
OTHER
NE?
OPTION TWO, YOU COME AND WORK FOR ME.
THE WORLD IS A BIG PLACE AND JUST GETTING BIGGER. I NEED ARROWS--*ARCHERS*--TO HELP ME GET COUPLES TOGETHER.
AND WHEN YOU'RE DONE, WHEN YOU WANT TO RETIRE, YOU STILL GET TO GO TO THE WHITE LIGHT DISTRICT.
YOU GET WHAT THIS LIFE DENIED YOU: A LITTLE MORE TIME. AND I GET A HELPING HAND.
I GOTTA ASK...
...WHY ME?
WHY YOU?
RICK, YOU DIED FOR LOVE. *FOR LOVE!* AND THAT'S AWESOME!
WELL, LESS SO FOR YOU RIGHT NOW, BUT IN THE GRAND SCHEME OF THINGS, AWESOME.
AND SOMEONE WHO DIED FOR LOVE IS WILLING TO FIGHT FOR IT, TOO.
C'MON, RICK. LET'S HAVE AN ADVENTURE.
LET'S DO IT FOR LOVE.

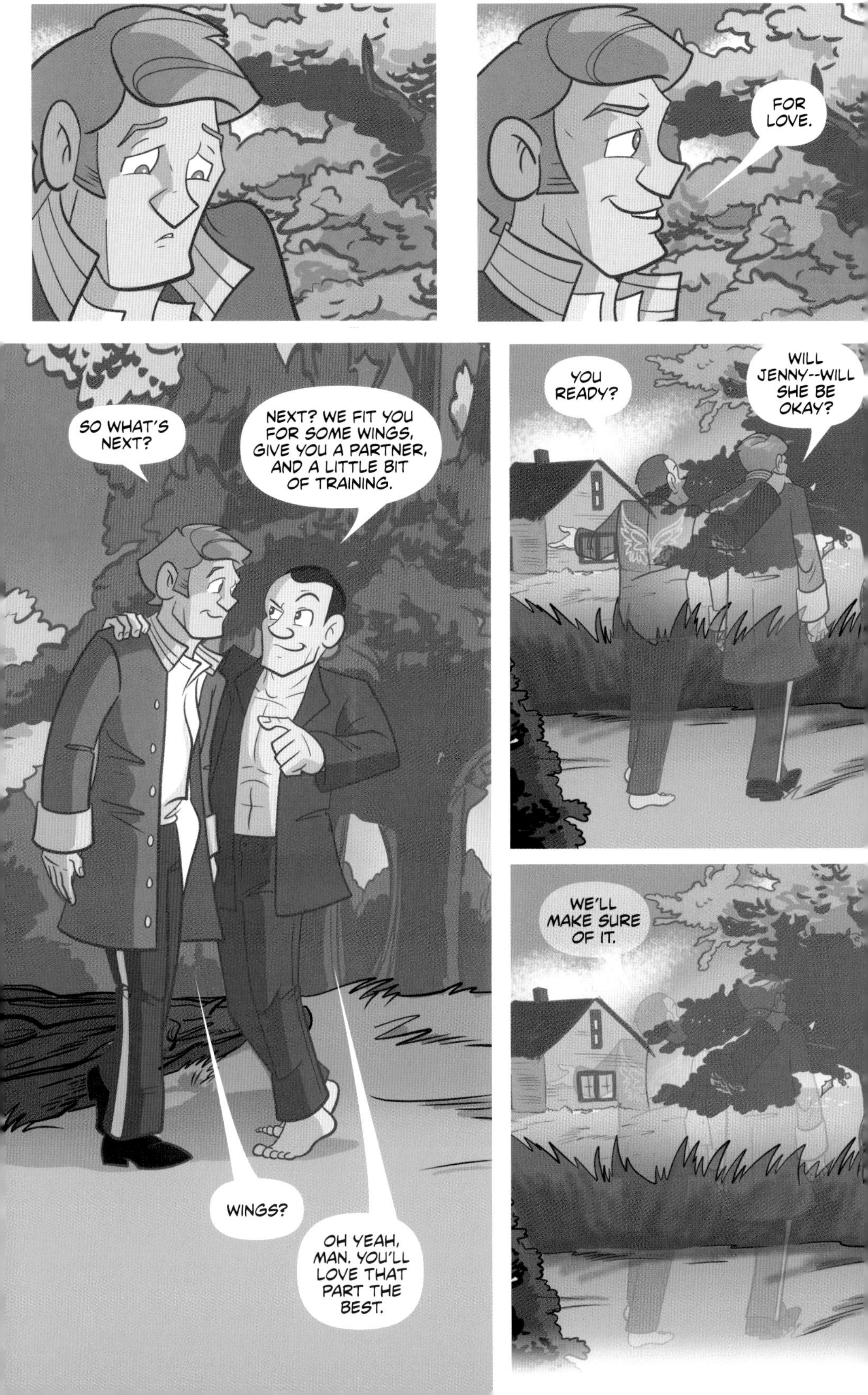
FOR LOVE.
SO WHAT'S NEXT?
NEXT? WE FIT YOU FOR SOME WINGS, GIVE YOU A PARTNER, AND A LITTLE BIT OF TRAINING.
WINGS?
OH YEAH, MAN. YOU'LL LOVE THAT PART THE BEST.
YOU READY?
WILL JENNY--WILL SHE BE OKAY?
WE'LL MAKE SURE OF IT.

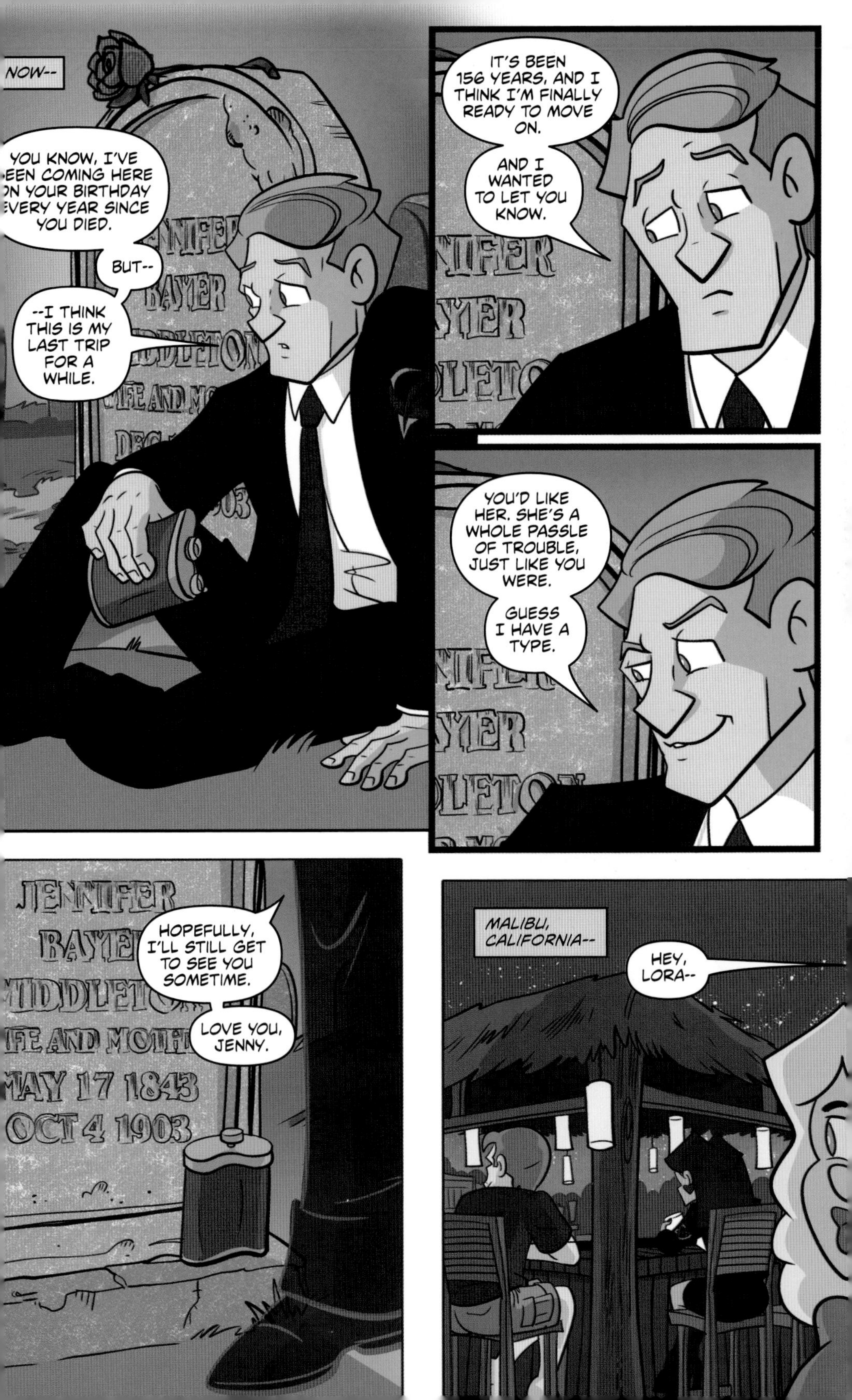
NOW--
YOU KNOW, I'VE EEN COMING HERE ON YOUR BIRTHDAY EVERY YEAR SINCE YOU DIED.
BUT--
--I THINK THIS IS MY LAST TRIP FOR A WHILE.
IT'S BEEN 156 YEARS, AND I THINK I'M FINALLY READY TO MOVE ON.
AND I WANTED TO LET YOU KNOW.
YOU'D LIKE HER. SHE'S A WHOLE PASSLE OF TROUBLE, JUST LIKE YOU WERE.
GUESS I HAVE A TYPE.
JENNIFER
BAYE
IDDLETO
FE AND MOTH
MAY 17 1843
OCT 4 1903
HOPEFULLY, I'LL STILL GET TO SEE YOU SOMETIME.
LOVE YOU, JENNY.
MALIBU, CALIFORNIA--
HEY, LORA--

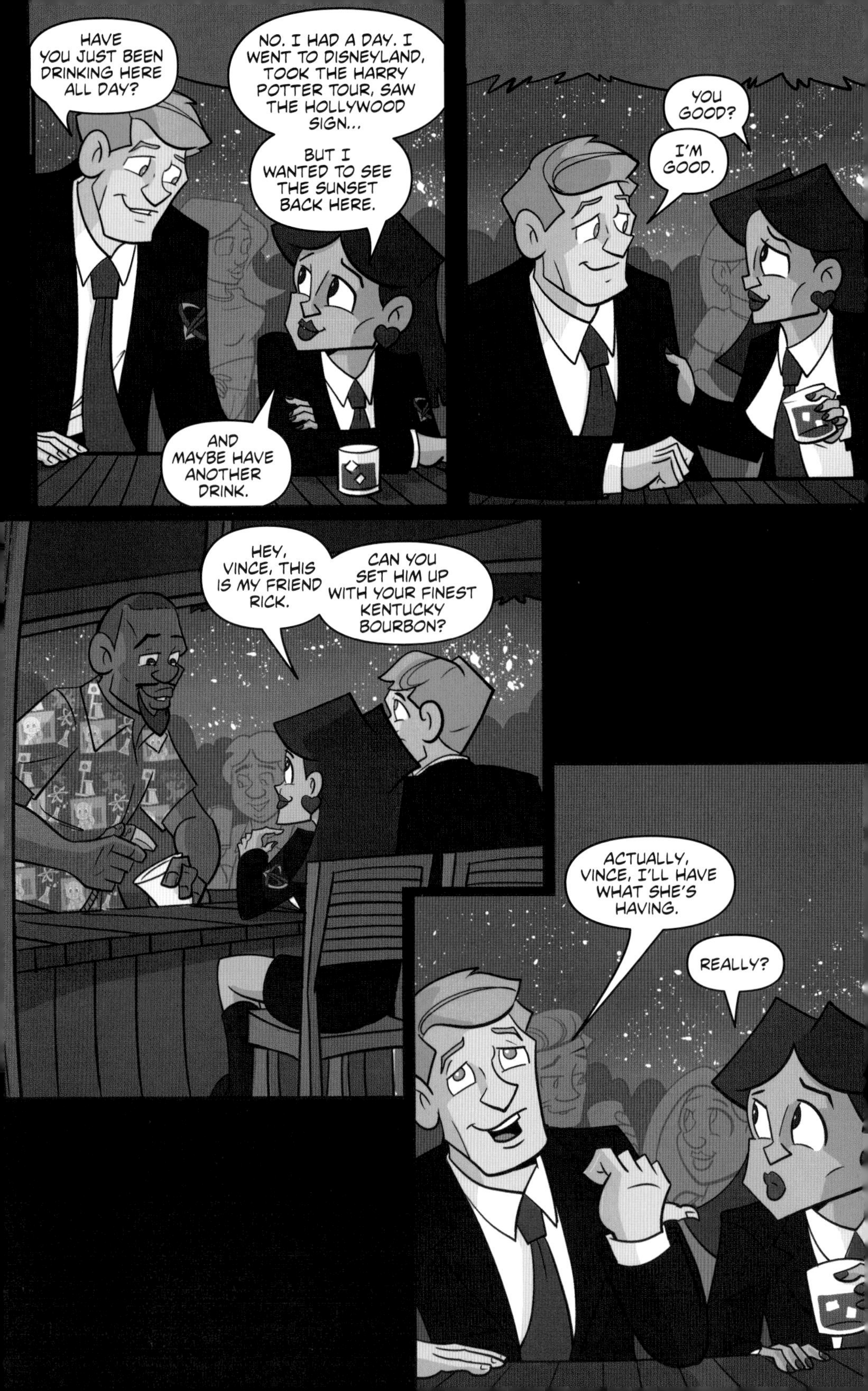
HAVE YOU JUST BEEN DRINKING HERE ALL DAY?
NO. I HAD A DAY. I WENT TO DISNEYLAND, TOOK THE HARRY POTTER TOUR, SAW THE HOLLYWOOD SIGN...
BUT I WANTED TO SEE THE SUNSET BACK HERE.
AND MAYBE HAVE ANOTHER DRINK.
YOU GOOD?
I'M GOOD.
HEY, VINCE, THIS IS MY FRIEND RICK.
CAN YOU SET HIM UP WITH YOUR FINEST KENTUCKY BOURBON?
ACTUALLY, VINCE, I'LL HAVE WHAT SHE'S HAVING.
REALLY?

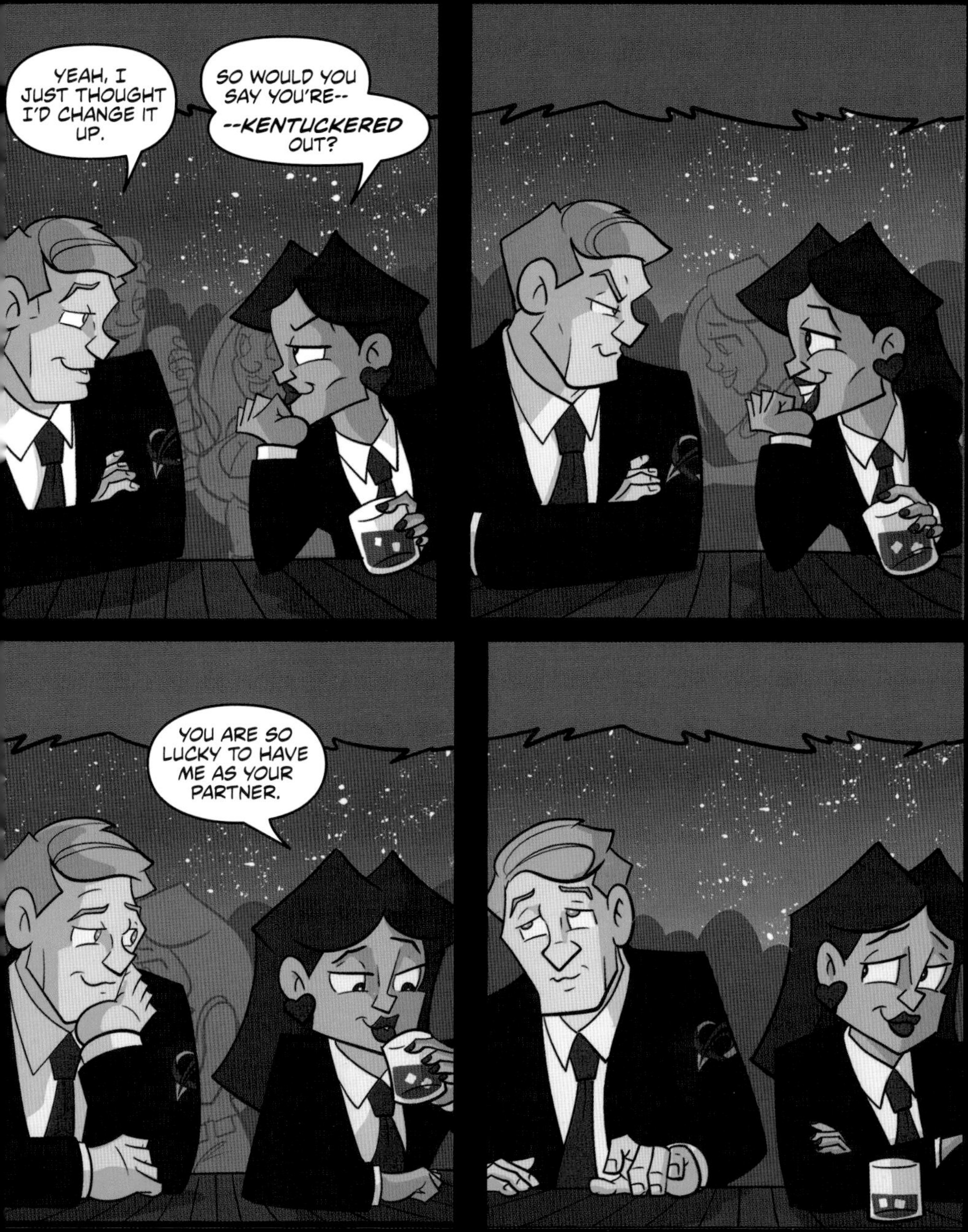
YEAH, I JUST THOUGHT I'D CHANGE IT UP.
SO WOULD YOU SAY YOU'RE--
--**KENTUCKERED** OUT?
YOU ARE SO LUCKY TO HAVE ME AS YOUR PARTNER.

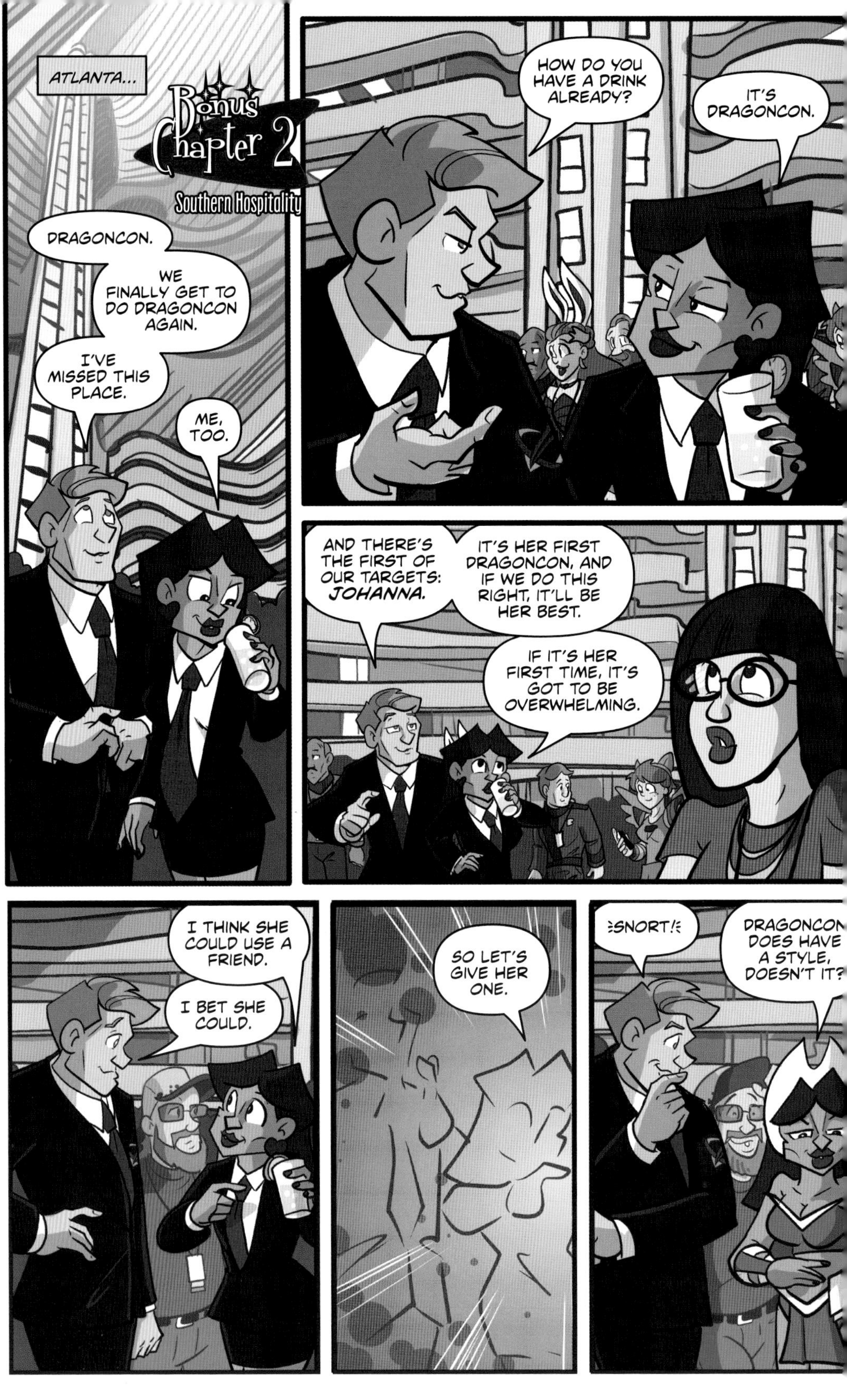
ATLANTA...
Bonus Chapter 2
Southern Hospitality
DRAGONCON.
WE FINALLY GET TO DO DRAGONCON AGAIN.
I'VE MISSED THIS PLACE.
ME, TOO.
HOW DO YOU HAVE A DRINK ALREADY?
IT'S DRAGONCON.
AND THERE'S THE FIRST OF OUR TARGETS: JOHANNA.
IT'S HER FIRST DRAGONCON, AND IF WE DO THIS RIGHT, IT'LL BE HER BEST.
IF IT'S HER FIRST TIME, IT'S GOT TO BE OVERWHELMING.
I THINK SHE COULD USE A FRIEND.
I BET SHE COULD.
SO LET'S GIVE HER ONE.
SNORT!
DRAGONCON DOES HAVE A STYLE, DOESN'T IT?

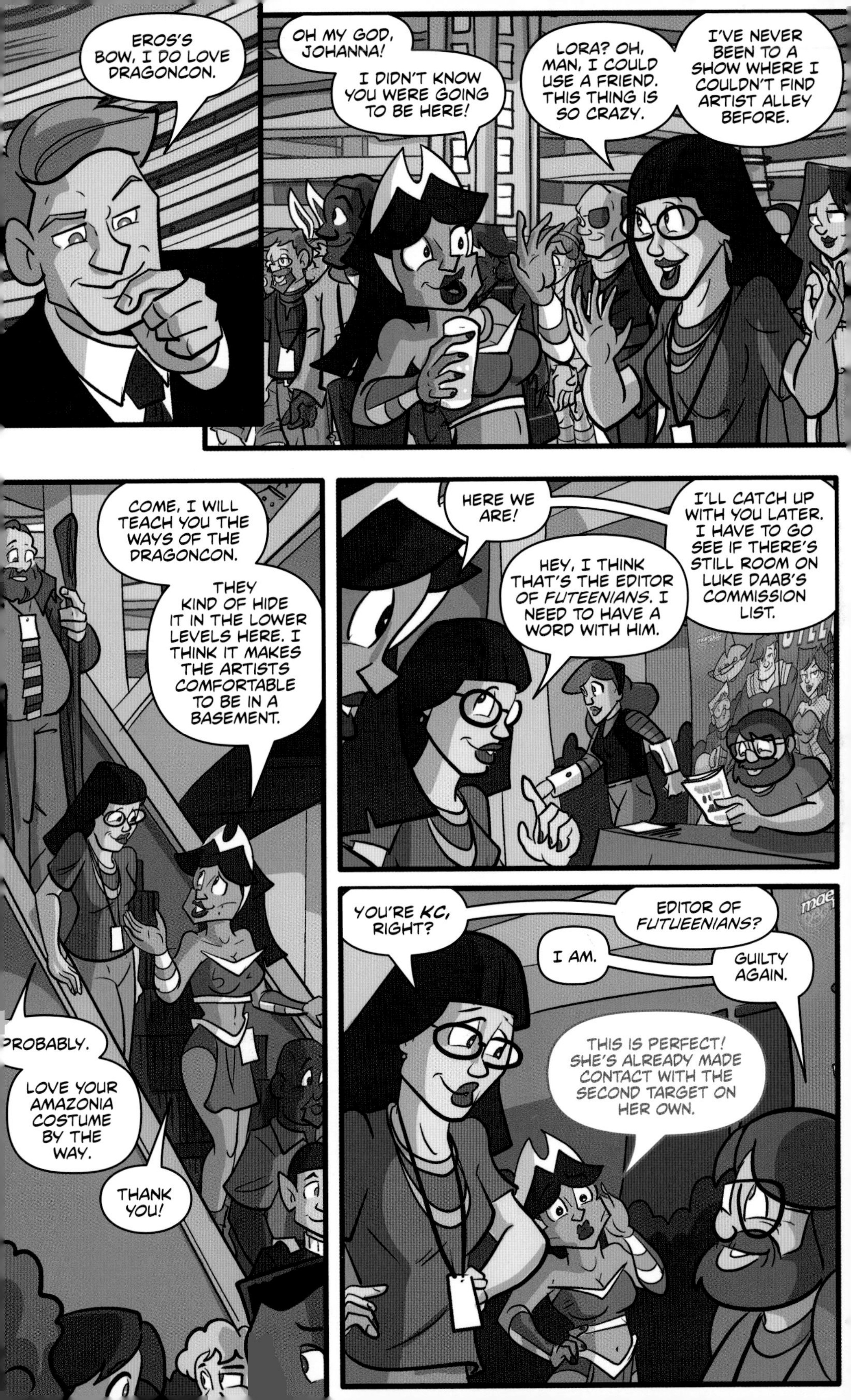
EROS'S BOW, I DO LOVE DRAGONCON.
OH MY GOD, JOHANNA!
I DIDN'T KNOW YOU WERE GOING TO BE HERE!
LORA? OH, MAN, I COULD USE A FRIEND. THIS THING IS SO CRAZY.
I'VE NEVER BEEN TO A SHOW WHERE I COULDN'T FIND ARTIST ALLEY BEFORE.
COME, I WILL TEACH YOU THE WAYS OF THE DRAGONCON.
THEY KIND OF HIDE IT IN THE LOWER LEVELS HERE. I THINK IT MAKES THE ARTISTS COMFORTABLE TO BE IN A BASEMENT.
PROBABLY.
LOVE YOUR AMAZONIA COSTUME BY THE WAY.
THANK YOU!
HERE WE ARE!
I'LL CATCH UP WITH YOU LATER. I HAVE TO GO SEE IF THERE'S STILL ROOM ON LUKE DAAB'S COMMISSION LIST.
HEY, I THINK THAT'S THE EDITOR OF *FUTEENIANS*. I NEED TO HAVE A WORD WITH HIM.
YOU'RE *KC*, RIGHT?
EDITOR OF *FUTUEENIANS*?
I AM.
GUILTY AGAIN.
THIS IS PERFECT! SHE'S ALREADY MADE CONTACT WITH THE SECOND TARGET ON HER OWN.

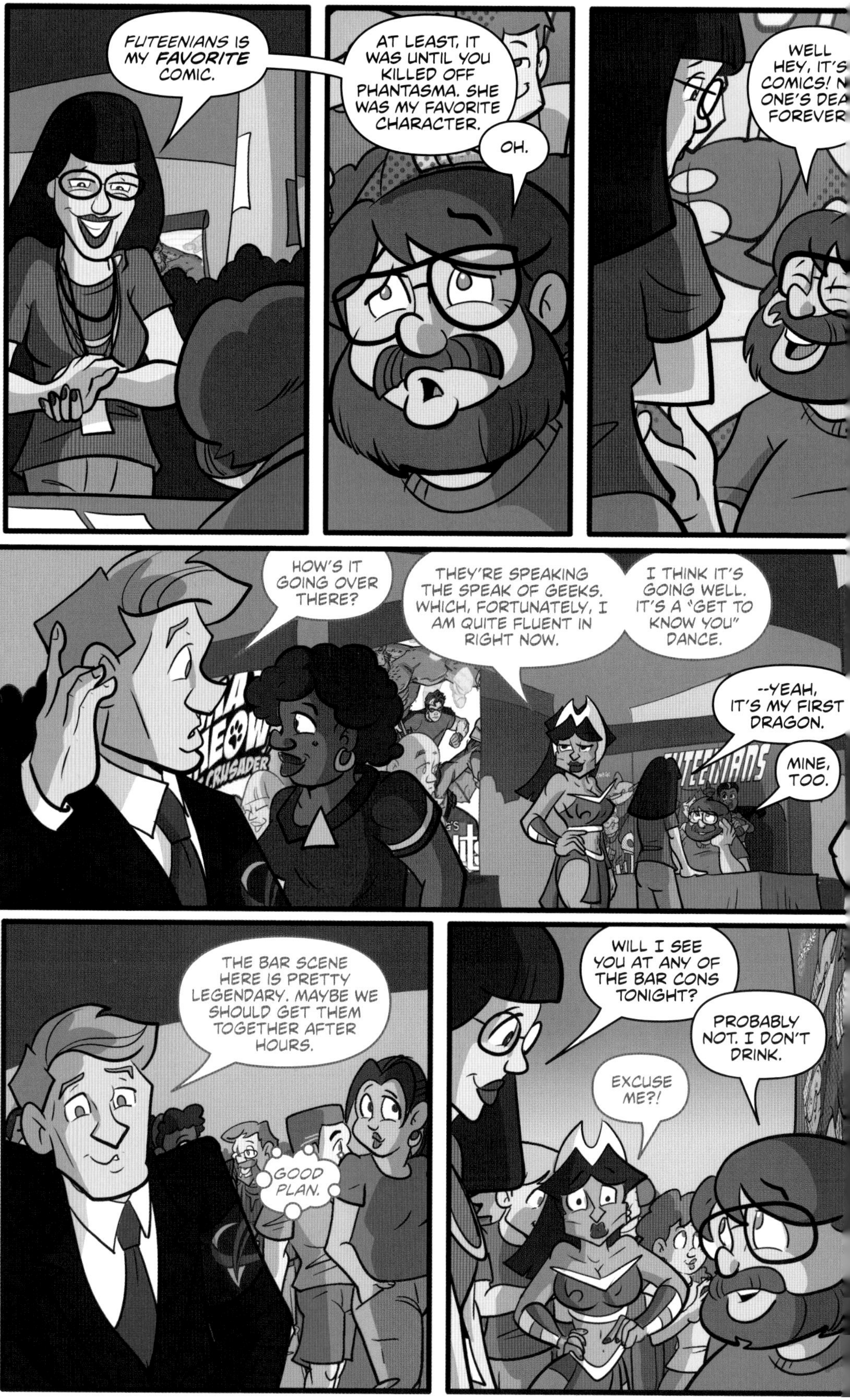
FUTEENIANS IS MY FAVORITE COMIC.
AT LEAST, IT WAS UNTIL YOU KILLED OFF PHANTASMA. SHE WAS MY FAVORITE CHARACTER.
OH.
WELL HEY, IT'S COMICS! N ONE'S DEA FOREVER
HOW'S IT GOING OVER THERE?
THEY'RE SPEAKING THE SPEAK OF GEEKS. WHICH, FORTUNATELY, I AM QUITE FLUENT IN RIGHT NOW.
I THINK IT'S GOING WELL. IT'S A "GET TO KNOW YOU" DANCE.
--YEAH, IT'S MY FIRST DRAGON.
MINE, TOO.
THE BAR SCENE HERE IS PRETTY LEGENDARY. MAYBE WE SHOULD GET THEM TOGETHER AFTER HOURS.
GOOD PLAN.
WILL I SEE YOU AT ANY OF THE BAR CONS TONIGHT?
PROBABLY NOT. I DON'T DRINK.
EXCUSE ME?!

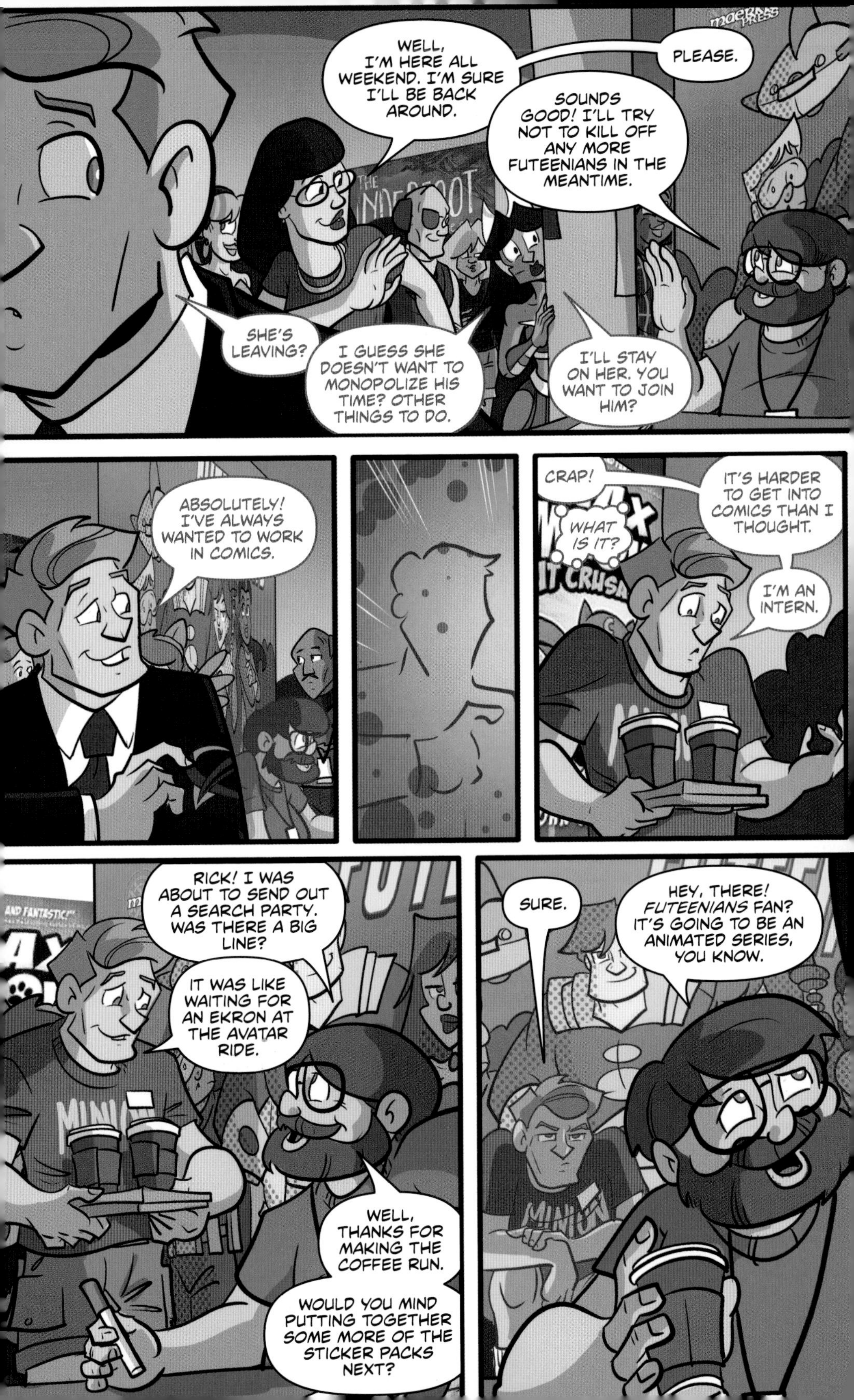
maerkle PRESS
WELL, I'M HERE ALL WEEKEND. I'M SURE I'LL BE BACK AROUND.
PLEASE.
SOUNDS GOOD! I'LL TRY NOT TO KILL OFF ANY MORE FUTEENIANS IN THE MEANTIME.
SHE'S LEAVING?
I GUESS SHE DOESN'T WANT TO MONOPOLIZE HIS TIME? OTHER THINGS TO DO.
I'LL STAY ON HER. YOU WANT TO JOIN HIM?
ABSOLUTELY! I'VE ALWAYS WANTED TO WORK IN COMICS.
CRAP!
WHAT IS IT?
IT'S HARDER TO GET INTO COMICS THAN I THOUGHT.
I'M AN INTERN.
RICK! I WAS ABOUT TO SEND OUT A SEARCH PARTY. WAS THERE A BIG LINE?
IT WAS LIKE WAITING FOR AN EKRON AT THE AVATAR RIDE.
WELL, THANKS FOR MAKING THE COFFEE RUN.
WOULD YOU MIND PUTTING TOGETHER SOME MORE OF THE STICKER PACKS NEXT?
SURE.
HEY, THERE! FUTEENIANS FAN? IT'S GOING TO BE AN ANIMATED SERIES, YOU KNOW.

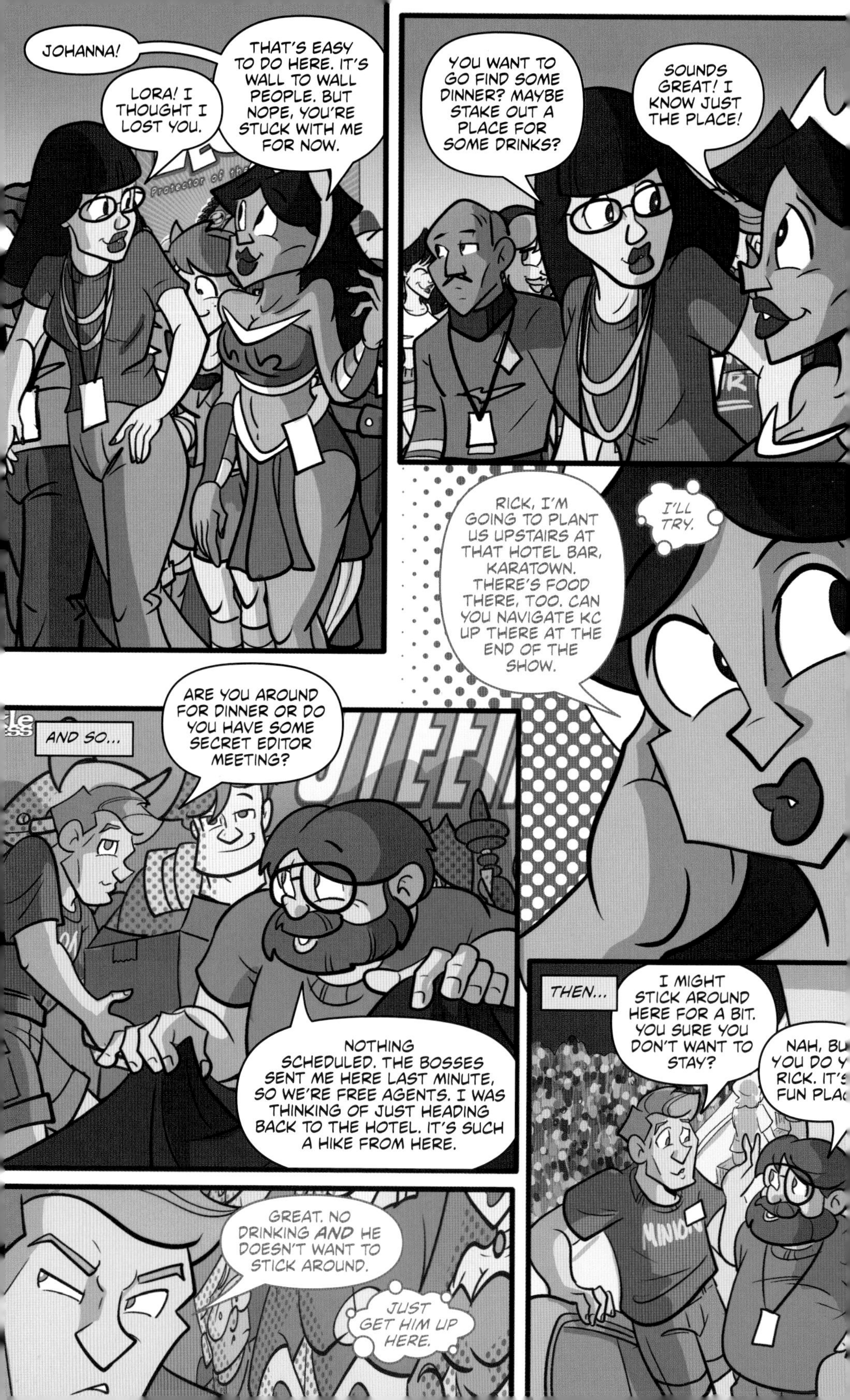
JOHANNA!
LORA! I THOUGHT I LOST YOU.
THAT'S EASY TO DO HERE. IT'S WALL TO WALL PEOPLE. BUT NOPE, YOU'RE STUCK WITH ME FOR NOW.
YOU WANT TO GO FIND SOME DINNER? MAYBE STAKE OUT A PLACE FOR SOME DRINKS?
SOUNDS GREAT! I KNOW JUST THE PLACE!
RICK, I'M GOING TO PLANT US UPSTAIRS AT THAT HOTEL BAR, KARATOWN. THERE'S FOOD THERE, TOO. CAN YOU NAVIGATE KC UP THERE AT THE END OF THE SHOW.
I'LL TRY.
AND SO...
ARE YOU AROUND FOR DINNER OR DO YOU HAVE SOME SECRET EDITOR MEETING?
NOTHING SCHEDULED. THE BOSSES SENT ME HERE LAST MINUTE, SO WE'RE FREE AGENTS. I WAS THINKING OF JUST HEADING BACK TO THE HOTEL. IT'S SUCH A HIKE FROM HERE.
GREAT. NO DRINKING AND HE DOESN'T WANT TO STICK AROUND.
JUST GET HIM UP HERE.
THEN...
I MIGHT STICK AROUND HERE FOR A BIT. YOU SURE YOU DON'T WANT TO STAY?
MINION

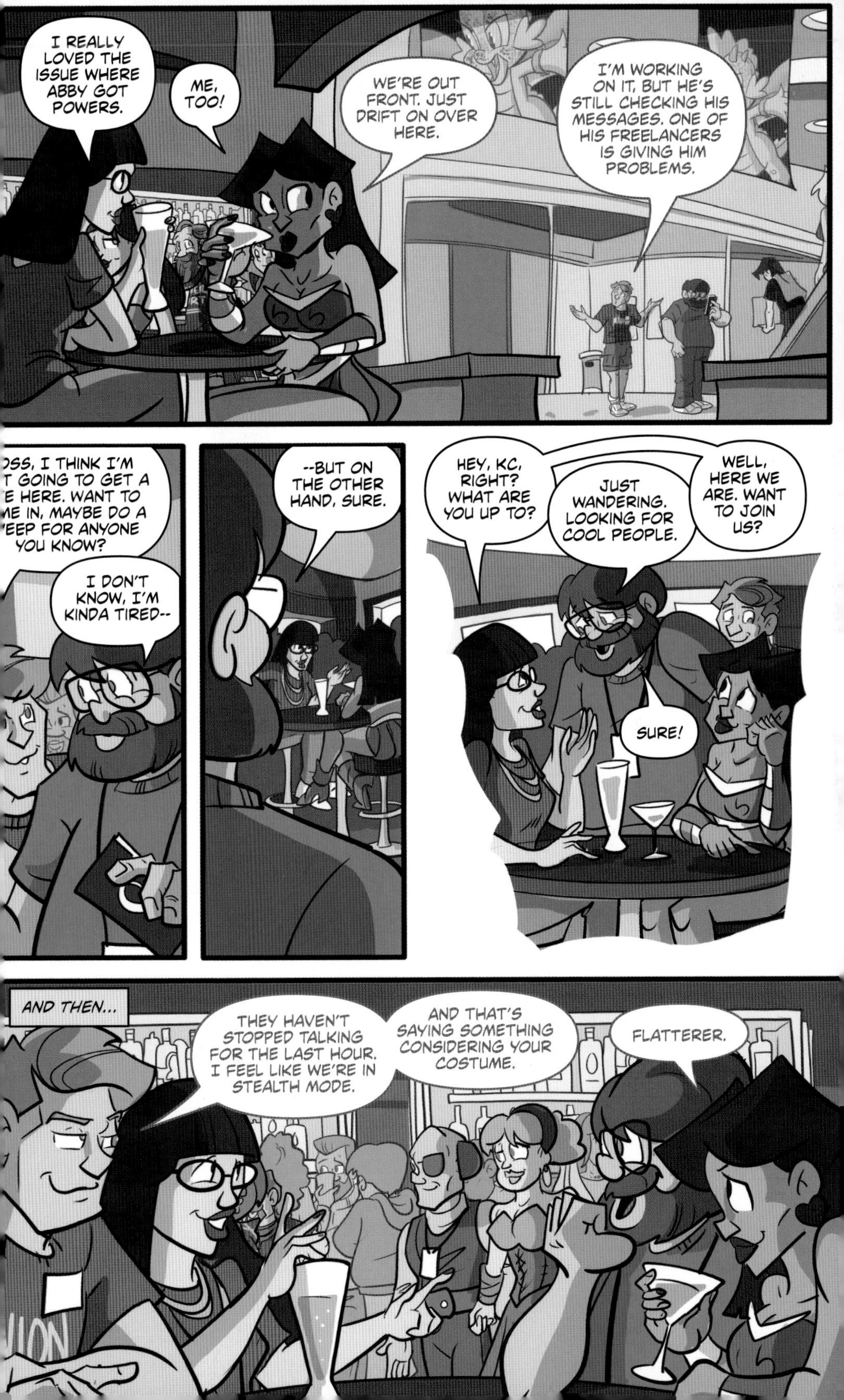
I REALLY LOVED THE ISSUE WHERE ABBY GOT POWERS.
ME, TOO!
WE'RE OUT FRONT. JUST DRIFT ON OVER HERE.
I'M WORKING ON IT, BUT HE'S STILL CHECKING HIS MESSAGES. ONE OF HIS FREELANCERS IS GIVING HIM PROBLEMS.
OSS, I THINK I'M T GOING TO GET A E HERE. WANT TO ME IN, MAYBE DO A EEP FOR ANYONE YOU KNOW?
I DON'T KNOW, I'M KINDA TIRED--
--BUT ON THE OTHER HAND, SURE.
HEY, KC, RIGHT? WHAT ARE YOU UP TO?
JUST WANDERING. LOOKING FOR COOL PEOPLE.
WELL, HERE WE ARE. WANT TO JOIN US?
SURE!
AND THEN...
THEY HAVEN'T STOPPED TALKING FOR THE LAST HOUR. I FEEL LIKE WE'RE IN STEALTH MODE.
AND THAT'S SAYING SOMETHING CONSIDERING YOUR COSTUME.
FLATTERER.

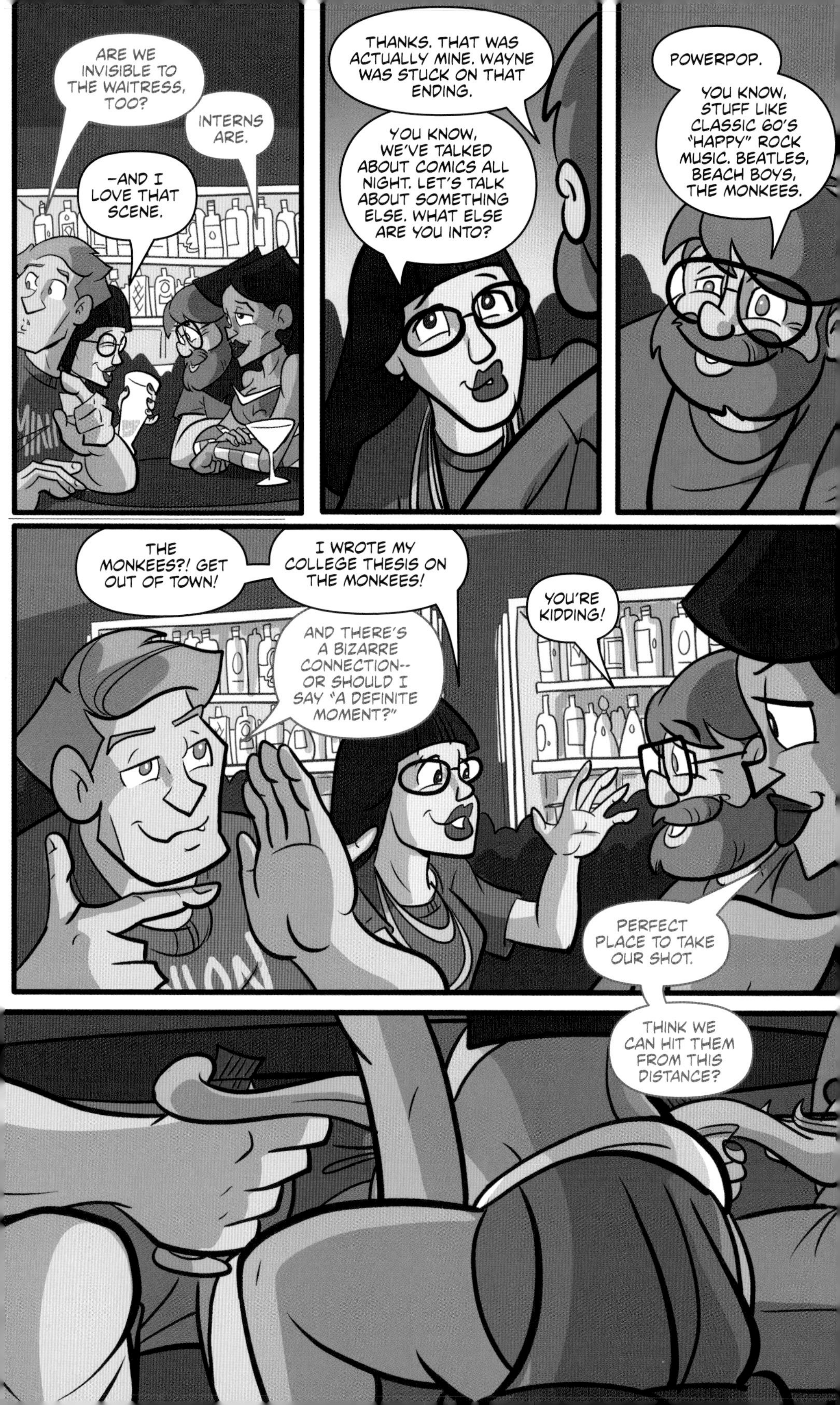
ARE WE INVISIBLE TO THE WAITRESS, TOO?
INTERNS ARE.
–AND I LOVE THAT SCENE.
THANKS. THAT WAS ACTUALLY MINE. WAYNE WAS STUCK ON THAT ENDING.
YOU KNOW, WE'VE TALKED ABOUT COMICS ALL NIGHT. LET'S TALK ABOUT SOMETHING ELSE. WHAT ELSE ARE YOU INTO?
POWERPOP.
YOU KNOW, STUFF LIKE CLASSIC 60'S "HAPPY" ROCK MUSIC. BEATLES, BEACH BOYS, THE MONKEES.
THE MONKEES?! GET OUT OF TOWN!
I WROTE MY COLLEGE THESIS ON THE MONKEES!
AND THERE'S A BIZARRE CONNECTION-- OR SHOULD I SAY "A DEFINITE MOMENT?"
YOU'RE KIDDING!
PERFECT PLACE TO TAKE OUR SHOT.
THINK WE CAN HIT THEM FROM THIS DISTANCE?

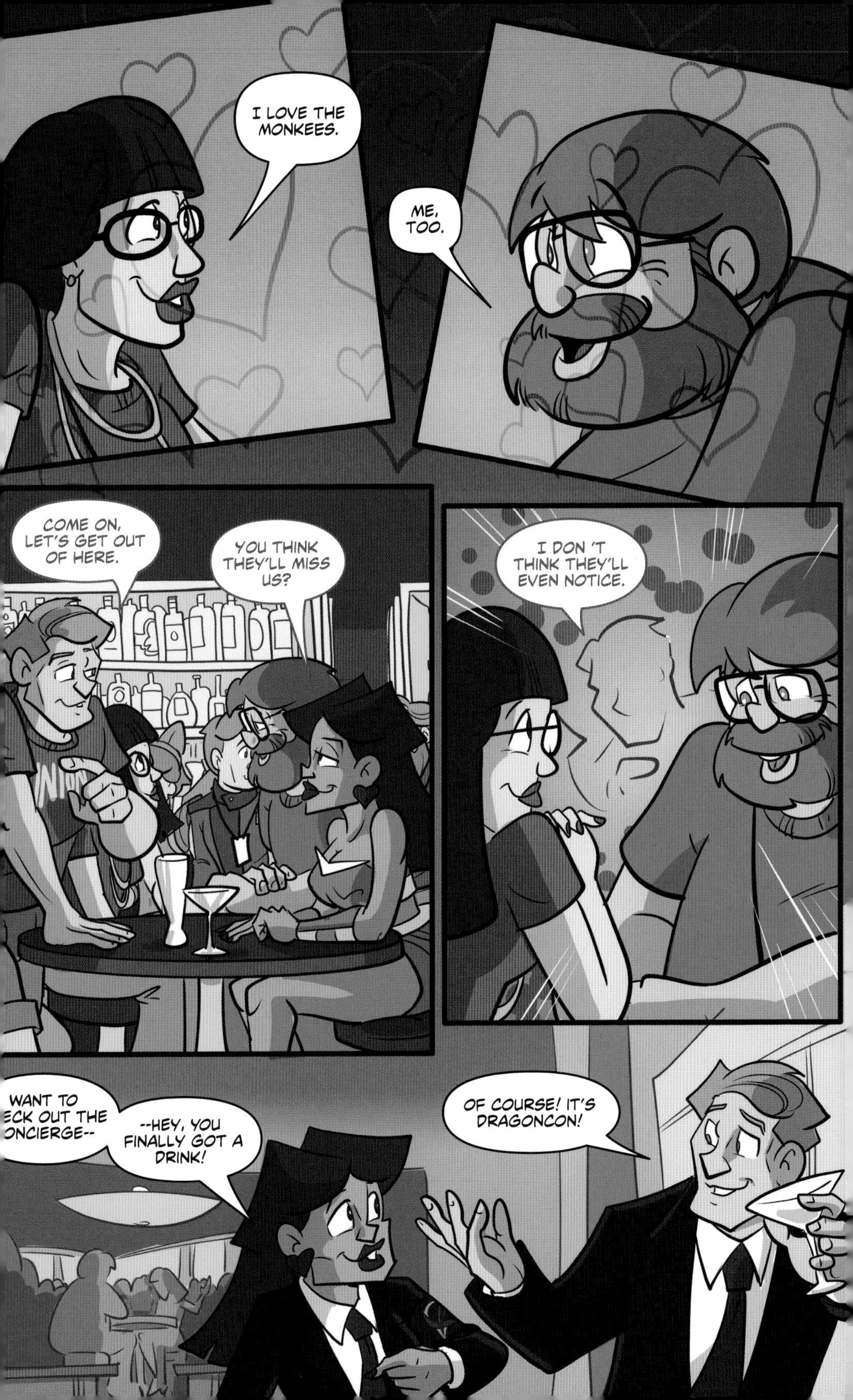
I LOVE THE MONKEES.
ME, TOO.
COME ON, LET'S GET OUT OF HERE.
YOU THINK THEY'LL MISS US?
I DON 'T THINK THEY'LL EVEN NOTICE.
WANT TO
ECK OUT THE
ONCIERGE--
--HEY, YOU FINALLY GOT A DRINK!
OF COURSE! IT'S DRAGONCON!

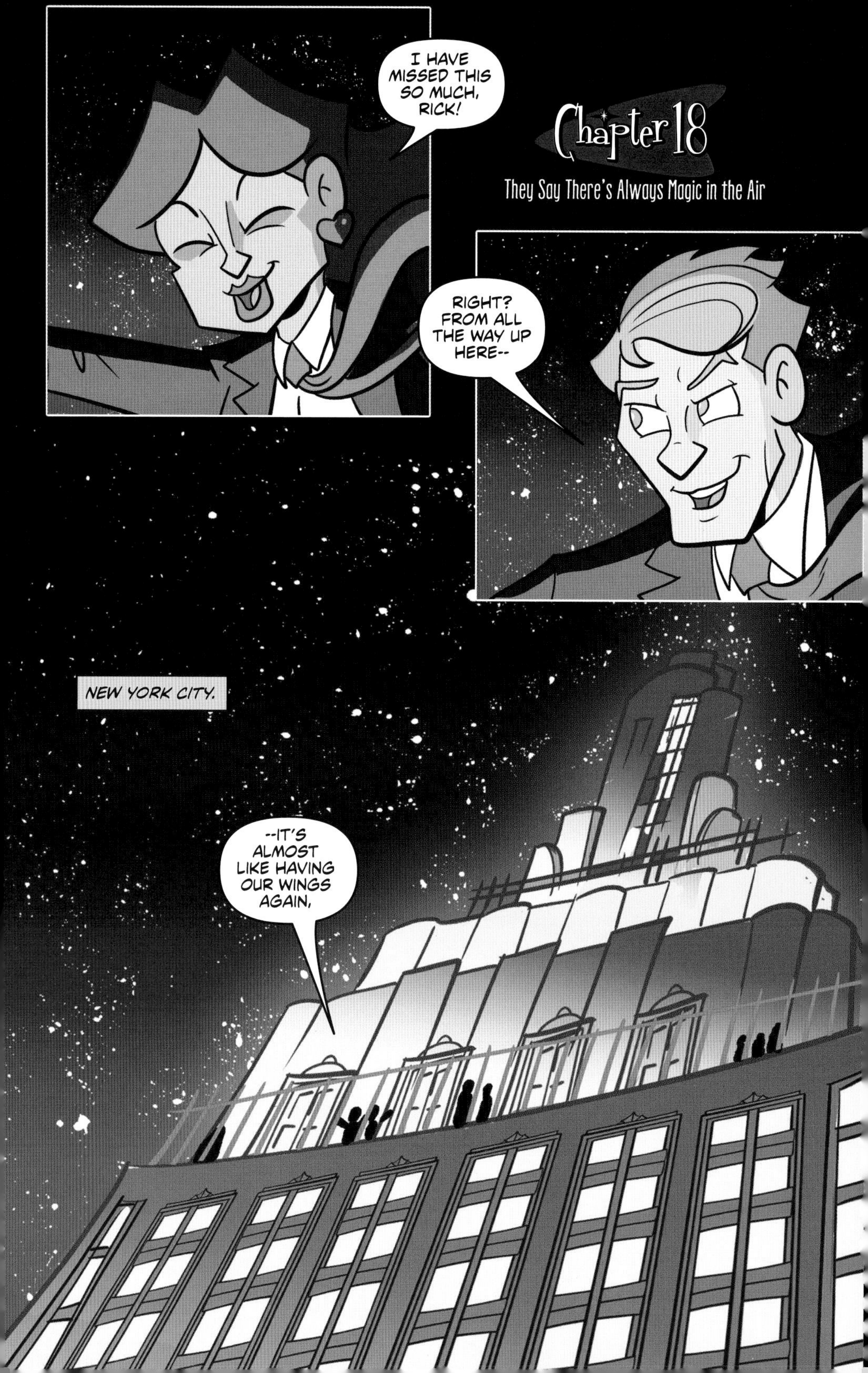

I HAVE MISSED THIS SO MUCH, RICK!
Chapter 18
They Say There's Always Magic in the Air
RIGHT? FROM ALL THE WAY UP HERE--
NEW YORK CITY.
--IT'S ALMOST LIKE HAVING OUR WINGS AGAIN,

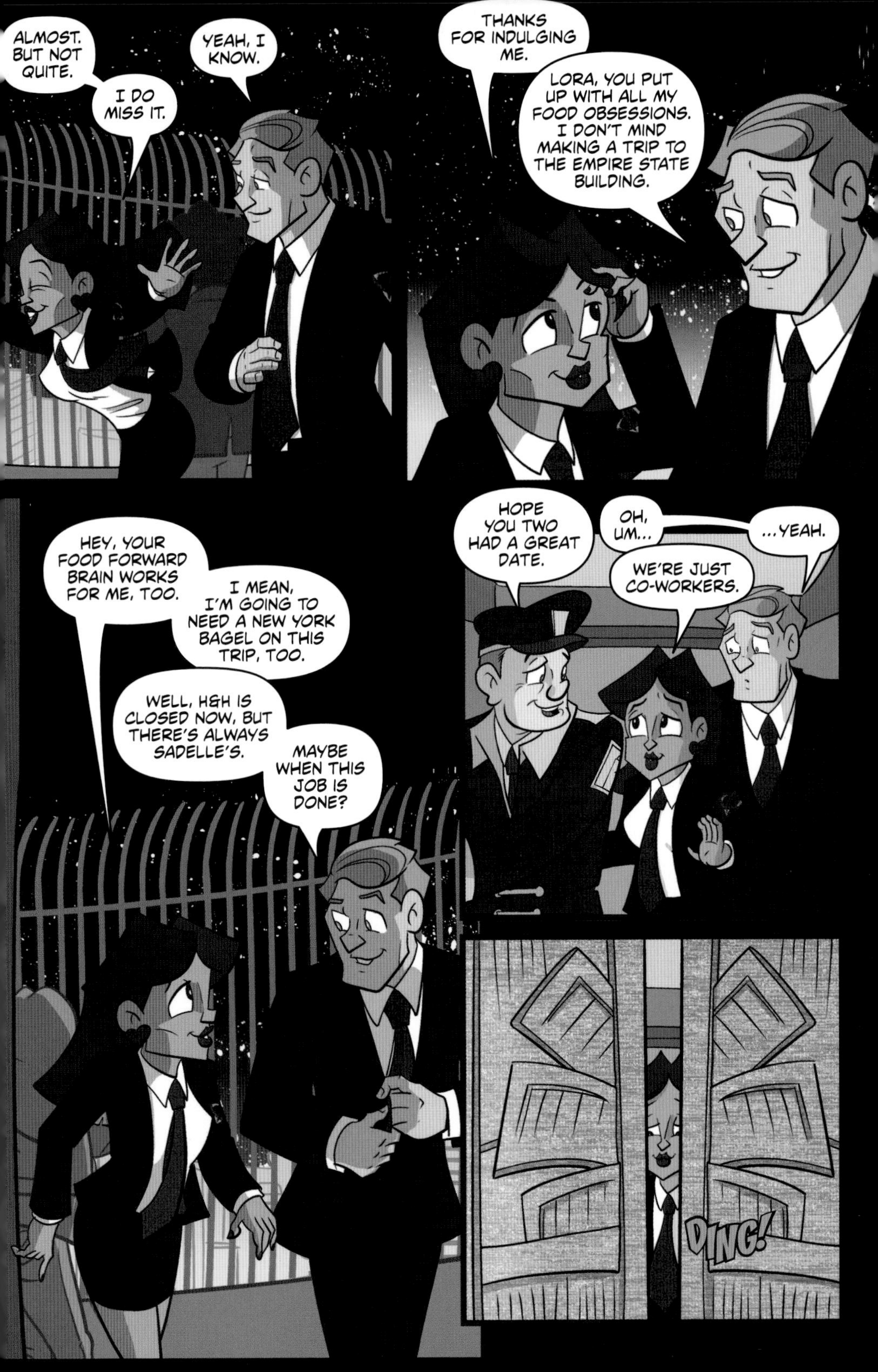
ALMOST. BUT NOT QUITE.
I DO MISS IT.
YEAH, I KNOW.
THANKS FOR INDULGING ME.
LORA, YOU PUT UP WITH ALL MY FOOD OBSESSIONS. I DON'T MIND MAKING A TRIP TO THE EMPIRE STATE BUILDING.
HEY, YOUR FOOD FORWARD BRAIN WORKS FOR ME, TOO.
I MEAN, I'M GOING TO NEED A NEW YORK BAGEL ON THIS TRIP, TOO.
WELL, H&H IS CLOSED NOW, BUT THERE'S ALWAYS SADELLE'S.
MAYBE WHEN THIS JOB IS DONE?
HOPE YOU TWO HAD A GREAT DATE.
OH, UM...
...YEAH.
WE'RE JUST CO-WORKERS.
DING!

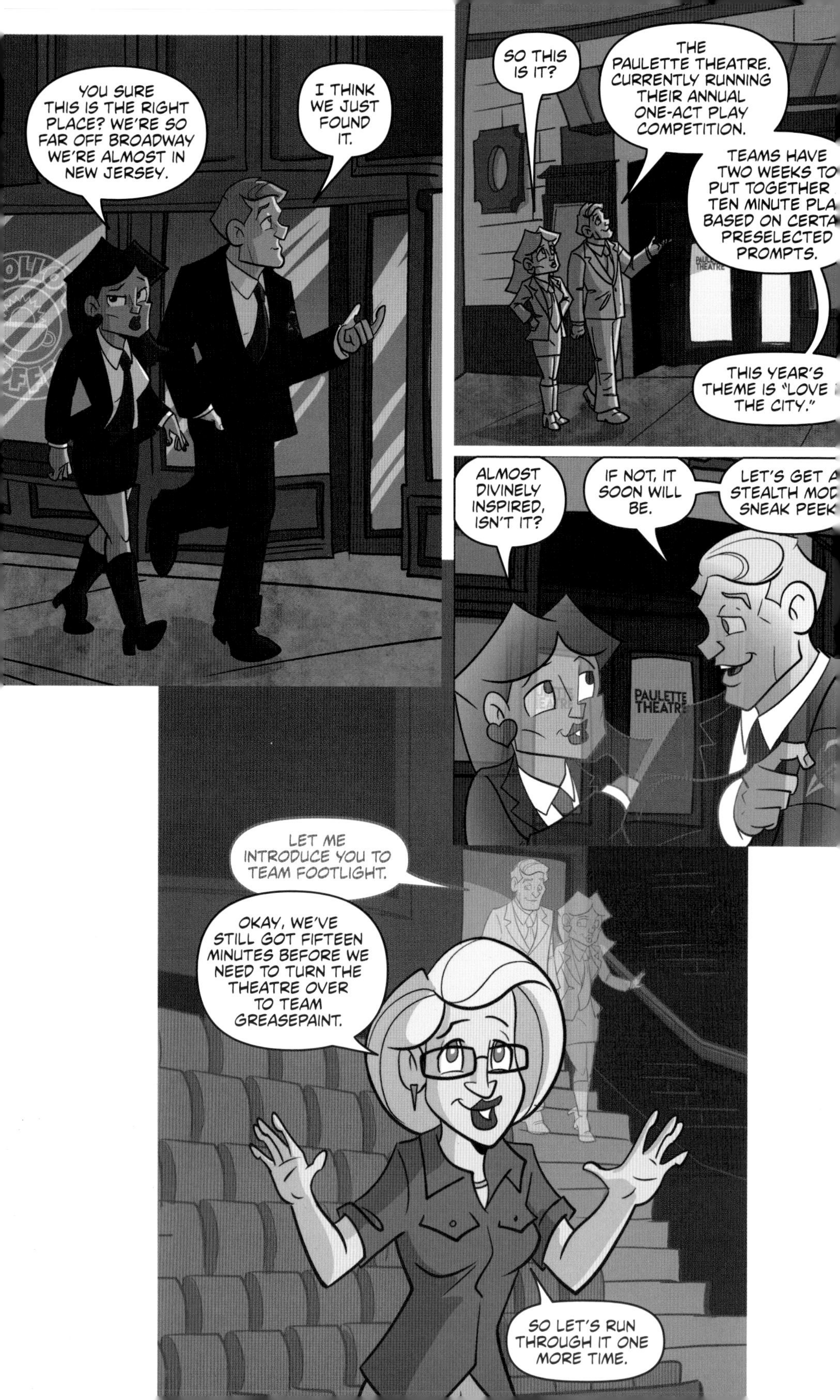
YOU SURE THIS IS THE RIGHT PLACE? WE'RE SO FAR OFF BROADWAY WE'RE ALMOST IN NEW JERSEY.
I THINK WE JUST FOUND IT.
SO THIS IS IT?
THE PAULETTE THEATRE. CURRENTLY RUNNING THEIR ANNUAL ONE-ACT PLAY COMPETITION.
TEAMS HAVE TWO WEEKS TO PUT TOGETHER TEN MINUTE PLA BASED ON CERTA PRESELECTED PROMPTS.
THIS YEAR'S THEME IS "LOVE THE CITY."
ALMOST DIVINELY INSPIRED, ISN'T IT?
IF NOT, IT SOON WILL BE.
LET'S GET A STEALTH MOD SNEAK PEEK
PAULETTE THEATRE
LET ME INTRODUCE YOU TO TEAM FOOTLIGHT.
OKAY, WE'VE STILL GOT FIFTEEN MINUTES BEFORE WE NEED TO TURN THE THEATRE OVER TO TEAM GREASEPAINT.
SO LET'S RUN THROUGH IT ONE MORE TIME.

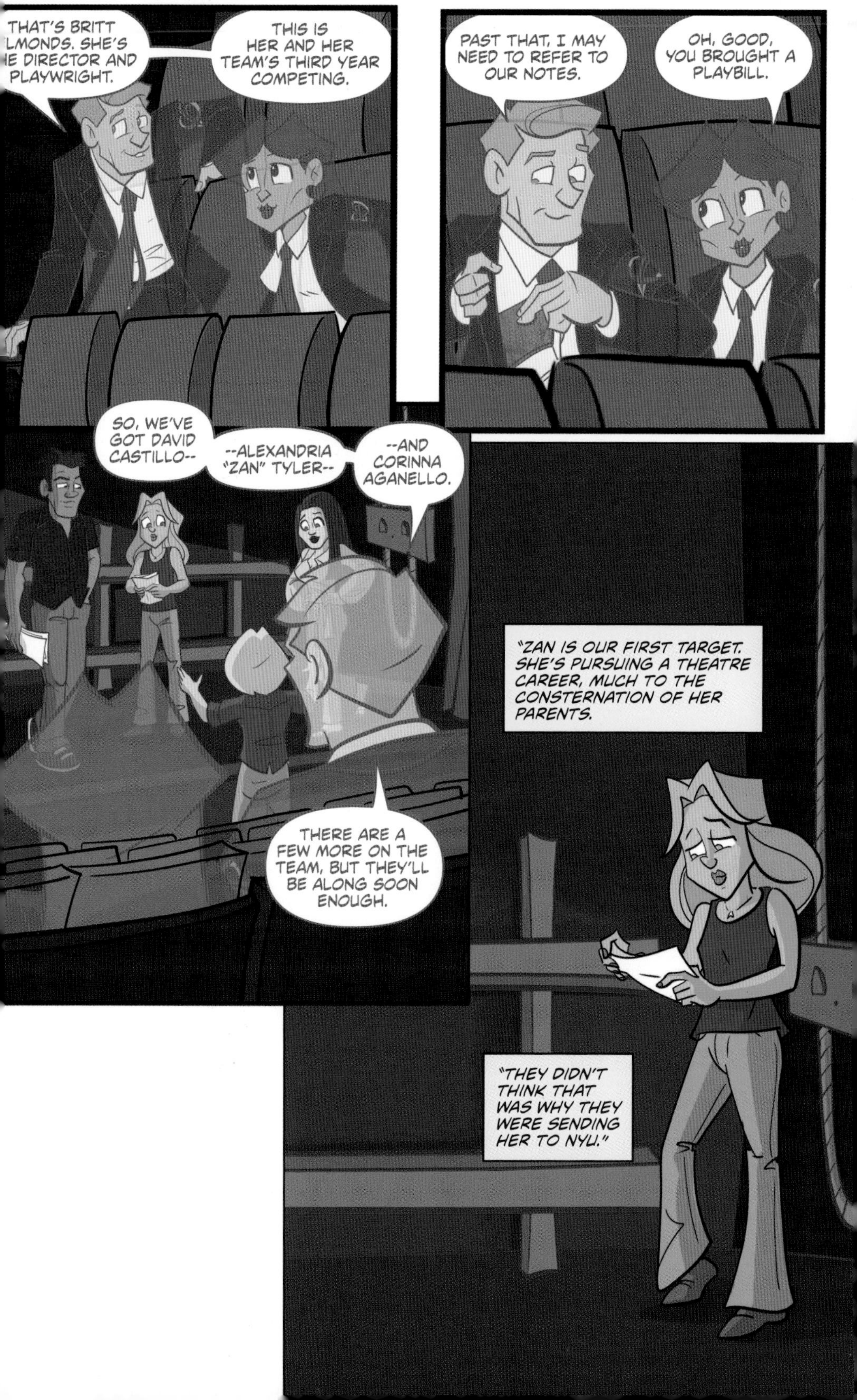
THAT'S BRITT
LMONDS. SHE'S
E DIRECTOR AND
PLAYWRIGHT.
THIS IS HER AND HER TEAM'S THIRD YEAR COMPETING.
PAST THAT, I MAY NEED TO REFER TO OUR NOTES.
OH, GOOD, YOU BROUGHT A PLAYBILL.
SO, WE'VE GOT DAVID CASTILLO--
--ALEXANDRIA "ZAN" TYLER--
--AND CORINNA AGANELLO.
THERE ARE A FEW MORE ON THE TEAM, BUT THEY'LL BE ALONG SOON ENOUGH.
"ZAN IS OUR FIRST TARGET. SHE'S PURSUING A THEATRE CAREER, MUCH TO THE CONSTERNATION OF HER PARENTS.
"THEY DIDN'T THINK THAT WAS WHY THEY WERE SENDING HER TO NYU."

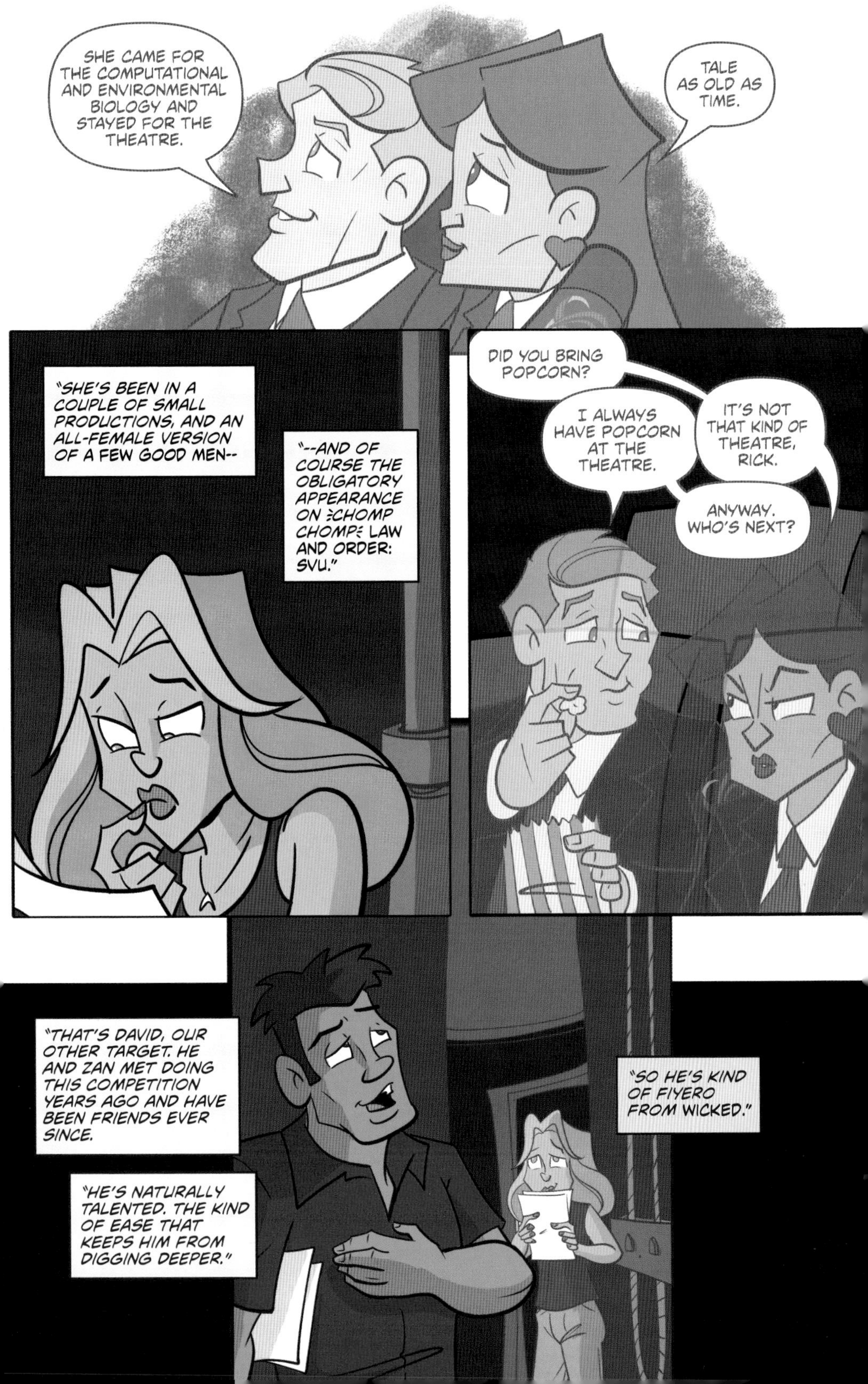
SHE CAME FOR THE COMPUTATIONAL AND ENVIRONMENTAL BIOLOGY AND STAYED FOR THE THEATRE.
TALE AS OLD AS TIME.
"SHE'S BEEN IN A COUPLE OF SMALL PRODUCTIONS, AND AN ALL-FEMALE VERSION OF A FEW GOOD MEN--
"--AND OF COURSE THE OBLIGATORY APPEARANCE ON ≥CHOMP CHOMP≤ LAW AND ORDER: SVU."
DID YOU BRING POPCORN?
I ALWAYS HAVE POPCORN AT THE THEATRE.
IT'S NOT THAT KIND OF THEATRE, RICK.
ANYWAY. WHO'S NEXT?
"THAT'S DAVID, OUR OTHER TARGET. HE AND ZAN MET DOING THIS COMPETITION YEARS AGO AND HAVE BEEN FRIENDS EVER SINCE.
"HE'S NATURALLY TALENTED. THE KIND OF EASE THAT KEEPS HIM FROM DIGGING DEEPER."
"SO HE'S KIND OF FIYERO FROM WICKED."

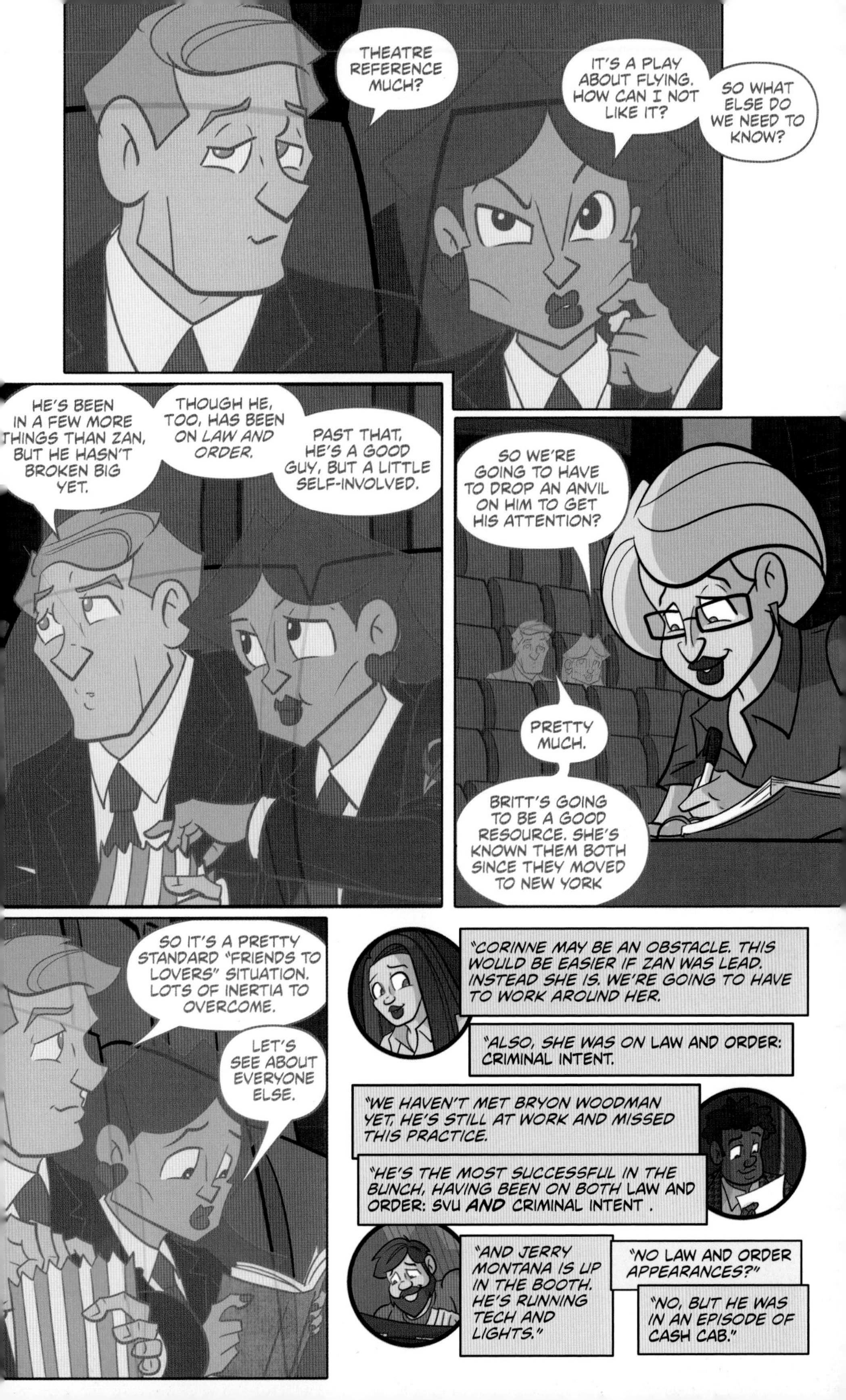

THEATRE REFERENCE MUCH?
IT'S A PLAY ABOUT FLYING. HOW CAN I NOT LIKE IT?
SO WHAT ELSE DO WE NEED TO KNOW?
HE'S BEEN IN A FEW MORE THINGS THAN ZAN, BUT HE HASN'T BROKEN BIG YET.
THOUGH HE, TOO, HAS BEEN ON LAW AND ORDER.
PAST THAT, HE'S A GOOD GUY, BUT A LITTLE SELF-INVOLVED.
SO WE'RE GOING TO HAVE TO DROP AN ANVIL ON HIM TO GET HIS ATTENTION?
PRETTY MUCH.
BRITT'S GOING TO BE A GOOD RESOURCE. SHE'S KNOWN THEM BOTH SINCE THEY MOVED TO NEW YORK
SO IT'S A PRETTY STANDARD "FRIENDS TO LOVERS" SITUATION. LOTS OF INERTIA TO OVERCOME.
LET'S SEE ABOUT EVERYONE ELSE.
"CORINNE MAY BE AN OBSTACLE. THIS WOULD BE EASIER IF ZAN WAS LEAD. INSTEAD SHE IS. WE'RE GOING TO HAVE TO WORK AROUND HER.
"ALSO, SHE WAS ON LAW AND ORDER: CRIMINAL INTENT.
"WE HAVEN'T MET BRYON WOODMAN YET, HE'S STILL AT WORK AND MISSED THIS PRACTICE.
"HE'S THE MOST SUCCESSFUL IN THE BUNCH, HAVING BEEN ON BOTH LAW AND ORDER: SVU AND CRIMINAL INTENT .
"AND JERRY MONTANA IS UP IN THE BOOTH. HE'S RUNNING TECH AND LIGHTS."
"NO LAW AND ORDER APPEARANCES?"
"NO, BUT HE WAS IN AN EPISODE OF CASH CAB."

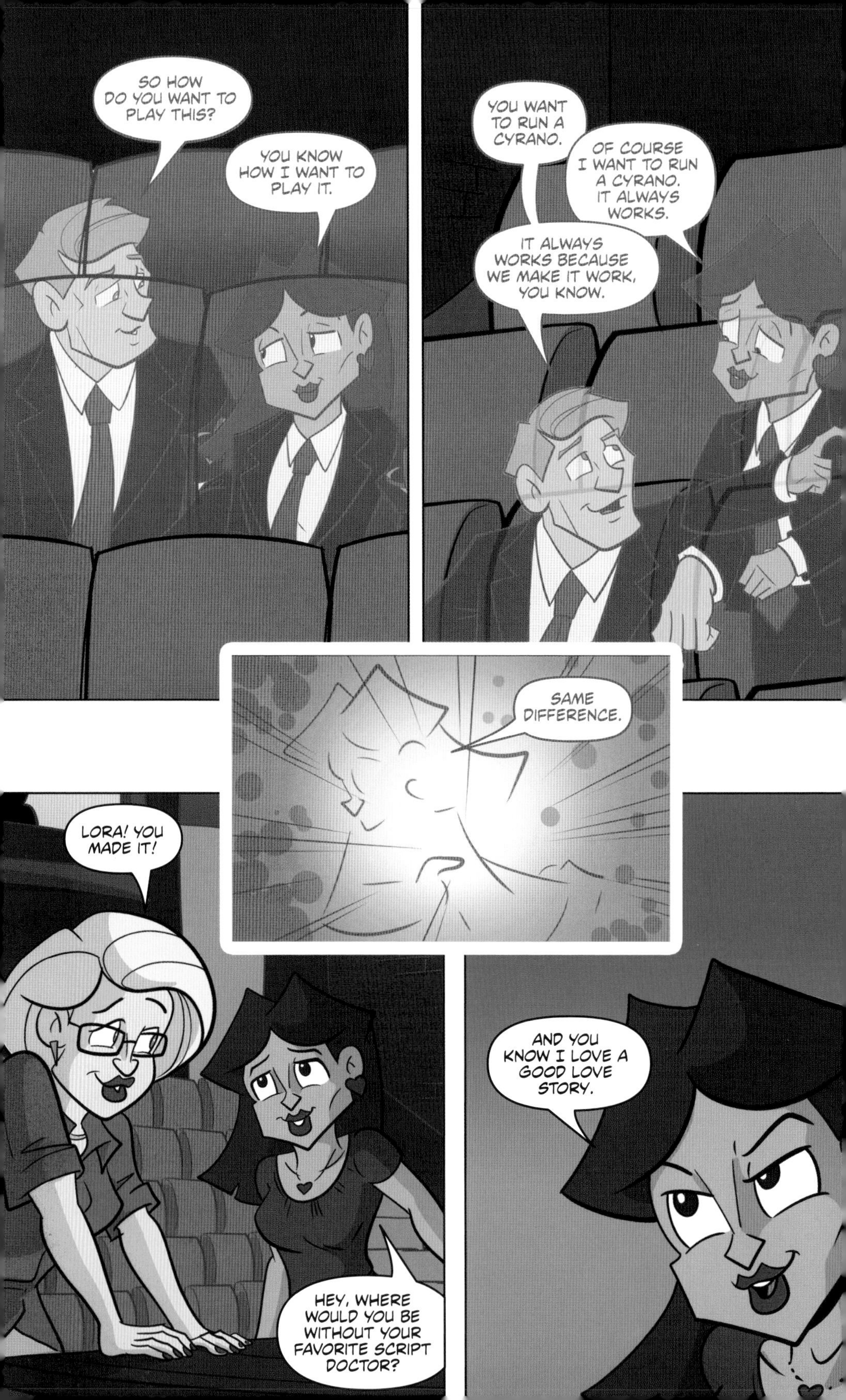
SO HOW DO YOU WANT TO PLAY THIS?
YOU KNOW HOW I WANT TO PLAY IT.
YOU WANT TO RUN A CYRANO.
OF COURSE I WANT TO RUN A CYRANO. IT ALWAYS WORKS.
IT ALWAYS WORKS BECAUSE WE MAKE IT WORK, YOU KNOW.
SAME DIFFERENCE.
LORA! YOU MADE IT!
HEY, WHERE WOULD YOU BE WITHOUT YOUR FAVORITE SCRIPT DOCTOR?
AND YOU KNOW I LOVE A GOOD LOVE STORY.

Chapter 19

Everyday I Write the Book

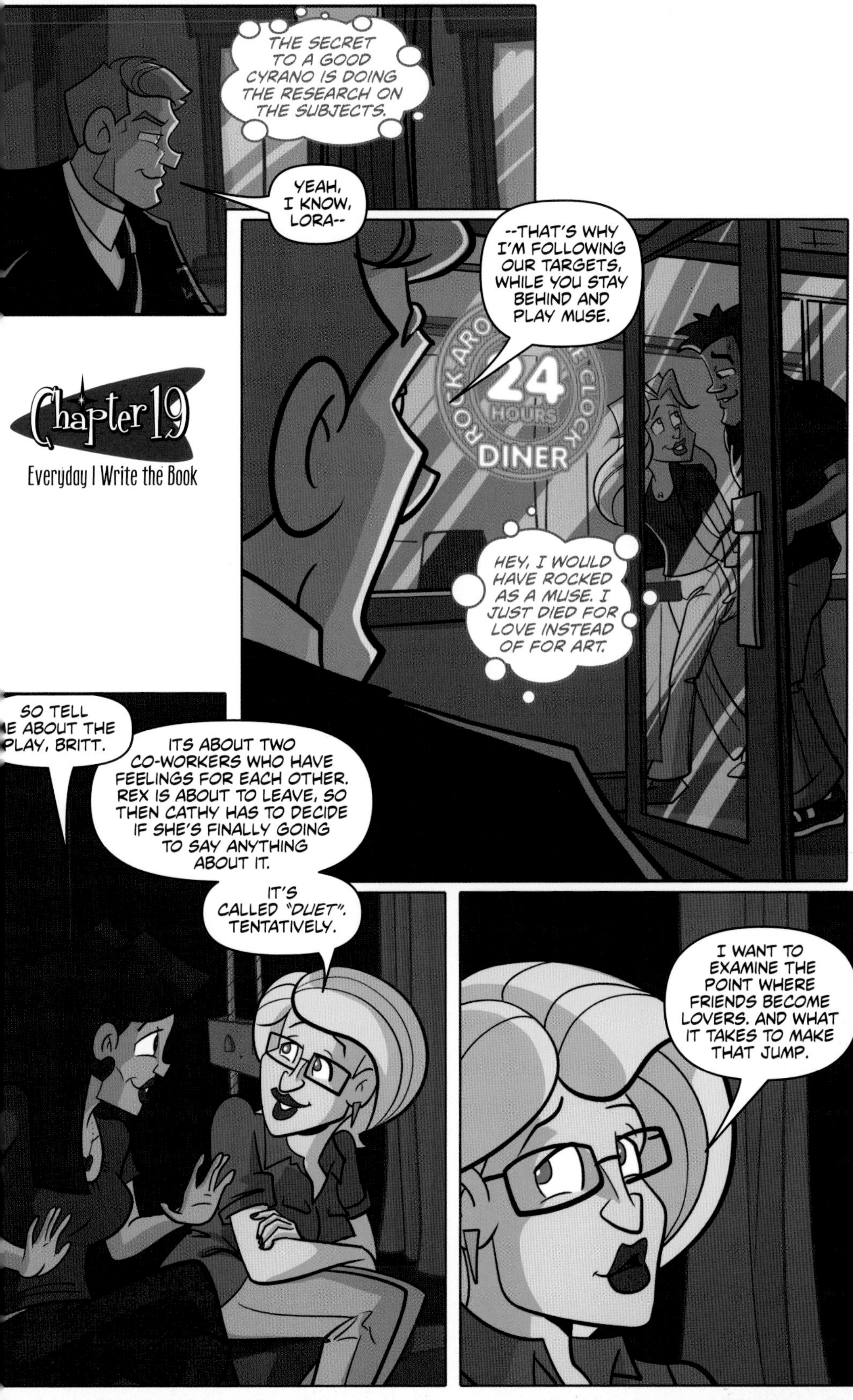

THE SECRET TO A GOOD CYRANO IS DOING THE RESEARCH ON THE SUBJECTS.
YEAH, I KNOW, LORA--
--THAT'S WHY I'M FOLLOWING OUR TARGETS, WHILE YOU STAY BEHIND AND PLAY MUSE.
24 HOURS DINER
HEY, I WOULD HAVE ROCKED AS A MUSE. I JUST DIED FOR LOVE INSTEAD OF FOR ART.
SO TELL E ABOUT THE PLAY, BRITT.
ITS ABOUT TWO CO-WORKERS WHO HAVE FEELINGS FOR EACH OTHER. REX IS ABOUT TO LEAVE, SO THEN CATHY HAS TO DECIDE IF SHE'S FINALLY GOING TO SAY ANYTHING ABOUT IT.
IT'S CALLED "DUET". TENTATIVELY.
I WANT TO EXAMINE THE POINT WHERE FRIENDS BECOME LOVERS. AND WHAT IT TAKES TO MAKE THAT JUMP.

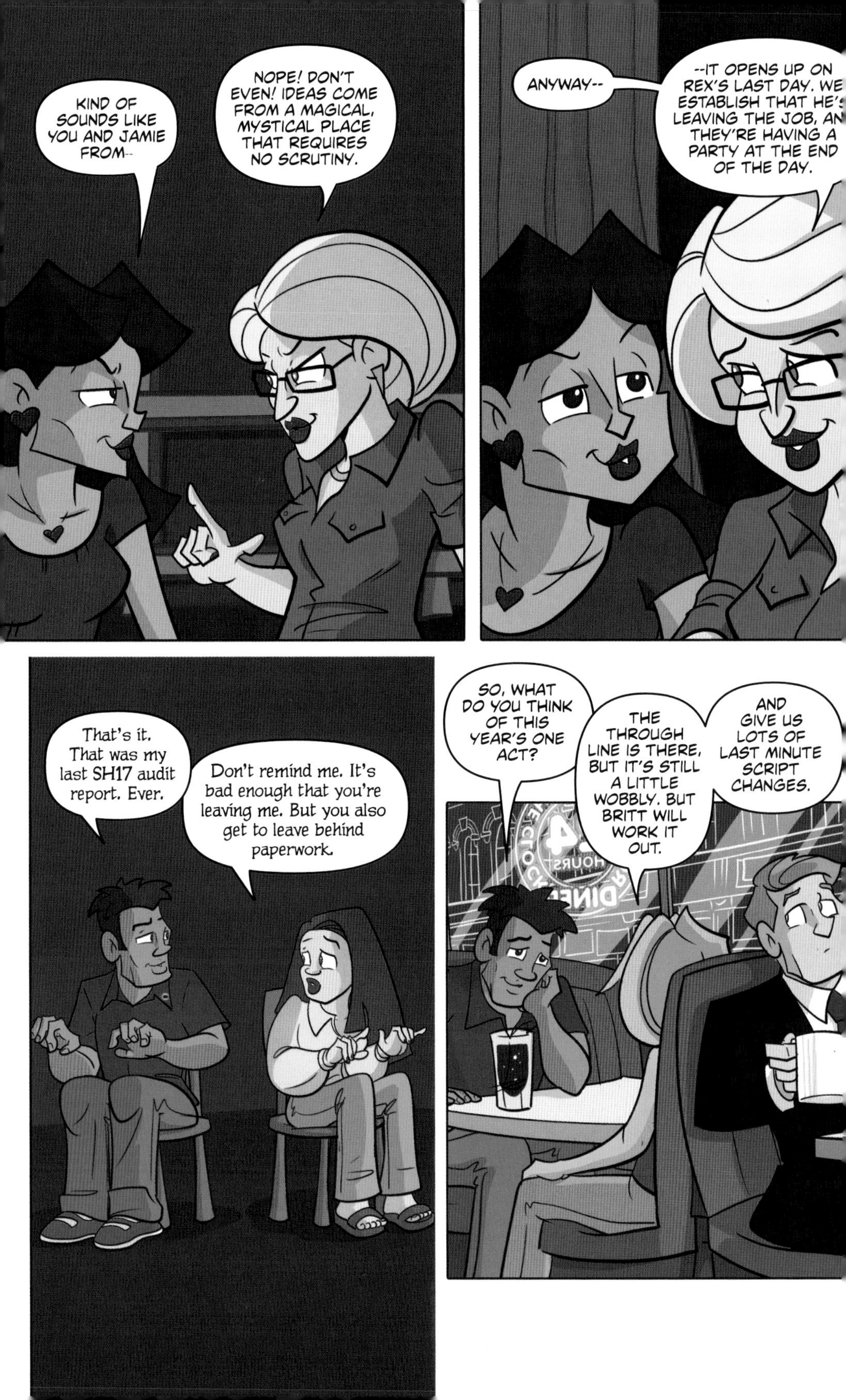
KIND OF SOUNDS LIKE YOU AND JAMIE FROM--
NOPE! DON'T EVEN! IDEAS COME FROM A MAGICAL, MYSTICAL PLACE THAT REQUIRES NO SCRUTINY.
ANYWAY--
--IT OPENS UP ON REX'S LAST DAY. WE ESTABLISH THAT HE'S LEAVING THE JOB, AN THEY'RE HAVING A PARTY AT THE END OF THE DAY.
That's it. That was my last SH17 audit report. Ever.
Don't remind me. It's bad enough that you're leaving me. But you also get to leave behind paperwork.
SO, WHAT DO YOU THINK OF THIS YEAR'S ONE ACT?
THE THROUGH LINE IS THERE, BUT IT'S STILL A LITTLE WOBBLY. BUT BRITT WILL WORK IT OUT.
AND GIVE US LOTS OF LAST MINUTE SCRIPT CHANGES.

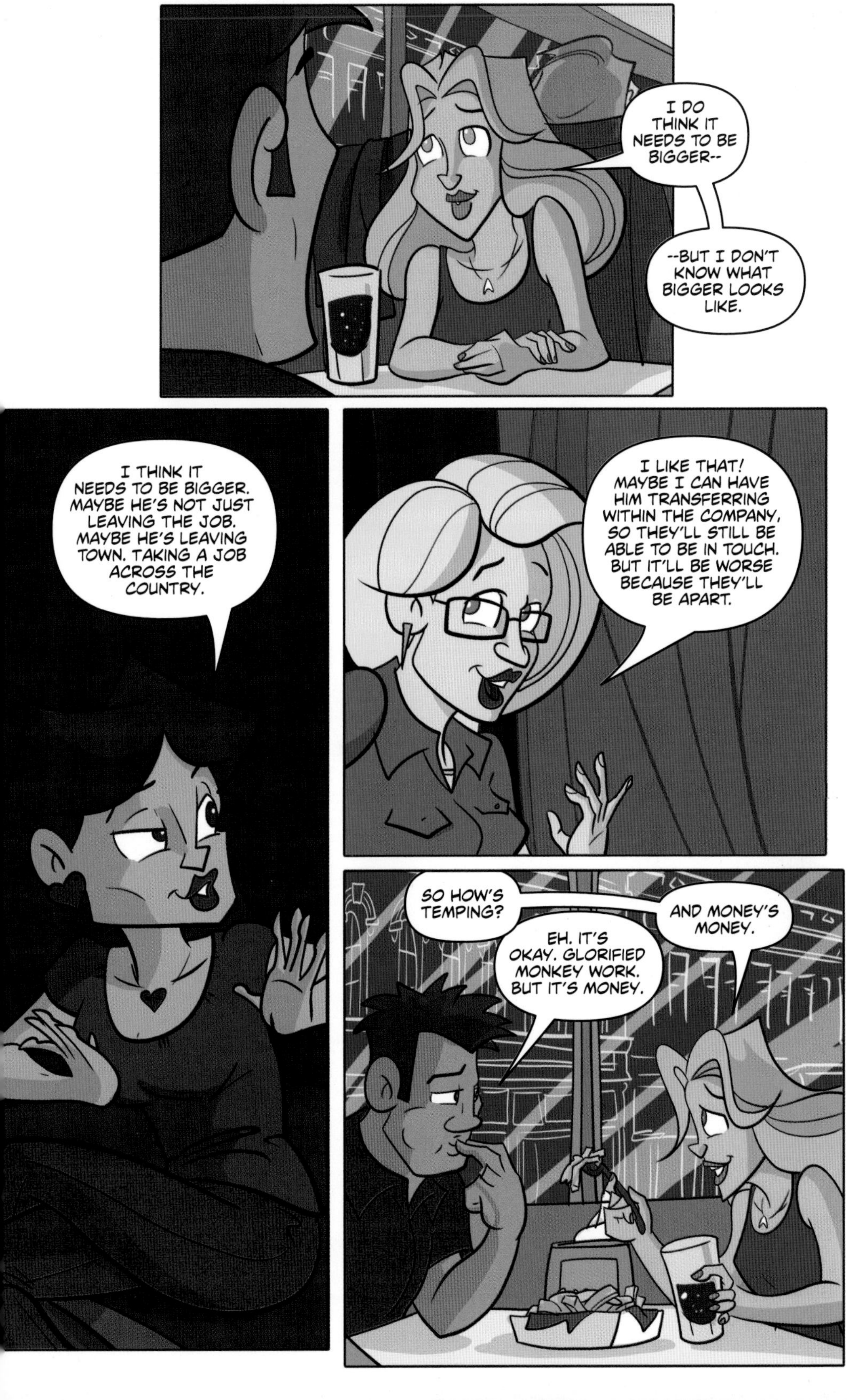
I DO THINK IT NEEDS TO BE BIGGER--
--BUT I DON'T KNOW WHAT BIGGER LOOKS LIKE.
I THINK IT NEEDS TO BE BIGGER. MAYBE HE'S NOT JUST LEAVING THE JOB. MAYBE HE'S LEAVING TOWN. TAKING A JOB ACROSS THE COUNTRY.
I LIKE THAT! MAYBE I CAN HAVE HIM TRANSFERRING WITHIN THE COMPANY, SO THEY'LL STILL BE ABLE TO BE IN TOUCH. BUT IT'LL BE WORSE BECAUSE THEY'LL BE APART.
SO HOW'S TEMPING?
EH. IT'S OKAY. GLORIFIED MONKEY WORK. BUT IT'S MONEY.
AND MONEY'S MONEY.

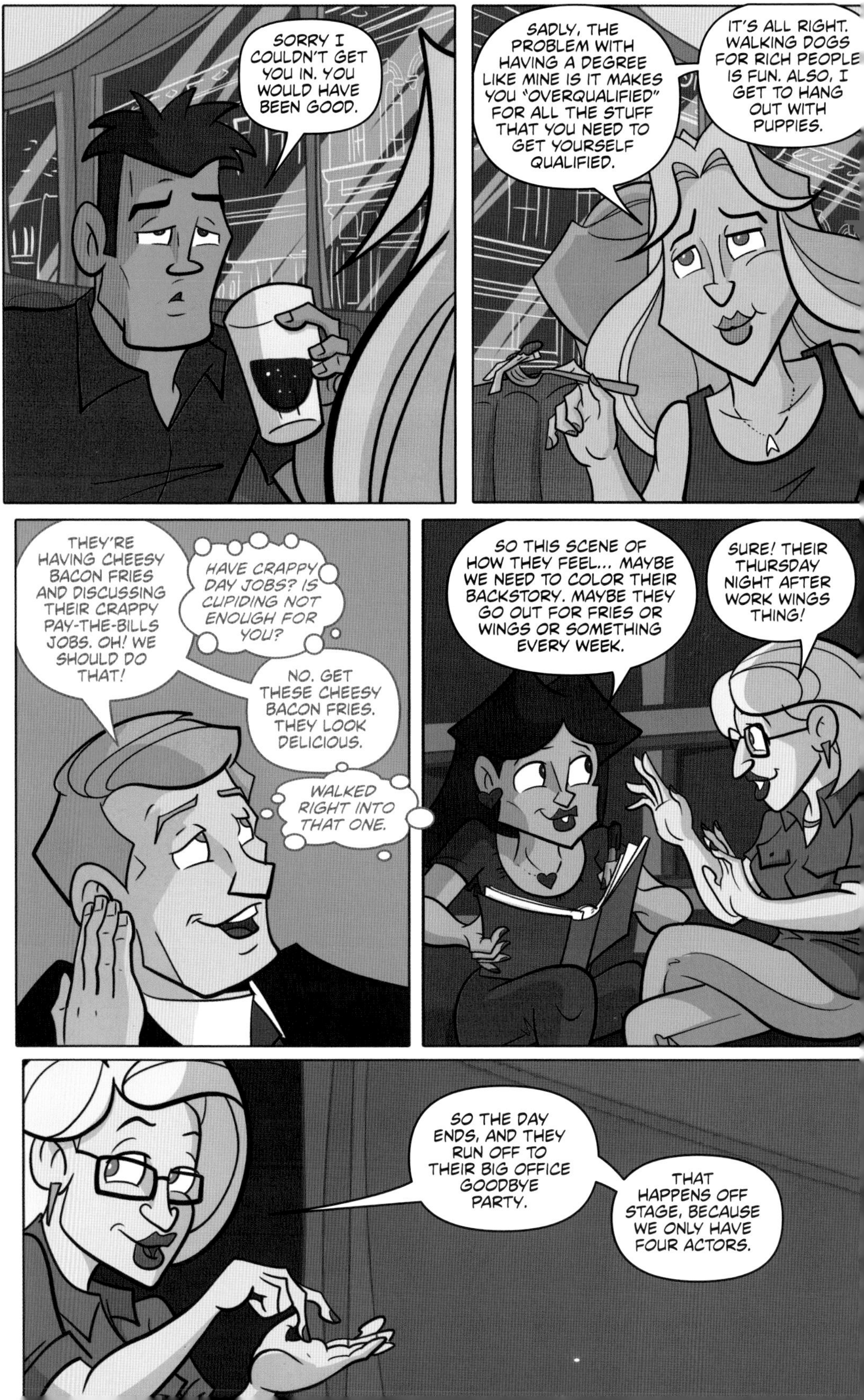
SORRY I COULDN'T GET YOU IN. YOU WOULD HAVE BEEN GOOD.
SADLY, THE PROBLEM WITH HAVING A DEGREE LIKE MINE IS IT MAKES YOU "OVERQUALIFIED" FOR ALL THE STUFF THAT YOU NEED TO GET YOURSELF QUALIFIED.
IT'S ALL RIGHT. WALKING DOGS FOR RICH PEOPLE IS FUN. ALSO, I GET TO HANG OUT WITH PUPPIES.
THEY'RE HAVING CHEESY BACON FRIES AND DISCUSSING THEIR CRAPPY PAY-THE-BILLS JOBS. OH! WE SHOULD DO THAT!
HAVE CRAPPY DAY JOBS? IS CUPIDING NOT ENOUGH FOR YOU?
NO. GET THESE CHEESY BACON FRIES. THEY LOOK DELICIOUS.
WALKED RIGHT INTO THAT ONE.
SO THIS SCENE OF HOW THEY FEEL... MAYBE WE NEED TO COLOR THEIR BACKSTORY. MAYBE THEY GO OUT FOR FRIES OR WINGS OR SOMETHING EVERY WEEK.
SURE! THEIR THURSDAY NIGHT AFTER WORK WINGS THING!
SO THE DAY ENDS, AND THEY RUN OFF TO THEIR BIG OFFICE GOODBYE PARTY.
THAT HAPPENS OFF STAGE, BECAUSE WE ONLY HAVE FOUR ACTORS.

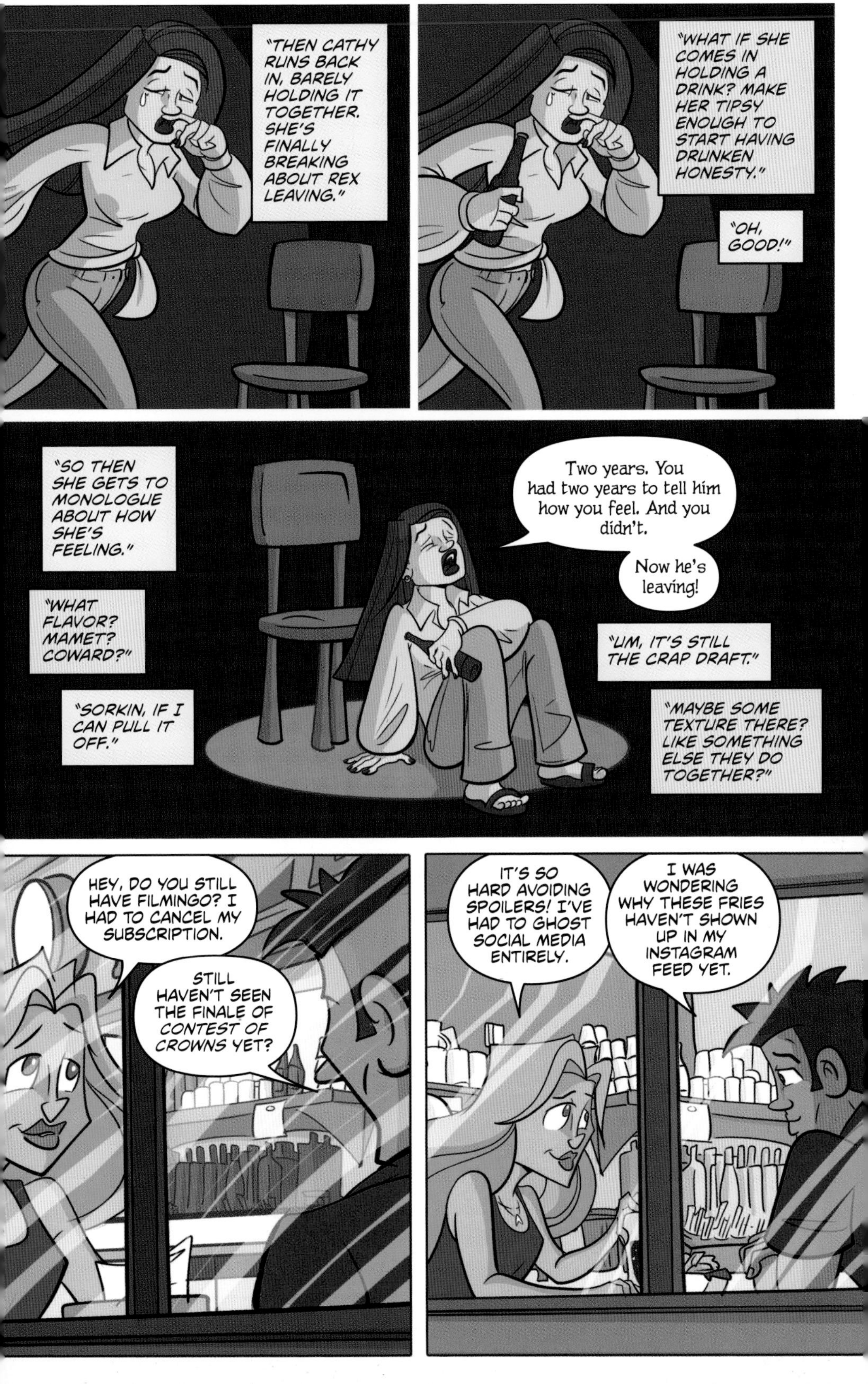
"THEN CATHY RUNS BACK IN, BARELY HOLDING IT TOGETHER. SHE'S FINALLY BREAKING ABOUT REX LEAVING."
"WHAT IF SHE COMES IN HOLDING A DRINK? MAKE HER TIPSY ENOUGH TO START HAVING DRUNKEN HONESTY."
"OH, GOOD!"
"SO THEN SHE GETS TO MONOLOGUE ABOUT HOW SHE'S FEELING."
"WHAT FLAVOR? MAMET? COWARD?"
"SORKIN, IF I CAN PULL IT OFF."
Two years. You had two years to tell him how you feel. And you didn't.
Now he's leaving!
"UM, IT'S STILL THE CRAP DRAFT."
"MAYBE SOME TEXTURE THERE? LIKE SOMETHING ELSE THEY DO TOGETHER?"
HEY, DO YOU STILL HAVE FILMINGO? I HAD TO CANCEL MY SUBSCRIPTION.
STILL HAVEN'T SEEN THE FINALE OF CONTEST OF CROWNS YET?
IT'S SO HARD AVOIDING SPOILERS! I'VE HAD TO GHOST SOCIAL MEDIA ENTIRELY.
I WAS WONDERING WHY THESE FRIES HAVEN'T SHOWN UP IN MY INSTAGRAM FEED YET.

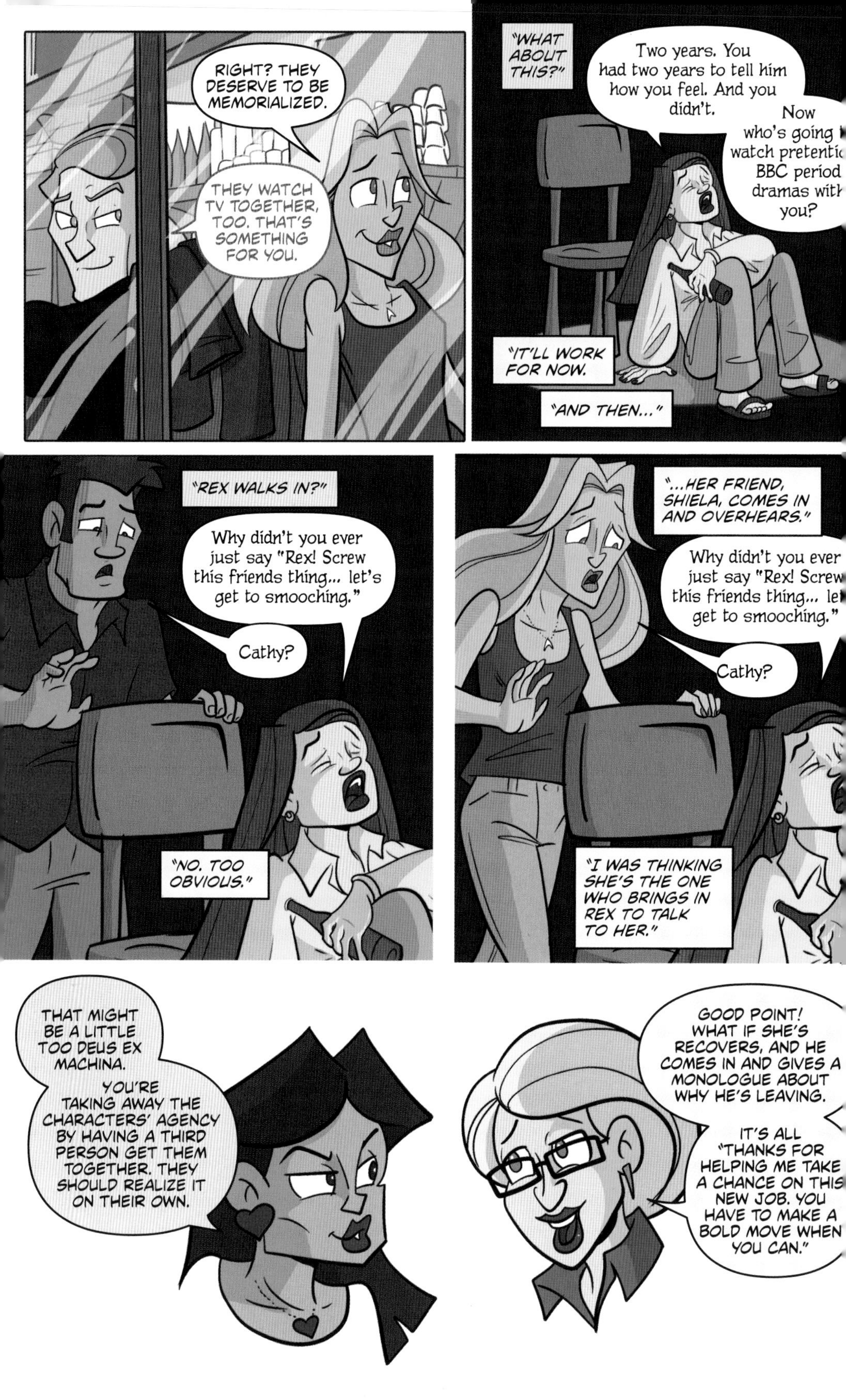
RIGHT? THEY DESERVE TO BE MEMORIALIZED.
THEY WATCH TV TOGETHER, TOO. THAT'S SOMETHING FOR YOU.
"WHAT ABOUT THIS?"
Two years. You had two years to tell him how you feel. And you didn't.
Now who's going
watch pretenti
BBC period
dramas with
you?
"IT'LL WORK FOR NOW.
"AND THEN..."
"REX WALKS IN?"
Why didn't you ever just say "Rex! Screw this friends thing... let's get to smooching."
Cathy?
"NO. TOO OBVIOUS."
"...HER FRIEND, SHIELA, COMES IN AND OVERHEARS."
Why didn't you ever just say "Rex! Screw this friends thing... le get to smooching."
Cathy?
"I WAS THINKING SHE'S THE ONE WHO BRINGS IN REX TO TALK TO HER."
THAT MIGHT BE A LITTLE TOO DEUS EX MACHINA.
YOU'RE TAKING AWAY THE CHARACTERS' AGENCY BY HAVING A THIRD PERSON GET THEM TOGETHER. THEY SHOULD REALIZE IT ON THEIR OWN.
GOOD POINT! WHAT IF SHE'S RECOVERS, AND HE COMES IN AND GIVES A MONOLOGUE ABOUT WHY HE'S LEAVING.
IT'S ALL "THANKS FOR HELPING ME TAKE A CHANCE ON THIS NEW JOB. YOU HAVE TO MAKE A BOLD MOVE WHEN YOU CAN."

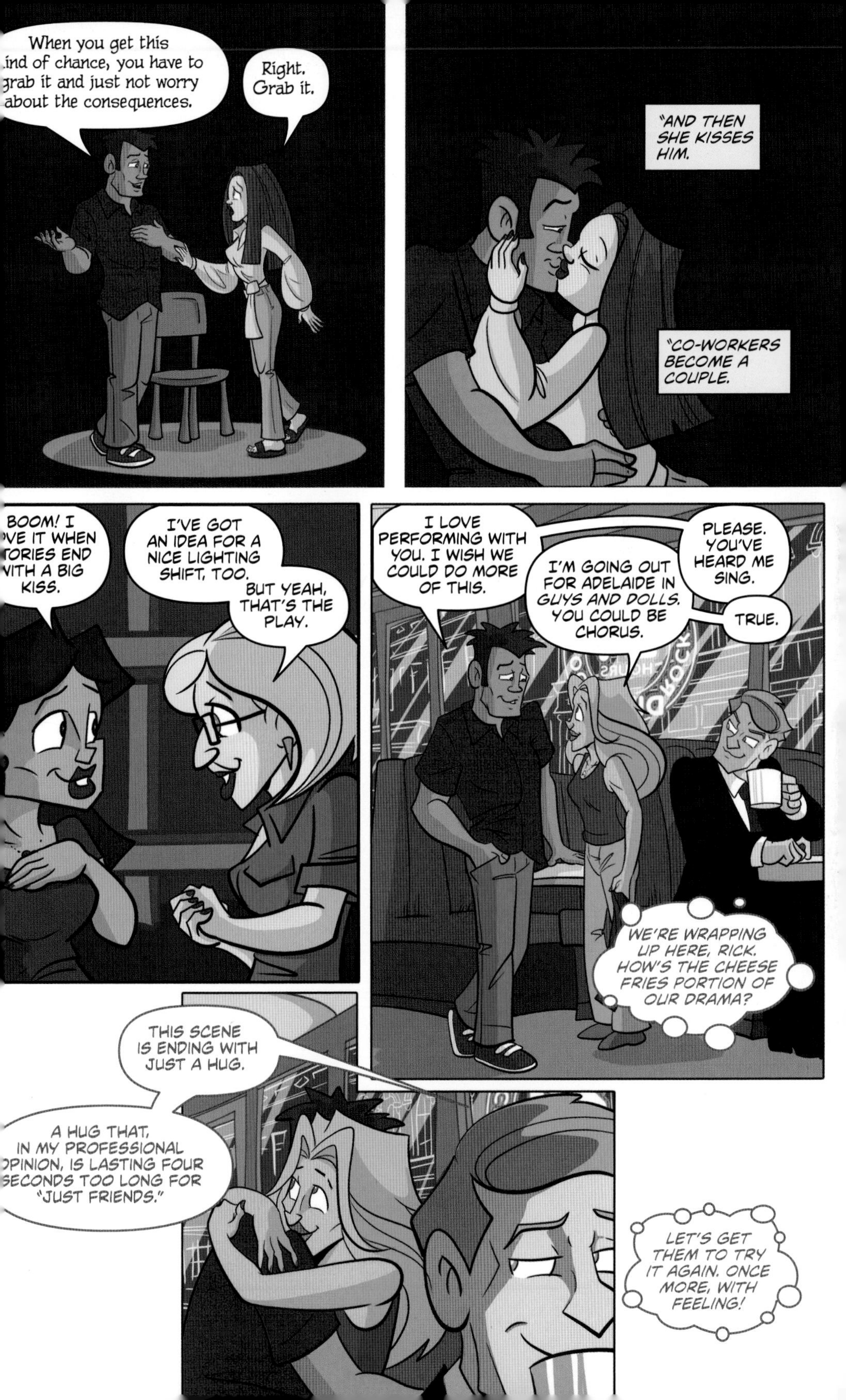

When you get this
ind of chance, you have to
grab it and just not worry
about the consequences.
Right. Grab it.
"AND THEN SHE KISSES HIM.
"CO-WORKERS BECOME A COUPLE.
BOOM! I
ve IT WHEN
tORIES END
WITH A BIG KISS.
I'VE GOT AN IDEA FOR A NICE LIGHTING SHIFT, TOO.
BUT YEAH, THAT'S THE PLAY.
I LOVE PERFORMING WITH YOU. I WISH WE COULD DO MORE OF THIS.
I'M GOING OUT FOR ADELAIDE IN GUYS AND DOLLS. YOU COULD BE CHORUS.
PLEASE. YOU'VE HEARD ME SING.
TRUE.
WE'RE WRAPPING UP HERE, RICK. HOW'S THE CHEESE FRIES PORTION OF OUR DRAMA?
THIS SCENE IS ENDING WITH JUST A HUG.
A HUG THAT, IN MY PROFESSIONAL
PINION, IS LASTING FOUR
SECONDS TOO LONG FOR "JUST FRIENDS."
LET'S GET THEM TO TRY IT AGAIN. ONCE MORE, WITH FEELING!

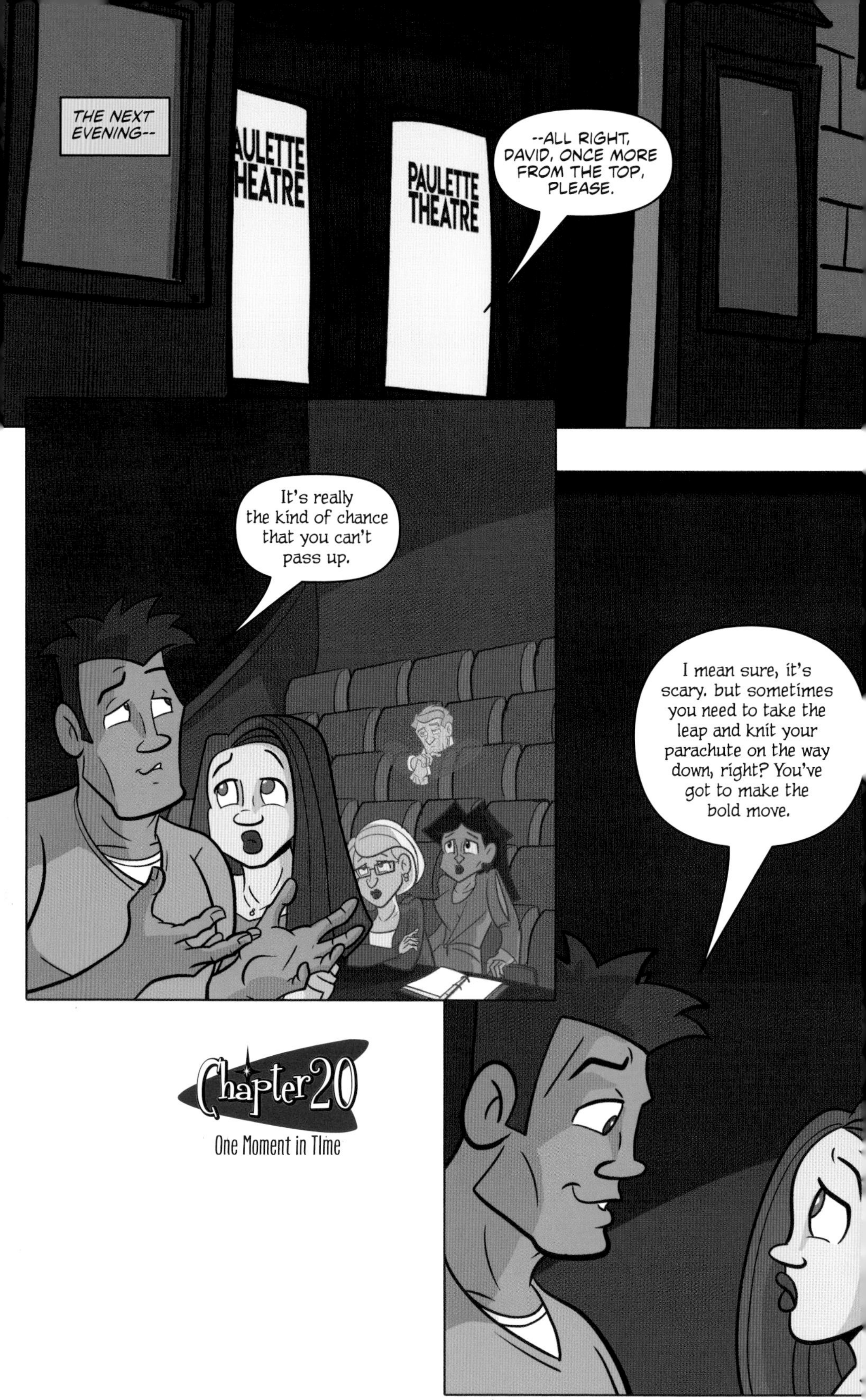
THE NEXT EVENING--
PAULETTE THEATRE
PAULETTE THEATRE
--ALL RIGHT, DAVID, ONCE MORE FROM THE TOP, PLEASE.
It's really the kind of chance that you can't pass up.
I mean sure, it's scary. but sometimes you need to take the leap and knit your parachute on the way down, right? You've got to make the bold move.
Chapter 20
One Moment in TIme

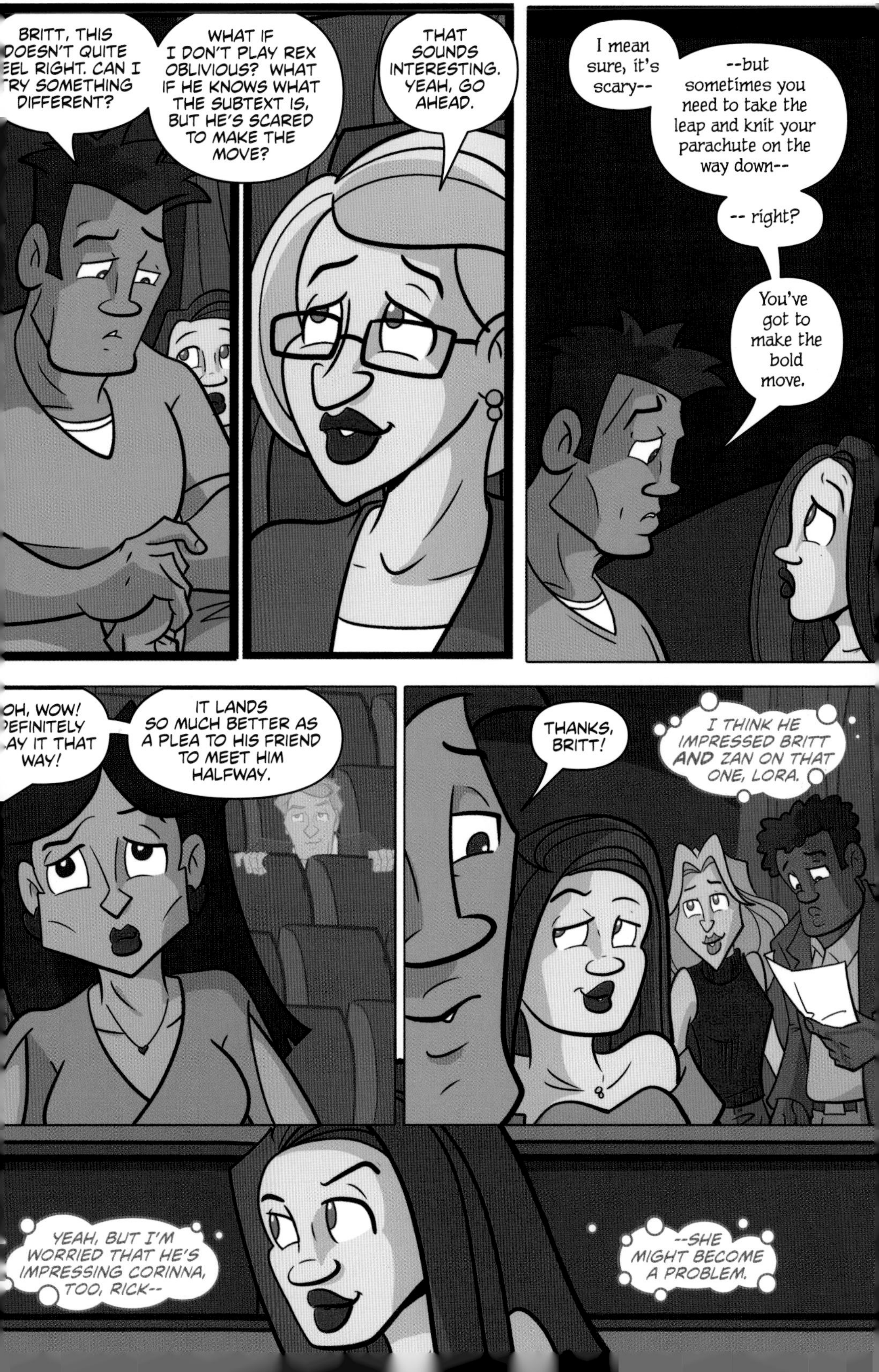
BRITT, THIS DOESN'T QUITE EEL RIGHT. CAN I TRY SOMETHING DIFFERENT?
WHAT IF I DON'T PLAY REX OBLIVIOUS? WHAT IF HE KNOWS WHAT THE SUBTEXT IS, BUT HE'S SCARED TO MAKE THE MOVE?
THAT SOUNDS INTERESTING. YEAH, GO AHEAD.
I mean sure, it's scary--
--but sometimes you need to take the leap and knit your parachute on the way down--
-- right?
You've got to make the bold move.
OH, WOW! DEFINITELY AY IT THAT WAY!
IT LANDS SO MUCH BETTER AS A PLEA TO HIS FRIEND TO MEET HIM HALFWAY.
THANKS, BRITT!
I THINK HE IMPRESSED BRITT AND ZAN ON THAT ONE, LORA.
YEAH, BUT I'M WORRIED THAT HE'S IMPRESSING CORINNA, TOO, RICK--
--SHE MIGHT BECOME A PROBLEM.

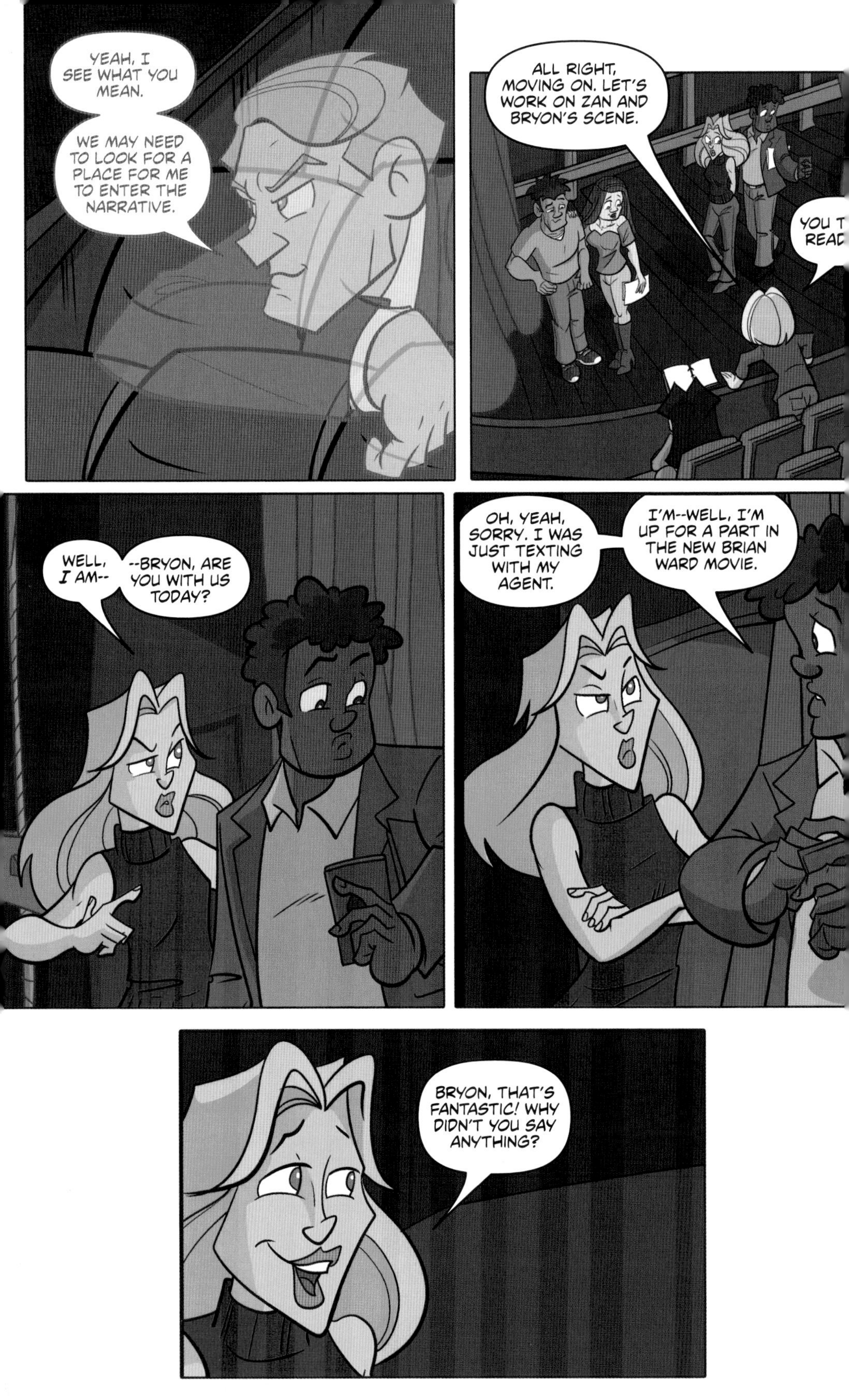
YEAH, I SEE WHAT YOU MEAN.
WE MAY NEED TO LOOK FOR A PLACE FOR ME TO ENTER THE NARRATIVE.
ALL RIGHT, MOVING ON. LET'S WORK ON ZAN AND BRYON'S SCENE.
WELL, *I* AM--
--BRYON, ARE YOU WITH US TODAY?
OH, YEAH, SORRY. I WAS JUST TEXTING WITH MY AGENT.
I'M--WELL, I'M UP FOR A PART IN THE NEW BRIAN WARD MOVIE.
BRYON, THAT'S FANTASTIC! WHY DIDN'T YOU SAY ANYTHING?

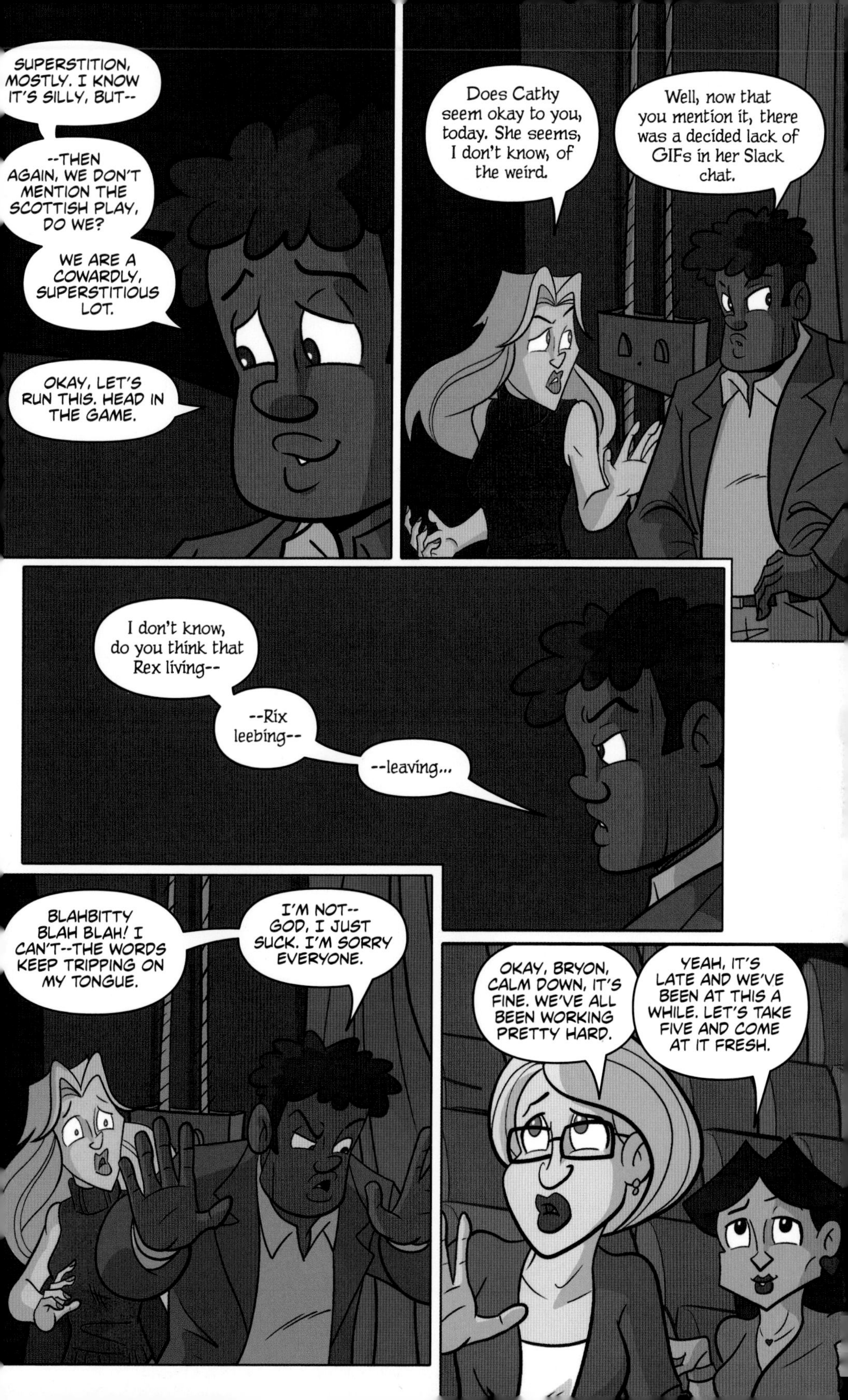
SUPERSTITION, MOSTLY. I KNOW IT'S SILLY, BUT--
--THEN AGAIN, WE DON'T MENTION THE SCOTTISH PLAY, DO WE?
WE ARE A COWARDLY, SUPERSTITIOUS LOT.
OKAY, LET'S RUN THIS. HEAD IN THE GAME.
Does Cathy seem okay to you, today. She seems, I don't know, of the weird.
Well, now that you mention it, there was a decided lack of GIFs in her Slack chat.
I don't know, do you think that Rex living--
--Rix leebing--
--leaving...
BLAHBITTY BLAH BLAH! I CAN'T--THE WORDS KEEP TRIPPING ON MY TONGUE.
I'M NOT-- GOD, I JUST SUCK. I'M SORRY EVERYONE.
OKAY, BRYON, CALM DOWN, IT'S FINE. WE'VE ALL BEEN WORKING PRETTY HARD.
YEAH, IT'S LATE AND WE'VE BEEN AT THIS A WHILE. LET'S TAKE FIVE AND COME AT IT FRESH.

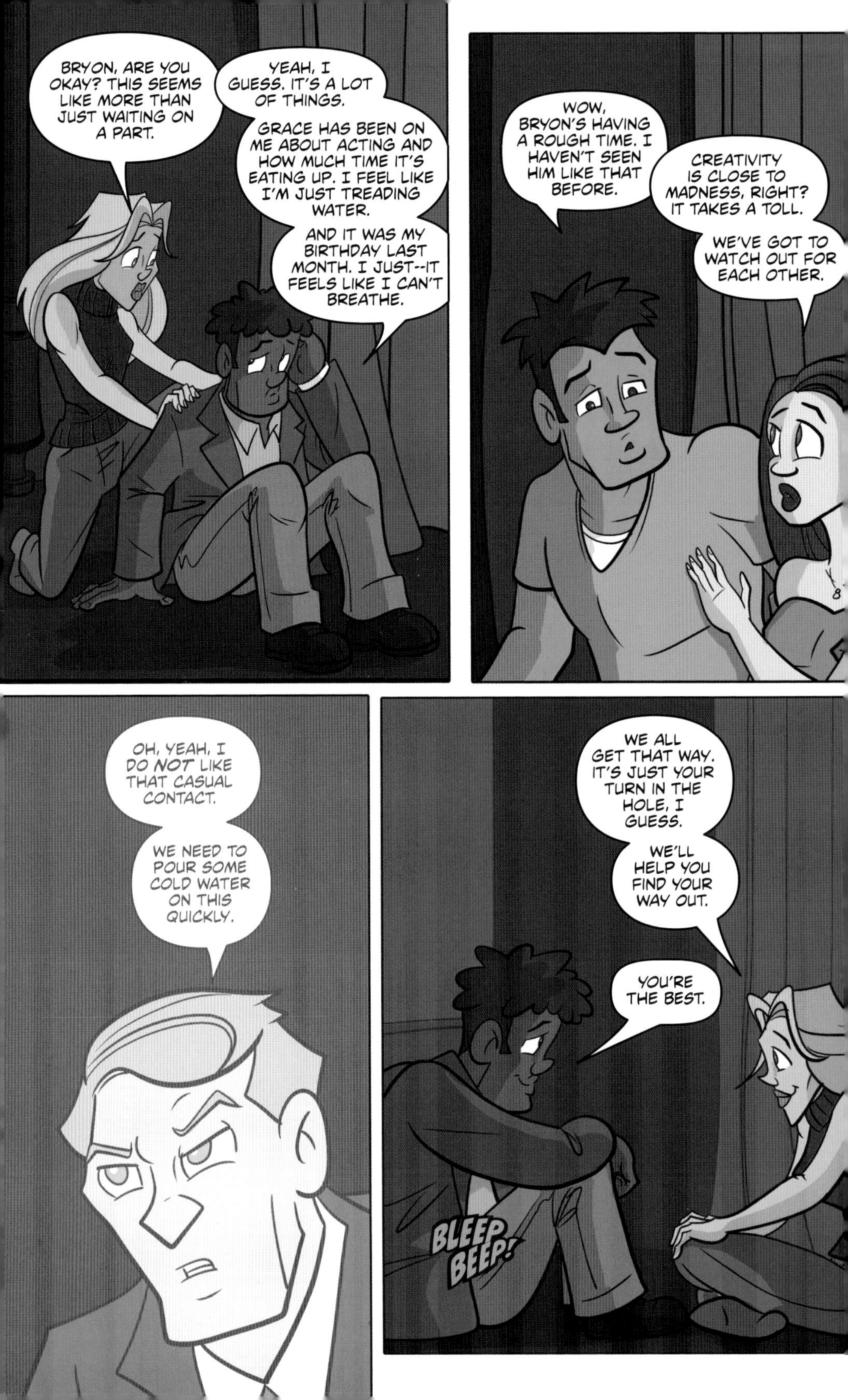
BRYON, ARE YOU OKAY? THIS SEEMS LIKE MORE THAN JUST WAITING ON A PART.
YEAH, I GUESS. IT'S A LOT OF THINGS.
GRACE HAS BEEN ON ME ABOUT ACTING AND HOW MUCH TIME IT'S EATING UP. I FEEL LIKE I'M JUST TREADING WATER.
AND IT WAS MY BIRTHDAY LAST MONTH. I JUST--IT FEELS LIKE I CAN'T BREATHE.
WOW, BRYON'S HAVING A ROUGH TIME. I HAVEN'T SEEN HIM LIKE THAT BEFORE.
CREATIVITY IS CLOSE TO MADNESS, RIGHT? IT TAKES A TOLL.
WE'VE GOT TO WATCH OUT FOR EACH OTHER.
OH, YEAH, I DO *NOT* LIKE THAT CASUAL CONTACT.
WE NEED TO POUR SOME COLD WATER ON THIS QUICKLY.
WE ALL GET THAT WAY. IT'S JUST YOUR TURN IN THE HOLE, I GUESS.
WE'LL HELP YOU FIND YOUR WAY OUT.
YOU'RE THE BEST.
BLEEP BEEP!

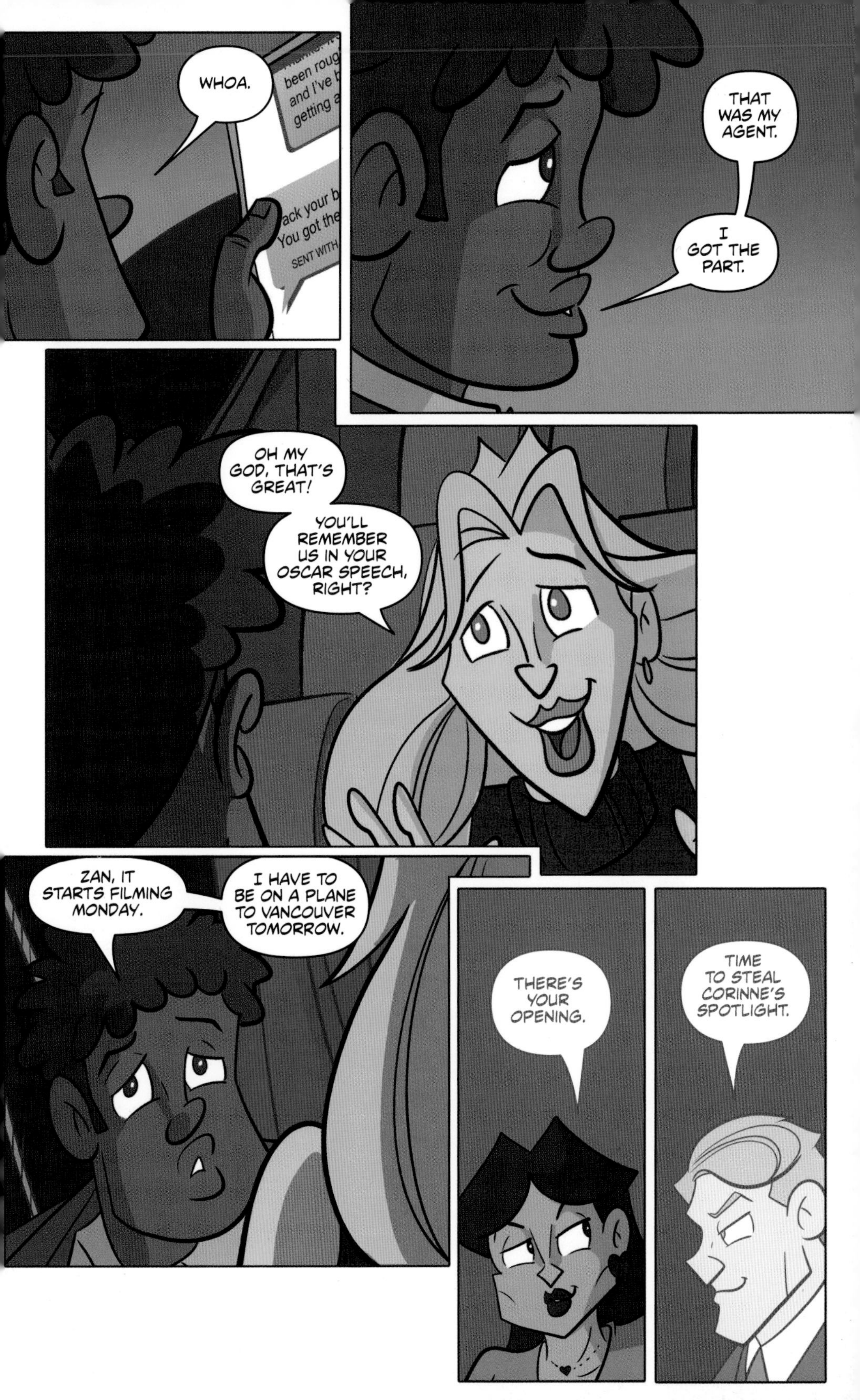
WHOA.
THAT WAS MY AGENT.
I GOT THE PART.
OH MY GOD, THAT'S GREAT!
YOU'LL REMEMBER US IN YOUR OSCAR SPEECH, RIGHT?
ZAN, IT STARTS FILMING MONDAY.
I HAVE TO BE ON A PLANE TO VANCOUVER TOMORROW.
THERE'S YOUR OPENING.
TIME TO STEAL CORINNE'S SPOTLIGHT.

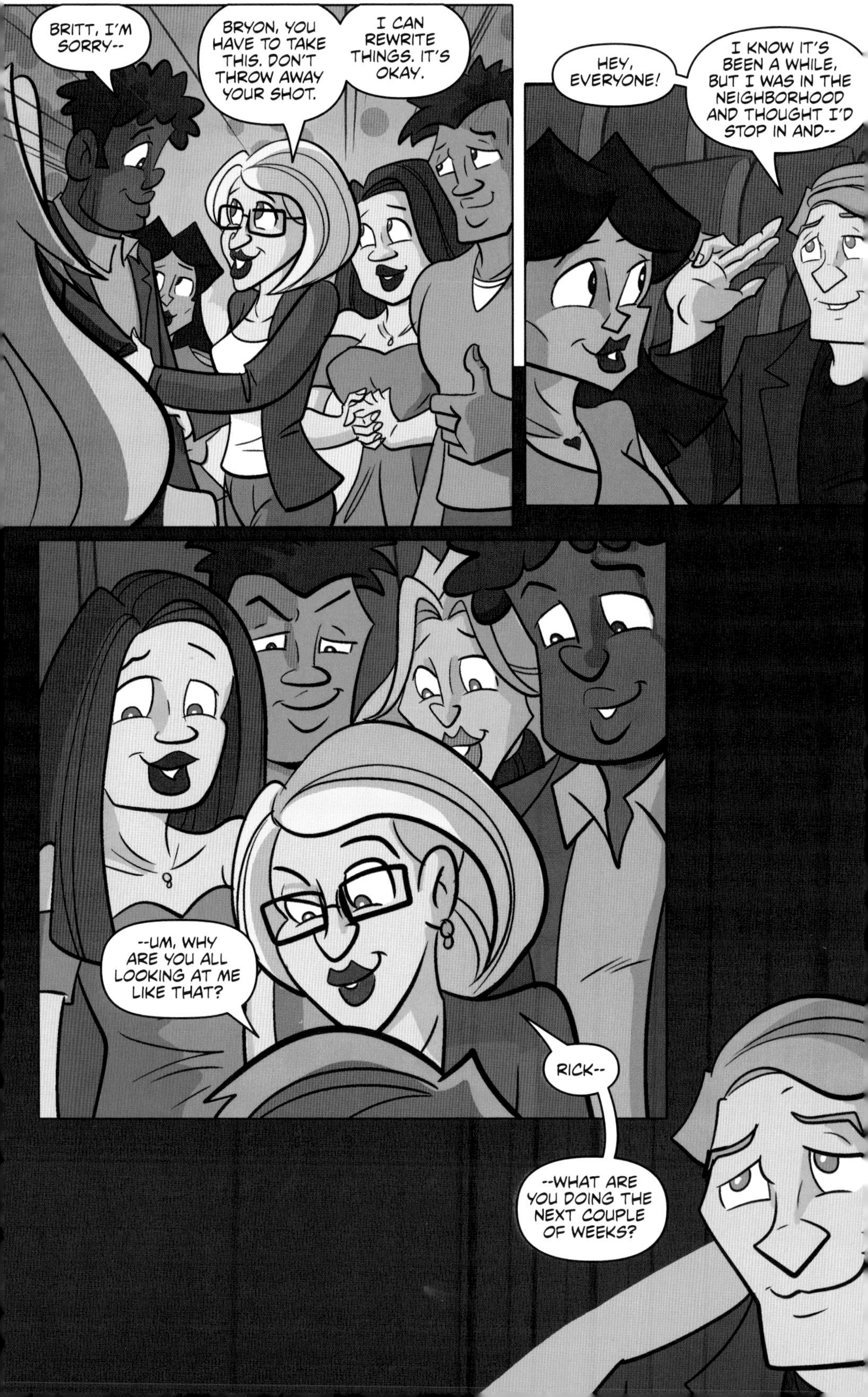
BRITT, I'M SORRY--
BRYON, YOU HAVE TO TAKE THIS. DON'T THROW AWAY YOUR SHOT.
I CAN REWRITE THINGS. IT'S OKAY.
HEY, EVERYONE!
I KNOW IT'S BEEN A WHILE, BUT I WAS IN THE NEIGHBORHOOD AND THOUGHT I'D STOP IN AND--
--UM, WHY ARE YOU ALL LOOKING AT ME LIKE THAT?
RICK--
--WHAT ARE YOU DOING THE NEXT COUPLE OF WEEKS?

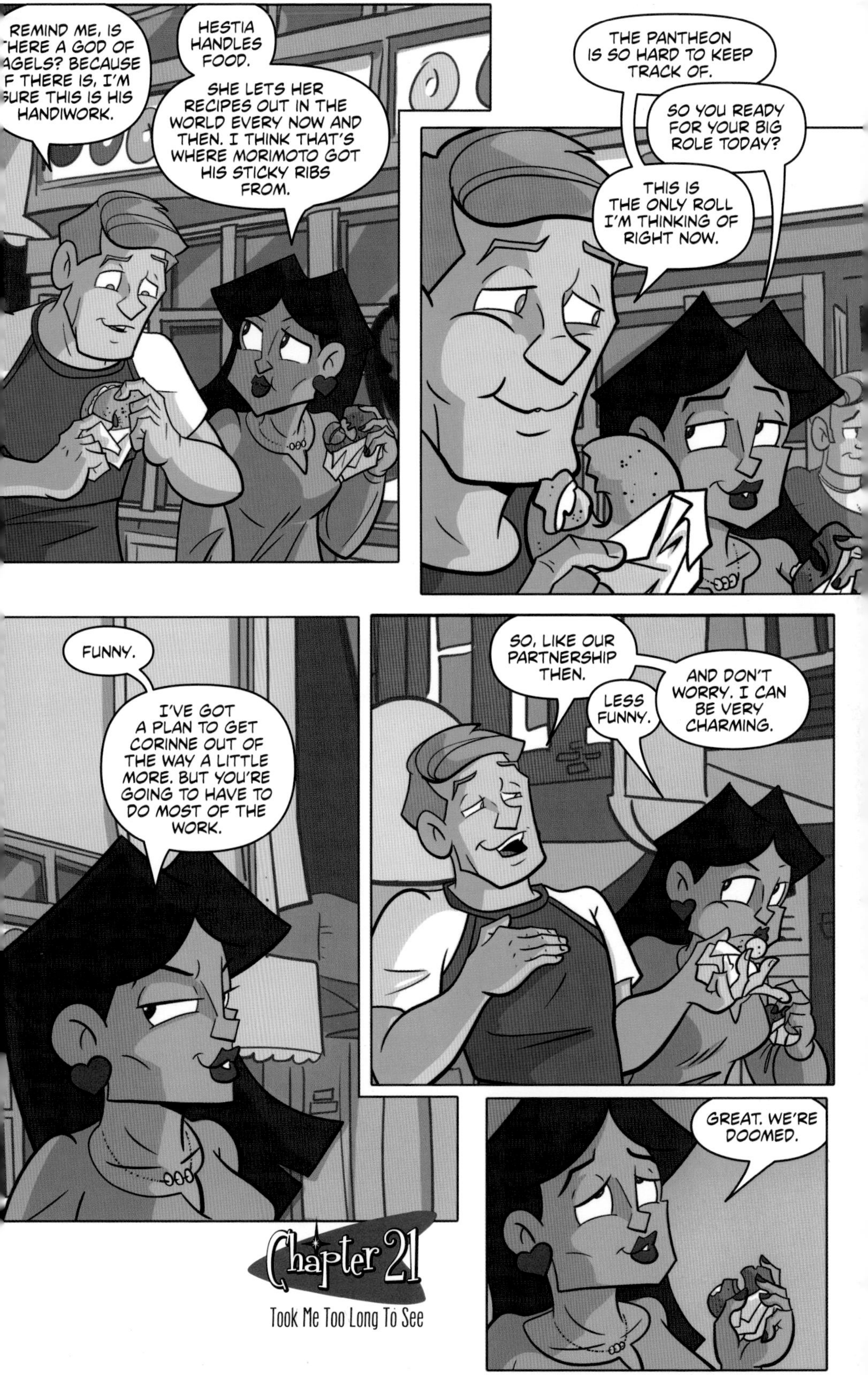
REMIND ME, IS THERE A GOD OF BAGELS? BECAUSE IF THERE IS, I'M SURE THIS IS HIS HANDIWORK.
HESTIA HANDLES FOOD.
SHE LETS HER RECIPES OUT IN THE WORLD EVERY NOW AND THEN. I THINK THAT'S WHERE MORIMOTO GOT HIS STICKY RIBS FROM.
THE PANTHEON IS SO HARD TO KEEP TRACK OF.
SO YOU READY FOR YOUR BIG ROLE TODAY?
THIS IS THE ONLY ROLL I'M THINKING OF RIGHT NOW.
FUNNY.
I'VE GOT A PLAN TO GET CORINNE OUT OF THE WAY A LITTLE MORE. BUT YOU'RE GOING TO HAVE TO DO MOST OF THE WORK.
SO, LIKE OUR PARTNERSHIP THEN.
LESS FUNNY.
AND DON'T WORRY. I CAN BE VERY CHARMING.
GREAT. WE'RE DOOMED.
Chapter 21
Took Me Too Long To See

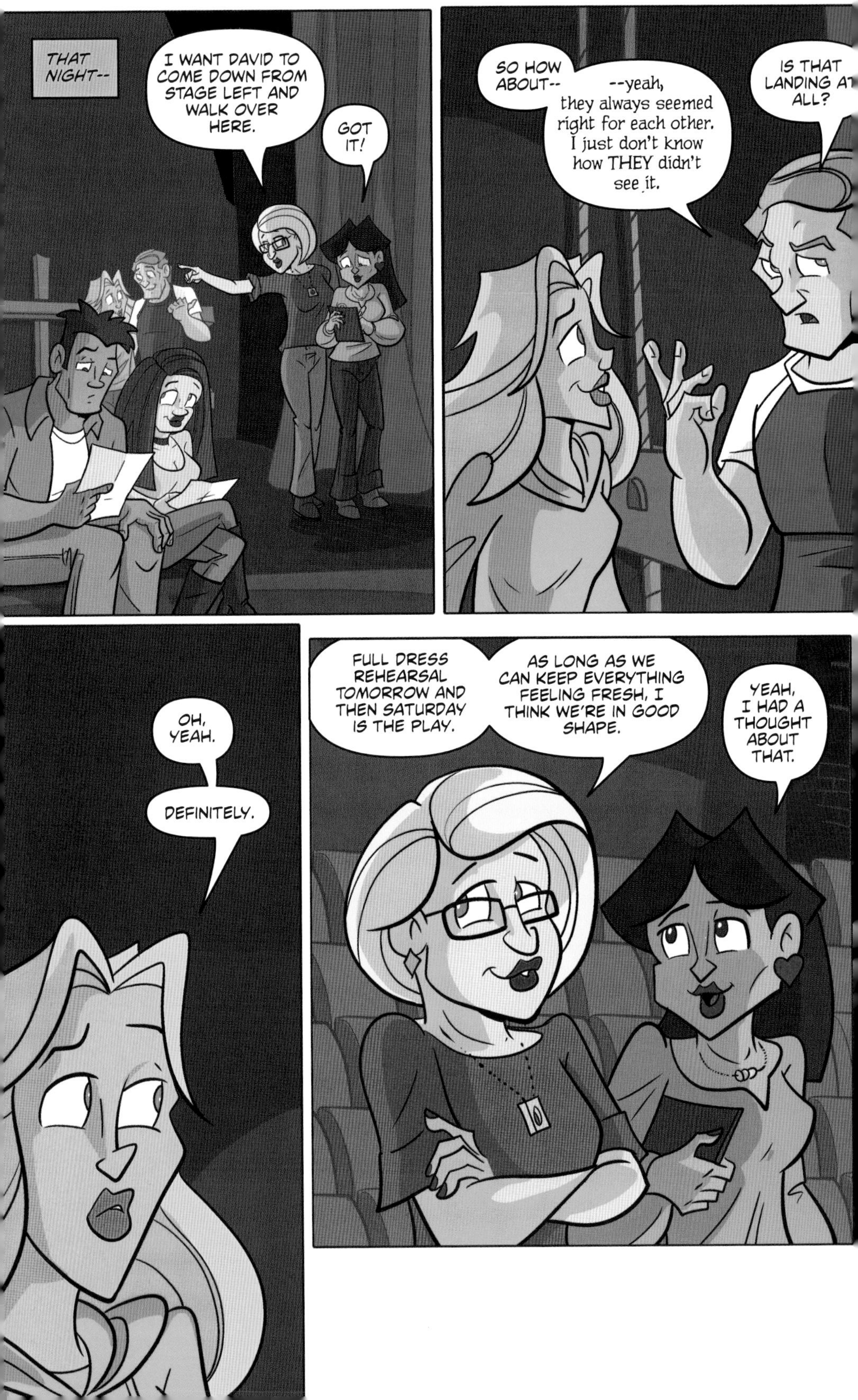
THAT NIGHT--
I WANT DAVID TO COME DOWN FROM STAGE LEFT AND WALK OVER HERE.
GOT IT!
SO HOW ABOUT--
--yeah, they always seemed right for each other. I just don't know how THEY didn't see it.
IS THAT LANDING AT ALL?
OH, YEAH.
DEFINITELY.
FULL DRESS REHEARSAL TOMORROW AND THEN SATURDAY IS THE PLAY.
AS LONG AS WE CAN KEEP EVERYTHING FEELING FRESH, I THINK WE'RE IN GOOD SHAPE.
YEAH, I HAD A THOUGHT ABOUT THAT.

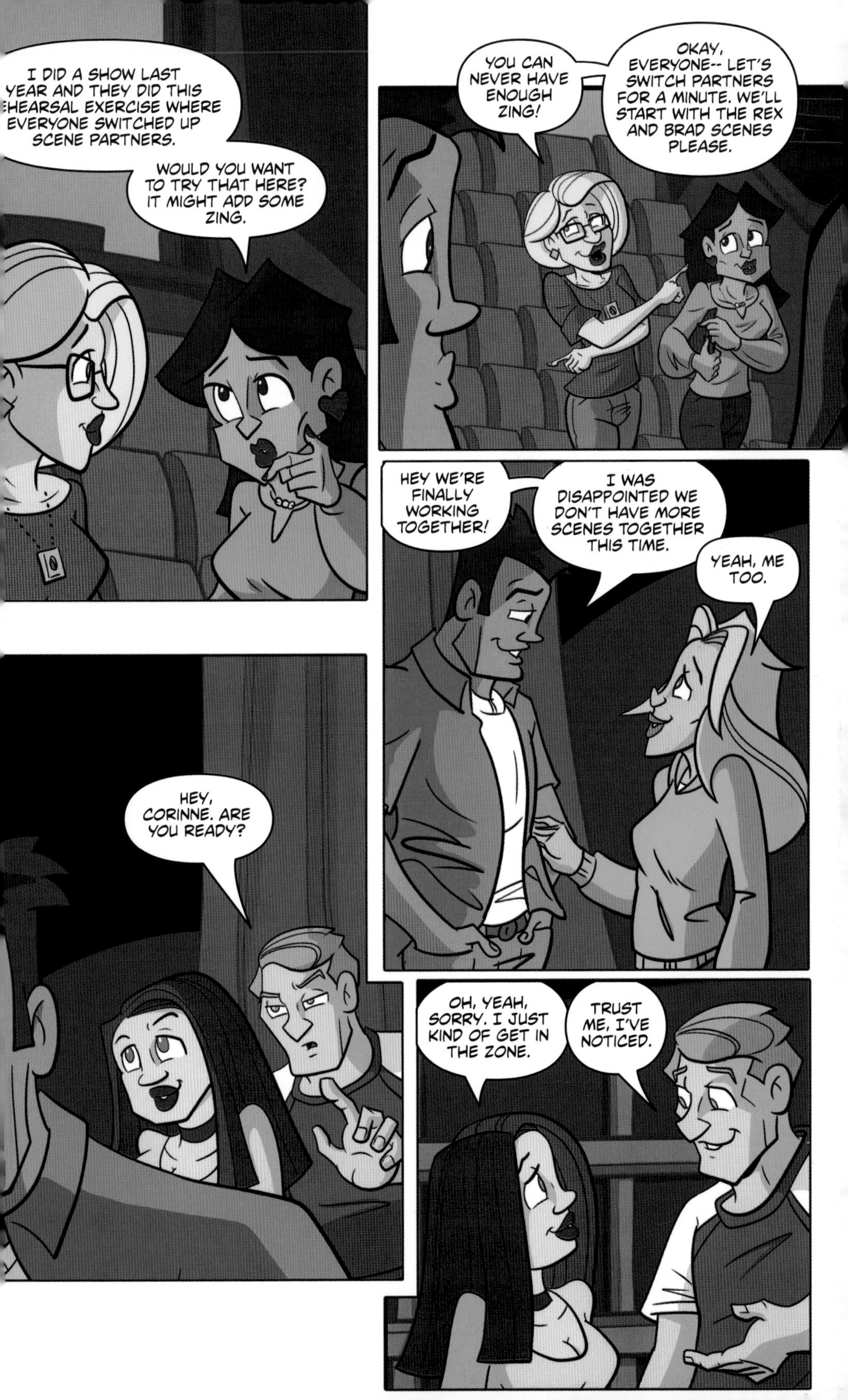
I DID A SHOW LAST YEAR AND THEY DID THIS EHEARSAL EXERCISE WHERE EVERYONE SWITCHED UP SCENE PARTNERS.
WOULD YOU WANT TO TRY THAT HERE? IT MIGHT ADD SOME ZING.
YOU CAN NEVER HAVE ENOUGH ZING!
OKAY, EVERYONE-- LET'S SWITCH PARTNERS FOR A MINUTE. WE'LL START WITH THE REX AND BRAD SCENES PLEASE.
HEY WE'RE FINALLY WORKING TOGETHER!
I WAS DISAPPOINTED WE DON'T HAVE MORE SCENES TOGETHER THIS TIME.
YEAH, ME TOO.
HEY, CORINNE. ARE YOU READY?
OH, YEAH, SORRY. I JUST KIND OF GET IN THE ZONE.
TRUST ME, I'VE NOTICED.

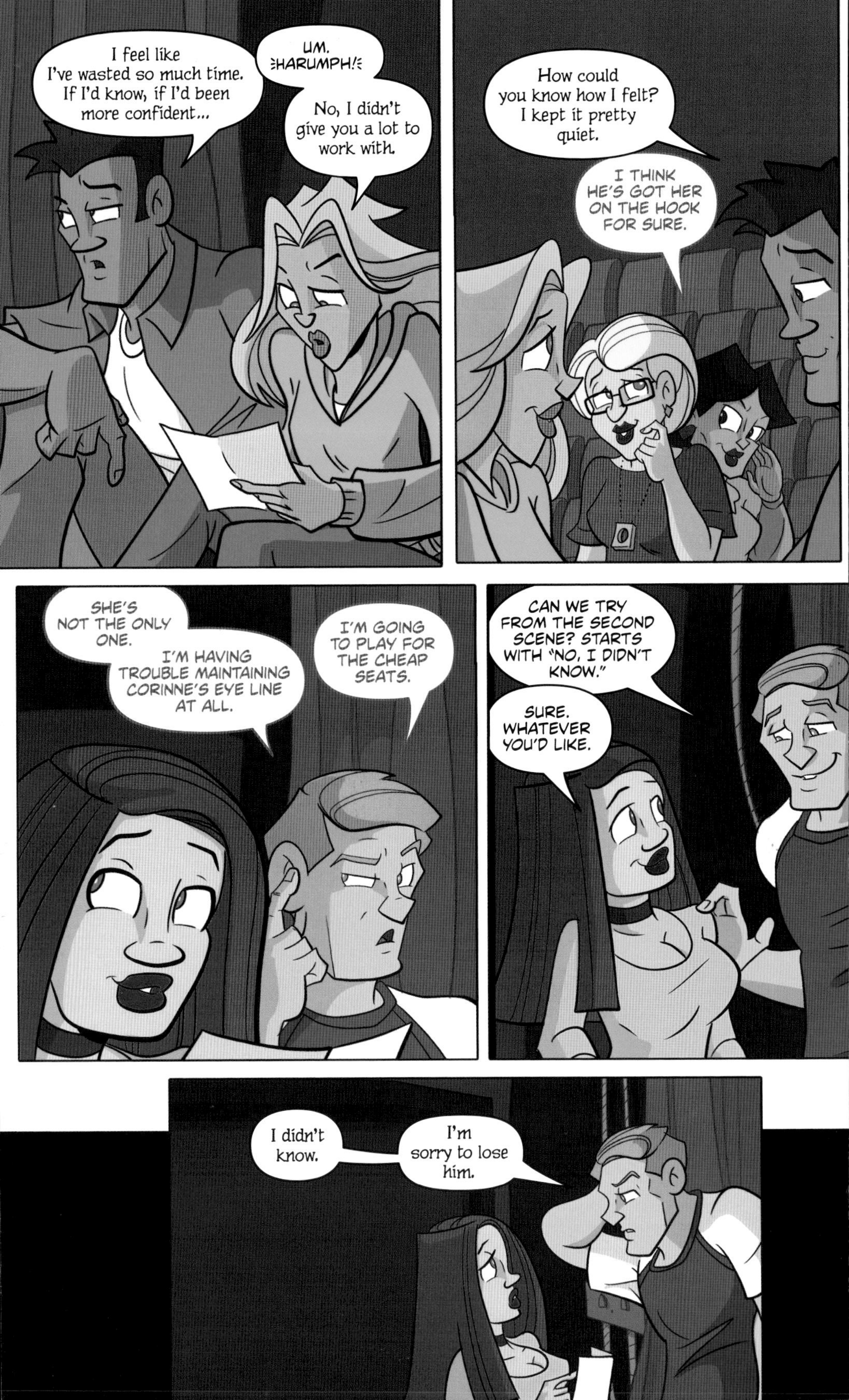
I feel like I've wasted so much time. If I'd know, if I'd been more confident...
UM. HARUMPH!
No, I didn't give you a lot to work with.
How could you know how I felt? I kept it pretty quiet.
I THINK HE'S GOT HER ON THE HOOK FOR SURE.
SHE'S NOT THE ONLY ONE.
I'M HAVING TROUBLE MAINTAINING CORINNE'S EYE LINE AT ALL.
I'M GOING TO PLAY FOR THE CHEAP SEATS.
CAN WE TRY FROM THE SECOND SCENE? STARTS WITH "NO, I DIDN'T KNOW."
SURE. WHATEVER YOU'D LIKE.
I didn't know.
I'm sorry to lose him.

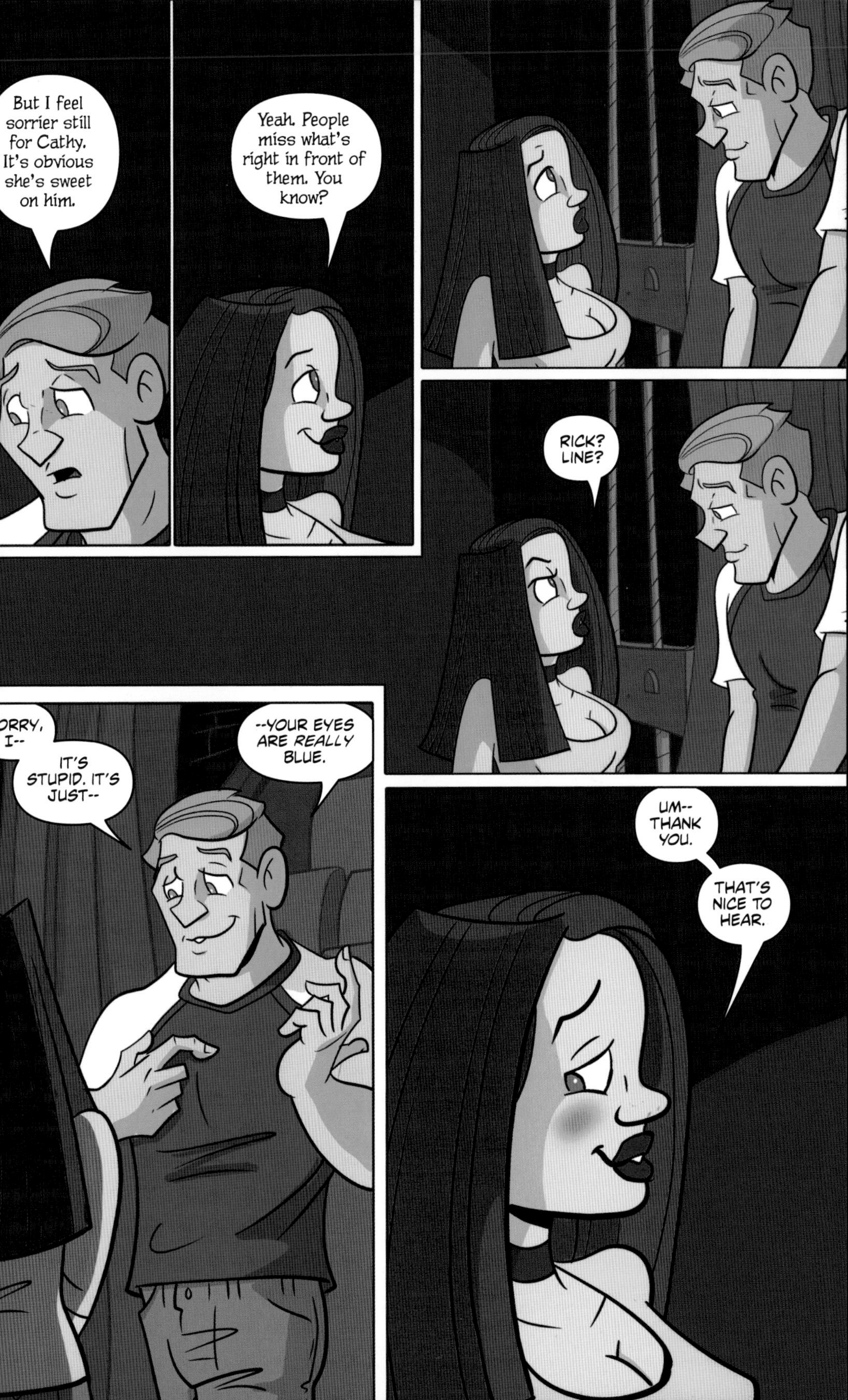
But I feel sorrier still for Cathy. It's obvious she's sweet on him.
Yeah. People miss what's right in front of them. You know?
RICK? LINE?
ORRY, I--
IT'S STUPID. IT'S JUST--
--YOUR EYES ARE *REALLY* BLUE.
UM-- THANK YOU.
THAT'S NICE TO HEAR.

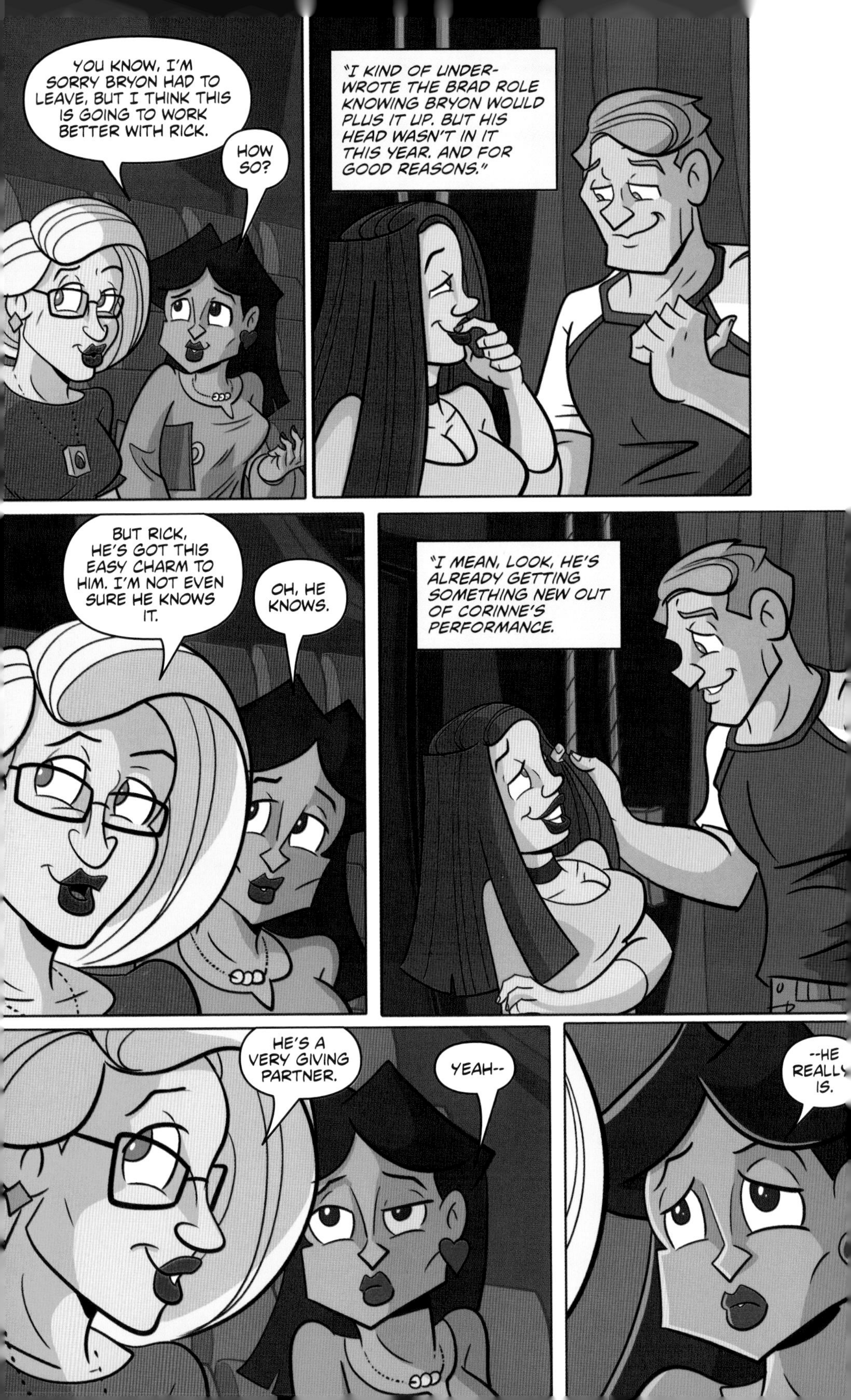
YOU KNOW, I'M SORRY BRYON HAD TO LEAVE, BUT I THINK THIS IS GOING TO WORK BETTER WITH RICK.
HOW SO?
"I KIND OF UNDER-WROTE THE BRAD ROLE KNOWING BRYON WOULD PLUS IT UP. BUT HIS HEAD WASN'T IN IT THIS YEAR. AND FOR GOOD REASONS."
BUT RICK, HE'S GOT THIS EASY CHARM TO HIM. I'M NOT EVEN SURE HE KNOWS IT.
OH, HE KNOWS.
"I MEAN, LOOK, HE'S ALREADY GETTING SOMETHING NEW OUT OF CORINNE'S PERFORMANCE.
HE'S A VERY GIVING PARTNER.
YEAH--
--HE REALLY IS.

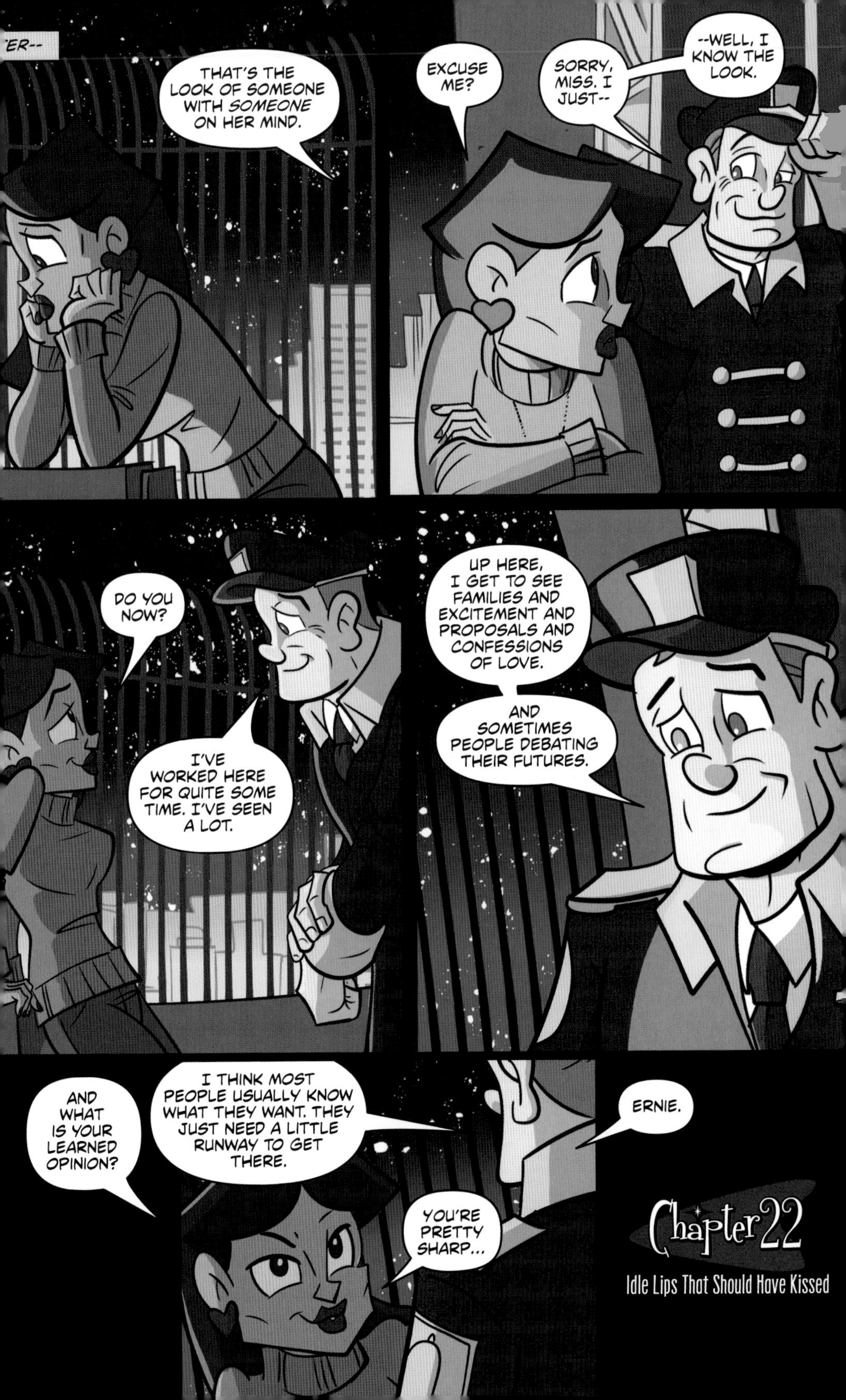

ER--
THAT'S THE LOOK OF SOMEONE WITH SOMEONE ON HER MIND.
EXCUSE ME?
SORRY, MISS. I JUST--
--WELL, I KNOW THE LOOK.
DO YOU NOW?
I'VE WORKED HERE FOR QUITE SOME TIME. I'VE SEEN A LOT.
UP HERE, I GET TO SEE FAMILIES AND EXCITEMENT AND PROPOSALS AND CONFESSIONS OF LOVE.
AND SOMETIMES PEOPLE DEBATING THEIR FUTURES.
AND WHAT IS YOUR LEARNED OPINION?
I THINK MOST PEOPLE USUALLY KNOW WHAT THEY WANT. THEY JUST NEED A LITTLE RUNWAY TO GET THERE.
ERNIE.
YOU'RE PRETTY SHARP...

Chapter 22

Idle Lips That Should Have Kissed

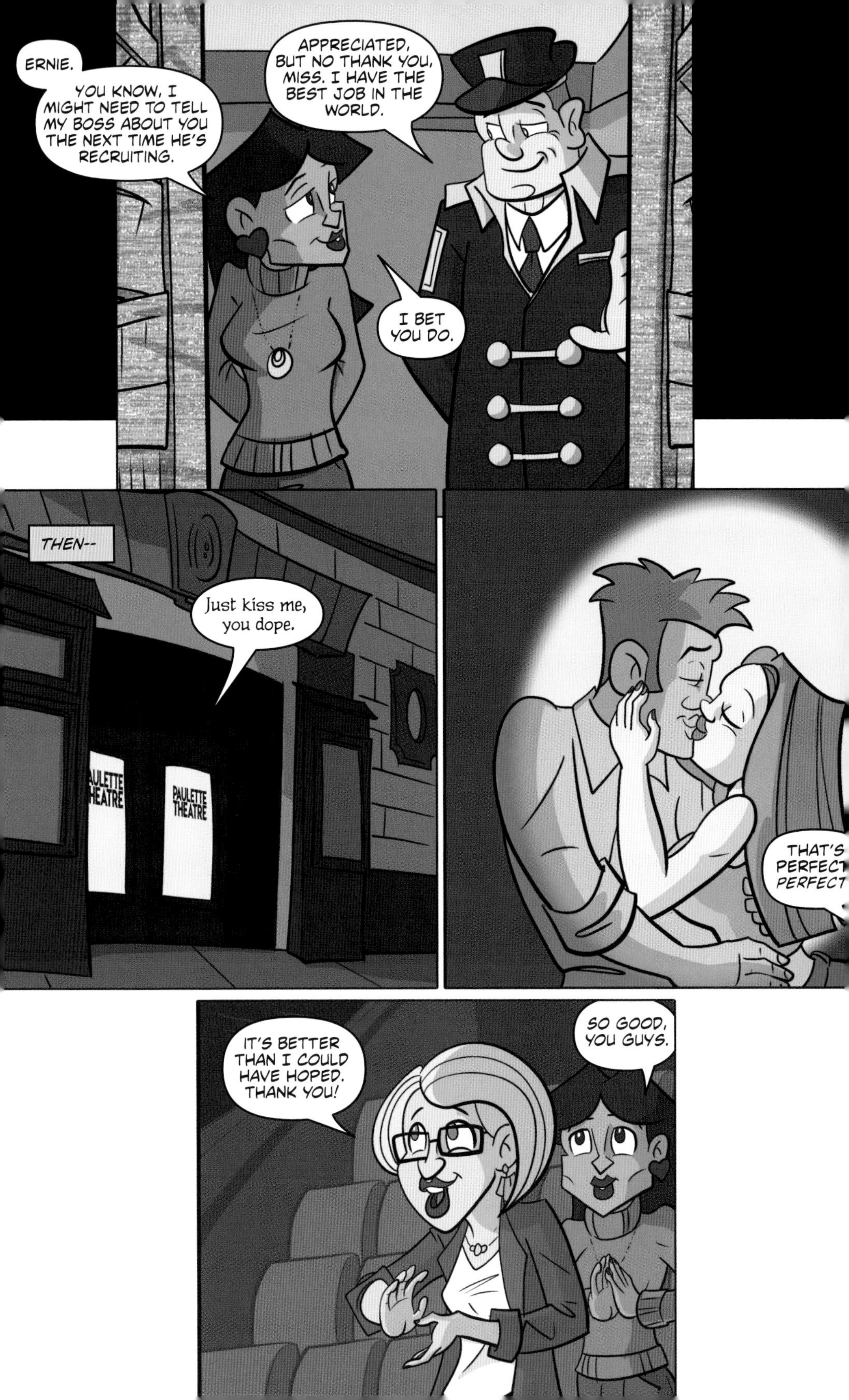
ERNIE.
YOU KNOW, I MIGHT NEED TO TELL MY BOSS ABOUT YOU THE NEXT TIME HE'S RECRUITING.
APPRECIATED, BUT NO THANK YOU, MISS. I HAVE THE BEST JOB IN THE WORLD.
I BET YOU DO.
THEN--
Just kiss me, you dope.
PAULETTE THEATRE
PAULETTE THEATRE
THAT'S PERFECT PERFECT
IT'S BETTER THAN I COULD HAVE HOPED. THANK YOU!
SO GOOD, YOU GUYS.

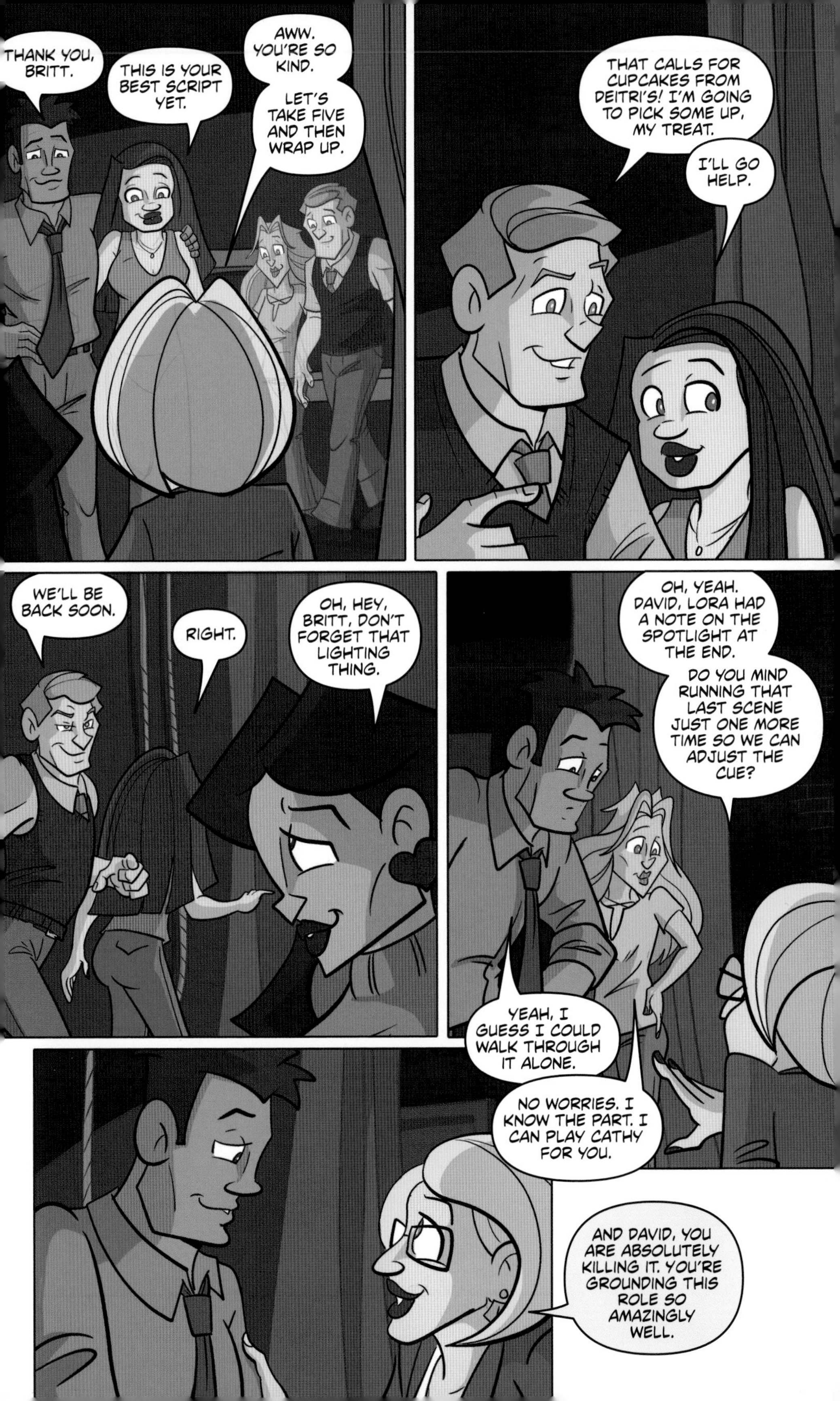
THANK YOU, BRITT.
THIS IS YOUR BEST SCRIPT YET.
AWW. YOU'RE SO KIND.
LET'S TAKE FIVE AND THEN WRAP UP.
THAT CALLS FOR CUPCAKES FROM DEITRI'S! I'M GOING TO PICK SOME UP, MY TREAT.
I'LL GO HELP.
WE'LL BE BACK SOON.
RIGHT.
OH, HEY, BRITT, DON'T FORGET THAT LIGHTING THING.
OH, YEAH. DAVID, LORA HAD A NOTE ON THE SPOTLIGHT AT THE END.
DO YOU MIND RUNNING THAT LAST SCENE JUST ONE MORE TIME SO WE CAN ADJUST THE CUE?
YEAH, I GUESS I COULD WALK THROUGH IT ALONE.
NO WORRIES. I KNOW THE PART. I CAN PLAY CATHY FOR YOU.
AND DAVID, YOU ARE ABSOLUTELY KILLING IT. YOU'RE GROUNDING THIS ROLE SO AMAZINGLY WELL.

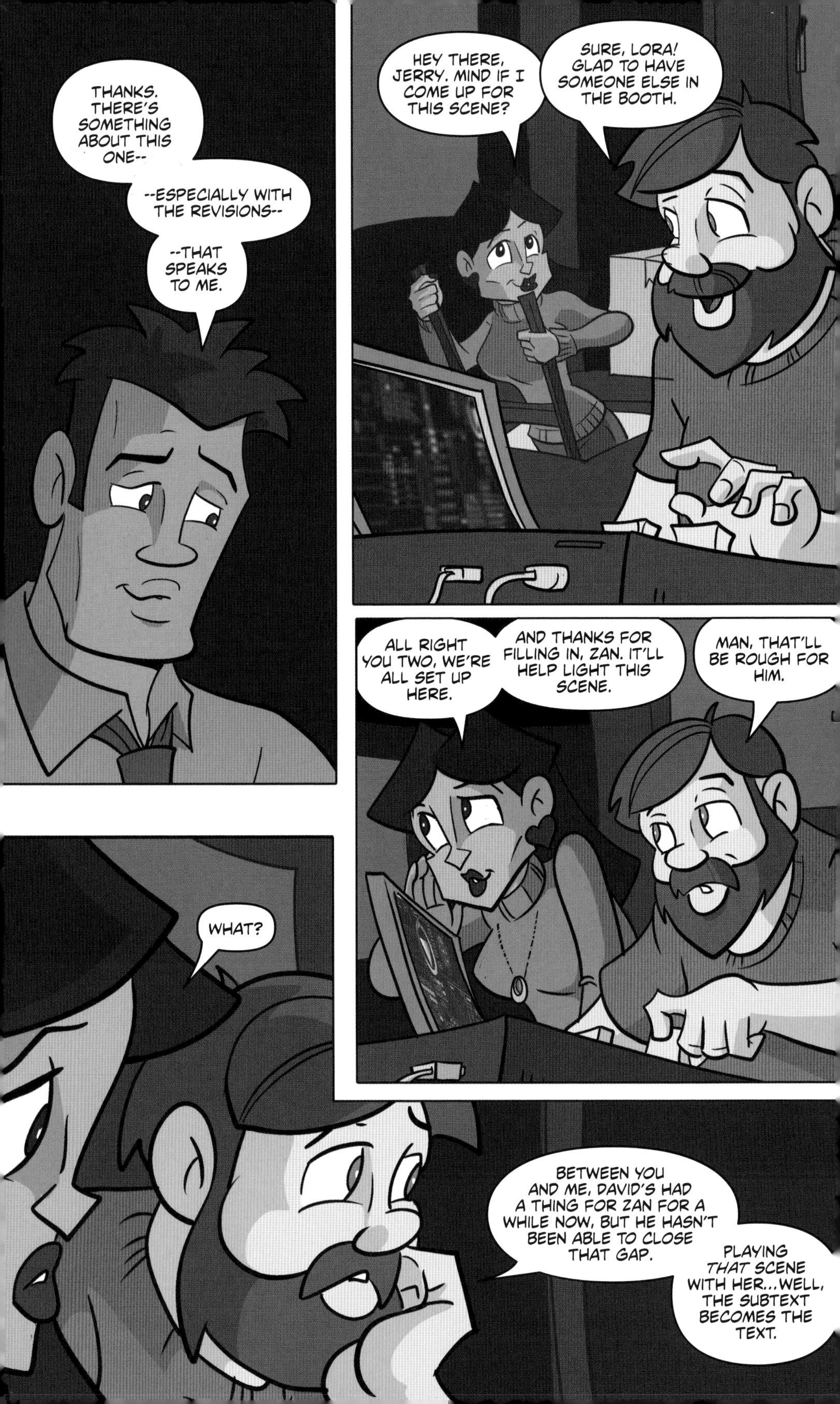
THANKS. THERE'S SOMETHING ABOUT THIS ONE--
--ESPECIALLY WITH THE REVISIONS--
--THAT SPEAKS TO ME.
HEY THERE, JERRY. MIND IF I COME UP FOR THIS SCENE?
SURE, LORA! GLAD TO HAVE SOMEONE ELSE IN THE BOOTH.
ALL RIGHT YOU TWO, WE'RE ALL SET UP HERE.
AND THANKS FOR FILLING IN, ZAN. IT'LL HELP LIGHT THIS SCENE.
MAN, THAT'LL BE ROUGH FOR HIM.
WHAT?
BETWEEN YOU AND ME, DAVID'S HAD A THING FOR ZAN FOR A WHILE NOW, BUT HE HASN'T BEEN ABLE TO CLOSE THAT GAP.
PLAYING *THAT* SCENE WITH HER...WELL, THE SUBTEXT BECOMES THE TEXT.

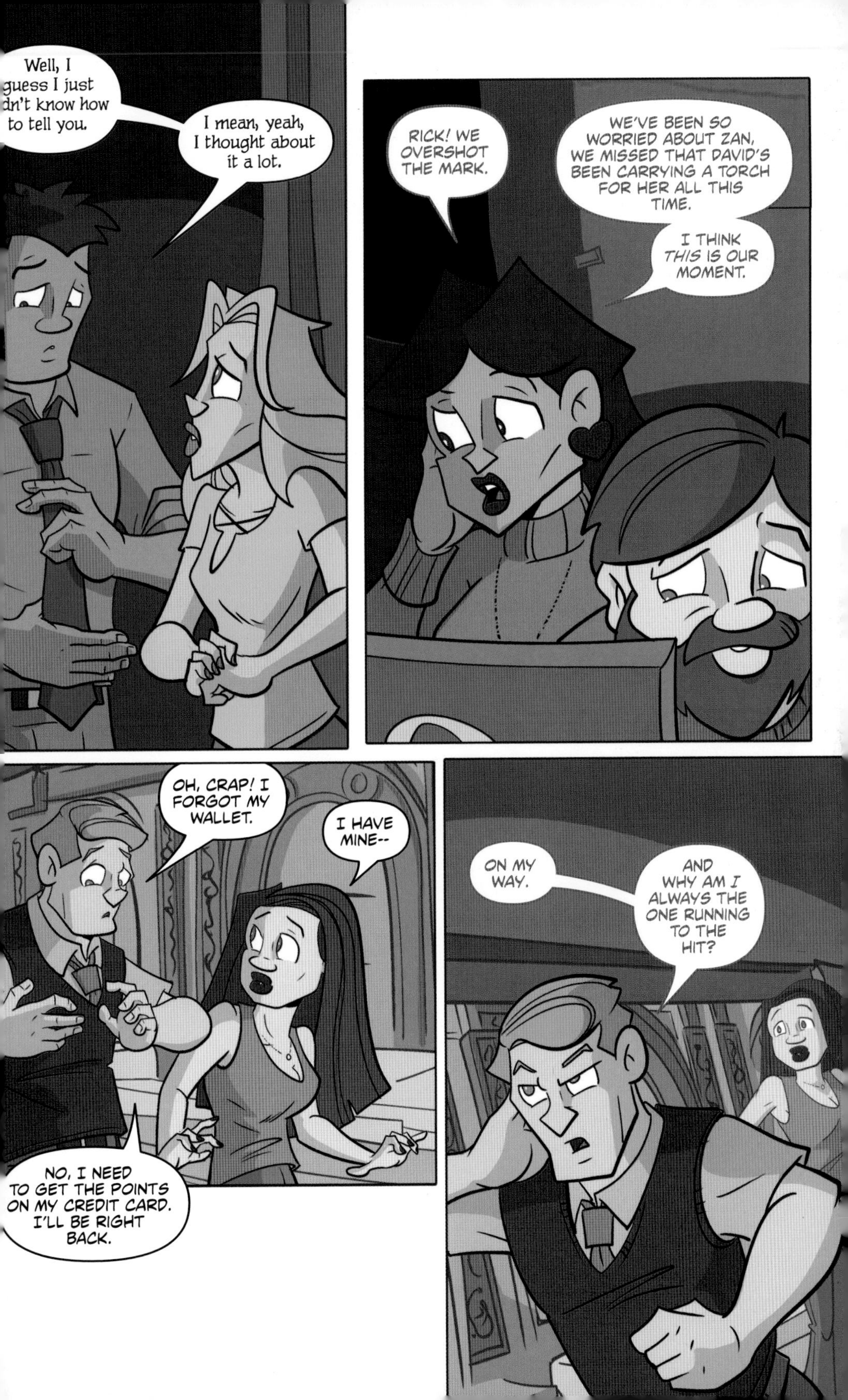
Well, I guess I just dn't know how to tell you.
I mean, yeah, I thought about it a lot.
RICK! WE OVERSHOT THE MARK.
WE'VE BEEN SO WORRIED ABOUT ZAN, WE MISSED THAT DAVID'S BEEN CARRYING A TORCH FOR HER ALL THIS TIME.
I THINK THIS IS OUR MOMENT.
OH, CRAP! I FORGOT MY WALLET.
I HAVE MINE--
NO, I NEED TO GET THE POINTS ON MY CREDIT CARD. I'LL BE RIGHT BACK.
ON MY WAY.
AND WHY AM I ALWAYS THE ONE RUNNING TO THE HIT?

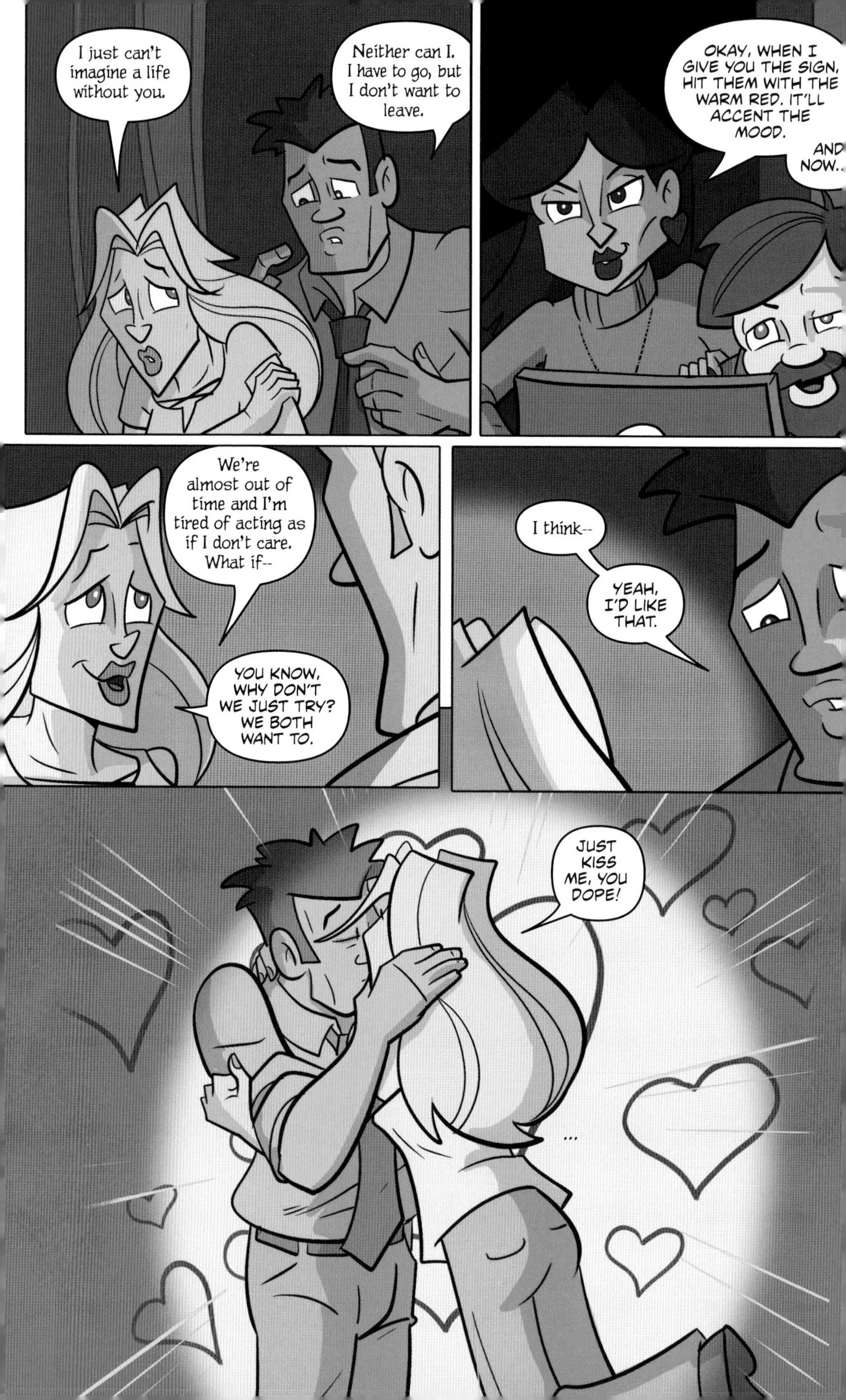
I just can't imagine a life without you.
Neither can I. I have to go, but I don't want to leave.
OKAY, WHEN I GIVE YOU THE SIGN, HIT THEM WITH THE WARM RED. IT'LL ACCENT THE MOOD.
AND NOW..
We're almost out of time and I'm tired of acting as if I don't care. What if--
YOU KNOW, WHY DON'T WE JUST TRY? WE BOTH WANT TO.
I think--
YEAH, I'D LIKE THAT.
JUST KISS ME, YOU DOPE!
...

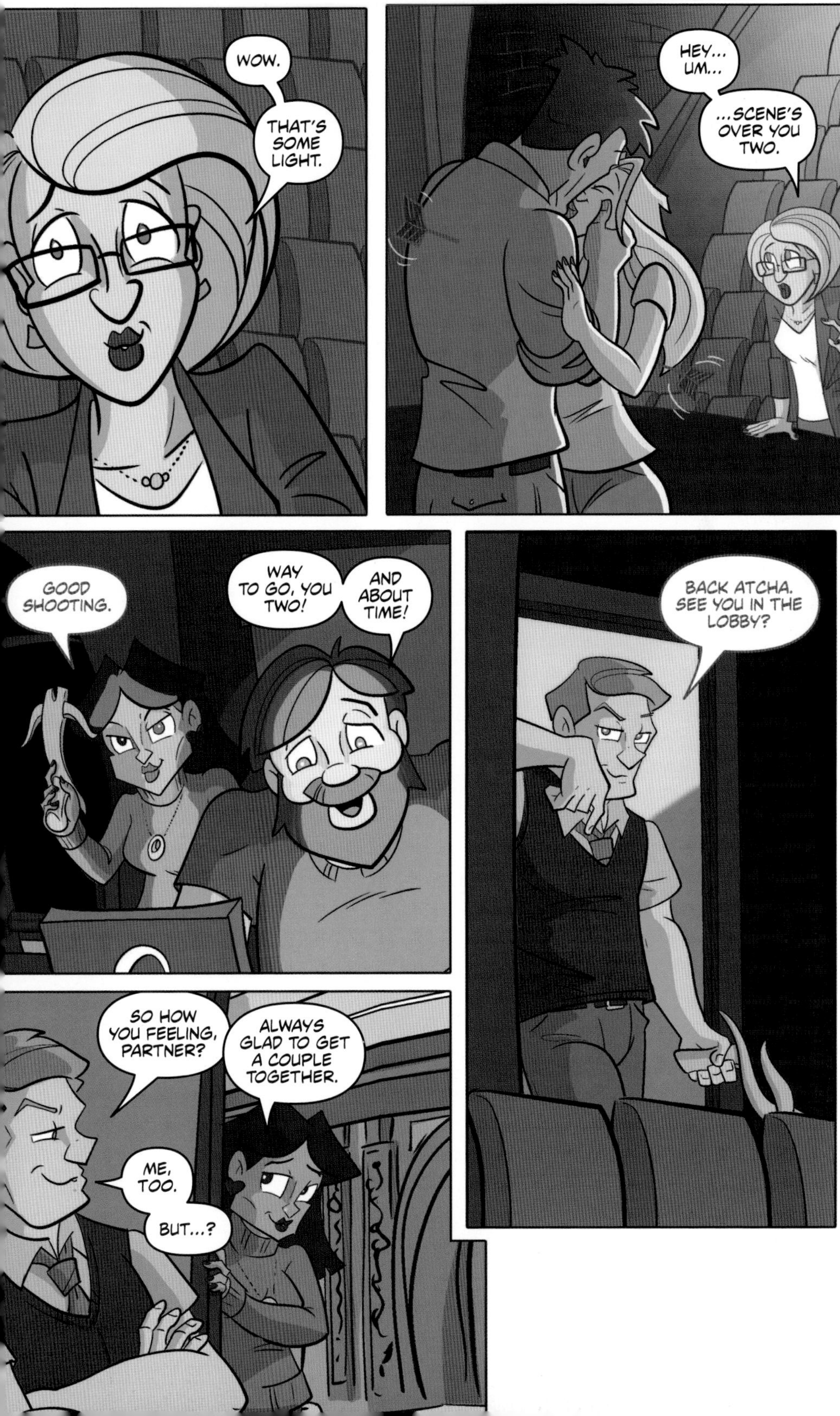
WOW.
THAT'S SOME LIGHT.
HEY... UM...
...SCENE'S OVER YOU TWO.
GOOD SHOOTING.
WAY TO GO, YOU TWO!
AND ABOUT TIME!
BACK ATCHA. SEE YOU IN THE LOBBY?
SO HOW YOU FEELING, PARTNER?
ALWAYS GLAD TO GET A COUPLE TOGETHER.
ME, TOO.
BUT...?

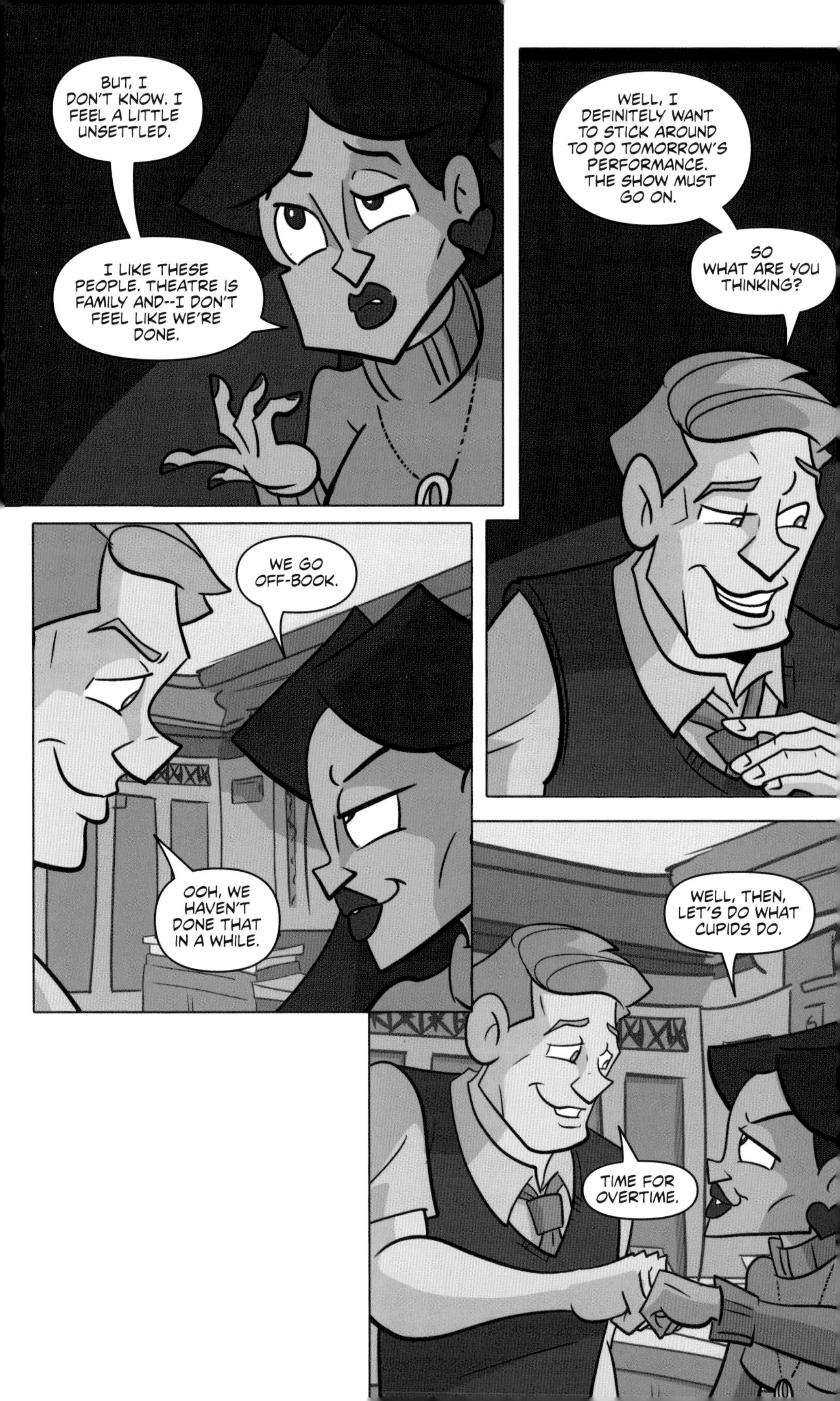
BUT, I DON'T KNOW. I FEEL A LITTLE UNSETTLED.
I LIKE THESE PEOPLE. THEATRE IS FAMILY AND--I DON'T FEEL LIKE WE'RE DONE.
WELL, I DEFINITELY WANT TO STICK AROUND TO DO TOMORROW'S PERFORMANCE. THE SHOW MUST GO ON.
SO WHAT ARE YOU THINKING?
WE GO OFF-BOOK.
OOH, WE HAVEN'T DONE THAT IN A WHILE.
WELL, THEN, LET'S DO WHAT CUPIDS DO.
TIME FOR OVERTIME.

Chapter 23

When Arrows Blocked the Sun

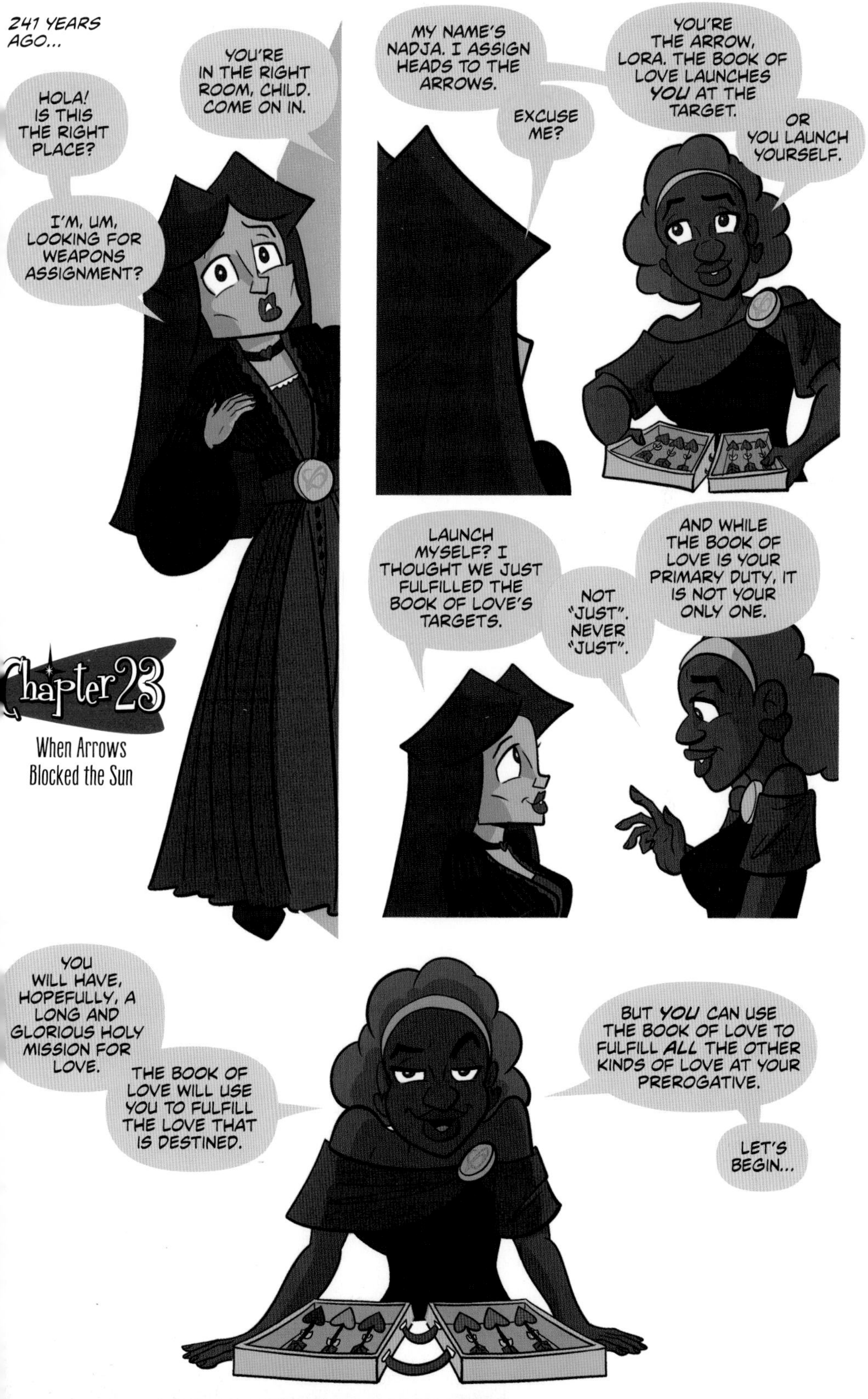
241 YEARS AGO...
HOLA! IS THIS THE RIGHT PLACE?
I'M, UM, LOOKING FOR WEAPONS ASSIGNMENT?
YOU'RE IN THE RIGHT ROOM, CHILD. COME ON IN.
MY NAME'S NADJA. I ASSIGN HEADS TO THE ARROWS.
EXCUSE ME?
YOU'RE THE ARROW, LORA. THE BOOK OF LOVE LAUNCHES YOU AT THE TARGET.
OR YOU LAUNCH YOURSELF.
LAUNCH MYSELF? I THOUGHT WE JUST FULFILLED THE BOOK OF LOVE'S TARGETS.
NOT "JUST". NEVER "JUST".
AND WHILE THE BOOK OF LOVE IS YOUR PRIMARY DUTY, IT IS NOT YOUR ONLY ONE.
YOU WILL HAVE, HOPEFULLY, A LONG AND GLORIOUS HOLY MISSION FOR LOVE.
THE BOOK OF LOVE WILL USE YOU TO FULFILL THE LOVE THAT IS DESTINED.
BUT YOU CAN USE THE BOOK OF LOVE TO FULFILL ALL THE OTHER KINDS OF LOVE AT YOUR PREROGATIVE.
LET'S BEGIN...

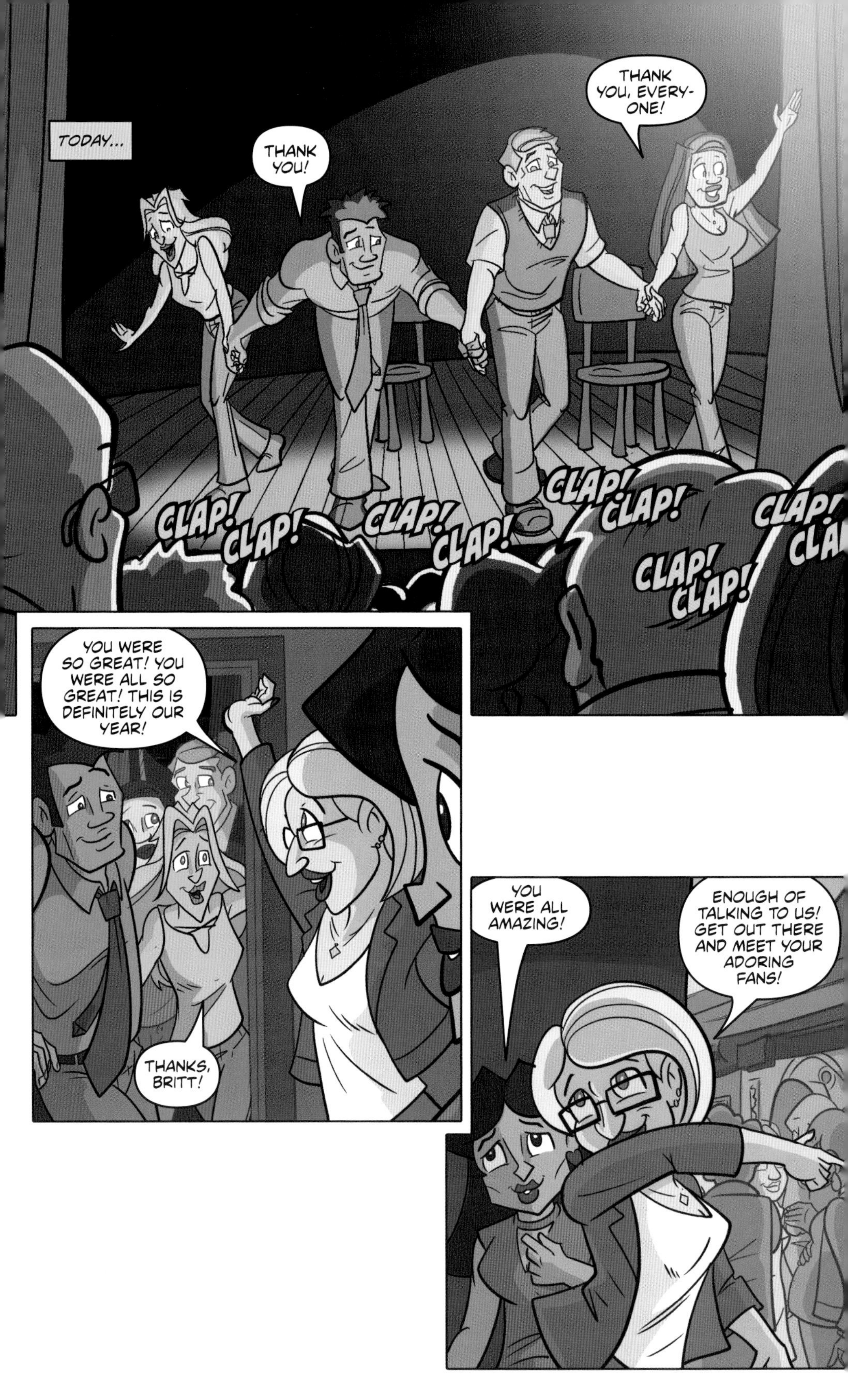
TODAY...
THANK YOU!
THANK YOU, EVERY-ONE!
CLAP! CLAP! CLAP! CLAP! CLAP! CLAP! CLAP! CLAP! CLAP!
YOU WERE SO GREAT! YOU WERE ALL SO GREAT! THIS IS DEFINITELY OUR YEAR!
THANKS, BRITT!
YOU WERE ALL AMAZING!
ENOUGH OF TALKING TO US! GET OUT THERE AND MEET YOUR ADORING FANS!

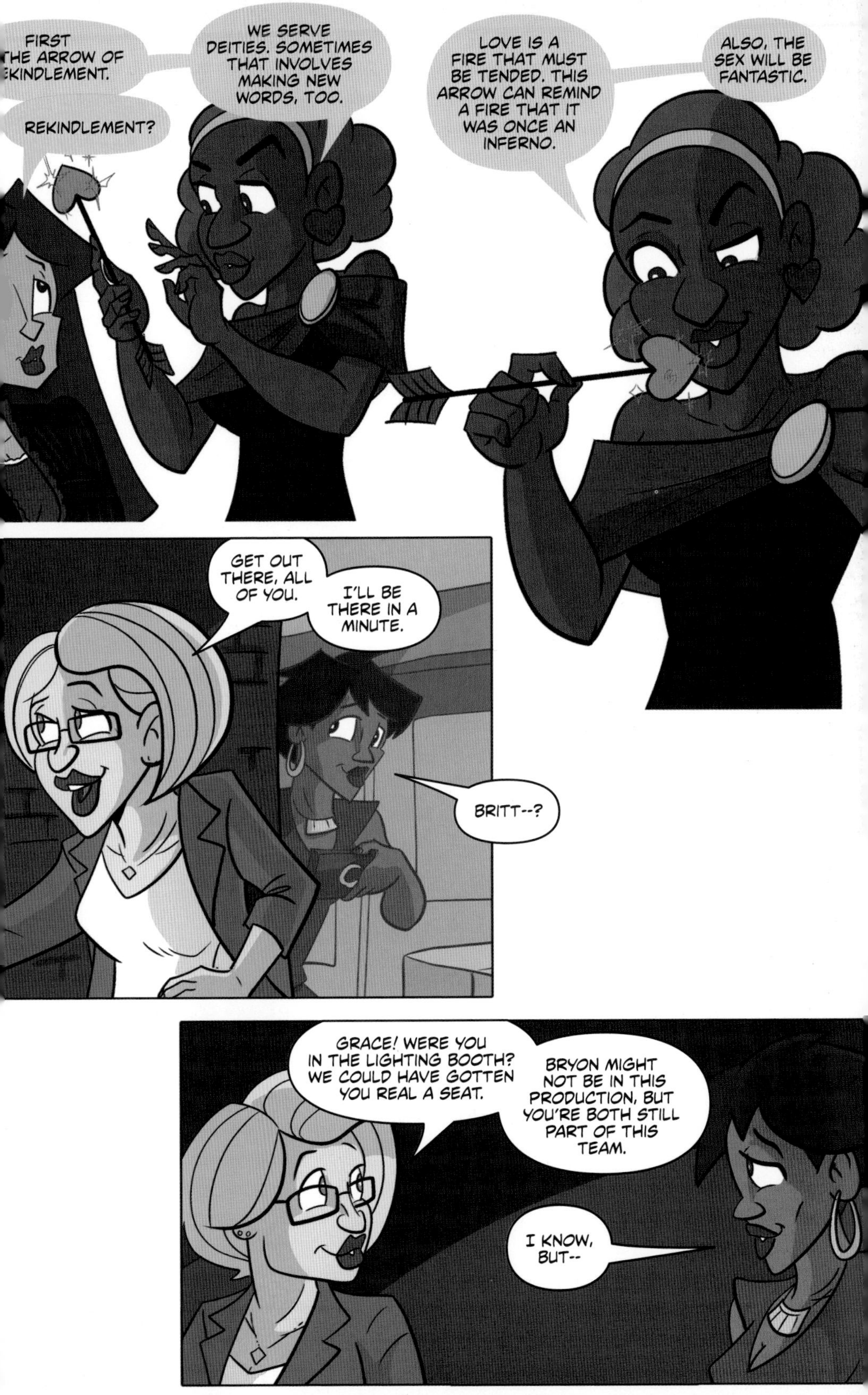
FIRST THE ARROW OF REKINDLEMENT.
REKINDLEMENT?
WE SERVE DEITIES. SOMETIMES THAT INVOLVES MAKING NEW WORDS, TOO.
LOVE IS A FIRE THAT MUST BE TENDED. THIS ARROW CAN REMIND A FIRE THAT IT WAS ONCE AN INFERNO.
ALSO, THE SEX WILL BE FANTASTIC.
GET OUT THERE, ALL OF YOU.
I'LL BE THERE IN A MINUTE.
BRITT--?
GRACE! WERE YOU IN THE LIGHTING BOOTH? WE COULD HAVE GOTTEN YOU REAL A SEAT.
BRYON MIGHT NOT BE IN THIS PRODUCTION, BUT YOU'RE BOTH STILL PART OF THIS TEAM.
I KNOW, BUT--

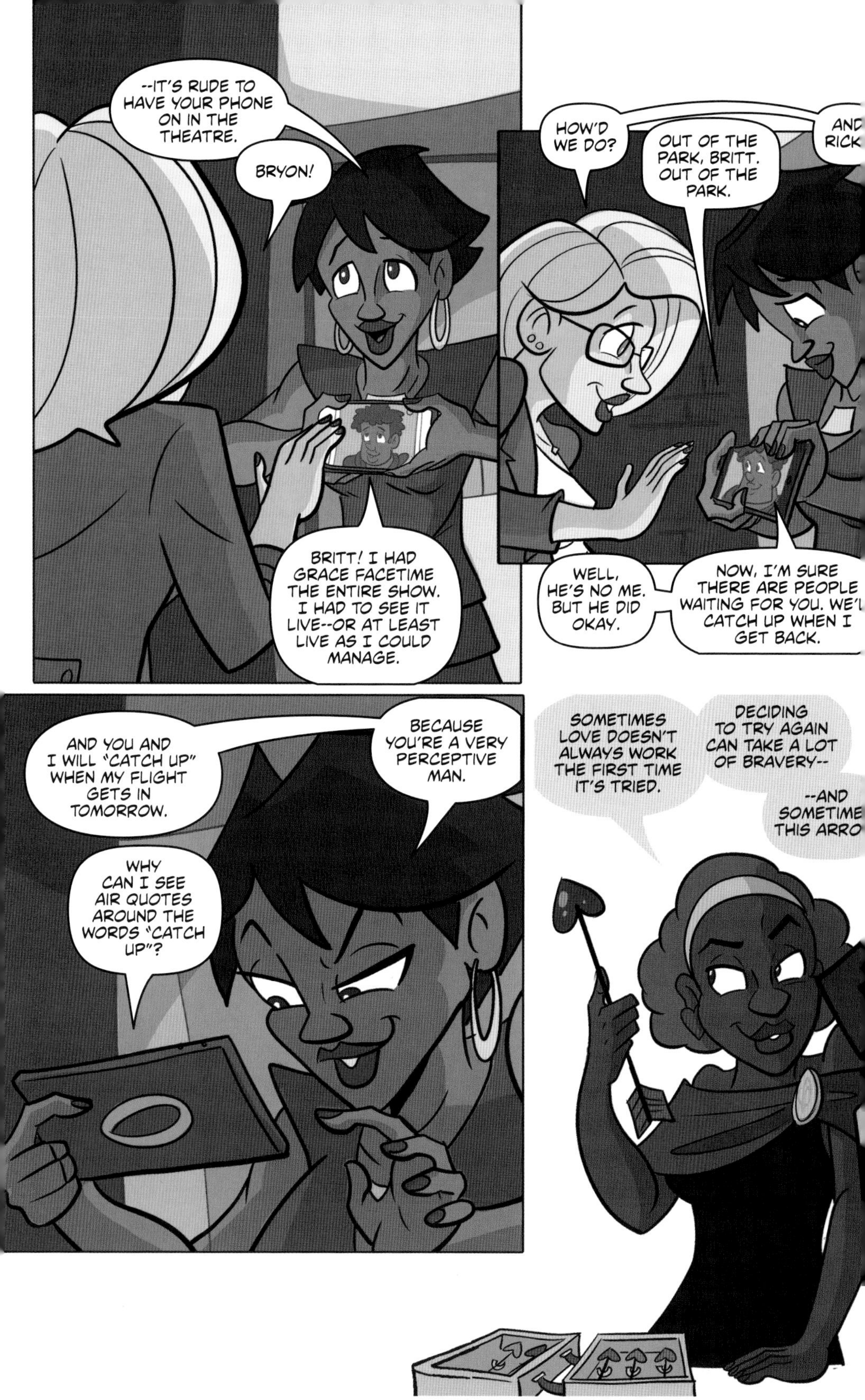
--IT'S RUDE TO HAVE YOUR PHONE ON IN THE THEATRE.
BRYON!
BRITT! I HAD GRACE FACETIME THE ENTIRE SHOW. I HAD TO SEE IT LIVE--OR AT LEAST LIVE AS I COULD MANAGE.
HOW'D WE DO?
OUT OF THE PARK, BRITT. OUT OF THE PARK.
AND RICK
WELL, HE'S NO ME. BUT HE DID OKAY.
NOW, I'M SURE THERE ARE PEOPLE WAITING FOR YOU. WE'L CATCH UP WHEN I GET BACK.
AND YOU AND I WILL "CATCH UP" WHEN MY FLIGHT GETS IN TOMORROW.
WHY CAN I SEE AIR QUOTES AROUND THE WORDS "CATCH UP"?
BECAUSE YOU'RE A VERY PERCEPTIVE MAN.
SOMETIMES LOVE DOESN'T ALWAYS WORK THE FIRST TIME IT'S TRIED.
DECIDING TO TRY AGAIN CAN TAKE A LOT OF BRAVERY--
--AND SOMETIME THIS ARRO

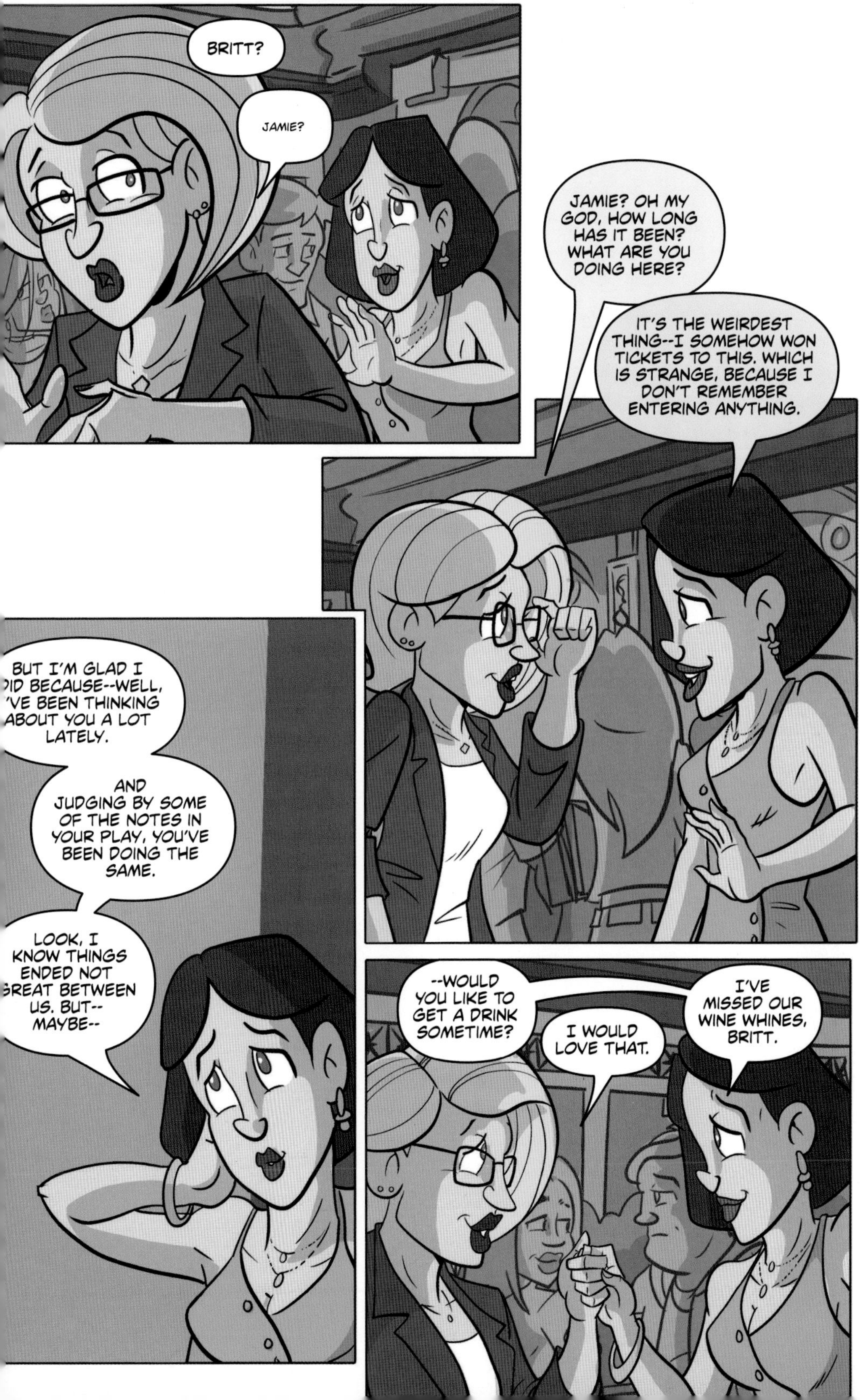
BRITT?
JAMIE?
JAMIE? OH MY GOD, HOW LONG HAS IT BEEN? WHAT ARE YOU DOING HERE?
IT'S THE WEIRDEST THING--I SOMEHOW WON TICKETS TO THIS. WHICH IS STRANGE, BECAUSE I DON'T REMEMBER ENTERING ANYTHING.
BUT I'M GLAD I ID BECAUSE--WELL, 'VE BEEN THINKING ABOUT YOU A LOT LATELY.
AND JUDGING BY SOME OF THE NOTES IN YOUR PLAY, YOU'VE BEEN DOING THE SAME.
LOOK, I KNOW THINGS ENDED NOT REAT BETWEEN US. BUT-- MAYBE--
--WOULD YOU LIKE TO GET A DRINK SOMETIME?
I WOULD LOVE THAT.
I'VE MISSED OUR WINE WHINES, BRITT.

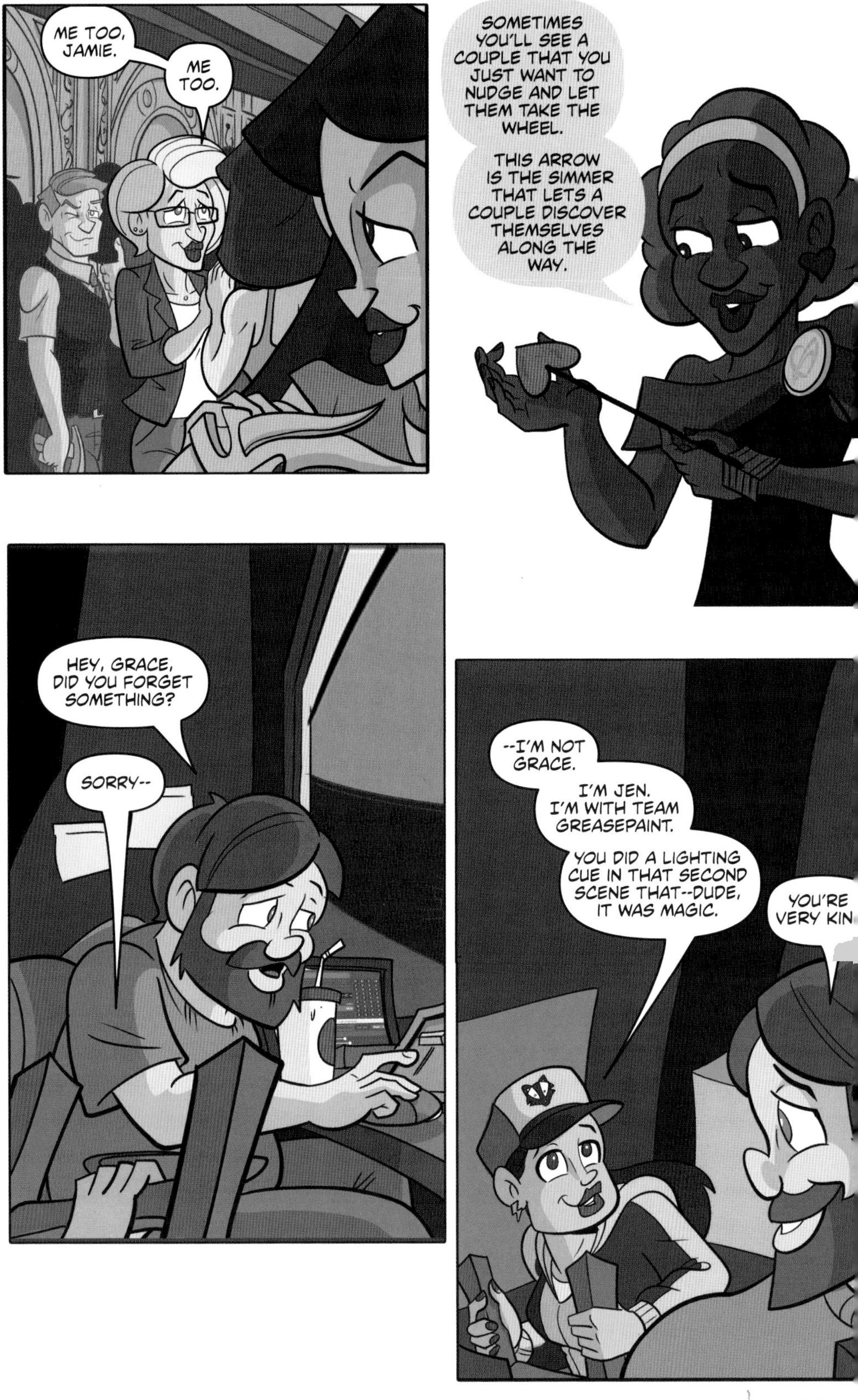
ME TOO, JAMIE.
ME TOO.
SOMETIMES YOU'LL SEE A COUPLE THAT YOU JUST WANT TO NUDGE AND LET THEM TAKE THE WHEEL.
THIS ARROW IS THE SIMMER THAT LETS A COUPLE DISCOVER THEMSELVES ALONG THE WAY.
HEY, GRACE, DID YOU FORGET SOMETHING?
SORRY--
--I'M NOT GRACE.
I'M JEN. I'M WITH TEAM GREASEPAINT.
YOU DID A LIGHTING CUE IN THAT SECOND SCENE THAT--DUDE, IT WAS MAGIC.
YOU'RE VERY KIN

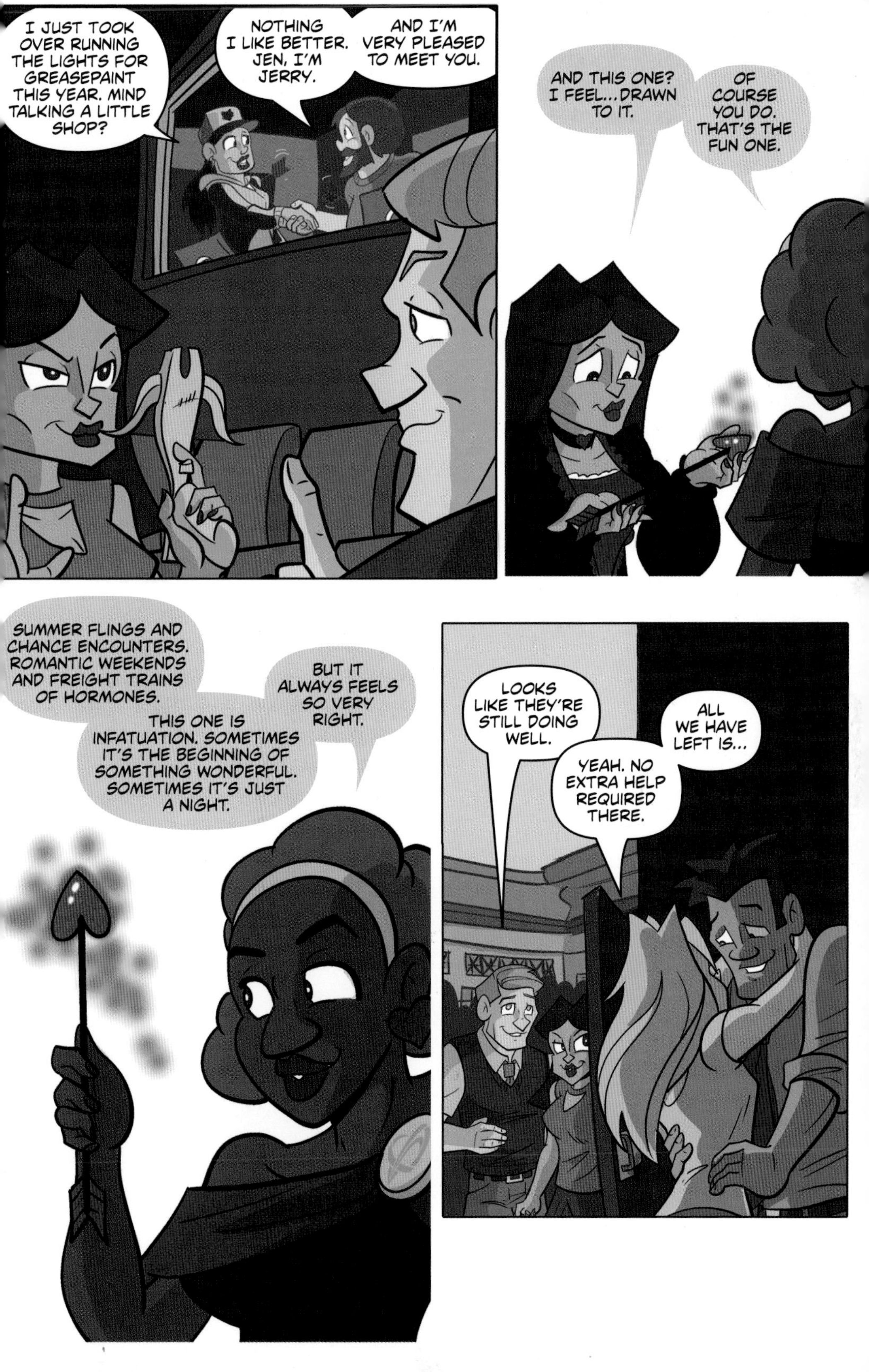
I JUST TOOK OVER RUNNING THE LIGHTS FOR GREASEPAINT THIS YEAR. MIND TALKING A LITTLE SHOP?
NOTHING I LIKE BETTER. JEN, I'M JERRY.
AND I'M VERY PLEASED TO MEET YOU.
AND THIS ONE? I FEEL...DRAWN TO IT.
OF COURSE YOU DO. THAT'S THE FUN ONE.
SUMMER FLINGS AND CHANCE ENCOUNTERS. ROMANTIC WEEKENDS AND FREIGHT TRAINS OF HORMONES.
THIS ONE IS INFATUATION. SOMETIMES IT'S THE BEGINNING OF SOMETHING WONDERFUL. SOMETIMES IT'S JUST A NIGHT.
BUT IT ALWAYS FEELS SO VERY RIGHT.
LOOKS LIKE THEY'RE STILL DOING WELL.
YEAH. NO EXTRA HELP REQUIRED THERE.
ALL WE HAVE LEFT IS...

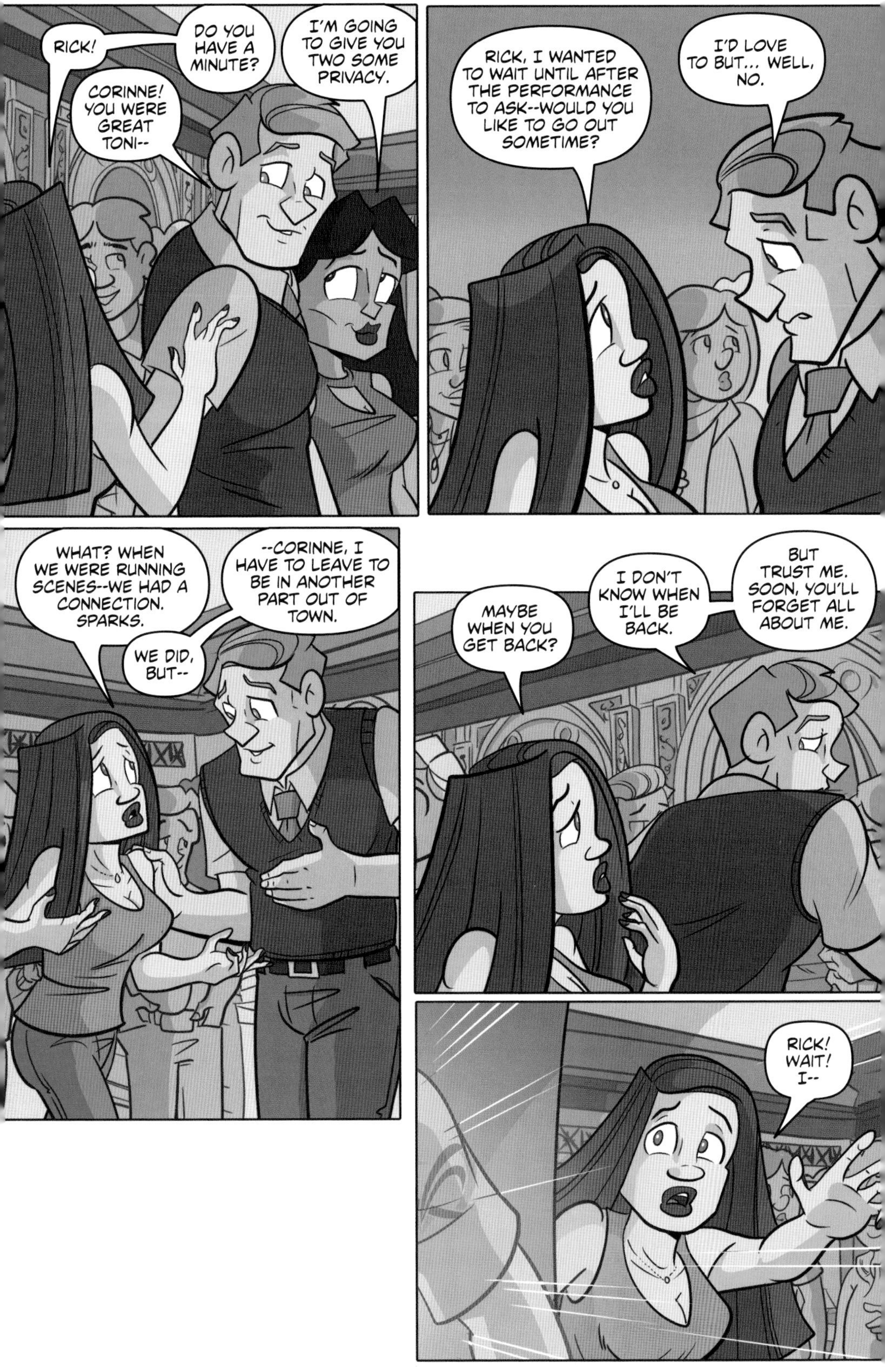
RICK!
DO YOU HAVE A MINUTE?
CORINNE! YOU WERE GREAT TONI--
I'M GOING TO GIVE YOU TWO SOME PRIVACY.
RICK, I WANTED TO WAIT UNTIL AFTER THE PERFORMANCE TO ASK--WOULD YOU LIKE TO GO OUT SOMETIME?
I'D LOVE TO BUT... WELL, NO.
WHAT? WHEN WE WERE RUNNING SCENES--WE HAD A CONNECTION. SPARKS.
WE DID, BUT--
--CORINNE, I HAVE TO LEAVE TO BE IN ANOTHER PART OUT OF TOWN.
MAYBE WHEN YOU GET BACK?
I DON'T KNOW WHEN I'LL BE BACK.
BUT TRUST ME. SOON, YOU'LL FORGET ALL ABOUT ME.
RICK! WAIT! I--

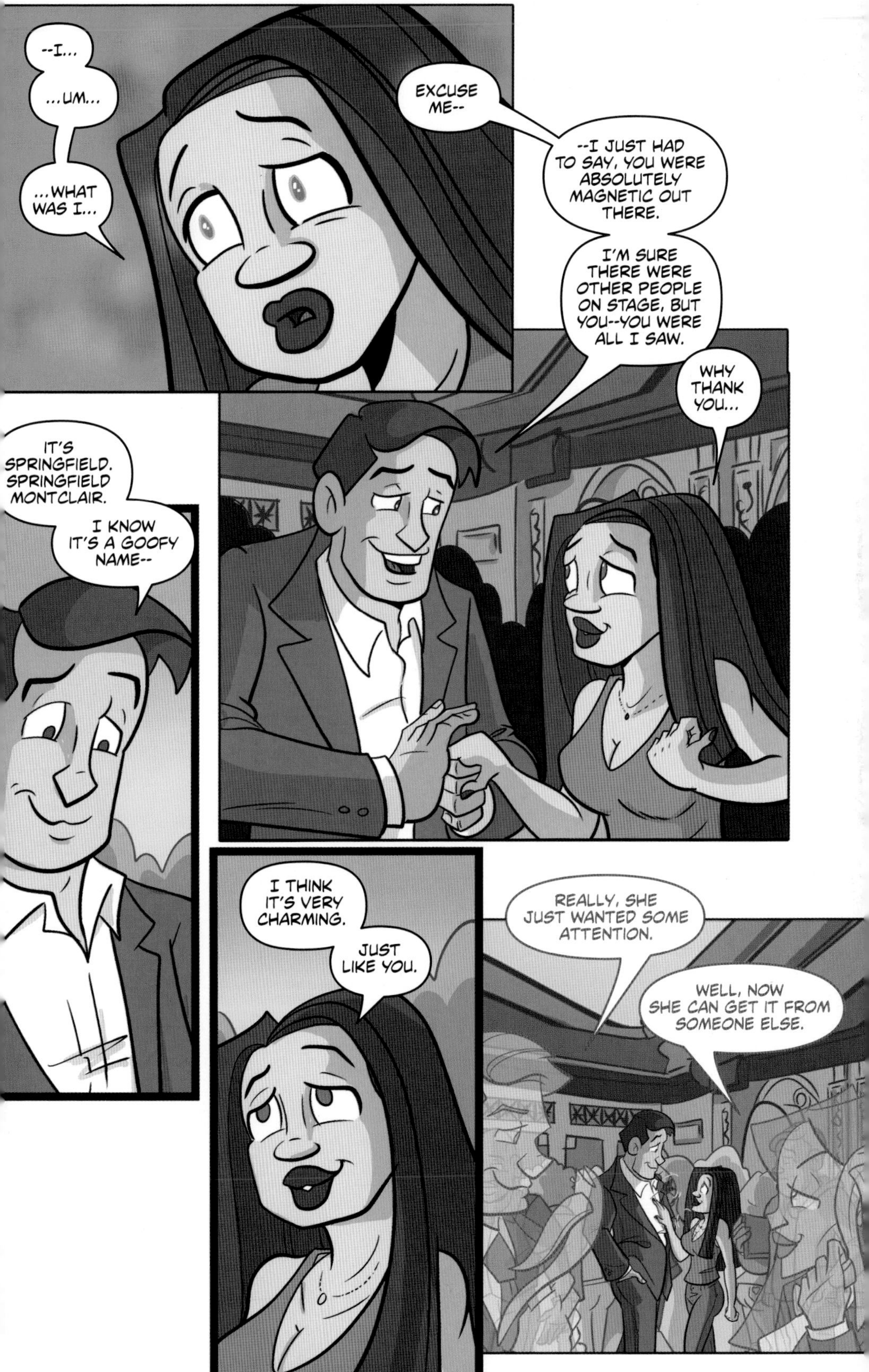
--I...
...UM...
...WHAT WAS I...
EXCUSE ME--
--I JUST HAD TO SAY, YOU WERE ABSOLUTELY MAGNETIC OUT THERE.
I'M SURE THERE WERE OTHER PEOPLE ON STAGE, BUT YOU--YOU WERE ALL I SAW.
WHY THANK YOU...
IT'S SPRINGFIELD. SPRINGFIELD MONTCLAIR.
I KNOW IT'S A GOOFY NAME--
I THINK IT'S VERY CHARMING.
JUST LIKE YOU.
REALLY, SHE JUST WANTED SOME ATTENTION.
WELL, NOW SHE CAN GET IT FROM SOMEONE ELSE.

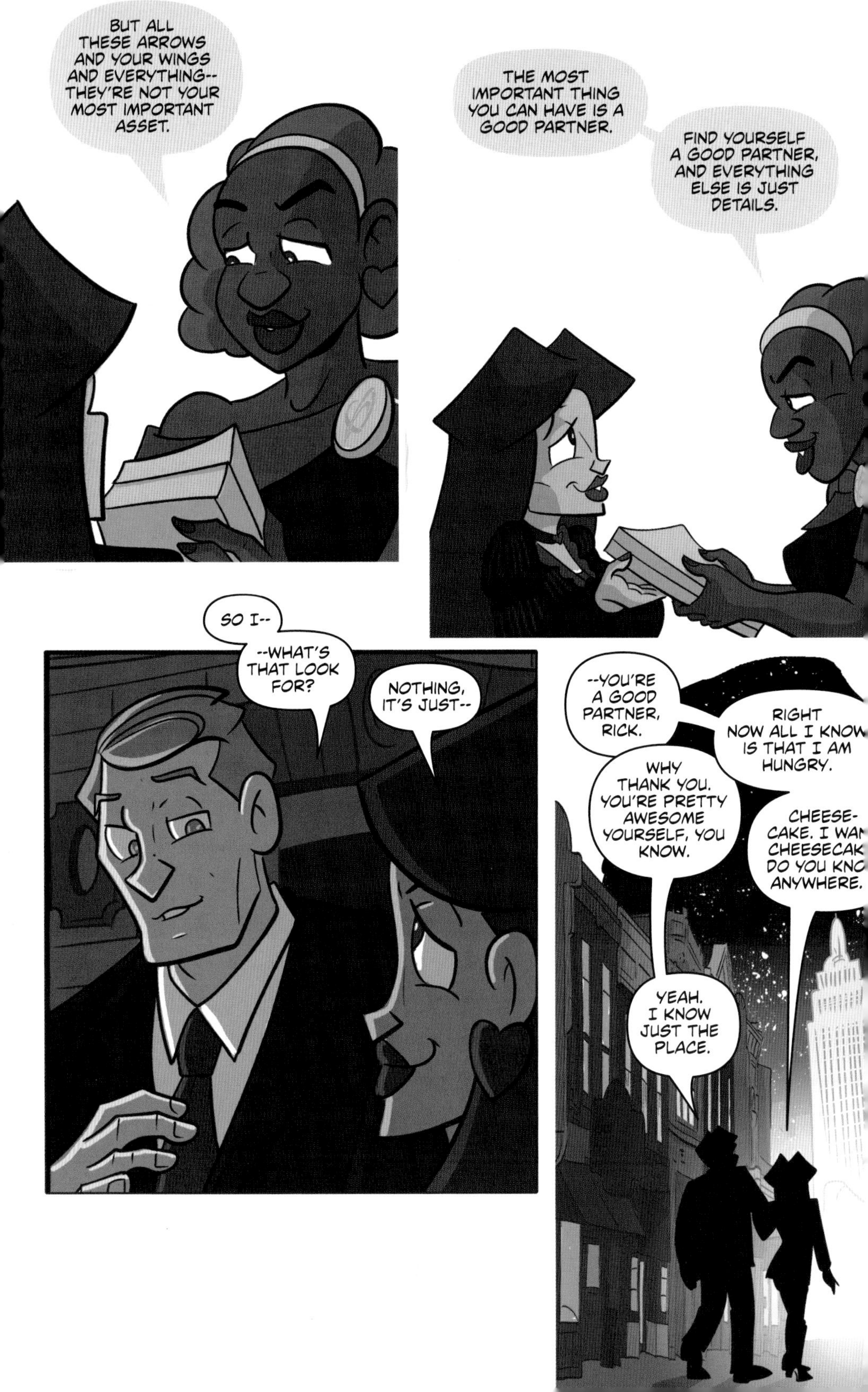
BUT ALL THESE ARROWS AND YOUR WINGS AND EVERYTHING-- THEY'RE NOT YOUR MOST IMPORTANT ASSET.
THE MOST IMPORTANT THING YOU CAN HAVE IS A GOOD PARTNER.
FIND YOURSELF A GOOD PARTNER, AND EVERYTHING ELSE IS JUST DETAILS.
SO I--
--WHAT'S THAT LOOK FOR?
NOTHING, IT'S JUST--
--YOU'RE A GOOD PARTNER, RICK.
WHY THANK YOU. YOU'RE PRETTY AWESOME YOURSELF, YOU KNOW.
RIGHT NOW ALL I KNOW IS THAT I AM HUNGRY.
CHEESE- CAKE. I WAN CHEESECAK DO YOU KNO ANYWHERE.
YEAH. I KNOW JUST THE PLACE.

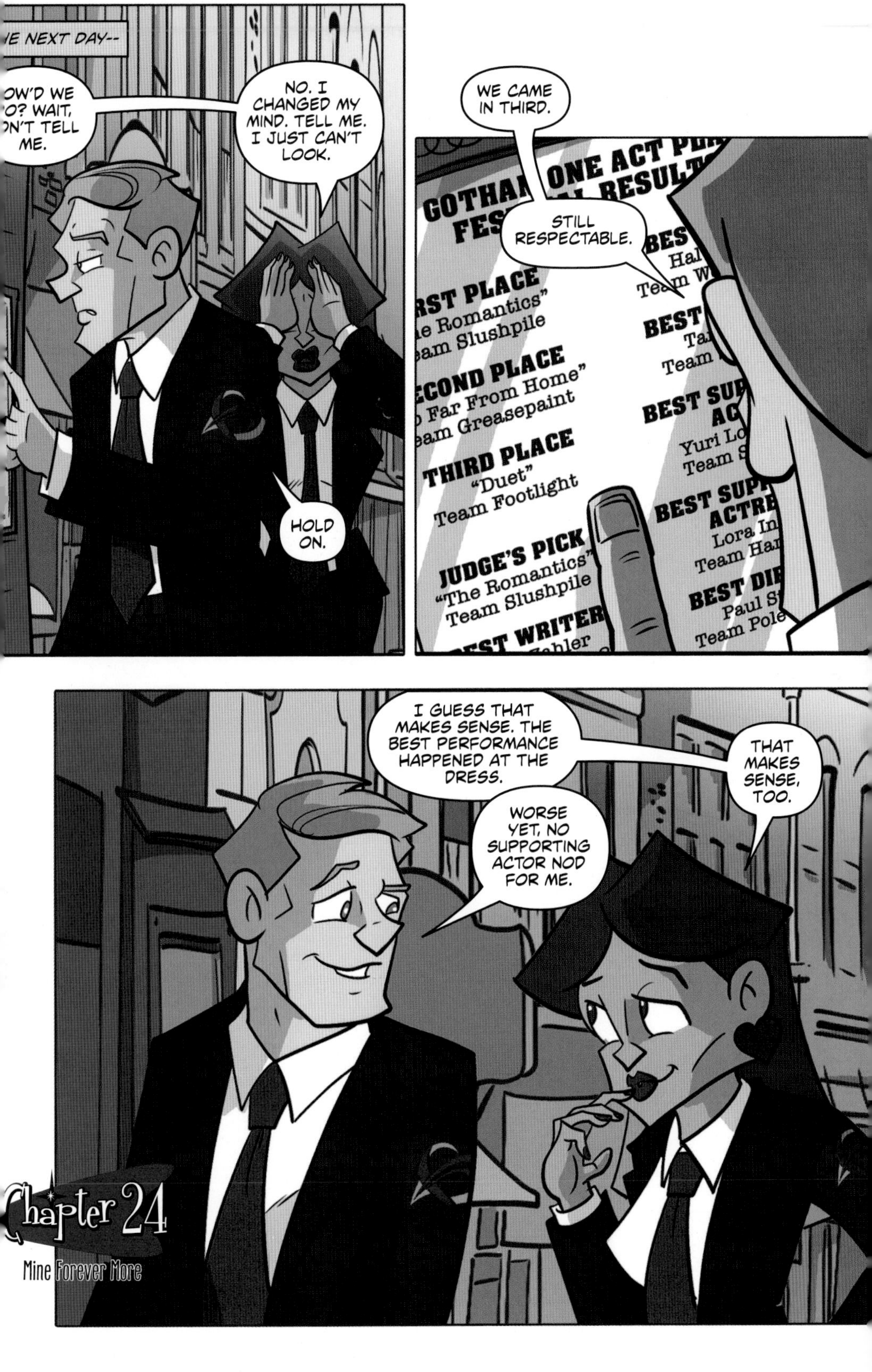
E NEXT DAY--
OW'D WE O? WAIT, N'T TELL ME.
NO. I CHANGED MY MIND. TELL ME. I JUST CAN'T LOOK.
HOLD ON.
WE CAME IN THIRD.
STILL RESPECTABLE.
THIRD PLACE
"Duet"
Team Footlight
JUDGE'S PICK
"The Romantics"
Team Slushpile
SECOND PLACE
Team Greasepaint
I GUESS THAT MAKES SENSE. THE BEST PERFORMANCE HAPPENED AT THE DRESS.
THAT MAKES SENSE, TOO.
WORSE YET, NO SUPPORTING ACTOR NOD FOR ME.
Chapter 24
Mine Forever More

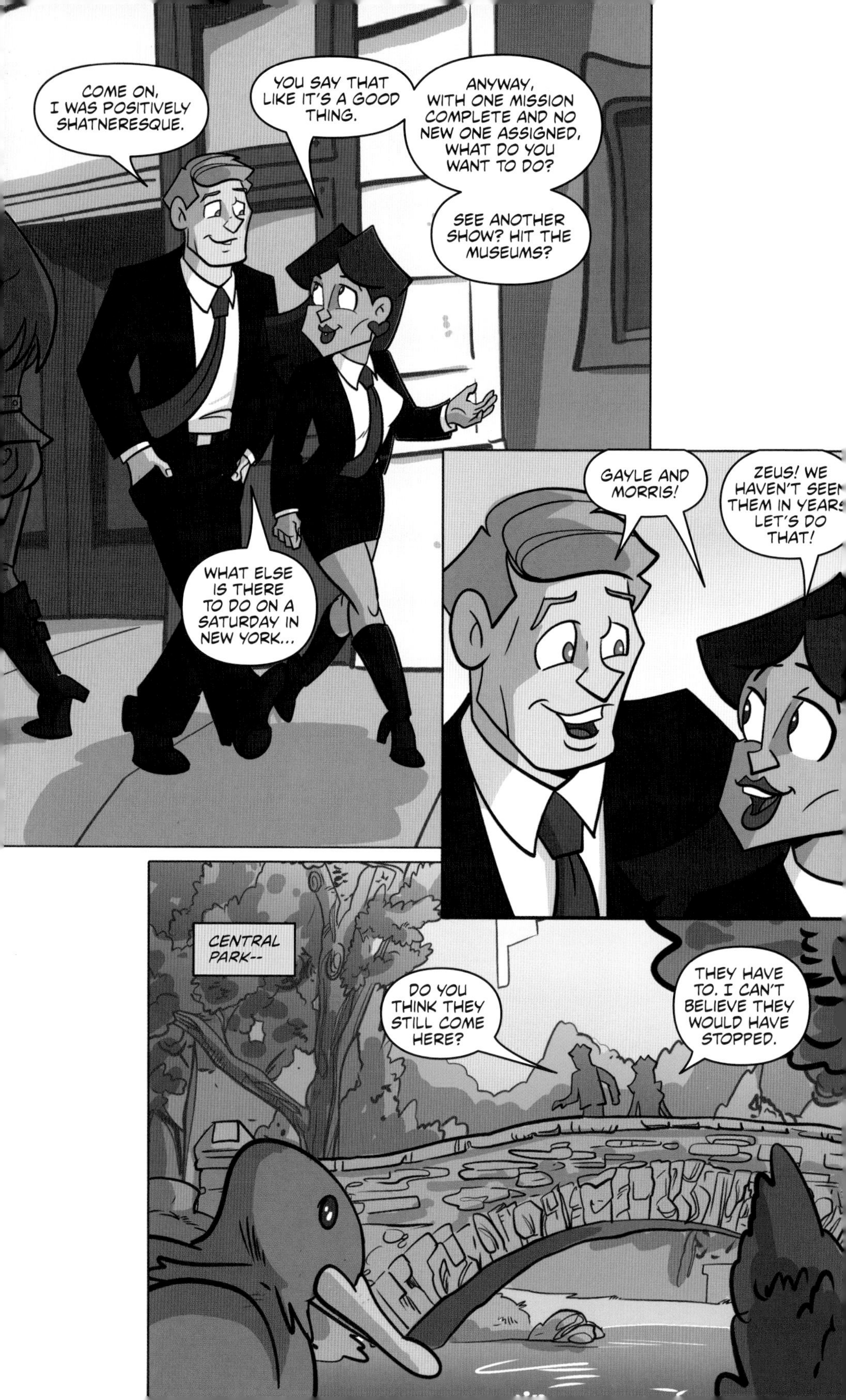

COME ON, I WAS POSITIVELY SHATNERESQUE.
YOU SAY THAT LIKE IT'S A GOOD THING.
ANYWAY, WITH ONE MISSION COMPLETE AND NO NEW ONE ASSIGNED, WHAT DO YOU WANT TO DO?
SEE ANOTHER SHOW? HIT THE MUSEUMS?
WHAT ELSE IS THERE TO DO ON A SATURDAY IN NEW YORK...
GAYLE AND MORRIS!
ZEUS! WE HAVEN'T SEEN THEM IN YEARS LET'S DO THAT!
CENTRAL PARK--
DO YOU THINK THEY STILL COME HERE?
THEY HAVE TO. I CAN'T BELIEVE THEY WOULD HAVE STOPPED.

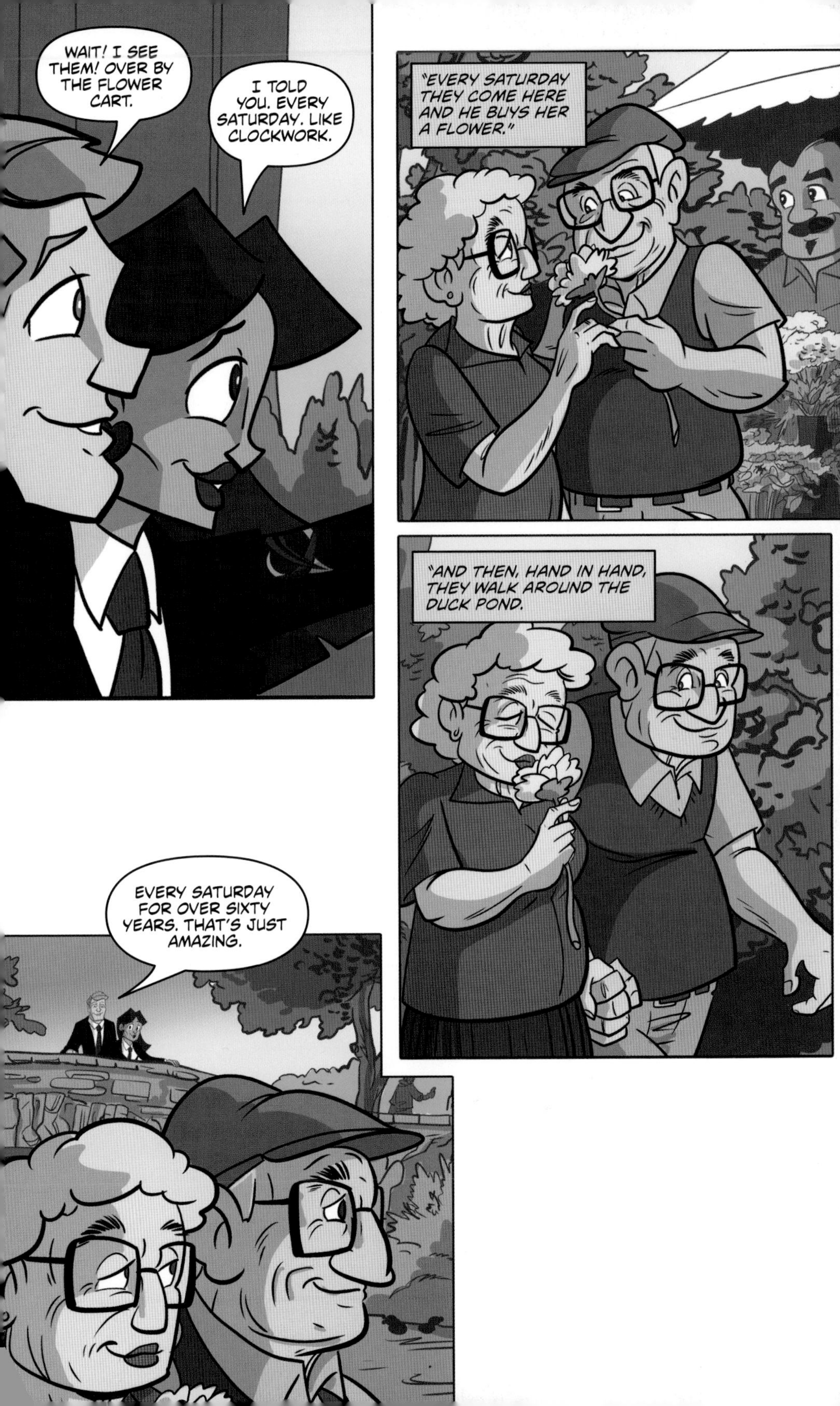
WAIT! I SEE THEM! OVER BY THE FLOWER CART.
I TOLD YOU. EVERY SATURDAY. LIKE CLOCKWORK.
"EVERY SATURDAY THEY COME HERE AND HE BUYS HER A FLOWER."
"AND THEN, HAND IN HAND, THEY WALK AROUND THE DUCK POND.
EVERY SATURDAY FOR OVER SIXTY YEARS. THAT'S JUST AMAZING.

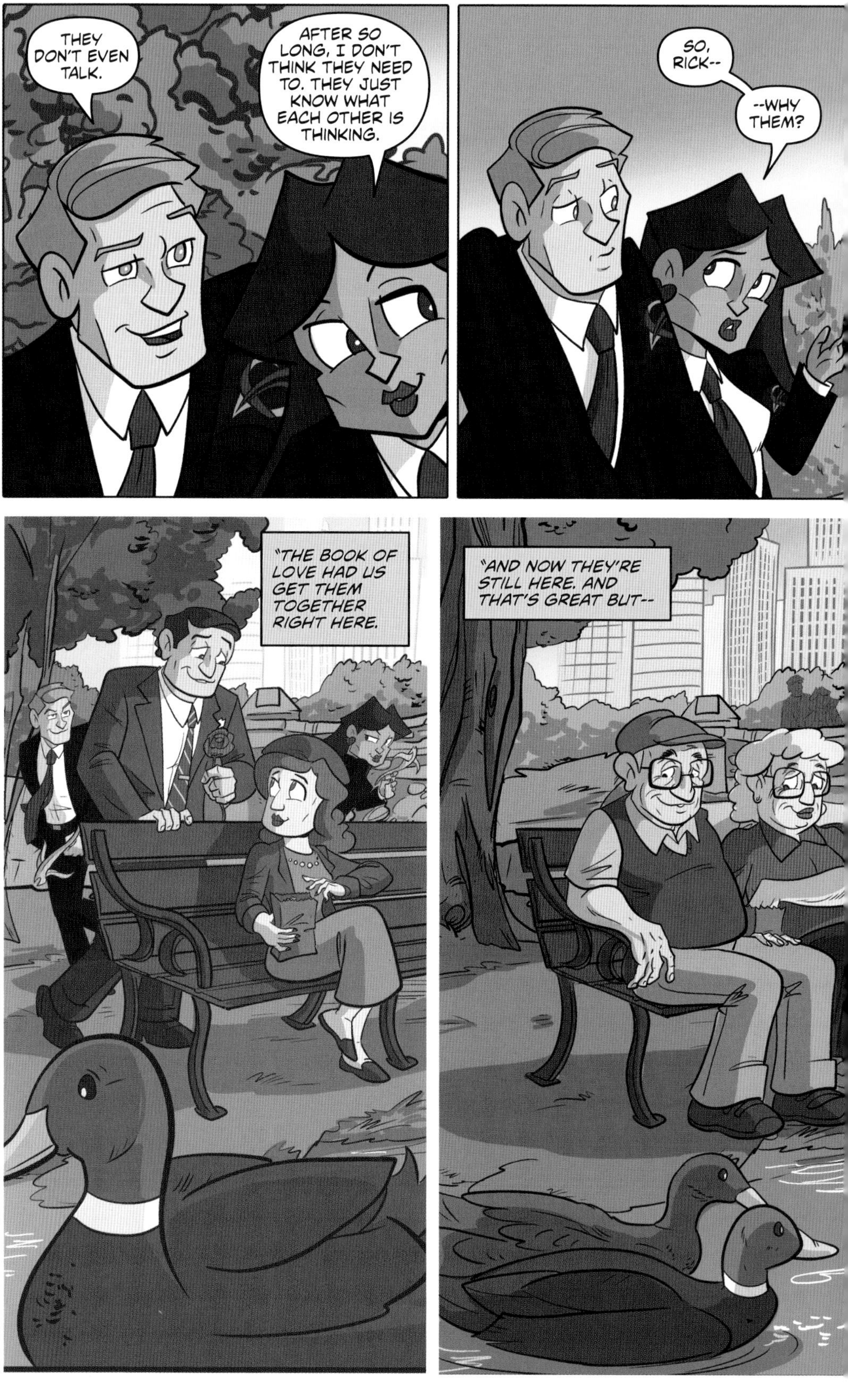

THEY DON'T EVEN TALK.
AFTER SO LONG, I DON'T THINK THEY NEED TO. THEY JUST KNOW WHAT EACH OTHER IS THINKING.
SO, RICK--
--WHY THEM?
"THE BOOK OF LOVE HAD US GET THEM TOGETHER RIGHT HERE.
"AND NOW THEY'RE STILL HERE. AND THAT'S GREAT BUT--

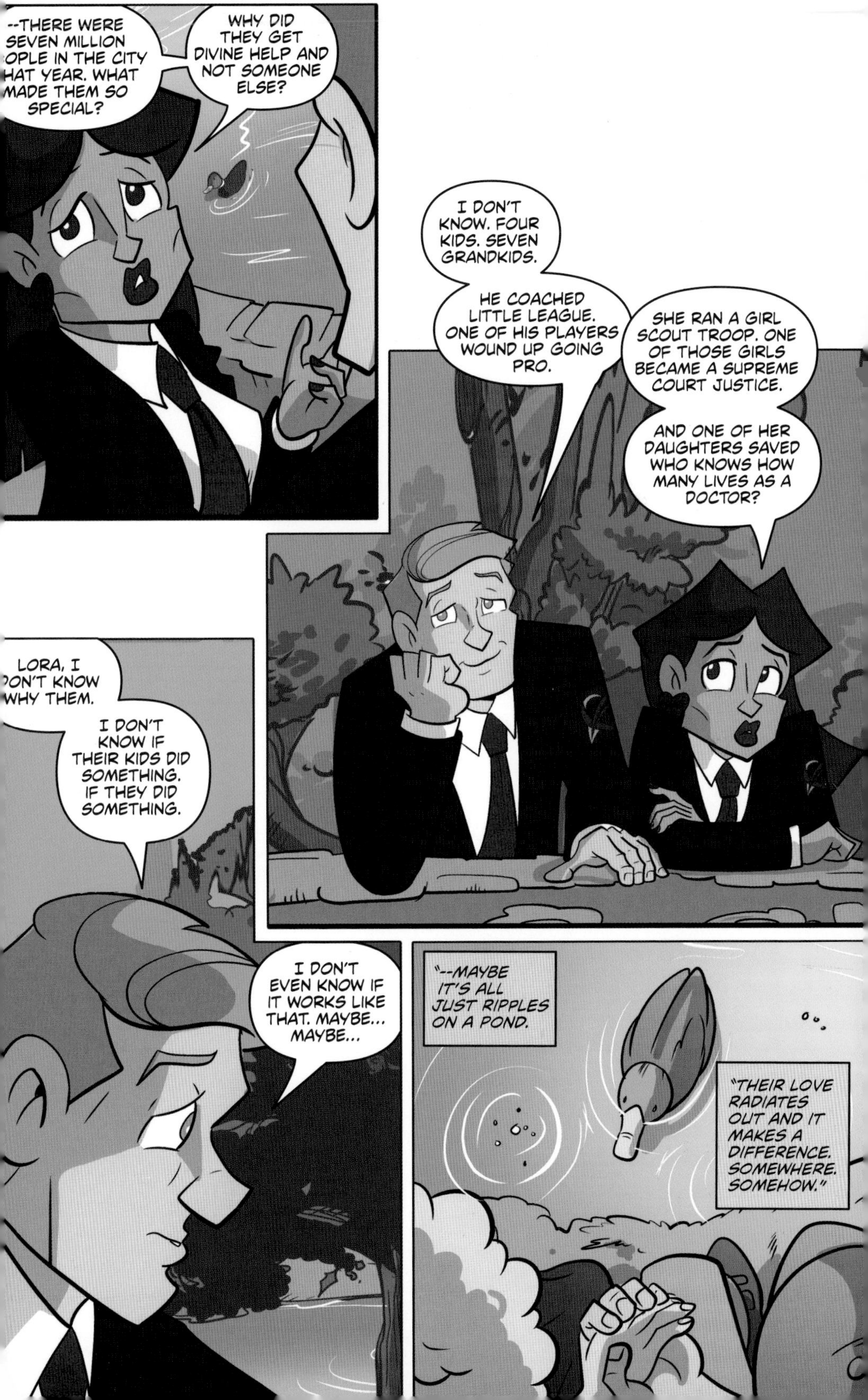
--THERE WERE SEVEN MILLION OPLE IN THE CITY HAT YEAR. WHAT MADE THEM SO SPECIAL?
WHY DID THEY GET DIVINE HELP AND NOT SOMEONE ELSE?
I DON'T KNOW. FOUR KIDS. SEVEN GRANDKIDS.
HE COACHED LITTLE LEAGUE. ONE OF HIS PLAYERS WOUND UP GOING PRO.
SHE RAN A GIRL SCOUT TROOP. ONE OF THOSE GIRLS BECAME A SUPREME COURT JUSTICE.
AND ONE OF HER DAUGHTERS SAVED WHO KNOWS HOW MANY LIVES AS A DOCTOR?
LORA, I ON'T KNOW WHY THEM.
I DON'T KNOW IF THEIR KIDS DID SOMETHING. IF THEY DID SOMETHING.
I DON'T EVEN KNOW IF IT WORKS LIKE THAT. MAYBE... MAYBE...
"--MAYBE IT'S ALL JUST RIPPLES ON A POND.
"THEIR LOVE RADIATES OUT AND IT MAKES A DIFFERENCE. SOMEWHERE. SOMEHOW."

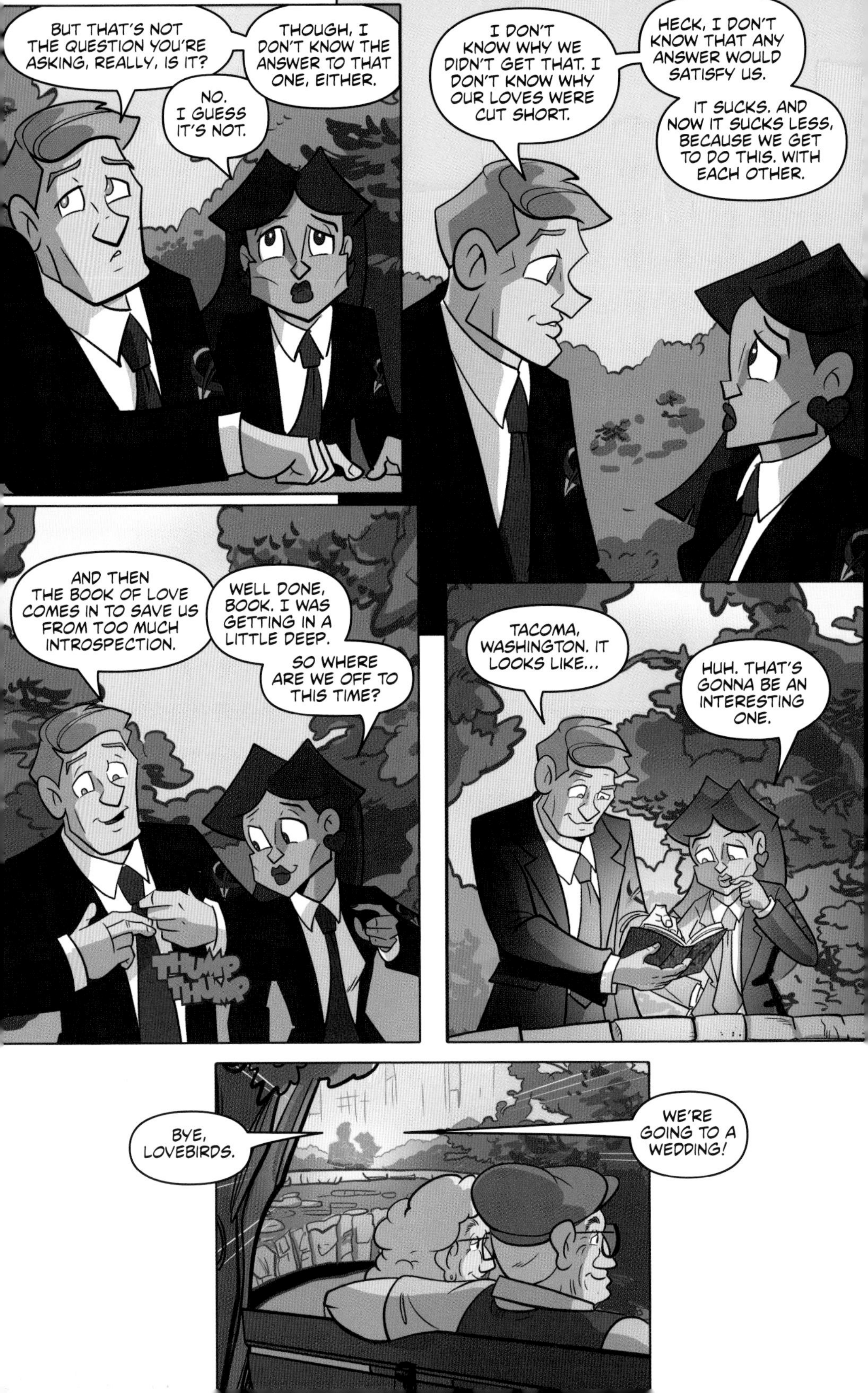

BUT THAT'S NOT THE QUESTION YOU'RE ASKING, REALLY, IS IT?
NO. I GUESS IT'S NOT.
THOUGH, I DON'T KNOW THE ANSWER TO THAT ONE, EITHER.
I DON'T KNOW WHY WE DIDN'T GET THAT. I DON'T KNOW WHY OUR LOVES WERE CUT SHORT.
HECK, I DON'T KNOW THAT ANY ANSWER WOULD SATISFY US.
IT SUCKS. AND NOW IT SUCKS LESS, BECAUSE WE GET TO DO THIS. WITH EACH OTHER.
AND THEN THE BOOK OF LOVE COMES IN TO SAVE US FROM TOO MUCH INTROSPECTION.
WELL DONE, BOOK. I WAS GETTING IN A LITTLE DEEP.
SO WHERE ARE WE OFF TO THIS TIME?
THUMP THUMP
TACOMA, WASHINGTON. IT LOOKS LIKE...
HUH. THAT'S GONNA BE AN INTERESTING ONE.
BYE, LOVEBIRDS.
WE'RE GOING TO A WEDDING!

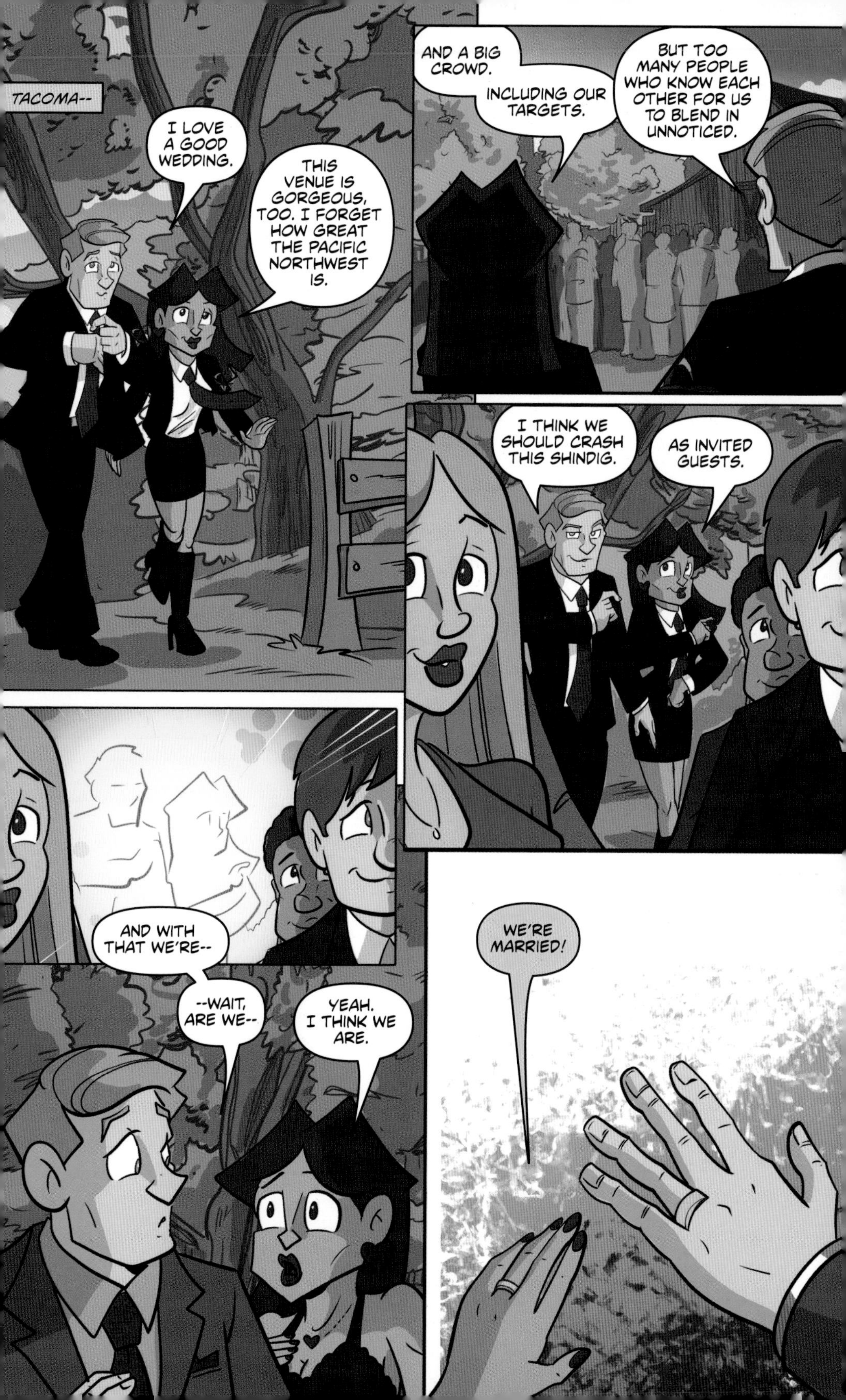
TACOMA--
I LOVE A GOOD WEDDING.
THIS VENUE IS GORGEOUS, TOO. I FORGET HOW GREAT THE PACIFIC NORTHWEST IS.
AND A BIG CROWD.
INCLUDING OUR TARGETS.
BUT TOO MANY PEOPLE WHO KNOW EACH OTHER FOR US TO BLEND IN UNNOTICED.
I THINK WE SHOULD CRASH THIS SHINDIG.
AS INVITED GUESTS.
AND WITH THAT WE'RE--
WE'RE MARRIED!
--WAIT, ARE WE--
YEAH. I THINK WE ARE.

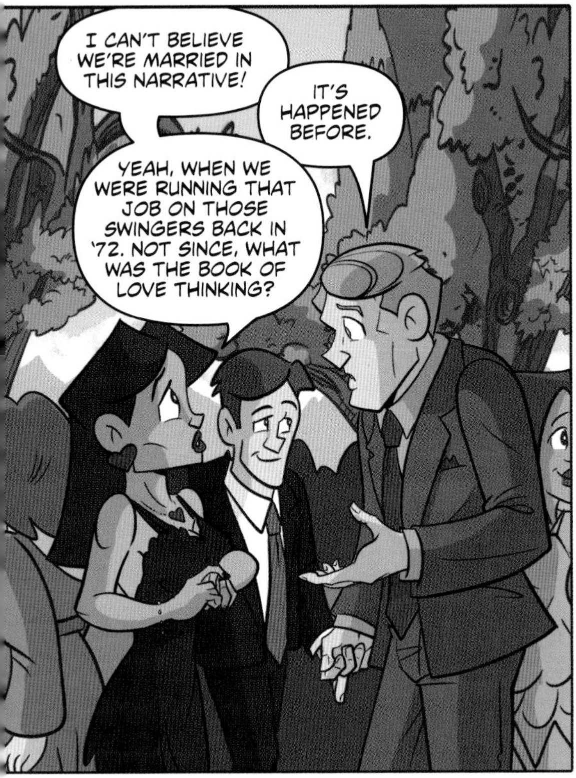
I CAN'T BELIEVE WE'RE MARRIED IN THIS NARRATIVE!
IT'S HAPPENED BEFORE.
YEAH, WHEN WE WERE RUNNING THAT JOB ON THOSE SWINGERS BACK IN '72. NOT SINCE, WHAT WAS THE BOOK OF LOVE THINKING?

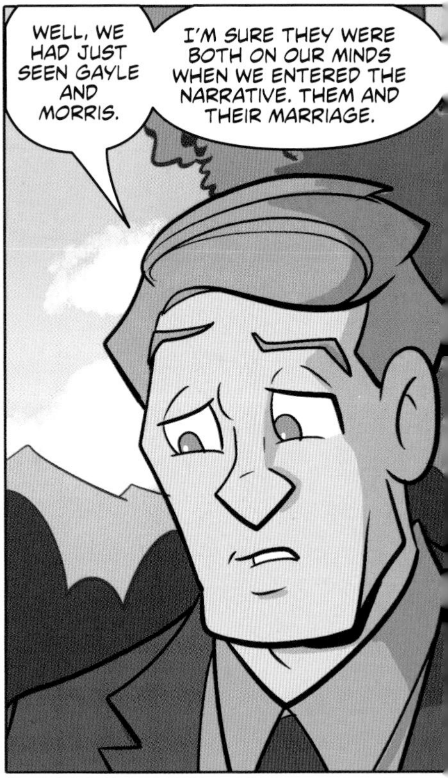
WELL, WE HAD JUST SEEN GAYLE AND MORRIS.
I'M SURE THEY WERE BOTH ON OUR MINDS WHEN WE ENTERED THE NARRATIVE. THEM AND THEIR MARRIAGE.

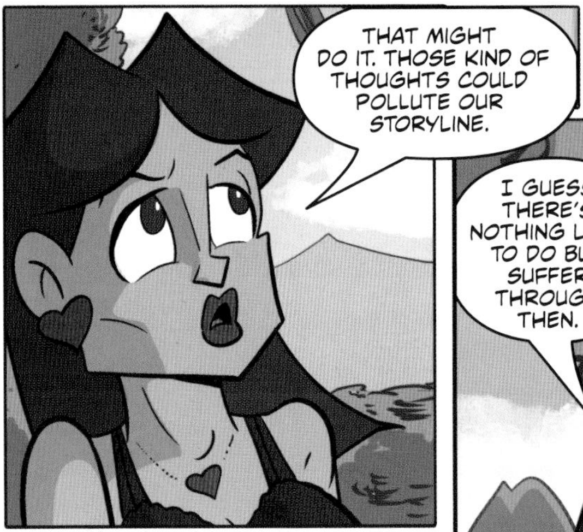
THAT MIGHT DO IT. THOSE KIND OF THOUGHTS COULD POLLUTE OUR STORYLINE.

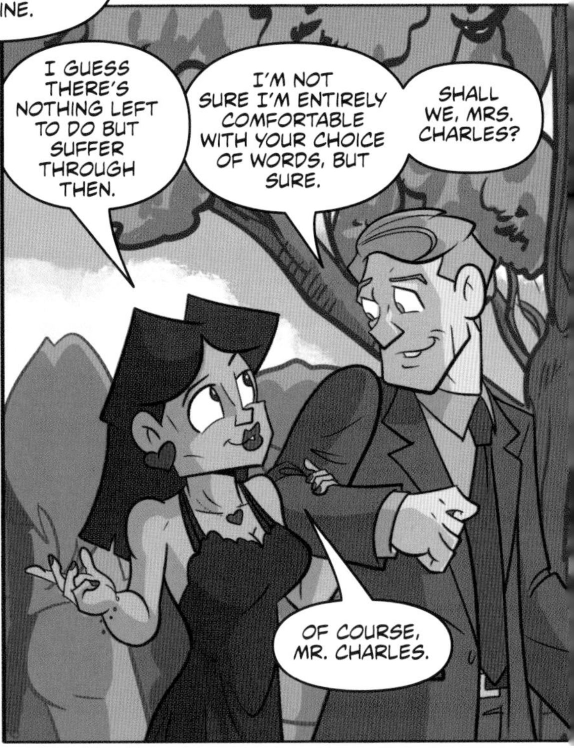
I GUESS THERE'S NOTHING LEFT TO DO BUT SUFFER THROUGH THEN.
I'M NOT SURE I'M ENTIRELY COMFORTABLE WITH YOUR CHOICE OF WORDS, BUT SURE.
SHALL WE, MRS. CHARLES?
OF COURSE, MR. CHARLES.

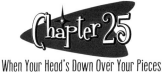

Chapter 25

When Your Head's Down Over Your Pieces

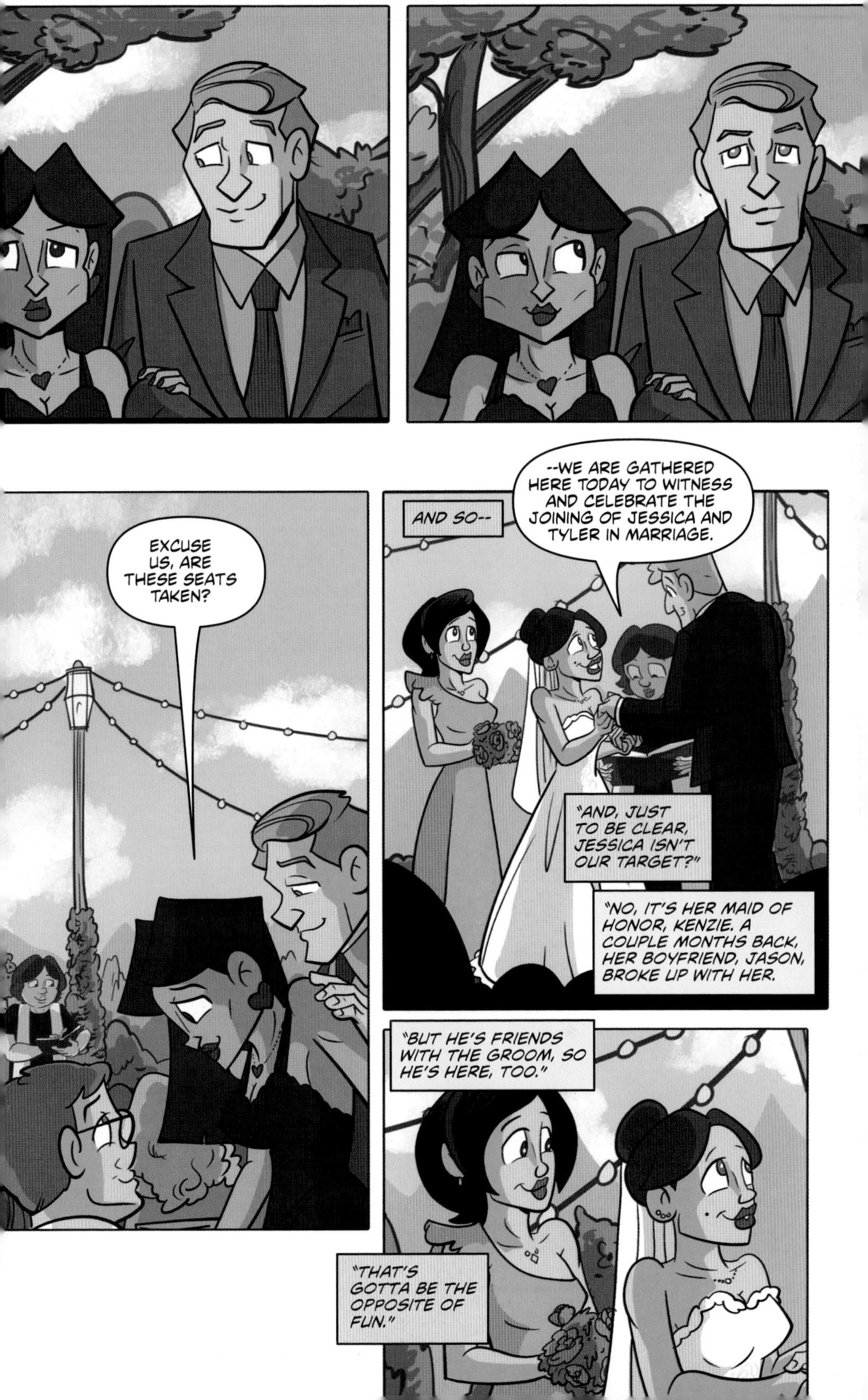
EXCUSE US, ARE THESE SEATS TAKEN?
AND SO--
--WE ARE GATHERED HERE TODAY TO WITNESS AND CELEBRATE THE JOINING OF JESSICA AND TYLER IN MARRIAGE.
"AND, JUST TO BE CLEAR, JESSICA ISN'T OUR TARGET?"
"NO, IT'S HER MAID OF HONOR, KENZIE. A COUPLE MONTHS BACK, HER BOYFRIEND, JASON, BROKE UP WITH HER.
"BUT HE'S FRIENDS WITH THE GROOM, SO HE'S HERE, TOO."
"THAT'S GOTTA BE THE OPPOSITE OF FUN."

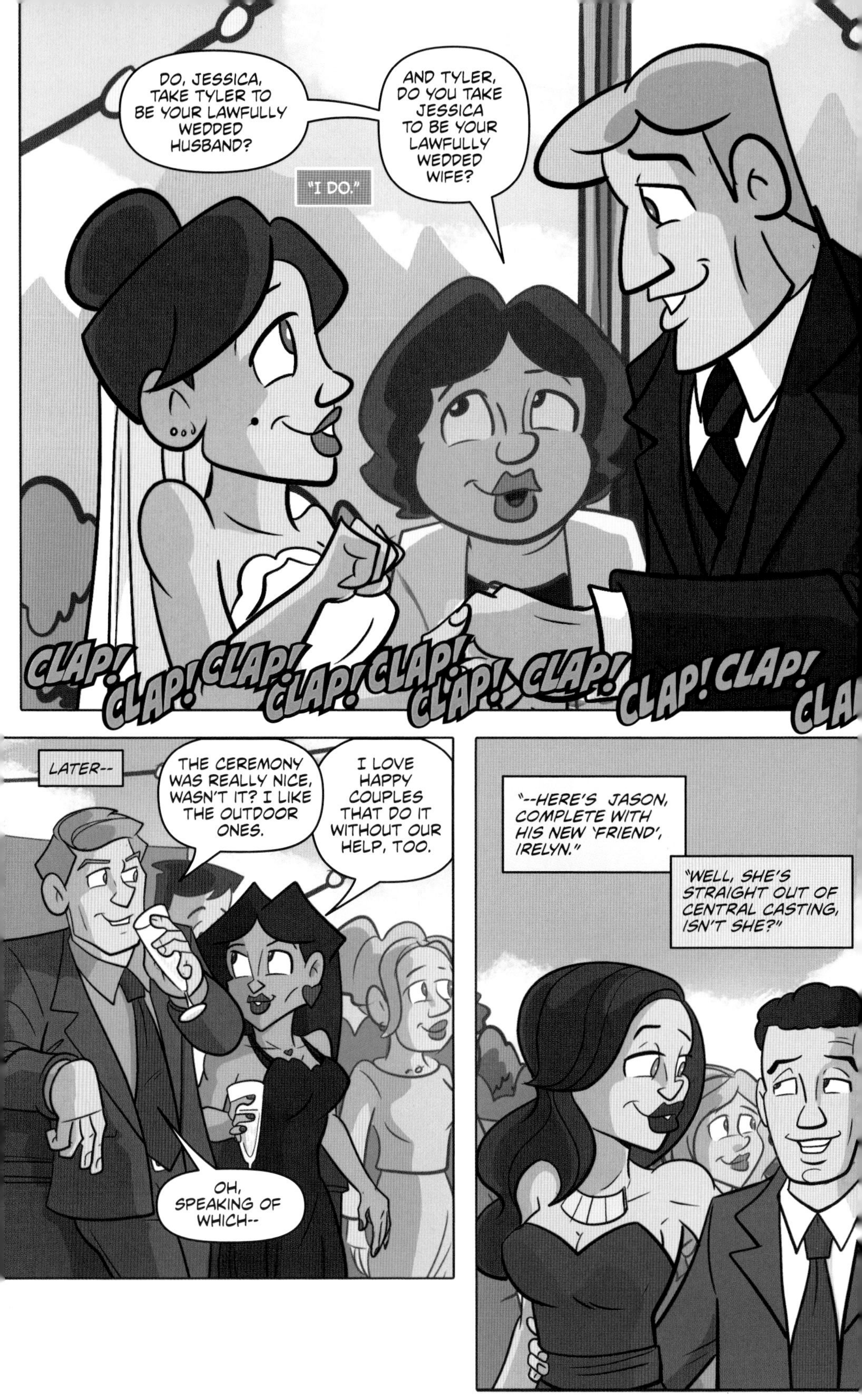
DO, JESSICA, TAKE TYLER TO BE YOUR LAWFULLY WEDDED HUSBAND?
AND TYLER, DO YOU TAKE JESSICA TO BE YOUR LAWFULLY WEDDED WIFE?
"I DO."
CLAP! CLAP! CLAP! CLAP! CLAP! CLAP! CLAP! CLAP! CLAP! CLA
LATER--
THE CEREMONY WAS REALLY NICE, WASN'T IT? I LIKE THE OUTDOOR ONES.
I LOVE HAPPY COUPLES THAT DO IT WITHOUT OUR HELP, TOO.
OH, SPEAKING OF WHICH--
"--HERE'S JASON, COMPLETE WITH HIS NEW 'FRIEND', IRELYN."
"WELL, SHE'S STRAIGHT OUT OF CENTRAL CASTING, ISN'T SHE?"

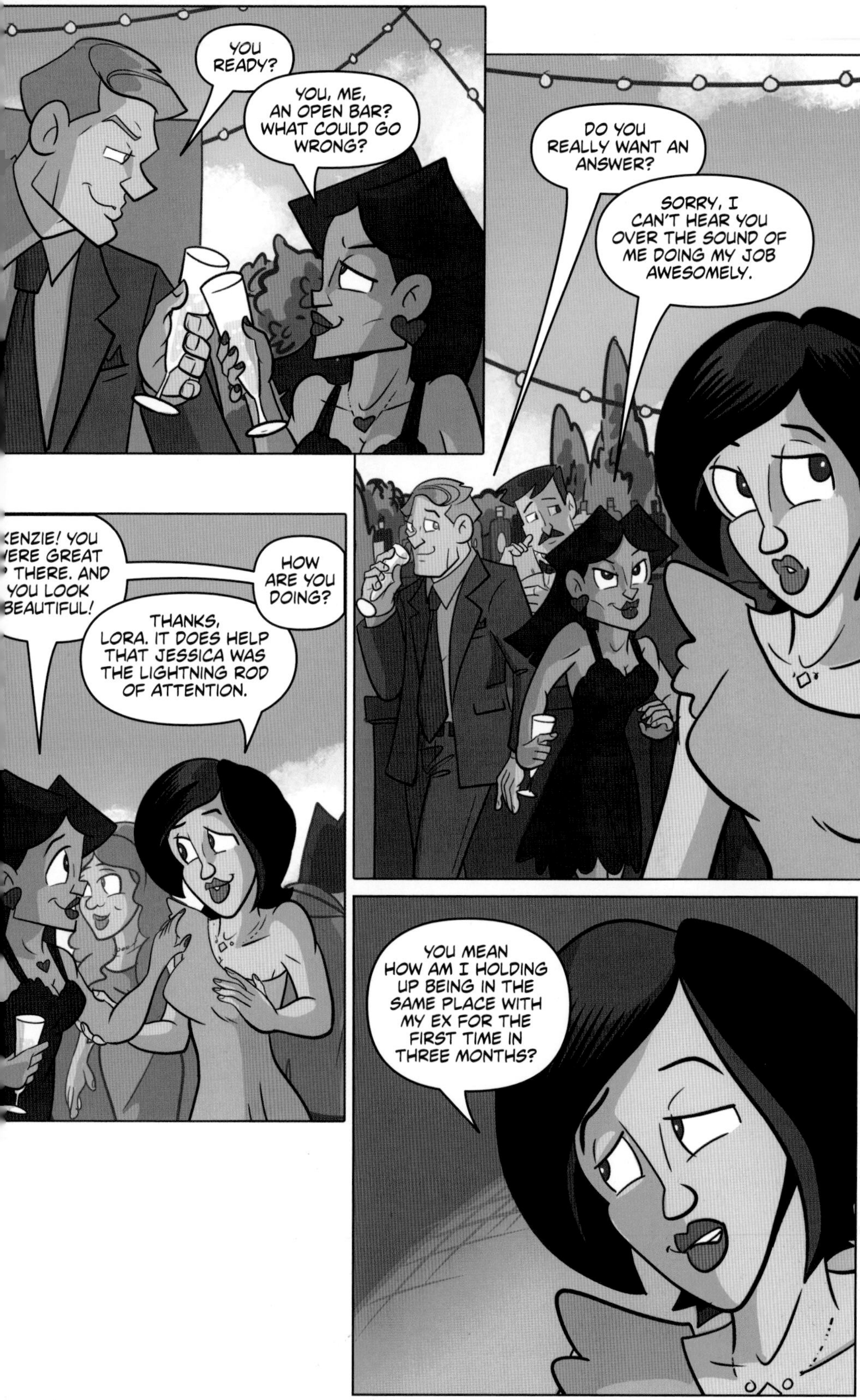
YOU READY?
YOU, ME, AN OPEN BAR? WHAT COULD GO WRONG?
DO YOU REALLY WANT AN ANSWER?
SORRY, I CAN'T HEAR YOU OVER THE SOUND OF ME DOING MY JOB AWESOMELY.
KENZIE! YOU WERE GREAT THERE. AND YOU LOOK BEAUTIFUL!
HOW ARE YOU DOING?
THANKS, LORA. IT DOES HELP THAT JESSICA WAS THE LIGHTNING ROD OF ATTENTION.
YOU MEAN HOW AM I HOLDING UP BEING IN THE SAME PLACE WITH MY EX FOR THE FIRST TIME IN THREE MONTHS?

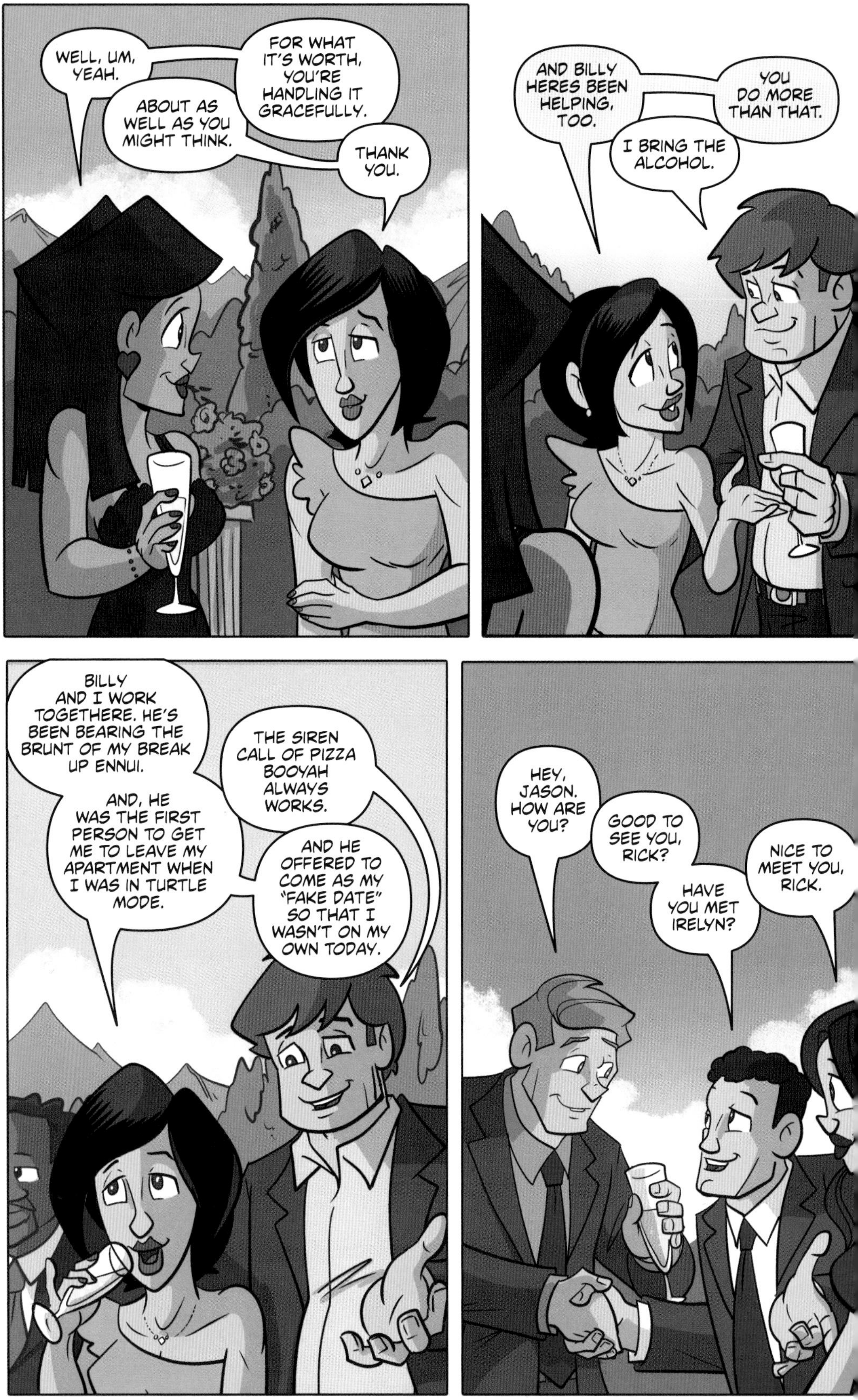
WELL, UM, YEAH.
FOR WHAT IT'S WORTH, YOU'RE HANDLING IT GRACEFULLY.
ABOUT AS WELL AS YOU MIGHT THINK.
THANK YOU.
AND BILLY HERES BEEN HELPING, TOO.
YOU DO MORE THAN THAT.
I BRING THE ALCOHOL.
BILLY AND I WORK TOGETHERE. HE'S BEEN BEARING THE BRUNT OF MY BREAK UP ENNUI.
THE SIREN CALL OF PIZZA BOOYAH ALWAYS WORKS.
AND, HE WAS THE FIRST PERSON TO GET ME TO LEAVE MY APARTMENT WHEN I WAS IN TURTLE MODE.
AND HE OFFERED TO COME AS MY "FAKE DATE" SO THAT I WASN'T ON MY OWN TODAY.
HEY, JASON. HOW ARE YOU?
GOOD TO SEE YOU, RICK?
HAVE YOU MET IRELYN?
NICE TO MEET YOU, RICK.

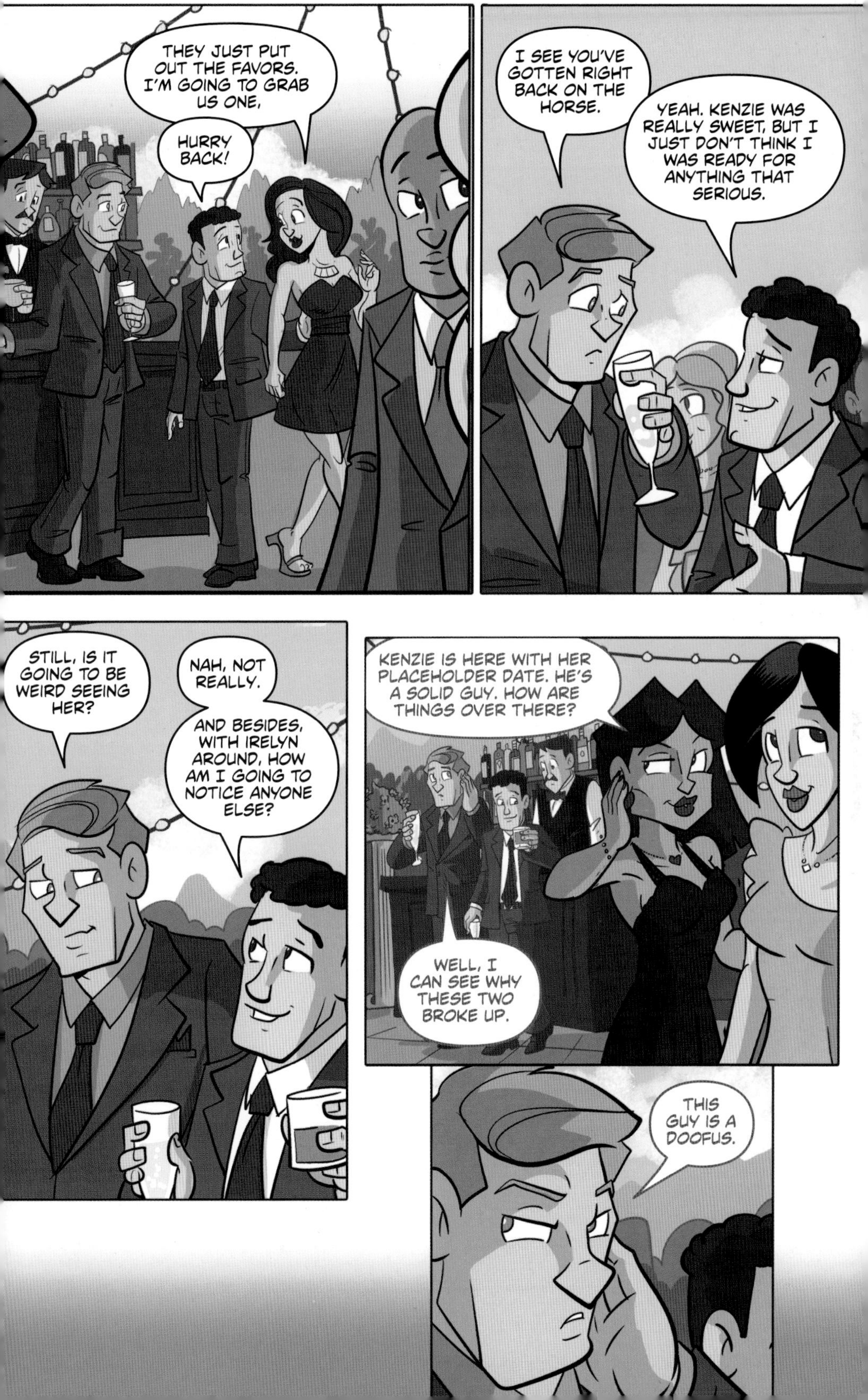
THEY JUST PUT OUT THE FAVORS. I'M GOING TO GRAB US ONE,
HURRY BACK!
I SEE YOU'VE GOTTEN RIGHT BACK ON THE HORSE.
YEAH. KENZIE WAS REALLY SWEET, BUT I JUST DON'T THINK I WAS READY FOR ANYTHING THAT SERIOUS.
STILL, IS IT GOING TO BE WEIRD SEEING HER?
NAH, NOT REALLY.
AND BESIDES, WITH IRELYN AROUND, HOW AM I GOING TO NOTICE ANYONE ELSE?
KENZIE IS HERE WITH HER PLACEHOLDER DATE. HE'S A SOLID GUY. HOW ARE THINGS OVER THERE?
WELL, I CAN SEE WHY THESE TWO BROKE UP.
THIS GUY IS A DOOFUS.

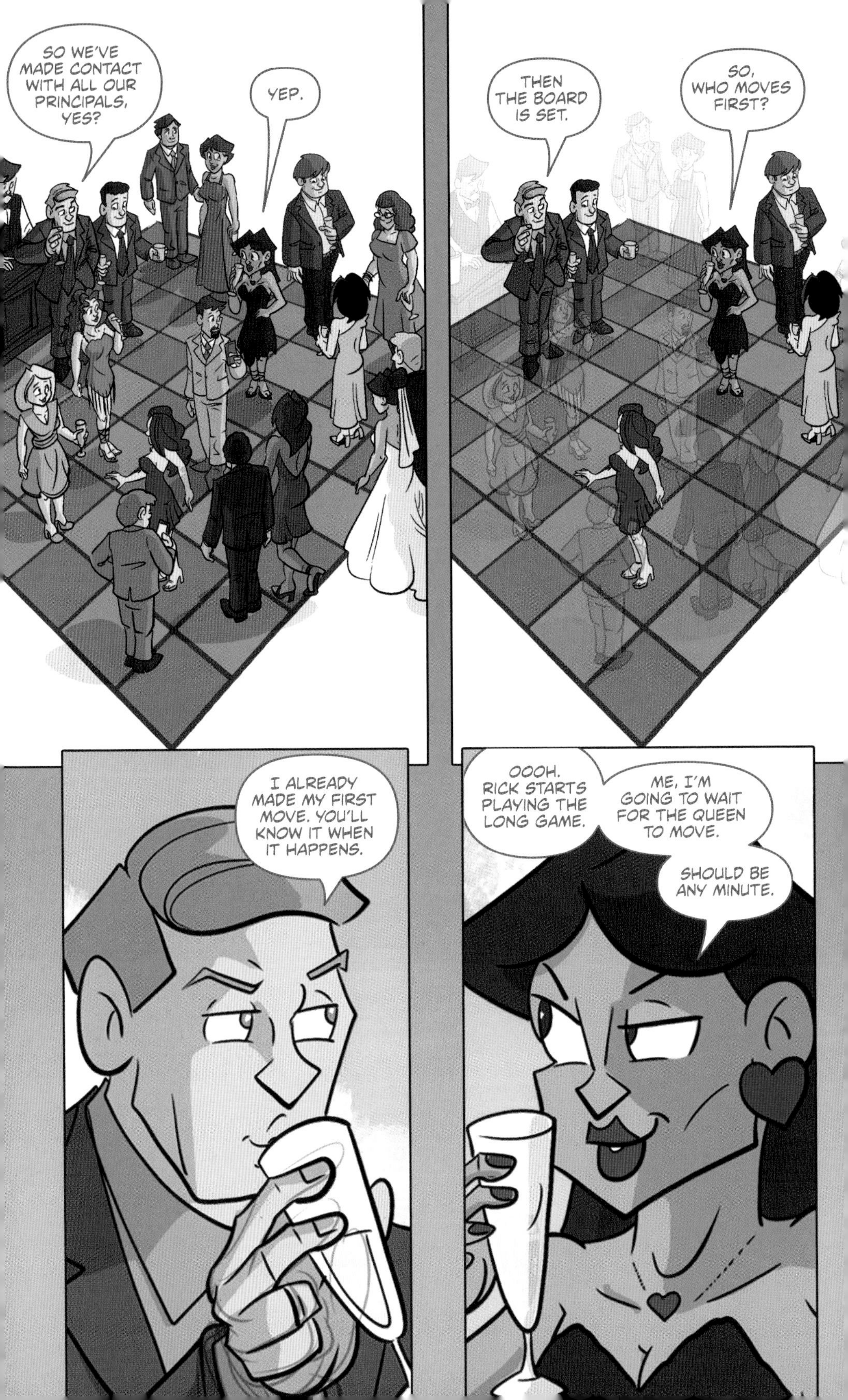
SO WE'VE MADE CONTACT WITH ALL OUR PRINCIPALS, YES?
YEP.
THEN THE BOARD IS SET.
SO, WHO MOVES FIRST?
I ALREADY MADE MY FIRST MOVE. YOU'LL KNOW IT WHEN IT HAPPENS.
OOOH. RICK STARTS PLAYING THE LONG GAME.
ME, I'M GOING TO WAIT FOR THE QUEEN TO MOVE.
SHOULD BE ANY MINUTE.

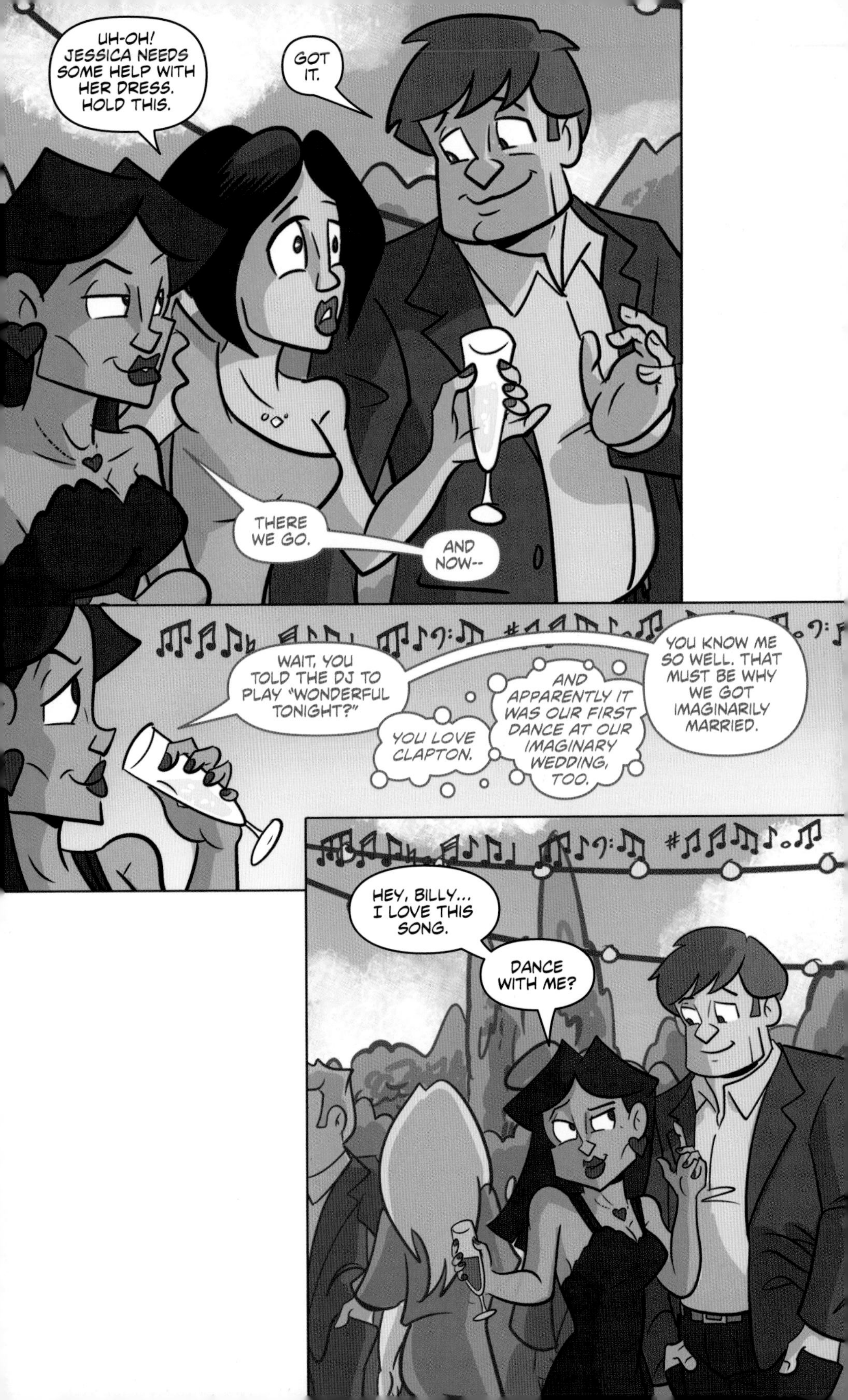
UH-OH! JESSICA NEEDS SOME HELP WITH HER DRESS. HOLD THIS.
GOT IT.
THERE WE GO.
AND NOW--
WAIT, YOU TOLD THE DJ TO PLAY "WONDERFUL TONIGHT?"
YOU LOVE CLAPTON.
AND APPARENTLY IT WAS OUR FIRST DANCE AT OUR IMAGINARY WEDDING, TOO.
YOU KNOW ME SO WELL. THAT MUST BE WHY WE GOT IMAGINARILY MARRIED.
HEY, BILLY... I LOVE THIS SONG.
DANCE WITH ME?

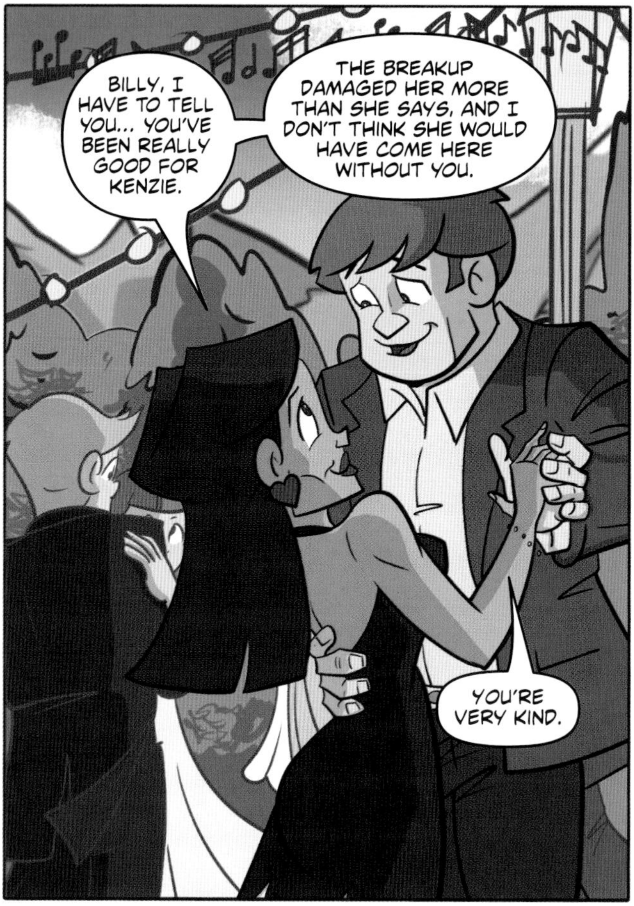
BILLY, I HAVE TO TELL YOU... YOU'VE BEEN REALLY GOOD FOR KENZIE.
THE BREAKUP DAMAGED HER MORE THAN SHE SAYS, AND I DON'T THINK SHE WOULD HAVE COME HERE WITHOUT YOU.
YOU'RE VERY KIND.

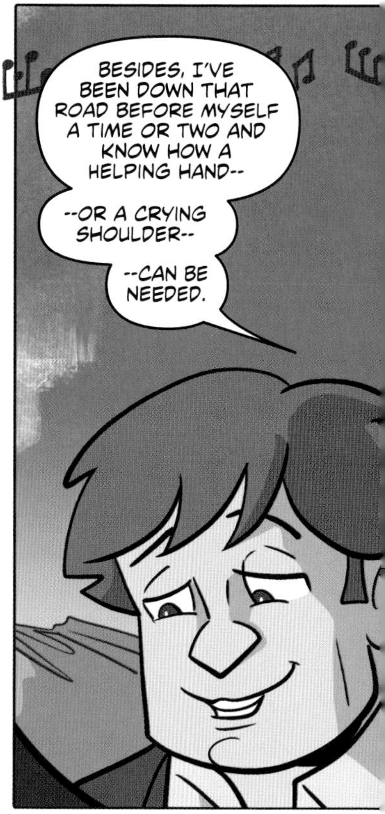
BESIDES, I'VE BEEN DOWN THAT ROAD BEFORE MYSELF A TIME OR TWO AND KNOW HOW A HELPING HAND--
--OR A CRYING SHOULDER--
--CAN BE NEEDED.

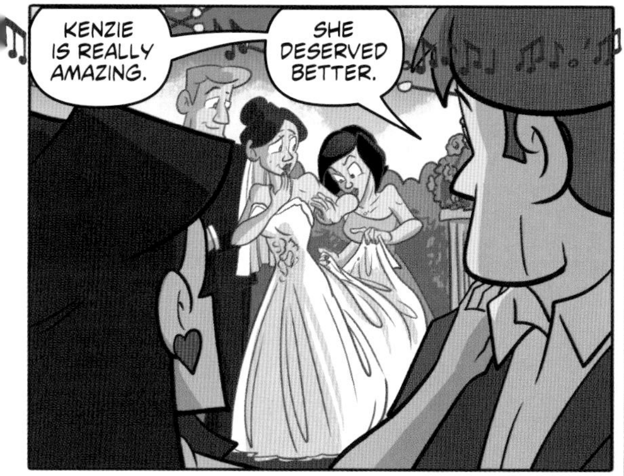
KENZIE IS REALLY AMAZING.
SHE DESERVED BETTER.

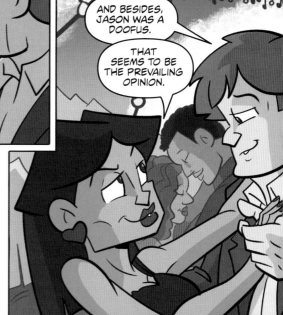

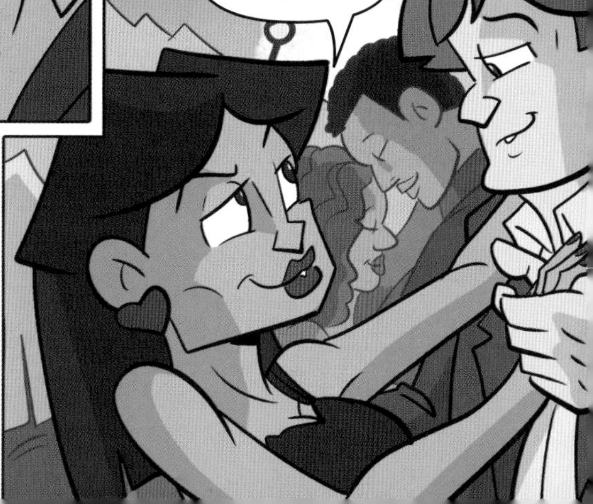
AND BESIDES, JASON WAS A DOOFUS.
THAT SEEMS TO BE THE PREVAILING OPINION.

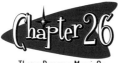

Chapter 26

Those Dreams Move On

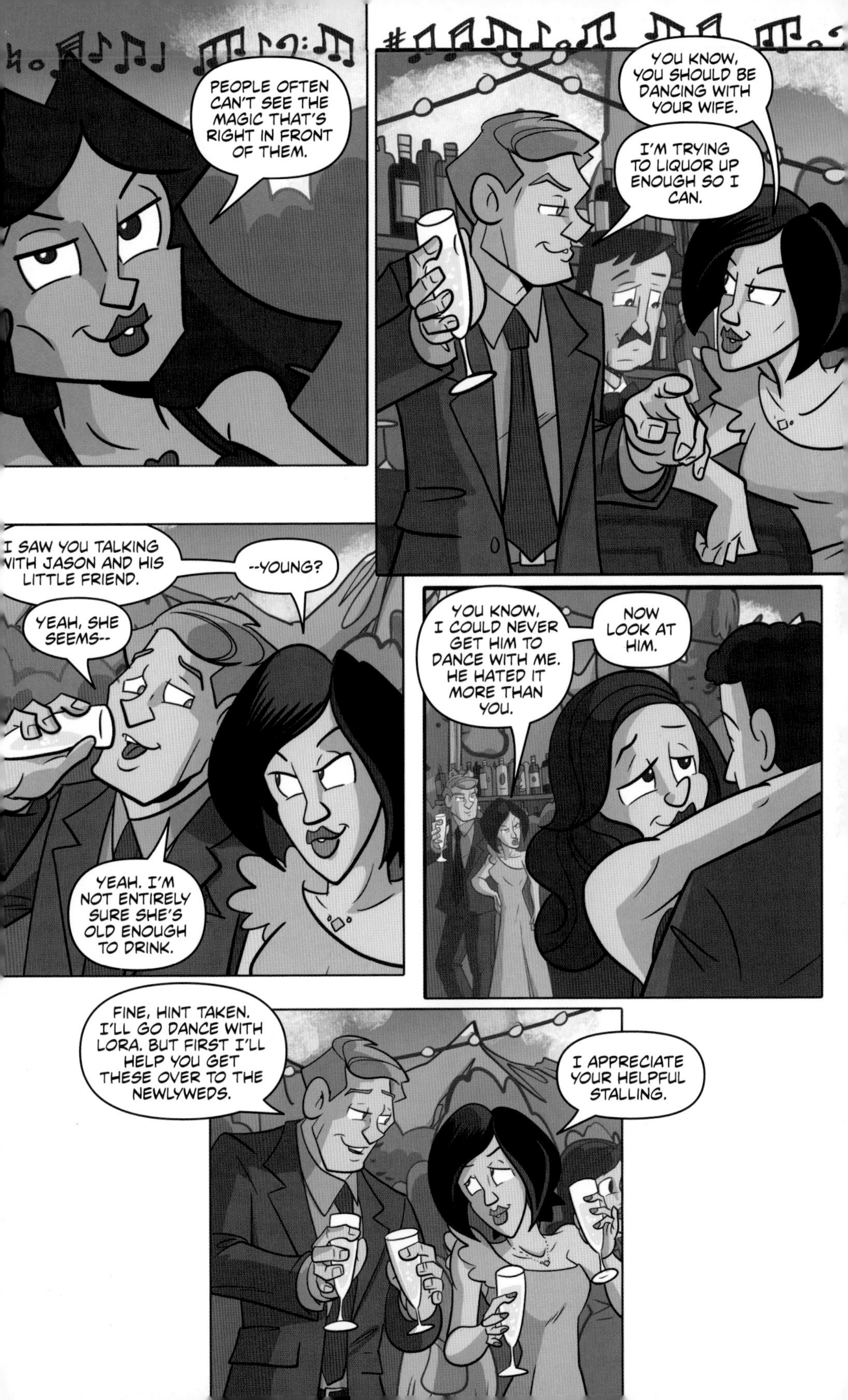
PEOPLE OFTEN CAN'T SEE THE MAGIC THAT'S RIGHT IN FRONT OF THEM.
YOU KNOW, YOU SHOULD BE DANCING WITH YOUR WIFE.
I'M TRYING TO LIQUOR UP ENOUGH SO I CAN.
I SAW YOU TALKING WITH JASON AND HIS LITTLE FRIEND.
YEAH, SHE SEEMS--
--YOUNG?
YEAH. I'M NOT ENTIRELY SURE SHE'S OLD ENOUGH TO DRINK.
YOU KNOW, I COULD NEVER GET HIM TO DANCE WITH ME. HE HATED IT MORE THAN YOU.
NOW LOOK AT HIM.
FINE, HINT TAKEN. I'LL GO DANCE WITH LORA. BUT FIRST I'LL HELP YOU GET THESE OVER TO THE NEWLYWEDS.
I APPRECIATE YOUR HELPFUL STALLING.

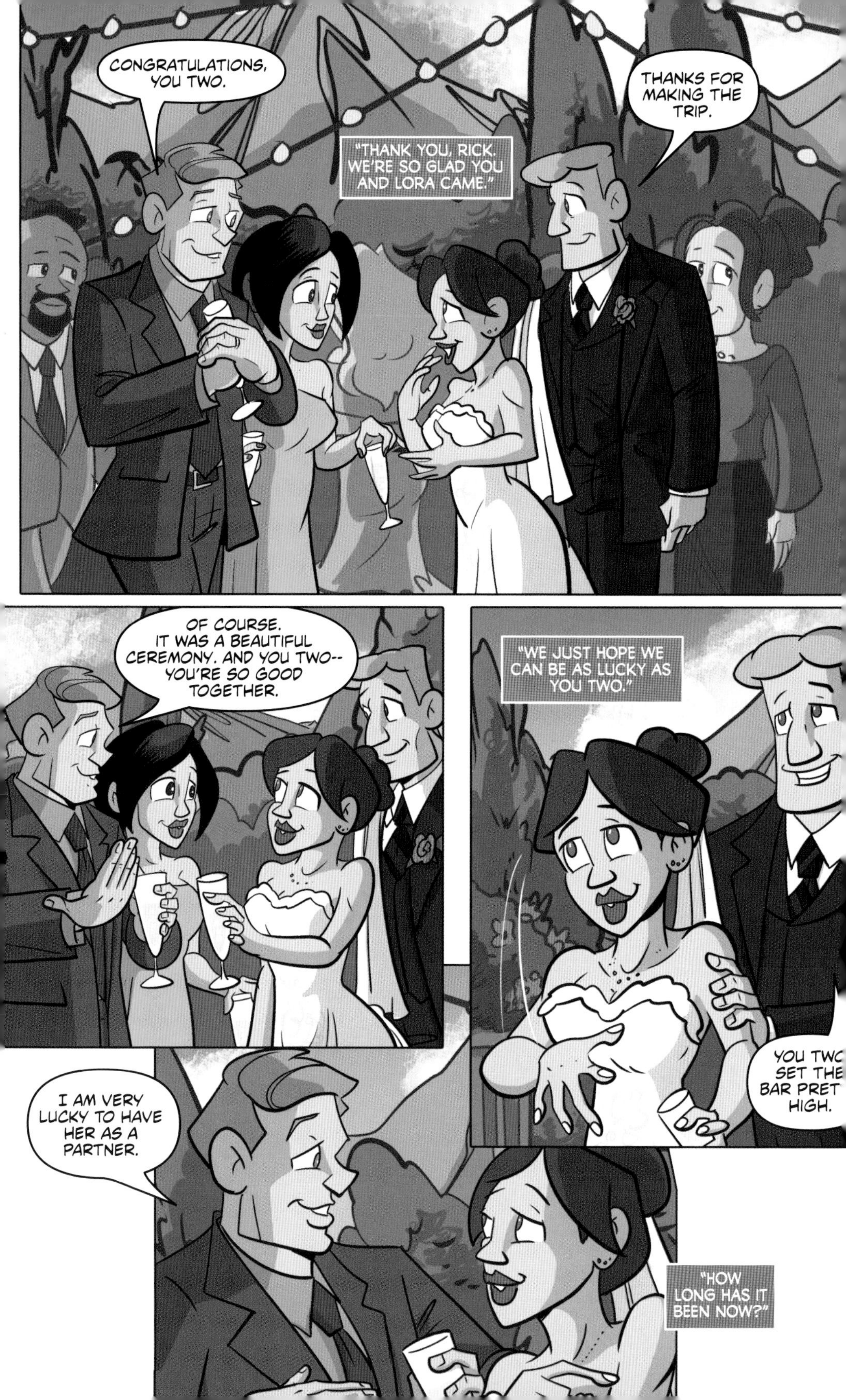
CONGRATULATIONS, YOU TWO.
"THANK YOU, RICK. WE'RE SO GLAD YOU AND LORA CAME."
THANKS FOR MAKING THE TRIP.
OF COURSE. IT WAS A BEAUTIFUL CEREMONY. AND YOU TWO-- YOU'RE SO GOOD TOGETHER.
"WE JUST HOPE WE CAN BE AS LUCKY AS YOU TWO."
YOU TWO SET THE BAR PRET HIGH.
I AM VERY LUCKY TO HAVE HER AS A PARTNER.
"HOW LONG HAS IT BEEN NOW?"

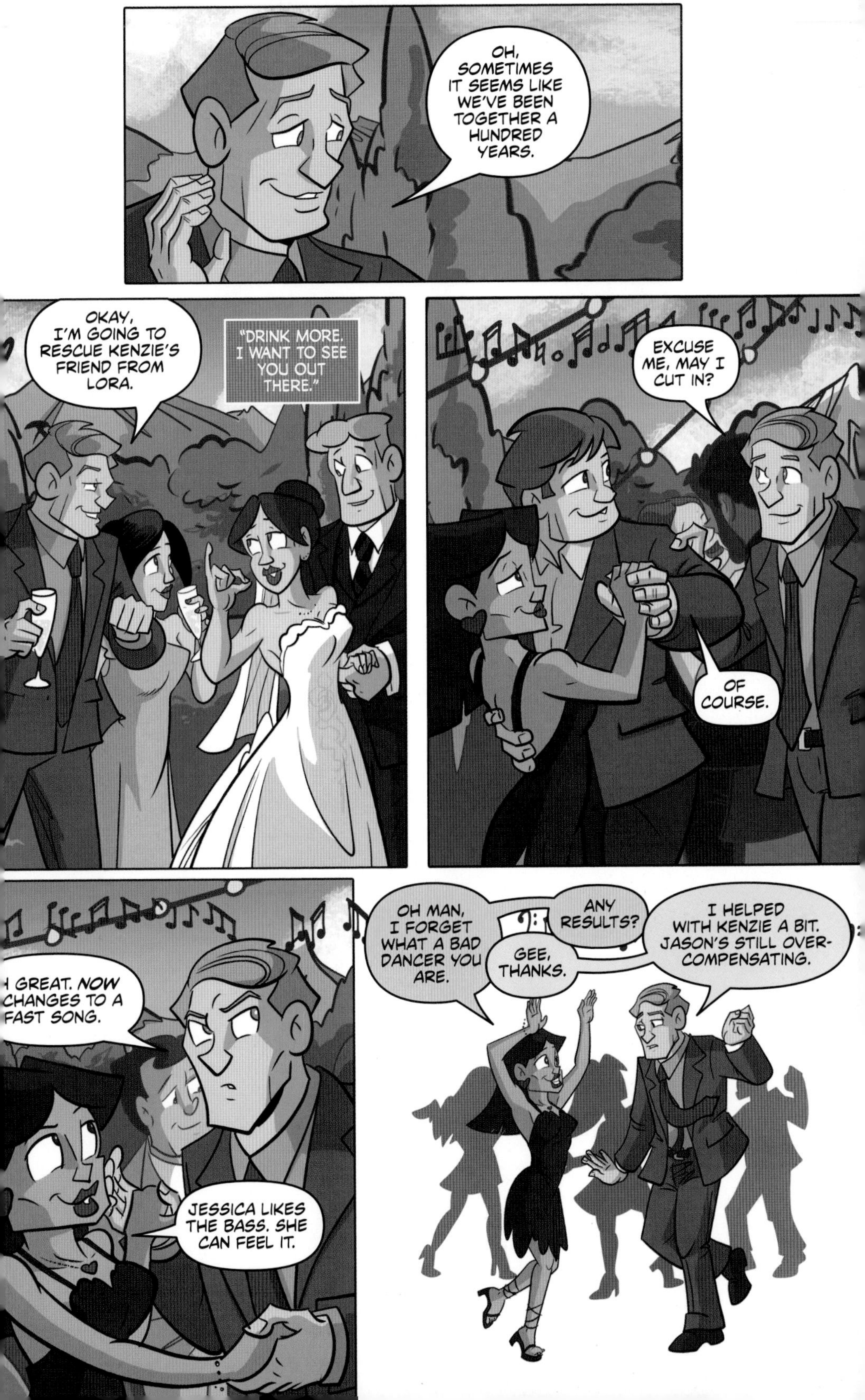
OH, SOMETIMES IT SEEMS LIKE WE'VE BEEN TOGETHER A HUNDRED YEARS.
OKAY, I'M GOING TO RESCUE KENZIE'S FRIEND FROM LORA.
"DRINK MORE. I WANT TO SEE YOU OUT THERE."
EXCUSE ME, MAY I CUT IN?
OF COURSE.
H GREAT. *NOW* CHANGES TO A FAST SONG.
JESSICA LIKES THE BASS. SHE CAN FEEL IT.
OH MAN, I FORGET WHAT A BAD DANCER YOU ARE.
GEE, THANKS.
ANY RESULTS?
I HELPED WITH KENZIE A BIT. JASON'S STILL OVER-COMPENSATING.

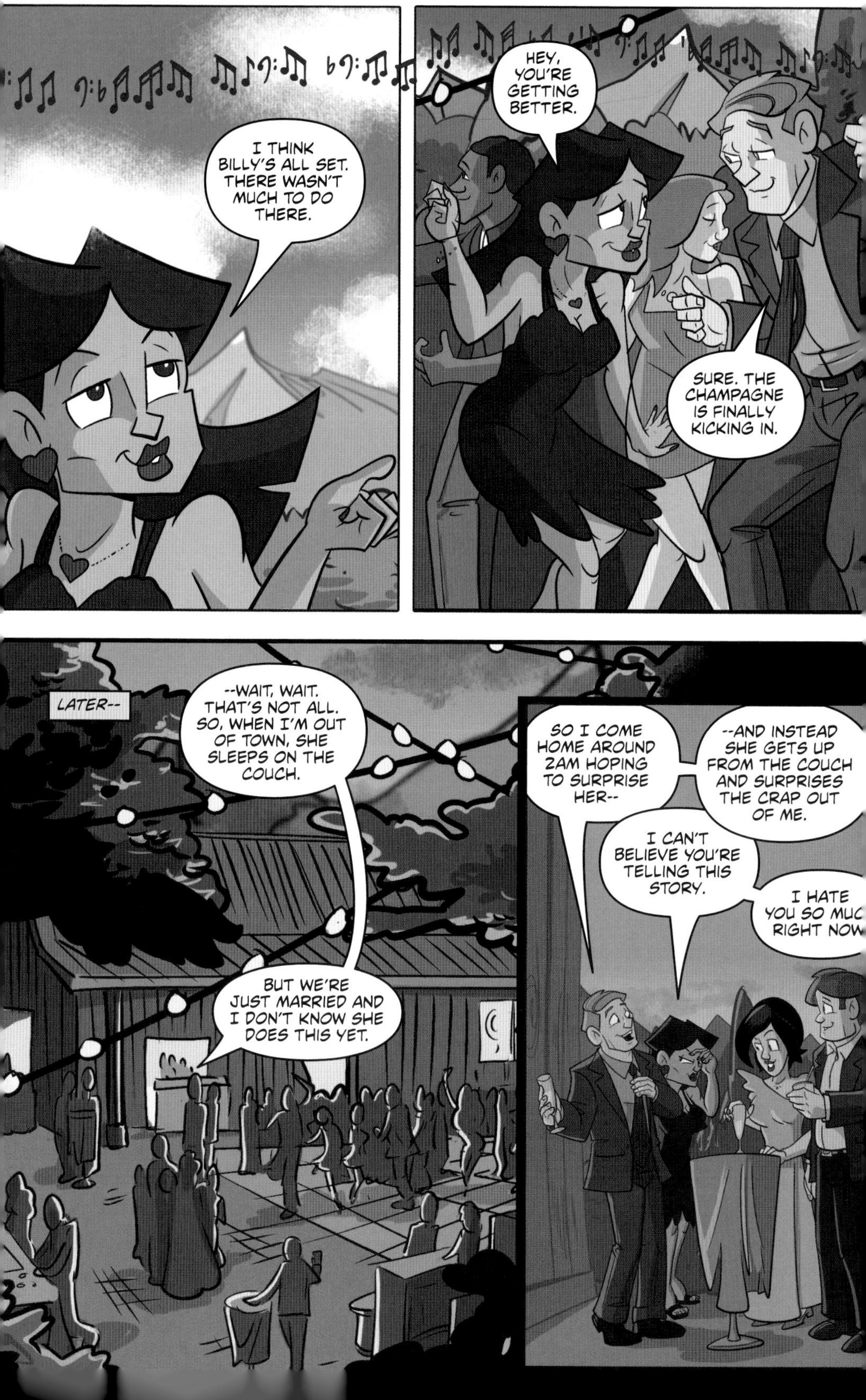
I THINK BILLY'S ALL SET. THERE WASN'T MUCH TO DO THERE.
HEY, YOU'RE GETTING BETTER.
SURE. THE CHAMPAGNE IS FINALLY KICKING IN.
LATER--
--WAIT, WAIT. THAT'S NOT ALL. SO, WHEN I'M OUT OF TOWN, SHE SLEEPS ON THE COUCH.
BUT WE'RE JUST MARRIED AND I DON'T KNOW SHE DOES THIS YET.
SO I COME HOME AROUND 2AM HOPING TO SURPRISE HER--
--AND INSTEAD SHE GETS UP FROM THE COUCH AND SURPRISES THE CRAP OUT OF ME.
I CAN'T BELIEVE YOU'RE TELLING THIS STORY.
I HATE YOU SO MUC RIGHT NOW

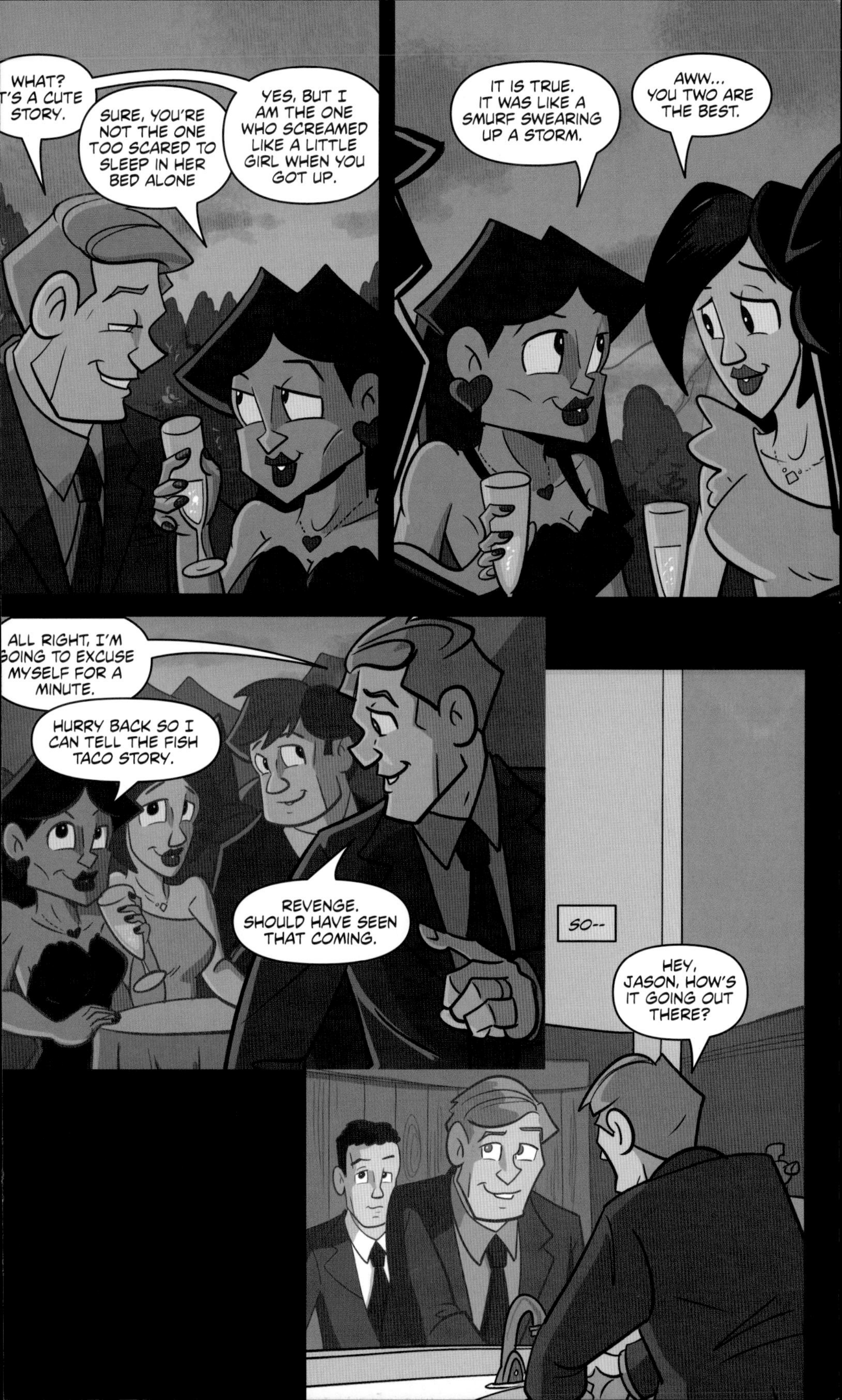
WHAT? IT'S A CUTE STORY.
SURE, YOU'RE NOT THE ONE TOO SCARED TO SLEEP IN HER BED ALONE
YES, BUT I AM THE ONE WHO SCREAMED LIKE A LITTLE GIRL WHEN YOU GOT UP.
IT IS TRUE. IT WAS LIKE A SMURF SWEARING UP A STORM.
AWW... YOU TWO ARE THE BEST.
ALL RIGHT, I'M GOING TO EXCUSE MYSELF FOR A MINUTE.
HURRY BACK SO I CAN TELL THE FISH TACO STORY.
REVENGE. SHOULD HAVE SEEN THAT COMING.
SO--
HEY, JASON, HOW'S IT GOING OUT THERE?

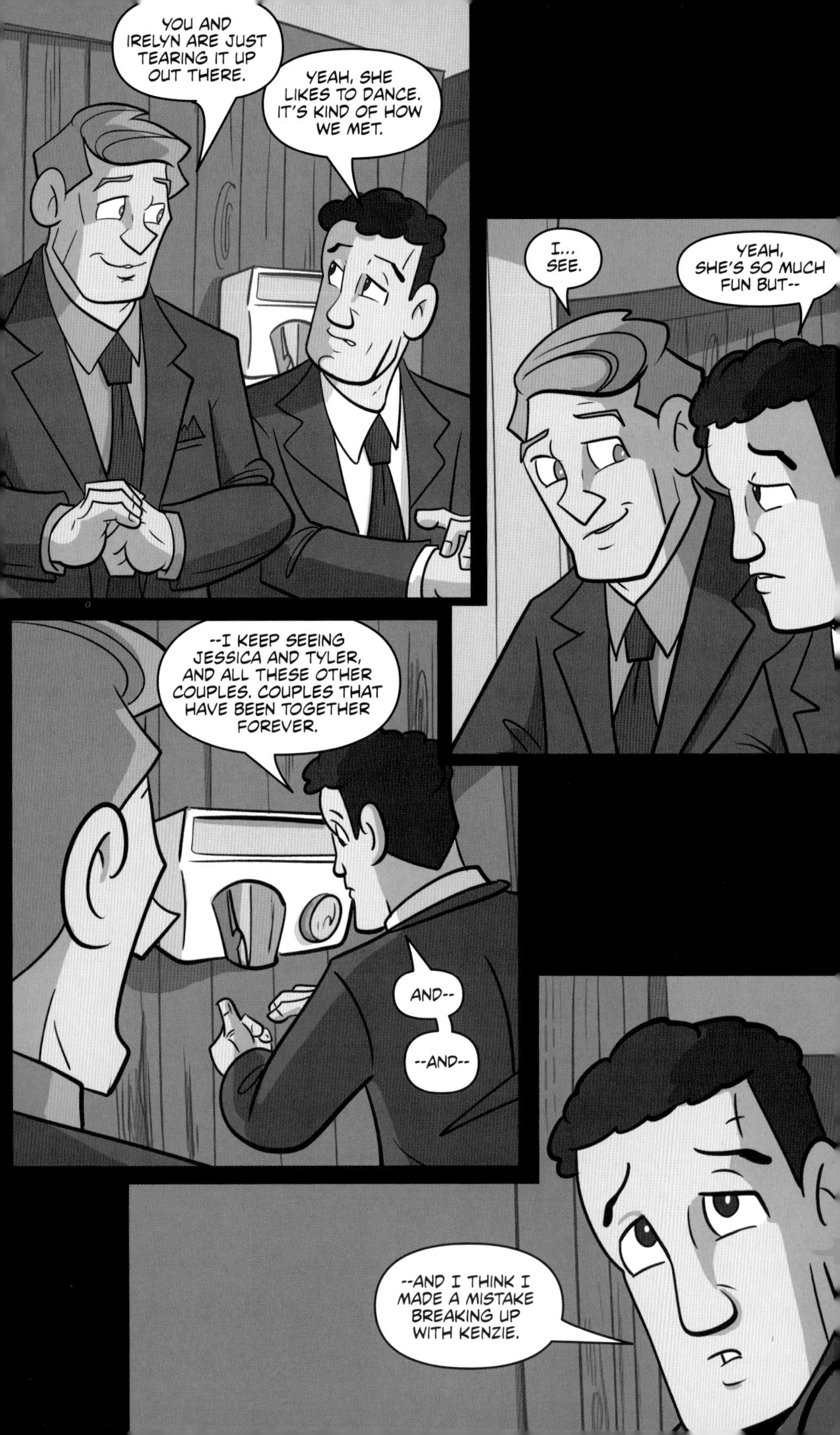
YOU AND IRELYN ARE JUST TEARING IT UP OUT THERE.
YEAH, SHE LIKES TO DANCE. IT'S KIND OF HOW WE MET.
I... SEE.
YEAH, SHE'S SO MUCH FUN BUT--
--I KEEP SEEING JESSICA AND TYLER, AND ALL THESE OTHER COUPLES. COUPLES THAT HAVE BEEN TOGETHER FOREVER.
AND--
--AND--
--AND I THINK I MADE A MISTAKE BREAKING UP WITH KENZIE.

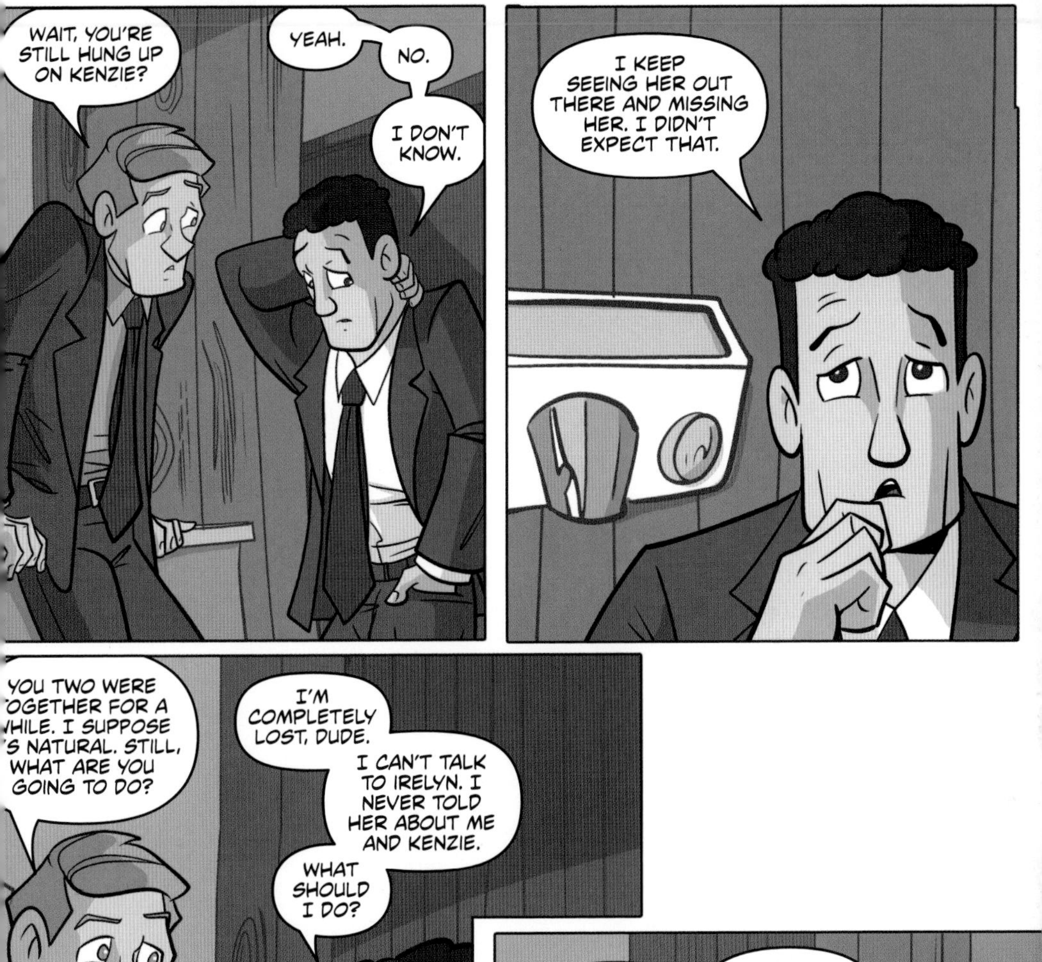
WAIT, YOU'RE STILL HUNG UP ON KENZIE?
YEAH.
NO.
I DON'T KNOW.
I KEEP SEEING HER OUT THERE AND MISSING HER. I DIDN'T EXPECT THAT.
YOU TWO WERE OGETHER FOR A HILE. I SUPPOSE 'S NATURAL. STILL, WHAT ARE YOU GOING TO DO?
I'M COMPLETELY LOST, DUDE.
I CAN'T TALK TO IRELYN. I NEVER TOLD HER ABOUT ME AND KENZIE.
WHAT SHOULD I DO?

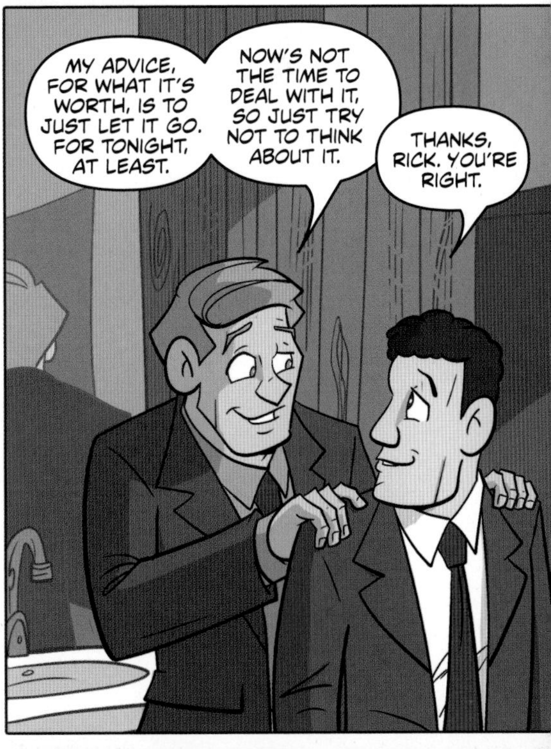
MY ADVICE, FOR WHAT IT'S WORTH, IS TO JUST LET IT GO. FOR TONIGHT, AT LEAST.
NOW'S NOT THE TIME TO DEAL WITH IT, SO JUST TRY NOT TO THINK ABOUT IT.
THANKS, RICK. YOU'RE RIGHT.

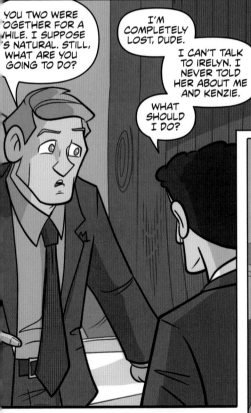

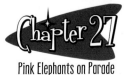

Chapter 27

Pink Elephants on Parade

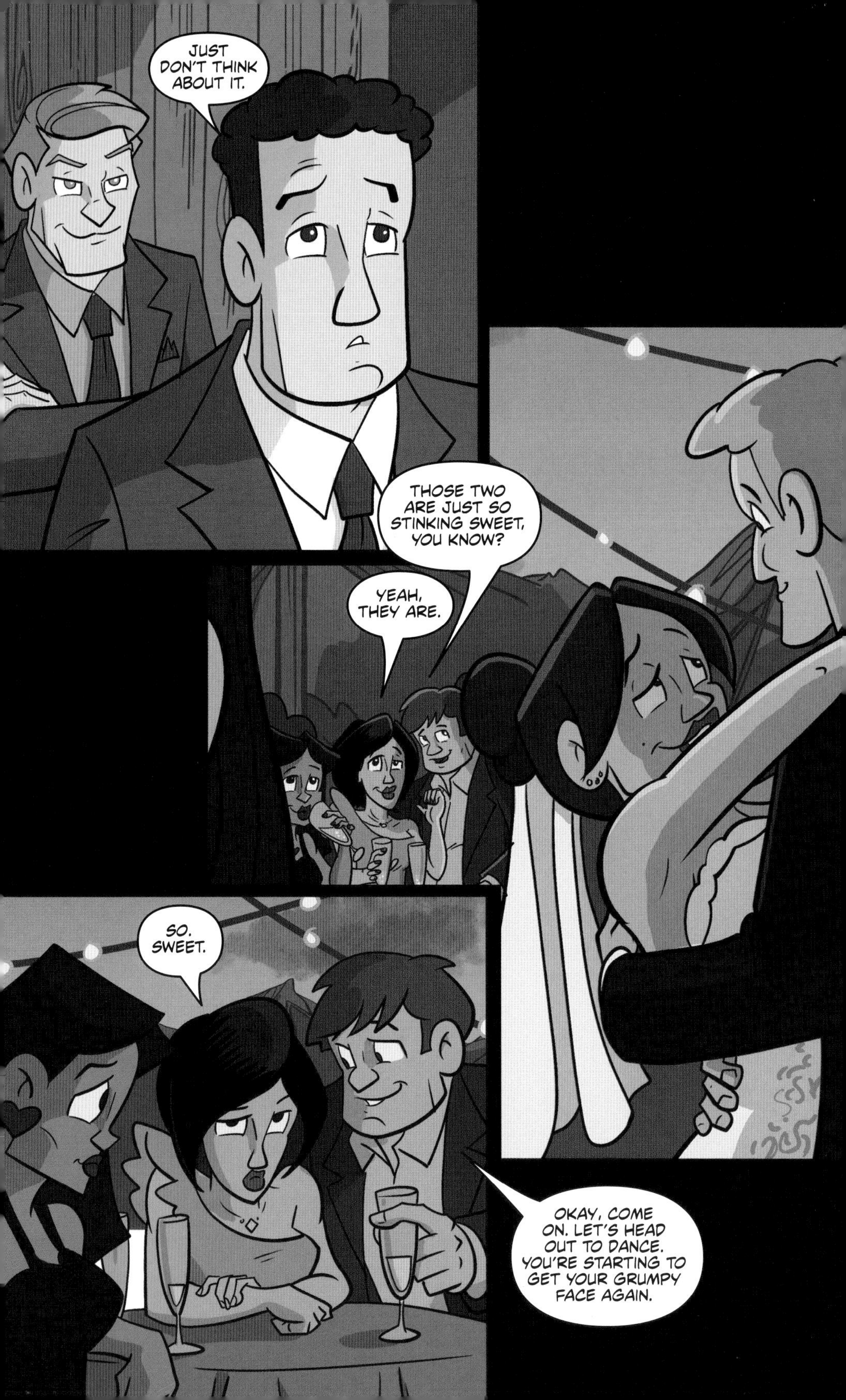
JUST DON'T THINK ABOUT IT.
THOSE TWO ARE JUST SO STINKING SWEET, YOU KNOW?
YEAH, THEY ARE.
SO. SWEET.
OKAY, COME ON. LET'S HEAD OUT TO DANCE. YOU'RE STARTING TO GET YOUR GRUMPY FACE AGAIN.

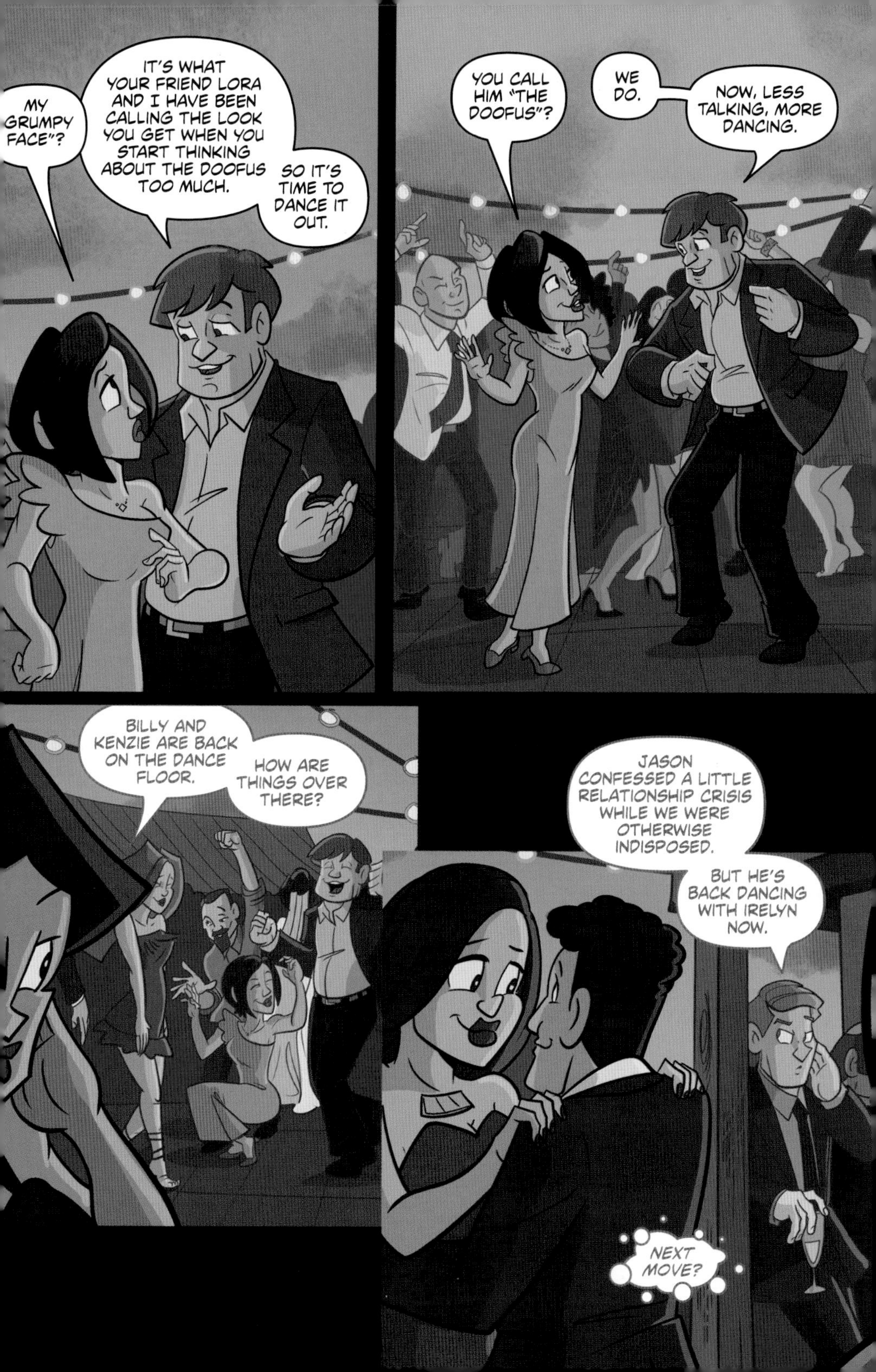
MY "GRUMPY FACE"?
IT'S WHAT YOUR FRIEND LORA AND I HAVE BEEN CALLING THE LOOK YOU GET WHEN YOU START THINKING ABOUT THE DOOFUS TOO MUCH.
SO IT'S TIME TO DANCE IT OUT.
YOU CALL HIM "THE DOOFUS"?
WE DO.
NOW, LESS TALKING, MORE DANCING.
BILLY AND KENZIE ARE BACK ON THE DANCE FLOOR.
HOW ARE THINGS OVER THERE?
JASON CONFESSED A LITTLE RELATIONSHIP CRISIS WHILE WE WERE OTHERWISE INDISPOSED.
BUT HE'S BACK DANCING WITH IRELYN NOW.
NEXT MOVE?

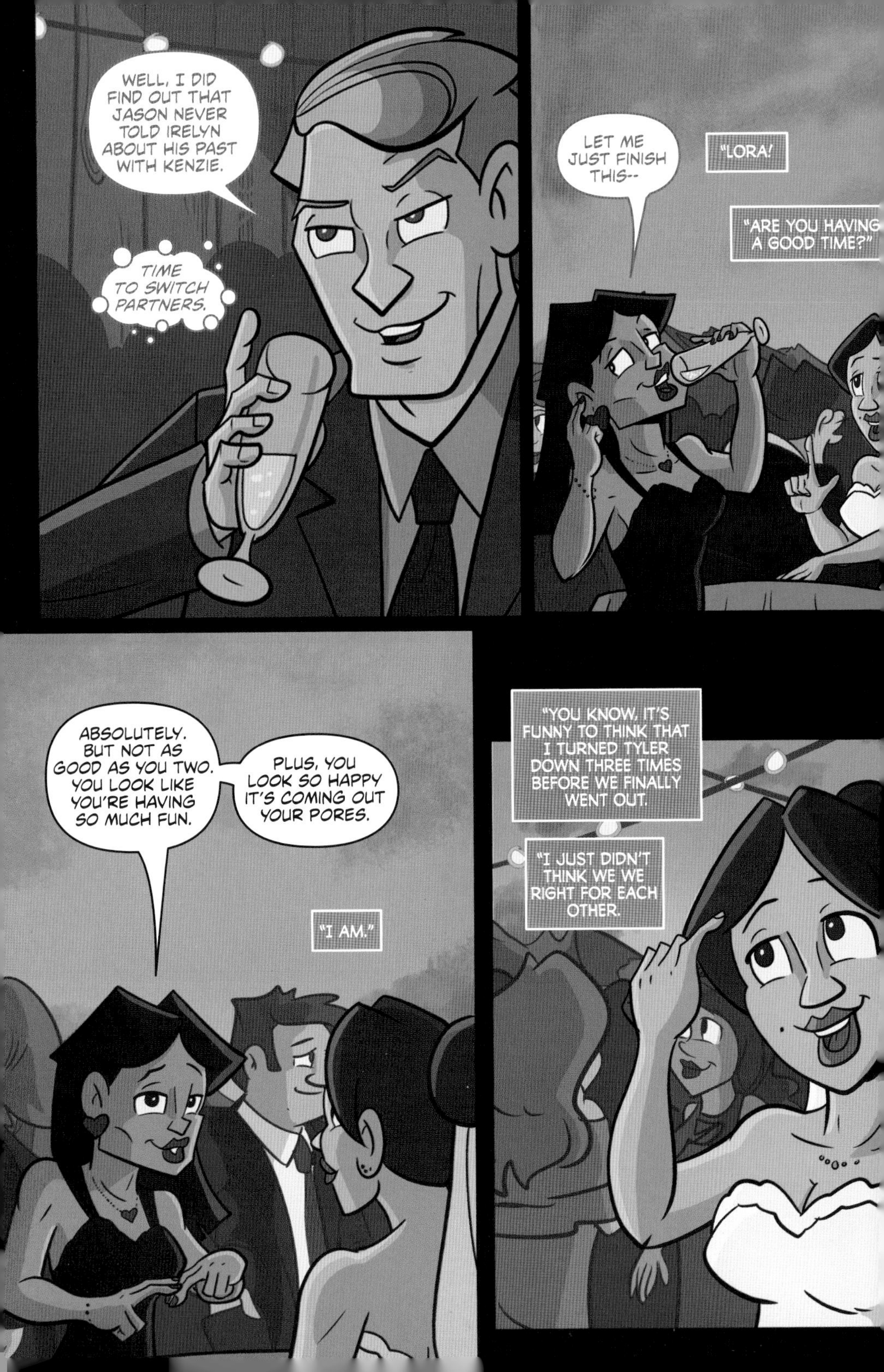
WELL, I DID FIND OUT THAT JASON NEVER TOLD IRELYN ABOUT HIS PAST WITH KENZIE.
TIME TO SWITCH PARTNERS.
LET ME JUST FINISH THIS--
"LORA!
"ARE YOU HAVING A GOOD TIME?"
ABSOLUTELY. BUT NOT AS GOOD AS YOU TWO. YOU LOOK LIKE YOU'RE HAVING SO MUCH FUN.
PLUS, YOU LOOK SO HAPPY IT'S COMING OUT YOUR PORES.
"I AM."
"YOU KNOW, IT'S FUNNY TO THINK THAT I TURNED TYLER DOWN THREE TIMES BEFORE WE FINALLY WENT OUT.
"I JUST DIDN'T THINK WE WE RIGHT FOR EACH OTHER.

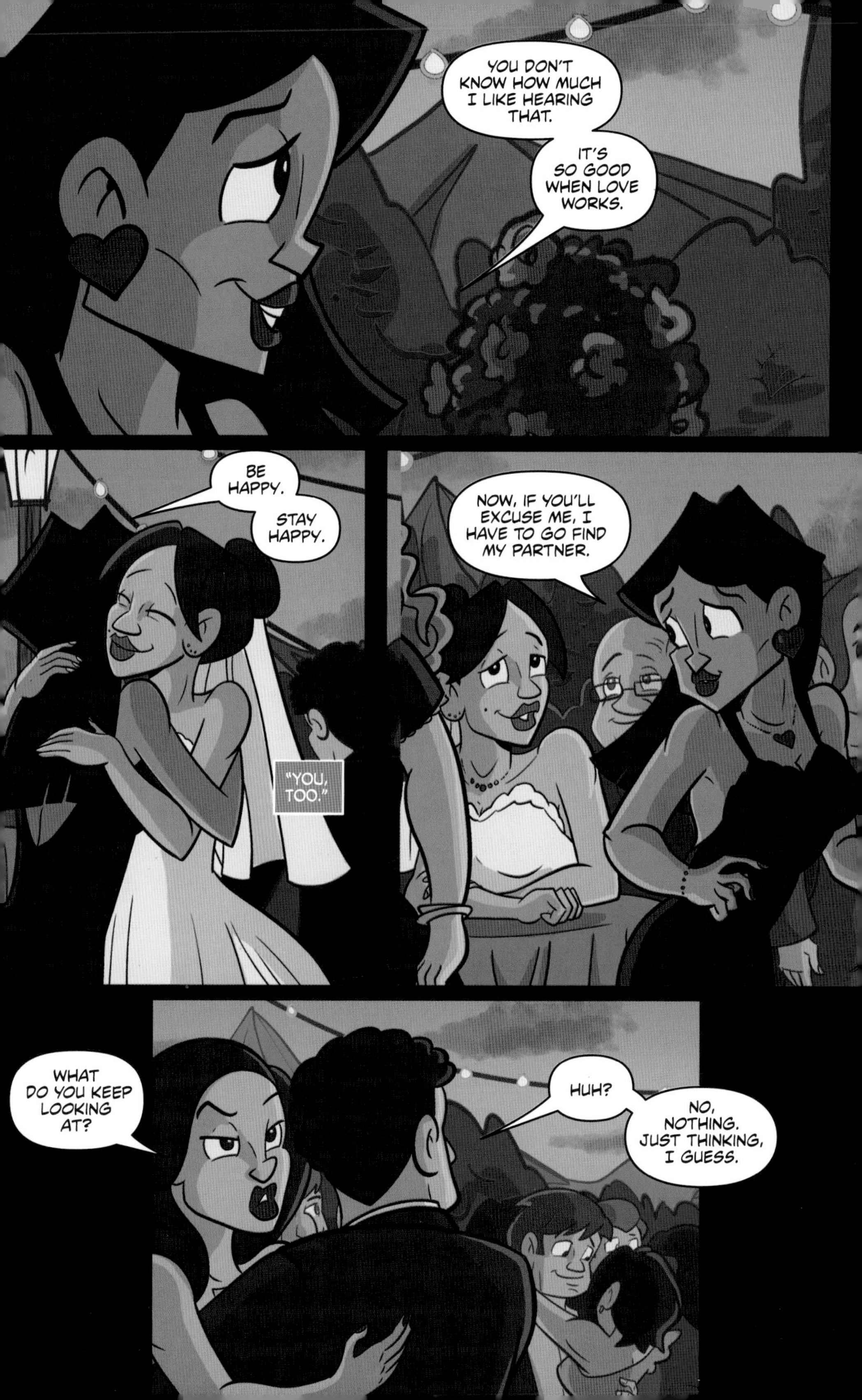
YOU DON'T KNOW HOW MUCH I LIKE HEARING THAT.
IT'S SO GOOD WHEN LOVE WORKS.
BE HAPPY.
STAY HAPPY.
"YOU, TOO."
NOW, IF YOU'LL EXCUSE ME, I HAVE TO GO FIND MY PARTNER.
WHAT DO YOU KEEP LOOKING AT?
HUH?
NO, NOTHING. JUST THINKING, I GUESS.

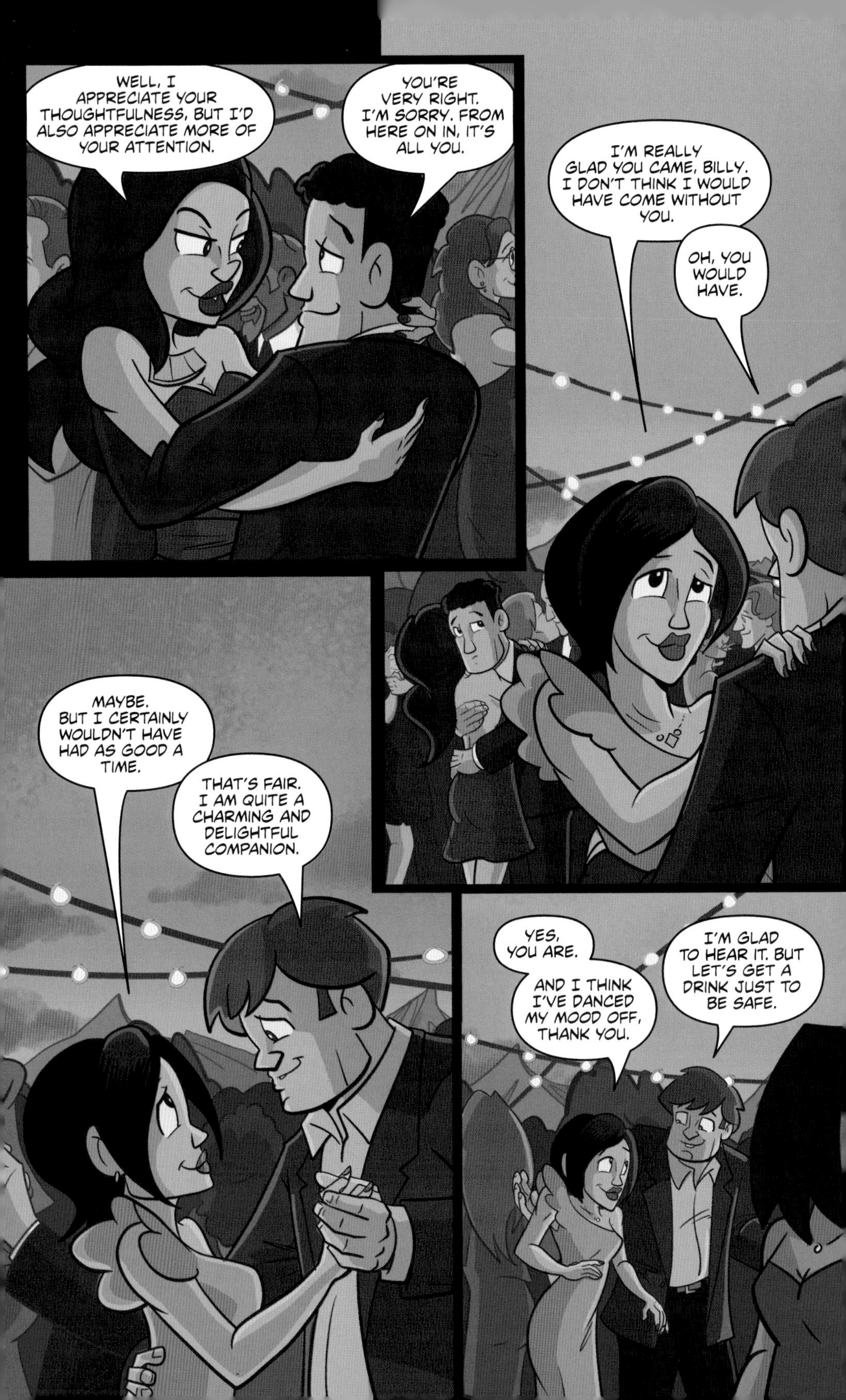
WELL, I APPRECIATE YOUR THOUGHTFULNESS, BUT I'D ALSO APPRECIATE MORE OF YOUR ATTENTION.
YOU'RE VERY RIGHT. I'M SORRY. FROM HERE ON IN, IT'S ALL YOU.
I'M REALLY GLAD YOU CAME, BILLY. I DON'T THINK I WOULD HAVE COME WITHOUT YOU.
OH, YOU WOULD HAVE.
MAYBE. BUT I CERTAINLY WOULDN'T HAVE HAD AS GOOD A TIME.
THAT'S FAIR. I AM QUITE A CHARMING AND DELIGHTFUL COMPANION.
YES, YOU ARE.
AND I THINK I'VE DANCED MY MOOD OFF, THANK YOU.
I'M GLAD TO HEAR IT. BUT LET'S GET A DRINK JUST TO BE SAFE.

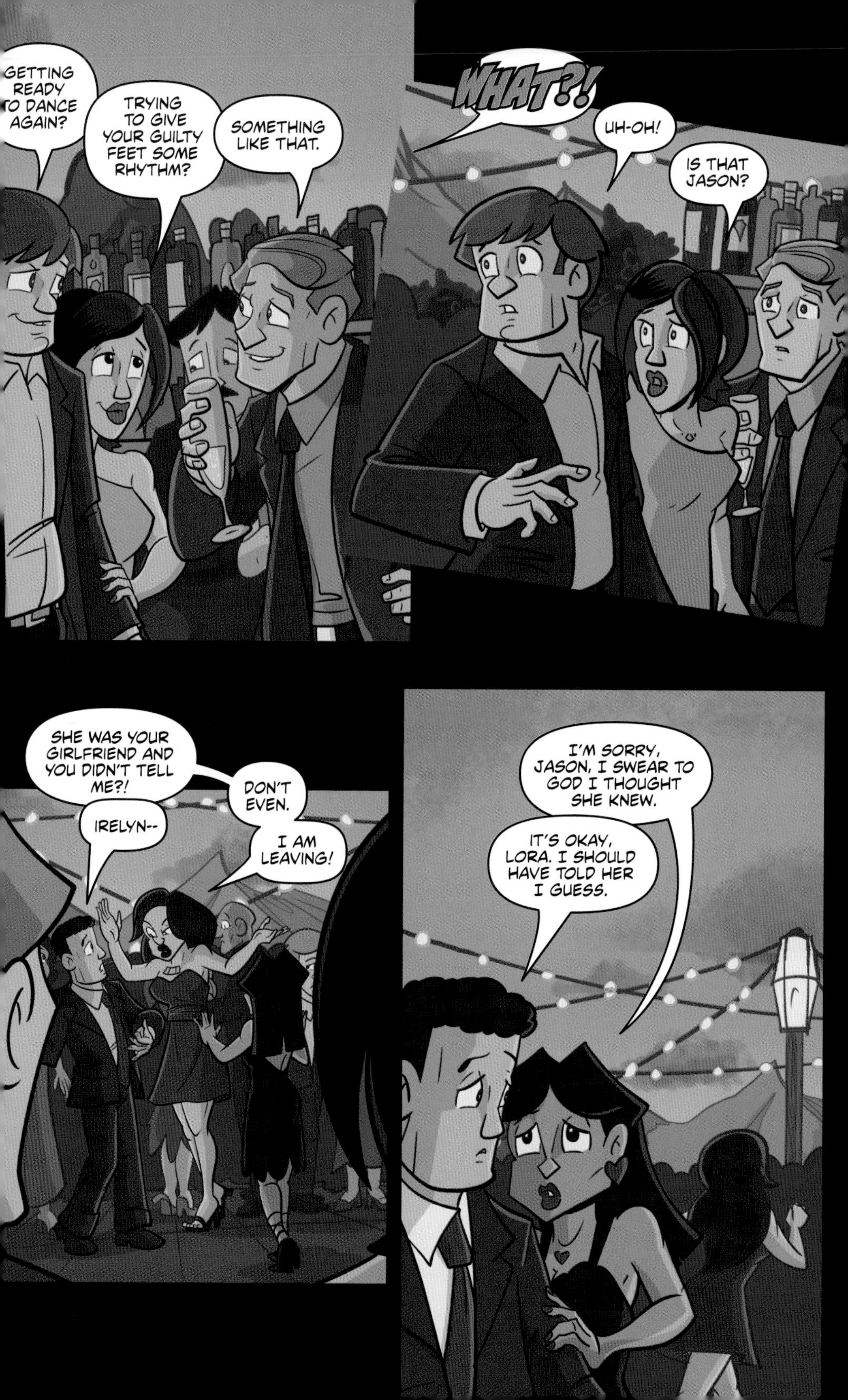
GETTING READY TO DANCE AGAIN?
TRYING TO GIVE YOUR GUILTY FEET SOME RHYTHM?
SOMETHING LIKE THAT.
WHAT?!
UH-OH!
IS THAT JASON?
SHE WAS YOUR GIRLFRIEND AND YOU DIDN'T TELL ME?!
IRELYN--
DON'T EVEN.
I AM LEAVING!
I'M SORRY, JASON, I SWEAR TO GOD I THOUGHT SHE KNEW.
IT'S OKAY, LORA. I SHOULD HAVE TOLD HER I GUESS.

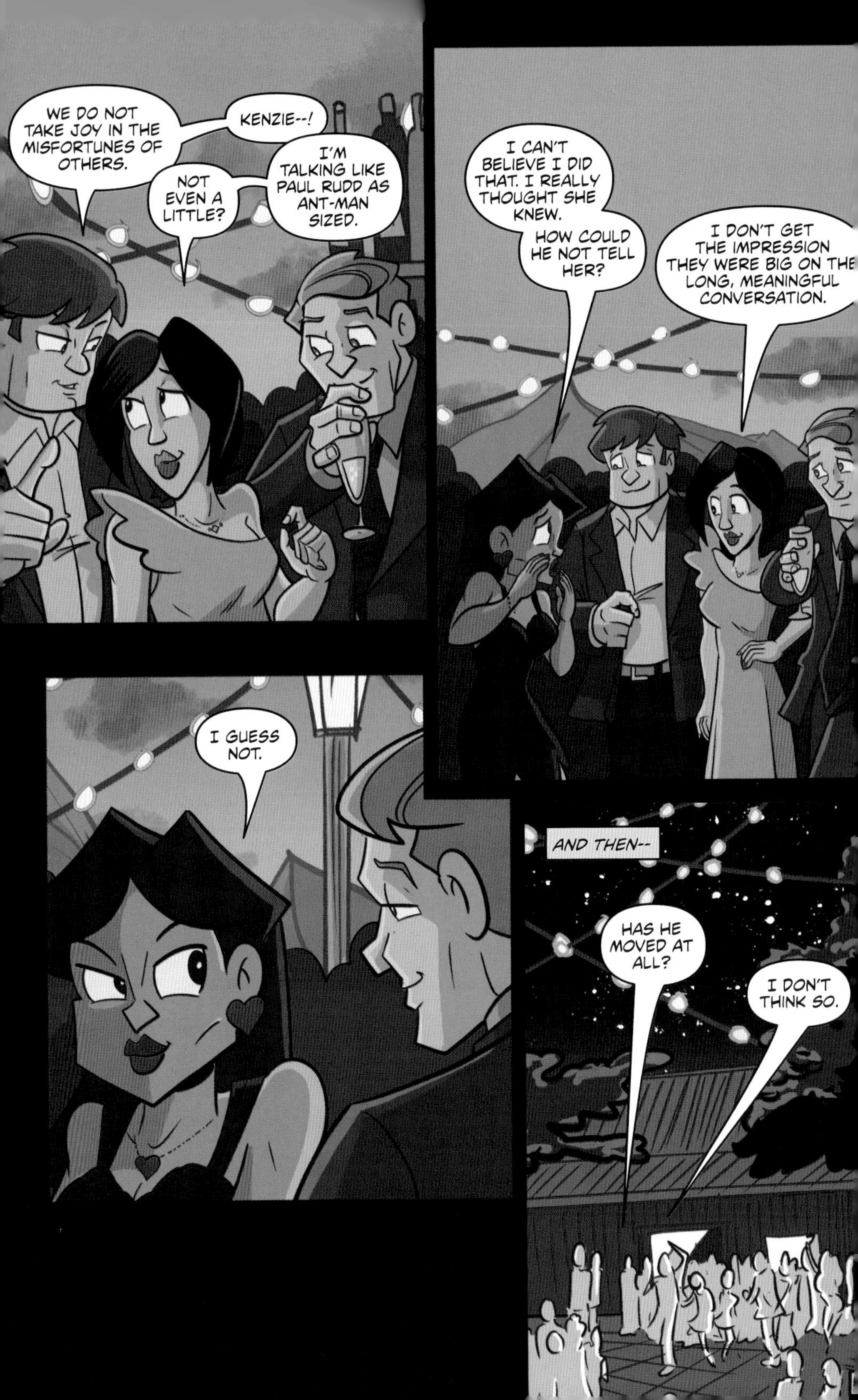
WE DO NOT TAKE JOY IN THE MISFORTUNES OF OTHERS.
KENZIE--!
NOT EVEN A LITTLE?
I'M TALKING LIKE PAUL RUDD AS ANT-MAN SIZED.
I CAN'T BELIEVE I DID THAT. I REALLY THOUGHT SHE KNEW.
HOW COULD HE NOT TELL HER?
I DON'T GET THE IMPRESSION THEY WERE BIG ON THE LONG, MEANINGFUL CONVERSATION.
I GUESS NOT.
AND THEN--
HAS HE MOVED AT ALL?
I DON'T THINK SO.

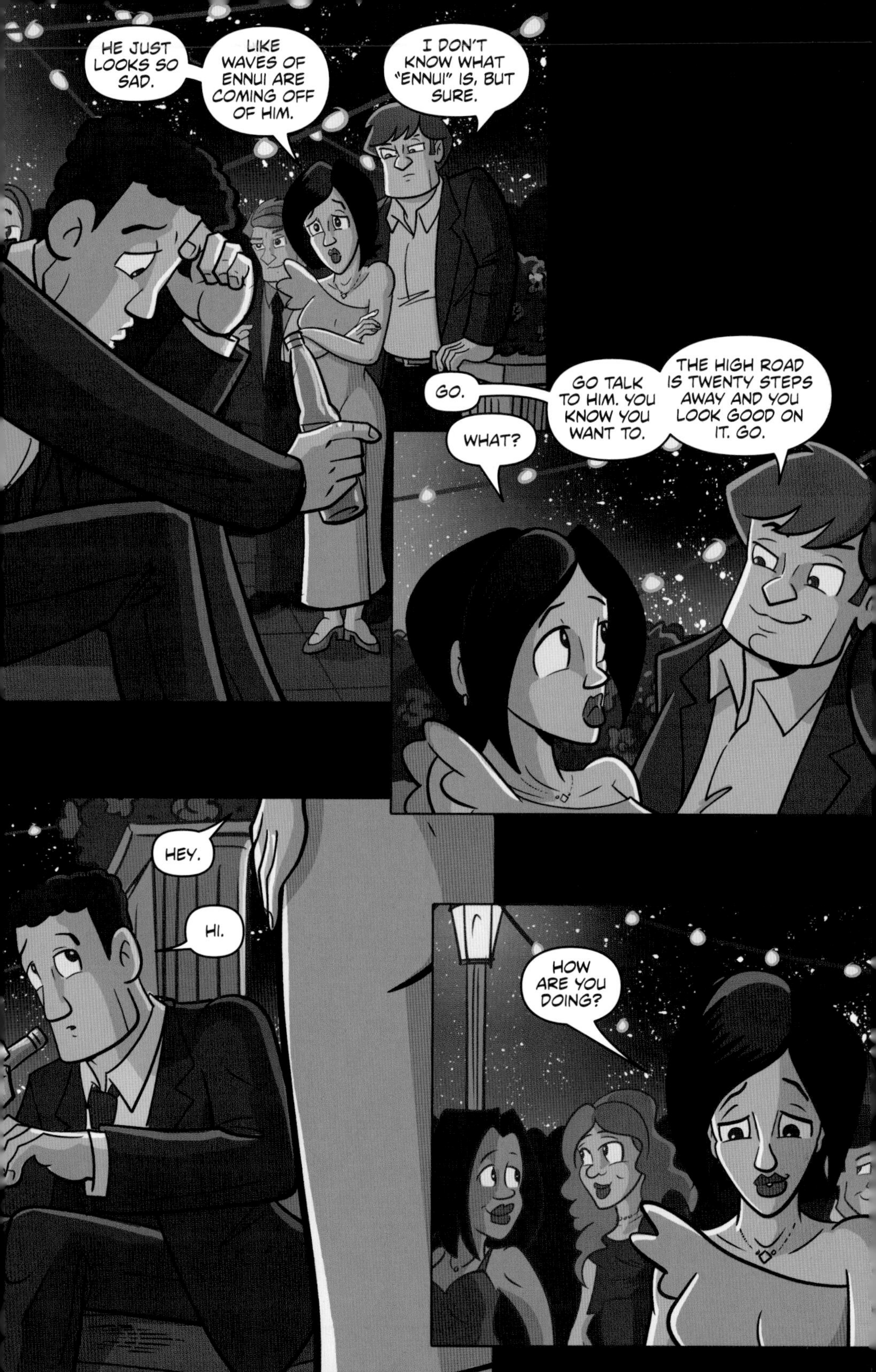
HE JUST LOOKS SO SAD.
LIKE WAVES OF ENNUI ARE COMING OFF OF HIM.
I DON'T KNOW WHAT "ENNUI" IS, BUT SURE.
GO.
WHAT?
GO TALK TO HIM. YOU KNOW YOU WANT TO.
THE HIGH ROAD IS TWENTY STEPS AWAY AND YOU LOOK GOOD ON IT. GO.
HEY.
HI.
HOW ARE YOU DOING?

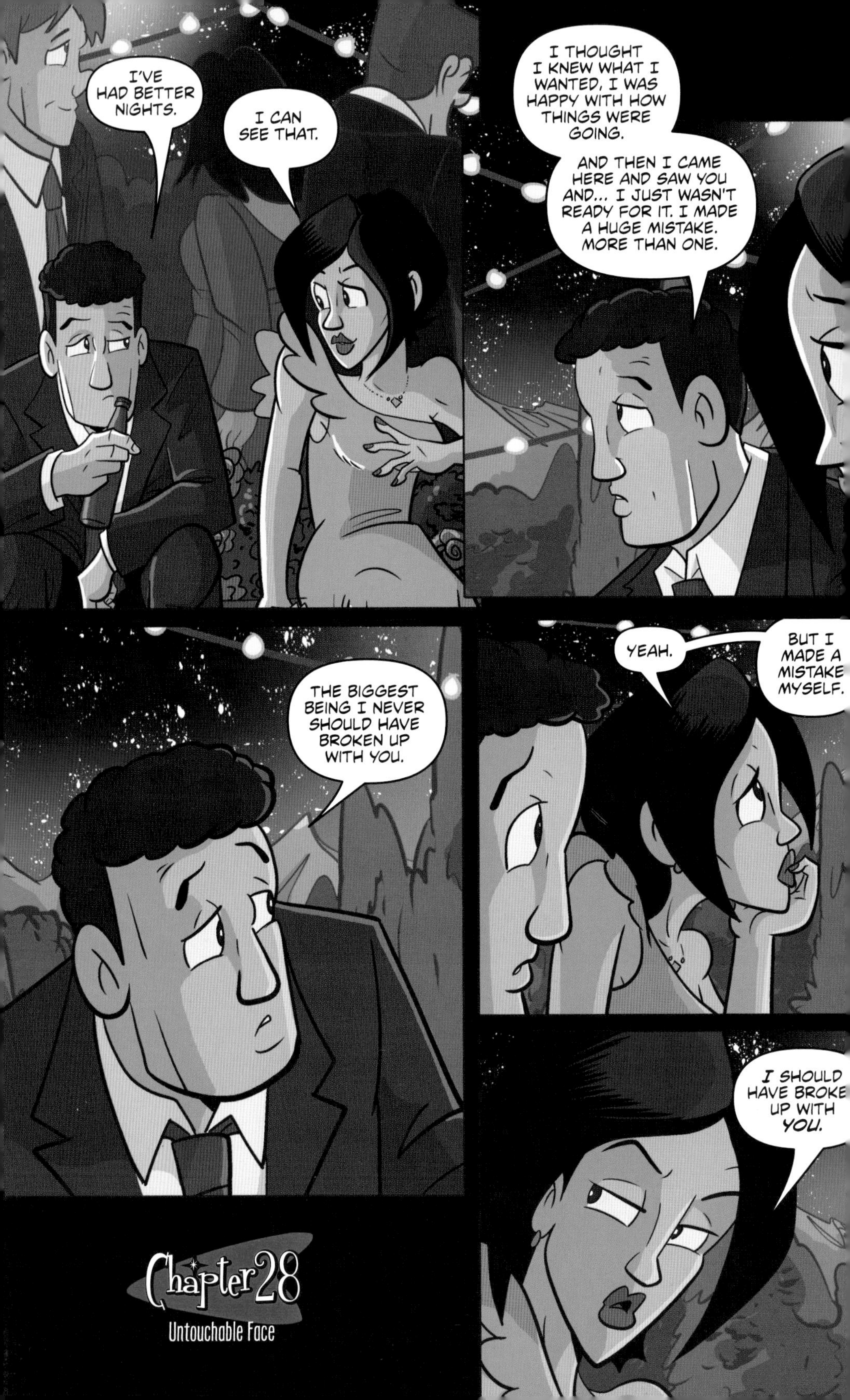
I'VE HAD BETTER NIGHTS.
I CAN SEE THAT.
I THOUGHT I KNEW WHAT I WANTED, I WAS HAPPY WITH HOW THINGS WERE GOING.
AND THEN I CAME HERE AND SAW YOU AND... I JUST WASN'T READY FOR IT. I MADE A HUGE MISTAKE. MORE THAN ONE.
THE BIGGEST BEING I NEVER SHOULD HAVE BROKEN UP WITH YOU.
YEAH.
BUT I MADE A MISTAKE MYSELF.
I SHOULD HAVE BROKE UP WITH *YOU*.
Chapter 28
Untouchable Face

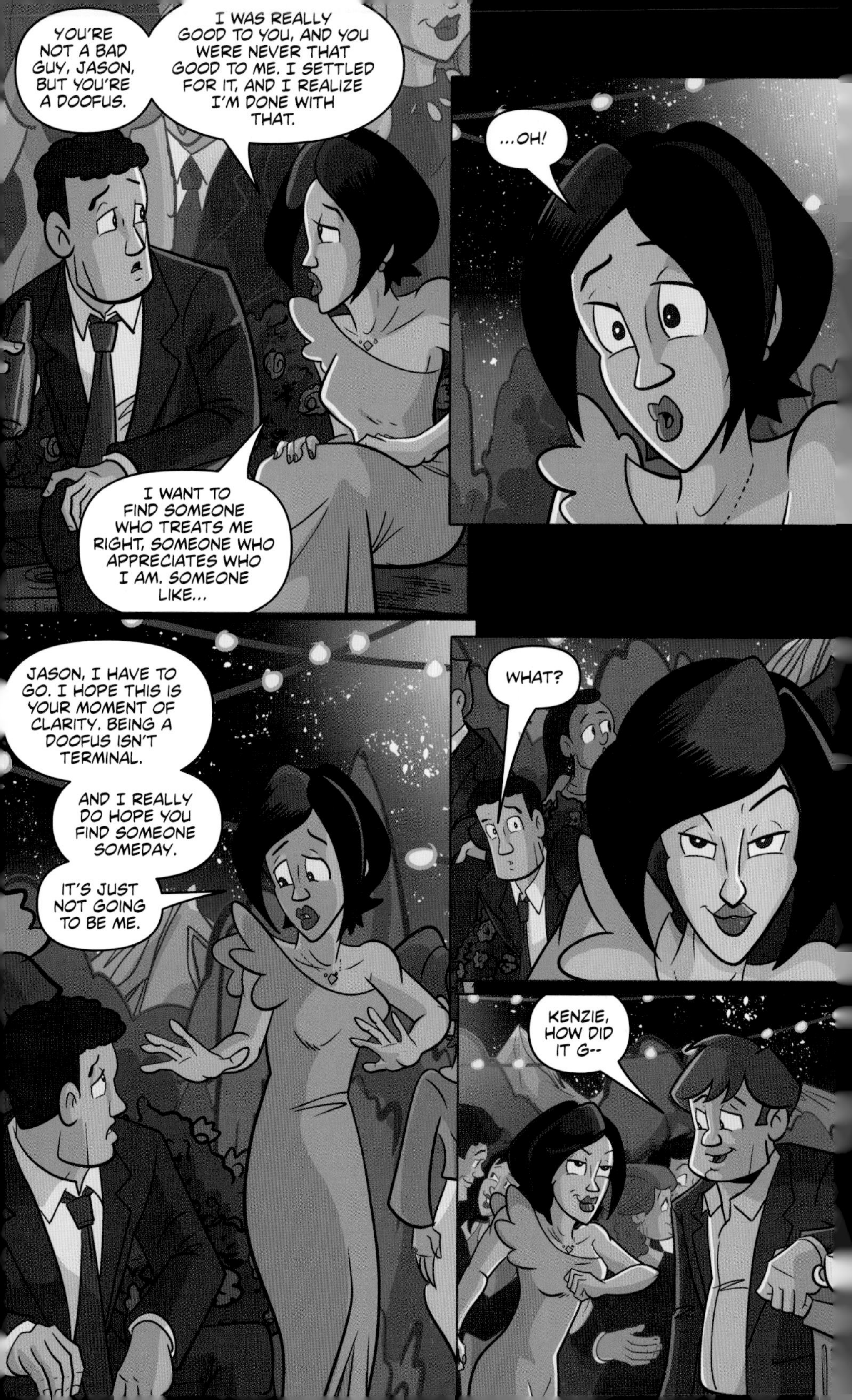
YOU'RE NOT A BAD GUY, JASON, BUT YOU'RE A DOOFUS.
I WAS REALLY GOOD TO YOU, AND YOU WERE NEVER THAT GOOD TO ME. I SETTLED FOR IT, AND I REALIZE I'M DONE WITH THAT.
I WANT TO FIND SOMEONE WHO TREATS ME RIGHT, SOMEONE WHO APPRECIATES WHO I AM. SOMEONE LIKE...
...OH!
JASON, I HAVE TO GO. I HOPE THIS IS YOUR MOMENT OF CLARITY. BEING A DOOFUS ISN'T TERMINAL.
AND I REALLY DO HOPE YOU FIND SOMEONE SOMEDAY.
IT'S JUST NOT GOING TO BE ME.
WHAT?
KENZIE, HOW DID IT G--

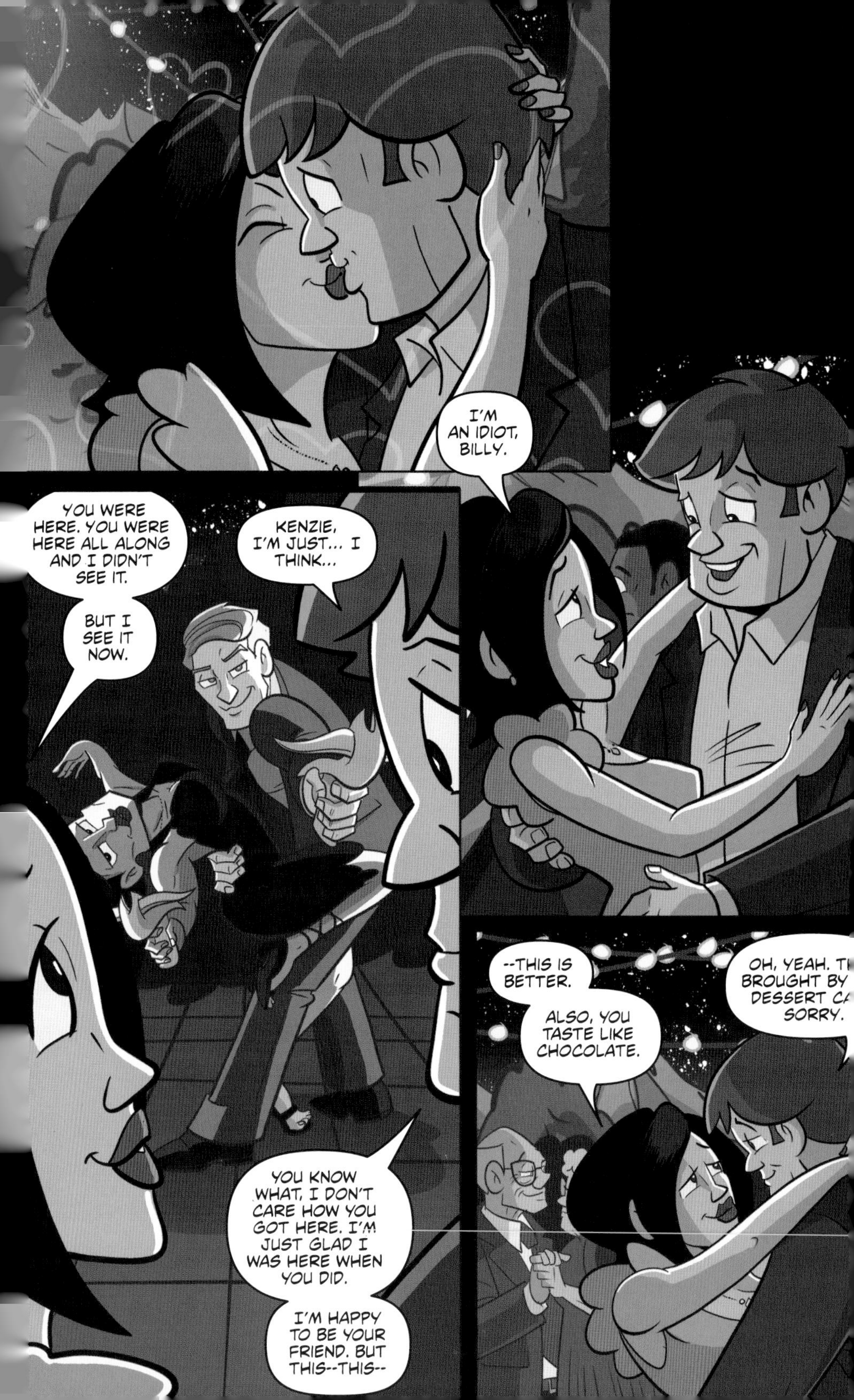
I'M AN IDIOT, BILLY.
YOU WERE HERE. YOU WERE HERE ALL ALONG AND I DIDN'T SEE IT.
BUT I SEE IT NOW.
KENZIE, I'M JUST... I THINK...
YOU KNOW WHAT, I DON'T CARE HOW YOU GOT HERE. I'M JUST GLAD I WAS HERE WHEN YOU DID.
I'M HAPPY TO BE YOUR FRIEND. BUT THIS--THIS--
--THIS IS BETTER.
ALSO, YOU TASTE LIKE CHOCOLATE.

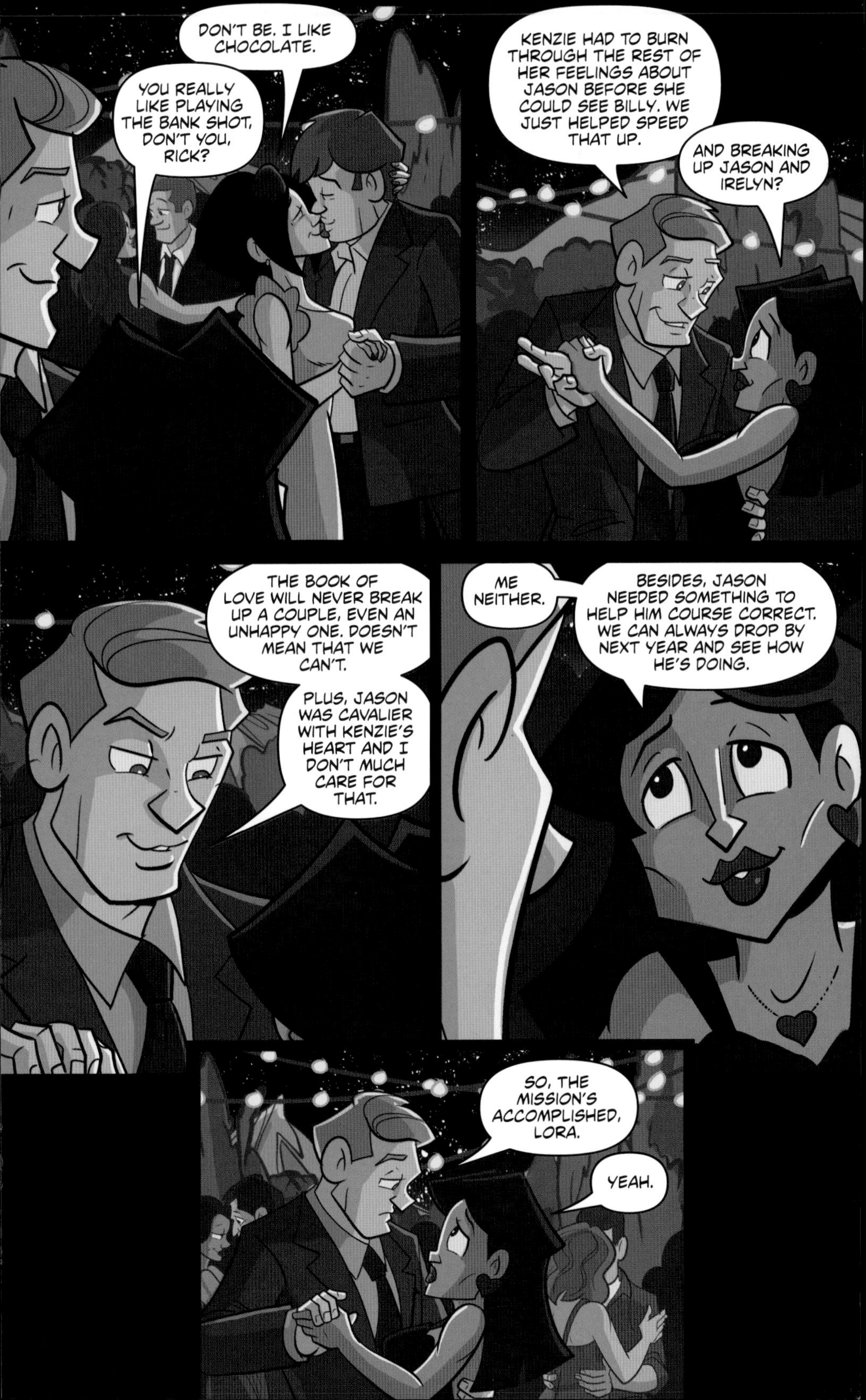
YOU REALLY LIKE PLAYING THE BANK SHOT, DON'T YOU, RICK?
DON'T BE. I LIKE CHOCOLATE.
KENZIE HAD TO BURN THROUGH THE REST OF HER FEELINGS ABOUT JASON BEFORE SHE COULD SEE BILLY. WE JUST HELPED SPEED THAT UP.
AND BREAKING UP JASON AND IRELYN?
THE BOOK OF LOVE WILL NEVER BREAK UP A COUPLE, EVEN AN UNHAPPY ONE. DOESN'T MEAN THAT WE CAN'T.
PLUS, JASON WAS CAVALIER WITH KENZIE'S HEART AND I DON'T MUCH CARE FOR THAT.
ME NEITHER.
BESIDES, JASON NEEDED SOMETHING TO HELP HIM COURSE CORRECT. WE CAN ALWAYS DROP BY NEXT YEAR AND SEE HOW HE'S DOING.
SO, THE MISSION'S ACCOMPLISHED, LORA.
YEAH.

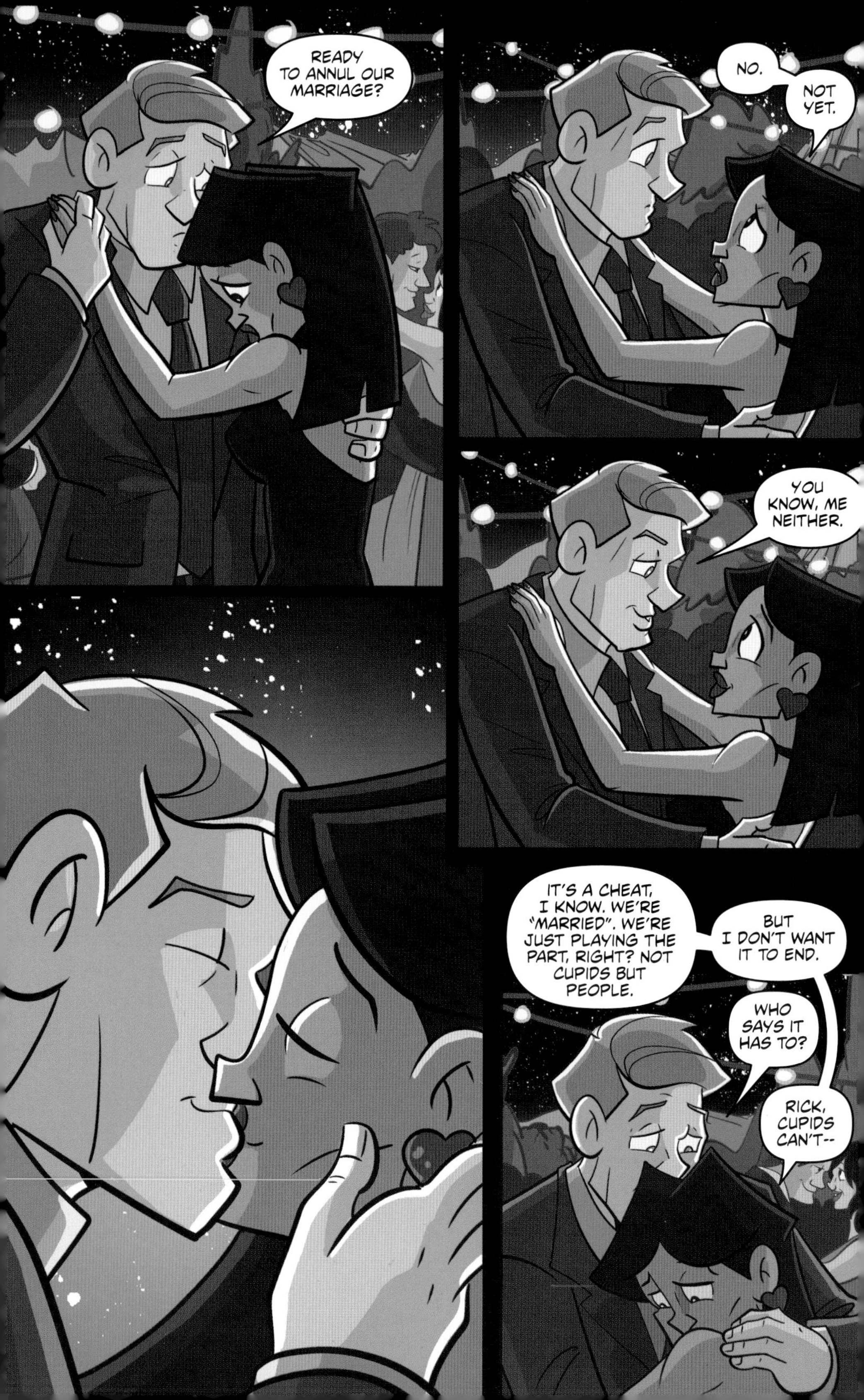
READY TO ANNUL OUR MARRIAGE?
NO.
NOT YET.
YOU KNOW, ME NEITHER.
IT'S A CHEAT, I KNOW. WE'RE "MARRIED". WE'RE JUST PLAYING THE PART, RIGHT? NOT CUPIDS BUT PEOPLE.
BUT I DON'T WANT IT TO END.
WHO SAYS IT HAS TO?
RICK, CUPIDS CAN'T--

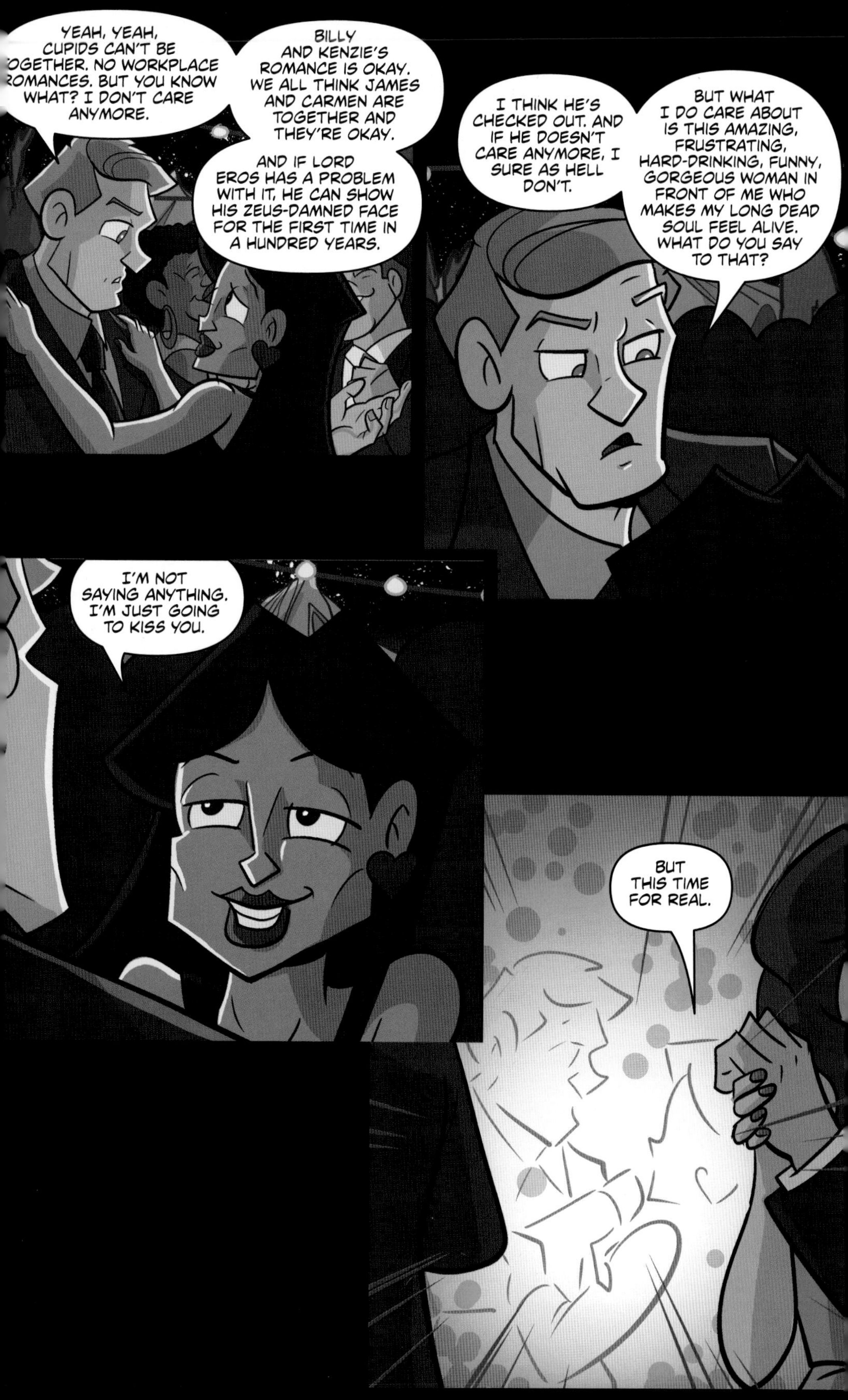
YEAH, YEAH, CUPIDS CAN'T BE TOGETHER. NO WORKPLACE ROMANCES. BUT YOU KNOW WHAT? I DON'T CARE ANYMORE.
BILLY AND KENZIE'S ROMANCE IS OKAY. WE ALL THINK JAMES AND CARMEN ARE TOGETHER AND THEY'RE OKAY.
AND IF LORD EROS HAS A PROBLEM WITH IT, HE CAN SHOW HIS ZEUS-DAMNED FACE FOR THE FIRST TIME IN A HUNDRED YEARS.
I THINK HE'S CHECKED OUT. AND IF HE DOESN'T CARE ANYMORE, I SURE AS HELL DON'T.
BUT WHAT I DO CARE ABOUT IS THIS AMAZING, FRUSTRATING, HARD-DRINKING, FUNNY, GORGEOUS WOMAN IN FRONT OF ME WHO MAKES MY LONG DEAD SOUL FEEL ALIVE. WHAT DO YOU SAY TO THAT?
I'M NOT SAYING ANYTHING. I'M JUST GOING TO KISS YOU.
BUT THIS TIME FOR REAL.

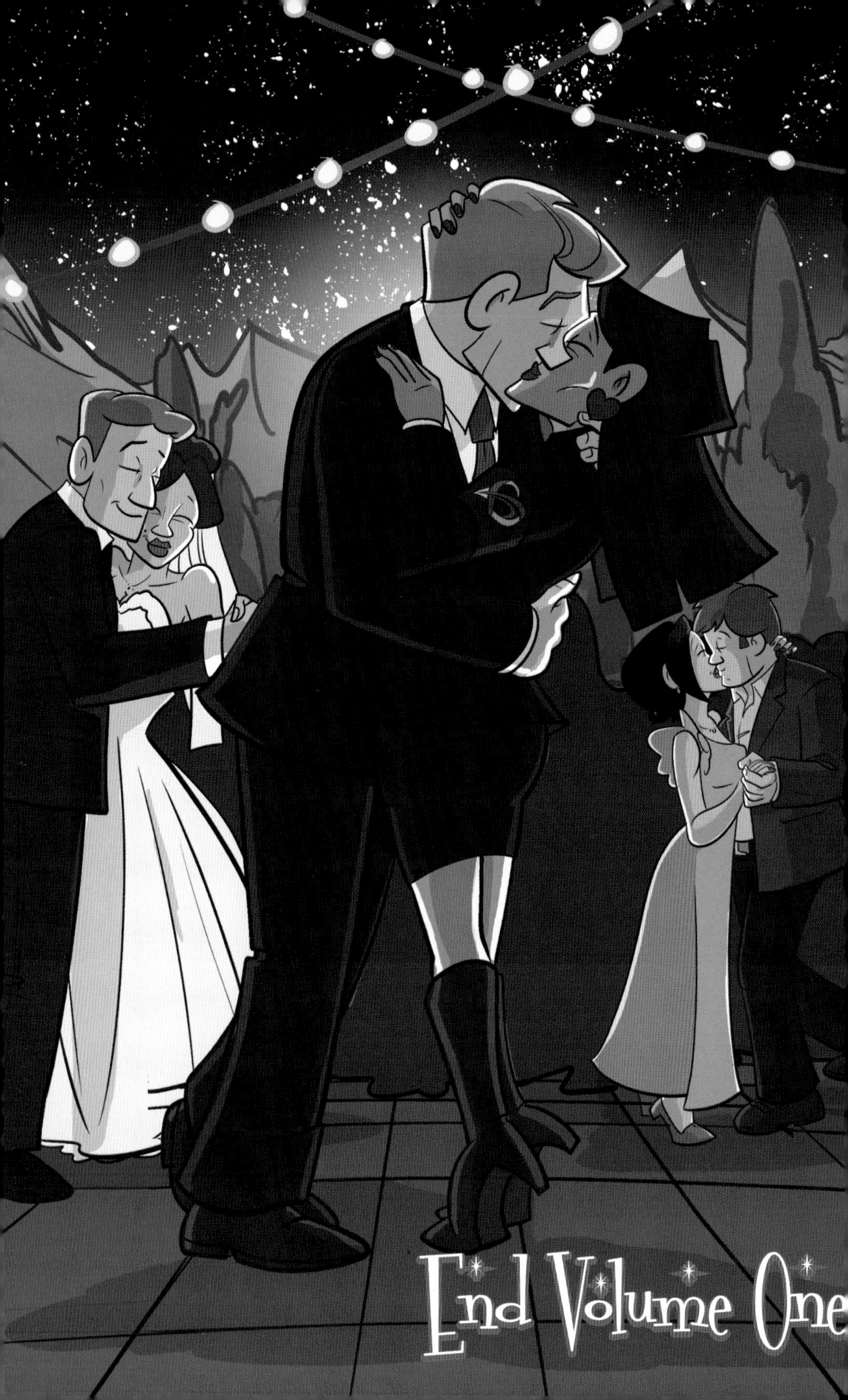
End Volume One

Taking Another Shot

It was Denver Pop Culture Fest in 2018 and *Warning Label* had just come out. I had maybe four chapters up, and three of them had come out the next week. I had no idea how things were going. WEBTOON was at the show, too. I went up to the booth and saw the smiling face of Tom Akel, my editor. This is the first time we'd really spoken since the launch. And he said:

"So, what are you going to do next?"

Next?!

Warning Label had only one real flaw in its execution and format... it was built to end. At some point, the story wrapped up. I couldn't keep putting Danielle through the wringer of her magical list of flaws. While that story went longer than I'd intended, it couldn't run forever.

I started coming up with new ideas. As per usual, the one I really thought would land didn't. (No, I won't tell you what. I'm sure it'll show up somewhere.)

This time I was going to fix that. I was going to pitch something open-ended that could go on for as long as fans were willing to read it. So, I thought and I worked and I scraped and... yeah, those ideas became ***Cupid's Arrows.***

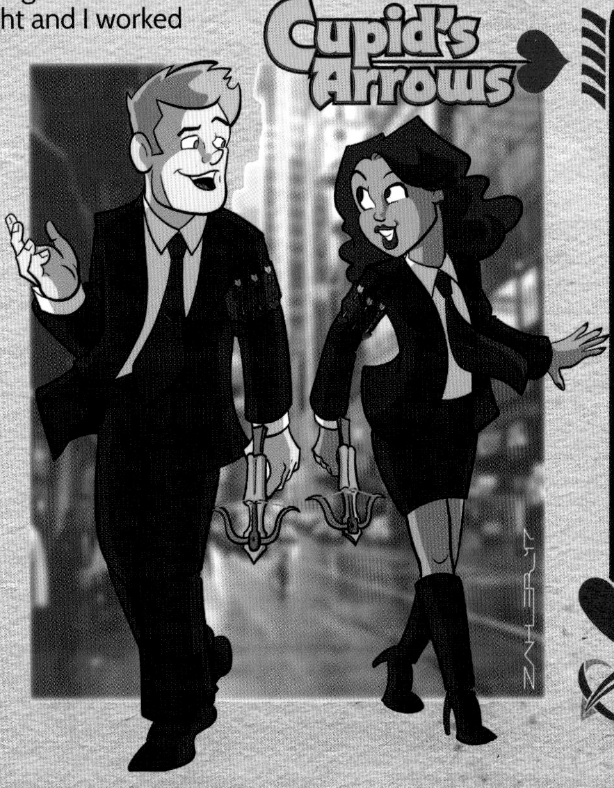
Cupid's Arrows

The story came from a bunch of places. I'd always wanted to do something featuring Cupid. I'd been a fan of the 1998 *Cupid* series starring Jeremy Piven and

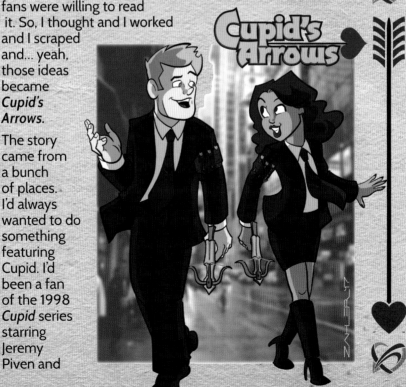

Paula Marshall where the fallen god of love had to get together one hundred couples.

The huge playing field of getting couples together had a lot to play with .And I'd done a Cupid-centric story in the *Batman: Brave and the Bold* spec script that I'd written which had led to me getting my first animation gig. In that, Batman and Wonder Woman were tasked by an ailing Cupid to get couples together using The Book of Love.

That script would never be produced, but it had more than a few ideas I could mine.

I also wanted to write a bantery, fun couple like Nick and Nora from *The Thin Man* or Dave and Maddie from *Moonlighting*. I like writing clever dialogue and chemistry.

So my initial pitch was:

> It's a big world. Long ago it got too big for just one Cupid. So the God of Love set up a private army of immortals to help him do his work (his "Arrows"). These two-person teams go out with targets selected by the Book of Love. They investigate and arrange meetings between couples, getting them to the perfect moment so the pairs can be struck by their arrows.

> The army is basically a cross between *Men in Black* and *Grosse Point Blank*, with a secretive team going around setting up "love hits".

> Rick and Lora are two of the best of Cupid's crew. They're not just a team but a couple, and have been for a thousand years. The two of them seek out these nascent couples, bickering and bantering all the way. Being members of Cupid's crew, they have some powers (invisibility, memory erasing and The Book of Love which is a near-infinite research tome) and they use this and their own experiences to bring love to the world.

> The series would be open-ended. We'd start out with one large arc, but their missions could vary greatly. Getting couples together is the obvious one, and would happen the most. Sometimes they act as confidants; sometimes they arrange situations; and sometimes they save existing relationships. But they'd also run into other Cupids and would come upon a team that is destined to become a couple, and help arrange that. A rogue Cupid could be getting the wrong people together, or breaking up relationships. The Cupids might need to rekindle a romance. And Cupid himself has become an absentee boss. Where did he go and can Rick and Lora find him? And we could do flashbacks to do period pieces, or how Rick and Lora's relationship or past missions went.

My editor had a couple of tweaks, the biggest was making Rick and Lora *not* a couple. The "will they or won't they" became a big story point and now I can't imagine doing the series without it. A different Lora, my friend Lora Innes (of *The Dreamer* series and *Wynonna Earp* fame) gave me a couple of other good suggestions, among them being that Cupid's power was fading and the teams had to be a little more resourceful to get couples together. That tied in nicely with my "missing god of love" setup.

I saw the Cupid teams as assassins for love, so I built a lot of their powers and setups around that construct. They could turn invisible, like a sniper trying to blend into his surroundings. And the idea that they could "enter the narrative" allowed them to go undercover without having to laboriously build out a backstory. Here, they could seamlessly enter their target's story, as if they've always been one of those background people in their lives. I gave them hitman type uniforms, black suits, red ties, and an armband that no one really seems to notice. (But it'd be great if anyone would ever want to cosplay these characters, right? Which did happen!)

And so I got to work.

Chapters 1–2: Setting the Stage

My WEBTOON editor explained their setup well to me. The series would launch with three chapters. Chapter one should hook them, two expands the story, and three hits the reader with a cliffhanger to make them need to come back next week.

I had done that well with *Warning Label*, and I saw no reason to change on this new project. So chapter one joined our heroes in the middle of a mission getting Angie and Derek together during Mardi Gras. And it was a struggle.

Rick and Lora's respective histories are indicated in their drink choices. Rick, a Southerner, drinks a southern bourbon, and Lora, a Spainiard, drinks a rum drink.

I had to figure out my characters, who visually were loosely based on Colton Haynes (Roy Harper from *Arrow*) and Melissa Fumero (Amy Santiago from *Brooklyn 99*) and how they stood and acted and what they looked like from every angle. I had to become comfortable drawing them. That's always a struggle, and only gets better by doing. But knowing that doesn't make it easier.

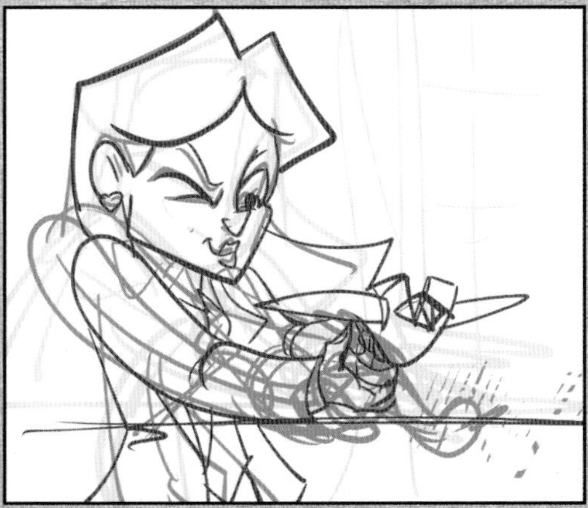

Foolishly, I also set it in New Orleans and Mardi Gras. It was nothing but crowds and exotic backgrounds and all sorts of stuff that made it hard to draw. Add to that an attempt to really dive into the infinite vertical scroll that is the WEBTOON format and... whew! It was a big mountain to climb.

Chapter two, thankfully, slowed down and allowed me to have a visual break. It also let me, through Ben the Bartender (who also appearaed in *Warning Label* slinging drinks a different bar), explain their mission statement and set up Rick and Lora's general conflict. Lora is a little more world-wearly and cynical, and Rick is a little more romantic and optimistic.

And it's here where we learn that the Book of Love has a reason for getting these couples together. The Cupid teams don't get together every couple. Plenty of people find love on their own.

Blue Line Coffee may be located in Chicago, but it's actually based on Madcap Coffee in Grand Rapids, which I visit multiple times during the Grand Rapids Comic Con.

Chapters 3–10: Kim and Fitz

When I pitched the series, I outlined four couples that our heroes would get together. The first were Kim and Fitz, a college couple bonding over coffee and conflicted over their determination and drive. But these arcs were delinieated in the most broad strokes. There was still lots of places to explore and play.

Making sure to end on a cliffhanger, I decided that having Kim have a boyfriend would be a great "oh no!" moment for the readers. Except, I was really uncomfortable having The Book of Love actually break up a couple. And that conflict became the hook of the story.

The story gave me lots of opportunity to show how our Cupids worked to get people together. Both of them would enter the narrative, so we'd see how that works. I hoped that the idea that they could only enter the narrative once per mission as a limiting factor would come through. without ever having the characters deliver the narrative transgression that is "As you know..." Because if you know, why do you need to say it, except to explain things to the readers? Lazy writing.

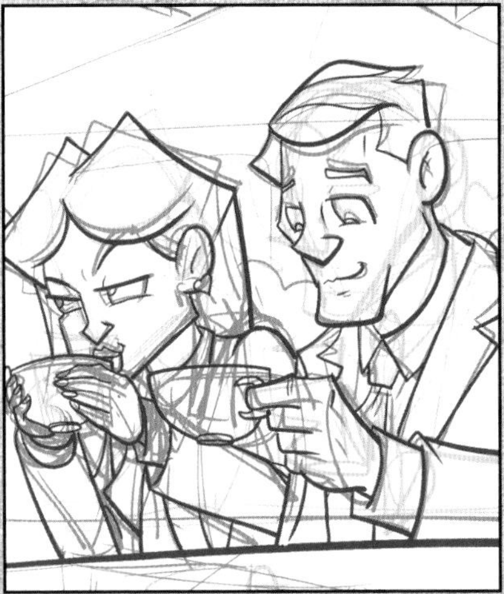

I set the story in Chicago, because I just love Chicago. It's fun to visit, fun to draw, and is a place I'm familiar with enough to not have to do a lot of reference.

It's at this point that I realized what a hole I'd dug for myself. I was going to have to create a brand-new cast of characters every seven chapters or so. Yikes, I hadnt thought of that. And I do a lot with digital backgrounds and reusing them. When Danielle was in her office at SpackleFlack, that was consistent. Why draw it more times than I needed to? But here, I'd be burning through backgrounds and settings, too. This was going to be a lot of work. *What was I thinking?*

That, along with the fear of starting a new project and trying to get comfortable in general, created for me a huge speed bump that made it really hard to plant my feet and get started with this. That, in turn, would cause me to burn up a lot of my lead time on the series. Not fun!

The point where I got over that fear and ennui was in Lora and Rick's late night pizza date. Based on my favorite pizza place in Chicago, Pizzeria Due, I got to make pineapple pizza and Chicago/New York references, but I also got to find my stride with their banter and relationship.

I also love the moment where Lora freelances on getting Sam and Monica together in the bar. It's a great character moment for her as it both shows her impatience after doing this for two hundred years and that she also still wants to help and get people together.

We also get references to other stories I've created, with Doctor Karma being a character in *Love and Capes*. Apparently, in the Cupidverse, Hollywood has seen how commercial my work can be... unlike the real world.

We also get one moment where Lora indicates a darker backstory when Kim says "She has plenty of later in front of her" and Lora knows how true that isn't.

Chapter 11: Interlude in Orlando

The TV show *Wiseguy* was one of the first shows I can recall doing very serialized storytelling and mini-arcs with the hero, Vinnie Terranova, bringing down different organized crime operations. The show was great for a lot of reasons, but one of the things I really liked is that it would actually take a breath between missions. The characters would have a moment to decompress before getting into another adventure.

That was the impetus for this moment. We needed a moment between missions.

It also gave me the opportunity to introduce James and Carmen. James and Carmen are based on friends of mine, and James was kind enough to support the Warning Label Kickstarter at a level where they got to appear in my new comic. It was supposed to just be a walk-on, but I decided that they'd be great as a fellow Cupid team. I could set up a lot of Rick and Lora's conflict against the rules by showing that there might be another couple breaking those rules.

James and Carmen are big Disney World fans,

All the chapter titles are taken from song lyrics. This one is, obviously, taken from the Tiki Room song at Disney World.

so setting this at a faux Trader Sam's seemed like a good fit. Plus it was fun to draw all the tiki backgrounds. If you look, you can see tiki versions of Spock and the Crusader in the tiki totem poles.

This is also the chapter that starts naming the Cupid's plays, including the Whitten, named after my girlfriend Emily, also the co-writer of the hamster-heavy *The Underfoot* series. (Check it out!)

This chapter also shows the Cupids getting a same-sex couple together. I wanted to show that love comes in all kinds of flavors, and putting this is so early addresses that issue. I hope.

Chapter 12–15: Asha and Isaac

It's no surprise that I do a lot of comic conventions, so setting a romance at one of these events was natural. And we all have crushes on actors or actresses and wouldn't it be cool if we hit it off with one of them?

Of course it also meant stupid, stupid crowd scenes, so I clearly don't think these things through.

I've been to Milwaukee once or twice, but setting most of the action in the comfortable confines of a convention center made it easy to make things feel

Chapter 14's title, "Telling Me Just What a Fool I've Been" is a lyric from The Cascades (and Dan Fogleberg's) "Listen to the Rhytym of the Falling Rain." Because rain was going to be an important factor in this part.

right. And it also helped create the running joke that Rick loves food and knows where to go in every town they go to. Because yes, cheese curds are awesome and do squeak on your teeth.

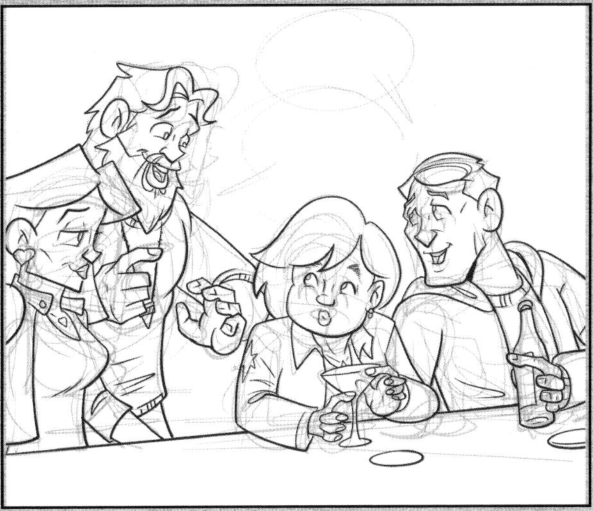

Danielle and Jeff make a very natural guest appearance here working at a convention. And they seem to recognize Rick and Lora. This crossover sent fans scrolling back through *Warning Label* to see if they appeared there.

Sorry, I'm not that good. It's a total retcon and a bonus for WEBTOON fans. But Rick and Lora do not appear in *Warning Label.*

Lots of my friends' projects and stores appear at this convention, too. See which ones you can spot and check them out. I'm always happy to highlight my friends' works where I can.

One of the things I learned too late in the writing process is that it wasn't enough to just have a couple, there had to be a reason for them to get together. There had to be some clicking, some chemistry, to make that sale. Doing that over and over through the course of a season isn't easy. You chew up a lot of ideas.

I made Isaac and Asha both Pacific Islanders because... well, first of all, why not? Honestly, that's why I make a lot of the choices I do. If there's no reason for someone not to be something, then why not do it? It leads to a more rich and textured world.

It also let me bond them, too. Isaac missed home because he felt like Los Angeles was a little plastic. Asha understood this feeling well, having gone home to see her mother's family every chance she could. You could see why they were going to make a good couple.

We also get more backstory on Lora and her ex-boyfriend, referenced in the last mission. I may not have seeded Rick and Lora in Warning Label, but I absolutuely knew that her Zephyr ex was going to come in and save the day here.

Sometimes, I will admit, that I throw things in planning to figure them out later. So in this chapter, we learn that Rick and Lora failed on one mission. How did that happen? What does that mean?

I don't know, but it sounds like a great place to start a story, doesn't it?

Bonus Chapter 1: Rachael and John

So, to make this Kickstarter, we had a reward level where I'd tell your story as a Cupid mission. Seemed easy enough. We wound up selling two, and these stories are presented here, and only here.

John and Rachael's story about being the only two to go see the Star Wars exhibit at COSI was lovely but... they didn't kiss on that first date. Which kind of robbed me of my traditional endgame. But what I did do was use that to establish that characters don't have to kiss to seal the deal. Asha and Isaac don't either, after all.

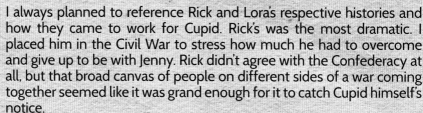

The "Frontier Partrol" series is actually a story idea I had in high school for a way-too-heavily *Star Trek* inspired series about the crew of the Starship Fantasia. The story references and designs are all from that.

But also I got to use it to build tension in Rick and Lora's relationship and build its inevatibility.

Chapter 16-17: Rick's Backstory

I always planned to reference Rick and Lora's respective histories and how they came to work for Cupid. Rick's was the most dramatic. I placed him in the Civil War to stress how much he had to overcome and give up to be with Jenny. Rick didn't agree with the Confederacy at all, but that broad canvas of people on different sides of a war coming together seemed like it was grand enough for it to catch Cupid himself's notice.

Cupid's look is very much based on Jeremy Piven (though he comes out looking for like Christopher Eccleston). I tried to capture some of that irriverent speech pattern, too. I didn't want him to be wearing the stereotypical Roman garb, so I did kind of borrow from Doctor Who. He'd have something like a sportcoat and pants which were kind of timeless. They come off more like silk pajamas, but that works well for Cupid, too.

I also wanted to be clear that the deal to become a Cupid wasn't a punishment or sentence or some kind of conscription. Rick was

coming from being drafted once before. It'd be cruel to do that again. Instead, it's a reward and a way to get some bonus time. But there's no downside to taking the deal.

This is also the moment where Rick stops grieving his past fianceé. If that's not clear enough, he forgoes having one of Jenny's favorite drinks to instead have one of Lora's.

> Vince, the bartender, is weaing an Atomicat Hawaiian shirt. The same one we saw in Orlando. Because why waste that kind of art element once you design it?

Bonus Chapter 2: Johanna and KC

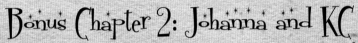

This was the other Kickstarter bonus story. KC and Johanna also had a long-term slow burn of a relationship. I was only promising five pages and went over on both of them!

They met at DragonCon, and while I was a little worried about having two convention-based stories in the same volume, DragonCon isn't like any other convention in the multiverse. I love it so, and in this pandemic year (as I write this) the convention was cancelled, so it was nice to revisit it, even if just fictionally.

> The Karatown bar is named after my friend Kara, who I met at DragonCon.

I again substituted my intellectual property for the real things. KC was not a comic book editor for Maerkle Press, my self-publishing imprint. Obviously.

Also, this chapter let me play with another running joke, that of Rick getting bad choices when he joins the narrative. Plus, getting into comics really is hard!

Chapter 18-23: Zan and David

Remember how I mentioned that I had all four couples for this first season sketched out? I threw those notes out here. This was originally a director and actor who got together at a college play. But there were issues with the director being in charge of the actor, I didn't want to do a second college story so soon after Fitz and Kim, and it just didn't work. So I called an audible and made this up as I went along.

I took the bare bones of it and set it at a quick, one-act play festival based on my time doing the 48-Hour Film Competition. I wrote for Team Slushpile (see our films at *www.slushpileentertainment.com*) and used that to create this competition. This arc also allowed me to show that

> The Paulette Theatre is named in honor of Elaine Paulette, the drama teacher at my hich school. I worked stage crew on *The Pajama Game* and it was one of the best experiences of my life.

Rick and Lora are far from perfect. They make a lot of mistakes in this mission. They misunderstand things and have to scramble to save the day at the end.

I have been to New York City a bunch of times and I love it lots. It's such an awesome and interesting and romantic place. I've been to the top of the Empire State Building more than a few times and I always thought it'd be cool to be one of the ushers up there because they see so many expressions of love. Being up there at night is a magical thing.

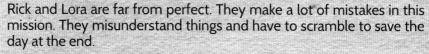

What I'm saying is that I could write a whole series about Ernie.

I also got to experiment with a lot of different storytelling techniques. The idea to change the lettering font when they were delivering lines of dialogue was a great visual to show what they were doing. And I also got to do a bunch of repeated images and minor changes to show the creative process of storytelling.

I love the Cupids freelancing and just giving everyone the mega happy ending. Very theatrical.

The pastor is drawn to look like my friend Jill, who is also a pastor. And a dear friend. So get to know me and who knows where you'll appear?

In art school, there's a theory called "When it doubt, leave it out." (Also, "black it out" or "white it out".) It means that you shouldn't fake what you don't know. Just delete it. Well, I was trying to figure out what the etherial plane looked like for Lora's flashback. I couldn't figure it out. And so it's all white, and I think it works great.

Chapter 24: Interlude in Central Park

Knowing that both my Cupids were in the place where they might finally admit they had feelings for each other, I needed another break in the acion so they could reflect on everything. Cue Gayle and Morris.

I think it was important for them to check in on a past couple and see that things were going well. And it shows that the Cupids kind of see relationships as a spectator

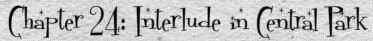

Check out the ducks! There's one when they're single and two when they're married.

sport, which I think is a natural evolution for immortal characters like them. Like a musician appreciating someone else's playing, they can see the work in a different way.

These two are loosely-based on one of my favorite casual couple encounters. I was at the Writer's Cafe coffee shop at Disney World. At Disney, everyone has the name of their hometown on their badge. I noticed these two older people had the same town, and I asked if they knew each other. They told me they'd been married for fifty years and now spent their retirement working at Disney and I thought it was the most awesome thing ever. So they're Gayle and Morris.

It also let me get introspective about the nature of love and why these couples are selected. I very much didn't want the couples themselves to be important. Like not every relationship ends in a successful Mars mission or cure for cancer. So making the Book's choice ineffable lets me tell the stories I want to and not have to add a layer of world-altering importance to everyone.

And it causes Rick and Lora to get delightfully philisophical about their own lives and tragic love stories. Putting them in the perfect frame of mind to go to a wedding in Tacoma.

Chapter 25–28: Kenzie and Billy

Your first question is probably, "Why Tacoma?"

I have relatives out that way, and the pacific northwest is just gorgreous, though it was a challenge to make all the greens in the mountains looks and shade different than all the ones last chapter in Central Park. (New York has more yellow in its scenes.) So when I needed a place, Tacoma was perfect.

This chapter also let me play with the format a lot. I very much didn't say who the targets were. I wanted people to guess. In every other chapter you

> Rick and Lora's married name is "Charles", showing my love of Nick and Nora Charles from *The Thin Man*.

know how it's going to play out. Here, you think you do and then, all of a sudden, you realize that you don't know who the principals are. Made things a little more interesting.

And yeah, it meant drawing *more* stupid crowds. But at least the backgrounds were easier.

Weddings can be crucibles for lives and relationships. It makes you take stock of everything, and I wanted to drive that home here. It was a great canvas to paint on. Running into an ex at a wedding feels like it's a universal experience, too.

It's a great reveal when Kenzie has her moment of realization about Jason and how they weren't right. It's liberating for her. And it's a nice different chord in the song of the series that while the stories are about people getting together, it doesn't mean that you don't get to expore why people are apart.

Having Rick and Lora confess their feelings in that crucible made perfect sense. It felt natural, especially pretending to be married. And let's pause on that.

The way I see the whole narrative and backstory working is that you have an entire life that appears, but you only remember the things that you need to. Like you, Dear Reader, have a third-grade teacher. Mine was Sister Borromeo. But you don't go around thinking about who your third-grade teacher was all the time. It's not until someone asks you that you recall it.

Similarly, Rick and Lora can recall their entire married life in the narrative, if they need to. Their stories are synced, they have the same memories, but they don't get burdened with them unless they need them. And further, all their memories come without the emotional resonance. So they remember getting married, but it's lyrics without music. There's no feelings of love that they'd have to ignore.

Except, of course, the ones they really have.

As for Jessica, the bride, she's another case of "Why not?" I thought it'd be great to have another character that was something different than central casting. I first toyed with giving her a prosthetic leg and being an former miltiary officer hurt overseas. But, that also came with the need to explain why she was like that, and that would give it more heft than I wanted.

See, my goal with these things is to just write interesting people that you care about, and not stop the story to call attention to the representation or diversity. Jessica's deaf, and it doesn't define her or become a story point or anything. She's just a person and that's the most important thing.

It did lead to as issue, though. You see, I draw and write in what's called The Marvel Method. I rarely have a fully typed-out, written script. I have dialogue in my head and take some notes and figure that I'll figure out the actual words later. Sometimes I'm specific, but not always.

With Jessica, I had to clearly have her signing words. But, I figured "of course I'm going to remember what I meant to have her say."

Write it down, people. Write it all down.

So, in a couple scenes, I had to go back and try to figure out what sign I'd drawn in hopes of having that word appear in the dialogue.

And then we end with, what I hope, is a strong ending. It's very much a Shakespearian "three happy endings" thing with Tyler and Jessica, Billy and Kenzie, and Rick and Lora. It was also important to me that they have a dramatic kiss outside the narrative.

So That's It...

...season one ends, Rick and Lora are happy and nothing bad ever happens to them. No evil Cupids or grouchy dolphins or... wait, no, that all totally happens.

But that's Volume Two.

Thank You to our Kickstarter Backers!

Aaron Jamieson • Adam Eaton • Aidar Bikmullin • Airadea • albone Alex • Alex • Alex Johnson • Alexander Zerbe • Alexandra A Alexis Sommerman • Alissa • Alyssa Sherry • AMA1 • Amelia Buchmeier Andrea • Andrea Trahan • Andrew Kaplan • Andy Smith • Anne Rose Dueñas • Ariana Rivera • Ariqua Furse • Arthur Penndragon • Ashley Ashley • Asia Hoe • Barbara Randall Kesel • Becky • Beena • Ben Hall Ben Thompson • Benjamin Kitt • Beth • Bill Schmidt • Bill Walko Billy Bolt • Blake Petit • Bob Ingersoll • Bradford Tree • Brenna Koeppen Brian • Brian (aka brainwise) • Brian Melcher • Brian Ward • Bryn Grunwald Brynn • Caitlin • Cari Simmons • Carla Santellano • Caroline Wax CartersFARM • Cassandra • Catherine • Catherine Fleming • Chelsea Christopher Daley • Christopher Morton • Claire Reisberg • Cleo Maranski Conan64ds • Crystal • Crystal Henderson • D Joseph forbes • Dan Tran dan_eyer • Dana Goddard • Danielle • Darrin and Ruth Sutherland Darryl Warcup • David • David Chuhay • David Kinsel • David Nett David Phelps • David Tai • Dee • Denise Panlaque • Dennis Dunkman Dirge • Dmessengah • Donny • Donovan Grimwood • Dustin Carr Dustin Hovatter • Ed Mattson • Ed Pogue • Eleora Bartsch • Elias Rosner Elizabeth Calienni • Elizabeth Lehmkuhl • Elizabeth S • Emilie A. Emily Groberski • Emily Shimano • Emily Whitten • Eric Gimlin • Eric L. Sofer • Eric Wilson • Erica Olivera • Erick Salinas • Esmeralda T Oliva Evan Meadow • Filiz Karahasan • Fish Lee • Flo_R • Gabrielle Camassar Gabrielle Laroche-Douhéret • Gary Phillips • James Santangelo Grayson Judd • Greg Morrow • Guest 775155227 • Hadara White Hayden • Heather Champe-White • Heidi Mangold Helene de Bettignies • Hilary • Hugo Vicente • Irene Wade • ItemCrafting J. Robert Deans • Jack • Jacob Wahlenmaier • Jakob • Jaminx • Jan Grzybowski Jane Sherbrooke • Jared Quante Libet • Jeffrey Smith • Jenah Blitz Jennifer Edmond • Jennifer Lefeve • Jenny Arioso • Jeremiah Avery Jerry Selinger • Jesse Jackson • Jessica Enfante • Jessica Magelaner Joe Cabrera • Joe Dube • Joe Murray • joe niffen • Joe Ryan • Joel Singer Joey Watkins • Johanna Draper Carlson • John C. Derrick • John Nacinovich Jon E • Jon Johnson • Joseph Adam Davis • Joshua • Judah Warshaw K Mark Landes • Kaity Sarsfield • Kaiza • Karana_Gemstone • Kat Kat Graves • Katariina Kurjessuo • Kate Swafford • Katz • Kayla Daniel Keith Bowden • Keith G. Baker • Keith Reid-Cleveland • Kelly Dale Kelsey S. Hoffman • Kevin Mitchell • KillaCam7010 • Kim • Kim Gianopoulos Krystina Caywood • Kylie Wells • lacey • Laurie Jacobs • Leah Stoddard Leeanne Krecic • Leslie • Liane Herzog • Lili Wong • Lillian Lillian R Eaves • lizzicle • Loisbet Castro • Luke • M J • Madeline

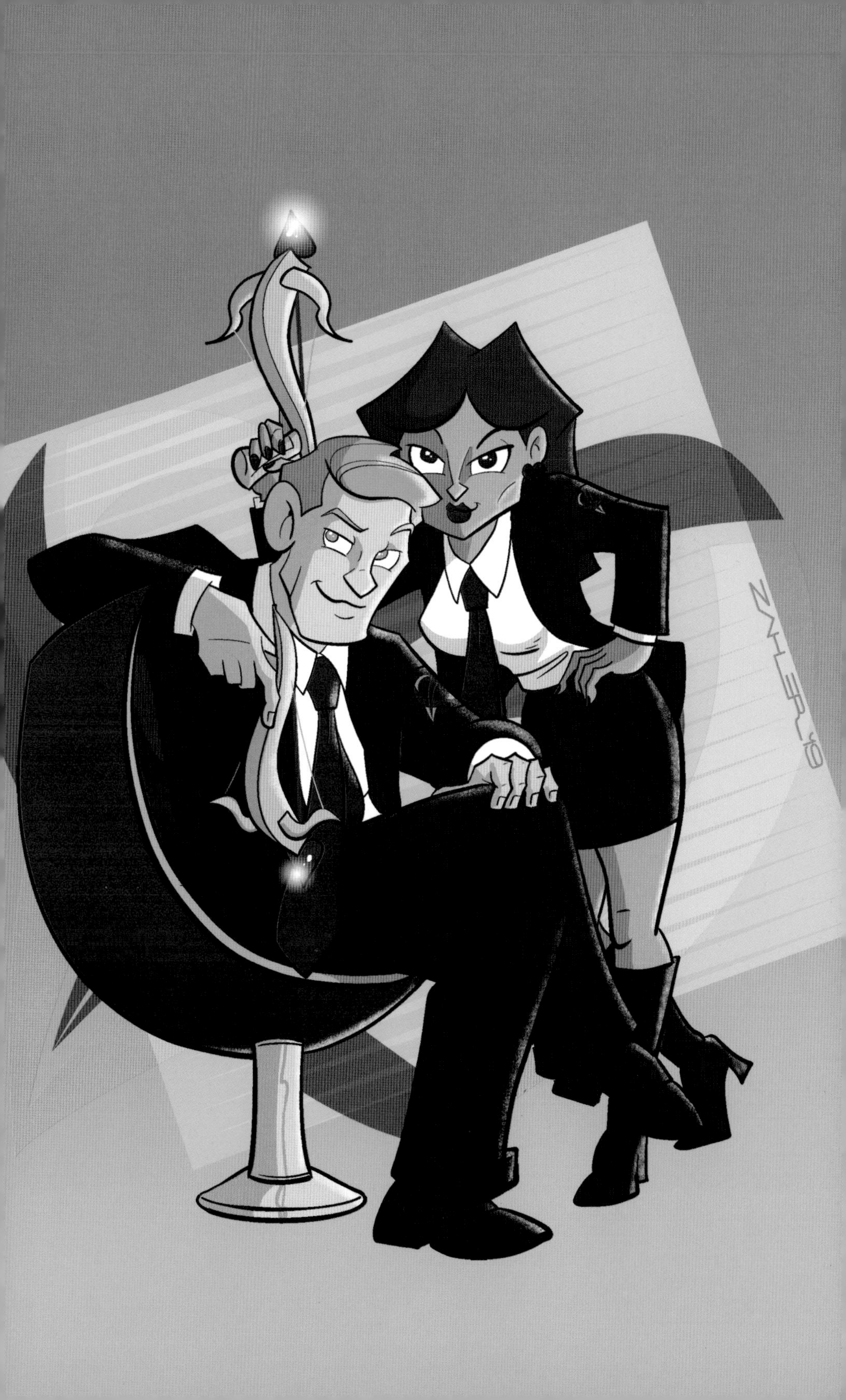
ZAHLER '19

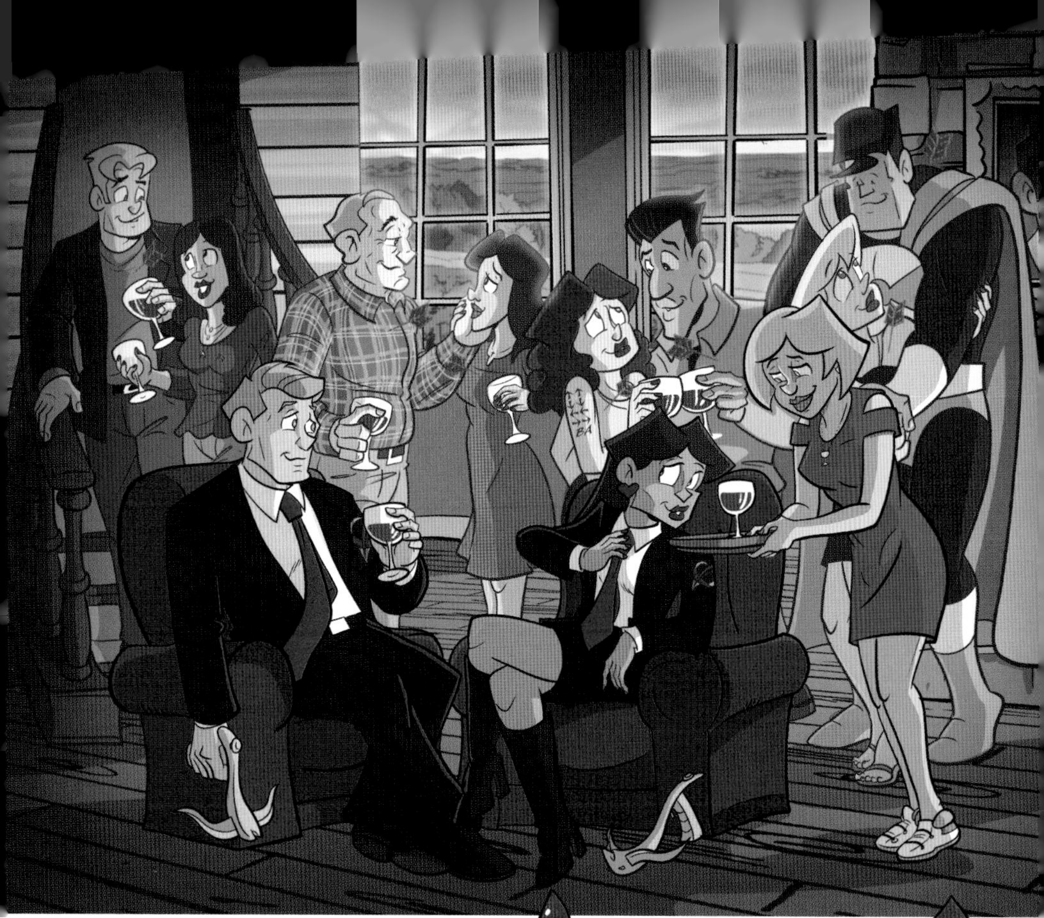

The "Busy Day" print featuring the Cupids and all my creator-owned couples. (Left to right, Carter and Lee from *Long Distance*, Jack and Teresa from *Time and Vine*, Danielle and Jeff from *Warning Label* and Abby and Mark from *Love and Capes*. Megan, currently unattached, from *Time and Vine* is serving drinks.)

Promotional art for the second season of *Cupid's Arrows*.

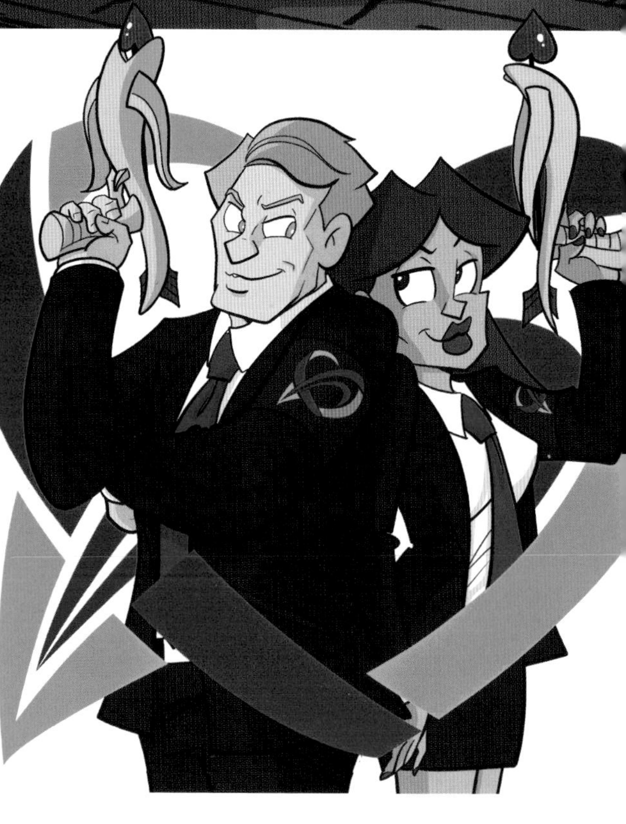

Poster for convention giveaways and reprinted and recolored for the Kickstarter. This is one of my favorite representations of Rick and Lora.

Manuel Moran • Mariah Healey • Marielle • Mark Boore • Mark Geier Mark O'English • Mark Pengryn • Mary Gaitan • Matthew G Mann Sr Matthew Wong • MelinaJulia Van Riet • Melinda Schmidbauer Michael • Michael Eckhardt • Michael Hancock • Michael I Michael Rhode • Michael Schiffer • Mike Aragona • Mike Marlow Mike Vrobel • Misty Bradley • Monica Schneider • MoonFromEarth Nathan • Nick Ulanowski • Nicole • Nightwing • Nolwenn Hoellinger Pablo Torres • pacman101 • Paige • Pate McKissack • Patricia Garcia Patricia Manning • Patricia Vanek • Patrick Martin Keane • Paul D Storrie Paul Engelberg • Purple Parfait • Purple Piece Games • Rachel Jurassic Park • Rebecca Leannah • Rebecca Oman • Rebekah Dawn • Rhys Morgan Rick Hansen • Rob Steinberger • Robert Armstrong • Robert Daley Robert Harrison • Robert N. • Robert Zahler • Roger Ash • Roger Price Romy Hofer • Ron • Rose Hannaford • Russel Dalenberg • Russell Rusty Meck • Ryan Drost • Ryan Emnett • S. Johnson • Samuel Millspaugh Sarah Anuszkiewicz • Sarah Elizabeth Koenig • Sarah Elizabeth Lawrence Sarah Grace • Sarah Humphreys • Satesh Charran • Scott Rowland Sean Tiffany • Sean Whelan • seanrabin • Sergio J Tuero • sg Shawn Van Dusen • Sherry Mock • Shimona Wong • Shleom Stephanie Davis • Stephanie Espinosa • Stephen Blanzaco Stephen Rose • Stephen Schneider • Steve Conley • Steve Dahl Steve Dong • Steve S. • Steve Sullivan • Sunyoung Chong Suzie Duncan • Switch • Tab • Tarini Konchady • Taylor Ness The Creative Fund by BackerKit • The Illustrious Q • TheAnimatedGamer Thomas Chick • Thomas Polok • Tim Garrett • Timothy Klaman Tony Isabella • TPGary • TR • Tracey Schmid • Trevor • Tyler Crone Tyler Mundt • Vanessa • Victor Lopez • Victoria Fout • Vijay Varman Vince Bayless • Wade Farley • Wayne Sung • Yusuke92 Zamien Tassinari • Zoe Weis

About the Author

Exceedingly dapper and relentlessly charming, Thom Zahler creates well-cultured superhero romances in a tuxedo and top hat, as a true gentleman would.

Working his way up from being a hired hand at Zahlerdu Abbey, the Irish Thomas began lettering for Innovation Comics and moved eventually to create *Love and Capes*, *Long Distance* and *Time and Vine*, published by IDW, as well as *Cupid's Arrows* and *Warning Label* for Line WEBTOON.

He is a frequent man of leisure at IDW's *My Little Pony* stables, and has gone on expeditions with the Disney *Tsum Tsums* and crew of the *Enterprise* as well.

He is now Lord of the Manor at Zahlerdu, where he frequently is heard asking "What is a weekend?"

No, seriously. What is a weekend? He hasn't had one since 2004.

Find Him on the Internets!

thomZ.com

@thomZahler 🐦 📷

Special Thanks to:

Amy Wolfram • Greg Weisman • Emily Whitten
Brian Ward • Bill Williams • Deitri Villarreal
Paul D. Storrie • James Santangelo
Jill A. Smith • Roger Price • Marc Nathan
Jon Monson-Foon • Jesse Jackson
Lora Innes • Kara Evans • Carmen Deluccia
Luke Daab • Christy Blanch
and Mike Bokausek